M.R. Lovric lives in London and Venice. *Carnevale* is her first novel.

Praise for *Carnevale*

'There is something irresistible about trying to trace a connection between notorious lover and memoirist Casanova and notorious lover and poet Lord Byron in Venice the seductive city where both men worked their way through galleries of women . . . Maybe Casanovrians play the same game that Byronists play, the search for the missing link, the one unknown woman who will make sense of some strange bits of Byron's life. M.R. Lovric, in her first novel, has gone one better, conjuring not only the woman who makes sense of Casanova's story, but who, thirty-odd years later, solves Byron's story as well . . . This is a lush book, dripping with opulent descriptions and elegant imagery . . . Ambitiously imagined' *Australian Book Review*

'Think gondolas and pigeons and *A Room with a View* . . . a dreamy, fantastical novel' *Sunday Business Post*

'Cecilia is a charming character and this is a touching . . . even moving read' *Independent on Sunday*

'Extraordinary, an intriguing, magical tale woven around the enigmatic character and grandeur of the Venetian Republic' *AXM*

Carnevale

M.R. Lovric

Virago

A *Virago* Book

First published by Virago Press 2001
This edition published by Virago Press 2002

Copyright © M.R. Lovric 2001

The moral right of the author has been asserted.

A CIP catalogue record for this book
is available from the British Library.

ISBN 1 86049 866 3

Typeset in Lapidary and Weiss by M Rules
Printed and bound in Great Britain by
Clays Ltd, St Ives plc

Virago Press
An imprint of
Time Warner Books UK
Brettenham House
Lancaster Place
London WC2E 7EN

www.virago.co.uk

Prologue

Before you hear about it at Florian, let me tell you what happened next.

It was night, and noiseless, except for the waves, the *brusio* of the mosquitoes and *brulichio* of the water rats and the secret corpses shifting gently in the dark silt of the Grand Canal.

I was cleaning the squirrel-fur brushes. I did not hear him enter. He was so slight that, in the long shadows of the room, I did not see him until he was standing with his small, white hand on the back of my chair. Then the air curdled around me, and he took my neck in that hand, hard.

'Show me your Casanova,' he said, seven years apart unacknowledged.

'Is that why you have come?' Neither, then, would I acknowledge them.

'Show me your Casanova, and I will show you why.'

'I have a hundred Casanovas here.'

'Then I want to see them all.'

I picked up a large portfolio and carried it to the table. Byron followed me with his dragging step. Then I felt it again, that pincer at the back of my neck, the way a cat mates.

'Open it.'

He did not loosen his grip on my neck. With his left hand he raked through the paintings and the sketches. He isolated six of them, sweeping the rest to the floor. There they lay, with their kind eyes and mouths upturned to the ceiling.

I saw the heel of Byron's foot descend upon a Casanova nose as he fanned out his chosen pictures on the table. The impossibility of this present scene released a memory: I saw myself painting by candlelight in the gondola, and the next day in my bedroom. I saw my small, unlined hand reaching out of its sleeve to dip my brush into the gallipot. I had painted every part of Casanova, while the waves jostled the steps of the *palazzo* and Casanova's cat lay beside us, refusing to be perturbed by the smell of oil paint, or the smell of us.

'This one. Did his eyes really burn you like this?'

'Yes, he made me hot when I painted him, just by using his eyes. It was a way he had.'

'Hot. I can imagine. And these hands – were they really so pink, so soft-looking?'

'But strong. You remember, he had fought duels with them, climbed the roof of the Doges' Palace with them. He could hold me around the waist with just one. However, Casanova was always gentle.'

'When he lifted you onto the bed. And I suppose he was a monster, where you she-creatures prefer monstrosity?'

I did not answer.

Byron continued, 'And those lips. Are you telling me that his mouth was so fleshy? Don't those lips look feminine to you?'

'That had not occurred to me. I do not kiss women as a habit.'

'You should try. I know your Casanova was happy with troilism. He was particularly fond of sisters, as I recall. And the Sapphic sorority, of course.'

'Yes, I know that too. But we were enough for each other.'

'You and I were enough for each other, once. Was it, with me, as it was with him?'

I did not answer. The pincer clenched my collarbone. 'Was I like him?'

I did not reply.

Suddenly, he released me. I skidded on the discarded paintings; I fell backwards to the floor. Then Byron was above me, and I was inhaling the vinegar of his breath.

Until we were both naked, the questions never stopped: 'Did he kiss you like this? Did he bite your nipple like this? Did he swallow your saliva like this? Did he enter you like this, or did he wait until you were ready?'

Afterwards, we lay still among the pictures. Charcoal and paint from Casanova's likenesses smeared our bodies. When it was over, Casanova's lips were to be found imprinted on Byron's thigh. Casanova's eyes were, as ever, on my breast.

Casanova's Recipe
for Chocolate Cake

First, you need the lips to eat it.
Lips of purple heather, lips of persimmon, lips like mandarin skins
scraped through honey.

And then the occasion to eat it.
The first time you make love to her, the last time you make
love to her, one of the times in between (may they be many,
or at least long).

Of course you also need the sweet wine to moisten it.
With the soul of a bottle inside you, your tongue sees more
clearly. This is true, be it Falernian, Scopolo, Tokay, Burgundy,
pink partridge-eye Champagne, or that liquid chalk they make in
Orvieto. No matter. Maraschino from Dalmatia, even, with
cinnamon and sugar. Or milk. Once I myself, on my knees,
suckled from the rose-pink spigot of a young mother in Milan.

In those days, I had teeth.
Where was I? O yes, chocolate cake.

Then you need a bed.
A bed to lie on, a bed to feed on, sleep on, in which to lose the
crumbs to lick off the next morning.

And a surprise is always acceptable, too.
A snuffbox with a secret spring, an unexpected dearth or
luxuriance of hair, a fruit preserved for just this moment, a virgin
who proves as amorous as a pigeon.

Oh, and yes, you need a chocolate cake, too.
Send out for one immediately!

Part One

1

La fame fa far dei salti,
ma l'amor li fa far più alti.

Hunger makes you jump,
but love makes you jump higher.

VENETIAN PROVERB

That is what I was doing when the cat found me. I was eating chocolate cake and drinking *fragolino*, a sweet swarthy wine distilled from the strawberry grape, in my bath. The sins of greed and sloth and the subsidiary peccadilloes of drunkenness and luxurious nakedness – as many as possible was my aim in the dark of that starless early spring night. Day by day, I had assembled what I needed for this entertainment.

My hands swam through the water until they came to rest like those of the Botticelli Venus. One arm reached down my belly. I curved my palm over the tokens of puberty that were beginning to show. The thumb, still more curved, I held for a moment motionless on the little jut of flesh which we Venetians call the *màndola*, the almond. How had she refrained, Venus? At that moment I thought of Casanova, and I welcomed the thought.

For I had seen him, in a doorway, with a girl, once. From my bedroom window at Miracoli, I saw a tall man moving as dogs do, but more slowly, and more tragically. The girl was hidden, except for exquisite doll's feet, which he had first raised to his lips, one by one. I saw the back of his head disappearing into the darkness that must have been the delta of her legs. Then I saw the head rise, disembodied in the darkness, and plunge towards what must have been her mouth. She was very small; he stooped. So all I saw then, for a long time, was the rise and fall of his buttocks clenched in sagging white pantaloons. The first time I heard his voice it was uttering a rich sigh and an extravagant endearment that put an end to the fascinating movements. After he had helped her to rearrange her clothing, he kissed her forehead, tenderly. I saw him hand her a coin. I saw her disappointment.

'Casanova,' she whispered. Through the still night air, I heard even her intake of breath.

'Yes, my soul?' He took her hand, and kissed it, then both of her eyes.

But she hesitated, and then slipped away without a word. What I still don't know is this: was she disappointed because the coin was small, or because he had offered her money for something she had in fact taken, and which he seemed to have given, with love?

'Who is Casanova?' I had asked as my family breakfasted the next morning.

My mother bit her lower lip and stared mistrustfully at a perfect red apple in her hand, as if it were the original fruit that led to all vice. My little sister, Sofia, stared fish-eyed over her bowl of milk at me. My father's stern face purpled. 'Casanova is not a name I want to hear from the mouth of a pure young woman. I will not have it uttered at my table.'

So I must find out at the convent, at the Caffè Florian, or on the street. *Va bene.*

'Don't say that to her,' whispered my mother. 'You know how contrary she is. Remember the caterpillars!'

It was the endlessly repeated family story, the one which, for them, had always defined my perverse character. One morning, years before, my sister and I had been told that the courtyard garden was infested with a species of stinging caterpillar. (These small, vivid plagues come to Venice sometimes.) We were forbidden to play there. I had immediately run downstairs to sit among the roses, allowing the beautiful green beasts to striate my arms and ankles. Sofia stood watching me, weeping for the pain. I did not make a sound, though the insects flayed and feasted on my skin. 'Why? Why?' my mother had lamented as she washed away the blood in my bath. I lay silent while Sofia sobbed at the keyhole. How could I explain that I had merely wanted to see what it was like? It was not nice, but it was something I had not experienced before. The caterpillars had been of such a *ravishing* green. And it *might* have been nice. The warnings against it had promised as much.

Certainly my father remembered the caterpillars, but he persisted, 'Casanova is not to be mentioned in this house again. I am shocked with you, Cecilia.'

He turned to my mother. 'How old is she? Thirteen? Fourteen? Is this what the nuns teach her?'

It was a fair question. Nuns, I was soon to discover, were a great speciality of Casanova's.

Before I can tell you about Casanova, there are some things you must know about Venice. I need to tell you how she was in the days when my account begins, for in her gaunt and ghostly decline, as you *poverini* must see her, you would not recognise the city of perfervid happiness which spawned both me, Cecilia Cornaro, and Giacomo Casanova, and our story.

Ah, we were a happy city! It was our entire occupation to be happy. We were mad with happiness, stuffed with it like truffles.

When I think of Venice as she was in 1782, I think of a hundred thousand souls all devoted to pleasure. Souls like that become insubstantial and faintly luminous. You see, we were in the *phosphorescent* stage of decay.

We were a happy city. We were harmless and slightly worn out, loose and languid in our frisks. We had a child's sense of fun, latterly a tired child's. We were always up to something. There was no viciousness in us, only the irresponsible trespasses that unfortunately happen when pleasure runs wild. We loved practical jokes. We were constantly in that exquisite, perilous state of happiness, the gasping moment before the belly-laugh jumps out of the belly. We were so happy that we could not bear tragedies in our theatres. The one sad play they tried was a tremendous flop. In the comedies, when the villains were despatched, we cheered the corpses: *Bravi i morti!*

The deepest of our philosophies was this:

> *A'a matina 'na meséta,*
> *Al dopo dinar 'na baséta,*
> *A'a sera 'na donéta.*

> In the morning a little mass,
> In the afternoon a little gambling,
> In the evening a little lady.

We gambled like lunatics. In Venice people staked their clothes and walked home naked. Others staked their wives or daughters. The poorer we were, the more extravagant we became. We lost the concept of the value of money because we did not earn it. At Arsenale, where we should have been building ships to defend ourselves, fountains of wine ran continually. We forgot how to sleep: we merely fell into stupors. We rose to start our routs when civilised cities were going to bed. Our masses were like gala concerts. Our very beggars spoke in poetry.

Yes, we were a happy city. Our morals were indeed somewhat *nimble*. And our dress might be called immodest, but this was because we considered it our *duty* to show the world every beautiful part of ourselves. And yes, our pleasures were spiced with a few picturesque depravities. Actually, we were ripe as old fish! There were lewd acts engraved upon our snuffboxes and calling cards. Certainly, we took no nonsense from our priests. Think on this: there were ten times as many courtesans as noble or respectable bourgeois wives like my mother. But Venice was not a bordello. It was a haven for women. Their *cavalieri serventi* – their gallant lovers – whispered into their pretty ears a light fare of compliments as continuously as the lagoon utters waves. We wore our hearts upon our sleeves all year round, for love-affairs were always in season.

Everything was decoration in that happy city. Luxury became us. In Venice, we were mesmerised by our own entrancing vision in the mirror: the mirrors of the water and the speckled mirrors in our sumptuous bedrooms. In Venice, every boat wore at the point of its prow a lacy little spume of foam. As the world closed in upon us, we used our depleted stocks of gunpowder not to arm ourselves but for fireworks! Fortunately, we were so beautiful that we *frightened* our enemies; they did not think themselves good enough to conquer us. When you hear that it was necessary to forbid the Venetian *laundry women* to wear velvet, satin and black fox fur, you start to understand what kind of city we were then.

Ah, we were a happy city! Venice had become so old that she had fallen into her second childhood and laughed at everything. We were voluble as parrots. Our hands conducted simultaneous conversations, eloquent as a pair of poets. With a flourish, we welcomed in all the self-styled counts and virgins, the fortune-tellers and the snake-oil salesmen. The very men who swept the streets sent the dust dancing in graceful arcs, tendering their brooms like slender ballerinas. We even made joy of *acqua alta*! We pirouetted over the *passerelle* with the water clucking underneath us like an old governess. We splashed and giggled even as the sea dragged our chairs and our underwear into the lagoon.

The sea took all our memories and our sins away. She bestowed upon us her strange mother-of-pearl light which changed every instant and gave us a taste for lightness and infinite variety in all things. She revived us with her fresh breath upon our cheeks after we had spent ourselves in our debauches. She was always behind us or ahead of us, winking at us, showing us the futility of caution or even planning. For us, the sea was a liquid stimulant like coffee or hot chocolate. And she was everywhere. You could not close your bed curtains against her moist, lascivious sighs. You could not stop up your ears against her saucy whispers.

We had *Carnevale* six months of the year. In our strange and beautiful masks we always had a choice of who to be. In our masks, we were accountable to no one, and we took full advantage of this. In those days Venice kept eight hundred and fifty mask-makers in business. For our masks were not merely for *Carnevale*. They were for the fairy tale of the everyday, to be worn every night.

We ate foolish foods: *meringata* and towering confections of spun sugar. We were so spoiled we thought cherries fell from the trees without stones. We drank pomegranate sherbet from Araby and herbed raspberry kvass. Afterwards we dabbed the corners of our greedy mouths with silk handkerchiefs and threw them away! We ground the detritus of our pleasures into the paving stones until they made a harlequinade of orange peel, confetti and pumpkin seeds under our slippered feet. In the crowds, the women were liberally fondled.

You start to have an idea of us, now perhaps. But don't even try to imagine the joy of being *born* Venetian in the time when Venice was a happy city. You would not come close to the truth. These things I knew in my bones about Venice before this story began, even though I myself lived in a family that tried to hold itself aloof from the happy city, that tried very hard not to be happy, but, instead, to be good.

Now this is what I, Cecilia, found out at the convent, at Florian, and on the street about the happiest son of the happy city – Casanova.

The Empress Maria Teresa of Austria took up a list of the deadly sins. Seeing that there were seven, she thought it possible to close an eye to six of them. But Maria Teresa hated Lust. Against it she unleashed all her passion, and sought it out everywhere for extermination. When Casanova was known to have entered Vienna in 1747, Maria Teresa set up an Emergency Chastity Commission. Girls walked the streets carrying rosaries to forfend him.

Giacomo Girolamo Casanova (the very words send the tongue dancing and the saliva swilling round the mouth!) – how does one think of him? As satyr of the bedchamber, necromancer, gambler, alchemist, spy; the only man ever to escape from the Leads, the dread prisons of the Doges' Palace. Not so much a man, was Casanova, as a trademark for louche behaviour. If he were rendered in stone – God forbid – it would be as the spouting priapus of the Grand Canal. You like to see him as universal human lusts written larger than life, complete with black cloak and foamy cravat. You have this sinister feeling about him: that he was irresistible, that he exerted occult sexual powers, that he devoured women as if sucking up a sherbet.

But only one third of Casanova's memoirs are devoted to his love-life. According to my present calculations, Casanova conquered one hundred and thirty times. He was erotically diligent for thirty-five years, so he conducted fewer than four love-affairs every twelve months: scarcely a matter for bringing out the rosary! The most vigorous organ of Casanova's was his *heart*. Intimate congress was rarely mere recreation for him. He made love with love. 'Without love,' he always declared, 'this great business is a vile thing.'

He was fifty-seven when I saw him in the doorway with that doll-like girl. He was African-skinned, large-eyed, taller than any other man in Venice. We would have some months together which will stay with me for the rest of my life. There was another man, later — between them, they cut me in two, like a magician's assistant. Always think of the numbers. Casanova did. He was a cabbalist: he believed in the spirituality of numbers, in the fusion of alphabet and algebra. His women and his trysting places were chosen scientifically, after delicious deliberations over charts and amulets, jujus and periapts. He loved the confluence of dates and times that brought him to his newest lover. If it did not work out, it was not meant to work out: thus he preserved himself and his lovers from pangs of disappointment or of self-doubt.

It was an astonishing and fine thing to be desired by a man like Casanova. All his courtships were Arcadian. To win us, he would suffer any kind of physical or moral humiliation, philosophically. When he had time, he would win us with the most assiduous attentions and deliciously elaborate scams. When he was in a hurry, then, yes, sometimes he had recourse to gifts and money. Love always cost him all he had. Casanova gave everything in the shop window; he left nothing in the store-room. But when he had conquered, well, *the women* were the true winners, for he devoted himself to our pleasure with the intensity of a vocation. Indeed he believed fervently in female pleasure, thinking it greater than his own. After all, he reasoned, *the feast takes place in our own house*.

The women he loved seldom hated him afterwards, and I believe we felt a kind of sisterhood. We knew about each other. This was a sorority of good fortune, of having known a man who was able to unite his heart, soul and sexual parts. A man who would say, 'You are bewitching. How did you get that way?' And truly want to know. He could tell you everything about yourself, every slightest motion of your soul, run a tender finger through every concealed fold of your

thought. Here was a man who would be aroused by watching you
eat a peach, write a poem about it, share the peach and the poem
with you, and lick the peach juice from your chin on his way to your
lips. And outside your window the next day he would leave a peach,
the sight of which would turn to soft sweet pulp both your memory
and the lining of your womb.

He would be faithful to you, with regard to the peach, that is. No
other woman would receive her tributes in this kind. One day he
would make you and your peach immortal, by writing your story in
his memoirs with breathless and renewing tenderness. In the meantime, he would sympathise with the monthly agitations of your
loins. He had memorised the swell of your cheek and the turn of
your leg. He knew the track of your life-line on your palm and
exactly which kind of kiss caused your heart to *fandango* inside you.
He would love your body odour, fresh or sour, and the sweat he distilled upon your skin during love was the sweetest smell of all to
Giacomo Casanova.

Of course my own womb was scarcely functional when we met.
I would like to say that our first encounter was something extraordinary for him – as it was for me – but Casanova courted me in the
ways long proven.

He used his cat. This cat has become famous among the women
of Venice, though the men know nothing of it. In the old days
Casanova was adroit at climbing in and out of windows. But by the
time he chose me for his lover, in the very young spring of 1782, he
was no longer so flexible of spine and limb. He sent a messenger.

Women first became aware of the cat in their dreams: the rhythmic throbs of its purr infiltrated their sleep. Eventually they would
wake one night to find the cat sitting on their pillow, with its paw
gentle upon their throat. The stroking of the throat was one of
Casanova's own signature gestures. The organ of ingestion was loved
by Casanova, who adored food and adored watching women eat.

For him, anyway, a throat was an amatory part, and one of his favourites.

The woman would not know that yet. The eyes of the cat would unnerve her. She could no longer stay in bed. She would become suffused with unbearable heat and sexual electricity. If she had a lover or a husband, she would turn to him. Thinking that she wanted attention, he would shrink from her in pretended sleep. For Casanova was always meticulous in his research. When a new affair was the talk of Florian, he smiled to himself. A neglected wife or lover awaited him, whether she knew it or not.

She would run feverishly down to the kitchen for wine or water, or to the canal, for air. There she would find Casanova waiting for her: Casanova would sweep her onto the kitchen table or into his waiting gondola, where they would shed their clothes like snake-skins, writhing in the dark. They would talk for hours in the tender intermissions, and she would return to her bed, happier than when she had left it. She might never see him again, or she might; she would know when the cat came to her in her dreams. Or she might find herself purring, and know that he was nearby, or ready for her. On summer nights, she might wake to hear Casanova's feline violin below her window and turn to find the cat looking into her eyes.

Sometimes the cat delivered love letters tucked in his velvet collar – charming leaves of paper in Casanova's clear hand, notes that sang like his violin. These notes gave times and places for assignations, the more risky, complicated and difficult the better.

As I have explained, I myself must have been chosen by number. He would never tell me which one. Was I, perhaps, the seventh convent girl to cross his path on the seventh day of the seventh month? Did my birthday or the hour of my conception run on a ley-line towards his bed? Was it my tough wit? (He would later explain to me that intelligence had become the medium that his blunted senses needed to enter into play in these depleted days of his middle age. In the old days, a pretty face or even a shapely elbow would have secured a hearty performance.) So it could have been my tongue, which was already sharpened on the tears of my sister, Sofia. Or was it something in my future – a dream, a child, a lover – that made me the *piatto del giorno* on May 1st 1782 for this hungry man?

In view of what happened afterwards, I think that this last may have been the case: I was chosen for the future I already contained inside me. But, knowing Casanova, it could have equally been my eyes, or my hands, or it could have been the way I ate *torta al cioccolato*. The performance with the girl in the doorway – was it a gentle education for me? At the time I thought I would never know. Indeed, even now, I truly know only what happened to me, that night I drank *fragolino* for the first time and took the bath that would become even more sinful than I had planned.

I had taken precautions. If I was to be discovered, I had reasoned, it would be through the door, and by my mother or my sister. I made sure the door was barred and bolted after the maid had filled the bath with water. The maid warned me, as she left, that my namesake, Saint Cecilia, had been boiled alive in her bath as a punishment for her wilful nature. How many times had I heard this? Through the steam and the candlelight, the maid looked insubstantial, like an annunciating angel. But she gave me a very earthy smile as I lifted my nightdress over my head and unloosed the sheaf of my hair with a subtle thud against my naked back. This was followed by a little nod, acknowledging my maturing body. Then she was gone.

It grew quiet. I entered the bath, sipped the *fragolino* from a crystal glass, and dipped the cake into it. The image of Saint Cecilia, thrashing like a lobster, faded, and I sank deeper into the water. I watched the candlelight posturing on the walls, like the warm ghosts of the watery reflections that keep us company by day in Venice. I assumed my Botticelli pose, a swag of my hair in my hand. The appearance of the cat, through the window, took me by surprise. I watched as he approached me, sat by the edge of the bath, and reached towards my throat with a soft paw. I am a lover of cats. I let him stroke me. Then I heard the violin.

To this day I cannot resist a violin. That night, the *fragolino* fluttered in my blood, heated by the steaming bath water. The window was big enough for me to climb through. Still wet, still naked, still streaked with chocolate and with *fragolino* sticky on my chin, I dropped from the window-sill into strong arms. The *fragolino* had made me drowsy – I must have been a dead weight for him – but, big man that he was, he swept me easily under his cloak, through our courtyard and water-gate and into the gondola. I felt the lurch as we left dry land together. I smelt his breath in the darkness: garlic, cinnamon and *prosecco*. I felt the hairs of his wrists on my back, and his cool porcelain buttons against my wet breasts.

All Venetian gondolas are black, by decree. In the extravagant days of our early splendour, they were every colour, darting like birds of paradise across the Grand Canal. Later, sumptuary laws had stripped them of their vivacity. But that was merely on the outside. Even the Inquisition could not penetrate the opulent secrecy of the *felze*, the surprisingly commodious cabin perched on the top of the boat. Inside Casanova's gondola, where the moonlight leaked in through the *felze*'s black curtains, there was refulgence of crimson velvet and purple satin. I distinguished a low divan, draped with a coverlet of squirrel fur. Onto this, he laid me tenderly as an egg. I looked up and saw Casanova's face. He kissed both my eyes, and both my feet. He laid his lips on mine, which fell open. After a long time, he drew away. His eyes never left mine while I watched him undress. I saw thighs and elbows emerging from brocade and velvet. I saw the unpeeling of stockings. I saw lace and linen discarded. When it was done, he kneeled in front of me, and reached for my hand, which he placed between his legs. My fingers curled around him and my thumb rested at the tip, where it seemed to belong.

'Saint Cecilia,' he said, his eyes swimming with tenderness, 'still hot from her boiling bath. My beautiful little martyr, you are about to make a more gentle sacrifice.'

He lowered his head but kept his eyes fixed upon mine. I kept my hand upon him while he licked the chocolate from my face, and the droplets of bath-water from my shoulders. He did not lose sight of my face for a second. I held my breath and felt the hot nudge of his tongue upon my ribs. I was not frightened. I was only afraid I might die of excitement before it was over. He bent to kiss my belly, my breasts and my throat, where he lingered a moment. When he moved up to my mouth, he whispered into it, 'Yes?'

Yes. I may have said it aloud. I cannot tell you if I did.

That first time was silent, apart from my small cries, and finally, his. Then he blew quick puffs of cool breath over my efflorescent face and neck until I stopped trembling and could hear above the noise of my heart.

The second time, he took inventory of my body. How grateful were his appreciations of my throat, my fingers, my breasts and my thighs! How grateful to my ear were those unfamiliar words: *beautiful*, *exquisite*, *adorable*! My feet were large, but in Casanova's fingers they felt such little delicate china ones, little whispers of white skin and coral enamel. He found reasons to love even the parts of myself I disliked: my long arms and legs – 'See they were built to be wrapped around a man!' He told me things about my face I did not know before: about the conch-shell curve of my closed eyelids, the cat-like triangle of my jaw, the pomegranate-seed translucency of my lips and the interplay of the Tiziano reds and Tintoretto browns in my hair.

'And you have Aventurine eyes, Cecilia,' he told me, finally. I thought of the goblets in my parents' *palazzo*: glistening brown Murano glass flecked with gold. *Aventurine eyes, that's what I have*, I told myself.

I had been addicted to beauty since I learnt, precociously, to distinguish one colour from another. Remember the ravishing green caterpillars! Now it occurred to me that beauty might also be found in my very own person. I held up my much-praised hand to the moonlight – yes! It was lovely! Casanova seized it and kissed it softly from fingertip to wrist, punctuating each touch of his lips with a new and more subtle compliment. Now he praised my unabashed curiosity and my instinctive skills in giving pleasure by accepting it. I was absorbent as muslin to this downpour of compliments.

Hours later, when we had poled to San Vio, and lay throbbing like lizards in the moonlight, I asked, 'Why me? How do you know me? Why did you want me?' I was still greedy for extravagant tributes and endearments. After that night I always would be.

But now Casanova took my hand and replied, very seriously, 'Does it matter, now? Didn't you find love a good thing, Cecilia? Must you question where it came from?'

My curiosity was not to be repressed. 'But why me? Was it because I was a virgin?'

'It's true that virgins are a delicacy, and that I love to pluck the first fruits. But then I have also loved brides-to-be, with their wombs ready in happy agitation, and even women with their bellies already swollen with a little passenger, which means that it's the safest thing in the world. But in your case, let us say that I saw you. And that it was you who seduced *me* in that moment. And because you were difficult to obtain. For me, love gains in strength when I see that the conquest will cost me an effort.'

'Do you ever fail?' I found myself hoping that he did.

'I prefer to relegate the possibility of failure to the category of impossibilities,' he said, with a flourish of his fingers. 'But yes,' he added, with his hand clenched in his lap, 'it has happened. It happens.'

He ran a gentle finger over my eyelids and kissed my nose. I thought about the violin, the cat, the waiting gondola, his foreknowledge of my bath via the complicity of the maid. I thought about the performance in the doorway. It was more attention than I had received in my whole life.

'I'm glad that you did not fail. I felt it very strongly. Something happened inside me.'

'Yes, I know it did, my soul.'

'But I loved it. I would like to do it again.'

'Yes, I know you would, Cecilia,' he said, and he stroked my throat down to my breasts. His fingers swam gently around my nipples. I writhed on the rug and he smiled. 'But my steed is presently resting in his stable.' He pointed at his depleted organ upon its bed of damp hair. I had never seen anything so fascinating. I could have gazed at it for hours. However, Casanova gently raised my eyes to his, with a handful of my hair. We looked each other fully in the face. 'This intermission is a good thing,' he continued, 'because it means we have time to talk. Talking is in many ways the best part of the thing.'

'But I can *talk* to anyone. I can talk to my *sister*.'

'You and I have the privilege of talking in a special way together. We can describe the pleasures we have just enjoyed. I believe that I can feel myself stirring again when I remember them. We can describe what we want, which will bring fire to our desires, and then we can make our wishes come to life.'

Outside the gondola, the moonlight wavered over the water and the pearly domes of Santa Maria della Salute. And inside I groomed the steed. Casanova talked in tongues to every part of me. Later, he asked me about my dreams. When I told him I wanted to be an artist, he stretched supine, opened his arms, and said, 'Paint me.'

'I have no brush.'

'Then use your tongue, Saint Cecilia, patroness of all musical instruments, and inventor, I believe, of the organ.'

Such confidence he had in his body! He showed no self-consciousness about the flowing sweat I licked up and the crepy crevices into which I, tentatively at first, but with increasing enthusiasm, inserted my tongue. He let me investigate all the little pouches of loose skin that hung at the base of his spine, the neat yellowed toenails, his sweet, tired hair-fringed nipples, the salty hollows under his arms. He did not stop me. I was welcome to everything. Where mere inquisitiveness might have stopped, a fervent new instinct took me further. For this kind body, author of such happiness in me that my skin now hummed with delight, I began to feel something I had not known before: a desire to *give* that same kind of pleasure myself. Casanova understood my epiphany the moment I did. He opened his eyes wide, grateful as a baby looking up at its mother before it takes the breast.

'I knew it!' he said, and turned me gently upon my back again.

The third time, when he suddenly withdrew and released his joy upon the well of my stomach, he traced a word in the drying stickiness. I realised that he had done this each time, but only now was I sufficiently composed to question him.

'What word is that?' I asked, straining my neck to try to read it.

'It is the word that I have spilled on you. The Creative Word. The Procreative Word. My Word.'

'I don't understand.'

'It's part of the poetry of life. God's Word created the world. Man's Word, this effervescing liquid that gushes out of us in our joyful congress, this makes the babies to repopulate God's world. For this reason, I spill it outside you, because, at this moment, we have no need of more Cecilias. This one in my arms is sufficient joy for me. We have other contrivances at our disposal, too, to keep our love to ourselves.'

Then he showed me a little device which he called 'my English Overcoat'. He explained that this pale pink transparent pouch fitted over the steed in its rampant state. Fastened with a satin ribbon at the hilt, it would capture the Word as it threw itself inside me.

'And we have this!' From a leather pouch he produced a small golden ball, shining like a firelit mirror. He warmed it in his palms for a moment, and then parted my legs and pushed it gently inside me. When he removed his fingers, without the ball, I could not feel it inside me at all.

'Why . . . Where's it gone?'

'It's deep inside you. When we use this ball the Word is dazzled by the gold, and forgets about its duties in your womb.'

I think we slept. Yes, we must have done so, for I remember waking and turning to him. It was the golden bells of Venice that tore us from each other in the end. Entwined like a pair of eels, fastened lip to lip and thigh to thigh, we heard the *mattutin* strike an hour before sunrise. Then, it seemed mere seconds later, *marangona* of San Marco intoned the dawn, calling people less privileged than ourselves to work. When it was nearly light, Casanova walked me home. We lurched a little. We were drunk with copulation, reeling with it, loose-limbed under its tooth-numbing influence. We passed through the streets where people stood muttering their morning prayers in front of shrines in tattered walls, pushing shabby flowers through the grilles, which framed paintings and small sculptures of the Virgin. Automatically, I curtsied as we passed. Each time, Casanova kissed the top of my head. 'My little saint!'

We arrived at the Campiello Santa Maria Nova at Miracoli, the street entrance to my home, and I wondered what would happen next. But Casanova had planned, in what I was to learn was his

meticulous way, every moment of our encounter, including the final
one, in which I, wrapped in his cloak, was to creep into the house
behind the sleepy servants arriving to make the fires. He delighted
in every detail of our night, including this final triumph of discretion. He, of course, already knew which was my room in our
palazzo, and the chamber of every other creature who dwelled in it
too.

'Will we be together again?' I whispered at the last moment. I
had no conception of modesty or coquetry. My new-found needs
were simple, and simple to express.

Casanova understood. He took responsibility for the desires he
had aroused; he knew their implacable nature. 'Do not worry. My
flesh will suffer too, Saint Cecilia, without yours. I have only the
beauty of Venice to comfort me until I can see you again.'

That, I was to find, was a lie, but like all Casanova's lies, it was a
beautiful and practical and necessary one.

Casanova was a true son of Venice in this. La Serenissima, as we
Venetians call our city, is as beautiful and practical as a peacock's tail:
her beauty is serviceable. It's a beauty that seduces people to
admire, respect – and to pay. Our beautiful Venetian *palazzi* are
pragmatic. My family's little *palazzo*, which now stood in front of us,
was a microcosm of those vast airy dwellings wading on the edges of
the Grand Canal. Like them, beneath the decadent, useless loveli-
ness of its facade was a kind of private manufactory, a living
creature, efficient as a battleship, economical as a convent.

So our *palazzo* consisted of four floors, starting with a *magazzino*,
or warehouse, at water level where my father's goods came in and
out at the landing stage on the canal. Above this was a low-ceilinged
mezzanino floor where his clerks slaved over the ledgers and the
precious articles were stored away from the damp depredations of
acqua alta. Above this was the *piano nobile*, which housed the frescoed

reception rooms and large, light bedrooms of my family. Finally, beneath the roof, the servants had their hot, high domain. The *palazzi* on the Grand Canal often had two *piani nobili*, one for public and one for private use. My family could afford such a *palazzo*, but our position, on a distant and relatively lowly limb of the noble Cornaro family tree, would have rendered that extra *piano nobile* ostentatious, something my father would never countenance.

Even before I met Casanova, I had claimed an eccentricity in my family's home. I had moved from my grand bedroom on the *piano nobile* to a large room on the lower *mezzanino* floor, just a few feet above the garden. There had been no little difficulty about it, but in the end my family consented. Perhaps it would be more truthful to say that I coerced them. After my first request was rejected, I spent hours of the night pacing the creaking floorboards of the *piano nobile*. I could not sleep, I told my parents, when they came with candles to take me back to bed. I told them that I dreamt monstrosities, and sometimes I hallucinated. I told them that I saw *pantegane*, huge water rats, swarming in front of me. Some nights I ran, as if flying over their soft pointy heads, into my parents' bedroom, where I would bite my mother's toes through the coverlet to wake her up. Still, they would not let me live downstairs.

I escalated my campaign. I told them that the *piano nobile* was most certainly haunted – that palpable evil spirits glided through its corridors at night. I even drew a few such horrors to show them. My sketches, which I still have, showed a precocious talent for obscenity. Many and bulbous were the extremities of my monsters, and I borrowed the palette of Tintoretto's apocalypses to colour their bruised and scaly flesh.

'She might show them at the convent,' my mother said to my father, in terrified whispers. 'Don't let Sofia see them.'

I told my parents that I was uniquely sensitive to these manifestations for they sought me out. After this, I was forced to submit to the ministrations of an exorcising priest. I endured his mumbling rites and prodding fingers with all the appearance of touching and hopeful acquiescence but the next night I was screaming in the corridors again. In the end, I told my parents that it had come to me in a dream that I would be safe from the floating spirits on the *mezzanino*, closer to the ground. I saw my mother clutch my father's arm; I concealed a smile as I watched their tired eyes meet over my head. A servant was sent for. The best room on the *mezzanino*, looking over the courtyard garden on one side and over the church of Miracoli on the other, was lime-washed and cleaned for me and my small chest of possessions carried down there. My victory was worth all the sleepless nights. Finally, I had my own little kingdom where I might draw and read all night if I wished. I knew that no one would hear me.

This was how Casanova had managed to find me and to catch me in his arms. I had just a few feet to drop into the garden, and no one to watch me. When he brought me back, I was able to return to my room without passing the chambers of my parents or my sister.

I was thirteen years old, and I had already claimed my privacy and my liberty. Now, in one night with Casanova, I had glimpsed the kind of happiness Venice offered her true children. I had taken my place in the happy city. I had no regrets for the innocence I left behind. My self-confidence and happiness were insuperable. It would be a long time before anyone made me realise that this feeling could be taken away from me.

In my room, that important morning, I stood in front of my mirror and saw that my body was entirely unmarked by its great and new experiences. Casanova had been so gentle. I wondered if the golden ball was still inside me. I investigated and decided that it probably was not. I smelt the Word on my fingers, smiled to myself, and rubbed it behind my ears. There was no time to go to bed. I dressed. I went to the convent, I studied the lives of two minor saints and three irregular French verbs, I came home, I ate, or at least the girl whose body I inhabited did so. My prim little class-mates, with their sensitive pubescent noses, must have scented something corrupted in me, for that day they avoided me more than usual. I had never been popular: my tongue was too mordant and my behaviour too erratic. But today they shunned me as if I were a Turk.

I took no notice. I myself was somewhere else, a good place. I passed the day in the company of my re-lived pleasures, each rec-ollection a wave of sensation crashing against my skin. I was over-sensitive to light, and to noise. I shrank back from the world and retreated inside my memories. There was almost too much to remember, of feeling, of taste, of words. So much of it had hap-pened in the dark that I had only to shut my eyes to re-enter the world of Casanova's gondola.

By the afternoon, when I returned home and to my mirror, my naked body had started to change again. Some slight bruising was marking my thighs. And my chin flaked, revealing tender shiny skin underneath; Casanova's kisses, his saliva, the rasp of his cheeks, the buffeting of his hips, had marked me after all.

By that night I was anxious. I had been awake for too many hours. My eyes felt peppery. Was I to know just once what it was to be the *morosa* of Casanova? Would I see him again? He had made many declarations, but no promises and no appointment. I remem-bered the doll-girl in the doorway. I wondered if she had seen him again. Perhaps she was with him that minute! I sniffed my bottle of *fragolino* and was swept with lust, and a sudden pain of a colour and quality I had never known before: erotic jealousy. I took my bath again, hoping childishly for the same results. The maid would not meet my eye as she left the room. When she had gone, I waited naked by the window. The water droplets cooled and dried on my skin, which became prickly with anticipation. Still, he did not come. Finally I went to bed, exhausted by disappointment.

But at midnight, cradling the *fragolino* bottle between my thighs, I heard the violin again. It was not easy for him, but for the entire duration of our time together Casanova would never again let me be lonely or insecure for him. When he saw how I hungered for them he would never willingly deprive me of a compliment, a caress or an endearment. He would never leave me wondering where I stood in his heart.

It was the same that second night, but more so. Because I had lost him, albeit for a day, I treasured him more.

Every morning, we were exhausted but not satisfied. Each night just taught us better how to love each other. Any night I did not spend with him was a mortification of my flesh.

And every evening, before I fell into his arms, I took my bath.

In it, like Saint Cecilia, I sang.

The Story of
Saint Cecilia

FROM AN *AGIOGRAFIA* (*LIVES OF THE SAINTS*), DATED 1780,
FOUND IN THE MARCIANA LIBRARY, VENICE.

EDITOR'S NOTE: *This edition is annotated with a variety of obscene sketches in colour. It has been put forward that the faces, remarkable for the sensuous pallor of the complexions and the unmistakably concupiscent lustre of the eyes, bear a marked similarity to the work of the famous Venetian portrait painter, Cecilia Cornaro, but this theory remains unsubstantiated.*

Saint Cecilia was a Roman noblewoman who lived in the third century of our millennium, under the reign of the Emperor Alexander Severus. Her parents, secret Christians, brought her up in their faith, and from childhood she was exceptionally devout. She was never without a copy of the Gospel concealed in the folds of her robe, no matter how uncomfortable it made her.

After a certain conversation with her mother, Cecilia made a secret vow of chastity. From that moment, she also shunned all the pleasures and vanities of the world. Instead, she devoted her considerable musical skills to the glory of God. She sang hymns of her own composition with such ravishing melodies that the angels descended from Paradise to hear her, and joined their voices with hers. She made herself mistress of every musical instrument they gave her. But she could find none noble enough to express the heavenly harmonies which flooded her soul. To relieve that frustration, Cecilia invented the organ.

When she was sixteen, Cecilia's parents married her to Valerian. He was young, virtuous, rich and aristocratic. His only defect – but it was a large one – was that he still practised the old heathen faith.

Cecilia accepted the choice of her parents. But inside her wedding robes, as she walked to the temple, her breasts chafed against a coarse hair-chemise of penance, smarting like the bites of a thousand caterpillars. Cecilia renewed her vow of chastity, imploring God to help her keep it.

At a certain moment on their wedding night, Cecilia told Valerian that her guardian angel, who fluttered constantly above her, required her to reserve her body for God. Valerian was instantly converted by her piety, empowered to see the angel, and to respect her vow of chastity.

Valerian soon introduced his brother Tiburtius to the true faith. Then all three went about together doing good deeds, including the honorable burials of Christian martyrs.

At this time, the Emperor was absent from Rome. A wicked prefect, Almachius, had taken charge of the State. He summoned the three young people to him, and forbade them to continue their public practices of Christian charity. They could not accede. The two brothers were thrown into prison, where they converted their guard. When the brothers refused to take part in the sacrifice to Jupiter, they were executed.

Poor Cecilia washed their bodies with her tears. Then she wrapped them in her own robes and buried them together in the cemetery of Calixtus.

Prefect Almachius now called for Cecilia, and commanded her to make sacrifice to the old gods, threatening appalling tortures if she failed to comply. She stood before him, pale, silent, doomed. The court wept to see such youth and beauty so stubborn and in such danger. She converted forty souls on the spot.

Almachius was enraged to see his court turning Christian under Cecilia's charms. He commanded that she should be carried back to her own house and plunged in a bath of boiling water. But for Cecilia the scalding liquid was as spring water.

So Almachius sent an executioner to decapitate her with a sword. But at the sight of her, the executioner's hand trembled. He struck her three times, clumsily, in the neck and breast. It was enough to mutilate but not to kill her. Cecilia took three days in dying, during which time she prayed and distributed her possessions to the poor. She sang sweet hymns until the moment she expired.

2

Bela coa, trista cavala.

Women with long hair can go either way.

Venetian proverb

'**P**aint me,' he had said. Well, I did. Many times, at first, with chocolate and *fragolino*. With peach juice, with crushed rose petals, with conserved plums from France, with dream-dusted jellies from Turkey, with white truffles from Piedmont, with Lucca oil, with Four Thieves vinegar, with honeyed almond orgeat, with plump opalescent oysters from the lagoon. These last we exchanged from one mouth to another. The saliva of a lover was the best sauce for an oyster, Casanova always said, and the act of exchange was rendered yet more delicious by its comedy.

I asked, as he fed me, 'But isn't it cruel to eat them? Aren't they alive?'

He licked a droplet of the salty nectar from my lip. 'Oh my darling, do not worry. They do not feel anything. They are sleeping.'

Once, I baptised him with water from my sister's bath.

'Where are you going with that?' screamed Sofia, attempting to cover herself when I burst in upon her and dipped my phial into the water.

'To Santa Maria Formosa, to the gargoyle, so his ghost can know your smell when he comes hunting through the city for virgin blood,' I told her, grinning implacably, holding the dripping bottle aloft. 'The expiring remnants of your virtue will stain his bloody teeth.' I left the *palazzo* with her cries echoing in the shuttered corridors. Above me, I heard the footsteps of my mother, hastening to discover what had befallen her pet, doubting not that it was at my hands, whatever it was.

Casanova enjoyed the story along with the bath water. '*Conversazione*,' he murmured, nuzzling my shoulder. 'But Cecilia, don't mistake a *lingua biforcuta* for wit. A barbed tongue is a sorry substitute.'

We lay naked within the close-lipped curtains of the gondola for hours, in between what he liked to call 'our delicious combats'. What sweet war we waged every night! We threw our bodies against each other, with all our strength. Once, when I reached for my chemise afterwards, he stayed my hand.

'There's no need to be ashamed of your body, Cecilia. Look at the cat – how he stretches and rolls, and enjoys his every muscle. Look at the dogs in the street: have you never envied the way they can lay their private organs upon the cool stones of the pavement when the sun roasts their fur? Don't you think they enjoy it? Why should we deny ourselves the pleasures of the beasts? Simply because we think we are better than they are?'

Casanova insisted we should accept our bodies the way the animals do, not judge them harshly or harass ourselves for the things they want and the imagined embarrassments they cause. He was not surprised to find indigenous erotic sapience in a thirteen-year-old girl. He found it natural.

He kept, in the gondola, a certain little book by Pietro Aretino, which demonstrated, in verse and illustration, the thirty-four ways in which we humans are more fortunate than animals. 'In the thirty-fifth, as you see, we are like the beasts,' said Casanova, pointing to a picture.

I lay on my stomach, gazing at each picture, aroused but also intrigued by the way the bodies were depicted upon the page. Aretino's protagonists were fine, vigorous beasts. I traced the fleshly curvatures and protuberances with my finger, pausing here and there.

While I did so, Casanova, smoothing my hair, told me about the supple young Jewess, Leah, daughter of his landlord in Ancona. He had tempted her with goose-liver and old Muscat from Cyprus, but what finally drew her to his bed was this very volume of Aretino. On the pretext of bringing him his hot chocolate each morning, she spent hours in his room. She induced him to discuss every picture in detail until he was palpitating with scarcely manageable lusts. Later, he had spied upon her trying out the positions with her would-be lover, without actually coming to the natural conclusion. Still a technical virgin, she had memorised every page.

I pushed the book aside and stretched luxuriously. I closed my eyes and let Aretino's images gyrate across my mind. With my face pressed against the squirrel fur, I felt Casanova lie down behind me and take me in his arms. He caressed me from my forehead to my flanks in long gentle strokes. Then he lifted my hair and fastened his warm mouth to the back of my neck like a mollusc, and sucked gently until I whimpered and revolved in his arms to face him.

'Even without art,' Casanova said, looking down on me with a smile, 'we have one additional pleasure. We can pleasure ourselves. A book like Aretino's can help. Perhaps you already know. Leah told me that all girls do that, though secretly, before they are married.'

Then Casanova taught me how to love myself, as expertly as he loved me.

When I was faint and crimson with my own pleasures, he stayed my hand. And he recited folio seventeen of Aretino softly in my ear as he covered me again with his body and moved sweetly over and inside me.

Afterwards, Casanova warned me against practising my new skill excessively or exclusively. 'It doesn't work well, Cecilia, don't rely on it. It may seem to relieve the pains of the loins for a brief moment. But it offends Nature and she takes her revenge by doubling the irritations of your desires.'

Night after night, while we rested from our lovemaking, Casanova fed me with more memories, washed me with happy, remembering tears. He loved to stroke my hair, his fingers nosing through the thick curtain to my scalp, which he massaged with firm strokes before gently raking all the way down to my waist, where the curls turned into damp tendrils. One night, while he hypnotised me with these caresses, he told me of Andriana Foscarini, whom he had loved so much and so hopelessly that he had *eaten* her hair, having first ground it to a powder, which he then worked into a pastille with sugar, flavoured with angelica and vanilla. He had sucked the blood from her finger, when she pricked it with a pin. She asked him to spit the blood into a handkerchief, but he had swallowed it like a cannibal. That was Corfu, 1745, nearly four decades earlier, when he was just twenty years old.

He told me about his own first complete act of physical love, a double act, with two sisters, Marta and Nanetta, in their attic bedroom at San Samuele. Later that night, as our gondola rocked in a little gasp of wind, soft and sudden as a cat's sneeze, he told me I reminded him of little Marcolina, a Venetian girl. She was a jewel: intelligent, mischievous, her long hair hanging in adorable ringlets like a mermaid's. Marcolina was both insatiable and omnivorous. She had promised Casanova never to be jealous of his other mistresses – provided that he let her sleep with them too. With an inexhaustible appetite for her own kind, Marcolina had given him inestimable pleasures, both in the witnessing and the sharing. Marcolina delighted, as he did, in initiating virgins. She raped them in a way that made them eternally grateful for the joy they had received. She tested every woman she met, with the petticoat password, a Florentine kiss, the cheek pinched between the thumb and third finger during osculation. At seventeen, when Casanova met her, she had already initiated more than three hundred girl sweethearts. Of men, the indefatigable Marcolina had not kept count.

I interrupted his story, 'So how can I remind you of her? You are my only lover, and I have never loved a woman.'

'I suppose it's your wit. And your hair. And the fact that you are Venetian. You know, I have not loved so many Venetian women. I was starved of them for years upon end when I was in exile.'

'But did Marcolina want to be an artist, as I do?'

'No, she confined her artistry to the bedroom. There she was a masterpiece. As you are. But you, Cecilia Cornaro, also have masterpieces inside you, waiting to be painted.'

The next day Casanova brought me a small wooden easel, a palette, a handful of graphite pencils, a stretched canvas and five slim paint-brushes. Like a magician, he flung open a wooden box, which was his final gift. Inside lay twenty-seven fat little bladders of paint pigments already ground and mixed with poppy oil. He lifted one out and pierced it with a fingernail. It yielded with a faint sigh. A droplet of vivid purple bled out. Together we bent over the box to inhale its rich vapour. There was never such a pungent perfume in the world, I tell you, as those first paints I owned.

It was a limpid night. The water breathed evenly under us, as if asleep. We set up the easel in the gondola under the light of a silver candelabra. With shaking hands I squeezed more droplets of colour upon the pristine palette and clipped the gallipot of oil to the edge of it; that little click sounded like a resounding kiss to me. I picked up a pencil and let my hand hover over the canvas, delaying my gratification for precious seconds.

'What shall it be, my darling?' asked Casanova. 'You see, I am waiting in utter confidence to be surprised by your genius.'

'It will be a portrait, of course,' I said grandly. 'It will *always* be portraits.'

He seized my left hand and kissed it deferentially, as if I were already a famous artist he scarcely dared approach. '*Ecco la qua!* Cecilia Cornaro! Painter of Faces.'

'But I have everything to learn.'

'It's inside you already, my darling. You must simply paint as you make love, which you do by instinct. And when you paint your subjects you must always imagine them naked under their clothes. Follow the imagined curves of their bodies with the devotion of a lover. If you become aroused by this, all the better. You will paint your desire into the picture. What portraits they shall be!'

'Nude portraits of lords and ladies, even? No! I don't believe you!'

'I have not finished . . . Then, when you have created the naked body, you must clothe it in close-fitting luxury. Be attentive to every enhancing detail. Now you are no longer the lover, you are the tailor, the *confidante* of all their bodily secrets. You must hide any pendulous flesh. Veil wrinkled necks in cobwebs of lace. Then, when you have finished concealing what must be hidden, then dazzle them with their own greatness! Give them clothes and jewels just a little better than those they can afford. If they wear satin, turn it into silk *Gros de Tours* with threads of silver. If they wear a golden bracelet, stud it with rubies.'

'Even though there are no rubies?'

'No one will criticise you for little inaccuracies like this.'

'Why not?'

'The portrait painter is the architect of their immortality! He – or she – does not need to be accurate as to the facts of his sitters, but he needs to pay attention to their *aspirations*.'

'Will they try to tell me what to do?' I imagined myself painting a doge, mindful of his dignity, or a fussy matron.

'Probably. But only little things. They know very little, and they are frightened of being ugly to the future. So when they ask you to add something to the portrait – an extra plume of hair, a little life to the cheeks – then you must give a little smile that implies that this is indeed the best news you have heard all day, and that you were simply waiting for permission to do so.'

'What if I find them repulsive? What if I don't like them?'

'Hated skin is your best training ground, as it's the hardest thing to paint. Paint lots of people you hate. Or dislike. When you have mastered that, you will know that you can paint anyone.'

Where he had learnt all this wisdom I never knew, unless it was from his brother, Francesco, who was an artist. They were not close, but they kept an eye on each other, if only to monitor that one had not superseded the other in material success. Somehow Casanova knew just when Francesco was prospering enough to hire his own colour-man to grind the paint pigments for him and mix them, drop by drop, with oil. And he knew when times were hard for Francesco, who had then to force the colour-man into hard labour, so that the excess pigments could be sold at a profit to more successful artists.

Casanova, of course, was my first portrait.

I remember grasping the brush and dropping the graphite pencil, which rolled away, pursued by the cat. I remember holding my breath until Casanova reminded me of the necessity to respire. I remember the first tiny slap of paint against the canvas and the moment the shape of his face took on the lines that I loved so well.

I remember the mixing of the browns to make his eyes. I remember the moment when I added the scintilla of humanity, the lustre, to the pupils. I remember how many attempts it took to shape his lips. Meanwhile I was learning other, more unusual skills. It was my fate to learn to paint afloat upon the water: the gondola was always in motion when I worked. I soon found a painting rhythm to compensate for the roll of the water, as I had for making love. My paintbrush would dip and meet the rising canvas just at the right moment.

I remember how often the painting of that portrait was interrupted. I would start purring in my throat, involuntarily, and the signal would be observed. Casanova's pose would dissolve. The few inches between us became an impossible perspective, and we fell upon each other. Or something about the way I stroked the paint with the brush aroused him, and I would be swept onto the squirrel-fur rug. The painting was accidentally knocked to the floor a hundred times.

It was a night-time portrait. I never saw Casanova during the day in those early times. But when it was finished, my portrait brought to light rather too much of the truth. The eyes were too large, and the mouth looked too hungry. The hands were too big. I was not yet skilful enough to hide the death of his hopes written on the sadness of his skin. I had wanted to paint him as I loved him, immortally, but I had not yet the cunning or the competence to do so. I painted him far too mortal. He flinched when I first allowed him to see it. But he recovered himself in an instant, and from somewhere deep inside the well of his tenderness he even extracted a compliment for me.

'Cecilia, you have painted a noble funerary mask for me. Now it's ready, whenever I need it.

'In fact,' he said, peering at it bravely, 'it's very glamorous.'

'Don't flatter me. Glamorous? You look like a ghoul. Forgive me!'

'It is glamorous, because death is glamorous. And death is the reason for all portraits in the end.'

'Why? What do you mean?'

'Portraits are mementoes of people who have passed through this life. When they die, their bodies decompose in the grave but their portraits continue to breathe as beautiful as life on the walls of the houses where they once lived. That portrait is their immortality. That's why the best portrait painters are rich and famous – people will pay anything to live forever.'

I pictured people, centuries ahead, gazing at my portrait of Casanova. I saw them lean closer, talk to each other, wave their fingers at it authoritatively, as I had seen people do in front of the masterpieces in our Venetian churches. I already hungered for their attention and their approbation, both for my lover and for my work.

'How can I please them?' I asked. 'Should I try to paint sitters whom they will love to gaze at?'

'That is your entire work. To make the audience curious, and regretful that they could never know this vanished soul in the flesh.'

'I should paint people so that the future will want to make love to them?'

'If you can do that, Cecilia, you will conquer the world.'

'But could anyone ever . . .?'

'It can be done. A portrait *can* arouse the senses just as Aretino's engravings do, even without showing the act of love. I remember a church in Madrid where there was a painting of the Virgin suckling the Infant Jesus. Her bare breast was exquisitely beautiful. That church was stuffed with golden candelabra and other pious donations from the aristocracy. At the door there was always a quantity of carriages and even a soldier with a bayonet to forfend quarrels among the coachmen who were constantly arriving and leaving. There was not a nobleman in the town who could pass the chapel without going to pay his respects, as he would say, to the Blessed

Virgin. Since I knew men, this devotion did not surprise me. It was obvious that every man in the church was there to worship not the Madonna but the breast.'

'And was it very beautiful, the breast?'

'It was ravishing. I knelt down in front of it myself once. One felt the breast breathing. The nipple had not inserted itself entirely inside the mouth of the baby, so one saw the darker flesh around it, softly puckered up with tender pleasure, and damp with the exhalations of the little infant. The breast was not large, just enough to rest in your hand, but it was possible to feel your palm tingling at the thought.'

'You went there only once?'

'Just once. For a few weeks later a tragedy occurred. A young abate claimed that the breast had started to debauch his dreams. He had a handkerchief painted over it. After that, the church fell into neglect and poverty.'

'Did the breast act on your own dreams?'

'There were times when I imagined it pressed against my back as I lay in my bed at night. That breast gave me the most voluptuous pleasure I ever knew without a woman in my arms.

'Now, Cecilia, imagine a whole portrait like that! A man or a woman caught in the ecstasy of their desire, a face with love written on the very pores of the skin . . . Do you think you can paint that, Cecilia?'

No one but a Vampyre could want to make love to my first portrait of Casanova. It was an appalling painting. But it was a start. It was also a statement of love and a declaration of my own desires. That first portrait spawned many successors, each a little better than the one before. I dressed him up. I painted him as saint and sinner, as angel and mortal. Into those portraits I painted my preferences for men like Casanova. I framed and sealed them. I painted into those portraits my love of individuality, of novelty. I painted my Venetian nature: my longing for something that was alive and imperfect, and not divine and perfect. I painted it all into his face. Other women might not recognise Casanova in what I painted. I painted what Casanova was to me and I to him. This changed with each new portrait — and there would be hundreds of them — as we loved each other better, and longer.

I know now that Casanova was right. Every painter is a lover in this way. For your subject you feel an inexhaustible curiosity about the flare of the nostril or the shadow of an eyebrow. No one but a portrait painter or a lover bestows such compulsive attention upon another human being, and not even a lover can memorise each eyelash, each crease in the webbing of the lips, the tenebrous arch of each nostril the way the artist does. You are looking for something intangible, an essential elixir hidden in the flesh of the face. When you find it you must find a way to lure it to your brush.

Certain portraits of certain faces, portraits which have captured that voluptuous essence, can make you fall in love, or go wild with desire.

Now my future was laid out for me.

For that was the only kind of portrait I wanted to paint.

The Cat Speaks

After that, she was always with us at night, and for a long time hers was the only female smell he brought into the gondola.

The only human smell, that is. Because after that I lived with the stink of paint and pastels in my nostrils for months and then years to come. When they were not mating, she was always drawing something, or painting it. I wrinkled up my moist nose at first, but I learnt to like it, because it meant titbits and caresses for me. Cecilia Cornaro was a good species of female; she loved cats.

It seemed to me that she was not a bad painter. At first she copied everything, but soon she started to make additions. I noticed that her saints often had Casanova's face, and her Virgins looked quite a lot like she did. She did not bother much with the Christ-child. Then Casanova put a mirror in the gondola and after that she was forever posing like the Botticelli Venus, or Tiziano's redhead on the sofa.

She was always painting faces. I considered this natural. Humans are defective in their sensory perceptions. They are mostly quite insensitive to the mien and manners of the *body*, the smells, the songs of the blood. Faces are all they give each other, and therefore what they are. I have even heard them describe the act of begetting their hairless offspring as 'face-making'.

My own suave features made an impression on Cecilia, in fact. In this time, she made a copy of Biagio d'Antonio's Saint Cecilia, and there you will see me, squatting on my haunches while the poor lady is boiled in her bath and everyone weeps. I incline slightly towards my mistress, in three-quarter profile, and this delicate restraint on my part is full of an aching tenderness.

Have you ever noticed how often, in a painting, a cat lends its ironic subtlety to a scene? By its mere presence, a cat gives a commentary, adds dignity and humanity to the direst of poor hovels, and pathos to the ridiculous deaths of gentle saints. Dogs and lions do merely what dogs and lions do, but a *cat* – his every gesture is there to be read.

3

*La fortuna l'è na vaca: a chi la mostra el davanti e
a chi el dadrio.*

Fortune is like a cow: to some she shows her good side;
to others her backside.

VENETIAN PROVERB

In the gondola, I was an apt pupil. But at the convent, I performed without distinction those crowded days. I had no sleep. All day, during lessons, I scribbled on my books. I decorated the borders with increasingly skilful sketches of my lover's face, breast and other parts. I made passable copies of my favourite positions from Aretino. The nuns, observing these last, were too embarrassed to reprove me or to mention the abomination to my parents. But my *Lives of the Saints* was confiscated.

As convents went in those days, ours was of the better class. It was more than a repository for unwanted or unmarriageable patrician daughters. The Abbess, a Dandolo daughter, presided over her echoing chambers of supposed virgins with a resolute hand. Many of the pupils were novices or young nuns but Sofia and I were not destined for the veil: my father's wealth was more than enough to keep us and to provide us with dowries. So we lived at home and attended the convent six days a week. We sang, we recited, we embroidered on silk, we learnt a little French. More than that it was not thought necessary to educate a Venetian woman of the upper or middle class.

Anyway the real lessons were to be had upon the streets of Venice. That was where we convent girls learnt that our eyes were not made to read but to lure and fascinate, that our fingers were not to sew but to caress, that our mouths were not for grammar but for the manufacture of dazzling fleet-footed smiles. Venice taught us how to be enchantingly capricious, how to wear out our slippers dancing upon Istrian marble and mosaic of mock lapis, how to talk about our dreams so that men hungered to be inside them. The love of God, they taught us at the convent, was our worthiest aspiration. But outside on the street, from the ballads of the gondoliers and the paintings in shop windows, we learnt that the kind of love that was prized in Venice was that which tasted as sweet and lasted only as long as a kiss.

I hasten to add that boys learnt little more, unless they were destined to be scholars. It's not that we were a stupid city. It was simply that for us education was just another form of entertainment. Our heritage was re-enacted in picturesque ceremonies on the streets all year long, giving us a chance to dress up and perform like beautiful puppets. Our churches were a feast to the eye: who needed to *read* the Bible when its most picturesque stories were painted upon our walls for us in such gorgeous colours? It was not that we despised the written word – oh no! The regatta laureates, the poets who made verses to inscribe on ladies' fans, the sonneteers, all flourished in our happy city, but in this last century of our ornate glory Venice was no place to be serious or studious about anything. In Venice, books were sold by weight, like sugar.

So there was no instruction for me in what I needed to know about portraits, art and artists. By the time I met Casanova I was already steaming with frustration at my unwanted and helpless ignorance about the things to which I was irresistibly drawn. Before

I met him I would roam the churches, gazing at paintings. I looked at them so hard that they were imprinted upon my eyes and I could still see them with my lids closed. I learnt, without knowing their names, what colours made skin and where shadows must fall on draperies. I learnt which lustre on the forehead makes a saint saintly. I learnt all the lies you have paint to tell the truth: the unlikely yellow the artist must drop into a pearl white eye-ball to make the sunset warm a velvet mantle! I learnt that to be true to the depiction of the truth you do not paint the truth.

I learnt so much that I became a philosopher of painting – as remote from the real work as a philosopher is from real life. My hands ached from the absence of a paintbrush, and sometimes I dawdled in the artisans' streets, my nose twitching like a cat's at the smell of oil and artists' colours. Casanova had already changed all that: now I painted nearly every night. When I left Casanova in the dim light of morning, we locked up my box of paints and laid my canvas upon its side in a small trunk in the gondola. Casanova himself wiped the worst paint smudges off my face with a faded silk handkerchief. I finished cleaning myself at home, in my boiling bath.

It was not entirely satisfactory, my floating nocturnal art, and we both knew it. I was ready to progress and I needed access to a teacher. Casanova introduced me to a friend of his brother Francesco, the artist, who now lived in Dresden. He had irascible relationships with his brothers. Of Francesco, Casanova was dismissive as only a sibling can be. 'Impotent, my brother. Imagine it. His poor wife loves him anyway, so she does not allow herself to look for satisfaction elsewhere. It's very sad. And Francesco's not particularly potent in the studio, either. But he's very good at painting smoke. And he has the wit to hide what he can't paint under expert billows of the stuff. I would not apprentice you to him, Cecilia, but he has a friend, Antonio, who paints portraits. Antonio's still here in Venice. He will see you, tomorrow afternoon. Tell your mother you're to help the nuns decorate the church for a wedding. Will that serve to explain your absence for some hours?'

I nodded.

I could not concentrate on my saints that next morning. I pushed my finger down the page, unseeing. The hours struck as slowly as if the hands of the clock were silted up. When I was released I pounded across the city to San Vio, where Casanova was waiting for me, leaning against the well, lanky as a collapsed marionette. It was the first time I had seen him in the daylight. He turned to me a little diffidently: he knew how his brittle skin and the thin lines mapped out upon his face would be cruelly exposed in the sunshine. He saw me looking at them, took my hand and ran my finger down the furrow beside his mouth. 'Look, it's worn away with smiling since I found you, Cecilia.'

I replied truthfully, 'Every inch of you is dear to me.'

On the way to Antonio's studio I tore off my linen cap and balled up its ribbons in my fist. I thrust them into my pocket and shook my hair free. With my hair around me I felt less nervous. Casanova smoothed it behind me as we walked. Antonio's studio was in San Barnaba, the *quartiere* of the impoverished nobles whom we call the *Barnabotti*. Some of them eked out their tiny pensions by renting their great rooms to artists. We climbed the stairs to the *piano nobile*. I hesitated at the door, until Casanova gently pushed me ahead of him. The first thing I saw was, floor to ceiling, portraits, sketches and empty frames. Then I noticed an exotic confection of tall broken columns, stuffed birds and velvet draperies in a sort of cage at the back of the room, and a little throne upon a raised platform.

Antonio came forward, drying his hands. He was a small, fair and well-favoured man of about fifty, exquisitely dressed. 'Tools of the trade, you know,' he said negligently when Casanova complimented him on his frock-coat. 'They come here looking for style. If I look stylish, it helps them feel confident.' Casanova watched me with interest as he introduced me to Antonio. He needn't have worried. The smell of paint on his hands was alluring, but Antonio had none of Casanova's magnetism. For me, erotic love was simply Casanova. I had not yet learnt to look speculatively at other men.

Casanova did not need to tell me what to do. During that first visit, I stole one of Antonio's miniatures, pushing it into my pocket when he turned his back. I protected the delicate surface with my hovering thumb. It was a minor but skilful study of a little boy. Antonio was proud of it. I had seen that pride in the way he dropped it down with a dismissive gesture when I praised it. I would have done the same myself. During the week I made a work-manlike copy of it, careful to show promise but no more. On our next visit I produced the original and the copy with a blush and a sigh. At the end of my stammering confession I exclaimed, 'How I wish I could paint like you . . .' I allowed my words to trail off on a hopeless, plaintive note.

'Cecilia, I shall give you lessons!' was the reply that I had sought and now received.

Within two months I had learnt all that Casanova and Antonio had to teach me. Antonio, like Casanova, was good to me. When he saw that I would not embarrass him, he persuaded friends and clients to sit for me. Everyone in Venice, not just Casanova, loved a novelty. The clients were happy to give an hour to a pretty young prodigy and were surprised at the result. At first I would be delegated to paint the clothes, draperies, child or dog of the sitter while Antonio worked on the face. But disparities began to appear: the dresses, curtains, children or pets would look more interesting than their owners.

Soon clients were asking for me to execute the main work and I was delighted to accept. Antonio started to look sullen, but I was earning well from my afternoons in the studio. I shared the proceeds with Antonio, but my growing reputation was all my own. I used my real name, Cornaro, and no one was any the wiser. In those days Venice was over-run with both Cornaros and Cecilias. Meanwhile my own family, far across the Grand Canal at Miracoli, lived in quiet retirement. The latest novelties, such as young female painting prodigies, to sweep the happy city went unremarked at our modest table.

You can outgrow an art teacher, as I did. Even before I mastered the paintbrush I developed a style of my own, which was both realistic and expressive of invisible feelings. I had taken to heart Casanova's words: I wanted to paint people in the heat of their desires. I wanted them to look as if they might fall from the frame into the viewer's arms. I would arrive at the studio with baskets of ideas. My little trick was to surround my subjects with the sensual things they loved or which excited them: I painted women with their new-born babies, or with cold white wine upon their lips, soldiers sniffing sulphur, merchants fingering rich fabrics. In the gondola, I continued to paint Casanova, too, surrounded by almost over-ripe fruit, and a hint of my own presence in his life: a laden paintbrush, a piece of *torta al cioccolato*, or a droplet of peach juice on his chin.

Skin was my subject: pale skin, from skimmed-milk blue to yellow cream; vivid skin stained by the Venetian sun to peach or terracotta. I luxuriated in it. I loved to paint skin against fur; my subjects were often portrayed with their pets upon their knees. Those fur-and-flesh couples often seemed to me happier than the ones made up of husbands or wives. I loved to paint the perfect amity between a young woman and her cat. I delighted in the sound of my sitter climbing the stairs with her yowling pet in a basket. I knew that I would soon make them both happy. Lifting the cat out of the basket, I would soothe it with long strokes before placing it on her lap. The cat would blink at me and understand. I also knew that a woman who had stroked a cat for an hour always looked ready for the attentions of a lover. All this was to my purpose. Casanova swore that I could paint cats *purring*. I will not be falsely modest – I could. I could also paint women purring; women come lately from their lovers' beds with a dull sheen of pleasure still upon their skins.

And water was my subject, whether beading a frosted glass or seen through a window behind my sitter. I painted it green, a colour that has to be invented in Venice, as it grows but sparsely here naturally. Water is colourless, so it steals its greens as reflections from the exotically flowering balconies or the verdigris pulverising upon copper domes. I found the other colours in water, too – on any one day the Grand Canal flows with molten jade, milk and honey, dark blood, champagne, nectar and poison. In Antonio's studio I was learning to paint the dewdrops upon a flower and the pearly ooze of fruit in a bowl. So convincing were they that when I placed my paintings in the courtyard to dry, small birds would come to peck at them. In the gondola I learnt to paint the moistures we humans emit in our times of joy. Those studies I dried discreetly inside the *felze* with the help of the curtains billowing tart air from the sea.

It seemed to me that I was called into the world for this – to drag a paintbrush across the canvas, just because flesh *is*, colour *is*, velvet *is*.

I had already learnt how to look into the bones of my subjects and expunge ten years from their ages by tightening their flesh infinitesimally here and there. My methods were a little crude in those days, but they worked. Really, I was erasing pain, though I did not know it at that point, because I did not know about that kind of pain. The unwanted grooves and sags had been carved into their flesh by bad loves. By removing them, I made my subjects feel lighter and younger, as if I had really cancelled from their lives the terrorising episodes that had disappointed their skins and scarred their beauty.

Casanova taught me what Antonio omitted, either through lack of understanding or a dawning professional jealousy. It was Casanova who urged me to learn what I could about the interior life of my subjects, and paint it afterwards. All really great portraits are astonishing likenesses, not so much of the physical truth but of the animating essence of the sitter. The true artist does not obsess to achieve technical likeness; he simply cannot avoid it. But the likeness is merely a raw material; it is thrown into the alchemical mixture of a portrait. Sometimes I would talk to my sitters for hours before as much as picking up my paintbrush. Antonio drummed his fingers and looked across at me in disbelief. I ignored him. I would hand them something to read, not to hear their voices, but to see how they held the book – either at nervous distance, or close up to their cheek like a lover's face. I was curious, but it was more than that. I did not seek to possess my subjects; I wanted to act as witness to their hopes and disappointments, their loves and their dreams.

Casanova had been right. What people want to see in their portraits is what they want to know, but cannot see in their own faces: some kind of inner truth behind their own eyes. The truth they seek is always this: *How much shall I be loved?*

Even these early portraits of mine had the depth and complexity of novels. Where they lacked technical perfection they showed the marks of my uncontainable curiosity. My pastels were sweet reminiscences, more diaphanous than remembered desires. My sketches were like love letters; my studies were poems in manuscript. I knew when I was successful: when their portraits were finished, my sitters walked away with them, hugging them to their breasts.

You make the road by walking on it. I made my road in Venice, and it started to lead me to money and fame. I was selling dreams, successfully. These were the dreams of people who wanted to look better than their best, to their lovers and families and to the generations who would succeed them. All of Venice knew about me. Eventually the stories even penetrated the private citadel of my parents' home, and were mentioned in our dining room. That day I lowered my head over my plate while I wondered what they would think if they knew that it was their own daughter who was causing such a sensation. I lived in fear that my father would decide to commission a painting of my sister and myself, to join the other sombre portraits on our walls, but fortunately an outbreak of pimples on Sofia's face preserved me.

When it was discussed at the table, I asked, 'Who would want to paint those?' pointing to the excrescences on her chin, neck and cheeks. Sofia fled, weeping, from the table. And the subject was closed, except that my mother redoubled her efforts to help Sofia. Now she applied the local remedy to Sofia's fiery face. When she lay in her minted bath she wore a soothing face mask of strips of veal soaked in milk. I am embarrassed to tell you the things I said when I first saw her bedecked like this. 'Don't be unkind,' Casanova would urge me. He gave me a phial of plantain water for Sofia, but when he was not looking I emptied it into the canal. This was not mere unkindness – though I admit that unkindness played its part. I simply did not know how to explain away its provenance at home, or indeed such a strangely charitable act on my behalf. Casanova, *invece*, believed in only the sweet side of me, and it was therefore all he saw.

By May that year my life had taken an entirely satisfactory shape. I was still creeping out of my bedroom window at night, for love, and spending my afternoon hours in Antonio's studio, for art. I had contrived a sustainable alibi for the time I spent at the studio: I was supposed to be at the Armenian monastery on the island of San Lazzaro with a blind old monk who had taken a liking to my voice at the convent and needed an amanuensis for his work. In return, he was, I said, instructing me in the rudiments of the Armenian tongue and faith. Although the Armenians were much respected in Venice, my parents were somewhat embarrassed at my new-found piety and studiousness. Though they clearly hoped that it was a passing development, like Sofia's pimples, they took no steps to interfere.

I was sometimes confounded that my parents had given birth to both me and Sofia. True, she had a passionate and precocious taste for sumptuous clothes, but otherwise she appeared to me entirely inanimate. I had this life that Sofia could not comprehend – ever. Her road was made without her needing to take a step for herself. She had the most inviolable aversion to novelty of any kind, unless she could wear it. She would marry her merchant, not from the higher echelons of the *Libro d'oro*, the golden book of Venetian patricians, but from a cadet branch of a noble family like our own. Her pimples would fade to pearly scars, her hips would become plumper, her brief bloom would be fertile, and soon her chins would increase. I would be a disinterested aunt in a few years. It was strange to live in the same house with such a bovine presence. But she could still be dangerous, being full of childish spite, so I was careful. At home tiredness now made me so meek as to be unnoticeable. It was, in fact, hard to muster up the energy, venom or interest to bicker with Sofia during that time, but I did, sometimes, so as not to arouse suspicion with my unwonted peaceableness. And so I managed to simmer Sofia's resentments without letting them boil over.

My mother always preferred Sofia. I heard her boasting as much to her women friends. 'Look! the Family Brow.' She pointed to an ancestral portrait. 'And underneath the Family Brow – no nonsense, and certainly nothing I didn't put there. She's like a little princess, she loves to be good! She never runs down stairs. She never answers back. She's a little slow, but men don't like them smart.'

The ladies congratulated my mother, who was a little pink from her long speech. Watching unseen from a corner of the room, I saw her touch her rigid, pomaded hair and straighten the little confection of flowers which had come askew above the sticky, powdered carapace. She put her arm around Sofia, who looked up at her, with a silent mew of satisfaction.

'And I believe her skin is starting to clear now,' added one of the kinder ladies.

'And Cecilia?' enquired one of the crueller ones.

I, Cecilia, was another story. My mother tried to dress me in identical style to Sofia. We were little adults, perfect miniatures of our mother in our dresses. Like all Venice we dressed in obedience to the law laid down by the *Poupée de France*, a doll on display in a shop window in the Merceria. *La Poupée*'s miniature fashions changed as often as they did in Paris, and, as we were rich, so did ours.

On Feast days we were crammed into brocade dresses with gold thread worked through the stiff bodies of flowered Pekin silk and half-sleeves foaming with lace. Sometimes we wore little side-bustles which protruded like small tables. Our necklines were V-shaped. We walked the streets in slippers of striped satin. For cold days we had little capes of camelot – goat and camel hair. We had gold buttons on our camisoles and silk ribbons to fasten our pearly stockings at our knees.

Sofia hankered for dresses with large panniers. She was duly reproved by my father, 'That is the most stupid fashion I have seen in years. Looks like a net for catching birds! A cauldron! I'm afraid that the noble ladies have adopted it as a good way of hiding bastards.' He wanted his daughters to be like our *palazzo*: unobtrusive on the outside and perfectly set up on the inside. We had furs and family jewellery but they were rarely aired. It was enough for my father to know that he had secured them for us. In the happy city, my father was one of the rare men who felt that way. He was a

Venetian, so he could not avoid a weakness for beauty, but he knew how to discipline it.

As little girls, Sofia and I wore our hair parted in the middle and coiled at the back. We both started the day with a white linen cap. Only Sofia came home with hers still on. My hair was always wild. No one was willing to withstand the screams and bites that ensued if they tried to untangle it. I refused pomade and demonstrated how powder made me retch and cough. I carried a feral smell, always. The nuns often seemed about to tell my mother something incriminating about me, but they could never quite bring themselves to the point. My body was always at fault. In my sleep my skin grew hot, bathing the sheets in sweat, so they had to be changed daily. In winter my hands were always cold. My mother would plunge my wincing flesh into hot water to unlock my coiled cold fingers and then she would clap them together. Then my fingers shuddered to life like little crab legs.

In Antonio's studio, I never had any problem with my hands, unless it was reaching too often for the same colour Antonio required. Too many sitters were asking for me, and there were days when he sat doing his accounts, while a family, former clients of his, sat for me. They would not meet his eye, even when they handed him the fat purse I had earned for him.

The situation with Antonio became too difficult. With Casanova's help, I found a studio of my own. It was a large room just off the courtyard of the Palazzo Balbi Valier at San Vio. From my mullioned windows, I could see the Grand Canal and the glory of the Palazzo Barbaro opposite. I could also step out between the three arches of the courtyard, onto the water steps, and bathe my feet in the iced flow of Venice's crucial artery on hot days. I could watch the seaweeds flapping slowly like aqueous bats around my toes and feel my blood cooling inside me.

It was convenient for Casanova, who would arrive by gondola when my clients had left and sweep me off. He was ever considerate of my work, preferring to wait, endlessly scribbling diagrams of duplicating cubes, a favourite obsession, while I finished something properly, even though his smell made my paintbrush perform distractedly. Sometimes we would stand, wrapped in each other's arms, looking at my work. And very often the same exclamation would rise to both our lips at once: *the left eye is too green! The right hand is unnatural! She has a bitter taste in her mouth!*

Casanova's cat came to live in the studio. The *pantegane*, the monstrous Venetian water rats, had easy access to my courtyard, which the cat now patrolled with severity. He was also useful in my work, posing as the winged lion for many a Venetian or tourist who wanted the symbol of Venice inserted in the background of their portrait. The cat posed willingly with his paw upon a stone Bible. I swear I came in to find him examining my portrait of him more than once. He seemed a little embarrassed and swaggered off. But I knew what I had seen. I did not laugh at him, because he honoured me with his love. Cat love is always conditional. He rejected all other cats, except the females he took and quickly fled from.

'You are selfish,' Casanova told him, 'there's enough love here for twenty cats. My friend Crébillon in Naples had eighteen or twenty of them, and none suffered a deprivation of caresses.' The cat twined knowingly around our legs, tolerant of our point of view, but absolutely resolute against the personal enactment of it.

I wanted to ask Casanova, 'And you have love enough for *how many* women?' For I had heard something that week about a woman named Francesca Buschini. But for the moment, though my curiosity was alerted, my sense of safety was stronger. Casanova had as much love for me as I could ever want. I would not be selfish, like the cat.

Sometimes Casanova took me to the island of San Michele, inhabited by the monks of the Camaldolese order. There was one particular grave where we loved to make love, feeling the cool moss upon our backs, each in turn. We most often went to the softly mossed tombstone of Fortunato, a young novice who had died a hundred years before. Sometimes we would be able to read sweet phrases from his epitaph afterwards, etched upon my shoulder . . .

>*Con culto d'amore*
>*spargono fiori e pregano pace* . . .
>
>In the name of love,
>Scatter flowers and beg for peace . . .
>
>. . . *diede l'ultimo de' suoi dolci sorrisi* . . .
>. . . he gave us the last of his sweet smiles . . .
>
>*Fortunato*
>*sempre estraneo alla terra*
>*anima fatta per cielo* . . .
>
>Fortunato
>Always a stranger upon this earth
>With a soul made for heaven . . .

The arrival at San Michele always excited me. The tall cypresses jutted out of the ground. Jade waves licked both sides of the church on its promontory. The baptistery was exactly like a large pale breast with an elongated white nipple . . . the sight of which started Casanova musing aloud about the milky delights that might be had with an albino lover – or two.

You would think I might have felt hurt by this but I did not. The trick with him, with the way he did this, was that I suffered no jealousy, for no man ever had more tact or gentleness in this respect.

Casanova made me feel that I was complicit in every enjoyment. He made me feel that I was the pinnacle of his pleasure, and everything else was merely an experiment in novelty. That being the case, one could not begrudge him his memories or his fantasies any more than a wine-lover's mistress can begrudge a drop of Merlot upon her lover's lips. They simply did not hurt me. In those days I was *potent* with love and happiness. My curiosity was stronger than my insecurity. More than that, I enjoyed Casanova's strange tales with him, for I was already starting to realise that we were the same: that I was an addict of novelty myself. Every story he told me was a novelty. Every woman he described was a novelty, a glimpse at another life.

I can picture him at the prow of his gondola, swaying slightly with the dipping waves. We had no need to make love in the graveyard. We made a special excursion to do so. It was the variety and the eroticism-in-death that excited both of us, and the picturesque ritual of our journey. We were not alone in feeling the seduction of San Michele. The island had not yet become our communal cemetery but its small graveyard had always held an unworldly lure for the Venetians, for we are all half in love with death. So there were always whispers, moist noises, exhalations and sighs of satisfaction from other graves, and other gardens, and pairs of hastening shadows stippling the moonlight. On damp nights, the tears of the evening trickled down the gravestones, and droplets wept gently from the needles of the cypresses, into the welcoming earth, and upon our naked skins. We loved those nights the best. Afterwards we carried an unearthly distillation of scents upon our skins, and made a pact not to wash until we saw each other again. I became unpopular at the convent in this period. My father would be disturbed by my smell at the breakfast table.

'You smell like a swamp, Cecilia,' said Sofia, who always smelt of milk and soap. 'A swamp, in which something died.'

'Wash yourself!' said my mother.

I went to the ewer in my bedroom and splashed water vindictively all over the floor. I touched myself with fingers still slippery
from Casanova, until I lay panting upon the marble floor. All day at
the convent, I would finger the embossing upon my shoulder and
remember.

Even when I go to San Michele today, I feel the erogenous tug of
the place – all the souls are there because of copulations; extensive
procreation alone has created the compost for this little field of
death. I often wonder how many of these cadavers had, in their lives
above the earth, made love as often as they wanted to? How many
of us ever do? How many have made love in a way that makes the
absence of it burn? When I was with Casanova, I was contaminated
with his relentless optimism, and refused to think of the obscure
future of our love. No, I thought only of the moment, of the sensation, and of the next novelty. I had not yet learnt to be afraid. In
those days I never asked myself, *But what am I that I should have your
love? Can I hold it? Will it last? Am I worth it to you?* I would learn to
ask myself these things. I would learn that unrelenting vigilance for
the first sign of ebbing love: that constant monitoring of the language of the mouth and the body, the first encounter with a hand
that no longer rises a millimetre to cup itself snugly under yours.
With Casanova I never needed to know such things. I had no sense
that my happiness was in danger. I was happy and I had no thought
that I could ever be otherwise.

Sometimes we even gave truth to my alibi; we went out to San
Lazzaro, once the island of the Venetian lepers and those unfortunates
merely suspected of being so. In 1717, the Venetian Senate had
granted the island, in perpetuity, to a small order of Armenian monks,
fugitives from La Serenissima's old Ottoman enemies. Within twenty
years the industrious Armenians had transformed the island into a
beautiful sanctuary, self-supporting and outward-looking. Visitors

were welcome to visit their quiet cloisters filled with oriental flowers and the library full of impenetrable documents rescued from the fragile but violent history of the Armenian civilisation. The monks devoted themselves to the scrupulous search for and rescue of any Armenian manuscript that could be saved. They kept their race alive by saving its words.

Sometimes I think we went to San Lazzaro for its silence, for the pleasure of hearing one hard green olive dropping from its tree and then the soft sucking noise of the dry earth welcoming back its seed. In the distance, we saw the fathers' terraced walks, their oleanders and cypress trees. We lay in the long grass of the foreshore in each other's arms.

'I feel good here,' Casanova announced. 'Paint it for me, Cecilia. Please, my darling.' He pulled a paintbrush from my pocket and traced the curve of my buttocks with it, slowly.

'But I don't paint landscapes,' I protested. He tapped the brush in affectionate admonition. I seized it and took my turn to reprimand the contents of his pantaloons with it. Through the squirrel fur of my brush I felt the steed raise himself for another race.

When we were replete with lovemaking, I painted. We talked about what would happen with our lives. We declaimed with equal enthusiasm upon this subject. The difference in our ages meant nothing. Casanova's plans were even grander and more complicated than mine. It was as if an endless pageant of life and possibility still stretched out in front of him. But he also saw ways of making use of the life he had already lived. Even then, for years in fact, he had been considering the idea of writing his memoirs. Why not? I believed in him. I had heard him speak and had fallen under the spell of his words. Others would too, I was certain of it.

My ambitions were of as tender concern for him. He continually plagued me to improve my French. 'Make yourself elegant in that language, my soul,' Casanova told me. 'With perfect French you are the equal of anyone in any dining room in the world.

'I shall, for example, write my memoirs in French, for the French can read. And will be permitted to read them. All civilised Italians, Germans and even the barbarous English speak French. I lived for months in London, barely needing a word of English. French is the language of exquisite snobbery, the private club of the rich, that same club from which you will draw your clients.

'Remember that when an Italian novel is published they print the lie on the frontispiece that it's "translated from the French", otherwise no *gentildonna* will want to be seen with it on her balcony! Remember your painting heroines, Angelica Kauffman, Rosalba Carriera – fluent in French, both of them. Try to be like them. And even English, brutish as it sounds, is going to be important one day. There are things afoot over there.'

'I would rather spend the time painting. I want colours, not words.'

In the new studio, after setting up my easel, I had painted a large screen with a recital of the colours I loved and prescriptions of the ways to use them. Casanova reminded me of the screen and of what I had written upon it.

'Darling, words are colours too. At least, they are in your mouth, in your words! That's why your portraits are turning into poetry. Love poetry. You feel colours the way other people experience their emotions.'

The Language of Colour

Ultramarine Blue, the queen and courtesan of the blues, the most noble and most flexible of hues, both common and royal. Buy it by the ounce according to its goodness, or by the grain, if exquisite. The most precious blues are ground from lapis lazuli, brought from Phoenicia in tall ships. The most sought-after demi-mondaines have eyes of this colour.

Cobalt Blue, a very bourgeois lady, cool and efficient, sometimes wanting to be greener. But she can be contained, with skill. You can add a little Lead White to maintain her blue intensity.

Cerulean Blue, charming the birds out of the trees with its transparency and luminosity. Good for the background skies of happy people.

Prussian Blue, of fighting strength, though, surprisingly, it can be softened to baby-slipper colours, when mixed with white.

Middle-aged men and small boys should be painted wearing this colour.

Indigo, a spicy pod, staining to dark blue-black. Think of the sky in the dead of a summer night. That's Indigo. Use it for backgrounds to suggest a mysterious past.

Cochineal Red, pressed from the carapaces of Mexican insects. From the corner of your eye, you sometimes see their ghosts writhing in the gallipot. Lips!

The genial family of Cadmium Reds, with tints leaning from yellow to blue. Not to be used for outdoor work as they fade in the light. But inside the studio, they glow. We have a whole dialect of reds upon our palates in Venice – *cremisino* (crimson), *scarlatto* (scarlet) and *sanguineo* (blood) for wool, silk and cotton. In other words, senators and cardinals and harlots.

Vermilion, oh so expensive, and how fickle in performance! It will turn black if not shielded from cruel light. Save it for the noblewomen in their dark cool parlours.

Rose Madder, or **Alizarin Madder**, like Merlot, red bleeding to purple-brown. The rubia tinctorum is extracted from the madder. Lovely on the shadowed crook of an elbow.

Carmine, a crimson as translucent as a licked lip.

Venetian Red, or **Red Ochre**, which lasts forever, and glows like lava.

Indian Red, or **Terra Rosa**, not unlike our Venetian Red Ochre, but blushing blue at the edges. For those too timid to wear Venetian Red.

Cassel Earth, brown juice of the ancient rottings of animals and plants. Unlike the Tuscans, we Venetians esteem the hues of brown. We prefer them for the shadows on our flesh to their greens.

Mummy Browns, from the crushings of Egyptian corpses, for the mortally ill and melancholy.

Burnt Terra di Sienna, a deceptively tame-looking brown that catches fire when mixed with oil so that flowing golds and ambers are born on pale sheets of background colour. Good for the hair of young men.

Terra Verte, blue-grey with longings only towards green, and of the earth. It can cling to Viridian, to remind it of the earth, and casts a brown undertone on all the colours it touches.

Lead White, or **Flake White**, like albino Parmesan cheese shaved by our cook. Outside Cremona, they sometimes call it Cremona White. I call it 'virgin skin'.

Titanium White, like the scum of cream on the pail of milk in the dairy. (By the way, will someone explain why lilies symbolise purity when the yellow stamens enfolded in the petals can stain you indelibly with their soft dust?)

Zinc White, pale and stark, like the cold blue on the lips of the dead. Like death, it slows the artist, for it drags out the time of drying.

Lamp Black, almost pure carbon. Perfect for visionless windows in the background and the eye-hollows of skulls placed on the table to show the futility and brevity of life. I do not like this kind of portrait. But this colour also works well on the dark ridges of velvet, to throw into relief the lights on the edges of the folds.

Charcoal Black, impurity incarnate, vegetable and mineral. Mixed in with white and other colours it makes the grey shadow we call *berettino*. Lurking in the shadows of white fabrics, strangely it makes for warmth.

Cadmium Yellow, ranging spicily from orange to lemon. A young woman's colour, a sherbet of a colour, shows excitement.

Naples Yellow, extracted from lead, and liking to be brackish amongst friendly browns and greens. Its use is now lapsing except among the glass-blowers. But good for a playful older woman's costume.

Yellow Ochre, from the earth, pure and good. Use it to make white satin *happy*.

Raw Sienna, the swarthier cousin of the Yellow Ochre. Uniquely transparent, and able to spread brown warmth, like goodness, over everything it touches. Adding it to yellow, you can make the wonderful fawn *lionato*, the colour of lions and angels' hair!

Viridian Green, like melted emeralds, and greedy for oil. It sucks up more than any other colour. You can marry it to one of the blacks to make your shadows verdant.

Violet and Red Lake, which make a tender mauve when mixed with Ultramarine, the way Bellini did it. Shadows under downcast eyelids. But be careful, for the Violet and Red Lakes drain away in the light, leaving only sighs of themselves.

And you want your portrait to last forever.

4

Ocio de pesse lesso, inamorà o fesso.

If you have fish-eyes, you must be either
in love or half-witted.

VENETIAN PROVERB

'To tell you the truth, I have always looked like a great sinner,' said Casanova, gazing fondly at my latest portrait of him. He felt complicit in its birth, as indeed he was. We were standing in the studio. The new-born painting stood glistening in the variegated light.

'Every speaking likeness has told truths of me. Even you, Cecilia, the first of my lovers to paint me, have painted my immortality as sinful.'

It was true. But when I look at that portrait now, it seems different. The sin has softened, somehow.

Even after you depose it from the easel, a portrait develops a life of its own. Casanova's portrait was at the beginning of its life, in those days; a young, immature portrait, its Rose Madders and Flake Whites still relative strangers to each other, its Violet Lake as yet unacquainted with its faded future.

A portrait is shaped just like a window. The subject looks out at you, locked in the past, his nose pressed against the invisible glass.

Locked inside the portrait is the story of the subject, and the story of the painter, and the story of their relationship. When a painter looks at a portrait she has made, years before, she re-enters that lost world. The process is rarely without a little pain. As the years pass, the pain becomes greater. The Vermilions, as I have told you, often turn black, the Zinc White desiccates and the Red Lakes hand their vibrancy back to your memory. You are left looking at nothing but loss. Believe me, these days it seems to me that the course of our lives is nothing but a gradual process of losing and of giving back.

So who was this man that I had painted? Was Casanova indeed a great sinner? Had he earned the patina of malefaction upon my canvas? Was it mixed in the sinews of my paint, or had it been applied like a varnish to him, now, at the end of his life?

Was he a beautiful man? That's what you want to know now. You already know he was interesting. I shall not tell you yet. There are more important things for you to know just now.

Apart from mine, which no one sees now, you will not find many portraits of Casanova. He was too busy being Casanova to sit still and allow himself to be captured. He himself had strong views on the importance of physical beauty. Love was more to do with curiosity and instincts than with the pure cold aesthetics of beauty, in Casanova's opinion.

'Women,' he used to say, 'are like a book. You begin with the title page. If that is not interesting, then you will not desire to read further. In fact, interesting is better than beautiful. A beautiful title page may attract your attention, but if it's not interesting, you will not continue with it.

'People who read many good books are always curious to read new ones, and sometimes, just for the novelty of it, they want to read works of a wicked or lower timbre. And so men who have loved many women, usually beautiful ones, become curious to try ugly women, if they are new to him.'

I asked him, 'But the object that always seems to be so new – is it really so in essence?'

'Not at all, for it's always the same story, with nothing new but its title page.' He laughed at himself and the number of stories he had read.

'So do you feel deceived?'

'By myself? Perhaps. But do I complain? No. While enjoying the familiar story, I always kept my eyes fixed upon the title page, the charming new face with which I had fallen in love. How could I fail to be happy?'

Of himself, he always said, 'It's not beauty that I possess. It's something better, but harder to define.'

Casanova's several portraits tried to define it for him, but I do not think they entirely succeeded. I never did, completely, with my own. I take every opportunity to stare at the other portraits of him, these days, to extract what those other fortunate artists saw, painting Casanova in his glory days.

How did he look? Everyone wants to know now, though most do not dare to ask me aloud. I read their need on their own faces. I, greedier than anyone for the human face, understand what they want to ask me.

To help them, I would send them first to the life-size alleged portrait attributed to Anton Raphael Mengs. I believe it was painted around 1760. I myself have stood in front of that portrait and tried to find my Casanova inside those lovely strokes of Mengs' brush. Casanova never mentioned the painting, but I am sure that he was involved in it somehow because his tender presence hovers around it still. Perhaps he did not like the portrait. He did not much like Mengs, who was a fair-weather friend and a cruel drunkard. Casanova perhaps remembered the man, and therefore could not like the picture.

But I do.

I love the creamy forehead, the little plumes of hair above his fleshy ears. I love the soft brown eyes brimming in pink bulbs of flesh above and below. I love the large nose: it has a look of generosity. I love the mouth that it was possible to imagine already preternaturally smoothed by kisses. I love the plump hands, not too large, their fingers not too long, throwing doubt, according to the traditional proportional calculations, upon the truth of the *eight* inches of best English contraceptive skins he would record in his memoirs. (I am not being coy. Who has the time to take measurements during love? Anyway, everyone knows that a man expands to the measure of his love.)

In Mengs' portrait, Casanova must be around thirty years old. He wears an Ultramarine velvet frock-coat, extravagantly buttoned in gold, and below it a waistcoat of Titanium White and Naples Yellow flowered brocade. *Ecco* – the discreet snowy cravat at his throat, and pleated spider-webs of lace at his wrists. *Please welcome me as one of your own*, his costume begs High Society. *I know how to dress. My minuet is the most exquisite you have seen. I have been embraced by popes and princes.* But he has a vulnerable air, as if he knows that he will probably be rejected. And he has a slightly skinned look about him. This is true in more ways than one, as this creamy portrait has stripped him of his vivid African colour. It has faded him or whitewashed him, depending upon how your see the loss of colour.

He holds a book open in a somewhat supplicatory way. *Please take me seriously*, says this pose. *I am the author of fictions and histories and pamphlets, articles and translations. I can talk knowledgeably of medicine, chemistry, alchemy, the* cabbala, *Descartes will praise my essay on the duplication of the cube. I have been a diplomat, undertaking missions for the French king. I set up the lottery that saved France! For my ingenuity and my philosophy I shall be known to the future.* But below the book, a bare-breasted woman, worked in gold, leers up at the unreadable shadowy text.

You can't help noticing her.

Casanova himself is almost feminine, and certainly passive, in his creamy softness. There's the merest shadow of a beard around the pretty pink jawline, picked out in Carmine and cream. Just behind him, next to a swarthy, thrusting column, a *putto*, with a slight suggestion of genitalia and feathery wings (in *cremisino* and white), offers a carnation. Casanova's own legs are comfortably splayed, but there is a soft sheaf of brocade strategically falling over the part of Casanova that has since become of greatest interest to the world.

I think that on the whole this is a good portrait of Casanova, even if it is not of Casanova. This pink man is no satyr. Sexual enthusiast, perhaps, but only on demand. There is a look of infinite kindness. There is no pleasure this man would willingly deny you. He is comfortable in his own skin and would like to share it with you. But only if you are disposed and preferably if you are urgent in your desire. He sits in a comfortable position to watch you undress, endlessly patient. He would prefer not to blow out the candle, for the darkness might deprive you of a compliment. All this I can read in Mengs' portrait, because it is a good one.

There's none of that invitation, in a slightly earlier portrait, by his brother, Francesco, done some time between 1750 and 1755. But I would send the curious to gaze upon it as I have done with Mengs'. For it, too, tells stories of Casanova. It is very different to the Mengs picture, which is full face, full colour; Francesco's portrait of Casanova is a left profile, sketched in various shades of pale terracotta and *berettino* grey.

It is a gentle face, the same face — again the large, guileless, slightly bulbous eyes — but now you see the pronounced hump of the nose, the generous nostril — again those smoothed lips, soft chin, and here also a sweet plumpness between the chin and the broad neck. The hair is again swept off the face in little puffs. A long ringletted ponytail, bound with a ribbon, rests lightly on his shoulder. His profile, in this sketch, resembles nothing more than a fish face — some benevolent, verdure-grazing fish, not a shark.

Francesco's is definitely a sibling's portrait. It is coldly and prettily executed, but with no breath in it, and certainly no fire. When I think of my sister Sofia (which is rarely) I would paint her like this: pale, the sibling of a central character rather than the protagonist of her own *spettacolo*.

So few portraits of Casanova remain. I cannot share with the curious those other visions of my lover, because I have not been able to look on them myself. In all my long journeys they have evaded me, though I tried to seek them out. But I run away with myself.

Somewhere in Portugal is the ring set with a miniature that Casanova had painted for the mysterious and adorable Pauline, whom he loved in London. The artist is supposed to be Jeremiah Meyer. Without seeing it, I could not tell you for certain.

I believe you can still see a miniature of him by Anton Graff in a private collection in Genoa. And another by Pierre Antoine Baudoin, with all the pleasures stripped from it. Then there is the engraving of Casanova, aged sixty-three, by Johann Berka. I have seen a reproduction. It makes me *spit!* He makes my Casanova look like an aged wild boar! Alessandro Longhi is supposed to have made two portraits, but I don't believe in them. Where are they? Let them come forward, so I can tell you if they are real.

And my paintings of Casanova?

I am sorry, but you won't see them.

Many things have happened to them, many things have been spilt on them, many fragments of colour are now chipped off their canvases on short journeys, and many contusions scar their surfaces from all the different kinds of damp that swelter out of Venice. Despite it all, they survive.

But you won't see them. The secrets of our gondola will die with me. We Venetians are good at secrets. We are the repository for any number of unspeakable, and unspeakably delicious, acts. Mystery hangs on our lips and dances in our eyes. A Venetian can disappear around a corner like a cat, leaving no trace but a sense of loss and a disturbing perfume in the air. In the last remnants of the happy times of which I write, it was *secrecy* that gave us a relish for the loves and intrigues we were almost too worn out to perform. Secrecy spiced up our pleasures so that we could taste them on our jaded palates. In the dark corridors of our city, our feet whispered along the flagstones and we hid our mouths behind our masks. Yes, we Venetians knew the art of silence and of withholding information.

Casanova was different. In this way alone, he was no true son of Venice, and indeed it was in part his candour that cost him his constant exiles. He liked to talk about his own delicious, unspeakable past. He withheld nothing, good or bad. So I soon pieced together the details, webbing his real words and sweet memories over the crude structure of his legend. There were no souvenirs: too heavy for a life-long refugee, always on the road. There were only his memories, tangible in the moonlight. As he spoke of them, he seemed to become again what he once was.

One night, rocked by a melodious *scirocco* in the lagoon, we lay enfolded in the gondola, and he told me about his early years. He took me to his past. He was an artist of a raconteur: Even in our intimacy, the whispers soon became a fully wrought story.

A song of love for all good things he sang to me that night. He painted pictures of the past for me, and where he himself entered the scene his memories turned from sepia to full colour and the canvas became fragrant with the scents of sweat, flowers, tears and crab soups.

Casanova's Chorus

I was conceived in the orchestra pit.
I have always performed.

They sent me to a boarding house.
I was starved there. I learnt to love food.

I was going to be an advocate, a clergyman.
But in the orchestra pit of my stomach, new notes were stirring.

I gave my first sermon at San Samuele.
There were love letters in the collection plate, afterwards.

I gave a second sermon at San Samuele.
Drunk, I performed ignominiously, but later I made a girl cry with delight.

I became the neolyte of a rich old man.
And what was his was mine, including his mistress.

I lived like a young god in the *palazzi* of the Mocenigo, the Barbaro,
   the Dandolo . . .
But I had not the blood or the gold for a palazzo of my own. I never would.

I started to be afraid of Time,
Of people being oblivious to me.

My pleasures were ritualised, I could concentrate better.
Then I'd make sure they would never forget me.

5

*Tuti quanti semo mati per quel buso
che semo nati.*

We all go mad for the hole from which
we were born.

VENETIAN PROVERB

Venice belongs to those who love her, and everyone who loves her bears their private map of Venice inside them.

While I painted Casanova, Casanova painted an indelible map of Venice for me. Even when he had gone, Casanova's secret itineraries remained to me.

For ever after, when I walked down the Calle della Commedia, I sniffed the crab soup that his mother, the actress Zanetta Farussi, demanded continually while she carried him in her belly. I heard the birth cries of Casanova and the screams of Zanetta, for whom the great Goldoni had once written a play. Amid the chaos, I heard the soothing voice of his putative father, Zanetta's husband, the actor Gaetano. And I detected another, more refined male voice – this belonging to an equal candidate for the honour of Casanova's paternity, the Venetian nobleman Michele Grimani. Or was it another rich patron, another lover of Zanetta's? It hardly matters. Casanova was born a woman's man, a mother's boy. Sadly, his mother lacked any maternal instincts towards him.

Casanova, as I heard that night, learnt early that he would have to go hunting for caresses.

As a child Casanova was mute. Only his nose spoke – volumes of blood. How could a child contain so much blood? The laundry looked like a convent after a massacre every day. Nobody believed he would live long. No one invested much in the silent child. He was only a year old when Zanetta and Gaetano left for London, where Casanova's little brother Francesco was born in 1727. Casanova they left at home, hardly thinking to find him there alive when they returned. But he was.

Casanova took me to this strange hushed childhood, so unlike the noisy luxury and discipline of my own. Casanova's nose became his eyes and ears and mouth at those times. As he spoke, I felt myself shrinking. Gazing through his memory, I crouched two feet above the carpet, on which I could smell the dust rising and the little reeks of old spillages. Enormous toys surrounded me, stiff with dried saliva and milk. I heard the cries of Casanova's baby brother and smelt the stench of his nappy from not far away. I saw the spines of the books flashing before my eyes, letters crammed into boxes, danced-to-death slippers kicked under shelves and forgotten. I smelt the sweat from inside them. I saw the knees of adults, passing to and fro. No one stopped to pick me up or caress my head. It was a strange, sensationless existence, as if living under water. This was how Casanova had seen the world until he was eight years old.

Then the picture changed. Now my eyes and nose were level with a large white apron. I saw *marmellata* and chicken blood printed on it, in the shapes of large strong fingers. I could smell the salt of armpits just a little higher than I was. Suddenly I was swept off my feet, and my nose was tucked into that armpit. I heard an elderly woman asking, in a rich Venetian accent, 'Who will be the most loved little boy in the world?'

When his nominal father Gaetano died, little Casanova went to live with his adored grandmother, Marzia Farussi, just a few doors away. From her, illiterate, passionate, maternal, the little Casanova received the fierce unconditional love that Zanetta was incapable of giving. And Nonna Marzia introduced him to the occult, which would ever after lure him into danger or into profit. We are practical, we Venetians, as you will see. *Venetians first, and then Christians*, as we say. We will borrow what we need to *arrangiarsi*, to get by, from whatever spiritual dimension offers succour, or opportunity.

At nine years old, blood still gushed from his nose and Casanova was still silent. So Nonna Marzia took him to a sorceress on the island of Murano. His earliest memory, which he loved to describe to me: the witch's cat-haunted hovel and her tender hands on him, the incense of fragrant herbs smouldering under his nose, and hot potions fed gently to him. The witch had undressed him, put him inside a wooden chest, whispered incantations, rubbed him with sweet pomades, and lulled him to a deep sleep. The next night, at home with his grandmother, a vision of a beautiful woman came down the chimney to caress him. The witch's spells appeared to cure the nose bleeds, except for moments of stress, when for the rest of his life his nostrils would express his fears in vivid torrents. Whatever really happened, Casanova learnt to talk and read in less than a month after that night at Murano.

Reluctantly, it seems, his mother started to realise that he was not an imbecile. Something had to be done with him. Zanetta took him by boat to Padua, where he was to study under a Doctor Antonio Gozzi. With little jabs and pushes, she marched him to a boarding house, and left him there with a small trunk and a deposit of six *zecchini*.

'Only six . . .?' I asked. He nodded.

The hirsute Slavonian landlady shrieked after Zanetta that she had not left enough money to feed and clean the boy. But his mother was gone. 'And that is how she got rid of me,' Casanova told me, sadly.

'Just like that?'

'She did not even look back.'

At the filthy boarding house, rats ran all over the attic where he tried to sleep, while three notorious species of insects roamed his body, punctured his flesh and drank at every orifice. He was so distracted by the insects eating him that his terror of the rats was diminished, and his terror of the rats distracted him from the torture of the bites. He had his first experience of what it was to be hungry. That, like his unsatisfied hunger for mother-love, would turn him into a wolf at the table and in the bedroom for the rest of his life.

After six months, his grandmother rescued him. His once pretty curls were so filthy that they had to be cut off entirely.

Finally, Zanetta left Venice for good. Her travels would take her to Verona, Saint Petersburg, and eventually Dresden, where she spent the rest of her life, showing little interest in her eldest son. Before she left she summoned him to Venice one last time.

'What was she like, your mother?' I asked him, so many times. He could not answer me coherently. It appeared that all these decades later he was still awe-struck by his mother's glamour and her beauty. Zanetta apparently was less impressed with her son when she saw him for the last time, complaining that the colour of his wig did not match his eyebrows.

But at supper Casanova found a way to impress his mother. He reeled off a witty Latin epigram of his own composition. I wish I could remember it now, for its cunning obscenity made me laugh aloud when he told it to me. But I cannot.

I do remember, however, his description of the result. I picture the little boy surrounded by his mother's elegant guests. After a short thunderstruck silence everyone guffawed or tittered. Affection was shown. His mother, for the rest of the evening anyway, appeared to love him. Choice items were handed to him from the table. His mother smiled at him more than once – definitely, directly at him. She even kissed him goodnight, which was also, of course, goodbye. It was the only time he could remember her touching him with kindness. His tutor, Gozzi, was given a gold watch.

But Casanova had been given something much more valuable. He was only eleven, but he had just learnt that with a clever mouth and good timing he could obtain kisses and other delicious things for that mouth. If he was clever, and outrageous, then pleasures, novelties, and late nights were in store for him. I think that there was born in him that moment the ambition to cultivate such skills as would make him attractive to any woman, including the most inaccessible of them, his mother. From that moment, I believe, he became an entertainer, like his mother. He would perform all over Europe, like his mother. She performed on the stage and in the bedroom, he would perform in the drawing room and the bedroom, the laboratory, the nunnery, the bordello and the casino. Most of all, he would perform on the world's most elaborately beautiful little stage: Venice.

And that eloquent nose of Casanova's, it had also been receiving an education. Even when they thought him an idiot, that large and sensitive organ was taking things in. Even as it bled, it was learning things, important things, to serve the rest of his body. It took in the smells of the canal, of the fish market, of sex and sweat and the streets around him.

'Cecilia,' he said, 'think how Venice smelt in those days. My senses were always on fire! I was that age, your age, where the blood is in constant agitation. Every new whiff sent me running like a puppy to nose out its source, and taste it.'

He told me how he smelt the darker scents of Venice, too – in Cannaregio, where the living were starving and the dead were rotting on the streets. In Padua, from his attic bedroom in the dreadful boarding house, he had smelt the smoked herrings, uncooked sausages, and raw eggs in the pantry, found them, and devoured them.

As his experience taught him more smells, he developed his own tastes. Soon he would learn to love the smell of a lover's sweat. He always adored anything on the redolent edge of corruption, its last flare of flavour soaring up his nostrils. He loved cheeses palpitating with little creatures, over-hung game, ragouts of sudorous truffles, garlic-haunted Spanish stews, Neapolitan macaroni, oysters, sticky salted cod from Newfoundland.

Casanova would bring me delicacies like this, when times were good for him, or, when times were bad, I would steal them from our kitchen for him. We always ate as we talked. It was a kind of communion of memory for him. The talk was of food and of love and of the life of the mind, and especially all three enjoyed together. There was one night where the Milky Way seemed to descend and hang just above our heads, in pinpricks of light. Under the luminous cobweb, Casanova and I chewed on pungent little flakes of salt-cod while he told me of his first unrequited passion.

In Padua Casanova had fallen in love with his tutor's pretty little sister, Bettina, who teased him with troubling caresses but refused to grant the favours her soft fingers had promised him. She was also conducting a clandestine liaison with a young student. The nervous nature of her secret love weakened her, and Bettina fell ill with the smallpox. The little Casanova sat by her bed as she writhed in a terrifying delirium. *This is what love can do*, he observed to himself. Even as her body festered, he loved Bettina more and wanted to protect her. Casanova drew no conclusions. He just knew he wanted more love, whatever it cost. He now knew that it could be expensive. He consented to the expense.

Bettina had survived, horribly scarred. Casanova left Padua and came back to Venice. He too was indelibly branded by the smell of love and now he took deep breaths of it everywhere. His guardians sent him to be a priest, but after his first sermon the offertory bag was filled with love letters. He was too drunk to finish his second sermon. He pretended to faint, to avoid humiliation. Then he was caught *in flagrante* with Teresa Imer, the favourite of his seventy-year-old patron, Malipiero, who beat him with a stick until he escaped through a window into the garden. The story made the rounds of Venice. The legend of Casanova, outrageous seducer of women, received its priming coat of varnish. When my father banished Casanova's name from our table, the escape from the Palazzo Malipiero was probably the first disturbing image of my lover that had rattled across his mind.

The young Casanova was clearly not intended for the Church. Thinking of the sufferings of poor Bettina, he wanted to study medicine and chemistry, but they sent him to be a lawyer. It turned out to be a useful way of meeting pretty women in distress, but no career for Casanova. He tried the army, travelled to Corfu and Constantinople. Again, failure. He returned to Venice.

So at twenty he became a violin player in the orchestra of the San Samuele Theatre. Gozzi had taught him to play and he found the instrument, like his voice, appealing to women. By his new work he was humiliated but not degraded. People might despise him, but he consoled himself with the knowledge that he was not despicable, and he was optimistic, as always. He told me, 'I was simply waiting for the wheel of Fortune to turn again in my favour, as it surely would.'

Whenever errands took me to the Calle do Spade at Rialto, I would stop outside the tiny bar where Casanova used to come for refreshment after long nights of short, piled-up pleasures. Masked young men would still arrive, creased and stained with the night's joys, and I could watch and imagine the young Casanova among them, his hot chocolate always drained first, and the cup eagerly held out for more. He never hoarded the liquid in his glass, or money in his pocket, or seed in his body – if he could help it.

Casanova's portrait of his young self had become so real to me that I could conjure it up in an instant, even now. But my memories of the names and places and the incidents he described have become diffused. These days I see just the broader canvas. My images of the happy city and of Casanova are mixed on the same palette and I no longer remember the details, just the outlines and the colours.

On that palette I see the great times, poor times, in which he and his friends haunted the alleys and the taverns of Venice, masked and mysterious or unmasked and outrageous. Casanova had the run of the city, which was the playground of Europe, a rich city, a golden city, a power in the world, a city of twenty thousand courtesans, and a powerfully bad odour sweeping up from her canals in the dog days of the summer. Truly, she *stank* like a city on the verge of ruin. New trade routes were opening to the East and America. As a serious commercial concern, Venice was being passed by. The city turned instinctively, convulsively to the frantic prostitution of her less respectable charms and, by the time Casanova reached his prime, La Serenissima had set herself up for one last decadent decades-long fancy dress party, a masked ball, to which everyone was invited. In Venice, everyone might now invent the role their fantasy desired for them and don the mask of their choice in order to play it to the full.

A mask is the portrait you choose for yourself.

Of course it was Casanova who first taught me what it is to wear a mask: the sense of sudden, dangerous freedom, when your face is hidden from those around you. Everyone should try it, in order to see what lies hidden inside themselves. For the mask, perversely, opens that side of you to the world. You can do anything! You can permit anything. You take more risks. You unmask your genitals to fornicate with masked strangers, but you do not remove the mask from your face. You put unknown foods into your mouth; you walk too close to the edge of the canal. You don't know how close because you have no peripheral vision, for the mask tells you what to see, just as it tells the others how much they may see of you, and what they should make of you.

One night Casanova and I went out together, masked, and he showed me the places he had roamed thirty years before. It must have been the first time I had worn a mask: I remember no previous occasion. Casanova had chosen Pulcinella, with a hooked nose and white skullcap. For me, he brought La Civetta, the flirt, with its elongated owl eyes and a ruffle of gold lace to hide my nose and lips. But I remember clearly how I felt when he tied the ribbons behind my hair and spun me around to face him. He gazed down on me expectantly. My inner transformation was instantaneous. Once inside my mask, I felt potent and dangerous. I felt I could commit rape, and murder. I felt I could enter the Doges' Palace and seduce the footman, and the Doge. I lost my own place in society. I was no longer Cecilia Cornaro, daughter of a respectable and prosperous merchant. I could be whoever I wanted.

'*Ecco!*' Casanova exclaimed, when I told him all this. 'You understand, Cecilia.'

With his fellow musicians, the masked Casanova had rampaged around Venice. After a night's performance they would retire to the tavern, leaving it only to spend the night in a brothel. If they found the bedrooms already in service, they would force the occupants to take to their heels, misbuttoning their pantaloons in panic and perplexity. Then Casanova and his friends would fall like werewolves upon the abandoned whores. They never paid the women, considering the pleasure they had given quite sufficient joy for the miserable creatures.

They passed their idle days thinking up scandalous practical jokes, and the nights in putting them into execution. They would wake midwives and send them to deliver women who were not even with child. They sent priests to deliver the last rites to perfectly healthy noblemen. In each street they passed they relentlessly cut the bell cord of every door. If they found a door unlocked they rushed in and terrified all the sleeping inhabitants, screaming that the street door was open. They would stand and laugh at the array of grimy night-caps and curl-papers that would come stumbling down the stairs.

Finally, one night during *Carnevale*, they pretended to be officers of the Council of Ten. They kidnapped three unfortunate weavers from a tavern and subjected them to a summary mock trial. The terrified artisans were dumped on the stony shore of the island of San Giorgio Maggiore. The pretty wife of one hostage meanwhile submitted with good grace and evident enjoyment to the amorous attentions of the masked pirates. The happy woman was thereafter safely returned to her door, where she thanked her escorts most sincerely and in good faith for their kindness. Her husband found her fast asleep in bed when he finally made his way home from San Giorgio at daybreak the next morning. No harm done. The wife would say nothing against her captors, who had, she declared, behaved like the gentlemen they evidently were.

'She did not mind so many men?' I remember asking. The story had made me feel uneasy. Casanova's reply has stayed with me, every word.

'It was a kind of mutual frenzy. We all consented to abandon the normal conventions of love. We all lived outside them that night. She was respectable, but given this chance, she let the animal side of her nature come to greet us. Then, when she went home, she went back to a normal, lawful married life, just a little happier than she was before, and with a joyful memory to sustain her.'

'I suppose I felt like that after our first night,' I said, thoughtfully.

There was no such return for Casanova and his friends. They had finally gone too far, not in the pleasuring of the weaver's wife, but in impersonating the officers of the Council of Ten. The exploit made them outlaws and put a price of five hundred *ducati* on their heads. Casanova told me that he was gratified at the amount. He had not worried unduly. 'You see, our leader was a member of the Balbi family, the Balbis of San Vio – the *palazzo* where your studio is now.' Not even the Inquisitors would punish a patrician.

However, the Group of Eight disbanded after this event, their nocturnal frolics at an end.

'We were not so foolhardy as to continue to tempt fate.'

'That time.'

'Yes, that time.'

Three or four months later, Casanova discovered that every detail of the truth was known to the Inquisitors, including the identity of each of the perpetrators. His name had been noted, his file had been opened, and he would not have to reach much further into the realm of misbehaviour to reap the full consequences of that night and every other night when, masked or unmasked, he had ruffled the serenity of La Serenissima.

'One more mistake and I would be in serious trouble.' Casanova told me.

My own family was of the upper merchant class. My father was handsome, hard-working and contented except in that my mother had failed to provide a male heir. One day, I hoped, I would surprise him, and soothe that pain, converting this sense of failure to pride. But not yet. For then I knew that my activities, if discovered, would put him out of countenance in the gravest manner imaginable: it would draw attention, unwelcome attention, to our family. I was biding my time, until I could surprise him wonderfully.

My father traded in fabrics and *objets d'art* from the eastern edges of the Venetian empire. Downstairs in the *magazzino* my father's men unloaded straw baskets of ostrich feathers, moulded caskets of pearls from Ormuz, shimmering rolls of Damascus cloth, Masulipatam muslin from India, and strange wooden cages of Armenian bric-a-brac. In turn, he exported the artistry of Venice to the far-flung cities that were hungry for our graceful luxuries. Sometimes I begged to go with my father on his visits to the Venetian artisans who worked for him. The weavers and pressers of silk unfurled their marvels with shy pride when we arrived and the lace-makers bent blushing over their creations, which were so delicate that they seemed like frosty breath. Under his direction the embroiderers made a simple red silk blossom with flowers of silver and gold thread. My father held up colours to the light for me to see, and he taught me their names. There are fabrics in this world that can only be Venetian, like the watered *marezzato* silk, mangled in the dyeing to make a pattern as wave-like and lucent as the surface of our lagoon. In Venice we make iridescent satins winking alternate colours as you turn it this way or that, like light on the surface of a canal. We cut deep designs into pliant velvet, *alto-basso* like the difference between high and low water. These colours and textures were the currency of our family wealth. He knew about beauty, my father, and in Venice this had made him rich.

My father also traded in jewelled and enamelled snuffboxes and with these, even more than with the fabrics, he secured and nourished our prosperity. It seems such a tiny thing now, a snuffbox, such an inconsiderable thing: a little trinket that would fit in the hand. But I talk of the great age of the snuffbox, which captured our desire for all things exquisite and concentrated in their beauty, things that would hold our flighty, promiscuous attention for a moment, and not demand more. For in those days Venice craved the pretty little things, not the solemnity of grandeur. We were fastidious and nice-gutted: nothing too crude, large or vulgar pleased us. We loved the Lilliputian domestic scenes of Pietro Longhi and Rosalba's winsome miniatures. The great Goldoni wrote poems about flies, beauty spots and silver spoons. Instead of churches, in those days it was the snuffboxes we decorated with elaborate mosaics. We had snuffboxes for every season: light blue enamel for the summer, tortoiseshell sprinkled with emeralds and topaz for the autumn. There were bone-china snuffboxes, and those worked in solid gold, others in silver inlaid with pearls. In my father's studios, the artisans fondled their tiny little tools, and every time we went there we found new and more beautiful boxes laid out upon little velvet pillows.

My father did not touch snuff. Not so many people did. That was not the point of the snuffboxes: it was the possession of this little share of the world's beauty and it was the grace with which the owner might flick his box open, with a flourish of jewelled fingers and manicured hands. Such things my father frowned upon himself. He did not care for ostentation, as I have told you. Our own pretty *palazzo* at Miracoli was decrepit on the outside. The mist and damp were allowed to gnaw their way through the painted facade, leaving blisters and scabs of paint and render. My father saw no point in trying to hold back Nature's voracity for the sake of pride. But inside our *palazzo* all was immaculate, beautiful, quietly luxurious – and private as the interior of an ancient seashell.

We knew our place in Venice, but barely. For in those years, even my father must have been conscious that behind the masks, the edges of society were starting to soften, as everything was, with the general corruption of Venice. There were noblemen managing the theatres! There were courtesans in the libraries! In the casinos threadbare aristocrats on the fall met ambitious parvenus on the rise. Just as Venice had no physical walls around her, she had no walls within her these days. Everyone and everything was for sale. Even entry into the *Libro d'oro*, the golden book of the nobles, was possible at a certain price. But the high nobility remained a small, tight circle. Amongst the oldest families the birth rate was almost null: the aristocracy was diseased and weakened by its century-long debauch. Moreover, when so many frantic pleasures beckoned, the domestic ones lacked allure.

But one person had been able, through coincidences and manipulations of chance, to enter that small, tight circle of nobility, and leave behind him, for a while, the threadbare truth of his origins. That person was, of course, Casanova. It was a tale he loved to tell, especially now that all involved were dead or senile, and he could safely reveal the stage-machinery behind the scenes that took him from the back streets and gave him a new position in the world: that of the cherished pet mystic of three affable, gullible and rich Venetian noblemen.

It took two nights, but he told me the whole story. This time we decided to tear ourselves from the squirrel-fur rug and enjoy the fruits and juices of Venice. We made a tour of the small bars in the dark streets, where men and women greeted Casanova by name and me with complicit smiles. We sat sipping *fragolino* from little earthenware bowls called *mezo boca'éto*, half mouthfuls. We went to the pastry shops and ate whipped cream with wafers. We went to a *magazén*, a strange combination of wine-shop, pawnbroker and bordello, where we took one of the rooms allocated for debauchery. I had started to ask Casanova, 'Why can we not go to your apartments . . .?' but he always closed my mouth with a gentle finger which I sometimes bit.

On our way up the dusty stairs to our room we passed two wretches hugging jars of dark liquid. 'Borrowers' wine,' said

Casanova. He explained that those who pawned their goods were obliged to accept a third of their payment in cheap liquor, drinkable only at times of desperation. We ourselves had our own picnic of stolen titbits from my family's kitchen secreted under my cloak. Upstairs in the dark shuttered bedroom, to the rhythmic music of the mattress next door, we laid out the *prosciutto*, bread and olives and wine on my scarf. Over these delicacies, talking with his mouth full and repeatedly knocking his wine-goblet flying with his extravagant gestures, Casanova related to me the crucial event in his young life.

It happened when he was twenty-one years old. It was on the night of April 21st 1746, at the wedding of Girolamo Cornaro della Regina and a daughter of the Soranzo family of San Polo. Casanova was fiddling in the orchestra at the Palazzo Soranzo.

'A cousin of yours, I presume?' Casanova asked. I nodded. My own family, one of the discreet minor branches of the family, had no doubt been invited for some secondary festivities. The party, a famous one, had gone on for three entire days.

As he left the wedding, in the dead of its last exhausted night, Casanova had passed by the red-robed Venetian nobleman, Matteo Bragadin. At that moment a letter fell from the senator's pocket and fluttered to the ground.

'Imagine that dropped letter,' Casanova told me. 'Fix your mind upon it. That piece of paper changed my life. To think that I might have walked past and left it! But I did not.'

Politely, Casanova had drawn the nobleman's attention to the letter. I can imagine the charming gesture with which he bent to pick it up and hand it to the older man, and the modest grace with which he accepted the grateful invitation of Matteo Bragadin to accompany him a way in his gondola, moored just outside the *palazzo*.

But in the gondola, Bragadin collapsed in sudden convulsions. Faintly, he complained that his arm was numb. His eyes were starting to lose their lustre. Casanova helped him home, shooed off the local doctor, and willed Bragadin back to life with a combination of vague medical knowledge and theatrical hocus-pocus. Fortunately, Bragadin survived. He refused to entertain the thought that his recovery had been anything other than a miracle wrought by the fascinating young man who had rescued him.

As witnesses to his miraculous recovery, Bragadin called in his loyal old friends, the nobles Dandolo and Barbaro. I can picture the young Casanova, his beautiful, vigorous body folded into a leather chair in Bragadin's study, his eyes modestly downcast while the three old men all but danced around him, whispering with childish excitement. When questioned Casanova lifted his large clear eyes to them, one by one, and spoke to them all so convincingly, with such obliquity and with such passion that the noblemen were entranced. He hinted that he possessed a magical mathematical formula with which he might know anything he wanted to. Bragadin explained wisely to Dandolo and Barbaro that Casanova's secret was to do with the cult of Solomon's clavicle, known as the *cabbala*. The others nodded wisely.

Casanova did not deny it. Nor did he confirm it. He had already divined that these three old friends beguiled their time with pleasant dabbling in the esoteric arts. He made sure that a charming and mysterious smile greeted their every rhetorical question. Ever after that night Bragadin and his friends would believe in Casanova's occult powers, and Casanova would allow them to do so. In this way, he became their indispensable oracle. They thought that, having him at their disposal, they would have the mythical Philosophers' Stone in their grasp: that they would therefore be able to turn the world upside down, and transform base metals into gold.

Of course, to have Casanova at their disposal, the three noblemen must perforce put themselves at his.

So Casanova was plucked out of the Calle della Commedia, out of his shabby class, out of the orchestra pit, and taken to live in the Palazzo Bragadin near Santa Maria dei Miracoli. Indeed, it seemed a miracle to him, for suddenly he had his own apartment, his own new clothes, his own servant, and his own gondola. He would share the luxurious table of his host, and enjoy an allowance of ten *zecchini* a month. He was not to feel beholden to his patron; he was a free agent. The Wheel of Fortune had indeed turned full circle.

'After all, I owe you my life,' Bragadin loved to say, fondly.

Casanova knew full well that this was not true, but he saw no harm in allowing it to be thought.

'If you wish to be my son, you have only to accept me as your father,' Bragadin would add, revealing yet again his innocence and good nature.

Casanova, not so innocent, knew that he would never be noble, a nobleman's son. He would always be the son of an actress and part-time courtesan. But this was the next best thing. The violin was cast aside; the humiliation evaporated. All he had to do was entertain his new father and his friends, and satisfy their avidity for knowledge of the occult. For this purpose, he invented a spirit, Paralis, whom he consulted on all obscure and difficult matters. The capricious Paralis spoke only in runes and double-entendres, and sometimes not at all. Sometimes Casanova and Paralis were occupied eight hours a day entertaining Bragadin, Dandolo and Barbaro. Paralis was a most possessive spirit and saw off all other pretenders to the noblemen's affections, including at least one potential wife.

It was just before dawn. We roused ourselves on the sordid bed. Some time at an early hour Casanova's voice had slowed and stilled to heavy slow breathing among the swags of my hair.

We exchanged sour-tasting but sweet morning kisses, at first with affection but soon with passion. The bells, as usual, forced us apart. He walked me home to Miracoli. Before I slipped into the house, we arranged to meet the next night at the church of San Geminiano.

My mother found me unconscious on my bed two hours later and could not rouse me. I slept the entire day and woke to the bitter herbal vapour of a tisane beside my bed and the shadows drawing in outside. I opened my eyes, sniffing. My father was looking down on me.

'Are you unwell, Cecilia?' he asked.

I started to smile, but retracted my lips instantly, trying to look wan and delicate. 'I shall be recovered after a little more rest. I shall not come to dinner tonight.'

'*Va bene*, Cecilia. That seems prudent. You are indeed a little pale. I shall tell your mother that you should not be disturbed.'

As soon as he had gone, I slipped out of the house. That night Casanova and I walked from the church to his gondola and floated away to San Vio to hear the rest of his story.

In that story my own image of Casanova merges with that which the poets of the pen and the paintbrush have left us in their records of the happy city in her happiest moments, those of Casanova's years as a rich young man about town.

Now Casanova was allowed his mad, extravagant, lustful youth, not unlike Bragadin's own. How life had changed for him! Now his playground was the costly society life of the Piazza San Marco, the meeting place of the intellectuals, the lechers and the women. Again, he went to the dogs, but this time in style. There was no end to his entertainments, scarcely any of them respectable. Under the shadow of the Church of San Geminiano, he muttered some prayers on his way home after nights of every kind of expensive debauchery.

As always, Casanova took the chance he had been given, and then took it to excess. Casanova's first leg-up to loftier social spheres had left him with a lifelong obsession with social climbing. But Venice knew his background too well. He could not charm or marry himself into the *Libro d'oro*. Among high society, in his mask (or with the mask he made of himself with his mobile features) he was the jester, the entertainer. He was almost an insider, but the young nobles who were amused by him now would never quite forget the poverty of his birth. Casanova never abandoned the friends of his violin-playing years. Among them, in his mask again, Casanova talked rough dialect, seduced the sisters of his friends. He was almost a glamorous insider, but his low-life companions could never forget that he had talents and refined tastes from beyond the back canals. Casanova was an unstable, fascinating brilliant element, a free spirit, rolling from pleasure to pleasure like a drop of mercury. In his mask, with gold in his purse, he tried everything. He was curious, famished for novelty, greedy for new faces and facts, and this curiosity was bound to get him into trouble, picaresque trouble. In those days of spies and censors, it made others, dangerous others, curious about him.

The Inquisitors showed an interest in the wild young man who kept proscribed books, consorted with foreigners, conducted liaisons with the women of men more eminent than himself. The practical jokes had become more extreme and less tasteful. There was the episode with the severed arm which Casanova excavated from a grave and placed in the bed of an acquaintance. The game ended badly, for the victim of this practical joke, Signor Demetrio, discovering the bloodied limb upon the coverlet, had suffered a seizure from which he never recovered.

Venice was becoming too small, too hot for Casanova.

So in 1748, aged twenty-three and just in time to avoid arrest, Casanova began to travel. He took himself to places where his pedigree was more shadowy, where the truth about him could be obscured in a miasma of charm. He also travelled in search of gainful employment or at least profitable entertainment, to taste new things, meet new people, not all of them women. In his time, Casanova would meet writers, priests, diplomats and adventurers. He would meet generals and charlatans. In the course of his travels he would make his extravagant bow to nearly everyone who was anyone from Catherine the Great, Madame de Pompadour, Farinelli il Castrato, several Popes. He made a point of it. Every new face was a treasured novelty for him.

Casanova himself, I am sure, was just as choice a morsel for the jaded palates of those he met. Charisma like his, potent as perfume-essence, was welcome in every yawning drawing room in Europe. To Casanova's youth and vitality there was an extra sheen: he was a Venetian. He was an unofficial ambassador from the mythical happy city. He had something about him they could not name, but wanted to touch.

Casanova told me, and I shall never forget it, 'When you say to a Englishman, a Frenchman, a Pole, a German, a Spaniard, "I am a Venetian," they always acquire a far-away look. This is because what they hear inside their heads is this: "I am tainted with corrupt splendour, I am a cipher for dark secrets, I am a creature apart, I was spawned in decadence and live upon the water. I am as unlike you as I can possibly be, and yet not quite a Turk or a fish."'

Of course, the Europeans were fascinated, attracted, and, more importantly, would pay for the privilege. Casanova was not the only Venetian abroad in those days. Joining him along the by-ways between Paris, Prague, London, Madrid, Vienna, Moscow, Dresden and Constantinople were Canaletto and Bellotto, Goldoni and Rosalba, the Ricci and the Tiepolos . . .

'One day, you will join them on those roads, Cecilia,' Casanova told me. 'With your talent, with your bathtub full of stretched canvases, you will see the world, and the world will see you. What a pleasure for the world!'

I laughed. But I was already beginning to think it was possible. I thought of the portrait currently on the easel in my studio. I thought of an easel in a foreign court, a throng of Frenchmen surrounding me, gesticulating with delight at my work.

Casanova leant over and gathered me up in his arms, pulling me on top of him. 'Do you love me, Cecilia?'

I raised my knees and spread myself over him like a little frog, nibbling his lips. I said, 'I love you enough to eat you entirely.'

'Don't say that, Cecilia,' he told me. 'I once knew a woman who did.'

The Milliner's Tale

BY Giacomo Girolamo Casanova,
Chevalier de Seingalt, Venetian poet

It happened in . . .
Did I ever tell you?
I had just escaped from Spain.
Three cut-throats had been sent to murder me at the border,
Probably the bravoes of the Duke of Ricla,
Whose wicked Nina . . . Or it could have been Manuzzi,
The anti-natural mistress of Ambassador Mocenigo,
Whom I offended by my indiscretion . . .
It was so easy for a man to make enemies in those days!
My gossip cost me the governorship of a colony
And nearly my life.
But I run away with myself. That's another story.
This one is about the milliner.

The mistress of la Pérouse:
A milliner. Pretty, slight, fair,
A look of rumpled linen about her pale face,

One of those blondes whose skin dimples like a ripening
     strawberry in her moments of joy.
So La Pérouse told us.
Anyway, when he left her,
Instead of the Eucharist, one Sunday,
She swallowed his portrait, and died.

First, she ate his mouth,
Whose lips she'd tried to swallow gently, so many times,
His nose, which she'd often sniffed for the perfumes of
     other women.
Then his hair, from which she'd combed the lice with
Her own small hands.
Last of all she ate his eyes,
Because they no longer looked at her
The way they did before.
Then, as I said, she died.
She choked on him, in her little shop
Full of hats, stockings and under-drawers of both types,
In one pocket, they found his love letters.
The other one was full of tears.

6

El leto xe 'l paradiso dei poveri.

Bed is the heaven of the poor.

VENETIAN PROVERB

Of course, during all this time when we were together, Casanova was living with another woman, in another part of town, and they sincerely loved each other. Francesca Buschini, a seamstress, kept his small house by the Barberìa delle Tole, near Zannipoli, in the northern edge of Venice.

Casanova rarely spoke to me of Francesca, but he hid nothing from me if I chose to ask him specific questions. But I did not wish to discuss it with him. I had preferred to find out about Francesca in other ways, much as I had distilled information about him before we became lovers: with my own subtle inquiries on the streets, in the convent, at Florian. So now I knew, from diverse sources, that he shared his little house not only with her, but with her brother and her mother. Francesca was devoted to him, and I understood that he needed the soft, gentle refuge of her after the wearying vagrant years that had finally delivered him back to Venice.

For I was beginning to see that Casanova, who seemed so vibrant to me, was living in the dog days of his life. To me, he was the emperor of my happiness, but I could not help noticing the thread-bare lapel of his frock-coat and the darning of his breeches. I had only ever seen him wear one pair of shoes, somewhat ignominious ones, gnarled at the toes. I saw the grey hairs that curled out from under his wig, and when I lay my head upon his breast after lovemaking I heard the slight wheeze above his heart. The days of his youth, which he brought alive for me every night, were almost impossible to rec-oncile with the poverty of his present. I understood that now that he had fallen upon hard times he needed to be with someone uncritical, unsneering and unaristocratic. His nerves were frayed by years of fawning and he had developed two tics along the lines of his much-practised sycophantic smile, the smile that said, 'But, of course, how utterly right you are, and what pleasure your insight gives us all . . .'

With women, I could see, Casanova might sometimes allow him-self to share his failure. With women, especially women like Francesca, I realised that he was permitted not to smile at all, to let his features relax and to allow himself even to drop his guard, even to weep, to stand vacantly by a window, clutching the curtain made not from some rich brocade, but from something simple, his, with-out graft or flattery. He could rest his head on the giving abundance of her breast, and sleep.

Of course he had no money. God knows how he paid for my beautiful paints and the exotic foods he brought me. All his life, apart from those precious few years as Bragadin's protégé, he had suffered from the lack of money, abased himself to obtain a little, and squandered it when he received it. He had never owned enough for long enough to support an honest woman.

With Francesca, I understood, he could be weak, old, fright-ened. He would sleep in her arms, whimper in his dreams, leave an old man's spittle on her shoulder, cheap make-up on the thin pil-lowcase, pomade on her nightdress, a grey hair and a thin laboured emission in her willing mouth. How could I be jealous of this?

With me he could be magic, tragic and potent. But dignified, never! And what cares a convent girl, half-depraved by her erotic awakening, for dignity?

Of course, I fell to daydreaming sometimes. I pushed my knuckles against my eyes to obstruct reality. Into the pulsing darkness comes Casanova. He comes to my bed. It is heaven there.

'Cecilia, I have something important to tell you.'

His shoulder shudders with a little sob, the pain of his final parting from the estimable Francesca.

'I give my life to you, Cecilia. I beg you to take it with both hands.'

He cannot say more, for his mouth is contorted with the effort of not weeping. He has stumbled here, his eyes full of tears, and has fallen somewhere along the way. His left garter lolls around his ankle, and the sagging stocking shows a trickling rosary of blood.

I rush to him. I kiss his nose, his eyes, the wound on his knee. I smooth down his rampant hair, tie up the garter. We are both kneeling. He pushes his head into my lap, and wraps his arms around my thighs.

'I will look after you, Casanova,' I tell him.

He holds me harder, and whimpers a little.

From his pocket spills a coil of pearls.

'These are for me?'

They are wedding pearls, such as all Venetian brides wear in their first year of marriage.

7

When I went to Casanova the next night I was voracious with new curiosity. And the first thing I wanted to know was this: why did he never marry? And the second one was this: would he ever marry me? In my pocket I carried a pair of little rings made of glass. I turned them on my fingers as we talked, and rubbed them against each other. As I listened, I became rough with them. They clattered like miniature castanets inside my skirt. Finally they fractured between my fingers. I emptied the shards from my pocket and gazed at the coloured dust, like entrails of a disembowelled kaleidoscope.

Casanova blew the fragments from my fingers. 'What is this, Cecilia?'

I never told him, because that night, when we tipped up the kaleidoscope of his memories, we saw Teresa, and we saw Henriette.

We had taken the gondola to the pleasure gardens of Guidecca and sat in the shadows of a gazebo. The tracery of the ironwork tattooed

Casanova's face with shadows in the moonlight. He looked as if he was wearing a mask. But his voice came, rich and familiar, from the mouth that had only just unfastened itself from mine. I held his hand and listened to the tale, stroking his fingers.

In 1754, when he was twenty-nine years old, Casanova met Bellino, an apparent castrato. The voice was exquisite, but there was something mysterious in the young man's aura, something alluring. Casanova found himself falling violently in love with the creature, without knowing which sex it really was. As he loved Bellino erotically, Casanova *felt* that Bellino's body was telling him that he was, in reality, a woman.

But every attempt to forage for the truth in Bellino's nether garments was energetically repelled. Casanova started to be tortured by doubts about the gender of the object of his desires, and by the nature of his own lusts. Bellino, meanwhile, hunted and cornered, tried to placate Casanova with his two little sisters.

At this, I raised my eyebrows. Casanova raised his hands in surprise.

'Of course I accepted, Cecilia. Imagine if you had been in my position. The first was another Cecilia,' he told me, 'like you, but younger, and a virgin. And then her sister, Marina, just as sweet. I loved them kindly for the nights I spent with them, and they are still adorable in my memory. But it was Bellino's virginity that I hungered for, and Bellino's love. Love is divine condiment that makes that little mouthful delectable. The little girls merely whetted my appetite for the main course, and I was glad to give them a tender education to serve in their future pleasures.'

I wrinkled up my nose, childishly. Casanova merely kissed it and went on with his story.

Deranged with lust, he schemed and planned to unmask Bellino's secret. Eventually he stole a glimpse at Bellino's private parts, and was devastated to see that the object of his desires was indeed, apparently, male. But even then he could not give up his obsession.

Casanova's optimism, as ever, eventually found a solution for his dolorous conundrum. He persuaded himself that what he had seen was merely a monstrous clitoris, and he was inflamed anew with curiosity and lust. For what a passionate nature must be endowed with such an expressive part!

Eventually – how could anyone withstand such assiduous attentions? – Bellino revealed himself as Teresa. She turned out to be an impoverished girl who pretended to be a castrato to further her musical career, so that she could support her family. In case of examination, to which castrati were often subjected in those days, she was equipped with a fascinating device. This was what he had glimpsed, and what had desolated him for a time. Now it delighted him.

Casanova described it for me, using his finger and thumb.

'It was a long soft piece of gut, the size of a thumb, white and with a silky surface . . . This contraption was attached to the centre of a very delicate, transparent oval-shaped piece of leather, five or six inches long and two inches wide. By applying this skin with some tragacanth gum, Teresa obliterated her female organ from sight.'

He told me how he begged her to put it on. With a gentle finger he found, to his joy, that the soft pendant offered no obstruction to the actual well of her fascinating passage. He was so aroused by the novel device that he made comical but delicious hermaphroditic love to her on the spot.

I could picture his avidity: I knew it well. When he wanted something, he would purse his lips in a little mew, with the most fervent twinkle in the eye.

'And I did not omit to thank the God who had brought me this new experience. As I thank him for you, Cecilia, now.' He kissed me.

Teresa set a pattern. Now Casanova knew that there was always something of interest to be found in the pockets of women. Be it

lies, love, or tears, Casanova wanted to know. He needed to know.
It might be something he had not tried before.

His greatest love, Henriette, a mysterious Provencal noblewoman, wore a military uniform until he prised her, and her secret
femininity, out of it. They spent three months of ineffable bliss in
Parma. He had never been so close to a woman.

'We went to sleep,' he told me, 'only to wake in the morning, see
each other naked and then we would fall like tigers upon each
other. Eventually, we would rise, more in love than when we went to
bed. Anyone who says a woman cannot make a man deliriously
happy all hours of the day and night can never have known a
Henriette.'

'Did you never quarrel? Were you never bored with her?'

'I was welded to her, mind, soul and body. Never a folded rose
petal came between us.'

But within three months the idyll came to an end. Henriette had
no more surprises for him. As she said herself, she had emptied the
sack. And then, when they parted, through no fault of either of
them, she left him a sorrow that is almost sweeter than pleasure.
Henriette wrote him a letter telling him to imagine that they had
shared a beautiful dream. She told him not to languish in chastity.
She wrote, 'I wish you to love again, and even to find another
Henriette.'

'Why did you not marry Henriette?' I asked him.

'Why, indeed. Sometimes I have been ashamed of loving other
women after God had offered me Henriette.'

'But marriage – no?'

'Cecilia, it's sacrament I detest. Marriage is the tomb of love. The
word "marriage" is used only as a respectable mask for the most
flattering of ideas – the passion of men and women. I prefer the
passion without the mask.'

'Even when it means that your love will end one day?'

'Even then. Always. And so I lost Henriette.'

'But you have me.'

'It's true, my darling, but will we always have each other? Will you always want me? You are a curious woman who loves novelties. Remember the caterpillars you told me about. Remember how you love new flavours, all my stories. The more bizarre they are, the better I please you. I am the same kind of man. It's curiosity that makes men unfaithful. If all women had the same looks and the same minds, a man would have no difficulty in remaining faithful. In fact, he would never even fall in love. He would take the first woman he found and remain happily with her till he died. But we are not like that. We are the slaves of novelty. She uses us to her own ends.'

Later that night, after heavy losses, we slunk out of a casino. Casanova held me under his cape, but he was not with me. He had left his heart in the little gold snuffbox he had handed over at the final count. Henriette had given him that snuffbox. The gondolier had been dismissed hours before. We would walk to my home, in the moonlight. We slipped past San Geminiano into the Piazza of San Marco.

It was *acqua alta*, the Piazza was afloat. The full moon in reflection laughed in the belly of it. Sneers and chuckles of water slapped the steps of the Procuratie.

'Shall we walk around to Rialto?' I asked. There was higher ground there.

'No, my darling,' said Casanova. 'We shall not be afraid of the water. We are Venetians. It is our element.'

He scooped me up in his arms and strode into the milky moonlit water. His legs disappeared into the dark, panting liquid up to his knees. He carried me diagonally across the square, held close against his breast. Over his shoulder I watched our slender wake, and then I turned to see the moon above us. The columns of the Piazza were reflected upon the water; we dizzied their reflections as we passed. Casanova warmed my ear with his breath. My left slipper dropped from my foot and was swallowed by the water like a delicacy. With my bare toe I caressed Casanova's thigh. He reached around with his hand and held my foot, smoothing my toes with delicate strokes. When we reached the Formosa end of the Piazza, we rose out of the water like a confection of Venuses.

At that moment a nun hustled past us, her white pinafore stained with blood. The blank expression on her hard young features frightened me. I told myself that at this hour she must have come from a childbirth or a sickbed. But what was she doing alone?

Casanova watched her until she slipped behind a column. Then she disappeared as if she had never been. For a moment I doubted if she had.

'Did we . . .?' I asked Casanova.

He was lost in his thoughts. Still he did not put me down. He held me tighter.

'Yes, it was a nun, my soul,' he said slowly.

'What are you thinking about?' I asked him.

In 1753, Casanova returned from his travels to Venice. He was now stuffed with information about the occult, the freemasons, astrology, astronomy, the *cabbala*. But he had brought with him a lucid cynicism about it all. More importantly, he intended to use this new knowledge not for philosophical pursuits but for pleasure.

Back in Venice, Casanova played the casinos, all one hundred and thirty-two of them, for the delights they offered and the opportunities to dazzle with his systems and keys. In those days the casinos or *ridotti* were small, unofficial clubs, meeting places for trysting, gambling, dancing and seditious conversation. They were also a place for the classes to mix, and as the Venetian republic gradually dissolved, the first places to melt were these casinos. Casanova, the man of indeterminate class, felt at home in the smoky depths, pungent with opium, of his chosen casino, curious always; even then his eager eye would raise each time the door opened, in a shower of cold air – would it be a new lover, a new protector, a gambler with a new game to teach?

And inside the pockets of women, there were still more surprises to find. Inside the robes of nuns, for example, Casanova found two of the most amorous bodies he ever touched.

C. C. and M. M. he called his nuns, covering their identities with initials that acted like Venetian masks. Their initials were drawn, for Casanova, from an intimate alphabet of semi-anonymous desire, free of convention, free of inhibition. In his stories, Casanova would often rechristen the real women like this, with liberating, concealing initials. He loved, in his time, M. M., C. C., Mlle XVC and Mesdames, it seemed to me, A to Z. Under their initials, as under their masks, women could be whomever they wanted to be.

Casanova was quite gratified to find that his rival with M. M. was no less than the French ambassador. The rotund de Bernis, a future Cardinal, spied on Casanova through a peephole as he performed his best with the nun in the small room at San Moisè decorated with encouraging erotic prints. Everyone knew who was watching whom, which heightened everyone's enjoyment. And best of all was the unforgettable night Casanova spent with both nuns. He told me about it, rejoicing in the geometry and in the violence of their tripartite pleasures. 'We ravished everything of each other's until we all three became the same sex.'

'But were you found out? You and the nuns?'

News of the nuns and other adventures seeped into the gossip parlours of Venice, and into more official ears. Casanova was living dangerously. He was larger than life, he made a noise, he attracted attention. In Venice the walls had not only ears but mouths. Around the city, stone lions' mouths in walls opened in grimaces of disgust to receive denunciations of Casanova. These letters were carried to the Inquisitors. Files opened years before were now fattened with incriminating reports and testimonials.

Casanova was becoming careless, thinking himself beloved by Fate. He was so in love with his own life that he could not look outside it and see the danger.

Finally, Casanova's outrageous luck ran out. He had received warnings in profusion, but he had refused to hear them. He had been too busy being Casanova. One night, his patron Bragadin embraced him sadly. 'I am going to lose you to the Inquisition, my son.' Casanova returned the embrace with true affection. How kind this man had been to him! Still he felt himself inviolable.

But the next morning, July 25th 1755, Casanova was arrested, denounced by a dozen secret spies for atheism, licentious living and freemasonry.

In his apartment the Inquisitors' henchmen found Ariosto, Horace, *Le Portier des Chartreux*, a magic spell-book, and Aretino's book of thirty-five useful sexual positions. Worse, they found all the ephemera of the freemasons, including *The Key of Solomon*, *The Zecorben*, the key work of the *cabbala*, and a *Picatrix*, a manual for creating perfumes and spells to conjure up demons of all classes.

For his arrest Casanova dressed in silk and lace, as if on his way to a wedding. The actor's son was still acting as a nobleman. No one itemised the charge against him, and he saw no reason to cut a *brutta figura* and creep around like one humiliated. Anyway, he would soon be out, he was certain. Bragadin, he thought, would see to things, as always.

But as he crossed the Bridge of Sighs and was ushered into his cell, Casanova suddenly realised that he was now not merely in trouble; he was in danger. There was no limit to the power of the

Inquisitors. In those days wrong-doers would simply disappear off the streets. They would be found maimed and strangled, hanging by one leg somewhere conspicuous, days or years later, a rare and stark lesson in consequences to the inhabitants of the too-happy city.

Casanova found himself making water every quarter of an hour, the first time such a thing had happened to him. He filled two large chamber pots with dark urine.

'My body was telling me the crisis I was in,' Casanova told me. 'I had refused to accept it in my soul. But suddenly it was all clear. I was destroyed. And I had brought it all upon myself entirely. I had such a bitter taste in my mouth as I have never experienced before or since,' he told me, kissing me for comfort against the remembered shock and pain.

As he withdrew his mouth from mine and looked down on me, a *pantegana*, a huge water-rat, scuttled across San Vio. He was the biggest I had ever seen. The cat growled, but even he did not attempt to follow the monster.

'A worthy ambassador from my old enemies,' said Casanova, pointing at the rat. 'They nearly got me that time.'

The Song of the Pantegane in the Prisons of the Doges' Palace, Venice

The culls come in all aflourish in their lace
They're bacon-fed and pasta-gutted
Silk waistcoats stretched over tripes and trullibubs
Stale drunk, tears of the bottle on their frock-coats
Pink and breathless from the pushing shop or
Trouser-ripe from lying in state with their regular harlots.
They think they'll soon be out.
Ha!

It's not long before they're
Dancing like death's head on a mopstick
Herring-gutted, weasel-faced,
Scratching at their scrubbados
And clutching at their eelish paunches,
Screaming that their great guts are ready to eat their little
  ones.

Some girls plead their bellies
But all the morts stop bleeding here.
Their fur drops off: they rub their nude pimply pelts.
Soon they stop talking, or mumble like a mouse in a cheese.
By then they all whiff the same, or more so.
So in the end we only know the fresh ones from the stale
     ones
And the dead ones from the dying.

You think we'd woffle 'em? Sniv that!
A wolf in the stomach would not persuade us!
We'd rather sail to the spice-islands in a privy-pot!
They are too dirty – we'd not stick our snaggs in 'em.
Slubber de Gullions not what we mange.
The slops they lush would give us rumpus in the chitterlins.

We draw the line in Rat-land
Nothing rotten, kickerpoo or still crawling or
Too damned sad on our red rags, our tongues.
Misery stinks most confoundedly.

Anyway there's too much competition
From the active citizens, by which I mean
the lice, the fleas, the flies and the mosquitoes.
They're sharp, the jointed beasts.
They know their trade.
They start eating
Before the culls have dropped their leaves.

8

Tute le volpe finisse dal pelisser.

All the foxes end up at the furriers.

VENETIAN PROVERB

In a sketchbook in my *armadio* I keep the illustrated rendition of Casanova's famous escape from the *Piombi*, the leadlined prisons in the attics of the Doges' Palace. For, as he told me about it, I reached for my sketchbook, and under the mesmerism of his words my hand hovered over the paper, spinning almost involuntary images.

It was not the first time Casanova had told the tale, and nor would it be the last. The story was already a living work of art. He had refined its pungent vocabulary, its knowing pauses and its sharp intakes of breath. I think we both knew that he was polishing it up for the account he would one day write, for the piece of his past he would put out for sale. Casanova would always be fiddling for his supper, long after he laid down the violin.

But this time he spoke the words just for me, and just for me to draw. It was a hot night in early June. We had taken the gondola to Santa Maria della Salute and moored it under a private bridge in a quiet canal. The waves flopped lazily, lucently around us, exhausting their small energies, as we exhausted our larger ones. Afterwards, a violin, Casanova's, could be heard floating over the waves. A little wind sniffled around the lagoon past Salute, and we had moments of relief as it nosed through the velvet curtains. It redefined the lines of sweat down our backs. Casanova reached up to touch the silky roof of the *felze*.

'Imagine a ceiling made of nothing but sheets of lead three feet square and wafer thin,' he began. 'Imagine living in there like a hunchback in a coffin.'

'You are the last man in the world I can imagine in confinement,' I said.

'I was the last man in the world to be able to bear it,' he agreed.

And so Casanova was plucked from his charmed life and put in a cell so small that he could not stand up. If he could have seen out, he would have looked down upon his magnificent former playground of the Piazza San Marco, still arrayed in its glory. Prisoners of State, however, had no such privileges. Casanova lived, viewless, under the roof of the Doges' Palace, for fifteen freezing or sweltering months. Rats as big as rabbits ran over his head, and insects feasted upon his flesh. It reminded him of the boarding house in Padua where he had suffered as a child. Indeed, he felt as helpless and as numb as he had then.

In the Leads, when Casanova lay on his bed, the only possible position, his feet hung over the end. He could not even pace the floor for fear of grazing his head. How to contain his anger in such a small space? How to feed his hungers, for women and good food? And most of all, for novelty? Every day was the same under the Leads. He itched all over with uncontainable desires. Sometimes, in his desperation, he imagined that the little lead nails in the room were nipples and he ran his finger along them.

After days of silence, still no charges had been brought against him. He interpreted the silence optimistically: the charges could not adhere, he thought, he would soon be free. He had been punished enough. Three weeks later, he still nourished hopes that his noble protectors would have him out at any moment.

But more weeks and then months went by, without explanation. He started to think of the noose and the fabled green poison of the Inquisitors. He already felt like an anonymous corpse.

Under the Leads, the heat was as intense as his fear. Casanova shed his finery and sat stark naked on his chair, while the sweat streamed off him into pools on the floor. He developed haemorrhoids, a gift from the Leads that would last for the rest of his life. A dangerous fever soon followed. A doctor visited, leaving him with a syringe and barley water. 'Amuse yourself with enemas,' the physician flung over his shoulder as he left.

But worst of all, in the Leads they would not let Casanova write. He felt, for the first time, that his sanity might abandon him. He heard voices. His dreams were contaminated with venomous fantasies. To read, he was offered only religious tracts of lurid fanaticism: Saint Cecilia and her brethren, all suffering the kinds of tortures he dreaded for himself. And, for amusement, he was allowed to cut his toenails, but not to shave.

The filthy, naked prisoner grew a matted beard. At Christmas, Bragadin was permitted to send luxurious presents: a dressing gown lined with fox fur, a silk coverlet stuffed with cotton, and a bearskin bag in which to put his legs during cold weather, which was now as cruel as the heat had been in August. And the nights were long. Each day that winter he spent nineteen of the twenty-four hours in profound darkness.

There was still no news. His cell was directly above the room in which the Council of Ten hold their deliberations. He heard the old men muttering indistinctly underneath him, like water in a cave, but no one came to tell him of his fate.

Casanova determined to escape, or die in the attempt.

He prowled his cage like a feral cat, tearing food from the arms of his guard. He needed strength to seize his freedom. After nine months confined to the same tiny cell a solitary concession was granted. He was allowed to walk in a corridor outside it for half an hour, and in those minutes he found and secreted a metal bolt.

Patiently, day by day, he set about making a hole in the floor of his cell. By August, the hole was nearly big enough to serve him, and then tragedy struck. The guard came to give him the happy news that he was to be moved to a better cell. There was a dangerous moment when the hole was discovered but Casanova persuaded the guard that discovery of the hole would cost him his own liberty, for his negligence.

Casanova hid his tool in his bible and it came with him to the new cell. A great privilege was granted there: he was given a pencil. And he had a neighbour, at last. He made friends with a cordial criminal next door, a Father Balbi, locked up for impregnating three virgins of his parish.

Casanova managed to pass the precious bolt to Balbi, who spent eight days making a hole in the ceiling of his cell. The priest was able to hide his work with the religious prints that he had been permitted to paper all over his roof. On the ninth night Balbi pulled his plump self up through the hole into the cavernous space between the roofs of the cells and the rafters of the Doges' Palace. He crawled across to Casanova's cell, tore open the ceiling and Casanova climbed up to join him.

Together they clawed a small hole in the ancient roof of the Doges' Palace. It was easy: the old lady was so ancient she was thinning on the top. They raked at the fragile wood with their fingers and it came away in their hands.

They climbed out into the open air. They were struck dumb by the sharp smell of the sea and the sight of it, so long denied. Below them, Venice played, strolled and slept. In his excitement, Casanova slipped and fell, as if for ever, until he was stopped by a rusty pipe, which opened a bloody seam in his leg. He hung there upon the roof, between life and death. It was clear that there was no way down the smooth facade. They must re-enter their prison and find another way down to the ground. They found a dormer window, tore it open and climbed back inside.

Like clever, agitated rats in a maze, the two men forced their way out through various rooms down to the second floor. They were still trapped. Dawn was starting to reveal the milky stones of the central courtyard of the Doges' Palace. Casanova, in desperation, pressed his face against a window. This elegant bloodstained apparition – for Casanova had again dressed himself with care, in his hat trimmed with Spanish lace and feathers – was seen by a guard, who hastened up to them, thinking them a pair of courtiers who had been accidentally locked up overnight. This had happened before.

Casanova drew himself up to his height, only the bandages on his knees detracting from his noble bearing. Casanova and Balbi accepted the guard's apologies graciously, and then walked with quiet dignity out of the courtyard, round the Piazzetta, over the Bridge of Sighs and onto the Riva degli Schiavoni. Once out of the guard's sight, they scuttled to the water's edge and took the first gondola they saw to freedom, to exile.

It was All Saints' Day, 1756. The first rays of the sunrise gilded the domes of Salute.

As he told me this story, I had filled page after page with tiny vignettes: Casanova on his too-small bed, plump Balbi holing his ceiling, the perilous moment on the roof. In my last sketch I showed Casanova and Balbi, standing in the gondola, and looking back at

Salute and the ghostly bell-towers of Venice emerging from the morning mist, like delicate stockings hanging out to dry.

I drew Casanova's thirty-year-old face, choked with an excess of emotion. In my picture Casanova looks like a child taken off to school by force. Leaving Venice, it seems to him, forever, he has broken down in tears.

9

La novità le piase a chi non ga gnente da perder.

Novelty pleases those who have nothing to lose.

VENETIAN PROVERB

All Venetians love a novelty! Venice craves novelty the way some cities crave war.

A pretty young novelty who can make the Venetians beautiful forever? Bound to succeed!

Within weeks of my opening the new studio, my sitters' book was peppered with noble names – ancient titles from the innermost circle of the *Libro d'oro*. I insisted on keeping my book myself, filling out the columns of down-payments given, paintings commissioned, finished, final payments made. Casanova looked over my book and shook his head with delight. He rejoiced in the fact that a young woman who could paint a dewdrop on a peach could also make so much money.

On Casanova's advice, I used some of my earnings to decorate my studio. I renovated the painted ceilings myself. I bought expensive furniture and carpets. The china was Sèvres and Limoges. A café next door provided French hot chocolate and dark aromatic coffee on silver trays. My divan was furnished with tapestried cushions and a yellow coverlet of flowered Pekin silk. The opulence of my studio was for professional gain rather than personal comfort: to attract even grander clients it had to be impressive. There were comfortable chairs for my rich visitors and a floor-to-ceiling display of faces already executed. I made sure that my studies of well-known subjects were prominently displayed. Young men, other artists, came to my studio. I realised with pleasure that they wanted to be seen there.

My clients, particularly the middle-class ones, came to my studio looking not only for a beautiful rendition of their own faces but for taste and style. They hoped that a little of my refinement would rub off upon them when they left. In their warehouses they stored luxurious silks. They knew which were the costliest bolts, but not whether one silk was lovelier than the other in an aesthetic sense. I showed them, by the silks I draped around them, by the colours I chose for their backgrounds. I gave them not just confident portraits, but also confidence.

My first-time sitters were very dependent upon me. They looked in grateful wonder at the classical busts and musical instruments I placed beside them. Sometimes I would ask them to rest an elbow upon a broken column and to stare into the distance. In this way I indicated a deep knowledge of the classical past on their part (whether they could read Latin or not). Or I would pose them next to a beautiful wooden globe to show their cosmopolitan *savoir faire*, or holding a kaleidoscope, to show the scintillating variety of their visions. Sometimes I painted them standing cross-legged, to show how much at ease they were in this learned elegant world. They liked to explain to their friends, as I had explained to them: 'You see, this foot planted solidly in the earth shows the stability of life. The other one, crossed and just tip-toeing the ground, shows the freedom and spirituality of my soul.'

More experienced sitters wanted to choose their own backgrounds and costumes. Venetians ladies chose strange poses sometimes. French fashion still dominated so I too endured our lamentable Marie-Antoinette phase of noble milkmaids. I was relieved when it was over. With their sophisticated coiffures and the luxurious adventures etched in their eyes, my high-born Venetian milkmaids were never completely convincing. The *Poupée de France* still reigned supreme in the Merceria. Whenever she appeared in a new costume the women of Venice ran mad to copy her within days. When I passed her, dressed in some almost unpaintable confection of lurid colours and exaggerated textures, I shook my fist at her. She wasted my time: my ladies' dresses might even go out of fashion within the period they sat for their portrait, and they would insist upon being repainted in the latest style. 'You're only a doll,' I sneered. Her glassy eyes glittered malevolently at me. She had dragged many Venetian husbands to their ruin with her excesses of lace and satin. No doubt she had also driven many other artists to desperation.

I still liked to paint my own landscapes and draperies, unlike some of my competitors who sent their paintings out to be finished by jobbing artists who specialised in such things, or employed little Cecilias with a specific skill. It was not unknown for a painting to be sent to three different addresses: to the expert in ladies' finery, to the foliage painter and to the specialist in ancient ruins. You could even buy paintings ready-made with an extravagant but enduring costume and a timeless background. There was just a vacancy for the head which the portrait painter would add in.

Casanova had taught me that these backgrounds were important. They were part of the character of the sitter, part of the portrait. Venice did not offer me the current fashion for rustic scenery from life, of course. So for my landscapes I arranged little fantasy models in my studio, with heads of broccoli for trees, and chess pieces for ruined towers. Or, where the sitters permitted me to be more imaginative, I tried to paint the feelings straight out of their hearts:

I tried to render their hopes, dreams and fears as clouds, mountains and birds of paradise.

An artist is an entertainer. In the studio I dressed myself pleasantly, to look older and worldlier than I was. I knew that I must present myself as the material equal and the aesthetic superior of my clients. When they saw me in a rich gown, of a fabric they could not quite name, my sitters felt comfortable, in safe hands. I had to guard my *lingua biforcuta* and groom my talents for *conversazione*. It was necessary to be gregarious to be a successful artist, to make people feel welcome, to be able to talk fluently while you painted. The act of being painted must be a pleasurable thing for my spoiled, bored and rich sitters. Anyway, it helped their faces, and so my portraits, if they were happy. Felicity is a great beautifier.

On prominent display I had all the artists' manuals. The French ones were particularly impressive. They showed exactly how drapery falls around the body and other such details that impressed the layman. In my opinion I had to know those things merely in order to know how to break the rules, but my sitters were reassured at the sight of them. They felt their money well spent.

I loved my tools. I was happy even to mix my own colours. In the corner of my studio stood a grindstone and jars of vivid powder, which would be liquified with the oil, drop by drop. But when I was very busy, I purchased paint that had been mixed already. The prepared paint lay waiting for me in oiled pigs' bladders, which sighed sweetly when I pierced them with a tack to release the nectareous colour inside.

I loved my brushes, either horse hairs wrapped with waxed string onto sticks, or little clumps of squirrel fur forced into the quills of birds and then these in turn forced onto narrow batons of wood. The brushes were graded according to the size of the bird that had suffered to provide them: crow, duck, small swan, large swan . . . I did not know if the birds were still alive when their feathers were plucked from them, but sometimes I heard their indignant squawks in my head when I picked up a brush made from their involuntary gift.

With some portraits I would stand fully six feet from the sitter and use a slender six-foot brush so that I was also six feet from the canvas. This enabled me to examine the painting from the same distance from which the viewer would eventually see it. The portrait painter often sees her subject and her painting too intimately. She needs, from time to time, to stand back and gaze upon it as the world will see it, before going back to the intimacy of close contact with the canvas.

I loved my pastels for quick sketches, but they did not last. I could not use them for my regular work or my popularity would not survive long. The pastels came from Switzerland and smelt of sterile efficiency. I soon humbled them to fragments. When in the *estro*, the full flamboyant flow of my work, I always pressed them too hard, and broke them in half.

I loved my palette, the curve of wood with what seemed like a bite taken out of it. This was where the swag of brushes would rest. When I was ready to work, I clipped my gallipot, with its measure of oil and turpentine, onto the palette. First, I reached for my twin-headed stick, with white chalk at one end and red or white at the other; with this I sketched in the highlights and lowlights of my portrait. Soon, I would gently blow the chalk away, as I approached with my paint.

I cannot really describe the process of applying the paint, because I do not myself know where it came from. I just know that I would sit in front of my subject, and a few hours later I would wake up, and the painting would be just a little more finished. In the *estro* of a portrait, I would stride around with my mahlstick, which stopped me from smudging my hand in oils that took days to dry. Sometimes I applied the paint with a brush, and feathered it with my fingers.

If you were to describe it to the inhabitants of another star, you would be obliged to say, merely, 'I drew the outline of a likeness and then I filled it in with colours.' But this process creates only pleasing marks upon paper. You need to make an individual who breathes, kisses, laughs, makes love. This does not happen until your colours meet and greet each other. At this moment, something new is afoot. The alchemy has begun.

You can paint a portrait *di getto*, achieve your final effect in one sitting. Or you can give it years of your life. There is not, in any case, a picture in the world that is really complete, other than relatively. When you put down your brush, the portrait is finished only until you pick it up again. If you worked upon it another day, the painting would seem more finished.

Even when you've signed and sold it, a painting continues to alter. Oil paint does not truly dry for many years, even though it may cease to be sticky within days. Linseed oil is touch-dry in three days, poppy oil in five and walnut oil about the same. But then the process of immortality really starts, with ageing. First the oil combines with the air to produce a solid film. That coating is at first sensitive and flexible, like baby skin, but it hardens and becomes more brittle as it gets older, and sometimes the oil secretes a yellow patina. Then comes the craquelure, the tiny cracks in the portrait's skin. Even when you work hard, painting fat over lean (creating a surface that is oilier and oilier), you cannot always avoid wrinkling in the old age of a painting. So it is better to know how it will look in its old age, and make provision for it to be loveable then, too.

As Antonio used to do, I seated my sitters upon soft chairs on little platforms. This raised their eyes to the same level as mine while I stood at the easel, but it also served to give them a sense of their own particularity. From their platform, they watched, with tiny swivels of their eyes, my own movements from paint table, to palette, to canvas. They always drew in a breath when I first raised my charcoal to the paper, and when I wiped away stray flakes with a silk handkerchief they always flinched as if I was erasing their soul. I could see them wondering . . . Was I inspired in that moment by their eyes, their fingers, their mouth? Did I want to kiss them? Did I like them? Would I make their immortal image beautiful?

Some clients demanded mirrors behind me so they could watch the progress of my work, and caution me. I was not discomforted by the mirrors. A sitter as anxious as that could be helped by the mirror. It would make sure he maintained his animation, his optimum level of attractiveness and alertness. He would monitor his attractiveness in the mirror and not slop into jowls nor slump into potbelly. The mirror kept my clients endlessly amused. No one ever tires of looking at themselves.

They were right to be anxious, my sitters.

They knew instinctively that when you paint a portrait you paint your reaction to the sitter, rather than the sitter himself. You paint your feelings on that day, your irritations, your bad night, your own cycle of the moon. Mixed with all these things are your impressions of the person whom you paint: how they look to you, how they smell to you. You swill in your ears the things they have said. You might even wonder how they will pay you. While your eye is noting the physical detail of their appearance, a more profound emotional transfer is being stamped on your spirit. When your eye has done its prodigious labours, you join all your perceptions together. Then you pick up your brush and load each hair upon it with what you now know.

So I was entirely occupied, in the hours allowed to me, in creating the immortality of others and making it beautiful. While I worked I had time to daydream on my own account. With all his talk of immortality, Casanova had inspired me to look to my own.

I wanted to be like my heroine Angelica Kauffman, twenty-seven years older than I was and already known the world over as '*die Seelenmalerin*' – the painter of people's souls. I monitored her progress jealously, watching as she realised *my* dreams.

I am indebted to Angelica for several reasons. Of course I owe her some technical matters and a few themes for backgrounds, for example, and some thoughts upon the construction of the human nostril.

But I also owe Angelica my talent for research, which would one day become almost more important to me than my painting. Upon Angelica I practised the art of learning all about someone else who obsessed me and possessing their story as if it were my own. You might call it spying. I call it research, or rather *distillation*. I learnt how to extract information about her painlessly, drop by drop from my clients who had also been hers. She taught me to scour the *Giornale* and the *Osservatore* for news of her successes and the scandals that pursued her. I would go to cafés to pay two *gazéte* to read the *avisi*, our gossip sheets. I learnt how to read English and French and even the Venetian newspapers, and press out from each sheaf of crumpled paper a new droplet of information about my quarry. I learnt how to distil truth from gossip. I learnt how to read her work, for a painter always reads a painting, and I learnt how to draw out of it what she had to tell me about what was important to me.

Angelica, unwittingly, had taught me something else: to be ambitious, to want to paint the people who shaped our time with their intellectual or physical charisma. That was a lesson which would one day lead me to hell.

But I run away with myself.

10

Al la puta oziosa el diavolo ghe bala in traversa.

The idle girl has a devil dancing under her apron.

VENETIAN PROVERB

Angelica Kauffman knew how to capture personality as well as features. In her long life she knew only two unsatisfied customers. Unfortunately, one of them was Goethe. But even he continued to adore her. She had started young, younger even than I had done. At eleven, the Bishop of Como, Monsignor Cappucino, engaged her to paint his portrait. Commissions followed from the Duchess of Modena and others. She was launched.

You groom your career as an artist by your choice of the paintings that you copy. You learn the skills of the other artists by tracing the paths of their paintbrushes. Angelica followed the path that my wistful imagination hewed for me. She had worked with my idol Piranesi on perspective and copied the great works in the Uffizi, as I longed to do. She had chosen the same paintings, the Raphaels and the Ghirlandaios, the same saints, and the same Madonnas that I craved to master.

Then, in 1765, three years before I was born, Angelica Kauffman had arrived in Venice. She stayed for a year, feasting upon our

Tintorettos and Veroneses, and painting visiting English Society who had developed a taste for her work. She moved to London and bought a tall house in the tight streets of Soho. Her London neighbours of the time included Lady Mary Wortley Montagu, former inhabitant of the Palazzo Mocenigo. In Venice, and in London, Angelica knew everyone. Her talent and the sweetness of her personality opened every door. The mad, impossibly talented painter Henry Fuseli was in love with her.

But instead she married a complete impostor, the so-called Count de Horn, who posed as a Swedish nobleman. The truth, as she soon discovered, was that her new husband was a bigamist called Brandt. When he was exposed, he tried to extort money from her, and then to kidnap her. He died, fortunately, in 1780. She was thirty-nine years old, and free again.

Except that she was never free, for Angelica, it seems, was always pushed by her ambitious father. Idleness was a sin, he told the newspapers, or at least it allowed sin to toy with you. So Angelica was endlessly productive and remained innocent. The King of England himself sat for her in 1768.

Then a second husband came to extract more work from her. She married a Venetian, Antonio Zucchi, fifteen years her senior, who had come to London to decorate ceilings, but who soon relaxed upon the earnings of his famous wife. Venice sometimes has this orientalising effect upon its men. *Venetians are*, as our proverb goes, *born tired and live to sleep*. Even our lovely buildings seem to be born frail and exhausted, so delicate do they appear in the morning mist, and within a few years they start to lean against each other for support.

During Angelica's engagement to Zucchi, Marat, the bloodstained French revolutionary, pretended to have seduced her. News of this scandal had come to Venice, and everyone thought the marriage doomed. The Zucchi relatives were to be seen purse-lipped and impermeable to friendly inquiries about their son. Nonetheless the wedding took place on July 10th 1781. Then the newly-weds came to Venice to share their joy with the family.

The Zucchis paraded their famous daughter-in-law around Venice. My parents were invited to a soirée. When they met her, no one could believe the Marat story. Even without her personal charm and obvious wholesomeness, there was Angelica's extraordinary work: her porcelain complexions, her deep, deep eyes, her exquisite hands. Everyone wanted Angelica to paint their souls. Clients pressed upon her, including the Grand Duke and Duchess of Russia, for whom all Venice had been transformed into a welcoming pageant, complete with bullfighting and extravagant processions. Venice was wild with rumours that the Duke had fallen in love with her. I saw her once, walking through the Piazzetta with a rich English client. I followed them at a discreet distance, staring greedily at her slender outline, the purity of her profile and the rigid tidiness of her coiffure. Her client gazed down upon her adoringly. I picked up his *carte de visite* as it fluttered from his topcoat pocket. I later heard that 'Mr Bowles, The Grove, Wanstead' had ordered dozens of paintings from Angelica.

I pressed my parents for details of their meeting with her, as far as I dared. I could not ask them the questions I wanted to ask. And even if I did, they did not have the language to answer them.

Angelica Kauffman left Venice in 1782, just before I, the unsaintly Cecilia, took my sinful bath and was interrupted by a cat. Angelica had been invited to Naples, where she painted the Royal Family. Sir William Hamilton, the English consul, commissioned a Penelope from her and was enchanted by her. He wrote to William Beckford, a young English friend: *As for Angelica, she is my idol.* Remember William Beckford, he is part of our story. Angelica, meanwhile, went on to Rome.

In time, Angelica would start to hear about me, never knowing how she herself had prepared my path for me. To me also would come those commissions from the Queen of Naples, the Hamiltons, Goethe and others. For the sitter who has once been painted beautifully, portraiture becomes an addiction. Having been painted by Angelica, they would, one day, want to be painted by me, to see what new beauties I could distil from their faces to display to posterity. I, moreover, was an Italian, so I had the insider's view of their paintable treasure. Angelica could paint their souls and make you wish for spiritual communication with them. But I – I could make you want to make love to them, to feel their fingers upon your own, their lips upon yours.

Enough of the cloudy future. We are talking of a green time when my favourite palette was the first one given to me by Casanova, when I was learning the truth of Casanova and his stories, when I was privileged to hear them from his own lips as I lay in his arms.

11

'After the Leads, I lived in exile from Venice for over eighteen years,' Casanova told me. 'That's longer than you have been alive, Cecilia. It's a long time to be away from home.'

I held him tighter. We were lying on the divan in my studio, on the yellow silk coverlet. He stroked my throat, and went on with his story. He was happy tonight. His first memory took him to a good place.

At first, after his escape, Casanova had returned to Paris. By staying silent at the right moments, and eloquent at even better ones, he had managed to take the credit for a bold plan to organise a state lottery. He had convinced the nervous ministers to back the lottery, and to make it as extravagant as possible. He knew the tastes of the French.

He explained, '"The thing," I told the ministers, "is to dazzle. It's an art that satisfies everyone. It's a correction of imperfect life that fails to offer sufficient excitement from time to time."'

France was dazzled. For the first time, Casanova was a rich man. He showed the Parisians how to live, how to eat and how to make love. Paris was laid waste by his charm. The Parisians devoured the luxuries he pressed upon them. But soon he was back on the road, in search, as always, of more love and more money. He traversed France and Italy, again and again, his strongbox laden with diamonds, watches, and Bills of Exchange.

He just needed one big deal to set him up for life now, he thought.

Just one.

In 1758, Casanova started to prepare for the elaborate scam on Madame d'Urfé. It would be the consummate act of dazzlement.

Jeanne d'Urfé was a rich, shrivelled Marquise obsessed with alchemy and the occult. She wore a large magnet round her neck to attract lightning. When they first met, she took Casanova to her laboratory, where he was astonished to be shown a substance that she had kept over the flame for fifteen years, and that was to stay there for another four or five. It was a projectile powder, which, when ready, she assured him, would be able to transform any metal into gold in a minute. Madame d'Urfé clutched his hand and stared at him avidly. Her chimney was full of black soot, her face lined with old lusts and bitternesses. She had quarrelled with her family. She had plans to replace them, magical plans.

As with Bragadin, Casanova entered into the spirit of it all, and added his own special talents to hers. Madame d'Urfé's great chimera was that she believed in communion with elemental spirits. Like Bragadin, she refused to believed that Casanova was an ordinary mortal. And, as with Bragadin, Casanova found it convenient not to disappoint her. He dazzled her.

He called up his old spirit-genius, Paralis, who once so effectively entranced his old Venetian patrons. With a series of charming small confidence tricks, Casanova put the Marquise utterly in his power, which is where she craved to be, and he became the arbiter of her soul, which she longed to offer him.

They spent five years in delightful negotiations, during which time Madame d'Urfé bailed him out of scrapes, sent him money, dressed him in fanciful costumes. She herself was sustained upon a continuous diet of elaborate and picturesque bunkum: mysterious manuscripts in invisible ink, ritual bathings, candle-lit ceremonies, naked nymphs and messages from the moon, all orchestrated with unctuous elegance by that talented spirit-oracle, Paralis.

It had to come to a head. Finally, Casanova agreed to impregnate Madame d'Urfé with her own reincarnation. He was to give her a 'Word' – an emission of semen, the issue of which creates life. By this operation, a union between a mortal woman and an immortal spirit, he would make her very own soul pass into the body of a male baby.

'Did you believe in this plan, even for a minute?' I asked him.

'No, not for a second, Cecilia.'

'But you proceeded with it, anyway?'

'Someone else would have done it, had I not. Europe was full of charlatans in those days! And I was at least gentle with her delusions. I enriched all her mysteries. I gave her something to hope for, secret plans to make, gorgeous ways to spend her money. She had more of that than she could use. She detested all her relatives. I was her family.'

'Family? Did you never feel guilty for what you did with her?'

'When I fell in with her crazy notions, I never felt that I was deceiving her. She had already deceived herself so thoroughly that I could not disabuse her, even if I tried. So I consented to enact her desires. I did not create them, remember. And indeed, I respected and even loved her in a way. You see, she was insane only because she had an excess of intelligence.'

There were several false starts to the reincarnation of Madame d'Urfé. One of the assisting nymphs proved venal. Anonymous letters arrived warning Madame d'Urfé against Casanova, but he defended himself with plumed gestures and soft words. He looked deeply into her eyes, and then lowered his own as if to say that what he had seen there was too profound to gaze upon a moment longer. Looking at the wall, he told her he needed more time and more money to prepare new and more esoteric rituals, to serve her better, to be worthier of her mystical gifts. The old lady clasped his hand, panting, and promised him anything.

Finally, in exchange for a vast sum of money, Casanova performed the long-awaited ceremony. Three times in succession he used his own body as a medium to impregnate Madame d'Urfé herself. In the magic world they conjured up, it was not, of course, Casanova undertaking the important business but Paralis, his immortal incarnation. His lover, Madame d'Urfé, also renounced her human form to become the goddess Séramis.

They met by moonlight in a beautiful bedroom and removed their robes, one by one.

'And was Madame d'Urfé very old and ugly?' I asked.

'Hideous, a monster, poor lady.'

'And so how did you manage to raise the steed to utter the Word, Casanova?'

'That time, I had my Venetian angel, Marcolina, to help me. In lewd postures, and with skilful manipulations unseen by the goddess Séramis, Marcolina prepared me for my role. And I kept my eyes shut when Marcolina was out of sight.'

*

In the first rite, Casanova worked for half an hour, groaning and sweating. Séramis wiped from his brow the sweat that dripped from his hair, mixed with pomade and powder. The second combat was of fifty-five minutes. Marcolina continued to treat him to the most provocative caresses, preserving the wavering tumescence that Séramis' withered body threatened to soften to a nullity. The third time, Paralis appeared to faint away completely at the climax.

It was a triumph: Séramis was surely sown with the Word. Flushed and serene, she thanked Paralis for her immortality and pressed another large purse upon him.

I asked Casanova, 'Could you really make her pregnant?'

'I doubt it. And I must confess that I cheated. Only the first transport yielded the Word. The second and third times, I merely feigned the final convulsions. In any case, she was thirty years beyond child-bearing age.'

When I thought about it afterwards, I fashioned my own theory about what had happened. I could not blame Casanova, even as much as he blamed himself, which was little.

After all, the aged Séramis had enjoyed the best orgasm of her life with the most famous young lover of her times, so perhaps nobody was deceived. Madame d'Urfé, I think, got what she had paid for.

When I suggested as much to Casanova, he grew thoughtful, and then smiled broadly.

'You may well be right, Cecilia. Everyone is for sale. Some people even advertise.'

. . . Lady, with or without a Servant, may be immediately accommodated with a genteel and elegant furnished first Floor with all Conveniencies; to which belong some peculiar Advantages; it is agreeably situated in Pall Mall, with boarding if required; it may be entered on immediately, and will be let on very reasonable Terms, as it is no common Lodging House, and more for the Sake of Company than Profit. Please to enquire at Mrs Redaw's, Millener, exactly opposite Mr Deard's Toy Shop in Pall Mall, near the Hay Market, St James's.

12

Amar e non venir amà,
xe come forbirse el culo senza aver cagà.

To love without being loved
is like wiping your arse without having shit.

VENETIAN PROVERB

'Did you ever lose heart?' I asked him a few days later.

Casanova had come to my studio again and stood slowly spinning my wooden globe with absent-minded hands. The globe slowed to a dragging dawdle. The pink outline of England lingered under his fingers. He looked down, grimaced, and flicked the whole country away. He turned his back on the globe and came to my easel.

'The heart is a fool,' he told me, with uncharacteristic bitterness. He explained dolefully, 'Yes, I lost mine, in London. Never go there, Cecilia. It's a cruel place.'

It was rarely that Casanova asked for my pity. I moved along my painting bench and made space for him to sit beside me. He put one arm around me, and with the other picked up my brush-hand. He placed it gently against the easel to indicate that I should continue with my work while he told me the sour-tasting story of how London had razed his happiness, and of the dark things he had encountered within himself when he went there.

It had promised so much, London. The goddess Séramis had made him rich. While Madame d'Urfé took to her curtained bed in Paris, awaiting her supposed confinement, Casanova proceeded to England, full of confidence, sure that he could re-enact there his success with the French lottery.

He took a house in Pall Mall, engaged a manservant, and awaited conviviality and good times, as he had found everywhere else. But in London Casanova dined, silent in the shock of loneliness, alone. The local delicacies must be sampled, of course, but tender lampreys in Worcester sauce and even the famed green goose gravy savoured of nothing when he could not share them. He looked for old friends, as always. But there was no such sustenance to be found. Even his former lover Teresa Imer, reborn as the London hostess Madame Cornelys, showed him only the most grudging hospitality. He advertised coyly for a lady lodger, which made him a laughing stock. But he amused himself interviewing the applicants. The advertisement brought him the mysterious Portuguese Countess Pauline, who reminded him of Henriette. He suffered acutely when she left, as Henriette had done, to pursue her destiny. More pain awaited him.

His heart, fragile from the loss of Pauline, was a mere plaything for the sharp Swiss whore La Charpillon with whom he fell precipitately in love. He wanted her to adore him. She hated him, made a fool of him, and nearly bankrupted him. He paid for her; he was promised her. A dozen times, she offered herself to him, only to trick him from his joy at the last moment. Then he found her *in flagrante* with her hairdresser. When she still refused him, he was reduced to violence, and hated himself for it. After he beat her, she pretended to be dying, and made sure that he heard about it.

In the cold, ugly streets of London, Casanova thought of suicide for the first and only time in his life. He set out for the Thames, his pockets lined with balls of lead. But a chance meeting with the affable Sir Wellbore Agar, a plate of oysters and the sight of three naked prostitutes dancing the hornpipe accompanied by blind musicians all combined to restore his will to live. (He was even moved to notice that, while dancing, the male prostitute maintained his conquering appearance, and he resolved to try this experiment upon his himself when he felt better.)

Then he found the supposedly dead Charpillon dancing a hectic minuet in the Rotunda at Ranelagh.

'Did you beat her again?' I asked.

As he had wanted me to do, I worked while we talked, painting a damask curtain, the background to my current portrait. Casanova gestured with admiration towards the sheen of my fabric, and replied, 'You know me, darling, there is little taste for brutality in me. Anyway, I was too weak, too destroyed by her machinations. I took to my bed to recover my health and hide from the humiliation she had thrust on me. Everyone in London was laughing at me, cold English snorts and giggles from behind their hands.

'While I lay in bed, contemplating my pain, I came up with another plan.'

In the bird market, Casanova purchased a pretty green parrot. In his bedroom, he taught it to deliver just one simple phrase: 'La Charpillon is a worse whore than her mother'. In less than two weeks the obedient parrot learnt the words so well that it repeated them tirelessly from morning to night. It adorned each performance with an improvisation of its own: after uttering the words, it gave a great burst of derisive laughter.

'La Charpillon is a worse whore than her mother!' sneered the parrot on Casanova's bed-post. 'Caaaaaaaaaaawah! La Charpillon is a worse whore than her mother!'

It was time to get out of bed and start living again.

Casanova put the loquacious bird for sale at the stock exchange for fifty guineas. Alerted to the danger, La Charpillon's latest admirer purchased the bird and silenced it forever on the spot. But the caper, which was the talk of London, exorcised La Charpillon's malevolent spirit from Casanova's breast. When he saw her in the street a few months later, he had difficulty in remembering her name.

However, it was a turning point for him. 'From the moment I met La Charpillon,' he told me, 'that was when I started to die.'

'But you were a young man!'

'I was thirty-eight years old.'

Certainly, after La Charpillon, nothing was ever the same. The hurts from the past started to join the hurts from the present in a mosaic of pain. Casanova reminded me how, reciting a sad litany of his failures. There was the stone-hearted Angela in Venice, the unheatably cool Marchesa G. in Rome. Andriana Foscarini – she of the dragee made of hair – had ever refused him access to the 'fatal vault'. Now there were women who took him to their beds only for him to find a hideous pesthouse under their chemises. He already felt, suddenly, that he had grown old. There were times when he found the pleasures of love less intense than he had imagined them before the act. After love, he no longer slept well. That is, when love could be obtained. Women no longer chose him, automatically, from among a field of rivals. For now he was made to feel it was a favour granted even to share a woman with another man. He could no longer expect that sacrifices would be made in order to spend one night with him. He was sometimes obliged to pay for the pleasures that had flowed into his life freely before. His schemes became more elaborate. The women were becoming more expensive to obtain, just when he had less with which to buy them. Worst of all, young men showed no offence when Casanova tried to steal their women from them. They did not see him as a threat.

'I had lost the power to please at first sight, which I had so long possessed in such vast quantities,' he told me.

'Except me,' I said, reminding him of our first night, pointing at myself with my brush.

Casanova gently diverted the dripping brush from my white *fisiù*. 'Poor laundry women, Cecilia!' He would not be consoled. 'But remember how hard I had to work, how much I had to arrange, in order to obtain you.'

After London, everything became harder for Casanova, not just the women. When we tipped the kaleidoscope to the years after La Charpillon I saw flight from debt in London, fruitless journeys to Riga and Saint Petersburg to curry favour at courts who were indifferent to his talents. I saw duels, banishments, humiliation in Paris and imprisonment in Madrid. I saw assassins on his trail and near escapes. I saw breathless concealments in wardrobes, stolen raptures in sordid attics and short excursions under insanitary petticoats. I saw the continual unlocking of his strongbox to bring out gold to pay for his pleasures and the pleasures of others. I saw him circling Venice, in ever-decreasing circles. He was homesick, tired, and almost penniless.

The Casanova of the recounted stories was getting older, feebler, less reliably potent. I was beginning to be able to reconcile the Casanova of his tales with the Casanova in my arms. This Casanova had started to feel his mortality and he had started to be afraid of time. By continuous travelling, he had tried to stop time. By wearing a mask, he had still tried to stop time, for no one could watch him withering behind it. With the love of a young women like myself Casanova tried to stop time. I began to understand some-thing – why his greatest loves were seldom older than Juliet – and I began to understand something else – why he had never chosen one woman, for alongside her, however much he loved her, he would start to grow measurably old.

I pictured Casanova living out his exile alone under high foreign skies, feeling vulnerable.

And so hopeless. He craved closeness, and was beginning to wonder if he would ever be close to anyone again. He knew he had love in him. He had known intimacy, and he knew how to love, properly. But his life now, in comparison to those past joys, was merely a candle flame against a dirty window, just a smear of warmth against a pocked mirror. He had made no impression upon the world; his only legacy was etched upon the transient skins and hearts of the women who had once loved him. There was a bad alchemy at work inside Casanova now, a corrosive inner acidity that was consuming his self-confidence and good humour. In his younger days, he never bore a grudge. But by now, too many evils had rained down upon him. On occasion, spleen bubbled from his fat lips, his pantaloons were sagging, over-loaded with loans, for which he hated to grovel.

I pictured Casanova, in increasingly shabby carriages, rapping his head against the glass to the rhythm of the horses, looking at the veins thickening on the backs of his hands, the bruises healing or emerging, the mosquito bites on the scars of old loves. Insults rotted in his memory, with no sweet new experiences to soften their blows now. Casanova knew, as he knew every hair on Madame d'Urfé's pendulous chins, the jaunt and jut of every road from Pisa to Paris. But nowhere, along the way, could he find what he was looking for.

Casanova, too many times now, knew what it was to clutch his last *zecchino* so tightly that when he paid it over for food he still had its impression etched upon his hand. He read his brand mark: MARC. FOSCARINUS DUX VENEZIA chased its tail around the circumference, while inside there was the square cross with floriated points. Venetian *zecchini*, Ottoman *piastre*, French *louis*, English guineas, Milanese *philipi*, Portuguese *reis*, Spanish *maravedís* had tumbled from his hands at pleasure houses and gaming tables, very few had made their way back to him.

Casanova started, shamefully, to profit from his own myth. The rich and curious would pay in coin to hear his stories. He would even tell them for nothing, so hungry was he, these days, for attention. Casanova knew the value of speaking French with his charmingly muscular Italian accent. He could plume the feathers of his words with extravagant gestures – imaginary flowers and jewels blossomed on empty fingers from which every ring had been pawned. When he spoke well, he was led to the trough to feed on rich foods. Behind his back, he heard the well-bred sniggers. And in his ears he always heard the metronome tick, the hourglass in his purse trickling away to emptiness. Then the smile of the knowing servant not lasting long enough to sugar-coat the last *Oui, Monsieur*, as he made his hasty exit from a noble house with his winnings in his shoes.

In the kaleidoscope Casanova was always wearing his *Arlecchino* costume, performing. He performed so well that everyone was fooled. No one sensed the slow bleeding of his tragedy. He did not want their pity, anyway. Pity carries sadness on its soft back. Casanova could not bear to inflict sadness, or to endure it. The one art he had continuously practised, against all odds, was that of happiness, given and received. He had made a cult of it. He was the last son of the happy city, and happy he would like to be.

He wanted to come back to Venice, where he could practise happiness as he did in the old days. He had had enough of being an outlaw in Europe, condemned, pilloried, ridiculed, cold-shouldered and even imprisoned, merely for being Casanova.

He scrabbled at the door, which seemed to be half-open.

'Let me in!' begged Casanova.

'Perhaps,' teased the Council of Ten.

And so Casanova waited in Trieste, longing for happiness, believing in it.

He swam against the tide with his display of relentless optimism. The very essence of Casanova was about to fall out of fashion. In 1774, as Casanova waited for a word of clemency from Venice, Goethe published his melancholy masterpiece, *The Sorrows of Young Werther*. Its pensive young hero commits suicide as a result of a noble and hopeless love. The book was a sensation. Napoleon Bonaparte himself read it seven times. It was banned by the Vatican. But it was already too late: the book had done its work. Suicides blossomed all over Europe that year. Happiness had fallen out of fashion. Something darker was falling into place.

Casanova was a man out of time. Still, he refused to be down-hearted, let alone suicidal.

While he waited for his pardon, Casanova called in his favours, as he had done everywhere else. These too were fewer in supply. His patron Bragadin had died already, leaving Casanova nothing but a Bill of Exchange for 1000 *ecus*. Like his protégé, he had lived to the full and spent everything he had. Signor Barbaro was dead too, and Dandolo was ailing.

But there were still women who had reason to be grateful to Casanova. He revisited ex-mistresses, and renewed affectionate and sometimes erotic ties. A pattern emerged, in which the grateful husbands of his former lovers repaid him the money he had used years before to arrange their nuptials. And if the first-born child, now grown up, looked something of a sinner – with what joy Casanova recognised his own happy handiwork!

He was still in Trieste, waiting for an answer from the Council of

Ten, when he was given some opportunities to do small services for the Venetian state. He strained to perform, and was rewarded, first with acknowledgement and even with payment.

Finally he received a safe conduct pass dated September 3rd 1774. When the longed-for document was delivered to him, he read it, he reread it, he kissed it many times, then he fell into a concentrated kind of silence. After that, he burst into tears.

Casanova could come home, at last. But it was a home-coming of mitigated joy, and no honour. When Casanova came back to Venice it was with a new name and in a new capacity. He was called Antonio Pratolini, and he was a spy.

The Cat Speaks

When we dislike one of our kind, or if he becomes old, or damaged, we kill him. Humans are more cruel.

They allow their outcast to crouch at the edge of their magic circle, looking in. They let him smell their fish roasting, they even let a few drops of hot oil splash on his tattered coat.

They talk about him as if he is not there.

And that is the worst thing that they can do to him.

Much worse than death.

This was what Casanova knew about women: give them assiduous attention and they will be yours. Give them the kind of attention they have never dreamt of, they will fulfil your dreams.

But without attention, women, cats and Casanovas wither and fade away.

13

A l'ostaria bever, o magnar, o zogar,
or bestemiar or far la spia.

At the tavern, either drink, eat,
play, swear — or spy.

VENETIAN PROVERB

Casanova arrived in Venice just nine days after he received his pardon. He had travelled with undignified haste, propelled by his rapacious hopes.

He was given a room at the Dandolo *palazzo*, and let himself be seen in his out-dated finery on the Rialto, the Merceria and of course in the Piazza San Marco. It was 1774 and the Inquisitors had just closed down his old playground of the *ridotto*. The necessary activities of gambling, flirting and drinking had now spread like impetigo to private establishments. Here Casanova tested his welcome, arriving with a flourish of not-quite snowy lace, sometimes finding wine and renewed friendship thrust into his hands, other times slinking outside in a convulsion of shame when no one recognised him, or worse, pretended not to do so.

'Here was Casanova, returned at last, the world conquered,' he told me wryly. 'I was barely fifty. I planned to spend what I had now decided would be the sweet flower of my maturity in the arms of La Serenissima.'

He was still, after all, the friend of the Mocenigos, the Memmos and the Grimanis. He was still welcome at the opulent casinos of Pietro Zaguri and Lorenzo Morosini. Everyone, it seemed, wanted to see him – and who did *not* want to hear from his own lips of his tales of European adventures, his travels, and not least, the famous flight from the Leads? Of his bloody duel in Poland with the Branicki? Of the French lottery that made him a millionaire? Of how he had spent his millions on hundreds, at least, of women. It was rumoured that even the Inquisitors asked him to dine, and Casanova did nothing to dispel these stories.

He presented a brave face, but in reality Casanova skimmed the edges of desperation. He could not live on just his monthly pension of six *zecchini* willed by Barbaro, and a similar stipend from the failing Dandolo.

Casanova had, in a trawl of his influential friends all over Europe, managed to sign up 339 subscribers to his translation of Homer's *Iliad* into Venetian dialect. But he had to abandon the work for lack of funds. His writing was not going to keep him in bread and cheese, let alone oysters and duck in marmalade sauce.

So Casanova, alias Antonio Pratolini, became a secret agent for the Inquisitors. He wrote them at least fifty reports, but it was obvious that he had little appetite for the work. Casanova's reports were dismally boring. He was constantly renegotiating his stipend with the Inquisitors, who were obviously satisfied neither with Il Signor Pratolini's attitude nor the diligence of his research. They had every reason.

Sometimes, during our time together, I helped Il Signor Pratolini write his reports for the Tribunal. The Inquisitors never knew how enjoyably Casanova's tongue filled his cheek when he wrote them.

Or perhaps, on reflection, they did.

'Let's see,' Casanova would say to me, 'let's do something *theatrical* today.' And we would concoct some little delicious thing for the Inquisitors, 'On *the scandalous freedom that takes place in theatres when the lights go out.*'

No one knew better than us.

Sometimes, feigning illness, I avoided the family dinner. I retired to my bedroom clutching my belly and plumped up my bed with pillows in a careful approximation of the shape of my body under the coverlet. I borrowed one of Sofia's discarded dolls whose hair flowed wildly as my own. (*Why did Sofia have a doll who looked like me?* I wondered.) A few of the doll's curls spilled out upon the pillow. I worked with deft hands; I had done this before. I slipped out of the house in the black domino Casanova had given me and met him at the doors of the theatre as agreed. Inside our red velvet box we kept one eye on the actors but both mouths and both pairs of hands entirely busy with each other. We never undressed completely, for one never knew when the mischievous actors would alarm the fornicators in the audience by brandishing a huge flaming candelabra aloft. How they knew the right moment I could not understand, unless they kept acute ears to the crescendo of sighs from the boxes.

Unfortunately the Inquisitors had not proved as stupid as Casanova thought. They had soon withdrawn his regular pay of fifteen *ducati*. Casanova resorted to a cringing letter, but fell into the direst poverty. Then he had tried to set up as a theatrical producer, publicity officer and critic. 'After all, the theatre is in my blood,' he told me. He hired a troup of French players and the Sant' Angelo theatre. Casanova was ahead of his time as usual: double bills, advance advertising and appetising hints and promises of perversions and atrocities, live on stage.

One night Casanova and I walked past the Sant' Angelo theatre on our way home to Miracoli. Now it was shuttered and dark. 'Tell me about your plays,' I asked.

'Nothing good to tell, I am afraid, my darling.'

Casanova had stood in front of the nut-spitting, groin-scratching audience, inventing distractions to cover the thin substance of the entertainments he had created. More than once he diverted the audience from their discontents with a fountain of bright blood from his reliable nose. He used all he had learnt to hold the crowd, to tease their desire for a performance and keep them in their seats until the end, waiting for that moment of dazzlement which he had so subtly promised them. At the end, he had to make sure that there was enough time for the actors to escape, before the curtain call, which would certainly be a festival of soft vegetables.

'Sometimes, I too, had to make a timely exit to avoid the spinach and the potatoes,' he told me. 'But it was better than London, where the mob would gut the theatre if the performance did not please them.'

He turned back to writing; set up a weekly journal of theatrical critique, which he personally distributed in his old haunts, the theatres and cafés. Only eleven issues were published. Casanova's career as a theatrical impresario was over. The theatre had not replenished his purse; it had drained it. His needs were still greater than those of the poor man he was. He was greedy for expensive foods. It hurt his soul to dine upon the sea-louse soup of the poor, or on polenta and a slice of watermelon, like the noblemen of San Barnaba who had fallen on hard times.

After we became lovers, I committed daily depredations on the kitchen at home for him. Sofia, astonished, caught me once, with six slender *fette* of *prosciutto* and ten quail eggs in my hand, only an hour after an ample dinner. There were a lot of good things to eat in our house that year. My father's affairs, unlike Casanova's, were prospering. Unlike his oldest daughter, he had no bad habits, and the family wealth rubbed against itself in our coffers. My father, though, still lived like a monk in a city aflame with ostentatious joy.

Stolen titbits did not nourish Casanova's soul. From my studio's courtyard he could look at the Palazzo Barbaro, scene of some of his most audacious episodes and the ingestion of the most luxurious delicacies. Even now, the chandeliers gushed light. Still the clink of glasses was muffled by the slow tears of the expensive wine inside them. The fragrant noise travelled over the water to my studio, to the exile who had returned from exile, and yet still found himself locked out of his home.

To the current inhabitants of the Palazzo Barbaro the great Casanova was a joke, an old joke gone a little stale. He was a slightly sordid adventurer, an extraordinary anachronism. But Casanova was so hungry for attention and complicated dishes that he would have accepted an invitation even on that basis, and would have gyrated, grimaced, caricatured himself to entertain them. He could have borne their curling lips and their asides, the laughter that they would not bother to hide. He would have borne all of this just for a taste of their supper, or even to eat their leftovers, provided that it was not in the servants' quarters.

Casanova was still this proud, though. He still would not gamble for a living. He maintained that he had never done so. He gambled as he talked and walked: naturally and with great *sprezzo*, nonchalant style. To live on his skill at the table, he would have had to cheat. It was a language, in Casanova's day, gambling, a passport into society. To know the game, and how to play the game, how to perform the rituals, was all important. Cheating, 'correcting fortune', was part of the game then, too, as fraud was part of fashionable society. The decadent dregs of our high society were permitted to ply their underhand trade, provided the 'correction' was carried off with a panache and skill that did not actually insult their dupes.

But Casanova was not, in general, a deceiver at the table or any-where else. He loved too much the endless novelties fortune offered the gambler; he loved it too much to corrupt it, even in his favour, even when he was desperate. So these days Casanova still gambled, as he had done all his life, in the spirit of extravagance and pleasure. Even if he lost, each card turned face up was, after all, a surprise. Every time he reached his hand into a velvet bag, to pull out a numbered ball, it fed his appetite for something he had not seen before, like the inside of each pistachio nut he slit, or every chemise he had once slipped off a lovely shoulder.

One night I plumped up the pillows on my bed again and we went together to a party at the Palazzo Mocenigo on the *volta*, the turn of the Grand Canal.

Casanova's history was littered with Mocenigos. In the 1750s, he had consorted with Alvise II, Venetian ambassador to Paris and the favourite of Madame de Pompadour. Alvise V, the Venetian ambassador to Spain, was the notorious bisexual whose male mistress, Manuzzi, had caused Casanova to be imprisoned. But Casanova always felt affection for Alvise V, born in the same year as himself, who had suffered, as he had, at the hands of the Council of Ten. After Madrid, an excuse had been found to send him to the fortress of Brescia for seven years. Alvise V had recently died, but there was still an endless supply of Mocenigos, Alvises and others. Indeed Alvise V had fathered two daughters. One of them had sent this rare invitation to Casanova.

We arrived at the lion-coloured *palazzo* by water, nosing through the ten gondolas that the Mocenigo family kept tethered to their blue-striped *paline*. I looked up and counted twelve lion heads carved in white rectangles above the windows of the *piano nobile*. The Mocenigo consisted of several *palazzi* threaded together inside and out. Our party was taking place in the apartments of the central *palazzo*. This part of the Mocenigo was not one of our Venetian Gothic fairy-tale constructions. It was low and, for Venice, plain. Put it on Pall Mall or Oxford Street and you would not look at it a second time. But on the Grand Canal, in its party regalia, with torches ablaze and flowers dripping from the balconies, the Mocenigo was *palazzo* enough for us that night.

The Mocenigo sea-porter, in a doublet of velvet and gold, directed us with a flourish through the dark entrance hall, strangely decorated with harlequins of mirror and red velvet, to the stairs where the lanterns were held in stone arms that seemed to have thrust themselves through the wall with violence.

Upstairs, the air in the crowded *soggiorno* was heavy with an essence of rose the young Madame de Pompadour had sent the Mocenigos from Paris. The perfume, the crushed souls of a million flowers, was still robust all these years later. We all wore masks. The cream of Venetian society was there, with the cream of the courtesans and the great ladies, some of which were one and the same. They were all dressed according to the stringent dictates of the *Poupée de France* and encrusted with cosmetics. In those days to make love to a noble lady was like breaking open an egg to let the sweetness gush out.

Marina Benzona was there, looking like her Longhi portrait, holding a Sèvres cup of chocolate, wearing a comet of a jewel in the rolling gold of her elaborately dressed hair. Her glittering vitality still disturbed the air. We looked at Rosalba Carriera's portrait of Lucrezia Basadonna Mocenigo, her beauty bursting out of her jewelled corselet. 'Poor lady. She was betrayed by a dog of an Englishman,' Casanova told me.

Faces I had painted swam in and out of the crowd. Maurizio Mocenigo loomed over me, as if he would like to swallow me up. Since I had painted his portrait, he had turned up frequently at the studio with a hungry look on his cavernous face. He was a friend of Casanova's but he seemed to think that I might be interested in another lover. I laughed in his face, but as politely as possible. I did not want to lose a client, particularly a Mocenigo.

Casanova joined a table of *Biribissi*. I stood behind him, warming his back with my breasts pressed against it. I looked down upon the toys of the game, particularly the vivid board with its thirty-six painted squares. Swimming before my eyes were delicious images of pears, cherries, eagles, pineapples, peacocks, unicorns, doves, tulips, owls, dogs, bears, angels, lions, harlequins of both sexes in decorous undress. On this board they were painted with a charming naiveté. I imagined how much better I could do it myself.

Casanova was losing horribly, and I was worried. I took his hand and we slipped out of the rose-coloured drawing room and into a strange dark study. We enjoyed each other thoroughly and consolingly behind an enormous empty frame that was leaning up against a wall, louche as a beggar. Pressed against a marble panel, with Casanova's warm mouth upon mine and my dress in foaming disarray around me, I abandoned all other thoughts but those of pleasure. If someone had come into the room and found us – and perhaps they did, for we were so lost in each other – our love would have seemed a living portrait.

'One day,' Casanova declared afterwards, helping me out of the frame and smoothing down my hair, 'people will sit all day in their own houses watching moving portraits like this and learn about the world.'

I shall always remember that night as one of the sweetest that we knew together. I remember standing with him upon the terrace in the tender quietude that followed our lovemaking behind the frame. Through the curve of a side canal, we saw the moonlight fingering the house of our great Venetian playwright, Goldoni. It reminded Casanova of his mother. His face fell and sad thoughts overcame him, spilling into the memory of his losses at the table. I soothed his hand, distracted him by pointing out Carpaccio's house near Rialto. I pointed out the noble steed-like towers of the Frari and Saint Barnaba and the obelisks sprouting like horns from roofs along the curve of the canal. I pointed up to the red lids of the curtains like our eyelids after a night together. Still, he hung his head.

Finally I slipped back into the party and plundered the table. I returned to him, still motionless on the terrace, and pushed a large crustacean into his mouth. He turned to me, and took me in his arms.

'You are a rare and precious person, Cecilia Cornaro. I love you, and I honour you. You will be great, and I will be known for having known you and loved you before anyone else did. That thought comforts me as much as your love.'

As usual, he traded my comfort for a story. He brought the past of the Palazzo Mocenigo to life for me. He told me about the English Lady Arundel who had stoutly confronted the henchmen of the Inquisitors here. She was accused of taking a traitorous Venetian as her lover. He told me of Angelica's one-time neighbour Lady Mary Wortley Montagu who had occupied one of these *palazzi* just twenty years before. Amongst the Venetians, she was famous for the malodorous wig that did not cover her greasy black locks hanging loose as seaweed, never combed or curled. Even when receiving guests she wore an old mazine wrap that gaped, revoltingly, open to show a dirty canvas petticoat. Her face was always swelled on one side with the remains of a pustule, covered partly by a rotting plaster and partly by cheap white paint. Nevertheless, Lady Mary had been a great seductress, and was reputed to have made love to the Sultan of Turkey. In Venice, she had waited, mostly in vain, for her Italian lover.

'This is a *palazzo* that attracts the English,' said Casanova. 'I don't know why. The Mocenigo does not seem to make them happy.'

We returned to the depleted gaming tables, and joined the addicts at their play.

Picture, as I do now, Casanova playing *Biribissi*, his face rapt, his whole body seeming to pivot upon the turn of the card, like the fall of a leaf. Picture, as I do, cards falling like a Bohemian autumn, turning, in my daydreams, to the papery touches of Madame d'Urfé. In those dreams, now turning to nightmares, Casanova was often on the edge of the game, chosen last to play, qualifying by his charm and fame rather than his purse. Or he was found wanting even in this, and was not invited at all. He was condemned to that dead realm of unwantables, the men with their brave stretching grins.

In seven churches in France there are frescoes of a *danse macabre* — a bishop, *un mort*, a nobleman, *une morte*, a woman, *un mort* in comical dance upon the walls. The dead smile grotesquely and contort their bodies. Those who have fortune and a place in society stand serene and dignified. Gambling is just like that, every night. Ring round the table in the casino — *un mort, un signore, un mort* . . .

I watched the tides of loss and victory that flowed across the Mocenigo party. It's a cruel thing, a party. You are always winning and losing something and not just at the table. You can lose the gold, a lover flits out of your eyesight and returns flushed, you play, you throw the dice, reach into the velvet bag. At stake is your fortune, your reputation . . .

That was the night I myself learnt to play *Biribissi*, and then went home and painted the whole board from memory, but each beast, each flower had the face of one of the noble guests. I had it delivered, rolled up the next day. What a stir it caused at the Palazzo Mocenigo! — I believe they always used it after that. And yet more noble clients came tripping into my studio on their impractical slippers.

Years later I would see that *Biribissi* board again but I would not be able to bring myself to touch it.

The Cat Speaks

So Cecilia's star is rising in the world but Casanova's is falling and falling and falling.

The *Poupée de France*, that vixenish arbiter of female fashion, has a toy cat, you know, and its collar changes to match its mistress's finery. It even wears tiny mouse-skin mittens! (This despite the well-known saying *gatta guantata non piglia sorci*, a cat in gloves grabs no mice.)

Some people come to look at the doll, but I think most of them really want to see the cat. You see, it has a dazzling triangular smile. It knows something.

The cat knows the doll is as old as the shrivelled Madame d'Urfé, and that under her velvet and silk lurks a very shabby pair of underdrawers. And inside those drawers, the cat knows, there's a pesthouse. The woodworm are nibbling at the private parts of the *Poupée de France*. They are quiet and industrious, those woodworm, unlike the party-loving Venetians.

By 1797, the toy cat calculates, the *Poupée*, like the Serene Republic of Venice, and all who gamble in her, will fall to dust.

14

Chi ghe n'à ghe ne sémena.

One who spends money like semen.

VENETIAN PROVERB

'Beckford is back!' Casanova burst into my studio like a laugh opening a face. He came to stand behind me, with his arms around me, admiring my new portrait of Maurizio Mocenigo.

'Beck Ford?' I asked, swivelling my head to kiss him. I tasted excitement on his lips. 'Ah! Yes, *Beckford*. The Englishman.'

'Yes, The only one I ever warmed to. And he has a book with him!'

'Well, imagine that,' I said, turning from Casanova with a smile. I picked up my brush again. I was feathering the wings of a *putto*, the final touch to an allegorical background. The nobleman was coming to collect the painting himself the next day, one more excuse to present himself at my studio.

'Come now, Cecilia! Don't be so satirical. It's a book Beckford has *written*. I have persuaded him that the one thing he must do at this moment is come to you for a portrait. The face of the new author must be immortalised! Will you paint him, Cecilia? Will you make him beautiful, my angel? Will you do that trick of yours with the skin? And the eyes?'

'Let me meet him first. From all that I have heard about him, he may be absolutely impossible to paint. Remind me . . .'

Casanova refreshed my memory. While I finished the *putto*, he recounted once more his story of that highly original young man, William Beckford.

William Beckford was young, spoiled and over-excited. He was the only legitimate son of a wealthy political rajah. Everything in the Beckford household was done on the grandest scale. The most rigorous classical education was inflicted on the child in the gilded halls of his opulent home. The little prodigy Mozart was hired to give him music lessons. When his father died, the boy was left with a hundred thousand a year and a million in cash.

There emerged from this rarefied childhood a febrile little personage full of wild affections and dark humours. Whatever was most fearful and putrefyingly excessive, *that* roused the most delicious giggles in the boy. He became addicted to volatile romances like *The Thousand and One Nights* and everything exotic and escapist.

By the time he was thirteen, he spoke fluent French, Italian and a most exquisitely satirical English. His sensibilities were finely tuned. He was mad for music. He sang himself, in a high eunuch's voice and with a eunuch's effeminate affectation. He had a woman's plump hips, too, and a long feminine nose, which would one day sharpen to a dowager's beak. But in those days he was young and with all the supple attraction of youth.

As he blushed and stammered through puberty, Beckford found himself *imbroglio*ed in a wayward passion for William, the dainty eleven-year-old son of Lord Courtenay. As if this were not drama enough, or perhaps to prove something to himself, he then commenced a neurotic love affair with his cousin's wife.

Beckford took the only option then available to wealthy young Englishmen who had got themselves into trouble. He fled for an eleven-month Grand Tour, setting off on June 19th 1780. He determined to spend his millions like a poet, and to plumb the depths of everything gothic, taboo and masochistic that could be found to disgust and delight him in Europe.

He set off via Falmouth and Spain. (Years later, my fate would follow in his footsteps.) Beckford reached La Serenissima in August that year. Venice was already an old acquaintance in his eyes from hours spent in his library with innumerable prints and drawings of her domes and islands. But he knew her even better from his daydreams of dark murders in her narrow alleys and duels upon her sinuous bridges, not to mention the unspeakable acts he imagined, in some considerable detail, taking place in the gloomy chambers of her rotting *palazzi*.

He first arrived among us at sunset, under a cloudless sky, with a faint wind breathing on his cheeks. The caress seemed to promise him that Venice would make up for the loss of the pretty little Courtenay. In La Serenissima's sin and sensuality, he foresaw all kinds of compensations.

The next morning, before five o'clock, Beckford was roused by the din of voices and the splashing of water. Stumbling to the terrace, he beheld the Grand Canal entirely transformed. The water had disappeared. Now it was covered with fruit and vegetables rocking on rafts and barges. There was scarcely the sliver of a wave to be seen between the jostling tear-shaped trays of bright food. Lithe figures leapt deftly from boat to boat. Joining the amphibious *contadini* coming from their island farms were more mysterious figures, masked and dressed in black. These were tattered remains of those high-born and low-life pleasure-seekers who had spent the night at the table, following the frenzy of the dice. As the vivid darkness faded on their dreams a pale dawn showed the disappointments etched upon their paler faces. These people always had a craving for fruit, a quick restorative intake of sugar before they went home to their daytime beds, to nightmares of ill-fortune, love-disease, and encroaching old age. Like the *pantegane*, at dawn, depraved and self-abused Venetians were always to be found by the water, where the algae fondled the peeling paint at the ancient feet of the *palazzi*.

The sun began to paint the day's colours upon the town. Slabs of stone turned the pale gold of fresh fish *frittata*; others warmed to the fleshy pink of crab soup. Beckford found his belly scoured by a ravenous emptiness and he was drawn out of his hotel and into a gondola. He tried to purchase his own provision of grapes, little cakes and Schiraz wine. But the low fellow on the fruit barge refused to understand him, no matter how loudly he expressed his desire for just that bunch on which he had set his heart. The impudent fellow waved rotten truffles in the air and spilled droplets of brandy on Beckford's white cravat. The vendor had already disappointed him by being tall and blond, instead of small and swarthy. His accent, far from quaint, sounded suspiciously like something Beckford had once heard on Lord Courtenay's pig-farm. All Venice was ruined for him in that moment; her mysteries unwound, her wild glamour ruffianised. It took so few things and such tiny things to cast young Beckford into the sorriest gloom. He was so sensitive to each brutal nuance.

It was at this point that Casanova had come to his rescue.

'You were very kind to Beckford,' I observed, pointing my paintbrush at Casanova. 'Too kind, if you ask me.'

'You want grapes, my lord?' Casanova had asked him, a warm purr from behind Beckford's left shoulder. 'Allow me.'

The grapes were paid for with a flourish, and handed to the young man. Beckford, I thought to myself, could have had no idea what those few *zecchini* cost Casanova in those dark times. He would have seen only Casanova's enormous, inclusive smile. The smile was surely widening because Casanova had found in Beckford another undoubted novelty.

'The sweet fruit of liberty,' announced Beckford. Thrilled to be in receipt of attention, the deflated Beckford became tumescent with good humour.

'Liberty is sweet indeed,' said Casanova. 'Have you heard of the Venetian Leads?'

'Why, of course. The dreaded Venetian prisons from which no one escapes.'

'I escaped.'

'But no one ever escaped from the Leads except . . .'

Casanova swept a low bow. 'Giacomo Girolamo Casanova, at your service, my Lord. Soldier, violinist, gambler, poet, priest and servant of women. Venetian.'

'William Beckford, gentleman, seeker of the miasmic redolence of the past, fugitive from society, writer. Reluctant Englishman, Dreamer in Magic Slumbers.'

There were more smiles and pressings of hands. The two men went to sit on the steps of San Giaccomo in the shade of its wooden portico. They shared the grapes while they exchanged stories. Inside their skins the grape-pulps were already jellied by the warmth of the sun. Casanova and Beckford sat side by side, puncturing the sweet globes inside their mouths and nudging out the tart seeds with their tongues. Those moments, Casanova now told me, were the beginning of the intimacy that would bind them to each other. It was in every way an unlikely friendship.

It was a year and a half before the as-yet-unknown-to-me Casanova took me from my bath, but in this meeting with Casanova, the as-yet-unknown-to-me William Beckford had entered my own life. That morning, as Casanova befriended Beckford at Rialto, I was waking up in my parents' *palazzo*, where I lived like a little stranger among my family. While Casanova and Beckford shared a handful of fruit, I lay in my bed, thinking about squirrel-fur paintbrushes and how to get my hands on them. Later, as Beckford roamed around Venice, I sat at my desk in the convent, sketching unforgivable caricatures of the nuns on the borders of my *Lives of the Saints*. As Beckford and Casanova coddled their friendship, I conducted the normal schoolgirl vendettas. I grew further apart from my mother and Sofia. I watched the pink circles round my nipples grow. I noticed some unexpected hairs. That month the maid was obliged to bring me some linen rags and explain their use. I felt no *brividi*, no shivers of anticipation. I was entirely insensitive to my fate.

So Beckford entered my life. He was about to enter it in person and he would do so again, more profoundly, later still, in his absence. I would be haunted by Beckford, abused by his black humour and the darker reaches of his imagination. I would paint him. I would hear his own story from his own lips while I did so. I would not need to spy on Beckford or distil him from a painstaking research. The loquacious young man would push information into my ears. He would fill them with strange things which he imagined. By those imaginings he would draw something dangerous to me.

If Casanova had known any of these things, he would have protected me, he would have walked right past Beckford. He would have ignored his obvious need. He would not have brought Beckford to my studio. He would have left that dangerous boy alone.

But Casanova did not know anything of this. How could he?

15

L'amor non l'è amor, se no'l se desgusta sete volte.

Love is not love if it doesn't disgust you seven times.

VENETIAN PROVERB

William Beckford spent a month here on that first visit, a welcome guest in every high society *conversazione*. Tales of his millions had come before him and the Venetian nobles were interested, in their languid way, to see this novelty from England. But Beckford was disappointed in us. In vain, he awaited a passionate quarrel, a thrown glove, a flash of a jewelled stiletto, an aristocratic corpse dragged on velvet curtains, leaving a dark smudge of blood upon the pale terrazzo flooring. The noblemen yawned over their coffee, and seemed barely to move. Beckford took to tourism, looking for something, in the monasteries, palaces and islands, to frighten or disgust him.

Finally, at the Doges' Palace, Beckford found in the ghosts of Venice past a frisson very much to his taste. He observed the walls, covered in grim visages. What kind of tyrant, he wondered, could revel at his opulent balls, conscious of the prisoners consuming their hours in lamentations in the leadlined prisons above his head? What kind of sovereign could dance upon a floor beneath which lay damp and gloomy dungeons, the inhabitants of which were wasting away in the watchful company of rats?

An idea was beginning to take shape in Beckford's head.

At the Bridge of Sighs he sighed over the prisoners who had been led across it. Kind Casanova had been among them. Yes, he had already heard from his new dear friend of the fleas, the sensory deprivations and the unspeakable enema!

He told Casanova how he had rushed home, shuddering, unable to eat, and was gratified to view his dreadful pallor in the mouldy mirror before retiring to bed. In the morning, he had awoken to find his diary full of detailed drawings depicting fearful landscapes not known on earth. And looming above everything, five sinister roof-lines, surely of palaces, palaces more decadent even than anything he had found in Venice.

With persistence, and with Casanova's help, Beckford started to find the true darker side of Venice and did not need to invent it any longer. At a church he saw a font filled with bat's blood masquerading as the vital fluid of our Lord. In the musky quarters of the city where he roamed in search of Turks and Infidels, Beckford was able to spend some of his father's legacy to experience for himself a few exquisite forms of Oriental cruelty and debauchery.

Then Beckford created a dark drama for himself. He fell in love with a young male member of the most aristocratic branch of my own Cornaro family. I knew of the boy – a distant cousin – he was an experienced seducer. Beckford apparently thought him innocent but shuddered as he recounted to Casanova all kinds of soft delights unconsciously insinuated in the boy's lithe whispers. He knew that eternal infamy lay in giving way to that alluring tongue. The danger rendered the temptation even greater. Meanwhile, one of the fatal boy's two sisters fell in love with Beckford. She was married and bought poison to despatch her husband so that she might be together with the young Englishman. He tried to explain that he loved another member of her family. She thought her younger sister the fortunate object of his desire and swallowed the poison herself. It proved unpleasant but not dangerous. However, it was too late: the story was abroad. Venice was convulsed.

That must have been the first occasion I heard Beckford's name. I am sure that I heard my mother gossiping about it with her lady-friends. At the time, I'm sure I thought of him as nothing more than another foreigner fallen in love with our city and gone mad with it. Of the other matter, the boy matter, I heard hints, but I did not at the time understand them.

Beckford fled in disarray to be comforted by his friends, the Hamiltons, in Naples. But by December he was back among us. Casanova saw in the New Year with him and the dark early days of January. A year would pass before Casanova could find me and we would become lovers. I still remember that my family celebrated New Year, 1781, with a quiet dinner in our elegant dining room. Afterwards, my mother, father, Sofia and I went to watch the fireworks on the Riva degli Schiavoni and walked soberly home. I love to think that somewhere in the crowds we must have passed Casanova and the desperate young Beckford, saying their farewells. Beckford knew now that he must hurry back to England to turn away from the fascinating eyes of the young Cornaro. Casanova and Beckford parted, reluctantly, swearing to renew their brotherhood within the year. Beckford returned to England.

But Venice called him, with her ineluctable charms.

So in May 1782 he set off again for Italy, via Paris. As he drew closer to us, Venice began to invade his soul again. The idea born amid the horrors of the Doges' Palace began to take material shape. The ideas began to breed words. The words breathed pages. It became a book. It poured out of him, in Paris, in a single sitting that lasted three days and two nights. When he arrived in Padua on June 11th, he had in his trunk not just the travel diaries of the previous year, but a fat little manuscript, close-written in French.

It was *Vathek*.

At sunset, on June 13th 1782, Beckford returned to Venice, just in time to see his favourite haunts illuminated in the dying light. He beheld a troubled sky, shot with vivid red, the lagoon tinted like an open wound and the islands glowing embers.

It was in the red light of that sunset that Casanova burst into my studio to tell me that Beckford had come back. It was in the full sun of the next morning that he brought Beckford to my studio.

'I'm delighted to meet you,' I said, trying not to sound ironical. 'I have heard so much about you.' I ran my eyes over the soft complexion, grey eyes, long nose. *Flake White, Naples Yellow and Rose Madder*, I thought. *Viridian Green for the shadows under the chin*.

'Likewise, Mademoiselle Cecilia. I understand that you are the alchemist of human faces and the poet of human skin. I believe that your paintbrush discovers souls and the secrets of men's desires. I see for myself now that all these virtues come in a form so *viciously* lovely as to break men's hearts at first sight. I understand that I must be a little careful of your tongue. Ah yes, though, I see it now as you smile at me – it, too, is beautiful.'

He bowed. 'Have I omitted anything, Casanova?' His voice was pitched high, but I thought this an affectation. He seemed a man in other ways.

'Only that I love her more than my own eyes,' said Casanova, who was standing at my side and now kissed the top of my head.

'But of course,' said Beckford, with a smile, 'that is entirely understandable.' I warmed to him, habituated as I was to the nervous flattery of those about to be painted. I liked the flourish of his French, and the dark nuance of his humour.

He became entirely serious when he discussed how we were to style his immortality. We had different ideas, but I knew better than to argue in words. I would argue with my paintbrush, later, silently and invincibly. He had brought his thick little manuscript with him. He wanted to be painted beside its frantic pages. In the time it took me to paint his face, Beckford read me the entire story of *Vathek*. I *heard* the book before anyone ever saw it.

Vathek would not be published in English until 1786, anonymously, and then not again until 1809, a year that would become important to me. The English public would be convulsed by the young, extreme Oriental potentate, Vathek, with a liquorish taste after good dishes and young damsels, whose eye could kill with a single glance. They would shudder at Vathek's mother, the wicked Queen Carathis, whose own liquorish taste was for dead bodies strangled, with amiable smiles, by her team of mute and murderous one-eyed Negresses. They would marvel at her gigantic camel, Alboufaki, who could infallibly scent dead flesh in distant graveyards. Their mouths would water for the apricots from the Isle of Kirmith and their eyes for the lustre of the enamel of Franguistan. They would strain to admire Vathek's awful tower and the five sumptuous palaces he had invented, one for each of his raveningly self-indulgent senses. They would sigh at a voluptuous vision of Vathek's great love, Nouronihar, whose venality and carnality matched those of her prince, and whose lust for the glittering Carbuncle of Giamschid and the other treasures of the pre-adamite sultans probably exceeded even his own. *Vathek*'s diabolical levity and joyous licentiousness would not find another imitator until . . . but these musings do not serve at this moment.

Yes, I should have guessed that *Vathek* would seduce the English public, dying to have the strings of its strait-lacing cut and its chemise ripped asunder. But I could have no idea of its effect upon one young Scottish aristocrat, George Gordon, heir to Newstead Abbey . . . Now my tale runs away with me yet again.

Certainly, *Vathek* kept me amused while I worked, and it helped me paint a more accurate portrait of the author. It provided me with a literal and metaphorical background for my painting. For amidst all the horror was a delicious humour, which somehow intensified the abomination. There was more to Beckford, I thought, than met the eye.

Even then I thought that.

I painted Beckford in his favourite green coat with porcelain buttons and his buff-coloured striped waistcoat, which caught the grey of his eyes. To please him, I inserted into his portrait chess pieces in the shape of the five palaces, and a large terracotta model of the camel, Alboufaki. Casanova, looking over my shoulder, laughed in delight. He too had listened to the tale of Vathek, and had made suggestions, mostly in the realms of gastronomy and sensuality.

I knew too much about Beckford, and I forgot to hide it in my work. And I was mistaken in my reading of him. I thought a man with such black humour would be able to laugh at himself.

Beckford had the classic dark English wit, and at his fingertips all the gorgeous vocabulary of the *seraglio*, the *bagnio*, the barrack room, the *caravanserai* and the crow's nest. There was no picturesque depravity that could not cause him to pour forth paragraphs of detached but delighted amusement. But about himself, Beckford lacked a sense of humour, a fact that, had he but known it, made him comical. As far as he was concerned, the tragic element of his persona smothered anything light inside.

And so when he first saw his portrait, Beckford sucked in his breath like a schoolboy, in joy. But on his second look, it horrified him, for into it I had slyly inserted a heap of mementoes of Venice and the Cornaro youth. In the background of the picture were unmistakable suggestions of a pink satin corset, a bottle of old wine, dice. I painted the Cornaro crest upon all his buttons. This was one of my special devices – something I would do with a magnifying glass after my sitter had left for the day. It would take a magnifying glass to find it again. But my masterpiece within this portrait of Beckford was a slanted mirror in the background. If you stood by the painting at a certain angle, you would see the mouth of the little Cornaro sucking his thumb, or possibly someone else's, with an expression of intense delectation. And I had painted, upon a little *cartello* lying unfolded on the floor, the Venetian proverb that expresses the devilish delights of sodomy.

> *L'ànema a Dio, el corpo a la tera,*
> *e 'l bus del cul al diavolo per tabachiera.*

The soul goes to God, the body to the Earth
and the arsehole to the devil, for his snuffbox.

When Beckford found his voice, it was small and reproachful. 'Cecilia, when I wanted a Venetian portrait, I thought you would paint me the way Tintoretto would, luminous, free from what besets me here,' he said, pointing at the offending portrait. 'Casanova told me that you would make me beautiful. He told me that you had magic fingers, that you made images that people could worship.' Then he looked at the ground, pouting like a schoolgirl. The *lingua biforcuta* uncurled inside my mouth.

Seeing the signs of danger, Casanova intervened. 'You don't need to take the portrait if you do not want it, *caro mio.*'

'I don't want to be that man,' Beckford whispered.

'And nor do you have to be,' soothed Casanova. He put his arm around Beckford and led him away. Over his shoulder he smiled at me reprovingly. I knew what he meant: I should not use portraits to cause pain. People like Beckford carry enough pain inside them without that.

How was I to know that the pain that birthed *Vathek* would become part of my own history? How was I to know that one day the book would creep into my life in a way that was too painful to bear? But I was not listening properly to the messages of *Vathek*, in the lines or between the lines. In any case, I was about to confront a more devastating sorrow of my own.

16

La lingua no ga osso ma la rompe i ossi.

The tongue doesn't have bones, but it breaks bones.

VENETIAN PROVERB

Why do we hate endings so much?

In my mind, I have an image of Casanova standing behind a slammed door, converting his pre-lacrimal contortion into an ingratiating grin. I could almost sketch on paper the inner process, the strength that grabbed those little muscles around his mouth and eyes and forced them up, not down. No wonder he ate like a wolf. The mere act of withstanding rejection – in other words, of being Casanova – consumed a *casino* of crab soup and croutons a day. That's what it took to pull the strings of that million-jointed puppet and to nourish his appetites, erotic, intellectual, alimentary, elementary. There was only food to power all these operations, and of course a supplementary diet of books and love. But even the reading and the lovemaking had to feed upon the food he put in his mouth.

I have an image of Casanova looking down the Grand Canal. I see him standing between the arches of the courtyard, silhouetted against the verdigris of the water. He seems not a man but a strange sorrowful punctuation mark, one that indicates pain. Behind him looms the tall palace of his dead patron, Barbaro. Casanova's shape is dark against the glow of all those chandeliers under which he used to gush and sparkle. They would not kindle for him again, now. Now he watches the animated silhouettes in the rubicund light of the *piano nobile*. He watches them from the darkness below. The conversations of the party float across the Canal but the words are unintelligible. An unimaginable distance of years stretches between the good times and now.

I have an image of him accepting his fate and reinventing himself for what comes next. I see him ransack his soul for some new reserve of energy and courage, some new mantra – sweet and nourishing – to succour him in his desperation.

With pen and ink, I drew him, from behind, the strangest portrait of Casanova. We Italians say white-and-black, not black-and-white; we are ever the optimists. My picture shows Casanova changing his prospects from black to white.

We have an expression – *ingoiare il rospo*, to swallow the toad – and, in my image, that is what Casanova is trying to do. He is trying to force down his gagging throat the poisonous fact of the new evil that has come to plague him.

Casanova was leaving me. He had fallen foul of the authorities in Venice. He had been incautious in his pride and in the only extravagances left to him – word and gesture. He had boasted and strutted one too many times in the Piazza San Marco. Perhaps, before he met me, he had consoled the wrong unhappy wife or the wrong daughter of the wrong patrician father, made too many incursions into the dwindling list of noble virgins in the *Libro d'oro*. One, or several of these crimes had caught up with him. Even though there was one obvious incident to explain why he had to go, the real reason was undoubtedly one of these. Since the death of his protector Bragadin, he had been vulnerable.

The superficial story of his new, last exile was this: when the last theatrical venture failed, Casanova was employed by the Genovese diplomat Carlo Spinola as his secretary. Spinola was rich and eccentric. He lived in a luxurious villa near Padua. He was amused by his new employee and encouraged him in his feats of raconteurship and gastronomy. At first, Casanova divided his time between Venice and Padua, happily occupied in small harmless intrigues on Spinola's behalf.

But, as usual, his felicity was not of long duration.

Some time before Casanova took up his appointment, Carlo Spinola had made a wager with a certain Carletti. Spinola had lost the wager, which was of some 250 *zecchini*. However, he chose to overlook the matter; Carletti remained unpaid. He approached Casanova, who agreed to mediate in exchange for certain pecuniary considerations. But the affair ended badly. Instead of paying him for the services rendered, when gently approached at a soirée at the Grimani *palazzo*, Carletti attacked Casanova both verbally and physically. Casanova, overcome with horror at both the violence and the indignity, backed away, and made to leave. He did not try to defend himself.

'Bastard!' Carletti screamed at him. 'Son of a whoring actress!' The blows rained down until Carletti had exhausted his vigour and his malice. The host, Casanova's supposed friend Carlo Grimani, stood by in silence. Splattered with his own blood and tears, Casanova limped from the house and back to Francesca Buschini. I did not see him afterwards for some days. It was Francesca, and not me, whom he needed until he could think of a way to save his face. He did not want to burden me with his weakness and his self-disgust.

But I knew what had happened. The incident was the talk of Venice. I prowled the cafés and the bars in my cloak to hear the news and tried to filter the truth from it. There was no account forthcoming without some kind of commentary. Some saw Casanova's point, others Carletti's, but all agreed that Casanova had behaved like a beaten dog. The epithet of coward was a new one for Casanova, but I was grieved to see that it stuck. Men were glad to point a disparaging finger at him. I knew that when he ventured to show himself in public again, the few doors that had remained open to him would now start to slam in his face. The Venetian bourgeois, the nobles and even the gondoliers would assume, as he passed, the closed expressions they wore under their masks, and he would again be a stranger in his own city.

The cat shut up becomes a lion, we say in Venice.

In this internal exile, shut up like a lion, Casanova found a voice with which to address his wrongs. He wrote a vengeful satire *Né amori, né donne, ovvero la stalla ripulita* (*Neither Loves nor Women, or, The Cleaned Stable*). Thinly disguised as the central characters were Carletti, depicted as a barking dog, and Grimani, as the illegitimate son. Casanova went further beyond the pale. He depicted himself as Grimani's illegitimate half-brother, the offspring of a liaison between a whoring actress and Grimani's father. Casanova had yielded to the temptation to vent his entire spleen. The Carletti affair had been one humiliation too many.

'Bastard, you called me,' Casanova said aloud, addressing the absent Carletti. 'Bastard I shall be.' Casanova wrote most of the book in my studio, stabbing at the pages and growling to himself. I heard him muttering and talking to the people who had raised this ire in him. I would go to him and lay my head against his. He would stroke my face with his left hand, but he continued to write with his right hand.

'I am sorry, my soul,' he said, looking up at me. 'You must allow me my say.' He opened his eyes wide in pain.

'Of course,' I said, backing away. He continued to murmur and curse as he scribbled, late into the night.

He would not permit me to read the manuscript before it came out. He worked like a maniac, bundling it off to the printer in days. This done, he was calmer. He was more himself, more affectionate, more confident. He needed a lot of love, both to give and to take.

No one took any notice of the anonymous slim volume when it first appeared in the printers' shop, but somehow its provenance became known. The mysterious twenty-two *fleurs-de-lys* upon the title page did not fool anyone. To anyone in Society, the *noms de plume* and the allusions were transparent and that was just what Casanova had intended.

As I had feared, the piece won him no more friends and the indignation of high Venetian society rose up against him. Belatedly, Casanova realised that he had gone too far. Instead of justifying himself, he had damned himself. Days later, he confessed as much to me, but it was too late. Everyone was abandoning him. With his noble friends went those hangers-on who had courted him for his contacts, and with those went his creditors. Effectively, he was about to be starved out of town, in the cruellest and subtlest of ways.

The first act of his life had ended with La Charpillon's attempt on his soul in 1763. Now, he told me, Venice was closing the second act of his life. She was making him a stranger to herself, even within her walls of water.

'What will be the third act?' I asked him.

'It will be my memoirs, of course. Then, when they are finished, this comedy will be ended. And if it's hissed this time, I shall not hear it.'

'It will not be hissed. How could they hiss you?'

He stood there for a long time, looking out of the window, his arms slack at his sides. Eventually I crept up behind him and inserted my fingers between his. He caressed them automatically. Casanova was not capable of withholding tenderness, even when the world had tried to strip him bare.

'I love you,' I told him. 'Don't forget that.'

These were the last loving words I spoke to Casanova. The situation was graver than we had thought. For that night, unbeknownst to me, Casanova received a summons from Francesco Morosini, in his capacity as Procurator. He was told that he was no longer welcome in Venice. Unless he left, and was quick about it, he would be back in the Leads.

He came to tell me as tenderly as possible. On the chair in my studio he took me on his knees and buried his face between my breasts. He smelled like a frightened animal, sharp and feral, but I held him close to me. I felt the warm moisture of his breath on my skin and stroked his stiff hair. I kissed his eyes. He did not look up. I felt him trembling in my arms. I felt tears on my bodice. He told my breasts that they were the most beautiful he had known. He took my hand, and kissed all my fingers. He told them that they were the fingers that men find at the end of their dreams. Still, he did not look up.

There was something so final in these tributes that I too became frightened.

I held him away from me to try to look into his eyes. He pushed himself against me again, clinging like a child.

'I must leave Venice, Cecilia,' he mumbled into my breasts.

I am sure Casanova was not thinking clearly. His despair had deranged him. I should have read it in his face the moment he arrived, in the flaring whites of his eyes, and felt it in the sweat of his palms. But I could not. I was lost in my own distress. For the first time, we did not turn to each other. For once, we did not look at each other as we spoke. We were in a state of panic; we could not concentrate. We made mistakes about each other.

Throughout his life, Casanova had always tried to attend to the long-term material needs of lovers after they were separated from him by fate or the implacable demands of opportunity. The lovers were handed on to someone who could look after them well, and love them to distraction. In my case, as if I were just another lover, he offered me to Maurizio Mocenigo, in whose palace we had played at *Biribissi* and disported ourselves behind the empty frame.

'Since I must leave you, go to him, Cecilia. He has loved you since you painted his portrait. I have talked to him. He will look after you while you paint. You will need to think of nothing but your work. You don't have to be his lover. He will be your Protector. He will wait for you.'

I pushed him away from me and sprang from his lap. Still, we did not look at each other. I paced up and down the room. Casanova sat on the chair with his head in his hands. His whole body personified abjection from the trailing hem of his shabby satin frock-coat to the sweaty pleating of his brow. The cat came out of the shadows to stand in front of him, with ears and tail erect as if to defend Casanova from my dangerous anger.

When my words finally came out, they were as cruel as I could make them. I tried to project an unbearable image into his mind: 'So that is the end of us, is it, Casanova? How neatly you have parcelled up my future for me! How kind you are!'

Then I whispered, 'Will you not be jealous of me in Maurizio Mocenigo's arms?'

Casanova swallowed and replied so quietly that I could barely hear. 'More in my mind than in my heart, where it matters.'

Still looking down, Casanova added quietly, 'I want to know that you are secure in a decent man's sincere love.'

I think it was his resignation that made me lose control of myself in the grievous manner in which I then did. He had already consigned our happiness to the past, without consulting me. I give this as a reason, not as an excuse for what I said next, or the brutality of its expression.

'Coward!' I screamed at him. 'Why can you not leave me honestly? Because that is what you are doing. You are leaving me. Why can you not admit it? Or have you found another novelty? A pair of sisters? A countess with her own Montgolfier balloon? Why pretend you are giving me a better life without you? I am not one of your passive little Bettinas or Henriettes.' He flinched at this but I went on, 'If I want a better life, I can make it one without your help. I am already doing so.'

I added, vindictively, 'What help could you give me, anyway? And if I want another lover, I shall find him myself. I don't imagine I shall have much difficulty.' I gestured at my breasts in reflection in the tall studio mirror,

In the same mirror, for I would not look at him directly, I saw his head sink lower, but he still said nothing. Then the cat clicked back his ears and began to sing. Loudly, he keened, and fulsomely. He filled the room with his yowls and squeals, his low moans and rasping cries. He pulled long agonised notes from the depths of his small body. He looked at me, and at Casanova, and filled his lungs to cry again. I had never heard him make a sound like this, not even when he fought the *pantegane* in the courtyard or went to war for his sleek lovers on the rooftops. He strained at his velvet collar till it seemed about to burst.

Over the din of the cat, I shouted. I still had more venom to expend with my *lingua biforcuta*. I said to Casanova, 'If you had loved me more, you would have been more afraid of losing me, and you would not have printed that book. But perhaps it's just an excuse, so you can go off on your adventures again. Go and find whatever woman it is whose scent has got you twitching, But don't show that long nose around here any more.'

The cat yowled louder. His hindquarters lifted from the ground with the effort of his song. He opened his mouth so wide that we saw the pale pink cathedral of little bones inside, all the way to the back of his dark gasping throat.

Casanova opened his eyes wide in pain, but he said nothing. I knew that he had no script prepared for women hurt by his actions. He had spent his life avoiding the need to say those words.

I said, 'You have nothing to say. You hang your head like a little boy who has disappointed his parents. You have never grown up and yet you are old. You make mistakes I would scorn to make. You are entirely pathetic, ridiculous! No wonder Venice doesn't want you any more. You're like a tired old doll from the nursery. You're falling apart and you no longer inspire love – you are tolerated only for sentimental reasons. But really you're now too shabby for us to bother with.'

I turned my back upon them both. The cat was still spending his tiny soul in plaintive cries. I stood a long time like that.

If I had known then that I would never see Casanova again, I would have turned around a second later. I would have pulled him to me and kissed his eyes. I would have licked his nose. I would have torn his poor frock-coat, scrabbling to get inside it and kiss his breast. I would have begged, 'Let me go with you!'

But I did not know. I stood in silence until I could swallow my tears. Then, still alight with anger, I turned around.

But Casanova was gone. I had not heard his departing footsteps over the screams of the cat, who still sat there singing his desperate aria.

I picked up the cat and held him to my breast, which was humid with Casanova's tears. I stroked his paws and his ears. I kissed the top of his head. The cat nosed my bodice and pushed his head close to me, finally silent but vibrating with his emotions. He gazed up at me, nudging my chin to make me look at him.

'I am sorry,' I told him. I was ashamed to meet his eyes. 'We will make everything good again.'

A week later a present arrived for me at the studio, a long flat parcel, tied with ribbon. When I tore it open, hundreds of pale pink English Overcoats slithered to the floor like the dried petals of enormous roses. They were followed by a tinkling gold ball. The cat pounced and batted it around the studio while I bundled the Overcoats into the *armadio*, the tall cabinet where I kept my canvases, finished and unfinished. I snatched the golden ball from the cat and threw it into the bath where my canvases lay soaking. The dark fluid swallowed it with a lascivious gulp. I was furious and ashamed. He still thought I could want a man other than him!

Seeing my anger, the cat opened his mouth again. I rushed to pick him up and hoisted him up to my shoulder, where he scrabbled in my hair until he found my ear. I soothed him with long hard strokes down the length of his back. He laid his muzzle against my earlobe and commenced a voluminous purr.

This time it was my turn to howl.

The Cat Speaks

Casanova generally had the knack of keeping his females affection-ate, even after they mated with him.

But even when we give satisfaction, male cats are subject to vio-lence and hatred after making love. We would be happy to stay for a little mutual grooming and a post-coital catnap. But we are hissed and scratched away.

It is a fault in the design of our procreative organ, which is spiny. In penetration, the little spines lie smooth, but as we withdraw they are brushed up the wrong way and tear the tender chamber of the female. It is the pain that makes them hate us when we leave them.

17

Fato el buso, pol passar qualunque sorze.

Once the hole is made, any mouse can get in.

VENETIAN PROVERB

I heard that Casanova left for Mestre the same day I flayed him with my rancorous tongue. Apparently he hovered near Venice for some months and even came through on a barge to collect some belongings from Francesca. I suppose he was still hoping for mercy from the Inquisitors. It was not forthcoming. Then, it seems, he took command of his exile and departed for Austria and France. While in Vienna he was able to infiltrate the diplomatic bag of the Venetian Ambassador to insert an anonymous letter to the State Inquisitors. The letter predicted, authoritatively, that on May 25th 1783, an earthquake would seize Venice and drag her to the bottom of the ocean. The letter caused such a panic that many patricians fled the city for their country estates. The rumour had touched the quivering part of the Venetian consciousness that still remembered the horrors of the earthquake that had destroyed Lisbon just thirty years before. Perhaps we also felt guilty, we Venetians. We knew it was our turn to fall. We had stayed up too late, played for too long and too hard. Like naughty children in a fairy tale, a bad end was due to us, whether by commotion of the stars, flood or fire. Our deep Venetian superstitions responded to the threat.

I sat on my steps at the Palazzo Balbi Valier, with my feet lost in the green broth of the water, and watched streams of gondolas laden with treasure lurching up the Grand Canal. By May 20th the value of property in Venice had halved. A week later I watched the boats sneak back in quiet ignominy. I spent a lot of time on those steps. I did not want to be inside my studio, which was still full of air breathed by Casanova, and canvases imprinted with his opinions. I could not believe that he had gone. So I did not let him go; I did not acknowledge his departure, or that it was forever. I merely waited for him.

I myself had received no letters except the parcel of English Overcoats.

I was now left alone in Venice, with only the education he had given me. Gradually I allowed my loss to infiltrate my thoughts, through my body. How many times I wished I was lying in the arms of Casanova, with his nose in my armpit, like a companionable kitten. Now I lay in the arms of no one, and felt a blankness which was without mercy. In agonies of frustration, I assumed the pose of Botticelli's Venus night after night. But Casanova was right: self-pleasuring only really worked as a supplement to more substantial joys. On its own, it merely preserved my lust.

My dissatisfaction was written on my face when I woke up in the morning. Passing boys and men would stop and look at me in the street, mutely offering to help. My mother was jealous. Sofia was jealous. The admiring looks and comments that had formerly been reserved for their more cultivated beauty were now directed at me. Both my mother and Sofia had the look of that pasty-faced *Giustizia* painting by Bonifacio de' Pitati, hair as fine and as limp as wet silk. They were both upholstered with thick pale skin, and both had impossibly small feet. Sofia loved to dress up like a great lady. Her hats spouted little stuffed birds and dead butterflies. She was starting to wear her hair piled up in a *pouf à sentiment*, with a lock of my mother's own hair inside it and sometimes a little portrait of her in a locket too. Her hair was now powdered and little puffs of sparkling white dust clouded her face when the wind blew. In spite of such allurements, the men looked at me.

Sofia complained, 'You make me feel invisible when I walk with you.'

My mother blamed my breasts. So did I. There had been a mistake. In the last few months I had grown the wrong ones. I had the temperament of a woman with small, independent breasts, the kind that require no thought, that do not draw attention to themselves and adhere to the ribs almost imperceptibly. Instead, I grew soft, white Madonna-like breasts, gentle, undulating as I walked. My breasts drew admiration out of men, and smiles out of babies. Like those of the Madonna in Madrid, my breasts were unmistakably carnal, to everyone else and to me. Every time I slipped a chemise over my head, and the fabric caressed them, I suffered agonies of frustrated desire.

One day a group of young men surrounded me, with their sticky bodies and their pointless commentary on my breasts, '*Stupendi!*' '*Perfetti!*' '*Complimenti!*' '*Fidanzata?*' I walked through them, scornfully, my eyes fixed on a point just beyond their heads. They parted to allow my passage. I myself held my *hands* in high regard: my hands had something to give this world. So I ignored the boys, which inflamed them, for there was something about my breasts that promised them more. From behind me, the boys made dog noises like the hounds of the Isle of Bones in the lagoon. They promised to fuck me to death. I would die smiling, they told me. In Venice, I reflected, our concepts and expressions of love and death are always very much mixed.

'*Le mani a casa vostra*,' I spat at them when they reached out to touch me. 'Keep your hands to yourself!'

But in the end, it was too much for me, the incessant call of sex in my blood. Other people had recognised it before I did. I had denied it too long. Three months after Casanova left, I opened the *armadio* and took out those English Overcoats. I would do as Casanova had told me, and enjoy the pleasures of beasts. But it would not be with the boys who called after me in the street.

I had no use for unskilled hands upon my body, or selfish firm flesh. For the rest of my life, with the exception of one, I preferred older men with cool hands, whose faces dissolved slowly in orgasm, whose foreheads were pleated with experience, whose lips were webbed with tiny folds, who bore a certain deep groove from nose to mouth, behind whose ears was a little vulnerable area of slacker flesh, sensitive as a petal, that was where I liked to rest my lips during the night. I preferred to hold these delicate men, rather than to be held myself . . . so I would always arrange myself behind them and hold them. At the last minute I would gently slide one knee between theirs and enfold their slackening limbs in my thighs. If they loved me their hand would reach out for mine at this point. If they had merely wanted me, and might want me again later, they would shuffle their hindquarters into my groin before relaxing into the contemplative sleep of the quite-soon-dead.

Of course, after Casanova had gone, I tried them all – all kinds of men, some young, some old, some mutilated, some perfectly constructed. Sometimes the cat would be there, watching. When a *corteggiatore* of mine left, the cat would shrug his tail into the very punctuation mark of irony.

The tail would say to me, 'A fine fellow you have chosen there!' Meaning exactly the opposite. We must hope that the cat found his own low loves more satisfying than I found mine.

Venice is a bad place to be with the wrong man, even if he is doing all the right things. So many times, for so many years since, I have sat in a gondola, gliding past painted *palazzi*, with the wrong man nibbling my shoulder or stroking my fingers. Years later I found the right man who would do all the wrong things, and he was worse.

I learnt then things that Casanova could never have taught me, things about pain, things about failure. I learnt that we stand for a long time in front of a door that has been slammed in our face. It takes a long time before we see that the walls of our lives are punctured with millions of doors. Sometimes, blinded with tears, we lurch into the nearest one. Is it a surprise that it sometimes turns out to be a bad choice?

After Casanova left, I found painful memories everywhere I looked. We had been able to stride about the back streets, me secreted under his arm . . . now, in his absence, I saw too many older men with their diminutive teenage mistresses under their arms. What a gesture! What an exclusive, inclusive gesture: excluding everyone else and almost swallowing the lover. I knew it so well, the exchange of looks as the arm of one is raised and the shoulder of the other is lowered, those quick pivotings of the bodies in to amity, the quick reassuring squeeze and then the infinitesimal nestlings. And then the kiss. Now I must talk of other things.

Double lives are lived twice as fast and twice as dangerously as others. Of course, in the end, mine was discovered. I grew careless. One day I accepted a commission delivered on parchment without checking the seal of the signature with sufficient care. A week later a friend of my father's duly marched into my studio with his corpulent wife, a friend of my mother's.

After three days locked in my room, I began to detect a new note in the family meeting upstairs in the *piano nobile*. I heard my uncles clapping my father on the shoulder. I heard the twittering of my mother's sisters. I heard the name of Angelica Kauffman mentioned more than once. Rosalba Carriera was cited several times. I heard the names of my satisfied clients from the high echelons of the *Libro d'oro*. The house was no longer disgraced. My parents had decided that they could be proud of me. So when I came out of my room. it was on my own terms. I could keep the studio at the Palazzo Balbi Valier, and my clients. Suddenly I was an adult, a business woman, a woman in charge of her own destiny.

The Cat Speaks

What did Cecilia mean, 'his own low loves'? She's hardly in a position to criticise, and it gets worse.

For myself, well, I admit it, I have my Persian harem but I also like a little rough. I like a thin little tabby from the ghetto sometimes, or the old spinster white from San Polo. Or the red cat from San Giobbe who's got a bit of a past. And the novelty is perpetual! Every cat's face is different, and then, when you look closely, you see that each feature has its own personality. Sometimes each eye has a different expression. And then there are the smells!

Alas poor humans who cannot smell the poetry that rises off a female cat in season! Poor humans who must be in the same room as one even to know that something good and juicy disturbs the air. We cats carry information in our blood and we know a ready female three roofs and two alleys away.

Among the male cats, there are four states of desire:

Andàr sui copi, to go out on the tiles

To have an urgent need to make love, in the manner of the Venetian cats who, when in heat, go meet each other on the rooftops where they MIAOW noisily.

Restàr imatonìo, to remain stone-like, impassive

To be out of season and uninterested in physical matters.

Mandàr in squero, to need to go to the gondola-workshop

To be in need of serious help, generally after fighting over females, or, in humans, after *Carnevale*.

El ze tuto un caìn de folpi, to be nothing more than a basin of octopus

An expression used for an old cat who believes he has the kind of sexual capacity on which, in his case, the sun has already set.

18

La colpa l'è na bela putela, ma nissun la vol.

Guilt is a gorgeous girl but nobody wants her.

VENETIAN PROVERB

N ow that I was free to practise my profession, my ambitions became more greedy. To be a better painter, I needed to know more. The more I wanted to know, the further I placed myself out upon a moral limb.

An artist, for example, needs to know what lies beneath the outer garb of the sitter; not just the skin, but the muscles and the bones. Otherwise your portraits are of well-stuffed dolls. If I was to progress I needed to draw the human figure from life. And this was a problem for female artists. Angelica herself, the first female Royal Academician, had been mocked for her inability to portray the musculature of masculinity. A poet suggested in a satiric verse that if she were to marry such a man as she painted that she would find her own wedding night a somewhat lacklustre occasion.

It was not her fault! Johann Zoffany's 1772 painting of the members of London's Royal Academy shows the two female members, not in the flesh with all their serious, self-conscious colleagues, *but in portraits hung upon the wall*. Angelica, you see there, and her rival,

Mary Moser. In Zoffany's painting, Angelica and Mary hang, pale and dull, behind the beautiful nude male model who is being examined by the male Academicians. The women are not permitted to see the frontal parts of the model, or to join in the discussion. They are silent, works of art themselves rather than participators.

Remember that in this world the word 'artist' automatically denotes a male, unless 'female' is additionally specified. Every woman artist is accustomed to be celebrated as an exceptional member of her species; she is a curiosity. Our paintings are worth less than those of our male counterparts. I would often have sitters referred to me who could not afford what they really wanted: an Ingres or a Jacques-Louis David. There is only one thing we women artists can look forward to in the dim future: after our deaths we generally have fewer inferior paintings attributed to us than our male colleagues do. More often, unfortunately, our best work is attributed to the master who originally taught us. Sometimes, I have wondered if this will happen to Antonio and me, but I doubt it now, in view of what has happened since. I doubt it.

Female artists have always needed to be careful not to be identified with artists' models, who are, in men's minds, looseness and depravity incarnate. Surely it is lubricious, people have always thought, for a woman to stare at a man for hours, or herself in a mirror? Up until my time, and Angelica's, if we painted ourselves, it had to be as models of virtue. You see, the more unlike men we are – the less virile, the less analytical, the less aggressive – the more prized we are. We women should, some male critics have claimed, paint only babies and flowers, as graceful and fresh and harmless as our lovely selves. We women artists have always been accused of taking an immoderate pleasure in colour, of applying it like cosmetic paints to skin. But as well as artifice, we women are also supposed to be dangerously close to nature, perilously instinctive.

As Casanova used to say with tender admiration, we bear an untamed uterus inside us, a voracious organ with no connection to our brains, and it frightens respectable men!

But it was still a good time to be a portrait painter, and even a woman, if you knew how to take your place, with style. The Parisian Académie Royale had just given portraiture its place in the hierarchy of true arts. We came second only to history paintings. Genre, still-life and landscape were numbered below us. And the new fluidity of our society also helped us. The rising bourgeoisie hired painters to give a patina of aristocratic heritage to their walls. By painting their portraits, we legitimised them. Their painted faces on the wall were the equal of any nobleman's. Some of these new sitters even asked for portraits in clothes of an earlier age. In this way, we helped them elongate their pedigree.

Now that I was free to do as I wished, I still wanted to paint portraits, but I wanted to get closer to the skin. I was still ambitious to equal and supersede Angelica. In the matter of painting desire, and desirability, I longed to claim the laurels. Casanova had been right, I realised: if I could do that I could conquer the world. But there were practical difficulties.

The female nude, I had mastered early. To learn my own body, I had always had access to mirrors and stolen candles. I knew how I looked in the heat of my passions. But how was I, without marrying, to obtain access to the male nude? I did not want to marry. After Casanova, marriage seemed somehow irrelevant, and possibly intrusive. So I set myself the task of learning male anatomy in a pleasurable way. Or mostly pleasurable. Or, to be honest, mostly tolerably pleasurable. And sometimes, only my appetite for novelty or information kept me from disgust.

These days, despite my personal preference for delicate older men, I chose my physical types to match my commissions. If my sitter — Count Alvise, say — was stocky and greying, then so was my current lover. They seemed to come in shoals, the kinds of men I painted. Sometimes I was condemned to a diet of lovers with stagnant eyes, sheltered by patient sparse lashes. Other times it was skinless young men with ugly, disproportionate organs and disappointing stamina. It happens like that.

I found my men in the fish market, where the smells made all Venetians come alive inside their clothes. There would be an exchange of subtle glances and they would follow me back to the studio. Or I found them in San Marco, surrounding the blue and white striped awning of the Public Lottery tent under the Campanile, or drawing the sun into their loins as they lounged on the stairs of the Procuratie. Or I would hear heavy breathing behind me and deliberately stop in my tracks to provoke a collision and the subsequent pleasantries. There seemed to be an endless supply of such men, waiting for women such as me to look them in the eyes, confident that we would come. Whatever the current phenomenon, I would sketch him afterwards, when he lay exhausted. Or coax him into the same pose that my sitter had requested. Most would do anything I asked, if his wife was not waiting for him.

I cannot pretend that I was as cold-blooded as I wanted to be. I never entered a man's arms without the hope that he would teach me something new of joy. But I rarely left them with that hope fulfilled, and disappointment embittered kisses I exchanged with them. They were shallow kisses, merely an exchange of currency to secure the final transaction. I never took nourishment from those kisses, as you do when you fasten your mouth upon the mouth of the man you really love, by whom you are loved. Unfortunately, in the hectic discomfort of a poor kiss, you always find time to be reminded of the rich joys of a proper one.

My system of flesh models led to confusion in the studio sometimes. Lost in a brush-stroke, I would forget, and imagine, under

my aristocratic sitter's clothing, the naked body I had already experienced. I would grow desirous, and this led to the real Count
Alvise, for example, climbing out of his breeches and onto my
divan, just as his unwitting body-double was accustomed to do. I
would refuse to accept payment for compromised portraits like
these; by doing this I ensured discretion. I couldn't afford to let it
happen too often.

But I liked the Count Alvises too, and I liked to feel them in my
hands. I liked their knowing fingers on my body, and their rich
grunts of appreciation. I liked their surprise at the things that didn't
disgust me. I liked to hear the soft plop of a droplet of their sweat
falling on my breasts. I liked helping them find their way inside me,
and I liked the faint apology when they fell out afterwards. I liked
the way their faces presented themselves for portraiture after lovemaking. More than once I obliged a man – an older one. I gave him
the opportunity to help me make him more loved-looking for posterity. I liked the way these noblemen looked at me in the street
when we met, as all Venetians meet, days later. What is she? I could
see them wondering. Artist, or lover? How should I greet her?
With a sinuous movement and a smile, I passed them quickly. I preferred to leave them wondering, in case I needed them again.

For the sake of my female portraits I undertook a few similar
Sapphic adventures. But I did not always have to make love to a
woman in order to make her take her clothes off for me. Sometimes
I just had to pay her. So I would haunt the slums, looking for physical doubles of my ladies and countesses among the *faxoléti*. I would
lure them back to my studio with a few *zecchini*. There I would have
them sling their great mealy bodies, naked, on the same velvet chair
where, a few hours later, their rich and pampered counterpart
would delicately alight, completely unaware that the rich fabric still
bore the fragrance of the streets. With what horror the noble ladies
would have viewed my earlier sketches of their flesh-sister's breasts,

bellies, knees and thighs. These graphite sketches, highlighted in white, were secreted in the cupboard for which only I had the key. Inside, what democratic orgies of skin! The naked bodies of the *fax-oléti* and the Count Alvises all smudged together with the supposed heads of *contessas* and *dogessas*.

Children could be a problem. Rosalba Carriera, painting the ten-year-old Louis XV, had fallen into despair. In the course of the first sitting alone, the young king's gun fell over, his parrot died, and his small dog succumbed to a violent fever. Other children, with fewer accoutrements, can torture an artist just as badly. Then there are the mothers. None is ever satisfied with the satin of their child's painted skin. I was never happy with . . . but . . . another time, another time.

You do not paint too many old ladies in my profession. Few of them crave it. But I painted women of every other shape and con-figuration. Like another of my idols, Ingres, as an artist I preferred women, for their textures, their accessories and their mysteries. I told tales on them in my pictures. I might let the candlelight fall upon the name of their secret lover on a calling card in a silver plat-ter beside them. I might try my trick with the painted porcelain buttons. On the other hand, I tried to help the ones I liked. They needed help, often.

Why is God so unkind to us? Why does he cork a sylph with a gorgon's head? Or bind an exquisite face to a lumpen form? In cases like these, I would help them with every device I could: the old Ingres mirror trick, for example, would distract the viewer from the imperfections that I could not hide. I would position my lady with her back to a mirrored fireplace. The mantelpiece would be bedecked with a vase of delicate wild flowers. Her front view was of a *décolletée* woman in an elegant salon, but the subtext, the picture behind the picture, showed her naked neck reflected as if in a meadow: sophisticated sensuality and the innocence of spring, both sides at once. The viewer, seduced by the neck, would not ask for more beauty in the face. I always loved to show these tell-tale arches of women's necks reflected in mirrors behind them. It was those necks, held bravely or slumped in defeat, that told their real stories.

Sometimes a man brought his new young mistress to my studio to be painted. I could read the faces of the recently violated, the wonderment, the speculation, and the anxiety with which she fondled the beautiful new doll she had received for her pains. So I would deck the confused little girl in the kind of clothes her older sister wore, and dress her hair like a sophisticated princess, but upon the white tablecloth beside her a pewter goblet would be overturned, and a trickle of red wine would signify her recent sacrifice. I already knew it was unlikely that her first experience had been as wondrous as mine.

I had ways to detract in paint, too, if the situation called for it. If my sitters were haughty, and liked themselves that way, I painted them from below. Then the 'reader' of the portrait would know his place, always forced to look up to the arrogant *contessa* or *conte*. I painted subtle punishments for the character flaws of my sitters. Their collars did not sit straight on their rigid necks. I would mock a proud old man by looping a gold watch chain twice across his chest. From a distance, two pendulous breasts appeared. I could rely upon the vanity of my sitter to get away with this trick: he would never stand far enough away from his portrait to realise what I had done to him. His friends would never tell him; his family would not dare.

A man might want himself shown as a model of virtue, when I knew him to be a cruel priapus. So I would paint him with the tools of rectitude at his desk. But in a little reflection on the polished wood of his chair, you could read a tiny sketch of the body of a bruised prostitute, lying upon a disordered and bloody bed. A tin-pot philosopher, who bored me to tears during the sitting, would be punished too. I would paint his orrery – the globe of circling discs that show the movements of the planets – with mud and hairline cracks, to mock his fractured, dusty thinking.

I knew the dreams and fears of my sitters by what they asked for. If a man requested a portrait of his fiancée with a pair of doves on her lap then I knew he doubted her chastity. If a woman posed with a love letter, then I knew she lacked one from her lover.

Sometimes I painted my subjects' futures – weddings, illnesses, successes, failures – into my backgrounds, the way a religious artist will sometimes show a sinister crucifix in the dim hinterland behind his Madonna and child.

I learnt to paint heat and cold so well that you could always tell the season of my portraits. This, too, was a way of revealing more about my sitters than they had consciously intended. My palette was the weather inside them. People who commissioned winter portraits had chosen to be brave. They held themselves against that special cold of Venice – the icy vapour rising from the canals, a pernicious cold that sidles inside your clothes and clutches at your limbs. In winter, you carry frost inside you in Venice; in summer you swell and fester. The winter light – it's different. In summer it pours itself without discrimination. In winter it gilds capriciously, one window of a *palazzo*, one stone in a mosaic. My summer pictures showed young women about to be married, already pregnant.

I continued to follow in Angelica's footsteps, because that is what people demanded of me.

As I have told you, portraiture is addictive. Some people commission a new portrait the way they order a new dress, or, if they are rich, sometimes just to celebrate a new dress. Some people like to be painted in mourning, because it shows their tender side, and an irreproachable opulence, for every extra jet button and dark flounce is but a further tribute to the dead. Like Angelica, like Ingres, I painted Queen Caroline Murat of Naples. In all three of our portraits she is depicted in sumptuous mourning for her sister-in-law, Josephine, wife of her brother Napoleon. Vesuvius smokes gently behind her, in all three portraits.

Queen Caroline, by the way, never paid any of us, and you can tell from the mean little glint in her eyes that she never intended to. It was a hazard of our business. The more elevated the sitter, the more difficult it was to extract payment. After Queen Caroline, I took to painting merchants for a while. The bourgeoisie always handed me the purse with their left hand as they took the canvas in their right. If they wanted their frames just a little too large, and with just a little too much gold leaf, *va bene*. I did not have to see it.

Most of all, I loved to paint my own people, the Venetians, the last Venetians of the Serene Republic, as it would turn out. My portraits would be the last word on their happiness, its final verification. I captured the waning spirit in the light in their eyes. I took the heaviness of their flesh and turned it into a fulsome jewelled light. I was painting the autumnal bloom, the final flare before the rotting begins, and perhaps the rotting had already commenced under the high colour of the cheeks. I did not know that I was painting the fall of a Republic in those vivid faces. I knew that I was painting an apprehension there, a fluttering awareness behind the eyes, a greedy need for the pleasures that would soon be confiscated. No wonder Venice hungered for my portraits as the rest of the world, and one Napoleon Bonaparte, closed in upon us.

I loved the diaphanous Venetian fabrics smoky over luminous breasts. I adored the shadow of a Rialto goldsmith's bracelet on a ripe arm. I liked the secret cleavages of elbows. I could make a mouth look soft and blurred as if kissed all the way out of clarity and into confusion, or hard and impermeable to the kiss of the most devoted lover. I loved to illuminate a pure complexion with the same sweet light Giotto had reserved for saints, and darken a corrupt one with the throbbing shadows perfected by Tiziano.

I painted my way through the *Libro d'oro*, sat in drawing rooms that my mother and Sofia only dreamt of, portrayed the men and women all Venice was talking about. One day, my clients flattered me, Venice would become too small for me. Casanova's prophesy would come true. My fame would spread. I would spend the flower of my womanhood on those roads of Italy, with my bathtub full of canvases.

But I would always come home.

It may seem unaccountable that I stayed there with those estranged beings, my family, after Casanova left and I became famous. But I am an Italian. I must have my blood around me. And I liked to hear their voices in the background. I liked to hear the house waking up above me. I liked the intimacy of day-to-day life. I liked watching the pimples come and go like migrating birds across Sofia's face. I liked watching my mother at her embroidery. I liked the salty smell of my father when he came home from the docks. Of course I never told them these things. I assumed they understood them from the fact that I continued to bestow my erratic and barbed presence upon them.

Perhaps I thought that the exposure of the years would weather my mother's reserve towards me, and mine towards her. I had no hopes of Sofia: she would soon get married and leave. For my father, I hoped merely not to disappoint him. I had been a strange daughter. He had not asked, at his daily prayers, for his house to be blessed with artistic genius. He had asked for more silk, more customers, more shipments from the east and more *Carnevale* balls to create the desire for his stuffs. He did not ask for more love in his life. I was sure he did not have a mistress. He was a sober man. I had never worried that I might meet him by accident at a decadent casino or in the wild dark streets at *Carnevale*, where the bodies juddered like drumsticks in dark corners and a wordy perfume lingered in the air.

So I did not leave home. Like Venice, I am pragmatic. I admit it, I took what I wanted from my family, and gave very little back. I left the role of dutiful daughter to Sofia. For myself, I took the role of barely tame house animal, something more ungrateful than a cat. My *lingua biforcuta* stabbed at everyone. I shall not tell you the horrible things I said. I forgive myself only because I lashed out in pain. I was lonely for Casanova. I was lonely for *conversazione*, intimate *conversazione*. Without it, my wit festered and turned in upon itself. Gradually, as my success continued, there came a point where no one dared remark upon me.

But I always came home, nearly always. There were few lovers, as I have explained, with whom I chose to spend the night. At the end of the day, I loved to walk from my studio at the Balbi Valier to my family's *palazzo* beside the church of Santa Maria dei Miracoli. I could not renounce the daily sight of the little doll's church that juts out of the surrounding sweet terracotta walls at such astonishing angles that it seems to have been placed there by the careful hand of a child. Of all the churches in Venice, Miracoli is my favourite and not merely because I was born in its shadow.

I loved my room. There was a golden light from the courtyard garden outside, especially after rain. It was a disturbing light, and I could not completely account for it. On the other side was the jade-green canal and the pink and grey marble of Miracoli and the cool shadows they painted on my windows. After Casanova left, I decorated the room with frescoes of the places where I had enjoyed my most exquisite pleasures with him: the grave of Fortunato at San Michele, the long grass on the foreshore at the island of San Lazzaro, the canal at San Vio where we used to moor the gondola, the opulent interior of the boat, with the coverlets banked in lustrous wrinkles after a night of hectic loves. I painted the empty frame in the study at Palazzo Mocenigo, where we had made such gorgeous moving pictures together. I painted a life-size copy of the *Biribissi* board from that same night at the Mocenigo. Around the window I had painted the fairy tale palaces of Beckford's *Vathek*, and yes, Alboufaki the camel. My room was my own world, private from the rest of the world. I could go there and live among my memories and my fantasies.

I sound unbearably selfish, I know, but in fact everyone was happy. It seemed to the outside world that I had remained respectably at home, despite my eccentric and potentially scandalous profession. Within the family, the shock of my discovery gave way to a quiet acceptance. Soon the little earthquake was absorbed by our *palazzo*. The walls closed in around my family again. No one knew of my midnight and dawn comings and goings, except the servant who still brought me the bath water. I did not speak to her, but in front of her I was entirely without physical inhibitions. It was she who took my sweaty or bloody clothes away to clean them. It was she who saw the tooth-bruises on my neck, and the abrasions of nails on my back. But I never talked to her.

My mother came down to my room just once after I had completed the frescoes. She had heard the servants talking about them and wanted to make sure I had done nothing to corrupt the maids, nothing more to put the Cornaro name on the lips of the gossips at Rialto or cause a whisper at the *Broglio* under the arches of the Doges' Palace when my father went there to discuss business with the noblemen.

She knocked quietly and came in only on my bidding. I stared at her, plump and anxious in her fine clothes. Like all adolescents I looked for my future in her drooping face. I imagined painting it. Better to die young, I thought in my arrogance.

My mother walked just a few steps into the room and stood still in shock as if the Medusa had just caught her eye. She shuddered. Gambling, lust, the corruption of the Orient, everything she feared was there to be seen in vivid, shameful colour on my walls.

'How did I make you?' she asked. She was not angry, just mysti-fied, and a little afraid.

I was sorry for her, but I could not make myself take her hand or comfort her. I merely said, 'I do not know, Mama. Perhaps it's not your fault.' We agreed it would be better for my father not to see the pictures.

'To think I named you for the gentlest saint,' she whispered as she left.

Poor Mama! My father certainly treated her as if I were her fault. He could not meet my eyes any longer; he was afraid of what he might see. He had always been brusque and dominating. In my father's presence my mother, whose background was nobler but whose fortune had been negligible, was the personification of acqui-escence. She had no detectable desires of her own. Or perhaps I just was not looking for them. My father still treated her like a daugh-ter. She took his pronouncements with downcast eyes. Only occasionally her little finger drummed against the fourth one, oth-erwise her gentleness was impeccable.

She was always touching Sofia, the way Italian mothers do, like cats; always licking a finger and smoothing down a pale eyebrow, or wiping an invisible crumb from those thin pink lips. The two of them had from the start a kind of milky conspiracy that had always excluded me. (Of course, I did not care.) Sofia developed delicately as my mother hoped. She was given to vapours and nerves and swooned prettily at dramatic noises or bad news, the fashion-able pose of the time. She looked like a little Madonna in her *zendaléto* of supple muslin, which wreathed her head, crossed her shoulders and encircled her waist. If I could be forced into mine, I looked like a madwoman escaped from an asylum.

Prim as she was, I suspected Sofia of rifling through my things, so I kept anything really important in my studio. Once, for her edifi-cation, I left her my copies of Aretino's more extreme positions. I knew she had found them when I saw her at dinner that night. She was pale and blotchy and would not meet my father's eye. I could see her thinking, *He has one of those things.* It was beyond her comprehension that he might use it with my mother as Aretino recommended. I thought to myself, *She will find out soon enough.* For Sofia was already betrothed to a respectable client of my father's. Soon she would be leaving home. After that I thought she would not spy upon me again, and I left everything I wanted in my bedroom. I was wrong, as it turned out.

I went to church with my family. To please them, I went to confession, where I recited the sins of my sitters, claiming them for my own, for the pleasure of hearing the priest pant and shift erotically inside his confessional. I made these vicarious confessions partly out of curiosity as to what kind of penance my sitters deserved for their sins (for I knew they would not confess such things themselves) and partly to avoid confessing my own. I already knew how I would pay for those.

I would pay for them by feeling alone. My cruelties to Sofia and my mother would be repaid by a numbing isolation. The cold sensual sins I committed in my studio would be replaced by a sharp longing for the loving embrace of Casanova. Even so, I teased my mother and sister by emerging from these false confessions with my face crumpled and dissolved in liquid mortification. They looked around, terrified that our neighbours would see the guilt on my face and that my precarious position in society — and theirs — would be further compromised.

Casanova was long gone — it would be eight years before Sofia found my annotated Casanova sketchbooks under the bed in my painted *mezzanino* room and delivered them to my parents. Before they had a chance to silence her, her ejaculations had been overheard by the maid and two gondoliers. By the afternoon, it was being talked of at Florian. That night, it was mentioned at a grand dinner given at the Doges' Palace. At the sumptuous table, two of my late lovers were convulsed in their soup.

At the time, I knew nothing of my exposure. I was at Asolo, painting portraits of the local dignitaries and their ugly wives. When I came back to Venice two days later I found myself famous in a new way. Somehow the news had got out: Cecilia Cornaro had been the last love of Giacomo Girolamo Casanova in Venice.

19

El baso xe 'l rufian del buso.

The kiss is the pimp of the hole.

VENETIAN PROVERB

Let me tell you how Casanova used to kiss me. It will do you good. It will do me good, too. It's been too long since I had a kiss like that.

This is how we would kiss if we stood upon the balcony at the Palazzo Mocenigo, for example, or by the well in Campo San Vio. This was a public kiss, which we did not scruple to share with those less fortunate than ourselves, those who do not know how to kiss. With our mouths fastened together we were anonymous as a statue of a tall man and a small woman.

We would stand for this kiss, which started with our arms encircling each other. Then our lips would touch and our eyes would close like those of two mechanical dolls. We would then withdraw for a second to look into each other's eyes. Then he would incline his head one way and I the other so our lips might meet without the interruption of our noses. Then I would put my hand behind his head like a baby's and draw him to me. He would put one arm around my shoulder and the other around my waist. Then the real kiss would begin.

This kiss had its own foreplay of lips and tongue-tips. First we sipped at each other like oysters. The kiss had its own gentle penetration and its own accelerating rhythm. All the time our hands moved slowly, pressing each other's shoulder blades, waists and flanks, as if to contain the richness of the kiss inside our bodies. Such a dangerously beautiful kiss must not be allowed to escape, at all costs.

This kiss had its own climax and its own other-worldly swoon afterwards, when we sank back into our skins, with my head against his breast, he with his chin resting softly upon my hair. We often wet each other's throats with tears then. We were more exhausted than if we had sported with steed and treasure, which, to be sure, roused themselves and moistened as we kissed like this.

But we did not make love after a kiss like this.

Other kisses were, as we say in Venice, merely the pimps of the lovemaking to come.

But a kiss such as this one was its own journey and destination.

It was these kisses that I hungered for alone in my studio, now that he had gone.

20

Gh'è più zorni che luganega.

There are more days than there are sausages.

VENETIAN PROVERB

Casanova did not forget me any more than I forgot him. His love for me was preserved, like the promise in our kiss, like the sun in a jar of honey, like the wild boar's musk inside the sausage.

I know this now, but for the entire lamentable duration of that first year without him I thought he must have expunged from his heart all memories of me. I knew that I deserved nothing better. In his moment of weakness and need, I had turned upon him with my egregious *lingua biforcuta*.

How do I know that he never stopped loving me?

There is evidence. I have it in writing. If you look in one place, in a wall, in the Balbi Valier, scratch a little, scrape a little, you will find it, my cache of precious letters.

Exactly a year after we quarrelled, the first letter arrived. 'My darling Cecilia, my soul,' it said. At the endearment, my eyes blurred with tears. 'I find that I cannot resist writing to you any more than I can resist breathing. I find that my love for you and my fears for you have conquered my desire to leave you in peace.' The letter was tentative and apprehensive. He continually apologised for writing. He wrote that he could easily understand if I did not wish to hear from him.

I hugged the letter to my breast. Then I gave it to my cat to sniff. He brandished his tail and vibrated it as if the letter were a she-cat with whom he was newly in love. I felt the same! I was in love with that letter. I carried it everywhere. All day, as I worked in the studio on my painting, I composed and revised my reply inside my head. While I painted with my right hand I fondled Casanova's letter in my pocket with the left one, running my forefinger down its grooves, tapping its stiff little corners with my thumb. Finally, that evening, I sat down at my desk at Miracoli, looking over the court-yard where I first dropped into his arms, and wrote fifteen chaotic pages without stopping. I wrote him loving thoughts and memories, but most of all longings. I told him how I missed the very hairs of his wrists and the half-moons of his eyelids. I reminded him of how we used to kiss. I told him how I missed his breath on my hair and the fold of his thoughts where I used to enclose myself.

But I stopped short of begging his forgiveness. I had no need to do so. It seemed that he had accepted what I had said; he had swallowed the toad. To withdraw my words now would have been unkind, for it would deny the pain I had caused him and the reason for our twelve parlous months apart. So I wrote as if that terrible day had never happened. Like Casanova, I pretended that it had not. I acknowledged no cloud between us, no break in our love. I smoothed it over. I did not ask him about his last thoughts, the ones that carried him so far away from me. I did not ask him why he had stayed silent a whole year.

Within days I had my reply. And so it went on. Casanova wrote to me, from all his exiles, his hiding places, the great and obscure corners of the world where disgrace, misfortune and old age now sent him. Like systematic cuffs to one side of his head and then the other, these hard strokes of fate, in the end, left him dizzy and weak.

After that first year of silence, the magnificent tumult of his handwriting spilled into my lap every few weeks. And I wrote to him, with the comfort I could offer. 'Casanova, try to see it this way: you love novelty. Fortune is using this time to demonstrate to you a sample of everything you missed on your previous journeys. She offers you the endings to stories left off in the middle. She offers you a chance to muse on what they all meant. You will write one day for everyone, as you write it now for me. How beautifully you write! I could not put this down in painting, this long adventure of yours, yet you have painted it in words.'

And he wrote back. 'Don't philosophise, Cecilia. I write my adventures for you because I want you in my arms. As I write, I see your face and feel your hand covering mine as if to blot the wet ink with its warmth. I write to you in order to be with you. And because, as you know, I fear for you. There are hard things in your path. Don't forget that, my soul.'

I came to know those letters as well as I know the streets of Venice. I came to know their turnings and their deviations, the places where the sun shone in them and the sad parts waterlogged with rainy tears. I could never understand why he worried so much about me, why pockets of anxiety opened everywhere I looked. It almost seemed as if he knew something, as if there was something I should already know, something evil and frightening about what lay ahead of me. But every word of warning was wrapped in so much love that in the end I came to see them as part of that love, proper love, which cares more for its object than for itself.

You might call them love letters, those letters of Casanova. Indeed they were perfumed, crammed and saturated with love. But they were also a rehearsal, for his memoirs. And these letters were part of a chain of love letters that unites so many lovers . . . a telling and a retelling of the desires that bite you. You hear a word, you savour a delicious phrase, you think, 'Aha! Why didn't I say it like that?' And the next time you write a love letter, you do. Whether you unconsciously mimic or you wantonly plagiarise, you take the good words which come your way and you send them on.

Thus I am certain that these love letters from Casanova represent one hundred and thirty-two loves apart from me, and the one hundred and thirty-two loves (or so) of those one hundred and thirty-two loves and all their written caresses. There is, in those letters from Casanova, a special tongue-trick he learnt from C. C., and another phrase he heard first on the soft lips of M. M. There's a scribbled sigh stolen from Henriette and an affectionate bawdy joke from Marcolina. I never saw the memoirs of course, but I would recognise them if I did, for in them I would also find my own words mixed with the others. Would I protest? No! I should be honoured. I should then be included with the chosen few: I have loved properly.

When I first heard from him again, Casanova was in Paris, city of his former triumphs. He was staying with his brother Francesco, the painter. But out on the streets now there was not a face to greet him. No familiar actress was named on any playbill. The rich had lost everything; the poor were parading their riches in the most vulgar of manners. Even the courtesans were brand new, as the old ones had gone to cut a fine figure in the provinces where their glamour made their wrinkles look alluring. Politics, not pleasure, was all he found. Even the police were not interested in Casanova now.

Picture him, writing to me in Paris, hunched with cold and rejection over a glass of cheap wine in a café in Avenue d'Italie – what was this place to do with Italy? With Venice? Where was the colour and the life? This pallid street had been sucked by a French vampyre

or bleached by a French laundry woman with arms like a *bastonada*.
Casanova reflected, in a frail attempt at optimism, even arms like a
wooden club have their pleasant applications.

'But every arm,' he wrote, 'let us face it, only makes me long for
yours, Cecilia.'

Picture him at a Parisian shop window. A painting, a very bad
painting of Venice, had drawn him to smear the cold glass with his
breath. Inside the shop, the bell tinkled emptily in his ears like an
old toy, spinning in a deserted nursery. Marble women writhed in
contortions to evade the amorous attentions of men and gods.
Stuffed monkeys hunched on poles. Casanova spun around like the
doll in a music box, the tails of his frock-coat floating in the air. He
saw mould-tainted mirrors bewildered with reflections. No one
came to serve him. He knew he had been judged unworthy of
attention. He was too shabby to fawn over. The painting that had
seized his stomach, through his eyes, was of San Vio, where we used
to lie in the gondola together.

'Take this letter,' he wrote, 'to San Vio. Hold it open in the sun
and warm it for me there.'

Picture him eating *foie gras* at the table of a rich patron waiting to
be amused. The vast expense of the meat melting on his tongue
soothed his insecurity: this vulgar French poodle was prepared to
pay enormously for the privilege of having Giacomo Casanova, the
self-styled Chevalier de Seingalt, at his table. Paying for one's food,
Casanova wrote to me, seemed like paying for love. It was a *faux-
feast*. Alone, he ate like an ogre. In company, his manners were as
exquisite as his rapacious hunger would allow. He described to me
how he would cherish each oyster, finger each peach, tear the
pheasant meat slowly from the breast bone. He craved expensive
foods: duck in marmalade sauce, pistachio nuts, crab soup.

'And so,' he wrote to me, 'at the tables of the rich, I cringe and
grovel and I tell my stories.'

But alone in the Place des Vosges Casanova gnawed on *salade frisées-lardons* at a table by a door that would slam after him when he left. He could not these days afford to scorn any kind of food, for he had been hungry. And perhaps he would try that bizarre dish with eggs and beetroot on the menu . . .

But he always remembered the better times, those times as a millionaire in Paris, that other Paris, the Paris of his youth, where his table was as famous as his bed. He wrote to me now of those rare fowl he used to keep in a dark room, fed on rice. Their flesh was as white as snow, with an exquisite flavour. To the excellence of French cuisine, he added the genius and nuance of Italy. 'After all, we have the most sensitive tongues in the world, we Italians. For our tongues there is a universe of difference between a pasta shaped like a ribbon or a tube. What other nation can make this subtle distinction? It's the same when we kiss . . .' He had delighted the palates of his guests – in those days *he* paid – with his *macaroni al sughillo*, rice pilau or *in cagnoni*; the sweet giblets in his *ollas podridas* were the talk of the town. Only butter from Vambre was served at his table, and his Maraschino came directly from Zadar in Dalmatia. That was in the days when he had set up the national lottery, when Madame d'Urfé was clay in his hands, when interesting women dropped into his arms whenever he opened them, when nothing had been impossible.

Now he was always hungry, carrying his emptiness from place to place, feeding it with travellers' impressions he could not share as there was no lover at his side. Alone, Casanova looked up at Place des Vosges palaces lit by chandeliers, under which he used to dazzle. He walked past prodigiously stuffed grocer's shops, which seemed to beckon him, intimately. *Come inside, come inside, there's an abundance of good things here for you.* It was not true. Another door slammed in his face.

I had the sense that he had risen to the top of the water for the last time, gasping in the cold current, determined to drown with his head held high. Many years later, when I was in Paris, I tried to find the door that slammed against him that night in the Place des Vosges. I walked around the square three times, like an old dog before it settles for death. With each relay, I was more sickened by the cruelty of it. Casanova was there in 1783 with his vibrant misery. I was there decades later with mine. What was this malevolent wrinkle in time that kept me and him alone, outside, when we might have walked together, with me under his arm, under his cloak, with the tiny hairs on our wrists entwined, and the steam of our breath joining in soft spumes against the black night?

The letters came, one after another. And thus I came to hear about his wanderings in Holland and Austria, his attempts to found a newspaper, to build a canal from Narbonne to Bayonne, his plans for a sailing expedition to Madagascar, his interest in the huge gas balloons of the Montgolfier brothers. I saw him reduced to subtle solicitation and worse, to begging, until finally, for a thousand florins a year, he accepted his last, saddest exile.

He had been expelled from the rest of the world, and it was time to stop; time to stop, and reflect. And it was time to write, not just to me but to the world, and to the world to come.

I sat on the steps of the Grand Canal, with Casanova's letters riffling in my lap. I smelt and smoothed and breathed in the fragrance of those letters. I tried to extract from them the answer to the one question that still haunted me.

The Cat Speaks

You see how she loves him. You see the question and the answer implicit in her last words. Why didn't he ask her to join him? Maybe you have guessed already. You know Casanova. He had already forgiven Cecilia before he left that room she poisoned with her *lingua biforcuta*. It wasn't that.

I suppose you think you are very clever. You have your theory about a letter that was never delivered to her. Well, yes, I suppose some things are obvious. Goldoni and the other playwrights have made incident and coincidence seem special when really they are just a part of everyday life.

So, yes, there was a letter. And no, it was not delivered, but you should be aware immediately that this was not through any lack of effort or competence on my part, but because she did not want it.

The day that they quarrelled she left the studio and hid herself away at Miracoli. I could not have delivered the letter in any case. It was not my fault. Not that I feel guilty for losing the letter. Guilt is not known in the world of cats. The letter fell between the gratings of a drain. Well, yes, I admit, I dropped it when I was distracted by a sparrow. That is my nature. I do not apologise for it.

Cecilia never knew how Casanova waited for her at San Michele, at the grave of little Fortunato, a whole miserable night, with only me for company. I know that by the end of that night Casanova had accepted, with his usual grace, a rejection Cecilia never gave. He accepted his new role – to be a lover from afar – and off he went, alone again, into exile again. He was afraid to ask her a second time; I think he thought Cecilia, with her talent, might end up keeping him, and that was a thought he could not quite bear.

Never mind.

One day a real *acqua alta* will dislodge the letter. Not a petty little *acqua alta* but a ferocious one. It will clean out the cluttered arteries and veins of Venice. It will make Casanova's letter float to the surface, and I will be ready to take it to her.

But back then, in 1782, I knew that I could not bring Casanova back to her. He was in disgrace. He would stay there. She knew that I would never catch the king *pantegana* who lived in the well in our courtyard, and she could never catch him for me. But I could sit on her lap, and she could stroke my ears, and we could dream a little together.

So much pain flowing in blood-red routes across Europe, while Cecilia stayed at home dropping useless tears into the Grand Canal, reading his letters, waiting for him to ask her, experimenting with cretins and sophisticates until they made her sick.

I watched her weep when she was lonely for him. Sometimes I howled a little, in sympathy.

When the day grows dim, I always make myself available for Cecilia. The Grand Canal, to those who can really hear, becomes noisy with tears at that time. As everyone knows, cats can hear what humans cannot. Our ears twitch even when we seem to be most profoundly asleep. We are sensitive to misery. There is a lot of it about.

Other cats join us, me and Cecilia. We sing.

The chorus thickens with song, and tears. We are voracious of the sadness, we devour it. Cats are absorbent of human misery. We take it away in our fur.

The hour of the cats draws near. The sun dies in the arms of the evening. We cats take to our roofs. We walk over the terracotta tiles with a delicacy you cannot imagine, lifting our paws high like Spanish horses.

Under the water, in Venice, the bones of dead cats and dead humans are joined in the sediment. In love, in joy and in loss, we cats are with the humans who deserve us.

It may seem just now that Cecilia does not deserve me. Be patient, though.

She will *earn* me.

21

La lagrema più grossa xe quela che va in carozza.

The biggest teardrop is the one that goes in a wagon.

VENETIAN PROVERB

Paris, October 10th, 1783

Darling Cecilia,

How are you? It's days and days since your last letter. I worry for
. you, as you know. Don't leave me without news. Since we started
this delicious correspondence I find I cannot live without it.

As you know, I am in Paris now, with my brother Francesco. I
shall stay here some months. One has need of family in times like
this. (God knows, though, my mother never felt that need!)
Francesco has been envious of me all his life, of course, but,
finally, he has managed to reconcile envy with affection. Francesco
should have been a rich man. Paris loved him once. Did you know
that the Empress Catherine bought one of his paintings for the
Hermitage! Ah, Cecilia! I see your triangular face all *pointed* with
envy at this! Francesco should have been able to look after us all,
but his life of luxury and two bad marriages have left him in
ruins. He's now twitter-boned and impotent in every way, as he
has always been in the bedchamber. I guess that God gave his

Word to me in such excess that my brother was bound to be deprived. Who knows? I must only be grateful for my share.

In any case, Francesco requests that you convey his regards to Antonio, if you see him – I don't know if he has yet forgiven you for taking his noble clients. But one day, I predict, Antonio will be proud to be the portrait painter who gave the famous Cecilia Cornaro a start in her glorious career.

Paris is cold and strange to me. There is no one here who remembers me in my great days here. No one ever remembers the women I loved. Every night I dream of Venice. Always that white light of the morning of my escape from the Leads. I see something dead floating under the surface of the water at San Barnaba. An eddy from a silent gondola divides the blank sheet of liquid behind me. Faces are withdrawn from windows as I pass. And nowhere do I see a beckoning smile or an outstretched hand for Giacomo Girolamo Casanova.

Of course, I meet celebrities as usual, the wise Mr Benjamin Franklin and a young man who was the son of the delectable Marie-Louison O'Morphy from a liaison after her time in the king's harem. Portraits, portraits! Remember it was I who brought La Morphy to the king. For I had her portrait painted; in it I had her pose naked, with the glories of her rump and thighs begging for the urgent attentions of a lover. The painter was so proud of his work that he made copies. When the king saw the portrait, he demanded to see the original, and having seen her, he took her. Sometimes it has seemed to me that I have travelled only in order to bring happiness to pretty girls in need of a little help. It was always tempting to sweeten the charity with a little love.

I finish this letter now, for I am summoned to the drawing room. I must smile, and bow, and declaim – the French that I learnt in Rome all those years ago still serves me here. My little teacher, Barbaruccia, what joy it gives me to remember her dressed in men's clothes for her elopement! And that makes me remember the nun M. M. in her male attire. I think of how I followed her trim buttocks in pantaloons through Zannipoli by moonlight. Ah! They have all become so ghostly.

Only *you* seem real to me now.

Goodbye, my little Cecilia. Paint well. Remember that I love you. Remember to take the greatest care of yourself.

Your Casanova.

Paris, November 21st, 1783

Cecilia, my Cecilia,

Today is the festival of Salute in Venice. In my mind's deep eye I see you with your candle entering the fairy-tale church, a fairy-woman yourself, but smelling richly of oil. And tomorrow, by coincidence, is your Saint's day. I hope that you will mark it. Don't be so lost in your work that you forget Saint Cecilia and her bath! Think on the bath you took on the night you met me . . .

It's so strange to realise which are the things that make you homesick. This morning I sat in a café in Montmartre. Suddenly the clink of a spoon against a coffee cup brought back to me a vision of Florian and our Piazza, and a thousand Venetians stirring sugar into their coffee, sweetening their already too-sweet lives. It was unbearably painful to know that you might be among them, and that I am not.

In three days I leave with my brother Francesco for Vienna. Francesco is to be taken under the protection of Prince Kaunitz, but I, my love, must look to myself. I must find work.

I kiss you. I need to know how you are.

Your Casanova.

PS Is it true that there are plans to send up a gas balloon in Venice during *Carnevale* this year? How I wish that I could see it.

Vienna, mid February, 1874

Dear Cecilia,

After sixty-two days of travel and it seems as many years of genuflection, I have found work. I have ended up here in Vienna again. I have become the secretary of the Ambassador Sebastiano Foscarini. I am to write his dispatches. He's a gentleman. I am indebted to him for the sum of 500 francs. I do not see how I shall pay it, but I am not dead yet.

I have met here a young girl who reminds me of you, my love. Caton M. has none of your talents, but I like her lopsided smile. I saw her nether garments fluttering on her windowsill yesterday, and became aroused, though without much vigour.

Without you beside me, my desires are running dry. Yours, I hope, are in their full flood. I know you hate to hear it, Cecilia, but I must say it to you: I wish you more love in your life, both given and taken. Our time together has been so short. You must have more than I could give you. Nature demands it.

Speaking of underclothes, Clement of Alexandra, who was a man of great learning, observed that the modesty that seems so firmly rooted in the minds of women is in fact lodged only in their underclothes, because as soon as they are persuaded to remove those, not a shadow of it remains.

I cannot remember your nether garments, Cecilia. But I believe this is because you never wore them.

But I do not know for certain. There are so many things about you I do not know. We never lived together; we never passed a winter in each other's arms, nor woke to kiss each other with cold noses. All we had were those drowsy before-dawn rousings,

the grittiness under the eyelids, those hasty farewells. I never
watched you sleep, never saw the hollowing and plumping of your
breast as you lay dreaming.

The next morning

Last night I dreamt that I was wearing your clothes, impregnated
with your smells. Then you appeared, and you treated me
masterfully, reaching into my neckline and pinching my nipple.
You bared your own breast and with it you entered my mouth and
stayed there as long as you wanted, while I gasped.

I am yours as you are ever mine.

But go carefully, my darling.

Your Casanova.

PS Tell me more about the balloon, darling. Was it painted like a
Tiepolo ceiling? Did it rise like a bubble from a garlanded
stage . . . ? That is how it happens in Paris.

April, 1784

You are saved, my dearest one,

The Dutch war against Venice is over! Almost as soon as it is
begun! I can tell you before you hear it from anyone else.

My patron, Foscarini, has met with the Dutch ambassador
here, and a settlement has been achieved. The Emperor Joseph
has intervened to help us. I myself travelled to meet the great
man and was instrumental in the rescue. Casanova has come to
the rescue again of La Serenissima and her beautiful women.

If only I could save you every time you are under threat,
Cecilia. You know that you stand alone and perfect in my
imagination, and you have the strength in yourself not to feel
threatened by other women who have taught me only to love you

properly. We are the same in this, darling, for although you are discreet I rejoice in the flushed cheeks I sometimes read between the lines of your letters these days.

A few months ago, at a dinner given by the Ambassador, I met a most interesting man, a freemason, Count Charles de Waldstein of Dux. He is not yet thirty, but mature in his ways, with a weakness for racing and gambling. We talked of many esoteric matters, of the Clavicle of Solomon and all things to do with magic and the occult. I felt so at home I exclaimed, '*Oh! che bella cosa!* All the things that are familiar to me!'

'So,' replied Waldstein, 'come to Bohemia with me. I am leaving tomorrow.'

I think he means it. He tells me that he has a library of 40,000 volumes in his castle in Bohemia. I am cordially invited there, not just as a guest, but to live, should I want. He offers me a position as his librarian.

Cecilia, can you imagine it, your Casanova as a librarian, that perambulating scarcely breathing symbol of pedantry and impotence – that laughing-stock among living souls? That false-monk? In some Bohemian backwater, with not even its own theatre and no casino?

Never.

Count Waldstein boasts of the splendour of his table (you see, he has divined my little weakness), the plenitude of Bohemian virgins, and the eminence of his own noble guests, but I am not seduced.

Except by you, as always.

Tell me you are safe and well, darling. I need to know.

Your Casanova.

Ah Cecilia,

   I have at last received a letter from you, and how I have
revelled in it!

   Your letter was brimful of your fragrance, your oils, your
juices – all the pleasure that you paint on this world by breathing
in it, my darling. I want so very much to look at you again. And
on Venice. I need to hold you in my arms and reassure myself that
my worries about you are groundless, that you are safe and whole
and that no one has come to hurt you.

   But I am so happy that your *work* has found success. You are
invited to go to London? Just like your idol, Angelica! You are
right to stay in Venice yet, darling. Travel can come later, when
you are ready. And I hope that you never taste an English cheese.
They are so much pap and cardboard with a sour smell. The
cheeses of the North are also a sorry lot. Barely any flavour. My
senses are as alive as ever. I remember the special stink of every
Italian cheese like the poems I still know by heart. I think I may
turn these memories to use one day . . . a *Dictionary of Cheeses*,
written from recollection.

   I am still in Vienna, as you see.

   Do you know, Cecilia, I begin to realise that wherever I am,
I feel as though I were in a strange country. All those years I
longed to be in Venice, and when I returned, she was not my
home and she treated me as cruelly and as coldly as my
mother did. My real home is where you are. All else is foreign
to me. You are my whole family, my court, my *palazzo*. Without
you, everything grieves. Even the windows are flooding with
tears! I see the everlasting Teutonic moisture trickling down
them in droplets of despair. Look! I have caught one tear on
the corner of this letter: see how it makes the ink weep on the
page!

Now write to me again, Cecilia, tell me what's nearest your
heart so that I can carry it near mine.

Your Casanova.

PS How goes it with my devilish cat? Is he still the monstrous
nightmare of the *pantegane*? Do their salty whiskers twitch in fear
as they dream of him, as even now he approaches the quiet
breathing of their lair with murder in his heart?
PPS Cecilia, you are well, are you not? Tell me the truth. I want
to know if there is something wrong.

Vienna, December, 1784

My dearest Cecilia,

Have you heard about poor Beckford? He has married, finally,
but he is also disgraced. Some keyhole-sniffing puritan lord has
caught him *in flagrante* with the little Courtenay and now, I am
told, the frightful English scandal-sheets are in love with the story.
I hear nothing from Beckford himself now. I believe he has
become some kind of hermit.

I wonder if his *Vathek* will ever see the light of day? Do you still
have that portrait? The one he would not take away? How I
would love to see your bedroom painted with his palaces! How
beautiful it must be. Your letter, with its sketches, stands propped
up on my desk, so I can imagine what you see by candlelight each
night.

However, I own myself nonplussed that you chose the scenery
of *Vathek* for the room where you dream. There is a dark side of
you that causes me to fear for you sometimes. Your bright black
wit sometimes hovers on the edge of danger. *Vathek* disquiets me
because it laughs so flirtatiously with the extremities of evil. It is
an *indiscretion* of laughter. It partakes of what is sublime and what

is horrific alike while sniggering behind the hand, condoning both without really experiencing them. To me, this is more 'obscene' than Aretino, for at least Aretino is sincere. Those thirty-five positions come straight from the heart and never hurt anyone. In the wrong hands, *Vathek* could do damage.

How I hate to write to you on this cheap paper. I wish I could send you parchment and watermarked card from Belgium. For I know how you will finger my letter, my Cecilia. And your letters, always on such gorgeous paper, smelling of Venice and you – can you guess how I devour them, and fold them, and unfold them, and bat them about my desk and squeeze them to death in my hand under my pillow at night?

So that old devil of a cat is a father once more? It's a shame that his *morosa* chose to kitten on that wet portrait, but I am sure you can repair the damage. Keep one of the *gattini*, Cecilia. The old tom will not last forever. He wants too much and fights too hard. One of the *pantegane* will catch him in a weak moment and he will be gone.

As I am gone.

Your Casanova.

Vienna, April 21st, 1785

My darling Cecilia,

My master the Ambassador is sick, and I think he will perish. I shall be on the road again very soon.

I had a daydream, Cecilia. You must tell me what it means. In my daydream I am being auctioned to a crowd of noble women. I wear my satin frock-coat, which you know so well, but it's worn and shabby. The women, however, are richly jewelled, expensively plump, and during the auction each is seated at a table of rich food. Every table is set for two, with one empty place. In the strange atmosphere of the room, each woman seems to *become* the contents of the plate in front of her.

First Lemon Sole bids for me, then *Foie Gras en sa Gelée*, and then finally *Crab Bisque*, with her melting eyes and her croutons bobbing gently in the shade of a linen napkin. But now *Foie Gras* is winning – a finger of sunlight quivers in her *Gelée*. I start to wonder about its flavour – *Sauternes*, perhaps? Those wizened but distended ampoules of gold beside the pale *tranche* of *Foie* must be the *Sauternes* grapes, I think. But *ecco quà* – she is not the winner. Another bids more fiercely. And *she* is just a lump of hard, coarse bread on a naked, dirty table top. The bread is too hard to break in half, I can see. I will have to earn the whole thing. Madame Bread looks exacting intelligent, cool. She has a book open on the table next to the bread . . .

I am looking at the tattered shreds of your letters to me. It destroys me to see them so shabby, just like the man to whom they are addressed. Sometime, alone in inns or waiting on roadsides, I re-read them. I find these days that I have to prise them open, for they cling damply to each other. Your crisp beautiful paper has become limp. With every reading, your lovely writing has become fainter. Sometimes only the flourishes remain. I can no longer bear all these sadnesses. Only fresh letters with your breath still hovering over them will do for me now.

So I am sending them home to you. Please keep them for me, darling, with your letters from me, if you still have them. I would like our love story to live in your studio. A part of Casanova will in this way stay in Venice. They could not exile my love for you, for Venice, only my body which is now becoming worthless in any case. You live for me now, enacting my desires.

Perhaps these letters, full of proper love, will protect you from evil. I hope so, my darling.

Your Casanova.

Vienna, April 23rd, 1785

This day died my master, Ambassador Foscarini. I am again
without a protector.

O my Cecilia, I am tired, tired to the bone, of this life where I
am never secure. Where I must always teach some new cook how
to make duck with marmalade sauce! Where the pistachio nuts
are ever cold, tightly closed, and I discover them already rotting
inside the shell when I force them open! Where the maid brings
me a watery tepid chocolate to drink in the mornings!

Everyone is dead – Father Balbi who escaped from the Leads
with me, my foolish young brother Gaetano. All I hear is of death
and loss. I taste bitterness in my mouth when I awake each
morning. This is not like me, as you know, Cecilia, but my exile
from Venice has exiled me from myself. The remnants of my
inner sweetness are curdling in my belly, the more so the further I
travel from Venice. I am frightened at this change in myself.

Do you remember last year I met Count Waldstein of Dux in
Bohemia? Even then, he pressed me to his employ – a dignified
position as librarian in his vast library. I refused him scornfully. I
swore that I would never be a librarian.

It is always easy to break one's word to oneself. The moment
has finally come for me to accept the offer. My resources are at an
end. My exile is confirmed. I shall die in far Bohemia.

But I shall have something to say, and the world shall hear of it.
While I am tending his forty thousand volumes I shall be writing a
few of my own. Yes, I think Casanova's memoirs will be born in
Dux. This fact will be Venice's shame.

Will I never hold you in my arms again? Or better still, be held
by you, in that way you have, behind me, with your knee thrust
gently between mine?

Your Casanova.

September, 1785

Cecilia, my soul,

I have arrived at Dux. I enclose a map. As you see, it's five miles
west of Teplitz, on the main road to Most and Plzn. It is pretty
place in the autumn sunshine, but I swear I shall die here in the
first winter. Perhaps by the time you have received this letter, your
unhappy Casanova will have ceased to live, for he will have been
poisoned by the servants. It's a dark and murderous state, this
Bohemia, and I do not like the way the cook looks at me.

I bless you, together with the children of my cat. Death
inspires me with no fear; I weep only that I die in a foreign land,
far from the woman I love, and unable to embrace you for the last
time. And with my memoirs still unwritten!

The next morning

I must have been exhausted last night. In the light of day, my spirits
rise. For the first time in a long while I awoke to find my steed in a
triumphant state. I thought of you immediately and enjoyed my
familiar fantasy among the sheets. I have survived my first and
second meal. My linen has been laundered and almost all returned
intact. Perhaps I shall continue to survive here a little longer.

I realise that for the first time in my life, my material needs are
taken care of. I am fed and paid without question. My fee, the
cost of Casanova in these skinny days, is a mere 1000 florins a
year. It has come to this, and, worst of all, I am even grateful.

I am rescued from my miserable contemplations by making
notes for my memoirs. Visiting my old loves makes me happy, as
you thought it would. I find that instead of growing old I am
growing up, as you told me I must.

You were always so wise.

I hope you know well enough how to take care of yourself.

'Herr Bibliothekar', Casanova.

PS They are apparently a race of dwarves here in Bohemia. All the blankets are too small for your tall Casanova. I have ordered two blankets sewn together.

October, 1786

Dearest Cecilia,

I am pleased to hear that your sister has married. The dress sounds like a masterpiece of vulgarity. You are a little cruel, Cecilia. I wish her happiness. How I loved to see the young Venetian women wearing their wedding pearls for the first year of their married lives. The bloom of the pearl and the bloom of the women were always in sympathy, one adding beauty to the other. It was one way of telling, for the connoisseurs amongst us, whether a woman was in need of a little extra attention. In the first year of marriage – rarely! That reminds me of the famous story of Caterina Querini, who burst her necklace of fabulous Oriental pearls while dancing too boisterously at a ball. Instead of gathering the jewels, she simply trampled them with her feet! But that was when Venice was a happy city, of course.

What kind of man is your brother-in-law? A gentleman, like your father, or a rascal?

Speaking of scoundrels, I send you my new work, *Soliloque d'un penseur*. As you see, it's a skilful polemic against adventurers like that swine Cagliostro. Read it with care, my Cecilia – and be wary of such men. Their hard natures are not contaminated with affection or guilt, which is why they can achieve their ends. But they are adept at persuasions of all kinds, and they are vain, so they may come to your studio to cajole you to immortalise them. Be careful, my darling.

No, I am not against your portrait of Goethe. I am proud that he sought you out at your studio. But he's an old goat, I hear, with a fondness for young women, so I hope that you did not let him take any unwanted liberties. The man is no doubt a genius, but I am sure that the humourless idolisation of the German nation has rendered him a posing piece of cardboard in the bedchamber. Pray do not try out my theorem, Cecilia. You know I am not usually jealous, but I draw the line here.

So he calls our Serenissima 'this beaver-republic'? And what is that ant-hill he comes from himself? After all those years as a civil servant in Weimar, his poetry reeks of the filing cabinet. I am amused to hear that he had a toy gondola when he was a child, and that you painted him with one in his arms. And now, reclining in his own grown-up gondola, I suppose he feels like a lord of the Adriatic!

He finds Venice crowded, does he? He finds our houses cramped? The Grand Canal is a 'snake'? I laughed aloud when I read what you told me of his ideas for new sanitary regulations in Venice, and his preliminary plan for a police inspector who is seriously interested in the problem. How typically Teutonic! How utterly impracticable! And he finds our dancers wanton? Our ballet deficient in ideas? The only play he liked was *Scuffles and Brawls in Chioggia*? (I must admit I always loved that one, too!) He finds us noisy? We Venetians talk all the time?

Why doesn't he just go home to silent, boring Weimar?

But I enjoyed his comment to you that people who decorate their own hats want to see their superiors elegantly dressed as well. This makes sense. And perhaps, yes, the Venetian dancers are a little bit wanton during *Carnevale*. But nothing like those Parisians. I remember the famous Camargo in Paris. She was already sixty years old when I saw her, and she could truly leap in a lascivious fashion. Nor did she trouble herself to wear drawers, so all her charms were continuously displayed for forty years. And

all this is nothing whatsoever compared with the barbarous
pastime of 'Morris dancing' performed in England!

Here, the servants continue to craze me with their subtle
tortures. The cook deliberately forgets my polenta or serves me
soup that scalds my tongue. The stable-man sends a dangerous
madman for my carriage. Another servant sets his dog to bark
under my window all night. They sound a hunting horn that is
out of tune just to fray my nerves. They laugh at me, they laugh at
me. The count does not discipline them sufficiently.

The other evening, I recited some Italian poetry, a full-blooded
performance. They giggled like nuns. I showed them my French
verses, hoping at least to earn some respect, but they continued
to laugh.

When I dress for a ball in my white plume, my suit of gold-
embroidered silk, my vest of black velvet, with rhinestone buckles
on my silk stockings, they laugh. They laugh at my Minuet – the
steps taught to me by Marcel, the most famous dancing master in
Europe, sixty years ago.

I stay in my room and write most of the time. When the
memoirs are published, they will stop laughing downstairs.

Your adoring Casanova.

                                                      June, 1787

Dearest Cecilia,

We were speaking about Goethe and dancing, were we not?
(For I feel we still speak to each other, in these letters.)

If the Count's servants could only see me dance the *fandango*,
as I danced it in Madrid! I shall never forget the first time I saw it.
The couples danced face to face. Without making more than
three steps, and armed only with castanets, the couple made a
hundred seductive poses, and a thousand lascivious gestures. And

their faces! The men's showed love fully requited in the deepest sense. The women's showed compliance, ravishment and ecstasy. In the *fandango* you see love in full, from the first whisper of desire to the last gasp of pleasure. After such a dance it would be impossible for the ballerinas to refuse their partners anything. The *fandango* produces a certain irritant to all the vital senses that must be satisfied. I wanted to scream when I saw it. The *fandango* distils desire on the skin the way *you* do when you paint a portrait. How can I better explain it to you than that? Anyway, I left the ball, found a dancing master, and did nothing else for three days until I could perform the *fandango* better than any Spaniard in Madrid.

Dancing is life, Cecilia. Alas, we never danced together! You say in your last letter that you do not enjoy it. I say that you simply do not know yet what joy is in your limbs. I say let your breasts dance! What can it matter that they draw the crowd? Resign yourself to their beauty! When you tell me how your breasts are grown in my absence, I become crazy with desire. I rush around the palace. I want to close my hands round anything that reminds me of your breasts. I try apples – too hard – and the pincushions of the maids – too lumpy. Finally I find a pair of peaches sun-warmed on a window ledge. Now I sit with them in my left hand while I write to you.

I am sorry to hear that your brother-in-law is already betraying Sofia even before she has taken off her wedding pearls. He is wrong to slight her. Be kind to her, Cecilia. Imagine how she suffers.

Here, it is not just the servants who slight me. The Count does not treat me as he should, and the servants notice this. More than once, I have been asked to eat at a side-table because the number of noble guests has filled the main table. I, Casanova, at a side-table, smiling and bowing from a distance at the jewelled pigs around the opulent feast from which I am excluded, apart from titbits!

The Count fails to present me to important visitors, and helps himself to the library without notifying me. I look around the revolting pink walls of the Great Hall and I feel sick. I remember reflections on the ceilings of the Palazzo Mocenigo and our airy *palazzi* dancing in the water, and my whole heart *fandangos* inside me with longing for Venice.

I hear someone coming now. I must stop and seal the letter before they see it. They spy on me continually, the servants, hoping to find something that they can use to hurt me.

Your Casanova.

PS I see that Beckford's *Vathek* has finally appeared in English.

September, 1787

Dearest Cecilia,

Here is the *HISTOIRE de ma FUITE DES PRISONS de la Republique de Venise, qu'on appelle les Plombs* — my account of my travails in and flight from the Leads. Rehearsed with you, in the gondola at San Vio, and now polished up and dressed in a leather jacket for the delectation of the public at large!

So you have been painting Angelica's old clients, the royal family in Naples? Make sure they pay you before you leave, Cecilia!

One day you shall meet with Angelica Kauffman, I know you shall. I hope you are not disappointed. For my money you are a better painter, Cecilia. And soon you will be more famous. You paint men with the Word inside them, and women desirous and capable of extracting it. Her people are so beautiful as to be without desires for any other human. In other words, they are dead. When the Count receives his guests, I tell everyone, beautiful and ugly — just so long as they are rich — about the famous Venetian portrait painter, Cecilia Cornaro, and how she turns their flesh to petals when she paints it; how she makes portraits that preserve the flush of passion forever. I shall send you clients from all over Europe until you will have more *zecchini* in your strongbox than I have seen in my whole life.

I have met again with my old friend, Lorenzo da Ponte. He's writing librettos for that Austrian kid-genius Mozart. You know, the one who taught young Beckford how to play the pianoforte! Da Ponte has asked me to collaborate on the words for the kid's new opera *Don Giovanni*. Who better than me? Perhaps he remembered that I was myself the author of an opera! I wrote it at Aranjuez during my cursed year in Spain. It took me just two weeks and it was rapturously received.

But back to the little Mozart. Two days before the premiere, and the opera was not yet finished! We met in Prague, on October 27th. Mozart was then forcibly locked in a room to complete the overture in time for the dress rehearsal, which was that very day.

I gave what help I could, but da Ponte's Don Giovanni is no Casanova. The Don is a hater of women, who revels in their tears. He's a professional seducer, who abuses his talents by using them to make women wretched. The very opposite of me! In examining the differences between myself and Don Giovanni, I realise suddenly and for the first time the true meaning of my tragedy with La Charpillon in London. She deliberately set out to make me love her and then treated me so that I suffered the pains of hell. She was Donna Giovanna, incarnate.

Anyway, the work was done and my advice was treated with respect. I had another thought when I watched the first night of the opera. It was about faces, and this is one for the portrait painter, for you, Cecilia. The singer who played the Don was painted in a fearful pallor, with ridges of infamy and shadows of corruption etched on his face. But La Charpillon, no, she was

worse. She did not look like the monster she was. She looked like
an angel, which proved tragic for me, and a hundred other men.

I hope you never paint a woman like her. Or her masculine
equivalent. Look hard at any handsome man who comes your way
and ask what he hides behind that beauty. Protect yourself, my
darling Cecilia. I fear that a beautiful human face could one day
be the most dangerous thing in the world for you.

Your Casanova.

1787

Dearest Cecilia,

So you have a baby niece, Cecilia. Does she look like Sofia? Tell
me about the christening. What did everyone wear? What
delicacies were served? You know how I love to hear about Venice
in festa.

I have sold the amiable Count Waldstein ownership of all my
papers. That is, the ones written till this moment. It is good to
feel coins in my pocket again.

I met a woman with a face cratered like the moon tonight. I
am happy, for at last I am no longer curious to make love to a
woman with a face cratered like the moon, just because I have not
experienced such a thing before. I am exhausted. I can no longer
perform the pleasures I used to. But this enforced passivity has
given me the leisure to savour my memories like old wines, which
have only just now aged to perfection and are ready to bring to
the table. I am still working on the memoirs, and up to my third
draft in some places. What a responsibility it is to create your
own literary tombstone! I work thirteen hours a day.

So the celebrated Mrs Thrale has come to Venice and you have
painted her? I hope you took the opportunity to improve your
English. I know it is a brutish language, which falls on the ears

like walnuts on a dry forest floor. But I have the strangest feeling that one day you will have need of it.

Your Casanova.

1788

Dearest Cecilia,

So you already have another niece! My compliments to your brother-in-law! Come, come, Cecilia, I am sure you have it in you to love the child.

I have a baby of my own to show. I present my *Icosameron, ou Histoire d'Edouard et d'Elisabeth qui passèrent quatre-vingts ans chez les Mégamicres habitans aborigènes du Protcosme dans l'intérieur de notre globe, traduite de l'anglois*. It's a novel about an imaginary journey to the centre of the earth. I had it printed in Prague. One day soon I hope to have sold enough copies to pay for the printing, which was cruelly expensive.

Do you like the blue-grey marbling of the fore-edge? I wanted to be reminded of the water at San Vio, and of 1782, and of you. That is how it seemed to me when I chose it from samples they fanned out before me at the printer's.

I apologise to you for the portrait of me in the frontispiece – what a smug brute I look! What hawk eyes, what a ridged forehead! What a jagged nose! The little haberdasher, Merci, who slapped it in Spa, would be proud of her handiwork. If only I could sit once more for a portrait painted by you! With a frontispiece like that, the books would fly out of the bookshop!

One day you will leave Italy and start painting the rest of the world. When it is safe again. One day you may even come here to Dux. If you only knew how I petition the Count to call you here. But he insists that he has not grown into his face yet, whatever that means.

Thank you for your description of the opening of the new Venetian opera house. I am amused at the *lingua biforcuta* in your account of who was there and how they looked in their finery. I hunger for such details and you have given me a perfect sketch of everything I miss.

Your Casanova.

1790

Dearest Cecilia,

So we are discovered? Sofia found your notebook? You tell me you are proud that the world at last knows the truth about us, but it is I who am proud. It cannot harm you, I hope, that all Venice knows I was – no, I *am* – your lover. Perhaps it will bring you even more clients, out of curiosity. I hope it does not attract anyone dangerous, unkind or obsessed. Your parents will soon recover from the shock, I am sure. You say our exposure to the gossips changes nothing between us. I feel the same, my darling. Gossip cannot corrupt the alchemy that still flows between us in these letters.

I open the drawer that holds my treasures. I look at my two peach stones, the oily little rag I stole from your studio, a sprig of your wild hair, your sketched self-portrait from San Lazzaro. I re-read your second-last letter and breathe its perfume. How sweet of you to decorate the borders with those colour sketches of our superb cat. What a marvellous beast he is! By the time it reached me the oil had soaked through it and parts of the letter were transparent. But I could still read your words and see those rampant whiskers and those lucent eyes. My faithful messenger! Please steal him a knob of butter from your mother's kitchen and present it to him with my compliments.

It has been a year without highlights. I have been again in Dresden and Leipzig (where the roasted larks are succulent as ever!)

I have counted books, in and out, in and out.

I have written.

I have been tortured by Feldkirchner, who tweaks rolls of manuscript out of my pocket and drops them on dirty floors for me to scrabble for.

I have missed you and worried about you.

Your Casanova.

September 13th, 1791

Cecilia,

Where is your letter? Why have I not heard from you? I hope fervently it is just the post-chaise that is delayed.

Next to me there is a brocaded chair, grander than the one I occupy with my shabby shelf. There, I thought, there Cecilia ought to be sitting, just opposite me; it was the finer seat, I left it unoccupied for you.

I have a companion, though, who keeps it warm for you – I have acquired a pet, a little terrier whom I have christened Melampyge. He watches me as I work and I can summon his affectionate presence with a glance or a soft word. He has disgraced me in Teplitz, by publicly impregnating a bitch in the street, and you can imagine the commentary his exertions drew regarding his master.

The servant Feldkirchner continues with his vendetta and it has broken out into violence. Just two weeks ago he had one of his brutish minions beat me with a stick in a dark street of Dux. I still limp. I have no recourse but my pen. I have now finished twenty-one letters to Feldkirchner, which, when published, will destroy his immortality. I am easy again, the way *you* feel when you finish a painting of someone you dislike.

After this distraction, I work tirelessly on the memoirs. I think the work is justified. One day, I think, they will be translated into all languages. As you know, I write in French – the libidinous French will buy it. We poor Italians cannot afford such works, and not enough of us can read. It needs a big, sophisticated readership, my book, of people who know the joys of life. Of course the nature of my life story means that some decent countries will forbid it, and its rarity will make it as desirable as pearls. How they will clamour for my book, hide it in their garments, read it secretly by candlelight!

It is only after uttering these three thousand pages that I suddenly realise the effect that I shall have. All my confessions of louche behaviour will be believed at face value but all the truths I tell that reflect well on me will be disbelieved. I shall be obliged to make enemies by revealing matters that show people I have known in a bad or immoral light. If I do not give their real names, they will be guessed. Either way, I shall make trouble! How the husbands and wives of Europe must be shuddering at the thought of these memoirs! Venice will not be able to forget me once they are published. They will make a mockery of this exile, for absent in body I shall still be on every lip. I suspect they will talk about me long after they forget the names of the doges.

Yet I do not wish her ill, La Serenissima.

You know, Cecilia, I loved it all, I loved to see our Venetian women, seeming always in masquerade. I remember those veils of glittering taffeta, from under which the women would dart a glance of fire. And the black veils of the married women, and the winter capes lined with fur from the bellies of squirrels . . . And the Jews, the Turks, the Armenians, the Persians, the Moors, the Greeks and the Slavs, all in their native costumes . . . How I miss the colours and the masks and the fairy-tale life of Venice! We were such a happy city!

Here everyone is pale grey, dressed in pale grey. They speak pale grey, they eat pale grey porridge, and we spend hours at the grey window pane transfixed by the slow grey rain outside. They tell me another hard winter is coming, all over Europe. I think of white winters in Venice and the softness of those freezing, forgiving mists.

Your Casanova.

PS I hear that Beckford's and my mutual friend Hamilton has married the delectable little Emma. How long before he is wearing the horns?

1792

Dearest Cecilia,

The grip of the ice must have loosened from Venice now? Tell me it has. What a tragedy! Since you told me of your father's death I have worried more than ever for you. You are without a real man to protect you. I do not like the sound of your brother-in-law. And your sister – how does she manage now? To lose a little child is the most grievous thing. Be kind to her, Cecilia. And your mother? She is young to be a widow, and in so shocking a circumstance.

Speaking of shocks, I hear stories from France that curdle my blood. I shall never return there. I am too much afraid of the executions of an unbridled people. They have gone mad for blood, now that they have tasted it.

Feldkirchner treats me as a drivelling old goat, a satyr, and he makes me feel like one. I hide from him. I sit under the white arches in the library and I dream of the high blue sky above Venice and the dark stars above us in the gondola.

When I close my eyes I think that you stand in front of me. Do you remember those kisses behind the frame at the Palazzo Mocenigo? And against the well in Campo San Vio? If only you could paint one for me, so I could keep it here and look at it.

Your Casanova.

1793

My darling Cecilia,

I am so glad you were not in Paris during the evil times. You are safer in Venice, where I can think of you in your studio. You are now so famous that the celebrities will come to you. Make them do that. It will add to your price. You will not have to pack your bath with canvasses and take them on the road. Unless you want to. Unless you seek novelty.

So I suppose you will, after all! One day, when Europe is a safer place, when the French have finally finished killing each other. But not yet.

Ah, I am so lonely, so lonely here. But I will not be alone. I have here my letter to you. And my memories. In my memoirs, I have found myself the author of so many delightful comedies. I can make myself laugh, even when alone in a room. I am satisfied to find that I have done more good than evil in this world. I have been able to make people happy. There is not a person in my life who does not owe at least a moment of contentment – if not ecstasy – to me. And I think of this: if I were such a moral leper as the world has painted me, why was I made so welcome in every court in the civilised world?

And there is good news – the Count has at last dismissed the evil Feldkirchner. May all your enemies be sent away likewise in humiliation. You never write to me of problems or wickedness, Cecilia, but I know that you must find them in your life. You are only a human being, like me.

Do not protect me. If there is something I should know, please tell me.

Your Casanova.

1794

Darling Cecilia,

I continue to revise my memoirs, this time for the honour of the Prince de Ligne, uncle of my host, who wants to read them, surely only to establish that he has indeed bedded more women than the great Casanova. Well, in the heart of his loins, the Prince knows that he cannot compare, because his combats are like so many notches on a stick, and mine . . . well, I have no need to tell *you*.

I have decided not to continue with my *Dictionary of Cheeses*. I don't want to dilute the *gravitas* of my true literary memorial, which will, of course, be my memoirs.

I am sending you a miniature of myself. I should explain that the satin jacket is the one I mention often in my letters. (It has rubbed up against minor royalty in several capital cities.) I have caused quite a sensation in it in drawing rooms on the Thames and the Seine. I have slept in it through entire nights on seats of carriages. It has travelled in diligences, cabriolets, diables, berlins, has been spattered with my vomit when I became sick with the constant motion. It is ageing with me. Like me, on closer inspection, it's no longer as good as in the picture. The cravat is a real showpiece; I bought it on a trip to Paris. By pure chance I happen to be wearing this cravat now, while I am writing. It, too, is getting older. Like me, it has outlived its time. Louis XV is dead. Louis XVI is fallen under the guillotine, but my cravat lives on, yellowed, but at least it is not spattered with blood and at least it is still overshadowed by my head.

I am glad you cannot see my breeches, as they are darned, which is a great shame to me. Looking at them, I recall the scandal of the newfangled breeches without codpieces in Spain. The only way the church could stop the fashion, which had spread like wildfire, was to proclaim that executioners alone were entitled to wear the unpieced trousers. I believe that the codpieces became yet more prominent after that edict, for no one wanted to be mistaken for an executioner!

Laughing at that memory delivers me another, of the Duchess of Villandarias, who was a famous nymphomaniac and utterly pious. When the uterine fury seized her, nothing could contain her. She attacked the man who had excited her instinct and he had to satisfy her, then and there. It happened several times in public places when I was in Spain, and all the people who were present simply had to take to their heels, or watch.

Any woman's womb, of course, becomes furious when it's not occupied by the matter for which nature has made it. The womb is an animal so self-willed and so untameable that a wise woman, far from opposing its whims, should defer to them. Yet the ferocious organ is susceptible to a certain amount of management, I have found . . .

My little Melampyge is no more. I have wept for hours and pronounced a funeral oration in Latin. Princess Lobkowitz has sent me a new dog from Berlin, and little Finette turns out to be as faithful a lover as I could want. I used to dislike dogs, with their eyes like reproachful saints and their stench like ancient sausages. But then I realised how often dogs are blamed for the eructations of their owners. Anyway, this new little dog is as delicate as a well-bred young girl. She leaves the room to spare me if she must perform any embarrassing function.

I used to think there were no embarrassing functions. I must have grown old, Cecilia.

Your Casanova.

1795

Darling Cecilia,

   The Prince de Ligne has now read the first volumes of my
memoirs. I quote his verdict: 'One third . . . made me laugh, one
third gave me an erection, one third gave me food for thought.'

   I have made an attempt to escape my prison. I requested letters
of introduction to the Duke of Weimar. I went there and waited
in antechambers; no one would place me as librarian,
chamberlain, anything. After six fruitless weeks I returned,
penniless, to Dux. I do not think to leave it again, Cecilia.

   However, I have been home scarcely a week and the insults
have started. This night there were strawberries for dessert, and
everyone was served before me. When the plate came to me,
there were none left.

   I was left looking at the empty plate and I tried to console
myself with its beauty. It's my favourite Sèvres service with
bluebells at the bottom of each bowl, leaving something to be
discovered at the end of each crab soup or berry compote, as if
to compensate for the sorrow that this one good thing is at an
end. I rejoice in the elegance of the diamond-shaped serving
plates and the coffee service with its vessels, tiny as egg cups,
seeming too fragile to hold their strong flavours. I know that I
am fortunate to live in a place where such things are still part of
everyday life.

   Love, kisses as always,

   Your starving Casanova.

PS I am distraught to hear that my miniature never reached you.
The artist is gone. I cannot have another made. This is the
footman's work. He hates me.

1796

Dearest Cecilia,

I am accused of fathering a child on the daughter of the gatekeeper! How potent remains the reputation of the great Casanova, even at seventy-one years of age! And Dorothy Kleer, the young woman in question, is one I would be honoured to impregnate. But, alas, I cannot claim the honour.

Still, it gives me pause for thought. I start counting. It is fourteen years since I was in your arms, inside your delicious flesh, Cecilia, and still I remember every sensation. I try to count the number of times and the number of places where we gave each other proofs of our ardent affection. I count the minutes I waited outside your window, that first night, for you to fall into my arms.

As I write this I hear news that Napoleon has occupied Brescia. How close he is to you now! So the noble Venetians think that he will deliver them from revolution? That he is the man of the moment? The latest novelty! How can they be so naive? *What* revolution? The factions in Venice are tiny; no one can take them seriously. But it's a good confidence trick on Napoleon's part, if he can get away with it. I fear he will. Then Napoleon will sell Venice like a gilded bauble.

Our city will not fall in glorious battle but will be sold to the first comer without even taking part in the transaction. Venice will become a harlot and Napoleon will be her pimp. Austria, I suspect, will be the client.

Your Casanova.

June, 1797

Dear Cecilia,

Your letters are heavy with horrors.

So the Great Council has voted itself into extinction? May 12th, 1797, then, marks the end of the known world for me. Venice is dead.

When you tell me that, at the end, Venice put up a tiny fight against Napoleon, I feel warm and proud. Of course it was the poor and dispossessed who rallied a little. They had nothing to lose, or rather, Venice was all that they had. I can picture them running around the streets, screaming for San Marco, spitting at the nobles . . . Yes, the People know very well who has betrayed them.

When you tell me that the French have entered the city, I think that it is a thousand and a half years since Venice saw an enemy on our stones.

When you tell me that Napoleon has ordered the *Libro d'oro* burned, I have mixed feelings in my breast. It is all summed up for me when you describe Marina Benzona dancing half-naked around the 'liberty tree' at San Marco wearing an Athenian petticoat split to the flank! A beautiful woman, gone to the bad, just like Venice! In burning the *Libro d'oro*, Napoleon has burned the list of all your clients, you tell me. He has also burned the characters in my memoirs!

I, too, preserve happiness and lust, as you do with your pictures. You see, I, too, am a portrait painter. You paint the faces of counts and princes who come to Venice to find you; in my memoirs I paint whole courts – the France of Madame de Pompadour, the Prussia of Frederick, the England of George. I lift the veil on all of them! And I am freer than you. For you confine yourself, by necessity, to the glittering cages of the rich who can afford you, while I move easily from garret to ballroom, from hovel to palace, from rich nation or gypsy encampment.

The panorama stretches in front of me now. For it is finished, the memoirs, the final revision – the record of my life until twenty-six years ago. I know now I will never touch the rest, and indeed the last twenty years, with the exception of loving and being loved by you, have been of little worth to me, or to a reader. So you will remain my secret, Cecilia. The way I won you and those nights of ours that I cannot recover will never be known to the world.

The more I write, the more I see that all things are linked together. I also see that we are the instigators of events in which we are not merely actors. Hence anything important that happens to us in this world is only what is bound to happen to us. By our actions, we consent to the consequences of them. I think now on my months in the Leads, and I realise that the punishment was not an outright act of despotism. I had abused my freedom, knowingly. I had stolen joy from fate. Fate stole freedom from me. It is like that.

That is what is happening to Venice. Poor fluttering little Venice, beautiful as a pleasure-craft, sunk under the warship of Napoleon's implacable will. Mark my words, Napoleon is not a good man for a happy city. Happiness is irrelevant to him. So is charm, beauty, lightness, richness, flirtation and rich food. He will grind our happiness under his little heel. But Venice consented to the sacrifice of her felicity by her heedless pursuit of it.

Your Casanova.

November 1st, 1797

Dearest Cecilia,

I feel detached, but diminished. How is an exile to feel about the Fall of the Serene Republic? It seems Casanova and Venice have succumbed together. I think we both have been ancient so long that no one thought we could grow feeble and die. We seemed to be immortal. I speak still, of course, both of Venice and myself.

I have summed up my age: I have been happy as only a Venetian can. I have slept in satin and walked through moonlit mud. I have unlaced silk to find pestilence. I have lifted a crude shift to find Heaven. But best of all I have known you, Cecilia Cornaro, heart of my heart. And that has been a pleasure unmixed with corruption, for once. I have known what it is to love someone greater and dearer to me than myself.

I am sick, darling. Nothing works any more.

Even so, death is not welcome here in my soul. I am not so curious to find out whether I am immortal: a truth obtained at the cost of the life of the senses is too expensive.

Now we are on the edge of something else. I don't like the smell of this new century. I shall have no truck with it. I sense something cold and selfish about it.

Love what is good and not what is dangerous, Cecilia, even if the bad thing is a novelty. You know how I fear for you. Do not be led into temptation by something that seems to be new. It may merely be an old evil dressed up in new clothes.

Your lover,

Casanova.

May 28th, 1798

Darling Cecilia,

I am ill. The pain is desperate.

The vultures are gathering. My nephew by marriage Carlo Angiolini is here, which probably means that I shall shortly die. He is kind, if stiff.

Elise von Recke has promised me crayfish soup but as ever I am disappointed. The rivers are swollen, and the crayfish will not

allow themselves to be caught. As I turn in bed I fancy that I smell
the *frittata* of fish in the Venetian *calle*. My taste-memories come
back, like truant lovers. In my dream I enjoy a meal of Venetian
fish dishes, one after another, *sarde in saor*, *baccalà*, crab soup.
From the kitchens downstairs comes, no doubt, the ineffable
stink of Bohemian cabbage, as ever, but I cannot detect it. My
senses have lost all sense of themselves; I am disoriented. By this
more than anything I know that the end is near.

Farewell. I fancy I am with you at San Michele, at the grave of
little Fortunato. I stand behind you, my arms around you, my
desire for you rising. I smell your hair, you turn to me, and the
words from his grave are embossed on your sweet forehead. You
smile and move towards me, Cecilia – I would give my life's
blood for one minute of that reality. I remember when we went to
see the Carpaccio paintings at the Schiavoni chapel, candlelit and
sweet beneath their glazes like blushing jellies. I showed you the
faces of the skeletal remains, those young men and women
devoured by the dragon. I think of us making the profoundest
love inside the frame at the Palazzo Mocenigo. I think of you
painting Beckford and of us listening together to his strange tale
while you do so.

If anyone had told me that I would spend thirteen years here in
Dux, I would have asked for a knife to drive into my gut. But they
have come and gone, those thirteen years, and I still am here. I
have extracted some joy from them, after all, because I have re-
lived my life, in the memoirs. The second time around you can
savour in your mouth the really good times and you can spit out
the bad times, with the knowledge that better times succeeded
them. Perhaps this second life was better than the first one,
because I can enjoy the laughter a second time, and I no longer
feel the pains. In fact, I laugh at them. My steed has become
unpunctual, my haemorrhoids bleed, my teeth drop on the plate,

like my old friends into their coffins. But still I look at what I have written and the past comes alive.

I spent all my glory in my living. There is none left for my dying. In this, too, I am like Venice. I am like an old lady selling off her furniture. I am more and more like Venice. Sometimes I think Venice sent me away not because of what I did but because of who I am. I grew old and decrepit: I reminded her of what she once was and the dismal contrast with what she had become latterly. Venice looked at me and said, 'Exile him! We don't wish to see ourselves that way.'

What disgrace and depression must fill the city now that she is sold. What a pitiful old courtesan Venice must look: it is the beautiful courtesans who wither most horribly. Now she must watch as her ragged possessions are wheeled away by efficient young men in uniform. Those men won't understand what her beauty was about. There is no poetry in their souls.

Ah, if they could but have seen Venice when she was a happy city!

The old Venetians could not bear the idea of submitting ourselves to one person. A doge was a kind of husband, Venetian style . . . a titular authority to be honoured with picturesque ceremony but comprehensively cuckolded behind his back. For the Venetians, the whole world was their *cavalier servente*, the lover who gave them all the breathless attention of which the old husband was incapable and to which he turned a blind eye. Now Venice is an old lady whose treasure is no longer between her legs but in her dwindling counting houses and in her past. Our happiness has tottered to the brink and tumbled over into the abyss.

I bid you farewell.

Benjamin Franklin said that a man is not completely born until he is dead. I am going to be born.

Perhaps I shall be reborn as a woman. I would like that.

I will love you forever and forever after, Cecilia. I worry for you. You seem strong but you are fragile. You feel things too deeply, and not always in order to paint them. Love and pain kill more women than they do men: keep away from the kind of man who will give you dangerous amounts of either. For my sake, Cecilia, think of what I have written here. Love, but do not get broken.

Your Casanova.

PS I hear that another ship has gone down in the Bay of Biscay, taking all hands and uncountable art treasures with it, including a painting of Angelica's. Never trust anything precious to the sea, Cecilia. The sea is hungry for art.

June 6th, 1798

Dear Madame Cecilia Cornaro,

I have found the enclosed letter to you among the effects of my uncle, Giacomo, who sadly passed on to a better world two days ago.

I know nothing of your relationship with him, but I assume that you would like to know that he died quietly, after a long illness. I was at his side. Despite his great age his heart remained vigorous till the last. It was a cancer of the bladder that carried him away. Nevertheless, he retained his taste for rich foods until the end. His last meal was of crab soup. My wife has told me that his mother, the actress Zanetta, had a craving for crab soup the day before he was born, and it seems that my uncle was born with the same craving, which has lasted from his cradle till his deathbed, no matter how many times it was satisfied.

My uncle has worked prodigiously, it seems, in the last years and there is a great quantity of paper here, close-written in French. I am obliged to clear his offices precipitately, before the arrival of the new librarian, and therefore shall burn what seems to be worthless immediately. The servants here are unkind and unhelpful. My uncle appears to have been on bad terms with nearly all of them.

His sole legatees are myself and my wife, Marianne, the daughter of the Chevalier's sister, Maria Magdalena, of Dresden. My uncle has left nothing of material value in this world, so I hope that something of worth is perhaps to be found among the debris here. I fear that I doubt it. It seems that all his life he kept nothing and saved nothing, and spent everything, even what he did not have.

My son is helping me to make big parcels of paper of what? We scarcely know. I only hope it can be an inheritance some day for my son. Glimpses of certain pages have been disturbing, and I do not wish my wife to see this work.

Madame,

I am yours most sincerely,

Carlo Angiolini

22

Morir xe l'ultima capèla che se fa.

Dying is the last stupid thing we do.

VENETIAN PROVERB

I went there once, long after he died, to paint a portrait of the young heir to Count Waldstein, Casanova's former employer. The castle had been built in the French style, elegant and harmonious, with a park and a lake. I asked if I could work in Casanova's bedroom. I wanted to spend some time in the room where Casanova had spent his last thirteen years. I wanted to sit in the brocaded chair he had reserved for me, the one beside his. The room was scrupulously clean, its curtains refreshed, its furniture in the latest style. The brocaded chair was no longer there and nor was there any trace of my lover lingering in the crisp, dustless air.

He is buried somewhere in the churchyard of Saint Barbara at Dux. The grave is unmarked, but a plaque outside the church wall reads:

Jakob
Casanova
Venedig 1725
Dux 1798

How ugly are those k's and g's! Where was my sweet Giacomo Girolamo? The liquid syllables inside the delicate web of Italian consonants? I pressed my back against the plaque to get the imprint on my shoulder, as we used to do with Fortunato's tombstone, those beautiful nights in San Michele. I felt nothing. I was merely empty of happiness, empty of him.

I told myself that this ugly plaque had nothing to do with Casanova. I knew that the memoirs would be his real tombstone, his monument, his key to immortality.

Or perhaps it will be the happiness of the women he loved. It is we fortunate ones who will show our gratitude by keeping his memory alive, each as we know best, in paint, on paper or in the stories we tell our children.

Far away, in Venice, there was another graveyard for me to visit.

In the winter of 1791, the Venetian lagoon had frozen over.

I remember the day it first started to snow. The cold slackened its clutch on us for a moment and the flakes started to float like tiny forgiving sighs from the sky. At first it lay upon the pavements and the canals, not dissolving but roaming over the glassy water like petals. But the cold crept up out of the depths of land and sea to seize it. Soon the Grand Canal and lagoon were impacted with dark ice. Then the snow turned angry. First, it fell from the sky in great clumps like pitchforks of hay. Then it snowed more, thrice and threefold more, as if the sky hated us and wanted to bury us forever like the fabled cities enfolded in the sand-dunes of Egypt. Then it snowed bandages across the windows of the city, binding our eyes so we could see nothing but whiteness. The *palazzi* were encased in ice that rendered into dead pastels all our vivid terracottas and porphyries. Finally it snowed in a great sheet of white, like a winding-cloth for the corpse of the frozen city. Then it stopped snowing and became still as death.

We hid our fears with mad revelry. What were we afraid of? I should explain, as no one who is not Venetian can easily understand this side of us. Venice is a walled city, but her walls are made from water. Walls of water are like the Emperor's new clothes: they exist only in the willing eye of the beholder. They are a confidence trick. With only a transparent, shifting wall to defend us, we Venetians learnt to play other confidence tricks. We fanned out our peacock's tail with ostentation and luxury. We presented ourselves as *invincibly* opulent. No one had dared attack us. Now the ice had stolen our walls of water. Our deepest fear was that someone might come marching across the solidified lagoon to claim us. Without our walls of water, we were as vulnerable as new-borns.

The lagoon had frozen over five times in my memory and on each occasion all Venice ran mad for entertainments wild enough to obliterate our anxieties. We held an extra-mural *Carnevale*. Anyone with use of their limbs threw themselves onto the ice and competed to glide as if footless or to make the most spectacular falls. People craned over balconies to watch young men wheel decorated carts to a launch point and then send them sailing in a blur of velocity to the limbo land between ice and water far out in the lagoon. Beneath us the ice groaned, full of our old, drowned sins. We peered down at it, looking for corpses and golden plates fabled to have been thrown from windows at the Palazzo Labia during antique *Carnevale* banquets. But the ice kept its dark heart, and our own, hidden from us.

That year, a grand tournament of horses was held on the solid green ribbon of the Grand Canal. The whole family had gone together to watch the event. We climbed the fragile wooden dais near the Carità church and found seats among a hundred other Venetians and a handful of dazzled snow-struck tourists. I sat with my nieces on either side of me, my mother and Sofia behind and my father in front of us. The little girls thrust their tiny hands inside their panther-skin muffs; my father's head looked pale and tender in the clear cold air.

With fanfares and flourishing of flags the race began. There was a plume of glassy splinters as the hooves rutted the ice. At first the racers galloped in a smooth arrowhead formation. But seconds later a single horse and its rider lost their footing and slid loose from the pack. We saw the pointed head of the horse hurtling towards us and the rider with his mouth open in a silent scream. As the rider and horse collided with it I heard the backbone of the dais snap and then felt myself flying across the ice. I landed on my belly with a rattle of teeth. I lay there face-down, my breasts throbbing, gasping for breath.

For long moments, there was nothing but the noise of the shattering of bones, thrashing of limbs and the hiss of blood congealing on the ice.

I sat up and swivelled around, spitting ice and a single wrecked tooth out of my mouth. I could hear Sofia's screams above the groans of the others. I pulled myself upright and looked quickly at my hands. There was no damage. Sofia was crawling towards the dais. My mother lay stunned and silent beside me. I took her hand and she opened her eyes like a doll. I covered them with my hand for I had just seen what was making Sofia scream.

When all the bodies were pulled loose of the wreckage, my father's was piled among the dead, along with the elder of Sofia's little girls, who still clung around the back of his broken neck and could not be separated from him.

Two days later, we consigned them to the shallow earth together in the *campo dei morti* at San Stefano. I mouthed the words to the prayers, thinking of my father. We had never had a conversation. But we had understood each other. We were both merchants of beauty. His love of lucent colour had been reborn in me in a new form. It was not grief that I felt but regret. I could not cry. I thought about my laughing little niece and her pale still face with a ribbon of blood from her mouth when we found her. One hand had been flung over her head as if she was asleep. Only the blood and the strange angle of her throat showed that she had been taken from us. I could not conceive of Sofia's feelings, but I decided I would paint a portrait of the child for her. I had a number of studies in my room. I was lost in these thoughts and forgot I was at a funeral. I wandered away from the solid little group, planted like black cypresses on the hard earth around the graves.

While Sofia and her husband wept with their arms around my mother, I stood a little way away, hollowed out by loneliness. I felt like a voyeur. Sofia and her husband had each other in their grief. My mother had them. Who had I?

I had my work.

My fame had spread, and finally I started to follow its trail with the turn of the new century. I began to look beyond Venice and even beyond Italy. I began to travel.

Like Casanova I had come to know the feel of flat hard earth and not the sinuous softness of the canals under my feet. I had inhaled the dusty stench rising from ditches instead of the sharp perfume of the sea. I too had laid my head down in anonymous apartments in innumerable inns: The Three Lilies in Berlin, The Crocelle in Naples, The Sign of the Crawfish in Vienna, À la Balance in Geneva, The Cheval Blanc at Montpellier, The Three Dolphins at Aix – all the same places where he had loved and schemed and played fifty years before. Every place recalled a different story he had told me. I lived his memoirs for him, again, as I had done in Venice, but this time without the enclosing warmth of his arms around me.

Soon the inns were replaced by apartments in noble houses and even at courts. It seemed that everyone in Europe wanted a portrait by the female Venetian painter who made such astonishing likenesses. Everyone was talking about me, and not only because I was a woman who practised a profession in a place and time when the uses of women were strictly confined. I was thought to be a prodigy.

People attributed supernatural skills to me because I knew how to paint people who seemed to breathe on the canvas. My portraits did not merely breathe: I painted them with a flush of unmistakable arousal or the pallor of satisfaction upon their skins. I had mastered Leonardo's technique of *sfumato*, the melting outlines that give a third dimension to a portrait. I knew to leave something to guess at in the corners of the eyes and the corners of the mouth. I could write the history of a person on their face. I could paint portraits that looked a little different every time you saw them, as if their features were freshly stained with a life still going on underneath the canvas. I liked to blur the edges. I liked to make the respectable women look like exciting whores, or at least to show a flicker of the hussy in them. This is an old artist's trick, to get people to give your painting a second look, to paint something slightly out of tune. People would always stop short in front of my paintings, and peer at them sharply. I smiled when I saw this. I knew very well what it was that I was doing: it was the subtle *perfume* of eroticism that I had used to capture their attention. When I saw people actually bend forward to sniff furtively at my work, I knew I had succeeded.

With the right alchemy of personality, talent and luck the rewards were rich for an artist like me. I could name my price. People were a little afraid of me. Not only was I an alchemist with faces but also of words. News of my *lingua biforcuta* had spread. I had taken Casanova's advice about languages: now I could exercise it in French, German, English and Italian. I could demand a retinue, luxurious coaches, stately apartments. I could have acted the *prima donna*. I rarely did, preferring to take my own bath of materials and to travel alone, and simply. I looked indifferently upon my increasingly luxurious accommodations. But it was gratifying to know that I could ask, within reason, for almost anything I wanted.

If only this had come to me earlier, I thought. *I would have asked to go to Dux.*

The Cat Speaks

Cecilia, when she is alone, goes to her cupboard and takes out her portraits of Casanova. She sits there with her head on one hand, stroking his eyes and nose and mouth with her finger. Sometimes I hear the fall and miniature splash of a single tear. Sometimes she moves her lips as if she is talking to him.

I too mourn my master. He was more like a dog than a cat, himself, but I mourn him.

He could be so *obvious*. When he wanted a woman, he was like a dog near a bitch in her season. He could think of nothing else except how to obtain her. His whole brain became a sex organ. And, as we say in Venice, *cazzo non vuol pensieri* (the prick does not want to think).

But he understood something that cats understand. The reason for our howls in our time of heat. Desires are nothing but torments. Whether to man or cat, Loves are true pain in the loins. We enjoy our lust because it frees us from those devouring painful desires, and gives us a little peace before we are roused to them again.

So he shared his last years with two little dogs? Well, I forgive him. They were effeminate little dogs, as near to cats as possible, from what I heard.

He made some mistakes in his life.

But he always had a soft hand for me, at all times, and he would share his oysters, his *foie gras*, and, in leaner times, his hard bread with me, or let me lick the sauce from his macaroni. He was a man a cat could love, Giacomo Casanova. It is not given to us cats to love very often.

Part Two

1

Novantanove a mi, e una per ti.

Ninety-nine for me, and one for you.

VENETIAN PROVERB

Ah Casanova, how can I speak to you, from this dim shaft of time? I can kiss you only with my fingers: I trace your lips as I have painted them, stinging fresh from my own mouth.
First of all, I give you numbers; you always loved numbers. Here are the important ones.

Welcome to the nineteenth century, Casanova. I write now of a time nine years into it, a perilous time for me. It is three decades since you first took me wet from my bath, since the last time I lay down with you in my arms. You were not old, never think it. Remember that our love is only as old as my first portrait of you, which is, of course, thirteen years younger than I am. I have painted six hundred and thirty-seven portraits in these long limping years without you. I have travelled to fifteen countries. I have painted Goethe again, and Napoleon himself. Your cat has sired and grandsired four hundred and eighty-five times. How many velvet collars have I bought? I simply cannot tell you. And yes, Casanova, they still speak of you in Venice. But your own memoirs, no, they are not yet published.

I too have my memoirs, unwritten but etched upon my skin. I cannot count the pages; they are not finished yet. But now I, too, can recount a catalogue of sensual and commercial disasters; even those are studded with their sweet moments. I know you, and you would not hate me for those adventures of my skin. You would not be jealous; you would rejoice in them. *You* taught me that ungainly human physical love is a gift from God. We humans could have mated remotely like salmon or spored like plants – instead we have delicious tangles of limbs and liquids. You loved all of them, the out-flung legs, the shapely feet, the soft arms, the sweat, the saliva, the seed, the tears of joy (*sweet, not salty*, you always said), the female juices. *What is a kiss*, you asked, *but the tangible effect of one's desire to eat and drink the one you love?* You taught me to love Love's noisy repertoire of display and gratification. The animals have their grunts, the plants their flowers – their ways of expressing sexual exuberance – while we have our music, art, poetry and the labora-tory of the kitchen. You, Casanova, gourmandised in everything.

You never made a conquest – you never had victims. Women were your *accomplices* in pleasure. As you always said, *when two people fall in love, both are Love's dupes; everyone wins a little, everyone loses a little.* You loved being duped in this way. You loved women. You didn't even hate the ones who rejected you, not for long, not even La Charpillon, who deserved your hatred. You craved not just the woman, but her desire for you. Mere consent made you disgusted with yourself. You never took a selfish orgasm. I remember you saying, again and again, as you gently wiped the sweat from my face, looking deeply into my eyes, *the visible pleasure I give you makes up four-fifths of mine.*

Your love had the shifting boundaries of our lagoon. It was always there, surrounding us, it would never dry up or pull away entirely. It was sometimes drawn to farther shores by the moon and adverse fate, but good luck and dawn light might deliver it back to us at any time. You could smell a needy woman the way other men smell stale beer or warm bread, the way women sniff the heads of their babies. The smell attracted you, the same way the smell of needy love repulses other men, worse men than you.

You took responsibility for the desires you aroused. But when the English Overcoats proved unobtainable or ineffective (the proof of course coming long after you had departed), you were always delighted and fascinated to meet the resultant progeny a few years later, but you were equally happy to allow other men the joy of their supposed paternity. And if you suffered from a love disease, you refrained from spilling your infectious *incense* inside one of us. That, to you, would be an unpardonable sin.

You used no ugly words for the private parts of our bodies. When you undressed us, you were enraptured to see our *treasure,* our *little pink jewel*, our *temple of delights*, our *little such-and-such*, our *retiring room* or our *sanctuary*. (You hated to hear it described by frigid Andriana Foscarini as 'the fatal vault'.) The hairs around our sex and under our arms were our *ornaments*. Your particular part was a *little fellow*, a *masked personage* (in his Overcoat), a sliver of *lightning*, but most often of all, your *steed*. When you were with us you wanted to *spread the columns apart*, and then *devour love's chamber*. When you entered us it was to *perform the gentle sacrifice*, or *pay respects*, but most of all, *to give the most ardent proof of affection*. Your tumescent steed was the most honest compliment you could give us.

In the case of passionate and prolonged lovemaking, it was always a *tender combat* or a *mutual transport*. In the case of virgins, you *plucked the fruit* or *picked the beautiful flower* (and it was always better than any other flower you had picked before). And finally you would offer a *liqueur*, a *nectar* or – my favourite, always – a *Word* in the mutual con-clusive ecstasy. Sometimes you gave so much that your Word was stained with blood. You made us understand that there was no more tender gift.

You liked to talk to us, before, during and afterwards. You loved each caress intensified with an endearment. Without words, you said, there was only a part of the possible pleasure. Like food without its beckoning perfumes, silent coupling was unsatisfying to you. You declined the attentions of England's proudest courtesan, Kitty Fisher, because you could not share the language of Shakespeare with her! You would spend whole days talking about your love to your lover. *Nature*, you said, *does not afford a wider subject*. Merely physical debauches always left you a little sad, a little diminished. But the prospect of a new, true love could always rouse you.

You hated lying to us, as you were sometimes obliged to do, in the fervour of the moment. You admitted to me, '*In the course of my life I have more than once found myself under the bitter necessity of telling a lie to the woman I loved.*' But you would do so to save our self-respect, and to keep love alive, and happy, just a little longer.

There could be nothing wrong in love, if it was the right love, you said. The right love was always reciprocal, joyful, unburdened with guilt. It was Original Love, without any concomitant sin. You had no respect for the moralisers. According to you, their reasoning was flawed. For does the flower do wrong that spreads its petals to the warm tongue of the sun? Does a wave do wrong that erects its crest in the soft breath of the wind? If so, then love was wrong, you opined. Love is the variegated God of all our natures, you argued. Anyway, we cannot help it, as far as love is concerned. And then we cannot help it, again. With love, there is no such word as *satiety*, positively no such word. Your desires were bigger than your capacity. All your life you feared that you might not be strong enough to satisfy the desires of those you loved.

Yes, you had your hundred and thirty women, and loved each in her turn, rarely several at a time. But yes, sisters were a speciality. You told me how you loved your way through a family of five, once, in London, saving the youngest and sweetest, Gabrielle, for last. But

you wanted only sisters who took pleasure in doubling your felicity
and tripling their own. You would let the woman lead, imperceptibly
or aggressively, you didn't mind, so long as she led you to happiness.
*'Seducing is not what I do. Or if I do it, it is unconsciously, something I do after
first being seduced myself'* was your own self-definition. I am sure you
have stamped it on your memoirs. (How I long to read them, as I
have already heard them. But I fear that this new century will find
them little to its taste. For times have changed, Casanova, and not for
the better.)

You never married: you knew yourself too well. The thought of
marriage made you shudder, even when you were crazily, wholly in
love. Because of your addiction to novelty, you knew you would
make a disappointing husband. So you spared the women you
adored by not marrying them. You *offered* the sacrifice from time to
time. You would promise, from your soul, to make Manon, or
Esther, or Teresa your wife, but Destiny was always, fortunately,
against it. You were plucked from the arms of your lovers, time and
time and again. You never rejected us. Separation was always by
force of circumstance, beyond our control. You left us intact, our
self-esteem untarnished. Or we left you, and felt ourselves enhanced
by profundity and tenderness of your regrets. You always, though it
broke your heart, encouraged us to accept an offer of respectability,
or a lifelong mate. (I understand this now. It has taken so many
years to do so.) You taught yourself to regard the lost woman as a
treasure who had belonged to you, and who, after making you
happy, was going to make another fortunate man so with your full
consent. *'It must be true that Fortune is a lady,'* you said. *'She is jealous
of other women and takes them from me.'*

Casanova, you loved your women, but you also liked to dance at
their weddings to good men who loved them, not with the feast of
passion you had laid out for them but with a quiet, post-prandial
domestic love, a serviceable love that would see them through to

the happy oblivion of old age. And all their lives those women would nurse a memory of a man who had created such a drama to spend an hour with them, who had, for a short time, been capable of dying not to be with them, who had regarded the touch of their lips as the pinnacle of achievable joy, who had given the act of love such a wild and sweet savour that for once they had known what it was that the poets write of. You left women with sacred memories of you, of themselves with you, and of Love itself. They all wished their children were Casanova's. And so did I. So I named my son for you . . . but I run away with myself.

While a woman was yours, you were hers, a happy timing leading to happy times for all. Love had always taken you to good places, with rare exceptions. Perhaps, best of all, were the bizarre loves, who took you to strange places on earth, and strange places within yourself. I remember all your stories. I remember Lepi the hunchback and her scarcely credible contortions and her miraculously sited vulva. I remember Roman Margherita with her false eye, which was a different colour from the other, and also larger. You had a matching porcelain eye made for her and were rewarded with the most tender gratitude. I think of the Negro maidservant you pleasured in Trieste, who taught you the falsity of one of your favourite maxims: *when the lamp is taken away, all women are alike*. There was the flatulent serving girl in Turin who accompanied each delicious thrust with a fragrant trumpet-solo from her posterior orifice. Each woman was for you beloved in her time, remaining beloved in your memory.

You loved one woman at a time, and properly, and then the next one, even better.

If only all love had begun and ended with Casanova! But there was another man, as I told you, who came afterwards. And he declared, 'I rather look on Love as a hostile transaction.' And made it so.

Each love was a bitter comedy, with lines that cut the skin, with the kind of sweetness that chokes, the kind of consuming passion that devours the lovers till they become spectral. He used only hard Anglo-Saxon monosyllables for our tenderest parts. From him I learnt, not because I wanted to, the ugly words *clack*, *cunt*, *piece*, *salt bitch*, and the uglier phrases *rut*, *join giblets*, *fuck*, *fuff-fuff* and *passades*. And he could not bear to watch a woman eat. And he could not bear to see an old lover again. We were already stale in his memory the next morning, and stinking the day after. He could smell lust on a woman like urine in an alley. It made him feel the same way: aroused and disgusted at the same time. He preferred as many loves as possible at once, all badly done. He dragged love out of women as if pulling an expiring flower out of the ground.

Love? A *transaction*? How my Casanova would have raged at this perversion. But then Casanova's loves were oceanic, curiously nourishing and pure; when ponds are stirred, they produce nothing but a bitter and unhealthy miasma. It has been variously said that this man was a great or a very poor lover. We are not yet at the point in the story where I am prepared to give my own account. But think on this: he was not even able to convey lust in his poetry, just mockeries of lust.

But you would be right in thinking that this pond-dwelling lover was successful with women. He was as successful, in his way, as my Mediterranean Casanova. He had small silken hands: women and money slipped into them, and then out again when he opened his little fist and let them drop. He made pleasure a sin, and sin a pleasure for his women. And when he had finished with them, he gave them a great appetite for suicide.

Women would have their period of success with him. He appealed to their egos with his haughty, tragic *froideur*: they wanted to warm it up. For a while he let them bathe in the delusion that they had done so, and that they had captivated him with their own particular gift, be it a fine beauty, an expert hand, a long eye, a sexual wit . . . In this he was like Casanova, who would always find that one special thing about a woman and make it his own. And, like Casanova, he was able to create, albeit on a temporary basis, an atmosphere of breathless tenderness around himself, an ambience that excluded all others.

How can I explain how he could make you laugh in ways you had never laughed? It was not a gentle laugh. It was more of a gasp, a crackle of air torn from your gut, because he *dared* so. His humour was as black as a November night, and as biting. How can I explain that you became complicit in his satiric, savage scorn against the rest of the world? How it seemed, sometimes, that all the gall evaporated in the convulsions of the shared, robust laughter? The laughter and the tears that would come later were part of the same insolent intimacy upon which he insisted. How can I convey the way he *knew* you, and made you ashamed to be yourself? How this shame made you need him all the more; you were enfeebled by it and so you craved the dispensation of his obliterating passion.

But I assure you that in the end it gives more joy to read about George Gordon, Lord Byron than it did to know him at close quarters.

Once, years after I first met him, I ransacked Byron's desk, when he had gone to his casino. I found an unfinished letter to his mentor, Lady Melbourne. By that time, my English was more than good enough to skim through it. But at first I was mystified by his code. I sat with the letter between my fingers, pronouncing the strange English consonants aloud. Suddenly I understood. Byron's leading ladies were designated by capital letters. Lady Caroline Lamb was 'C', his wife, Annabella, 'your A' and his half-sister, Augusta, 'my A' or sometimes merely a '+'. This code was different from Casanova's intimate alphabet of initials, of half-discretion and whole passion. In his case, to give them their full names would allow these women a complete entrance into his life, and a full part of it. That was not available. Byron invented a new mechanical system of love – of taking the parts that he needed, but never the whole woman. The result of this hostile transaction was a Frankenstein monster, a love that went bad and murdered happiness.

It is hard to say when Byron stopped being Byron and became Byronic. But I would learn from him that the cultivation of his own image, his romance with his own face in the mirror and on the page, was from an early age the central relationship in his life. Byron, rejecting the fat, unromantic mother he had been allotted, became his own, and nourished himself tenderly. By the time he grew to the age when we start to reach out for others, there was no room for a soulmate in that passionate and complex love story between Byron and himself. Of course, there *was* room for supplementary loves, and, oh yes, certainly, for a portrait painter . . .

Let me introduce you to the Byronic hero, recently delivered of Lord Byron. He is thin, pale, and wears black. Lacking ordinary parents, he is the orphaned son of the Gothic genre. His birthmarks are emotional cruelty, taboo-breaking and obsession. He terrorises women, engulfing them alternately in devouring fire and obliterating coldness. This is because there festers inside him great imprisoned love that no one has ever unlocked. The thought of being the object of that love is irresistible to women; it makes them shiver. The Byronic hero nurses a dread secret. But he cannot communicate with others and neither can they unravel what is knotted in his soul. Inarticulate in conversation, it is only when he soliloquises about himself that he is endlessly eloquent. He wallows in voluptuous but vaguely defined misery. He dies young: therefore his tragic emanation is all the more concentrated, and infectious. Like Casanova, Byron became a label, a metaphor. Casanova embodied, I now know, everything *di speciale* to the 1700s, and Byron, I hazard a guess, will mean something in this cold bright new century. If I am right, I pity the women to come. Our good times are past.

Yes, Byron was the new thing, the spirit of his age, the ornament and star of it, the *crème de la crème*. As with Casanova, I would sample all that was advertised, and I would be treated accordingly.

Perhaps he could not help it? I have sometimes tried to see it that way. The people who really knew him, Mary Shelley and Hobhouse, for example, told me that they could always distinguish something fatal and beautiful in his soul, down there amongst the bunkum, bathos and melodrama. His lovers would ever say the same. We were bound to do so. With every love-affair, the penetration was so deep, his grasp of your soul so thorough, that it became like incest. Incest and violation, they cross each other. Incest, the other side of self-love, the ultimate violation, was perhaps born into Byron.

He was born on January 22nd, 1788, the same day that my sister Sofia delivered her second daughter. Sofia's confinement was uneventful; the baby was perfect, except that she was a girl. After the midwife had left, we gathered in Sofia's room, to worship, as we Italian Catholics have always worshipped, the act of motherhood. Sofia was a little torn and pale, my brother-in-law somewhat aggrieved at the arrival of another female but trying to put a good face to it. He had already fathered two male bastards; he knew it was in him, the seed that sows sons. I watched him look at Sofia over the head of the new little girl. Yes, he would probably summon up the desire to beget the necessary heir upon my sister, I thought.

I held their first daughter wide-eyed in my arms while my mother dabbed the sweat from Sofia's face and kissed her a hundred times, little butterfly kisses, which Sofia seemed to absorb into her damp skin like a health-giving draught. She and my mother shared an air of potency, for once taking precedence over every other living thing in the house. Sofia grew more radiant every moment as she held her breast to the new baby. A wet-nurse hovered modestly at the back of the room. Sofia did not seem to want her. My father, awkward with tenderness, approached the bed and handed Sofia a jewel case of pink velvet. I saw a pale blue duplicate poking out of his robe; he had been prepared for both possibilities. My mother opened the case for Sofia, who, it seemed, could not bear to take her hands from her new baby. A golden bracelet slid onto the linen birthing coverlet and tangled in its silver threads. My brother-in-law lowered his disappointed face and stooped to pick it up. If it had been a son, there would have been diamonds.

My father laid a hand on his arm. He said quietly, 'Be happy, Giovanni. Even daughters can be great.'

My father did not look at me, but the compliment flowed over the whole room. No one dared to touch me or meet my eyes but I felt, for a moment, transformed from the aberrant spinster aunt to the warm pride of the household. Then the new baby began to mewl and I was forgotten again. I handed my niece to my mother and left quietly. I walked through the winter sunshine to my studio, where a count awaited me. Yes, it was a happy day in Venice, January 22nd, 1788.

Far away in London, in Byron's birth-room, everyone was scream-ing, his mother loudest of all. He told me afterwards that during Lady Catherine's labour her stays had cut into the fat flesh around her ribs and blood flowed down through the mattress. He told me that twenty she-cats sewn in sacks could not have made so mourn-ful and unpleasant a howling as his mother trying to expel him from her womb. She was in so much pain that she scarcely realised the creature who was apparently trying to kill her had lost the battle and left her body. At first the little scrap of skin looked barely human. His skull was shrivelled like an old corpse.

Then they realised that he had emerged with a caul over his

head, a mark of distinction and good luck – especially effective against death by drowning. Closer inspection revealed he bore an abnormally thin right leg ending in a foot that inclined markedly inwards: a club foot. Byron would swear afterwards that he could remember the shrieks of his mother when they showed her the twisted little limb. It seemed to prove everything she had feared since the best-forgotten moment of his conception.

Byron was born an Aquarian, then, with a club foot. He was an aristocrat, with no money, the only son of an obsessive mother, a father who was, it would turn out, worse than none at all. He was born both blessed and mutilated – perhaps it could not have been otherwise for him. George Gordon Byron would also remain an only child, something he always found significant. 'Looks like fatality,' he would tell me one day. 'The fiercest animals have the rarest numbers in their litters.'

That lucky caul was scooped from his infant pate and given to a family friend, who died in a shipwreck twelve years later. It was perhaps because of that caul that Byron was never afraid of the water himself. In fact, he loved it. When he entered it, it dissolved his deformity under its opaque or distorting surface.

Yes, he loved the water. And it was over the water he came to me, ten years ago now, in 1809. We were both far from home, in as wild a place as we would ever know, a cruel, luxurious place, a place I never hope to see again or hear upon the lips of any human being.

I speak now, only because I must, of Albania.

2

Se ocio no smira, cuor no sospira.

If the eye does not gaze, the heart does not sigh.

VENETIAN PROVERB

In the summer of 1809 I received a commission that was different from all the others.

A tiny messenger in a tasselled fez and both arms stiff with bracelets had arrived at our *palazzo* at Miracoli while we sat at luncheon. Since my father's death our household had become more luxurious. Sofia and Giovanni liked to use the silver plate that had previously lurked in large chests like pirates' treasure. French essences and wine sauces were now to be tasted at our table. My mother, Sofia and her daughter were as elegant as possible in their morning dresses. I, *invece*, looked like a beggar woman, with my clothes oily and multicoloured from an unsleeping night in my studio. But they had learnt to accept me as I was, and even my tradesman's smell passed uncommented upon these days.

Our flushed and nervous maid led our exotic visitor into the dining room where we sat together, Sofia, Giovanni, my mother, my surviving niece and I. The dark-skinned messenger — *Raw Sienna and*

Rose Madder, I thought — bowed deeply and lowered his heavy eye-lids over his moist chocolate eyes — *Raw Umber and Brown Madder*. I had not painted anyone of his hues before. It was impossible to determine his age, but I suspected it was close to mine. He pre-sented us with a basket of fragrant melons. Then he addressed us, first describing an elaborate spiral in the air with his long, elegant fingers, ushering the exotic perfume of his fragrant hair oil into our noses. He spoke a baroque kind of French, with such a long roll to his r's that by the end of certain elongated words I felt wrapped around his supple dark-red tongue.

'I, Mouchar, son of Mouchar, have the honour to bring graceful news to the honorable house of Cornaro in Venice. Ali Pasha, Vizier of the Three Tails, Veli of Epirus, Lord of All Albania and Western Greece, commands the pleasure of the artist Cecilia Cornaro's attendance at his court, for the purpose of rendering upon canvas the likeness of His Majesty himself and of diverse favourites among his children and wives.'

Only then did Mouchar son of Mouchar draw breath, panting a little. He looked at us with a charming, expectant expression, like a cat presenting a mouse to his beloved mistress. *Indeed*, I thought. *Vizier of the Three Tails. How Very Vathek! Rendering upon canvas. But, of course!* A smile was starting to jerk at the corners of my mouth.

'What's the dwarf saying?' Giovanni was asking. His French was poor. 'Does he want to sell us some silverware? We could do some-thing with those bracelets, perhaps. Who's his *capo*? I could swear he said it was Ali Pasha, that murdering rapist in Albania. But this little creature's the servant of some greasy Levantine merchant, isn't he?'

Fortunately Giovanni spoke, as usual, in dialect. The beauteous Mouchar continued to appear serene: he did not, apparently, number Venetian among his languages. I had already intuited that our guttural earthy dialect was not Mouchar's style. 'No,' I explained, 'he's not a merchant, he's a diplomat. I am invited to Albania to paint Ali Pasha. In fact, I believe I am *commanded*.'

My mother crossed herself. Sofia clapped a hand over her mouth and put her arm around her daughter. Giovanni spluttered, 'Well, how ridiculous. As if you would go to such a barbarous place, Cecilia . . . Cecilia? He kills women, you know. Fifteen women! Cecilia, *No!* You cannot!'

For he had seen my eager face. The word 'Albania' was now capering inside my head. I glimpsed whirling dervishes, turbanned princes, veiled princesses, desert landscapes, camels. I saw the world of young Beckford's *Vathek*, in real life. In my mind's dark eye I discovered dangerous lusts, scintillating secrets, stark palaces leaning over cruel abysses. Ah, my troublesome addiction to novelty, how it surged inside me at the thought of Albania!

'It's the caterpillars all over again,' said Sofia softly, without reproach and even with a little sympathy. She explained to Giovanni how, as a child, I had gone down to our courtyard and allowed the insects to bite me, simply because it was something I had not tried before, and because the little green beasts were beautiful. And also, of course, because I had been told that they were bad for me. My mother reached across the table for my arm and traced the tiny white scars with a gentle finger. I twitched my hand away and ran downstairs to start packing.

Two days later I left Venice, accompanied by the attentive Mouchar and a young Venetian pastry chef who had also been recruited to the Pasha's court. I travelled with just one small trunk of clothes but also with my bath full of canvas, pigments, oils and brushes. When Mouchar raised his fine dark eyebrows, I told him, 'All lady painters bring their own baths.' I could have told him that all lady painters eat their own first-born, so exotic did he think me, a Venetian, a woman, and an artist, with no maid or manservant of her own. My mother had pressed me to take one of the maids, but I had an instinct that I wanted to be alone. I felt a mysterious confidence in Mouchar, who had found his way to me in Venice and seemed unfathomably at ease in the ways of both the East and the West.

From the port of Mestre, we travelled by boat along the Dalmatian coast. I woke each morning at dawn to see an unrelenting sun rising on a black sea. *'What am I doing?'* I asked myself, standing on the deck. *'You are doing what Casanova would have done,'* I answered myself. *'Are you putting yourself in danger?'* I asked myself. And I answered, *'I don't care.'* The spicy smell of the shore excited me. The food on the boat was different to any I had tasted: strange-shaped spiny fish and damp salty biscuits. I passed my days on the deck with Mouchar, who proved a delightful companion.

We first saw Preveza, the southern port of Albania, at sunset. We had avoided the northern cities; they were, it seemed, at war with our host. Prevesa's towers and minarets, elongated by a purple sunset, seemed at first to be floating upon the water like Venice herself. Behind them, Mouchar pointed out the Suli mountains, brutal in outline and seeming to be hunched and ruminating darkly. As we pulled into the dock we were met by an ornate party of servants and musicians, who serenaded me and my bath. Suddenly I heard an ululation in the distance and the men, including Mouchar, frightened me by falling to their knees and scraping the ground with their dusty foreheads. After a few minutes they rose to their feet and continued as before. Mouchar explained, 'Ah, do not perplex yourself, Cecilia. This is how we pray in Albania.'

'Outside? And your churches? How are they?'

'Sadly you may not enter, Cecilia, being a foreigner and a woman. But they are different from yours. We have no images of God. We express our piety in the abstract; we do not show God in the paltry likeness of man. It is forbidden.'

'Yet the Pasha wants me to paint *his* face?'

'The ways of the Pasha are both great and mysterious, and not easily comprehensible, at times, to his humble subjects.'

I could not ride – few Venetian women acquire this skill. A little kadesh was rigged for me, and another for the bath full of canvases and paint pigments. Soon we were inland, jolting through arid countryside, which made me parched for our canals. The people were the most foreign I had seen or heard. Their harsh dialect had a Northern ring to it. Mouchar told me that the Albanians had five alphabets, and blood was still being shed over which was pre-eminent. When the Albanians spoke French, it was in the same baroque intonation as his own, and with the fairy-tale glamour of his vocabulary. In the crowds in the marketplaces, the Albanians mingled with Tartars in their high caps, the Turks in their turbans, soldiers, black slaves. The Albanian men strode in skirts to the knee, which reminded me of the Scottish kilts I had seen in engravings. But the exuberant twirl of their moustachios and the lascivious plumpness of their lips and the sensuous droop of their eyelids distinguished them from the thin-lipped, slate-eyed Scots. Over their white kilts, the Albanians wore embroidered tunics, gold-worked cloaks made of goatskin, crimson velvet gold-laced jackets and waistcoats, silver-mounted pistols and daggers. My hand fluttered in a blur over my sketchbook. Everywhere the noises put me in a constant state of expectation, like a child about to hear an exotic tale. The drums and the muezzin chanting in the towers seemed to promise old stories of wild loves and bloody revenges. I thought constantly of Beckford and his *Vathek*. It was all coming to life. At any moment I expected to encounter the monstrous camel Alboufaki and the wicked queen Carathis astride him, sniffing for corpses.

We arrived in the great moated city of Jannina on the last day of September, passing through a valley of mosques, goats and orange trees, with eagles, vultures and falcons hovering above us. The city huddled on an outcrop between the Pindus mountains and a stern grey lake. Before the city gates, our little cortege came to an abrupt halt. I observed what appeared to be a piece of dark meat hanging up for sale, opposite a primitive butcher's shop. As we approached, however, it became clear that what we beheld was a man's arm and part of his torso strung in bloodied cords from a tree. It was dangling by a broken finger impaled with a nail.

There was a muttering among the merchants, and the Venetian pastry chef fainted. I looked at the construction of the ribs protruding from the remains and tried to think of it as an exercise in still-life. In this way I contrived not to vomit. Mouchar slipped from his horse to make some enquiries. He came back quickly. The torso, I was told, belonged to a robber, whose other parts were to be found displayed in various quarters of the city. It was an example of the hospitality of the man who was my new employer.

We loitered six days in Jannina, where Mouchar disappeared briefly into the arms of his family. He explained to me that his mother needed to make sure that he had not been damaged or corrupted in some way by his dangerous visit to the infidel city of Venice.

I remained with the rest of our party in the kitchens of the airy mansion we had been allocated. I had already been freed from the normal limitations imposed upon my sex because of the strangeness of my profession. Now they let me join them as they crouched around their food, and I sat among their elbows and armpits, thinking how Casanova would have loved this wild garden of sweat. Mouchar, the shadow who had reappeared at my side, explained quietly that in their bathhouses the Albanians were subject to a superstition that meant that they could not pass soap to one another: to do so would be to wash away love. Stimulated by the almost edible sweat, I devoured plates of roasted meat, eggs and odd, angular vegetables. Someone handed me a hookah, and Mouchar taught me how to breathe in the soothing fragrant steam.

I drank tiny bowls of syrupy coffee. A merchant passed me a long-stemmed pipe. I tried that too. I could see Mouchar thinking, *female artists are truly a rare and wonderful breed*.

We went to watch a Jewish puppet show. The puppets, silhouettes of greased card-paper, rampaged round the tiny stage, rattling their loose limbs. Falsetto voices emerged from behind a dirty curtain, rousing the crowd to roars of laughter with a dialogue that appeared to consist mostly of threats and curses. It was easy to understand the storyline: the young protagonist was possessed of an organ so stupendous that it needed to be supported by a piece of rope hung from his neck. The organ proved wilful and had to be chastised, first by fist and finally with a knife. Indeed, it proved so recalcitrant that it had to be severed and rammed into his own posterior orifice. The behaviour of the lady-puppets was similarly and violently perverse.

Mouchar asked me, 'And how are the puppet shows in Venice, Cecilia?'

I smiled at him. 'Ah Mouchar, all Venice is just such a puppet show. Only we wear masks when we perform.'

He nodded wisely. I felt a little guilty.

At dawn the next day we set off for Tepelene, the Pasha's seat, seventy-five miles and four days away through rough terrain. The spines of the horses sagged under large leather trunks of provisions and, of course, my bath. Ali Pasha's gaudily caparisoned guards were with us to protect these valuables from robbers, or perhaps to keep the valuable Venetian artist under guard; it was hard to say. Perhaps the Venetian pastry chef was even more valuable to them. After all, he was a man. There was no question of travelling unescorted through the hills and crevasses, watched by felt but unseen eyes, and where even the tinkle of sheep bells sounded sinister in the thin air. Sometimes I heard an unholy howling in the night. The memory of the dismembered robber still hung before us.

On October 8th, my birthday, we descended from the passes and saw the towers and minarets of Tepelene piercing the yolk of the setting sun. Tepelene was yet more foreign than Jannina had been, and more exhilarating for it. The marketplace teemed with every exotic race. The air vibrated with kettle drums, and the thrum of the restless hooves of fearsome war-horses. I counted the black slaves and watched boys chanting their prayers in their low throats. A flag on the palace roof told us that the Pasha was in residence.

With persistence, I had found out more about my host. Mouchar would answer certain questions, and from his silence I divined the answers to the others. From the engraving I had seen in a traveller's account in Venice, it seemed that Ali Pasha himself was a small, corpulent man of around seventy, with a white beard and a gentle demeanour. Among his subjects, Mouchar told me, the Pasha was known for his profound knowledge of the human heart, and his ability to see through anyone who might try to deceive him.

'No one may behold his noble face without knowing that he knows all,' breathed Mouchar, fervently.

For all his spiritual depths, it seemed that Ali Pasha was also a man who would roast an enemy on a gridiron. I had seen the execution yard in Jannina: one of the merchants had told me that men died there with their skin stripped from their faces and hanging over their shoulders like peach peelings. Mouchar told me how Ali had hunted down and executed the ravisher of his sister after forty-two years. 'Neither time nor place can set bounds on his revenge when he has been traduced. In fact, the longer it is delayed, the more fatal are its effects, for his hatred increases with its duration.'

I dared not question Mouchar, for the sake of seeing pain in those beautiful eyes, about the fifteen murdered women. Of all the stories about the Pasha, this was the best known in Venice. Among us, he was said to have drugged his daughter-in-law in order to enjoy her body. She committed suicide when she woke to discover

the truth, sticky on her thighs. All the witnesses – fifteen women of
the harem – were drowned by his black mutes in the palace's ornamental lake. In another version of this story, it was whispered that
the women were executed for having caught the eye of Ali's son. Yet
another hinted that the massacre was ordered simply to defray the
expenses of the harem because it had become too large to run eco-
nomically.

About the origins of his fierce master I did dare to ask Mouchar
and he was most happy to reply at length. Between Mouchar's loyal
obfuscations of certain facts and his colourful effusions, I divined
that Ali had been born the son of a humble pasha in Tepelene. His
father soon died and he was raised by a fierce, dominating mother.
Then he was orphaned at nine years old. Not satisfied with his allo-
cation of glory, he had set himself up as a robber baron. By war and
bribery he had increased his domain to Arta and Jannina. He had
married his two sons to the daughters of Ibrahim Pasio of Avlonal.
Then he had made war against his in-laws, and had taken, by force,
all they had.

Ali Pasha was at the height of his power and luxury when he sent
Mouchar to find me in Venice. I understood from Mouchar's tales
that the Pasha wanted himself and his success immortalised by a
Western artist, who might bring images and tales of his splendour
to the so-called civilised kingdoms of Western Europe. He must
have commissioned some spy to find a painter who would make
him look beautiful for posterity, and who was also sufficiently
famous to have important clients visit her studio, where studies of
his image would confront them from the wall. Perhaps his inform-
ant had also discovered that I was the kind of woman who would
make a journey to Albania alone and without hysterics. Perhaps he
had heard even more intimate facts. I realised that it was unlikely
that my love-affair with Casanova had evaded the ears of the Pasha's
diligent spies.

At the same time it occurred to me that I had asked too few questions about the exact nature and term of my employment. I clung to my instinct that Mouchar would look after me, and I tried to persuade myself that our amity, which deepened daily, was my protection.

We arrived at the palace to be greeted in the courtyard by the massed servants of the Pasha. I nodded and smiled at the draped and turbanned multitude. Mouchar accompanied me to my quarters and waited respectfully outside while I arranged my few possessions in the airy stone room with its windows looking out on the bad-tempered mountains hunched above us. I fingered the white silk hangings of the bed and sniffed at the aromatic sheepskin rug on the floor. I touched the leathery petals of flowers I had never seen before. They looked like goat-heads and smelt of rotting fruit, a surprisingly delicious scent. When I had washed my face, changed my clothes, and dampened my suffering brushes, I met Mouchar in the corridor. He looked approvingly at my pink dress and the snowy *fisiù* tied at my neck, but he was much too polite to utter a compliment, for it would have meant that my previous appearance, dishevelled and dirty, might thereby have been insulted. There was no end to the subtlety of Mouchar's courtesy. Sometimes he made me ashamed of my *lingua biforcuta*.

He took me on a tour of the palace, at least of the parts that I was permitted to see. We passed though blue-tiled halls and marble archways. The Pasha's palace was crowded like a warehouse with gold, paintings, glass and silks. Some of these goods, Mouchar told me, were the inheritance of the Pasha's short-lived second wife, and the others were largely confiscated from his enemies. I saw what could be nothing other than a Carpaccio sketch of a dragon next to a watery English landscape. The whole building had the atmosphere of a tasteless millionaire's bazaar; the styles of the plundered goods were so diverse. There was no theme or style to its display.

Perhaps its very profusion was the point of it, I thought. Mouchar discouraged my tendency to linger in front of the art. 'Come, Cecilia, the Pasha is waiting.'

I dragged my feet, childishly. I was frightened. Such magnificence was not easy to maintain, I was sure. The unsettling atmosphere of the place seemed to whisper of crimes against the flesh. My thoughts ran in dark directions. I already knew that there were deep bitternesses to soothe within the Pasha's family. There must have been witnesses to the massacre of the women. There must have been people who knew too much, and who must be silenced. Then their silencers must have been disposed of to ensure secrecy. Mouchar had told me about hostile tribes and robbers in the hills whom the Pasha hunted, hanged, beheaded, dismembered, roasted and impaled, 'to preserve the safety of his beloved People'. It was a part of one of these robbers whom I had seen on my arrival in Jannina.

We walked deeper into the Pasha's domain. There were no doors in the core of the palace: Persian rugs, suspended on poles and ominously stained, served this purpose. The effect conspired to make the visitor insecure, wondering what daggers or delights lurked behind these fragrant hangings that undulated as one passed. There were few walls, but serried panels and grilles of delicately carved wood lined with rich, light fabrics that sighed as we walked along. I thought I heard the echoes of distant soldiers' footsteps, but it could equally have been the tapping of stealthy bare feet closely following us. Mouchar appeared unperturbed so I trotted along beside him, trying to suppress my imagination for the sake of the embarrassing growls of fear that emerged from my stomach.

I had a constant feeling of being watched. I could have sworn that I heard little intakes of breath just behind my ears at times. I heard disturbances in the air, like the wings of doves beating in a box. I

heard a snatch of a song. Once I heard a definite giggle. I spun
sharply around. 'What is that?' I demanded. Mouchar explained
that, at this time, Ali kept between five and six hundred women in
his harems, and, besides those, an equal number of effeminate
youths. These languid young people were kept locked up. It was
their laughter and their songs that I could hear from behind the
wooden and gilded grilles.

By the time we arrived at the receiving chamber I was completely
subdued. In fact, I was so nervous that I was afraid I would start
laughing at an improper moment.

Mouchar told me, 'When I introduce you, say nothing until you
are addressed by our Master. Speak in French, but slowly. Do not be
anxious. He mislikes nervous people. You will find him gentle and
kind, I know. He is ready to love you.'

'Love me?' My voice was high and thin.

'As a daughter.'

Mouchar walked though a tapestried aperture, motioning for me
to wait. I stood in the corridor, my throat dry and my hands hot.
There was a little flare of a headache hovering over the bridge of my
nose. As soon as Mouchar entered the throne room, genuflecting
and flourishing his wrist, I heard the Pasha utter a jolly command in
a flawed tenor voice, purring with goodwill and satisfaction.
Mouchar turned back to me, smiled and beckoned.

As instructed by Mouchar, I dropped into a deep curtsy immediately upon entering the room. Even as I rose, I kept my eyes
modestly lowered. I raised them very slowly. I noticed that the
Pasha was reclining on a velvet banquette draped with the rippling
skin of a prodigiously large lion. The first thing I saw was its
snarling maw, poised to snap. The first thing I saw of the Pasha
himself was his knees. They were plump as a grandmother's, swaddled in vivid silk. I saw the hem of his damask tunic, the colour and

crepy texture of dried blood. Then I saw a long dagger studded
with brilliants curved around his thigh.

'Rise, rise, my lovely dear,' said the Pasha, gesturing with his soft
fat palms. 'Let us look at you. Ah yes, very nice, very nice indeed.
You have done well, Mouchar, I am satisfied,' he said, without taking
his eyes off me. 'The portrait shall commence tomorrow, Madame
Cecilia Cornaro. I shall enjoy looking at you while you look at *me*.'

There was nothing menacing in his words but there was something sarcastic in his smile and something terrible in his chuckle. I
thought suddenly, *He has a lizard's eyes, Viridian and Cadmium Yellow*.
Now I examined my new subject further. Two ruffs of dark fur
bristled from his shoulders; he looked like an engraving I had seen
of a beast called a warthog. He wore a high turban composed of
many small rolls of fine gold muslin. His face was almost unlined,
his reptilian eyes small and brilliant in the context of his face. His
plump, baby-like body was rolled comfortably inside its linens and
damasks. He was easy in his skin, lounging on the lush red velvet of
the banquette. He fondled his hookah like a kitten.

In the role of artist, I was instantly at my ease. The usual involuntary processes had started inside my brain. I began to memorise
the planes of his cheekbones. His voice had already given me ideas
for the colours I would use: *Sanguineo Red, Indigo and Lamp Black*.
The engraving, I thought, had been accurate though it had not captured the child-like rosiness of his skin. *White, Yellow Ochre and
Vermilion*, I thought, *a little Rose Madder to tone it in*. Candour beamed
from his smooth countenance, and a little pleasant lechery. Even
this somehow put me even more at my ease.

The Pasha let me know – 'Go now, my lovely dear, as we have
matters here to discuss' – that I was dismissed. I was to repose in
my quarters until my work commenced the next morning. I
returned to my room and fell upon the beautiful bed where I slept
for seventeen hours without waking.

And so I settled in to the Palace of Tepelene. First, I painted one quick portrait of the Pasha as I had found him on our first acquaintance. When he saw it, he nodded to Mouchar again, and smiled at me. 'Yes, it is well done, a speaking likeness. Next time, you will show my teeth, please. They are very wonderful.' His mouth widened to a dragon-like snarl that showed plentiful white enamel inside. I suddenly suspected that the Pasha planned for my portraits to *frighten* his peers in the West.

After that day, he barely spoke to me. My instructions came from Mouchar. One day, for example, I was to paint a profile of the Pasha, in a green robe. He would be available to me, while meeting with his tax collectors, for two hours the next day. In the afternoon I was to paint a colour study of the favourite daughter, which the Pasha wished to see on his dinner plate that night. The next day, I was to make a pastel of the smallest granddaughter, and so it went on.

'Is that all?' I asked Mouchar satirically. I had never had the time and nature of my portraits dictated to me like this before. I was not too cowed to protest.

'There is this, Madame Cecilia,' said Mouchar with a bow. He handed me a heavy velvet purse. 'The Pasha wishes you to know that your genius will not languish unrewarded.'

Most days I painted the Pasha. I sat at my easel, watching as he terrorised and seduced the people whom he had enslaved. I saw him towering over a shivering miscreant, and laying gentle hands on a loyal servant. He stopped noticing me. I saw the comings and goings of his ministers and his lieutenants. I saw the cringing tax-collectors backing out of the room. I saw honoured guests arriving, I heard their downfall being plotted the next day. I saw him pawing at a shy new girl brought to the harem, and fingering the hair of one of his slender youths. The Pasha shared his life with me so that I could better paint him. I soon realised that my first instincts had been correct: unlike my other subjects, it was not his erotic bloom that he wanted me to capture, but his power.

In my quarters, rare and costly flowers were delivered every day. My ewer of water was always cool and fresh, with rose petals floating in it. I had found in an annexe to my room a bath sunk deep into the marble. Whenever I asked, it was filled with hot perfumed water and I lay there resting my shoulders from the exertions of my brush. I dined with the Pasha and his entourage. I enjoyed the new tastes and smells at the Pasha's table. Curried plover I tried, and snipe with black cherries, and pistachio-flavoured jellies of a firm and chewable texture. How Casanova would have loved to share this experience with me! I was happy in the work, particularly painting the pampered little princesses. The velvets and brocades of their tunics gave me hours of pleasure. The *Poupée de France* would have her delicate nose put out of joint, I thought – she would look almost shabby in comparison to the Pasha's women. The servants were bashful but kind, and very curious. I would often find clusters of them chattering in front of my easel. When they saw me they would disperse like a flock of sparrows, smiling shyly.

My own clothes were delicately cleaned and arrived in my room smelling of jasmine and lavender. More velvet purses arrived, and some jewellery.

It seemed to me that it was not such a bad thing to be adopted as the daughter of an Oriental potentate.

And so I was there in the receiving chamber the day that George Gordon, Lord Byron came to pay his respects to Ali Pasha of Albania.

Rumours of his arrival were already rife. Like me, he had already spent some days in Jannina where he had shown himself and his proclivities for all to see. Riders from Jannina brought new gossip every day. Of the young lord it was said that he was as beautiful as an angel and carnally voracious of both sexes. He swam like a turtle. His *equipage* was incredible: three beds and at least four leather trunks of staggering proportions. All this information the loyal Mouchar conveyed to me from the giggling ladies of the harem, who always, he told me, knew everything important before anyone else did.

'Does he not realise that he is in danger here?' I asked Mouchar. The English were little loved in Albania.

'I believe that the Pasha is disposed to be gentlemanly towards young lords – for it seems there are two of them. As you know, the English forces have just taken the Ionian islands from the French. It cannot hurt the Albanian cause to make welcome two noblemen from the conquering nation.'

'But Lord Byron is not a soldier?'

'Indeed not,' smiled Mouchar. 'I believe that the milord is a species of poet. The other one, his friend, also writes, but apparently looks less poetic.'

That afternoon the Englishmen arrived at the Palace of Tepelene, and within an hour they were brought to the presence of the Pasha. Ali had chosen to receive them in a large room paved with marble, a fountain playing over painted Dutch tiles at the centre. I could see that the whole court was titillated at the thought of the glamorous young visitors. I sat with my easel beside the fountain, working on a new portrait, with Mouchar beside me. All around the Pasha sat his officers and tax-collectors, in white robes and gaudy jewels, chattering and sighing like housewives.

A servant preceded the two visitors, who hovered in the entrance as gauchely as adolescents. In the dark archway I could not at first see them well. From their awkward postures they seemed very young. They started like ponies when Mouchar took up his post in front of the Pasha, bowed low, and began the preliminaries to which I was by now accustomed. Finally he announced, 'George Gordon

Lord Byron and his companion John Cam Hob House. You are welcome. You may approach our Lord.'

Then two men, one homely and the other beautiful, stepped out
of the shadows. Hobhouse came first, scarcely displacing the air
around him, he had so little grandeur to him. He was a tall man
with a large pale hook of a nose and a prim little pink pucker of a
mouth under it. *Equal parts white, Yellow Ochre and Vermilion, simple as
that*, I thought. Everyone was, frankly, disappointed. We looked
over his shoulder.

Did I imagine it, or did we all draw breath then?

When Byron entered the room, with a nodding bird-like lilt to
his step, it was as if everything fell to shadow around him. He was
like a lit alabaster lamp in a dark place – cool, pure, flawed and holy,
but with something erotically charged about him and something of
the grave, too.

In those first seconds, I learnt that face by heart, counting off a
rosary of its perfections. Mouchar had been right: Lord Byron
looked a poet. He looked like a poet from the tilt of his head to the
turn of his feet. I could see that there was something wrong with
one of them; he must have injured himself on the arduous journey,
I thought. He looked like a poet in his high-vaulted breast and his
narrow waist, emphasised by the full military regalia he had chosen
for his first interview with his host. He looked a poet as he bowed
subtly and sweetly to the Pasha. As he did so his magnificent sabre
grazed the ground as if caressing it.

Even if I had never spoken to him, I could have fallen in love with
Byron for the way his eye-sockets were moulded into his head at
such an exquisite angle, for the way that even the opaque jelly of his
eye was voluptuous. I could have fallen in love with him for the long
black shadow of his lash on the moonstone of his cheek. I could
have fallen in love with him for the slender curl of the groove
between his nose and lip. I could have fallen in love with him for the

chestnut corona of his hair, blooming in ringlets around his face and arranged so that the outline of his head was triangular as a kitten's. I could have fallen in love with him for the eloquence of his eyebrows and their quarrel with his eyes. For it seemed to me, even the first seconds I saw him, that those eyebrows arched in contempt, saying, 'This means nothing to me,' but the bright glossing of the eyeball said, 'The poetry of this moment is tearing me apart.'

He did not appear to see me.

'Your Honour,' he murmured, with his eyes becomingly downcast so that the pale lids curved over his cheek like shells. *Lead White, Rose Madder and Raw Sienna for the face*, I thought. *French Ultramarine and Yellow Ochre for the bluish shadows around the mouth and chin. In the lips, nostrils and ears, Purple Lake, reduced with white.* His lightish voice was marvellously tuned to his elegant French. I heard Hobhouse, gruffer and less graceful, echo him an instant later.

Ali Pasha had contrived to welcome Byron standing and now motioned to him to sit at his right side. Mouchar explained in whispers that both gestures constituted a great compliment, for no Turk would rise to meet a guest who was his social inferior.

The Pasha was gracious to Hobhouse, pointing to a small stool in a corner. A conversation ensued in slow, archaic French on the Pasha's side and careful compliments on the other. Like a benevolent old uncle trying hard to please, Ali showed the two young men all his favourite gold and silver toys, and urged them to look through an English telescope at a distant rider on the hills outside Tepelene. He told them, 'That man is the chief minister of my enemy Ibrahim Pasha, who has deserted his master and is on his way to me.' Hobhouse and Byron exchanged glances, obviously wondering what fate awaited the rider.

Without changing his expression, Ali suddenly posed his first question to his guests, 'Now, tell me what has brought you to my country?' His tone was no longer honeyed but dry and gelid.

Byron seemed to be rendered silent by fear and confusion. Hobhouse was quicker to absorb and manoeuvre through the danger, and answered, 'The desire of seeing so great a man as yourself.'

Ali smiled. 'So you hear of me in England? What do they say of me?'

Byron recovered himself. He replied, 'You are a very common subject of conversation in England. They speak respectfully of you in the places of power, and in the lower places, the women shiver as they whisper about you.'

Ali Pasha was not inaccessible to this kind of flattery. The conversation became more comfortable. Affection and affability flowed from the Pasha. He asked Byron why he had left Britain at such a young age. 'How can you bear to be so far away from your mother for so long?' When he saw Byron struggling to answer this fluently, the Pasha changed the subject. He complimented Byron upon his beauty.

'Had my people not brought tidings of you, had you travelled incognito, you would still be my honoured guest tonight. One lord always recognises another. I would have known your noble birth instantly by the smallness of your ears, your curling hair, and your little white hands.'

Byron blushed and bowed again. He was so delighted by these words that I saw his fingers clutch an invisible quill-pen to write them down. *The world will hear about this*, I thought. But in Albania, I wondered, could such personal compliments be separated from a sensual intent? Would Byron understand that? Would he find the thought revolting? Or arousing? Hobhouse fidgeted and chafed at his neck-cloth. The Pasha observed to Byron in a loud voice, 'Your friend has a plain face and a really terrible hat. How can you forgive him? Is it a Christian thing?'

I saw Hobhouse flinch and not only at the insult. I understood that Hobhouse felt that Ali Pasha looked a little too benignly at his friend. But Byron, clearly, was enchanted. He began to relax. Heedless of etiquette, he leant over and pointed to me. I blushed. My paintbrush was poised motionless at the surface of the canvas. I had held it like that since Byron walked into the room.

'Who is she?' he asked the Pasha. Mouchar frowned. The officials drew in their breath.

But the Pasha was inclined to be indulgent.

'No one, an artist. This one's from Venice. Now, my lovely young lords, I invite you to join us at our humble supper. We have lately engaged a Venetian pastry chef who makes, I am told, flowers and towers from sugar. You shall tell me if his skill merits the price I paid for him, or if I shall have to administer a little correction.'

At the words 'a little correction' a ripple of nervousness ran through the courtiers.

Byron and Hobhouse saluted the Pasha one more time and turned to leave. Byron limped to the door and turned back with one final graceful flourish of his sabre. The extravagance of the gesture wrongfooted him. He stumbled a little. Hobhouse reached out a discreet steadying arm. I realised then that the damage to his foot was permanent. The perfect young man was a cripple.

The Pasha, I could see, was making the same discovery. I saw his eyes flicker over Byron's leg. But he said smoothly, 'We shall expect you at our side again very shortly, my dear Lord.'

Byron bowed low again, his composure restored.

He murmured, 'I can think of nothing that I would desire more.'

But as he said those words, he looked at me.

3

El tempo, el culo e i siori
i fa quel i vol lori.

Time, arses and lords
do whatever they want.

<small>VENETIAN PROVERB</small>

In the Pasha's dining room I was placed between Hobhouse
and Byron, who laid his two large pistols on the table before he
sat down. He glanced around. Yes, everyone was looking at
him.

Turbanned slaves encircled us, bearing platters. Lying in beds
of scented rice were whole blackened lambs with their little
heads nodding gently. There were ragouts of flamingo flesh swimming with oil and sprinkled with cardamom seeds. There were
whole fish with cabochon emeralds where the eyes should have
been. The eyes were served separately impaled upon little sticks
with fresh herbs between them. There were suggestively curved
and swarthy vegetables stuffed with raisins and minced meat.
There were whole platters of cherries and more of white peaches
topped by black passion fruit, already slashed across the middle
so that the vivid seeds spilled onto the pale peach flesh below.
Silver jugs of pomegranate juice were poured into our glass goblets.

I was relieved to see that the Venetian pastry chef had surpassed himself. A miniature replica of the Tepelene Palace, entirely spun of sugar, was paraded around the dining chamber. As it passed him the Pasha snatched a tower and put it in his mouth. Everyone lowered their eyes while he sucked and crunched loudly.

'Very lovely,' he pronounced. Everyone began to talk and eat with gusto.

Byron touched nothing on his golden plate, which was continuously emptied by the servants who placed other delicacies upon it. They seemed to regard it as a challenge to tempt his capricious appetite.

The Pasha, clearly exhausted by the earlier long conversation in French, was seated with his ministers at some distance, and confined his attentions to Byron to flirtatious waves and winks. Fortunately, he did not notice how Byron spurned his food. Hobhouse helped himself only to bread and the more obvious cuts of meat. He talked to Mouchar, who listened attentively, even while the Englishman's stentorian voice sidled off into tortuous digressions and impenetrable pronouncements.

As for me, I was too agitated to eat. I still lived in the moment, an hour before, when Byron's eyes had met mine. It was a strange state of grace, in which I felt myself different but in ways I could not quite identify. I only knew that I heard a faint roaring in my ears and that I wanted to be with Byron, and to see if this hectic sensation was at work inside him, too. To my distress, he seemed to have moved into another state of being, a coarser, casual state. At first he and Hobhouse talked over my head, in English. At the time my grasp of that awkward language was quite imperfect and in any case they appeared to me to be talking largely in a code. I struggled to understand them. I heard 'Plen and Opt See', which seemed like Latin, but I could not make sense of it.

Then, reaching for my glass, my elbow grazed Byron's and I felt almost afraid to have touched him. But now he turned to me and looked me full in the face. It was the same avid look he had given me in the Pasha's reception chamber but now he was close to me, so close that I lost the perspective of his face and could look only at his eyes. In those, for one vertiginous second, I thought I saw something I had not seen since Casanova. I thought I saw something native to myself. But, unlike Casanova's, this instantaneous intimacy felt perverse and treacherous. I felt as if I had discovered an unknown brother in the skin of a ravishing lover, and that I had discovered the relation too late.

Byron's eyes said all this, and I saw his knuckles white against the table. But his voice was calm when he spoke.

'You must be Cecilia Cornaro,' he said in his beautiful French. 'I have heard of you. You have painted Goethe, have you not? And Napoleon?'

I answered mechanically, still exploring the element of his look. 'Yes, it is true.'

'And you are from Venice. It is my favourite place that I have never been. One day I shall go there.'

'We shall welcome you,' I said, trying to fit the conversation and the look together, hiding my hot hands under the table.

'Tell me about yourself. How can a female painter end up here at the Pasha's table?'

I told him briefly, and answered his questions about Goethe and Napoleon. They were the usual questions and I gave the usual replies; this calmed me. Yes, Goethe had provided hours of scintillating conversation while I painted him. No, I did not think he was the lover of Angelica Kauffman. Yes indeed, I was proud to be compared with her. Yes, Napoleon was indeed small and morose and no, his manners were not the most elegant. No, he had not ruined Venice, though he had left his mark upon us: dismantling our churches, suppressing the convents, filling in canals and numbering our streets. I told him how when I painted Napoleon's portrait just two years before, while he watched a Grand Canal regatta in his honour, the dull thud of falling masonry and the clanking of rising scaffolding was always in the background.

'Yes, yes. And now,' said Byron, 'I imagine you would like to know about me.'

'I can think of nothing that I would desire more,' I quoted.

He smiled at my slightly mocking tone and drew a little closer to me. I felt Hobhouse shift uncomfortably on the other side of me and his agitated breath upon the back of my neck. I did not turn around.

And so it was that I heard from Byron himself the strange story of his ancestry and childhood: the story that is now known to all who can pay a penny for a scandal sheet. He told it without embarrassment; he was cool and detached about everything, even his deformity. After a while he settled into the rhythm of his tale. He became animated. Anecdotes were embroidered with humour and melodrama. He spoke with a great outrush of breath, almost as if to relieve himself, physically, of boredom. He mimicked the voices of his mother, his butler and the other characters who had played walk-on parts in the drama of his early life. Even then I thought him more of a story-teller than a poet – or perhaps it was the story itself that was lacking in poetry and instead overspilling with more insolent incident than *The Thousand and One Nights*. It was a story anyone else would have hidden away in the dusty attic of the distant past. But Byron seemed to treasure the shameful as much as the good, perhaps more so.

Had Byron already decided that I would paint him? Because I had painted his hero, Napoleon? His future rival, Goethe? Was he merely presenting himself to me as a subject? Was he *deliberately* tempting me with the angles of his beautiful mouth and the graceful capers of his gesticulating fingers?

But his tone was almost impersonal. It seemed as if I was simply a member of an anonymous audience; the house-lights had dimmed and I sat in the dark watching him upon the stage. Yet I knew, because I had already observed him carefully, that he groomed his every smallest gesture for effect, and that the style and telling of this story was *intentioned*, and therefore it was directed at me. The rendering of himself he chose to give me was that of the protagonist of a wildly tragical farce. The question in my mind, floating like pollen upon agitated water, was this: did he tell it like this because he thought such a tale, told in such a way, would attract a woman like me? And if this was the case, how could he possibly know so much about me already?

Again, I was reminded of Casanova as we tipped the kaleidoscope upward and gazed together at the tumbling fragments of Byron's early memories.

It seems to me that the ancestry of George Gordon, Lord Byron, was a marriage of brutality misbegotten upon sensuality. The Gordon family was the cantankerous, miserable side, the Byrons the sexual and financial outlaws. Flowing together, those bloodlines, as Byron himself declared at the outset of his tale, had generated a history worse than that of the Borgias, and with as many casualties.

Byron was not destined for a high title. He was born in a backwater of his noble family. Then fortunate deaths, barren wombs and the imperative of fate put him next in line to the estate after his great-uncle, universally known as 'the Wicked Lord Byron'. ('Soon to be known as *the first* Wicked Lord Byron,' I was told, with a wink. His eyelid fell gracefully over his eye, extinguishing the blue-grey glitter for a moment.)

At the Aberdeen Grammar School the little Byron became the champion of all the marble-players, and nursed a truculent temper. He was, a neighbour declared, an 'ill-deedie laddie' and 'a wee crockit deevil'. As his mother prayed in church, he would prick her fat arm with a pin. A bracelet of plump red drops would burst on her skin, and later a bruise would flower on his thigh where she beat him. These were the kinds of gifts mother and sôn exchanged, from the outset.

Byron flexed his own soft white arm in front of me as he talked. I was not unaware of its graceful curve. His hand moved towards his thigh to finger a remembered hurt. My eyes followed it. He went on with his story, his hand still under the table.

Neither pain nor shame could contain the child, or the mother's anger against him. Byron was already skinless in sensibility to any insult from his mother, or anyone else. When Lady Abercromby advised his mother to beat little Byron for a misdeed, the child marched up to her and struck her face. 'That's for meddling,' he told her. When a woman in the street remarked upon his handsome face, and what a pity it was that he must limp, little Byron striped her with his child's whip, 'Dinna speak of it.' Now he mimicked his childish lisping vehemence for me, charmingly.

At home, the violence increased. The missiles changed from tongues and hands to tongs and pokers. On one occasion, mother and son were each seen to go secretly at night to the apothecary, to ask whether the other had purchased poison during the day, and to caution him not to accept such a commission if it came. Byron mimicked the sinewy Scottish accent of his mother for me. 'Lame brat,' Catherine had shrieked at him. Worse still, the worst she could fling at him, 'You are a true Byron.'

She had miscalculated her insult. Far from feeling the sting of these words, little Lord Byron-to-be was already revelling in the myth of his ancestors. He could not hear enough about the Wicked Lord, a murderer, a duellist who carried pistols in his pockets. Scarcely less colourful was Byron's own grandfather, the Wicked Lord's younger brother, known as Foulweather Jack. He had been shipwrecked off Patagonia, where he was obliged to eat the skin and paws of his pet dog in order to survive. Back in England, the Wicked Lord lived like a savage. Byron told me that when his black mood was upon him his great-uncle would throw the luckless Lady Byron into the ornamental pond at Newstead Abbey, the family home, and that he had shot the coachman dead in a fit of choler. Eventually he replaced his wife with a servant-girl. Then the Wicked Lord plunged his sword, fatally, into the liver of his neighbour, William Chaworth, during an argument about the best way to hang game.

Less forgivably, in his heir's opinion, the old Wicked Lord had let Newstead Abbey rot to ruins. He had stripped the forests to pay his gambling debts and killed two thousand deer unfortunate enough to graze his fiefdom. He built a miniature castle in the forest for his louche entertainments. He constructed two small stone forts at the edge of his lake, and would spend whole days there directing imagined naval battles. Sometimes, he would lie upon the stone-flagged floor of the kitchen and stage cockroach races up and down his body. The servants said that the black insects knew their master, who whipped them with pieces of straw to keep them in line.

'And then,' Murray, the old butler would recount to the young Byron – who now mimicked the speech for me verbatim, and in an almost impenetrable accent – 'the black beetles exhausted their wee black selves scrambling in the hairs on his Lordship's belly, which were considerable in number. Sometimes they got themselves all snarled up down there, and that drove his Lordship into such a rage that he would snap them in half, lengthways, like an almond, with his long nails, that were never cut, never, you know. Indeed, those beetles knew what it was to belong to a Byron, as did those poor deer in the forest, that ran red with their blood for a month in its entirety.'

The young Byron knew what it was to belong to the Byron clan. It was *untidy*, he told me, leaning closely and confidentially towards me. One never knew when one might meet one's bastard mirror image in the village, running cockroach races in the dust at the side of the road. It was to feel a rage in the blood that could not be contained. It was to have an ability to pick up and drop human relations at will, he told me.

'We are like that,' he told me, looking straight into my eyes. 'My father, for example.'

Byron's father, Mad Jack Byron, had previously fathered a legitimate daughter, Augusta. The mother died in childbirth. Mad Jack had deposited the baby girl with friends, never to be collected again, and went heiress-hunting in Bath. He found Catherine Gordon, a large girl with a strong Scottish accent, a reasonable fortune, and her own gloomy family history. Her father was a suicide. Catherine was her-self inclined to histrionics and bile. But she had loved Mad Jack on sight. She paid for a ring, and married him. In some ways she was no different from the other women who were rumoured to lay out cash for his company. Mad Jack, his son now told me, grinning, was said to have taken money for various stupendous sexual feats.

Mad Jack had run through Catherine's fortune in less than a year. Then he left her, pregnant, only returning episodically to forage for cash. The infant Byron's first experience of domestic life was of tears, bellowed oaths and doors slamming. Byron barely knew his father, who showed not the least interest in his small son. When his father was in the house, the little boy was nervous, pulling at the corner of his handkerchief until it frayed, and biting his fingernails. Eventually, Mad Jack went to live in France, in a strangely passionate relationship with his sister, Frances. He never saw his son again. Within three years he was dead of consumption, and the unstable Catherine Byron was left to look after her volatile young son entirely on her own.

'You may imagine, I did not make it easy for her,' said Byron.

The table was cleared around us. The Pasha bade us a good evening and explained he must leave to attend to 'a political matter'.

'But please,' Ali beamed, 'take advantage of the terrace and the moonlight.' He pointed through the arches to the wide balcony where the servants were laying cushions and glass bowls of green and black grapes.

He wagged his finger at me with a roguish smile. 'Do not exhaust the young English lords, Madame Cecilia.' Then he was gone.

Byron collected his pistols and made a supple gesture out of sliding them into his pockets. We walked out to the terrace. Hobhouse was still immersed in conversation with Mouchar. They appeared to be talking about votive sacrifices, a subject on which I was certain that Mouchar would have many elegant and horrifying things to say. Hobhouse was showing him a sketchbook. I flicked my eyes over it: yes, very creditable pen-and-inks of Jannina and an Albanian soldier. *A good eye for detail*, I thought.

Byron wanted my attention for himself. He said to me, 'Don't waste your time with Hobby. He is rather *tardy* in his appreciation of the fairer sex. From your face, you are not entirely shocked by my history so far. Perhaps you would like to hear more?'

'Yes, I would. It already sounds like a strange kind of fairy tale.'

'Not always a very charming fairy tale. There's more than a touch of horror to it. It's more like *Vathek* than *Cinderella*.'

'You know *Vathek*, my Lord?'

'It is my Bible. You know the book, too?' He looked at me appraisingly. 'Do you know it *well*?'

'Yes,' I said. 'And I painted the writer.'

Byron slapped his knees. With a flourish, he produced his own copy of *Vathek* from his pocket. He interrupted Hobhouse.

'Damn me! She knew William Beckford! She even painted him.' He turned to me. 'When he was in Venice?'

I nodded.

Hobhouse asked, 'Wasn't that before *Vathek* was published? I believe the first edition was in—'

I interrupted him. I did not want to think of the unimaginable stretch of time that had passed since those days. I said, 'It certainly had not yet been published at that time. In fact, I believe I was the first person to hear the story. He read to me from the handwritten manuscript. He wanted me to paint him beside it.'

'You heard *Vathek* in his own voice?'

I remember Byron's flushed agitation when I said, 'Yes.' He all but touched me in his urgency to extract information from me now. He leant close to me, as if to read on my face memories I could not recount fast enough. With my every word his smile grew broader. He twitched with a schoolboy's uncontainable excitement. I could see the questions crowding into his mouth.

The first one that came out was: 'Is it true that he wrote it in just three days?'

'Three nights, so he said, and he had the pallor of one who would abuse himself in that way.'

'Carathis, and Alboufaki, and Nouronihar – they were all there, then?'

I assured him that they were. Byron quoted favourite passages by heart until we were both gasping with laughter. Another thought occurred to him. He asked me, 'Did Beckford love Venice?'

'Yes, he adored it, but it was painful for him.' I told Byron and Hobhouse about the young Cornaro, and about my portrait of Beckford, and the poor reception it had received.

'I would love to see that portrait. And to have been in Venice with Beckford, when he was young and beautiful. Damn me, I can picture you, painting him. I can see him posing, dreaming. He was a beautiful young man, I'm sure, wasn't he?'

'I am afraid not.'

'But you made him so.'

'I am afraid not.'

This was not what Byron wanted to hear. His lower lip jutted a little. I changed the subject. I asked him why he loved *Vathek* so much, and how he himself had come across it.

'Ah, Madame Cecilia,' he replied with a mock sigh, 'that would be telling. *Vathek* really is the story of my life as a man.'

A light ticklesome rain had started to fall. Under the slender portico we drew a little closer together to avoid the straying droplets. The rain quickly settled into a delicate, regular thrum and sent soft moist breaths from the paving stones up towards our faces. I found my toes tapping inside my slippers in a sympathetic rhythm.

Byron settled back in the cushions, and started to talk. Again, he mimicked voices, mimed gestures. He talked without stopping. Occasionally Hobhouse looked up, startled, at the sound of certain names, and shook his head gently at Byron, who took no notice. Eventually the palace went to sleep around us. Even Hobhouse and Mouchar crept off, while Byron and I sat enclosed in his story. It was the early hours of the morning before Byron answered my question: 'Why have you come to Albania?' The answer, you see, was to be found in *Vathek*, and many other things beside. He was right: his history soon took a dark turning. I was astounded at Byron's impudent acts, committed without a thought to the consequences, as if people who loved him were made of stone. I was disturbed at the way he laughed about it. *If he has modelled himself upon* Vathek *then he must be pleased with his work*, I thought.

But I was more horrified at the abuse Byron had received, and even more so at the way he now described it. I must admit that sometimes I myself laughed at the black humour of his account. It was a nervous laugh, the way we Venetians laugh at the grotesque gargoyles that loom out of the dark at the water's edge. In the light of lamp, we smile at their mocking, brutish faces, but underneath our cloaks our hearts are beating like little birds. We have seen death, the grotesque humour of it. It is a joke against us.

So when Byron talked of himself, I saw the grinning gargoyles of Venice in front of my eyes. The deeds done against him were ugly, worse than ugly, but the fact that he could describe them as if they were a puppet show — that is what made me frightened of him. I remember thinking, *Is this what he wants, to frighten me?*

The story, like *Vathek*, started innocently enough.

Young Byron lived in Aberdeen with the smell of the sea in his nostrils. He dreamt of exotic voyages. That escape was as yet denied, so instead he became inseparable from his books, which took him worlds away from everyday life and away from his intolerable mother. He read while he ate, while he reposed. There was something about the sight of a book that fended off his mother. She would not scream at him if he was reading.

At first it was harmless. Byron read the histories of Rome and Greece and Turkey. He dreamt of a troop of Byron's Blacks — a fearsome platoon in black uniforms, mounted upon black horses. These imaginary cavaliers would, he told me, 'perform prodigies of valour'. Byron loved the letters of Lady Mary Wortley Montagu, the great and eccentric traveller, who had lived in the Palazzo Mocenigo in Venice (I nodded at this, but he did not notice) and in Constantinople. He also adored *The Thousand and One Nights*.

But most of all, Byron loved *Vathek*. He loved it all, the irascible temper and voluptuary excess of the eponymous hero, the malevolent flesh-eating mother, the fearsome camel, Alboufaki, the alluring Carbuncle of the Giamschid, and the grim living death endured by the pre-adamite sultans in the tragic Halls of Eblis. Byron spent hours absorbed in Beckford's little book, repeating the phrases, imagining the charms of Nouronihar, Vathek's lady-love, and the amiable stranglings performed by the mute grinning one-eyed Negresses of Queen Carathis. Love and cruelty, satire and pleasure, it seemed to me, had become deliciously mixed in the little Byron's head, as they had been in young Beckford's.

'Why can I not have a camel, Mama?' was his constant refrain in those days, he told me. He refused to dignify his small dog with the name Alboufaki. Lady Byron's reasonable demurs were met with a horrible stare. For Byron now practised to acquire Vathek's incandescent glare, in which one eye would become so terrible that no one could behold it, and any wretch caught in it would faint and expire. This did not, in fact, happen, when little Byron unleashed it, but he frightened the chambermaids dreadfully.

Vathek yielded to more palpable experiences, though the book was never forgotten. At nine, Byron fell in love with his cousin, Mary Duff.

'Really in love?' I asked.

'With all my heart.' He opened his eyes wide and pressed one small hand upon his breast.

The passion was pure and child-like until Byron was seduced by his nurse, May Gray.

'Seduced?'

'Ravished.'

Nurse Gray put him to bed every night after beating him thoroughly for the day's misdeeds. She did not spare his crippled leg. Indeed she beat it harder than the other one. She was probably the last woman Byron ever begged for mercy, he told me with an unfathomable smile. He re-enacted the scene for me, taking both roles. First he was the cringing little boy, the last sweet remnant of his innocent self.

'Nurse Gray, please dinna hurt me!'

Then he became the stringy young woman with her staring eyes all askew and her hard hands all over him.

'You have blasphemed against Our Lord in word and deed, you deserve no less. Look at ye! You are cloven in the foot like Black Beelzebub himself. Yer gimp foot is his sign.'

'Dinna hit me there! I am bleeding, look. My nose is dripping with blood. I shall tell my mother.'

'And d'ye think she will care? She will rejoice in her parlour to hear that Lucifer is being beaten out of ye at last. The more she hears ye cry, the more she likes it. Look, in your drawers, at the wee Prince of Darkness who lurks there.'

Nurse Gray had struck him a blow that sent him sprawling on his bed. Then she reached into his drawers and took the small Devil himself in her hand. She was not gentle, but even so, the little pink agent of Satan began to stiffen and shrug off its tiny foreskin.

'You see, the Devil!' she shrieked. 'Begone, Devil!' She kneeled and the little Devil disappeared into her mouth.

The little boy lay upon the mattress, choking on the blood surging from his nose. As she straddled him and lifted her skirts, Nurse Gray delivered a fiery Bible lesson. She continued to beat him, flailing her arms, striking first one side of his head, and then the other. He could not see – some merciful dark membrane had descended over his eyes, like a cat's. The little fiend was sucked up into a dark, hairy place. *Perhaps it would never return? How would he make water again if he lived?* He swallowed gulps of his blood and tried to breathe.

Byron told me that when he reached his first climax, he fainted, perhaps in ecstasy, perhaps in terror, perhaps in pain. Certainly, ever after, he said, hellfire and orgasm were confused in his brain, which was already teeming with *Vathek*-style eroticism. I asked him what had happened to Nurse Gray. The ululations of her own climax had brought the other servants running. When she had gone away, tied in a strange garment, I believe that she took with her any latent capacity for sexual tenderness that the bad Byron blood might have allowed him.

When Byron was ten years old, the Wicked Lord finally expired in Gibraltar. George Gordon, Lord Byron, became the sixth baron of Newstead. The first sign that the old Lord Byron was dead was a mass evacuation of the cockroaches from Newstead Abbey. The floor was black with departing insects. When the new little Lord Byron was told of his elevation to the peerhood, he ran to the mirror to see if there was any difference in his face.

Sadly, there was no difference in his leg. His mother wanted to make the new Lord Byron perfect. In proud silence he endured torturing treatments, wooden casts tightened to agony. Only once did he throw the hateful brace in a pond. To show weakness to his mother would be to fail. He would not do that.

Byron and his mother had taken possession of Newstead Abbey later that year. Infected by *Vathek*, he craved Gothic and grandeur. The ruined Abbey, the gargoyles crouching in the fountains and the vast haunted house all delighted him. But as the new century crept in, Lady Byron sent her son away to Harrow, which he described to me as a wondrous hot-bed of tantrums, masturbation and sodomy. Byron himself cultivated a ring of handsome stripling nobles. These were passionate, jealous relationships, especially with Lords Clare and Delawarr, the latter a sweet boy, almost too beautiful for his sex. Byron told me proudly that his fascinating influence was felt to be excessive by the headmaster, and at one point he was asked to leave the school.

But he could not bear to go back to his fat, bad-tempered, ridiculous mother. It was still a violent relationship. She would chase him around the house. When she had him pinned against the wall, when she seemed about to strike the fatal blow, Byron learnt to smile at her, full-lipped and charming, and say, 'If you love me, you will show it now.' Catherine would burst into tears. He had won.

He blamed her for his deformity for was he not crippled because she had muddled his birth, just as she muddled everything? He had attributed the withered leg to excessive and vain corseting during her pregnancy, and then some false delicacy in labour, that prevented him from making his full entrance to the world.

He had found another reason to hate her. His image of himself was plagued not just by lameness but by the unromantic plumpness he inherited from his mother, which reminded him hatefully of her when he looked in the mirror. At just five feet and eight inches, Byron weighed fourteen stone. With a drastic diet, and a regime of sweating inside seven waistcoats, he recreated himself as the ethereal Adonis I had first beheld that evening in the Pasha's reception chamber. This was the beginning, I understood, of his continuous struggle to elevate his personal beauty above that of common humanity. Often he failed and flesh clung to him, 'like damned tallow,' he said, but he would always start again with the purgative teas and provisionless days.

At fifteen he fell in love again, this time with his Newstead neighbour Mary Chaworth, the descendant of the man whom the cockroach-loving Wicked Lord Byron had killed. (In her home, he imagined the ancestral portraits glaring at him.) It ended unhappily. Mary loved another and would not take him seriously. He heard her words repeated back to him: *Do you think I should care anything for that lame boy?*

The frail young god with the embarrassing mother was afraid of women in those distant days. He snorted with laughter as he told me how when he saw them he would count slowly under his breath to keep calm. There was only one woman who did not intimidate him – his half-sister, Augusta Leigh, the daughter of Mad Jack's first marriage. Augusta, four years older than Byron, had been brought up separately. She was twenty when they met, a brief but warm encounter. They started a correspondence but it would be years before they saw each other again.

Byron arrived at Trinity College, Cambridge in 1805 with his public persona more or less complete. He kept three horses, two

menservants, a carriage and, eventually, a bear. Although he had one
of the most sumptuous allowances at Cambridge, thanks to his
mother's parsimony at home, his debts mounted to epic proportions.

It was at Cambridge, Byron told me with studied carelessness,
that he started to meet people. He mentioned John Edelston, a pale
slender chorister two years younger than himself. In his second
year at Cambridge, he published his first book of poetry, *Hours of
Idleness*. This fact, more than the bear and other eccentricities,
attracted interesting friends, like the estimable Hobhouse. But the
book was pilloried. Byron was wounded by what he saw as the gratuitous venom of the reviews. He had comforted himself,
thoroughly, he assured me, with laudanum and sensuality.

'There was a great deal of very good chastity to be got cheaply at
Cambridge in those days,' he leered. He gambled little; he hated to
lose money, he told me.

He took his seat in the House of Lords – for just a few minutes.
I deduced that Byron felt humiliated and excluded by the formal
proceedings. He would not think of taking it up as a regular pastime. A fortnight later, Byron published his *English Bards and Scotch
Reviewers*, a fierce satire on those who had abused or neglected his
earlier work. It was, he informed me, a raging success.

But he was feeling vulnerable. People, he told me with a little
shark-like retraction of the lips, were jealous. Far too many stories,
dangerous stories, were being spun. Malicious things were being
said that could damage him rather than promote him. Somehow the
story had got abroad about a wretched maid who had miscarried in
a family hotel in Bond Street and another who had been paid off,
having actually borne a child.

He felt trapped by his wretched circumstances. He could not live
with his mother; he could not afford to live in style in London.
There seemed no way to achieve the grandeur he had promised

himself in this small island of England, where he was just a young backwater peer, becalmed and sinking in his debts. It was time to leave, he had decided.

His guardian, Hanson – 'Old Spooney, slow as death' – had struggled to come up with the money for a long trip abroad. Byron had flayed him with increasing urgency, hinting at scandal if the funds were not found quickly. But in the end it was his gambling friend Scrope Davies who had lent him the money to travel.

It was time to follow Beckford, time to live like Vathek.

'And so you came to Albania?' I asked, stretching my legs, which had been curled under me all this time. Some time, in the course of the story, the rain had stopped and was replaced by a clammy warmth. My hot, tired head was alive with information. I felt precious, the repository of an extraordinary confidence. I felt privileged beyond the gods, but also, in a strange way, tainted.

'If only it had been that simple,' he said.

The dawn was starting to lighten the stones of the terrace. Byron suddenly rose.

'I cannot stay here with you any longer, Cecilia.'

'Why not?

'You know too much now.'

'Why did you choose to tell me?'

I felt an unaccustomed desperation. As Byron turned to leave me, I found it impossible to let him go. A compliment was due to me. I needed some acknowledgement of the intimacy we had shared. I was still at a loss, wondering if he had chosen me to hear his story because he wanted to become close to me. Was it because he was intent upon securing, at all costs, my rapt attention? Was it the truth, or had he, over-stimulated and insomniac after his journey, merely amused himself with a fanciful biography to beguile the time? He had asked me nothing more about myself. Obviously he did not yet know about Casanova. I wondered how long it would take him to find out. *Hours*, I thought.

In the meantime, I needed to know why I had received these extraordinary confessions. By laying his life at my feet in this unabashed way, he had in fact placed *me* in a strange, supplicatory position, which made me feel nauseated with anxiety. I was anxious because I already wanted, too much, to have been the subject of the storytelling style of seduction: the telling of such tales as weave invisible nets of desire around the listener, who finds herself longing to become not just a part of the story but its object. You see, whether it was idly or artfully done, it was well done. I was caught.

But Byron did not answer my question. He smiled, picked up his pistols and limped back into the palace. Two servants appeared from nowhere to escort him to his apartments, while I, transparent with exhaustion and something more tormenting, crept back to mine, where I lay, with my eyes wide open, on the silken bed.

4

El petegolo xe na spia senza paga.

The gossip is an unpaid spy.

VENETIAN PROVERB

I did not see Byron or Hobhouse the next morning, but the court was feverish with gossip about them. Everyone wanted to see Hobhouse's dreadful hat and, more importantly, Byron's beautiful face. It was as if an exquisite genie had been uncorked inside the palace and now floated through its corridors, convulsing its inhabitants.

Everyone seemed to know about my long night on the terrace. The little princesses, in one smooth seemingly choreographed motion, put their hands over their mouths as I entered their dayroom and sat at my easel. I pretended not to notice, but I, too, was pleasantly disturbed at the thought of seeing Byron again. It would clarify things, I told myself. He must have been spectral with exhaustion the previous night: that was why he had behaved so strangely with me. So I worked steadily, while my subjects chattered endlessly of his beauty, his drooping grey-blue eyes, his endearing limp, his delectably small ears and his delicate white hands.

One of those white hands I felt upon my own shoulder a few

hours later. The night's rain had delivered a clear morning which had now yielded to an unbearably hot afternoon. I was working on the nose of the Pasha's youngest *nipotina*, trying to diminish it without losing the likeness. I bent over my easel, feathering the paint with my fingers. I feared for the consequences if I did not depict the Pasha's granddaughter in a way that amply reflected her *nonno*'s proud love.

Without announcing himself, Byron undulated into the room, observed my work, and said, with his cold breath upon my neck, 'They are beautiful little animals, these granddaughters of Ali Pasha. You don't need to make them more delicate. When they are thrown on their backs in the *caravanserai* of their husbands, that sensual nose will only bring more children. Imagine it nuzzling under the arm of one of these great hairy brigands, or pushed into his groin.'

'Come now, old man,' protested Hobhouse, who had followed him into the room. 'Leave her to work. What if the Pasha hears about what you have just said?'

'He would confirm it. The old bastard is not above a bit of *famil-ial* love, as we have heard. I would have liked to see that daughter-in-law. If not touch her. Worth fifteen members of the harem, it seems.'

It was as if I was not there. My little subject, meanwhile, was sitting open-mouthed and silent upon her miniature throne, struck dumb by both the sudden appearance of the English milord and a faint grasp of what he had said. The French taught to the young Albanian ladies did not stretch to Byron's kind of vocabulary. I nodded kindly to her and she scuttled from the room. A single emerald earring spun on the floor.

Byron bent to pick it up. As he raised his head, he now looked at me for me for the first time. 'Your own nose, I understand, is used to more civilised sensations. Yes, I can see it wrinkling up at the *spussa* of the canal?'

How had he learnt the Venetian dialect word we use to describe an evil smell? Of course, then I did not know that Byron was an addict of languages, and could not bear to be near a country without a taste of its language in his beautiful mouth. 'I am a spice of everything,' I heard him say, afterwards, several times. He used his voice as a musical instrument, and he could move from language to language without effort. But English, remember, was what he chose to write in — English, that narrow language of whispers and insinuations, the only one I know in which the feminine and the masculine are not expected to be in accord.

That beautiful mouth was near to mine as he polluted the tent with his deft and dirty language. Certainly, with Casanova, I had learnt a natural sensuality and it was difficult to shock me. But I was shocked by Byron's words, not at the idea of sexual congress but the cold bestial picture he painted of it

Of course, I understood that he was flirting, in his way. It was nothing personal. This was only a debt he carelessly discharged to an attractive woman. It was as if we had not spent the whole night together, talking about the most private aspects of his past, as if we had not exchanged a look that had admitted an extraordinary intimacy between us.

He turned to me and said, 'Madame Cecilia, you know that I am an artist too in my own way, being a poet?'

I bowed. 'Indeed.'

'What a charming accent! I love to hear French with an Italian intonation. God, yes, Cecilia. I voyage, I taste, I taste *deeply*. I tear my heart and put it on a plate for the idle to pick at. I ride really *dangerous* horses. Of course I am a poet, woman!' He turned to look at my work, picked up a brush loaded with Cochineal and plunged it into the shell of poppy oil, where the red pigment clouded the yellow liquid. 'So you love it, do you, Madame Cecilia, your own greasy trade?'

He looked at the painting quickly, and then more closely. 'My god, there is something alive in here. It is so good, this portrait, that I could almost kiss you.'

The mention of a kiss, at a moment like this, as carelessly as this, pricked me cruelly. By proposing this kind of kiss, a commercial species of kiss, a pat-upon-the-head kiss, he had ruined the kiss I was starting to envisage in my imagination.

I looked directly at him and said, 'Until you spoke to me this afternoon, I could almost have thought you a gentleman.'

'Ha! D'you hear that, Hobhouse! Spirited piece! What a prodigy of courage!' Then he turned back to me.

'I want you to paint my portrait,' he said, looking not at me but at my easel. 'You will not find it easy. I sit badly. But there is something about your work . . . I like the little details.' He pointed to the emerald earring I had already painted with a tiny reflection of the Pasha alive inside its lustre. We haggled a price, he with a surprising vehemence. I had not thought that the English milord would be so mean, but in those days I knew little or nothing about Scots. He was also well aware of his own price, by which I mean he seemed to know already what kind of celebrity he could soon add to my portfolio.

Our exchange was hurried because he was on his way to meet with Ali Pasha again.

Byron informed me proudly that the Pasha had told him to consider him as a father while he was in Tepelene. Indeed, he treated Byron like a favourite son, sending almonds, sugared sherbet, fruit and sweetmeats to his apartments. Given the Pasha's well-known depravities with young boys and girls, the palace was afire with rumours that the pretty English milord was about to become his catamite. I blushed as I thought about the ways Byron and the Pasha would discuss me. The story of Casanova would be first on the list. I knew the gossip of men.

Hobhouse stayed with me after Byron left. He was not wanted at the Pasha's side that day. Hobhouse proved as amiable as he looked. With a little questioning it emerged that Hobhouse was, like myself, the child of a rich merchant. He had been born in another seafaring town, Bristol. He told me, as though I might understand it was important, that he was a 'Nonconformist' and a 'Whig' with an 'h'. I did not ask what these things meant. He continued smoothly. He was also a scholar and classicist. He was interested in the origin and aim of sacrifices. Hobhouse also had an outsider's taste for poetry, and for art.

He told me, as I cleaned my brushes, his entire history, particularly where it coincided with Byron's. He gave detail, to the point of being boring, which is why I know so much now. Details about Hobhouse are crowded into the repository I tend inside me along with other precious information. Thanks to Hobhouse I can never forget that the Jannina retsina is the worst in the world and, worse, that there is no one in the whole place who can mend an umbrella.

From that day forth, Hobhouse haunted my easel. He seemed at a loss as to what to do with himself while Byron dallied with the Pasha. But he also seemed confused in his response to me. After watching me spar with Byron, he accorded me a gentlemanly respect. He no longer urged Byron to watch his language in front of me. I was accepted as one of them. But it was more than that. He seemed fascinated. I could draw him to me like a baby to a mother's breast. He was a great big girl-boy anyway. I think he preferred boys, if anything. Whatever Hobhouse wanted from me, I hope he took it, because I certainly took from him, with both hands. I took information.

When I want to imagine Byron before I knew him, I have simply to conjure Hobhouse's careful voice, and summon our conversations in my memory. As I have explained, my discourses with Byron seemed more like performances, during which I sat stupefied in the pit, while he strutted the stage. With Hobhouse, it was a dialogue. I dared to ask him things that I could not put to Byron.

Now I asked him if Byron had been sad to leave England.

'Sad? I don't think so. Relieved, possibly. Things were becoming a little awkward for him.'

I asked if Byron did not miss his intimates, the women he loved? I knew he did not pine for his mother, but what of his sister Augusta and his friends?

Hobhouse told me ruefully that Byron often complained of an intense and picturesque loneliness, even in his own company. As for the women, Hobhouse explained, 'Cecilia, Byron always says that for him the word "friend" is the antithesis of "lover".'

I asked, 'So do you think he himself is much missed?'

Before Hobhouse could answer, the voice of Byron himself rang out behind me. He had returned from the Pasha.

'Well, by a certain group of them, those who attended my farewell party, I shall certainly not be forgotten.'

He looked significantly at Hobhouse, who abruptly rose to leave. Byron settled himself on a divan, stretched out like cat, and told what it had been like, that last party at Newstead.

5

Bisogna annegarse nel mar grande.

Better to drown yourself in a big sea
(i.e., Do it in style).

VENETIAN PROVERB

'I gave my last party at Newstead Abbey, the ancestral home of all the Byrons. Of that vast ruin, I had made just one or two parts habitable. The rest, including my garden, my lake and the fortresses, I left to rot. Nature, no doubt offended by the depredations of the Old Wicked Lord, had gripped her chance and strangled any sign of civilised life in my domain. The noble camel Alboufaki would have loved my garden. No graveyard ever stank as rife with the revengeful gases of decomposition. Molehills pustuled my old lawns. Lengths of wild vine rattled across my paths. Sometimes I used to go and scratch at the welts of lichen that disfigured the faces of my statues, whose thighs were chafed by nettles of primeval dimensions. When I inspected my flower beds, I noticed that the petals of the old Dutch roses had balled up in their buds and made no attempt to leave their carapaces. The roses knew: it was not safe out there.

'You want to know what the party was like?

'Imagine you are invited and you have travelled here to find me.

You arrive at the Abbey through its devastated forest, sweeping round a bend to see the magnificent ruin hooding the dark eye of its lake. The branches of my trees now meet over the drive. You probably have a somewhat nauseous sense of being swallowed into a long green alimentary canal. The empty arches of my ruined monastery send long shadows up to your feet. Four finials, strangled with vines, point up to a moist oysterish sky, for this is England, of course, not Italy.

'At the steps to the entrance you find on the right a chained bear, and on the left a frothing wolfhound. You reel from the foul, hot breath of one into, it seems, the yellow teeth of the other. But your host has judged the length of their chains to a nicety. An inch from your throat, the animals are yanked back to their tethers with a sickening wheeze. They crouch, whimpering their private sorrows. You stumble up the stairs and into the house, where you find yourself under fire from a group of strangely attired but rather lovely young men discharging jewelled pistols beneath the vaulting. It's practice time.

'I am afraid that the new Wicked Lord Byron does not appear to welcome you. Ribald suggestions are no doubt made to explain his absence. Never mind, the other young men, beautiful of face and foul of mouth, take you in their arms and kiss you, lusciously. Your travel-stained clothes will be removed, one by one, like the wrappings of a gift. Costumes, as if from the *ridotto*, will be given to you and you dress while the young men watch and caress you. They will tell you how it is here at Newstead, what is expected of you. Then, when they have prinked you up, they will leave you and run off to the cellars, where they splash and wade in old porter, their laughter echoing behind them, and blood-like footprints upon the stairs.

'There are the Abbey and its Gothic horrors to explore. There is, for example, the "Haunted Chamber", the small room adjoining my bedroom on the uppermost floor, looking over the ruined church. In this room, rumoured to be visited on occasion by the phantom of a headless monk, sleeps the handsome young lad, Robert Rushton, my page. Indeed, as you enter the room, there he is, flung naked and sleeping on his rumpled little bed, his hair feathered with sweat and his tulip skin stained with scratches. He looks like an angel but he smells of ill-use. Nothing can wake the boy when he sleeps like that, so I am afraid that you must leave him.

'Elsewhere in the house, you will learn that Paphian girls are reserved for the Lord's private pleasure. You think you can hear their giggling in distant corridors and their light steps on hidden stairs but you do not see them. For the moment. You hunt them in the dusty corridors, half-afraid of what you will find. In the end, you tire of this insubstantial sport and indulge less energetic curiosities. You look for the Old Wicked Lord Byron's murder weapon and his uniform. You might open dresser doors and drawers and find the latter full of the corpses of enormous black cockroaches.

'This party is a spectacle. You are a guest but also a participant. It is necessary to rise very late in the mornings. At breakfast you compare feats of alcoholic ingestion, projectile vomiting and copulation, for last night I will have shared my harem with you, my dearest friends, whom I am shortly to leave. You may remember me roaming among you at your sports in the candlelight. I appear last of all, having drunk, vomited and fucked more than anyone. Until I arrive, I suspect that there is a certain lassitude, a certain tendency to drink tea with milk and sugar, and very white bread with soft butter.

'Then I appear, in my stained nightshirt, brandishing my pistols. I might well shoot down a fragment of a ragged chandelier so that it drops into the salty oatmeal, where it will sink as if in quicksand. Everyone knows to applaud, and believe me some of the prettier young men also know how to curtsy. The maids come to clear the devastation from the table, and to be pinched. The day has officially begun!

'You fence, practise with your guns, write (preferably satire and love letters), torment the bear and wolfhound until you fear they will break their chains. So you go to the lake to see ruined fortresses where the original Wicked Lord staged his naval battles. You listen to old Murray, for hours, feeding him whisky to bring forth his stories of the old master. You must hear him describe the murder of the neighbour, Chaworth – he does it in such gut-wrenching detail!

'You dine, dressed in monks' habits, between seven and eight, downing quantities of claret and champagne. I promise you that your very elbow will become tired with the toasts. The wine is strong; you look at the great hall as if through the wrong end of a telescope. The voices of your friends sound metallic. Hot wax drips on your arms but you feel nothing. Tonight you address me as "The Abbot" and tonight I play the ghost of myself, rising out of a stone coffin to blow out your candle. The lovely Robert Rushton, or his reincarnation, appears as an acolyte to the noble phantasm, in transparent robes that reveal exactly, in tender rose-coloured silhouette, what endears him to your noble host. Indeed the subsequent picturesque ceremonies oblige me to cup my hand there, frequently.

'After the dead have risen and been admired, you pass around a human skull brimming with burgundy. It looks like black blood. You do not want to drink it.

'"*In estro*, plunge your lips," I command, implacably. This word "estro" – a corruption of *in oestrum* – I have adopted to describe all my own uncontrollable physical urges. So you bathe your tongue in the liquid and lap like a cat. Does the wine taste rusty? Is it hideously warm? Do you want to retch? Ha!

'While you drink, I explain in lugubrious tones, "My friends, you swallow from the skull of a monk dug up in the garden of Newstead Abbey. He was murdered, all for love, or at least for the bastards he begat. Drink, for it is his blood that you drink. Then eat, because tomorrow you may find your skull in a shallow grave, too. Or hacked by the surgeon, and spliced back together in a tin coffin. Drink! Death to the lip-lickers and the droplet-drinkers!"

'The skull is my pride and joy. I had it mounted on metallic legs and polished to the colour of mottled tortoiseshell. To christen it, I have written a poem that is now inscribed on it. Turn it in your hand, to read my lines as I intone them:

> . . . The worm hath fouler lips than thine.
> Better to hold the sparkling grape
> Than nurse the earth-worm's slimy hood;
> And circle in the goblet's shape
> The drink of gods, than reptile's food.

'At "slimy hood" I make a certain obscene gesture and crush Rushton to my breast. The boy seems dazed, or drugged. I warn you, "Drink, damn you! The last person who refused me is still looking for his testicles."

'Again, you raise the goblet to your lips, where my lips just were. The skull seems to move in your fingers. You tell yourself it is your own hands shaking, how, after all, you have abused your body these days! The skull is warm. Rivulets of claret are clotting on the polished bone. In the candlelight, it looks as though the arteries and veins, like Nature in the garden, are starting to reclaim their place. You could swear that you see something glint in the empty eye-sockets. You drink on. There is no doubt now, the skull throbs in your hands. You sense the soul of the monk flinching under this desecration. From the corner of your eye, you see a sudden strange phosphorescence in the garden. You think, with terror, of the dark corridor to your bedroom. But you drink on. You have no choice. I have commanded it.'

6

L'aqua de mare lava tuti i debiti.

The water of the sea washes away all debts.

<small>VENETIAN PROVERB</small>

After Byron delivered his monologue and left me without ceremony, I sat in silence for some time.

'That is what the English call a party?' I asked myself. 'It is not much like our *Carnevale*. It seems an unhappy way to be happy.'

Hobhouse came shuffling back into the room, uncertainly. He noted the expression on my face, my brush lying idle on the palette.

He asked me if I would be unhappy to paint Lord Byron. I asked him if I had a choice.

'Not really. Unless Ali Pasha forbids it. In that case, Byron will find a way to say that he did not wish it anyway. But if you do paint him, have a care to his nose, for God's sake.'

'Why?'

'He is very sensitive as to its length. Several portraits have been torn apart lengthwise that have not succeeded in conveying its delicacy and, well, *shortness*.'

I remembered Byron's comments about the nose of the Pasha's

granddaughter. Obviously it was only Byron's own nose that concerned him so. I began to be unwilling to do this portrait. I said as
much to Hobhouse.

'You may be right,' he agreed.

However, the Pasha approved the planned portrait enthusiasti-
cally. He even demanded a copy. Sittings were to commence
immediately.

The next day, Byron arrived in my apartments. He gave me a
business-like smile and began to set up the scene for his portrait. I
was not consulted about anything. Byron chose his chair, his costume, the angle of his head. I said nothing, but determined on the
usual revenge, to be extracted later in my detailings. Byron had
already decided what to wear. To further flatter his host, and to
indulge his taste for exoticism, Byron had ordered extravagant
Albanian costumes made for himself and his retinue. It was in this
guise, finer than a pheasant in its courting plumage, that he wished
to be painted. He carried in his arms a large bundle of papers, all
closely written.

'These, I shall explain later,' he said. 'You may begin to sketch me
now.'

I drew up my stool, and prepared to gaze. To put him at his ease,
I asked him to tell me about his journey to Albania.

The last party at Newstead took place in May. Byron and Hobhouse
left in June.

Preparations for the journey had been eccentric, expensive and
extreme. There was no hope of paying the creditors so Byron made
his debts deeper and more glamorous. Hobhouse had quarrelled
with his father and had no money. No matter! Byron would cover all
the costs, and more. Filled with *Vathek*-style visions of his journey,
everything became an allegory for Byron. Vathek's sumptuous
progress towards the Jewel of Giamschid was always at the back of

his mind. Danger, filth and disease did not frighten him. He was terrified only of the tiny humdrum inconveniences of travel. Hobhouse was to shelter him from these.

Byron took with him painted miniatures of his beautiful boy friends, and the living, breathing version of the young page boy Robert Rushton, with whom he posed for a full-length portrait while they waited for their ship at Falmouth. It was a fine picture, he told me. Byron also took with him his unprepossessing little valet, William Fletcher, whom I had met that morning. I could not understand a word Fletcher said. After that, I would often come across him, scuttling around the palace, muttering incomprehensibly to himself in some strange English dialect.

At the end of June Byron and Hobhouse embarked from Falmouth for Lisbon, just as Beckford had done thirty years before. Byron, now safely on his way, had announced in letters to his friends his intention to help Hobhouse with a book project. He would contribute a chapter on the state of morals and a treatise entitled 'Sodomy simplified or Paederasty proved to be praiseworthy from ancient authors to modern practice'. Falmouth, a sailor's town, had proved a delectable region, with plenty of opportunities for what he described as *Plenum et optabilem Coitum* – usually abbreviated to *Plen & opt C* – that is, full and desirable acts of sexual intercourse. It was a phrase, he explained, that he had borrowed from Petronius' *Satyricon*, in which it is used to describe the provision of a boy for sexual use.

Silently, I marvelled at how heedlessly Byron had set off into a Europe still embroiled in war and bloody revolution. I myself had not dared to visit Spain or Portugal during this turbulent period, though I had received invitations from their courts. It seems that this prospect of danger merely added spice to Byron's excitement. His concerns, like Beckford's, were reserved for his internal journey, the alchemy that the new environments would work on his own state of mind. Physical danger seemed something clean, something raw, which might wash away the unpaid debts and compromising memories. As the sea carried them further from England, Byron, he told me, felt calmer.

In Lisbon, where the Inquisition had not yet ended, they saw horrors. Byron described how corpses lay in churches with begging bowls upon their breasts. Until enough money was put inside these bowls, the priests would not bury them. They visited Montserrat, the Moorish palace where Beckford had sheltered in the wake of his scandal. Then they travelled to Seville on horseback, passing the crosses of the murdered on every hill. They continued to Cadiz, Gibraltar and then by boat to Malta.

In Malta Byron took lessons in Arabic from a monk. He enjoyed what he told me was a platonic love-affair with the cultured, exotic, sylph-like Mrs Spencer Smith. She was hard to leave, but the East beckoned, even more strongly than before, because now Byron could smell spicy breads baking on the Turkish boats moored in the harbour, and hear their crews at night keening their homesick songs as they crouched around their fires.

Robert Rushton had been sent home because 'Turkey was in too dangerous a state for boys to enter'. Byron was moody, missing his beautiful playfellow. In Malta, they heard stories of Gothic horror about Ali Pasha, the vizier who ruled Albania and all western Greece with Vathek-like cruelty. It was Byron's passion to meet him, though no Englishman had yet done so.

In the middle of September, Hobhouse and Byron embarked on the brig-of-war *Spider*, bound for Albania. The nature of the journey had suddenly changed for Byron, he told me. He was writing all the time as the little boat crested the blue Ionian Sea. Each hour he fattened his portfolio of scribbled lines and verses on assorted sheaves of paper. One windless evening, he laid them out on the deck, and paced around them. There seemed to be a pattern, a framework, waiting to accept a decoration of poetry. It was suddenly obvious to Byron what was needed: a single, long heroic poem. *How like Beckford*, I thought. I understood immediately the design and purpose of the proposed poem: it would transform him, turn this voyage into an epic and Byron into an epic hero.

I imagined how Byron, as he folded the scraps of paper to his breast that night, must have breathed a new life into them. A new Byron was being born.

Byron was tired of sitting still, and jaded with talking. He rose and came to examine my sketchbook, where I had pencilled a dozen likenesses of him, and also vignettes of the journey he had described. I showed him sitting on the deck, quill in hand, at work on his poem while the sun swooped into the sea behind him. I did not sketch the languid beauties of Mrs Spencer-Smith.

'A good start,' he said condescendingly, looking at my pictures of him. In my mind, I promised him a little blemish on the final portrait for that.

We walked out on to the terrace, to stand in the last glimmer of the dying light. Byron clutched his manuscripts to his breast. I have always been vulnerable to that time of the day. Byron, too, looked frail in that keen light. How narrow his outline seemed against the evening glow of the hills! The sunset came suddenly and violently. As we watched, the sun seemed to suffer a black cloak thrown over it from behind. Shafts of loud orange darted from the black sky; it seemed as if the shrouded sun were being dragged, screaming, off to prison.

Hobhouse joined us, with his new admirer Mouchar beside him. Byron became animated again.

'Ah Hob, you have arrived at just the right point. I am telling Cecilia about the moment I became a romantic poet. Quite possibly *the* romantic poet.'

Hobhouse, Mouchar and I slapped at mosquitoes on our arms. Byron was untroubled. I had already noticed that the insects never feasted on his skin the way they had devoured Casanova. *What did they know?* I asked myself.

Byron unfurled his manuscripts. I saw that he had sketched a rough approximation of a frontispiece. 'I present Childe Birun, Tragic exile, Adventurer, Lover, the Young Poet of the new century.'

Hobhouse explained in more details than I needed that 'birun' was the antique spelling of his friend's name. Then he asked, 'Are you really going to use your own name for this poem?'

I remember Byron looking out over the mountain passes as he replied, 'I use my real pain, my real sweat, my real seed, when I write, so why not?'

Hobhouse remonstrated, 'Think of your mother, Byron.'

'You're right. That fat bitch does not deserve to be immortal. Let's call me Childe . . . Harold.'

'That's not what I meant, Byron, but yes, Harold will do very well. May he make you rich and famous, and enable you to pay your creditors.'

'Lords do not take payment for literature. And if I did, I would not use it to pay the damned tailor.'

'Or the carriage-maker, or the furrier, or the vintner . . .'

'None of them. Women, though. *Plen & opt C*, cunts at any price. What I earn with my brain, I shall spend on my bollocks.'

'Byron!' exclaimed Hobhouse, turning to look and me; then, 'Cecilia!'

For I could not help myself. I was laughing. It was a bare, dark laugh, ringing out like a slap upon the face.

7

Al lume de candela
no se varda nè dona nè tela.

By the light of a candle,
you do not judge women or paintings.

VENETIAN PROVERB

I f you ask me today why I fell in love with Byron then, I would
tell you that it was because I could not paint him. He eluded
me. And therefore won me. I, the *cacciatrice*, the huntress of
men's faces, could not capture his on canvas, and perhaps that was
because his essential personality was verbal and not physical. His
words hung around me, refusing to be lured to my brush. It is a
problem we portrait painters have. We always paint a still, silent
image. The act of speaking splits the human face in half. So we do
not paint it, though we may elongate the mouth a little and expand
the wings of the nose just slightly to suggest its possibility. But we
cannot capture the act of conversation, which is the act in which we
know each other. Even the best portrait is therefore always a likeness in which something is just a little wrong around the mouth.

There is another aspect of portrait painting that conspired to
make me unable to paint Byron, and unable not to love him. When
you paint a portrait you sum up a life. With Byron, you could not
do this, because he was one person one instant and of a completely

different species the next. His nature was irreducible. For an addict of novelty, such as Casanova had taught me to be, this aspect was irresistible. It was impossible to be bored by Byron, though you might easily be outraged by him. Every quality was spiced by an infusion of its opposite. Every sentence was a confessional and a mockery of that confession. A portrait must reveal all the qualities that are the sitter's alone. No one painting could express that of Byron. Even a triptych, of angel, devil, man (which I considered, and then feared the consequences of this profanity in Ali Pasha's violent court) would not have expressed it properly. Byron, Hobhouse warned me, delighted in the failure of others, so he constantly dangled his image in front of portrait painters. Now it was for me to try to grasp him.

Casanova had not liked overmuch to be painted; he was not sufficiently fond of the shape of his own skin to keep it constantly in his sight. He offered himself humbly as a model, to help me. When he studied the results, he was looking chiefly at the progress of my technique. I think Casanova felt that it had been enough, by the time I met him, to carry about that image of himself, which he had not designed, and merely accepted, let alone to have it carried around for posterity. Remember, he had told me, 'To tell you the truth, I have always looked like a great sinner.' And there was a weariness in his voice, as if his appearance had forced him endlessly to enact the sins it promised.

Byron was exactly the opposite. He wanted himself stamped all over the future. He had mirrors everywhere, to catch himself. He loved any kind of water, particularly water in which he could see himself. He loved the dusty windows at Newstead, which trapped his image in reflection. But those mirror-portraits were merely ghosts of Byron's present reality. When he did not look at them, they vanished.

So he commissioned portraits: oils, engraving, pencil sketches. From his earliest years, he collected images of himself. And these portraits gave him access to himself: to angles he could not always capture in the mirror; to poses he could not always hold; to a youth that would not ever fade. They could preserve forever a sexual attractiveness that would never fatten or slacken from its glamour. Portraits caught him at his moment in time, and stretched that moment of supremacy into the infinite. No one could ever forget George Gordon, Lord Byron, with a portrait of him in the room.

I had finished my preliminary sketches. I was ready to start the main work.

Byron thought he had set his own scene, but, experienced sitter that he was, he did not see my infinitesimal adjustments to what he thought he had prescribed. He wanted a life-sized picture. But I did not paint people to their full size. I always painted them a fraction smaller. This is because, even in sociable Italy, we tend to stand a little distance from each other, so we see each other just a little smaller that we really are.

I usually painted with three-quarter light upon the face. This is the most flattering illumination because it avoids the asymmetry usually revealed by a full-face view. Asymmetry is antipathetical to our notion of perfect beauty. I hasten to add that almost no one is perfectly beautiful, in a technical sense, and those who are often in fact appear to have something lacking.

Sometimes I lit my subjects from underneath, which could create a sense of drama and even of the occult. To imitate Rembrandt I would hang a chandelier directly over the head of the sitter, perhaps two and a half feet above it. For people with a luxuriant coiffeur, this was a gift, for it made of their hair a spun jewel. I always worked in the dim light of a candelabra so that I could exaggerate to myself and therefore lie convincingly in oil about the beauty of my sitters. Candlelight erases wrinkles but preserves the essential structure of

the facial bones. It enables the painter to be faithful and to flatter at
the same time.

So, although it was morning, I drew the curtains, and lit the
tapers when Byron came in and assumed his pose with studied
carelessness. His body was comfortably disposed on the Pasha's
sofa. He presented his left profile, upraised to eliminate the incip-
ient double chin I had already detected. He turned his head this way
and that in the wash of candlelight till he found the place where the
little flames burned out the shadows of his nose, leaving it pure, delicate, tulip-like. As if unconsciously, he ran his fingers through his
hair. Afterwards, a feather of hair crested his delicate ear and a small
curl lay upon his neck like a caress. *He knows all the tricks*, I thought,
he has left me no blemishes to subdue.

I myself had one more trick to cajole a dazzling portrait out of
him. I put on my hat with little clips around the crown. To each clip
was affixed a tiny lighted taper. Now I approached Byron, gazing as
languidly as a Madonna. I did not meet his eyes, but let mine slide
slowly over every angle of his face.

Without actually touching him, I nuzzled him with the pinpoints
of light on my crown of thorns. The tenderness of my examination,
the caress given only in silhouette upon the wall, had its effect. I felt
the coolness on my throat when he drew in his breath. He forgot to
be beautiful. He let me describe him in light. I circled him, gentling
touching his eyes, his eyelashes, his brows, his lips, with the points
of my light. Then, as I had hoped, he raised his eyes to me in what
seemed a visionary gaze. That was what I would paint, and I knew
that it would sit well with him afterwards.

When I withdrew to paint my first colour sketches of Byron, he
seemed dazed. He had watched me all morning, with tiny motions
of his eyes. He was too expert a sitter to move his head. He had
some hours to recover his thoughts. As I opened the curtains to
show him that the first sitting was over, he announced his own

findings: 'Today I studied your mouth – it was more inviting than I had thought before. You know, Madame Cecilia, you should allow me to kiss it, for the sake of the painting. How can you paint my lips unless you know how they feel?'

The kiss again, traduced again, I thought. I said, 'You can tell me about how they feel. When I am painting your eyes, or some other part.'

'Some other part? Which other part? May I choose? We ought to talk less and feel more, Madame Cecilia.'

'But you are a writer, my Lord – your trade is words. From your own lips, of your own lips, I will believe what you say of them, and paint it. Other than that, you must allow me to practise my own trade as best I can.'

'But you need my help. Take my lips. Your painting can show the world how they looked in the moment of execution, but it cannot show how they got to be that way. You see my lips: they are full, they are bruised with kisses, they turn slightly at the corners because of the tragedies I have suffered. Now that you have heard this from me, and also because' – he was so sure of himself – 'you have already heard these things about me, you will paint those lips better than before.'

He paused. 'But you are still not doing your best work, because you have not kissed them yourself.'

Byron did not like sexual aggression in his women. He was stupefied when I calmly put down my brush and conducted a perfunctory act of research upon his lips. I already knew from my long researches that beautiful lips do not always taste ambrosial. I found Byron's tinny to taste and unyielding in their surprise. There was a faint smell of vinegar. I returned to my easel and said, 'Now I continue in full knowledge of your lips. I hope you will be satisfied with the result.'

His voice was high and agitated. The words spilled out of him. 'No I am not satisfied, you have not given satisfaction, you have not even taken it. It was a horrible kiss. I thought you Catholic women kissed better than anyone. I thought that worshipping your little idols made you experts in osculation. How could you kiss me like that? It was a cold kiss. Perhaps you prefer your own kind?'

I ignored the question. He waited for a second and then almost whimpered, 'A kiss as cold as that could hurt a loving heart.'

To this, I replied, 'Your own organ is safe, in that case. It was a cold reason I kissed for. And, I feel, a cold heart that I investigated.'

Byron drew himself into *Childe Harold* pose. 'It has become that way,' he declaimed, with a tragic sigh. 'I am cursed. I was born a poet, a nobleman, but the world has had its way with me. My fate has been confounded by the horrors of the love of women. My fortune is persistently evil. Everything is against me. If I had been born a pimp, whores would have been born without clacks. As it was, I was born with too much heart, and I find everywhere women who love me with just fragments of their being. This is what it is to be born a Byron.'

He pronounced his name as if the nectar of an oyster had trickled onto his tongue. He sank back in his chair, his eyes electrical, his colour high. He was waiting for me to capture this moment. But I turned my back on him and started to clean my brushes. When I looked around, he was gone.

My victories over Byron were tiny in the scheme of things. When I examined my painting, I found that I had failed to capture him. The man, yes, I had him – on his terms, of course – if I wanted him, but the portrait eluded me. I wanted him. Now that he was gone, I felt a commotion in my bowels. My hands were dry. The stem of the paintbrush trembled between my fingers. The hairs pricked on the back of my wrists. For all my bravado, I knew that I was falling into the danger of worshipping a graven image. I had not painted anyone so beautiful before. For the allure was not just the perfections of his features but the excitement trapped inside them.

He was back in my studio an hour later, with the smell of porter upon his breath, determined on revenge. I could see that he considered our physical intimacy already begun.

In what I was to learn was his usual way, Byron seduced me with a double-pronged attack of coldness and heat. That afternoon, he turned the mosaic of his character to the light and let it glitter selectively for me. One minute, he was the English milord, commissioning a portrait for his new book from a tradeswoman-artist. Next minute he was an adolescent, breathing hotly in my ear as I bent over him, whispering endearments to my neck, his hands reaching almost shyly for my breasts, saying to me, 'You've painted enough men. Look at this face. This man's in love. You know the smile. And I know *this* of *you*, Cecilia. I've been asking about you. For all your frigid kisses, what you don't know about the love of men could be written on your paint rag, with room left over for all of Pietro Aretino.'

So he had found out about Casanova; he had done a little research of his own. I chose to find this flattering. I laughed at him and pushed him away, but a ghost of my arm reached out of my body to pull him back to me. Then I saw a smile on his lips, a real smile, his first.

And truly, under that smile of Byron's, my life came to life. I found out that day that Byron had this ability to create a private climate, where the sun shone episodically, and was to be cherished all the more for it. I knew that he was *particolare*. Not everyone could endure him. Not everyone would want to do so. But he seemed special in a way that included me. His very originality somehow rendered the difference in our ages, cultures and experience all irrelevant. What was more important was that he included me in his consciousness, as a part of himself. When I was there he made me realise that I had been lonely, perhaps for years. I was still lonely. The difference was that I knew it now.

At the thought of Byron my celibacy — of the heart and of the skin — suddenly rattled inside me. Since Casanova's death, nine years before, I had not found anyone to love properly. While he still lived I had at least rejoiced in my flesh as he had counselled me to do, while glutting my heart on a continuous diet of loving words from Dux. But after he died I no longer had much enthusiasm for adventure. I felt that my body had been ransacked by careless use. So I kept it more often to myself, and I had little use for recreational intimacies, even with older men. It seemed to me that when I tried them, I was conscious of a shadow falling upon my skin when I returned from wherever the anonymous hands, mouths and members had taken me. It was rarely anywhere far outside myself. It was a shadow of what real lovemaking is, muffled in the grey timbre of a second-best experience. I could never escape the cold feeling it carved upon my skin. So I avoided careless loves — mostly.

Only occasionally I would take on a pupil, turn him into Casanova's unwitting disciple. Whether I did this simply to satisfy the hunger of my skin or with secret hopes of something more, I don't know. Perhaps I needed their faces to protect me from my own, or from the loneliness that lurked in waiting for me since Casanova died. Hobhouse, always the expert on obscure tribal matters, had given me cause for thought on this. In Bengal, Hobhouse told me, the woodcutters wear mask portraits attached to the back of their heads. This is because tigers will only attack from behind. They will follow a woodcutter wearing a mask, but they will not attack him. Many a Bengali woodcutter has been saved by his portrait. In the same way, once or twice I had been saved from the solitude stalking me by making the beast with two backs, with an unsuspecting man. But I had never opened my heart. I had not once fallen in love with one of those sitters, neither one of those tiresomely avid young men or those excitingly cool old counts.

And what else had I to do with my heart? I had withheld it so carefully for all those years, since Casanova. I was forty years old. Since Casanova died, I had never once been foolish. I had always been perfect. My problems were confined to souring in the gallipots and stiffenings of my brushes. I had taken no risks. I had never been in physical danger. I had walked the *passerelle* during *acqua alta*, not pushed my skirts through the dark sinews of the water. I had become a famous artist, but I had not left the coddle of the nursery. I did not know how to make a *risotto*. I had never chased a rabbit across a field, leaving my shoes in the long grass. I had now carried my bathtub of my own canvases all over Europe but I had never tried to create my own new colour. I had not risked a foreign frame.

For what had I been withholding myself? For Casanova? For a dead man? For a memory? For nothing. I would not withhold myself any more. For two decades I had been a conduit for other people's lives as I saw them written on their faces. I had painted their joy and their pain, as an anonymous scribe. *It is sad to be like that*, I suddenly thought, *I should have something for myself.* There was something about Byron that promised me something real, visceral. It might be infernal or it might be sublime. Byron made me feel that, with him, I might experience something that would make my *own* life worth painting.

Even as I philandered with these ideas, I knew what I was doing. This is how an addict of novelty, who holds everything new in too high a regard, persuades herself to do something dangerous.

By the next morning, our game had advanced. We sparred as old lovers, gave each other small wounds. Within a day, we had scars to make gentle over, or to lacerate anew. Byron had this way of penetrating your consciousness and extracting a return. He was the champion of the sulkers. But hours of sullen silence would end with an exquisite compliment, which answered your exact need of him, to which your insecurities rendered you doubly absorbent.

He said, 'How have you been able, so suddenly, to charm this warmth into my heart? It was free and empty, and cold as chastity, before I met you.'

He said, 'Since I have known you, the world is beginning to become bearable, even loveable again.' At the word 'love', my blood ran dappled inside me.

He said, 'Our conversations cannot possibly date just from yesterday; we have been thinking the same thoughts, in our separate worlds, for years.' I thought, *Pietro Aretino, conversazione, empty heart.*

What defence can you make against such an attack on your soul? My self-restraint lay down and expired under his sentences.

It seemed to me another compliment that Byron was intensely curious about Venice. He had read much about it, and wanted to see it, but he was already almost too involved with it. Venice was in his plans. But it became clear to me that he wanted to see it when his own splendour was fully realised and not before.

'I think that I have conjured you, Cecilia, out of the air,' Byron said, laughing. 'I come to Albania, and I find a beautiful Venetian woman who knows the secrets of *Vathek*. I am magical, you know!'

And he clicked his fingers three times in the air, like castanets.

In Venice, we say:

> *Chi varda la luna casca in fosso.*
>
> If you look at the moon you fall in the ditch.

That night, while I waited for him – his hand had promised me this visit in the language where masculine accords with feminine – I went out to consult the moon about this new event in my life. I paced the terrace, my bare feet rustling like beetles on the cool stone.

How often we consult the moon. How many decisions we take under her! It is as if we believe that the crystalline light she throws can cut through the dark canals of our thoughts. When we see the moon we instinctively clutch for the hand of our lover. If our lover is absent we say, 'Look! the moon has my lover's face! How kindly he looks down on me tonight!' The Orientals say that the moon has the face of a rabbit upon her. I say, yes, probably, she is as blank and timorous. She gave me no help. The moon and I suffered each other to soliloquise for a few moments, nothing more. But the cool air cleared my head and I was able, possibly for the last time, to think clearly about Byron.

I knew well that he had several interests in me, none of them disinterested. The first was simply that he wanted me to paint him: *Childe Harold* needed an image to illustrate it. He might never again be so beautiful as he was now, slender, healthy and vigorous from his travels. He wanted his beauty captured. He trusted me to do this; he acknowledged my artistry. My love for him would polish all my gifts.

The second was a sense of needing to prove himself against the most famous lover the world had yet known. A man who had given his name to a life of sexual splendour . . . an outlaw, an exile, a writer, a man whom history would not forget. Although he refused to discuss it with me, I was sure that this was a part of his thinking: whatever Casanova had had, Byron wanted some of that, too.

Then there was Beckford and my connection with *Vathek*. I suspected that even if Byron had not found me personally attractive, he would have wanted me for that.

And I knew that I was worth having on my own account. I still had the audacious sensuality that Casanova had detected when he saw me eat *torta al cioccolato*. I was amusing, vivid to the ear. My breasts still caused disturbances. The Pasha himself had indicated at dinner, addressing my bosom rather than my face, that I might be made very happy by him.

But as for me, I was vulnerable. We all create the image of our new lover out of our own needs, and not from what exists in front of us.

Crede Biron, said his motto. And I believed him when he told me that we two exotic outcasts should be together. I believed him when he told me that he had not given his heart to anyone for years, and that it lay, throbbing with his need for me, inside the open wound the world had slashed in his breast. All I had to do was plunge my hand inside and take out his heart . . . it was mine, if I wanted it. His very need made me want him. I heard again and again his words to me: 'It is fatal to love me. I never could keep alive even a dog that I liked or that liked me.' I wanted to be the woman who rescued him from this pain. He released a compassion in me that I did not know I possessed. Taught by Casanova, I was never the kind of woman to torment an aspiring lover who was going to succeed. Casanova always used to say, 'He who arouses desires is probably destined to satisfy them.' I consented my part in what would happen, and my culpability in it.

And yes, I had my less sentimental motives. Byron was a man whose contempt froze everything around him. I rose to the challenge of making his warmth shine upon me. I wanted to be included in his party of one against the rest of the world. And yes, maybe in me, there was an answering egotism: I had been loved by Casanova; now I wanted to be loved by this beautiful man who seemed to me to embody the cut, style and strange sexual omnivorous nature of this selfish new century.

And yes, Byron had beautiful hands and delectably small ears. He had eyes that melted my hands in my pockets. Yes, for those things alone I wanted him, the way I once wanted *torta al cioccolato*, the way Casanova had once wanted me.

I lay in my bath and thought all these things as my hands swam through the water. After a while I lay motionless like a little reptile preserved in a bottle. When I finally rose from the bath all its perfumed oils seemed to have leached into my skin. I secreted musk and lavender from my every pore. I fluttered a linen chemise over my head and lay on my bed. I blew out the candle.

But that evening, in anticipation of our tryst, Byron's foreplay was one-sided. He went to a Turkish bath, where the washing was performed by beautiful young men. He was frightened away by a fierce and unprepossessing old masseur, so he came to me dirty, with regrets for the slim fingers of boys upon his lips. It was part of his play for power. For how could I compete? He was already discounting what we were to do together, before we had touched one another. His flesh was already alight when he walked into my room, but I was to know at once that it did not burn exclusively for me.

He came to me, with the sweat of the day and the semen of the last days upon him. He did not knock. He opened the unlocked door to my apartment where I lay sleepless in the dark.

He carried his own candle. He held it under his chin so the full lips swelled to Nubian proportions.

'It is very kind of you to bring me a candle, my Lord,' I said, from inside the curtains of my bed.

'Yes, very kind,' he said, and blew it out. I heard him lay his pistols on the table.

'I reek to hell,' he said in the dark.

'It doesn't matter,' I said. The smell did not matter — it had spiked my nostrils as he walked in — but the insult had already stained this first night indelibly.

Now he leant against the carved bedpost. He was in no hurry. I understood this parry. I was to know from it that his passion for me was not insuperable. In the foamy moonlight, I saw the white swivel of his eye. I was also to realise that he did not wish to see my face. I felt them, suddenly, the small grooves and sags that he did not want to see. My hand swam, involuntarily, to my chin so I could stretch the skin back. I snouted my shameful too-large feet away under the sheet.

I was disheartened. I had been loved properly. I suddenly realised why people prefer to make love naked only with those who really love them. Only with love can the flaws of the body be forgiven. I was about to be judged on the coolest of criteria. I knew that it was wrong to invite this sophisticated coldness into my life. If I could not have love then I should find something closer to the animals, and enthusiastic like they are. I told myself to send Byron away and send a servant for one of the merchants from my journey. That would be safer than this.

I did neither of those things.

Meanwhile Byron mouthed the prepared text, 'I am your slave tonight, Cecilia. Make me your king.' I said nothing, hoping he would fill the space with words specially for me. I wanted him to leave the words in the room when he left, for me to cling to. I longed to inspire them. I did not. Somewhere in the dark corridors outside, a door slammed. It was the last noise I heard. Then the tongue of his dagger parted the whispering silk hangings of my bed.

'And so, Cecilia, I come in quest of the Carbuncle of the Giamschid. I think I spy it there all rosy on the sheets. I should per-haps have brought the balm of Mecca to lubricate it. But I did not.'

He was showing me his empty hands and laughing when he entered my bed.

He unbuttoned but he did not undress. He did not look at me. I felt more lonely than I had ever done in my life, in the moment when Byron became my lover.

He humiliated me. He made me lift my own chemise to bunch in a soft 'u' an exclamation above my genitals. He made me do it out of my own desire for him. He made me do it by not doing it himself.

His tongue was hard. I smelt English vinegar. He was small, but it was almost another reason to love him. He so needed not to be small, and he so needed me not to know that he was. He did not let me touch him before he entered me, distracted me with lunging bites and pinches, and in the moments afterwards, he let my own desire and imagination magnify him inside me. He said nothing, so I said nothing. It did not last long, the first time, but neither did the pause before he pulled me on top of him again. It took all night for him to exhaust himself, because he gave so little each time. He snatched at my chemise, my hair, but never my skin. I hungered and scrabbled for him in the bed, but he was not mine, not for a second.

We did not sleep; we were never at peace. But at the last minute, before he left, he laid a finger gentle as milk across my eyes, as if erasing what I had seen of his naked needs in the darkness. I pulled the finger down to my mouth. I sucked, looking up at him. I met a faceful of pain. He tore my lip with his fingernail in his panic to pull his finger from my mouth. He stumbled as he took the heavy pistols from the table and did not look behind him.

Why did I fall in love with Byron? I told you, already. Because he emptied me. It felt like fainting.

'Your love is not like love,' I told him, as he walked away. My mouth tasted of blood.

'What is it like?'

I said, 'It is like death.'

This pleased him. He stopped for a moment. With his back to me, I saw him measure the words in his ears. I knew I would see them some day upon the page. Then he asked me, as he opened the door, 'Did I not give you pleasure?'

But what little he gave, he took back later.

8

La dona xe come un indovinélo,
dopo spiegà no 'l xe più quelo.

A woman is like an oracle:
once explained, she loses her delectation.

VENETIAN PROVERB

From that moment, Byron lost interest in me, and I fell in love with him. 'I am your slave, make me your king,' he had whispered in the folds of the sheets. 'You are my slave, you are my slave,' he meant. I had known this, but I consented to it.

And so, I suppose, I had consented then to all that followed. For had I ever believed, even for a moment, that his heart was free and disposed to love me? He had seemed to offer it to me, but I always knew he kept it on a string fastened to his skin. By what right, then, did I feel pain to see that, when he rebuttoned himself, he jerked his heart back into his pocket? How pointless was it to grieve when he put it away so that I might never see it again?

'Cecilia, be careful,' Hobhouse said, gently. It was not in me, or in Byron. But it was only then that I remembered that Byron had not used an English Overcoat. My golden ball lay dry and smooth in its leather pouch in my trunk. I did not care. My desire for Byron already exceeded my interest in the consequences.

Desire. I know now that it is better to be without its sharpening beak between your legs. The point at which a painfully beautiful love becomes only painful is hard to recognise and by then, of course, it is too late.

I saw it first with Byron when, the next day, we sat together in my studio, discreetly observing in each other the lineaments of the night before. It was a quick transaction. I asked nothing and received nothing, except recognition of my outer shape. Soon Byron was gazing not at me, but at my portrait of him. I ventured my hand on to his thigh – he let it stay there as he would a fish that had not yet commenced to stink. I could not believe it. I left it there a little longer, so that he would have a chance to redeem it, but no, there was no responsive gesture. His hand did not arch up to meet my palm. He did not enclose my hand in his. He did not stroke my fingers.

Then, as we say in Venice, a devil attached itself to each of my hairs. I knew the right thing to do was to remove my hand casually, as if it had only accidentally occupied his thigh, but my delinquent limb lay there upon his knee. I stared at it, my five-fingered enemy flattened like a dehydrating fish on his immaculate linen. My beautiful hand! For the first time, I looked at it and it did not please me. It seemed to me that it no longer glowed with the liquid petal-pink of a conch shell's private interior. The skin, I thought, had tessellated, like the surface of the Grand Canal in a tight wind. My hand was not tender; it was waxy. It was still a beautiful hand but nothing could make it what it had once been. The light no longer suffused it. It needed to be held to have pleasure, and warmth. I removed my hand and bit my fingers to hide the sad outline of my mouth. But I put it back there on his thigh. I had, after all, consented to be treated like this.

I knew immediately this was to be the pattern of our days together. I was already exhausted by my longing for his touch. My exhaustion stole the strength I needed to stop wanting him. I was hollowed out with bravery. I was *excavated* with being brave. I was taut for any expression of affection, outside of the bedchamber. I realised that for some time now I had been panting quietly when-ever I was with him. My hand stayed on his thigh. Now I hung my head like a dog that has begged and been ignored.

Yes, love is a hostile transaction. He was right, Byron. You win if you don't say, '*I love you.*' You win if you make the first move to leave.

I swallowed the tears clenched in my throat, because I could not utter them. But then those Venetian devils started to ruffle my hairs, to pull and tangle. I could not help myself. I did not consent after all! I refused to be condemned to a meagre portion of love: I had been loved properly. The little Venetian fish on his lap curved itself and then pinched hard.

Even as I pinched Byron, I raged at myself: *be careful you will lose him*. There was an angry exclamation from those full lips. My hand was shaken off his knee. My time with him was already curtailed. A minute later, he turned me on my stomach, lifted my petticoat, and unfurled his arms like wings around me. But the end of his interest in me was looming closer.

Whichever Byron was, dog or prince, the other was always in my mind, tormenting me with doubts about my position in his heart. I hovered over that debatable land between adoration and obses-sion. My Libran scales tilted violently, one way and another. You see it too, with his poetry. There is this same contrast between Byron's reverential concept of Man, and his contempt for men themselves, and for women. People reading his poetry are alternately sunk and elevated, as if the hand of an invisible being pulls them up or down, without compassion for their disappointments or their joys. People in love with Byron felt likewise.

What could I do? Byron was so addictive. With Byron in my arms I felt an insolent happiness. In the rare moments where we lay together in the bed, the sheen of our lovemaking cooling to droplets on our naked bodies, our hair tangled together, I felt an intimacy I had not felt with anyone since Casanova. I realised how I had longed for a head on the pillow beside me, a head with which I could share thoughts and not just kisses. Byron continually challenged me and made me angry with a good cleansing rage. Then he softened me with a little hand clutching mine like a child's. He made me think. He made me aware of myself. He was the only person who ever said to me, 'Cecilia, how would *you* feel if someone painted *your* portrait?'

'Possessed, violated,' I said, wonderingly.

'Then be gentle with me,' he said.

'But you write poems that are *self*-portraits.' I said. 'Is there not a particular word for that?'

'Manustupration, you think?'

'Perhaps you don't trust anyone else to make an accurate portrait, one that is sufficiently beautiful?'

I stopped myself there. The sentence that hovered unsaid in the damp air between us was this: *Because there is no one who loves you with the passion that you feel for yourself.*

I could have said it. He would have liked me for it. Byron loved the effrontery of the truth. He was capable of moments of astonishing honesty. He was capable of seeing himself as he was. He could be as savage with himself as he was with others. He was afflicted with a scorn for himself as strong as any he inflicted on others. Sometimes he looked comically thunderous, like a monstrously naughty child who had hurt himself and needed to be kissed better.

He said nothing at all that could be counted as a declaration of love. But he seemed so painfully on the verge of it that I felt sorry for him. He would start, 'Cecilia, you are . . .' and stammer to a standstill, blush, busy himself with a curl or a cuff. Or he would limp from the room with his small ears on fire.

Without him, I waited. I was old enough to know the value, the shame and the pity of those hours I spent waiting for Byron. It was the first time in my life that someone had kept me waiting. And his reasons for leaving me waiting were so diminishing – a horse needing attention, a meeting with a man who sold embroidered felt slippers. All these were more important than being with me. Sometimes it was not the substance of the excuse but the careless way in which it was delivered that corroded my self-confidence. I was not used to this, and I was undextrous in handling it. Instead of fighting, I went down in an instant. If Byron thought less of me than a horse or a slipper, I felt that I must consent to my new place in the world, and the result of this was that I was even more grateful for his attention when it came to me.

Between my legs my desire swung backwards and forwards like a lighted censer.

I remembered something Goethe had told me, a German proverb: 'Desire enfeebles her slaves.'

Of course, I fell to daydreaming sometimes. I pushed my knuckles against my eyes to obstruct reality.

Into the pulsing darkness comes Byron. He comes to my bed; it is heaven there with him.

He is not limping. He is whole, and perfect.

'Cecilia, I have something important to tell you.'

His shoulders shudder with a little sob, the pain of his final parting from the vagabond life of his heart. He lays his head down upon the pillow. I cover him with my body in a warm embrace.

I fasten my mouth to the back of his neck like a mollusc and suck gently until he whimpers and turns around to reach for me.

He says, 'I give my life to you, Cecilia. I beg you to take it with both hands.'

He leans forward to kiss me, but first he licks my lips, tenderly.

He has brought me a gift – a peach. To celebrate the marriage of our

*souls, we eat the peach together, bite by bite, and lick the juice from each
other's chins.*

And so I betray you, Casanova.

Byron was never late for a portrait session.

No one had ever caught the sensuality of his lips before. I loved
that challenge, and even when kissing I was grasping a paintbrush in
my imagination. I sometimes had the curious sensation that he was
himself directing his kisses towards that paintbrush, too. He was
even more desperate than I that the result of our lovemaking should
be an enhancing portrait of him: he wanted my love for him to glaze
the image he could show the world. He scratched his name on my
palette with a quill, scoring through the dried paint. I tried to see this
graffiti as a declaration of love, but I knew it was something different.

And, as I had guessed, I shared his passion for me with his passion for my past. When we made love, I felt as if he was always
sniffing my skin to detect the musk of Casanova's. I was a vessel: just
as I interpreted his beauty, so I should also transmit his desire
instead of receive it.

I was aware of this, aware of the coldness and impersonality of his
love, even at its most hectic moments, and I feared that I would lose
him when the portrait was finished. So I spun it out, sketching
study after study, each with something not quite satisfactory to his
vanity, but with beauty which teased his ego. He was never tired of
looking at all these pictures of himself, and refining the exact image
of himself which he wanted to survive him. I realised that with my
evening sketches I was re-enacting for him *The Thousand and One
Nights* he had loved as child. Maybe he was aware of this process.
Perhaps he saw how I prolonged my love-life with him through my
creativity, and he perhaps enjoyed the knowledge.

Our words never revolved in those magic configurations of 'us'
and 'we'. And we never strayed into the Elysian fields of words

with a future; we forswore 'shall' or 'tomorrow' or 'always'. Byron was a brilliant strategist when it came to sleeping. Whenever I summoned the courage to say something important to him, not daring to look at his face while I did so, the silence at the end of my words would force me to turn to him. He would be catnapping.

Even then, I knew I had to fight for his attention, forage for anecdotes to amuse him. I faced him after lovemaking, finding, each time, my physical peace shattered by the utter detachment on his face. But whenever he felt me giving up, he refreshed my hope and my despair with a slight caress. He would not quite let go. He would never allow me to finish the question: 'When . . .?' He would say, 'Cecilia, my darling, do not spoil my dinner. I dine with the Pasha tonight. Don't be selfish.'

The Pasha was only rarely in the palace now. His political troubles had exploded into violence and he was often absent with his men and commanders. Byron was fretful when the Pasha was away. Sitting with him on one of the deep palace window-sills, I once took his hand and kissed it. He looked over my head, out of the window, as if someone had called him.

I asked, 'Byron, are you restless now?'

'I wasn't, but you have put me in mind to be so.' Then he commenced an inhuman howling. I recognised the noise. It was the same howling I had heard in the hills of Jannina on my way to Tepelene. He, too, must have heard it and been moved by it.

He wants to leave, I thought. *He wants to get away from me already.*

The more I painted him, the more I loved him. I, of all people, should have known the dangers of worshipping graven images. I should have realised why we are warned against them. In early Christian times, the evil spirits were supposed to be possessed of huge eyes that never closed, and to glide up and down with their feet together, as if propelled upon the wind. This was very like Byron's undulating slither.

I looked at my Muslim hosts, worshipping their abstract images, and envied them their independence of the human face. Surrounded by their art, their colours, their ceremonies, I absorbed the incense of their faith through all my organs of perception. I was infected with a spiritual unease: I had broken the spiritual law of their country by worshipping Byron and lived in an abstract fear of my punishment. Of course, we all turn the person we love into the person we worship. The artist does this in a simple way, with each successful portrait. But we all do it in more complex ways, for religious faith has lately become subsidiary to personal adorations in this world. Byron had converted me to this new cult with his beautiful face. Now I would pay for my heresy.

We sat together in an open-air marquee where the Albanians performed a primitive tragedy for the entertainment of the foreigners. It was so simple there – the villain wore black, the whore wore red. But what to do with the villain sitting next to me, as indifferent as lead? The players cast their huge shadows on the wall, the projections of their larger-than-life passions. The problem with Byron's was that they were smaller than life. I had learnt not to put my hand on his knee.

Love hurt increases the value of the loved one by the amount of the hurt: this is as true as Pythagorean theorem. Despite the pain, I wanted no more independent existence than Byron's shadow had. I loved him more than my own skin. My heart was eaten by love. I ate nothing. I was eating my own flesh to appease my hunger for him. Byron hated fat women like his mother. I was thin already, but I would become a wraith to please him. It turned out that I had miscalculated sadly. Byron also hated thin women! As my cheeks hollowed, he looked upon them critically. He told me that excessively slender women looked like dried butterflies mounted upon pins; he swore he could hear the rustle of their wings. As for *older* women who tended towards emaciation, he said ominously, they looked like nothing more than ancient spiders tiptoeing around the parlour.

I washed myself obsessively, so as not to smell of myself. I felt myself dissolving, turning to a slight feminine miasma, folded and gathered in his possession, like a genie in a lamp. No one else should have me at their disposal. Only then would I feel safe in him. I found myself hating anyone else who came near Byron. I, who had never been jealous, not even of Casanova's one hundred and thirty loves, envied Hobhouse for the time he had spent alone with Byron! I was even jealous of my own piece of canvas when Byron traced his finger down it.

I still did not worry about the difference in our ages. It remained irrelevant. I remembered what Benjamin Franklin had told Casanova. Older women were better, he had said. '*They are so grateful*,' he had pointed out. '*All cats are grey in the dark.*' I knew that what separated me and Byron was not age, or language, but love. It was the difference between what I felt for him and what he felt for me.

My portraits were love letters to him. They grew larger, more colourful. I used all the canvas I had brought with me from Venice. There was no canvas to be had in Albania that was big enough for my love. Even Byron, when he beheld these mirrors, saw in them only half the beauties that I found in him. I no longer painted what I saw. I painted what I loved. At night, now, with closed eyes, I abandoned myself to him whether he came to me or not. I could not tear myself from certain hopes and dreams.

But Byron could tear himself away from me.

9

Un baso e 'na forbia, e 'l baso scampa via.

A kiss, wipe your mouth, and the kiss is gone.

VENETIAN PROVERB

There was no parting scene, as Byron did not tell me that he was leaving. I was oblivious to the preparations. I pined for him, but I had sufficient impressions of his skin upon my own to feast myself to delirium for hour after hour. I assumed that the Pasha had commanded his time that day. Hobhouse had disappeared too, so I could not talk about Byron to him. But I had my paintings of Byron to stroke, caress, and perfect. I had my memories to edit into a bearable sequence. When he did not come to me that night, I assumed the neglect was just a new phase of the hostile transaction Byron made of love. I had no revenge to plan. There was nothing I could do to hurt Byron, or at least nothing I could imagine at that moment. ·

The next morning I awoke early in that house of gently sleeping women. Among the female quarters of the Palace of Tepelene, it was pink all through. The air lay still in pink marble halls and hung over pale, pink sleeping princesses. Fern-feathers of hair thrummed against soft necks humid with invisible exhalations of their skin. Their moist breath floated from their sleeping lips, nestled under their languid arms and trailed around their warm limbs.

I, too, felt pink and soft that morning. I had woken in the mood to kiss and forgive. After all, what was a night? Then one of my little princesses came to my room and whispered, 'Do you miss the beautiful English milord, Madame Cecilia?' I ran in my chemise through the vertiginous corridors to Byron's rooms. Suddenly my nails were blades, my shoulders were teeth, and my breasts were mica.

In Byron's room I found a scene of paper carnage. The bright skins of Ali Pasha's fruits were flung among letters and used linen. I knew that he had gone. I found the hat he had worn for my last portrait on the floor. 'No!' I screamed. It was the hat he had worn for me. I could not bear to see it thrown down, just like that. With that loose gesture, he had gone. I lay down among his discarded linen. I took a mouthful of his nightshirt and crushed it in my teeth. It smelt and tasted of me, rich, salty, sweet, abandoned. I wrapped his pillow around my head, breathing the scent of his hair. I tried to choke the emptiness and silence of the room. Inside the pillow, I prayed, *Help me*, but I heard only my own breathing in the whiteness. I wrenched the pillow from my face and flung it at the door from which he had left me. I looked for the paintings he had insisted on taking to his room 'to study their defects'. They were gone. But my little notes to him, now running with the sticky blood of a red orange, were still there, among bills from the Tepelene jewellers. A fly settled on my lip, as if drawn to the things going to the bad within me.

Byron had left some words for me in the room. They were unwritten words. I heard them, even as my imagination heard the hooves of his horses in the distance.

It just went away, he said, *that love I had for you.*

Yes, it was quite wonderful for a while.

But no, it doesn't matter now what I said then, because now it has gone, and it is as if it had never been.

I tried to argue with the words, but they were implacable. They fell on me, like blows.

What are you still there? Are you still talking about my love as if it were still important?

No, I am not interested in seeing where it went, and if it will come back. I am going away. It is your fault for driving me away with all this talk of my love for you that doesn't exist.

What about your love? Well, that is your problem, isn't it? And you know I cannot discuss emotional problems. Anyway, I have no emotions which are to do with you.

Women look ugly when they cry.

The room became hostile. The words continued to force their way into my ears.

Now go away. I don't love you, so you can't even make me feel uncomfortable.

I fled, spattering the marble floors with traceless footprints. For I had become what he had made of me: nothing.

Help me, I cried aloud to Casanova. *Help me*, I cried to his cat, who used to carry away my tears in his fragrant coat. I hungered for the cat's fish-breath, his muzzle thrust into my hand, his little red rag of a tongue on my fingers and his paws kneading my belly. *Help me*, I cried to my work. *Help me*, I cried to the minarets of Tepelene. And days later, I was still begging, *help me*, mutely, to motherly women in the street; to men who looked like Casanova, even fleetingly; to any cat, however it fled me. *Help me.* A messenger came to the palace to tell us that the author of this pain now stood on the deck of a boat bound for Greece. Hiding in the marble bathhouse of the palace, I tried to rearrange my *help me*'s into a more effective prayer.

There are people languishing in prison who have not paid their jewellers' accounts, but the promissory declarations and letters of love – no one ever punishes their violation! They go free, the perpetrators of those little murders, those capital offences against happiness, those crimes of lack of passion. There are many kinds of murder; the victim does not actually have to die. It kills not to know where someone is, or what is going on. To be denied information about the lover is to have the very air around you stoppered in the bottle where it grows stale and poisonous. That is another death. That was my death, in those days.

Why doesn't one simply die when left by the person one loves? *Insopportabile*, we say in Italy: we cannot support pain like this. It would be kinder to be left to die. But I could not suffocate my grief. I could not breathe for the invisible kick to my stomach. But what drove me to madness was the recollection of times that were no more, and could not be, for there could be no other lover for me like Byron. I had committed a few moments of intimacy and understanding with Byron to memory, where they replayed themselves like an opium-taker's dream, but more vividly.

I did not know anything about this kind of pain, for I had been loved properly. I caught sight of myself in the bathhouse mirror. My mouth looked like a doll's, caught in a pout, rigid as china. I heard the door click shut behind me, and it felt like a confirmation. I was to be incarcerated with my grief. I could only contemplate another hour of it, if I could use that hour to destroy myself. I was indivisible from the pain. It already clung inside my body like a tumour.

Mouchar came to me, full of soft concerns. The ceremonial had vanished from his voice. He took my hand. 'Cecilia, perhaps it is for the best. There are things about the English milord that you should perhaps know, or should perhaps never know. We have an expression here: "Still a goat, even if he flies." Think on it.'

I screamed, 'I'd rather be dead than be without him!'

But in the end I knew that I would not commit the double murder of myself and the child inside me.

I knew that I was pregnant within days of Byron's departure, when he was still within reach of a messenger. Only once had I ventured to suggest the English Overcoats and he had dismissed the idea with a laugh. Why? I had secretly hoped that this refusal was a pledge for the future; I soon realised that it was careless contempt for the consequences of the present. Then, I too had become complicit in the carelessness. My little golden ball had remained inside its pouch.

The fact of my pregnancy was very different from the vagrant idea of it. I retched and vomited continuously and not just in the mornings. Mouchar came to me with a healer woman, who burned bitter herbs under my nose. The vomiting continued. I wondered how to tell him the truth. Then, suddenly understanding, he arrived in my room with a gnarled, kindly midwife, who opened a leather sack of fearsome instruments and spread them out upon the bed beside me. In his subtle way, Mouchar let me know I had a choice.

At the sight of the silver tools, an animal whimper of horror escaped from me. This was how we all knew that I had chosen to keep the baby. A look passed between me and the midwife, and she shrugged her shoulders. *Your blood has spoken*, she seemed to say. *We must listen to the blood and consent to what it tells us.* She gave me a smile that promised that she would be back to tend me in eight month's time. In the meantime, the women of the palace would look after me.

Mouchar asked, 'Shall I send a messenger to him now, Cecilia?'

I shook my head and my tears flew around the room. I knew how Byron had paid off the maid who bore his child. I had no desire to tell him about the baby. I had learnt how he transacted love and it

was not for me, or my child. Mouchar unfurled his own silk handkerchief and held it to my nose. I longed to weep against his
shoulder but I did not wish to frighten him away with the ferocity
of my grief. I felt that if I received tenderness from a human being
now I would become as wild as an animal and that I might hurt
someone.

I would need some years before the broken things inside me
stopped hurting when I moved. But I had art, and that would not
hurt me. And by then I was starting to fall in love with the creature
growing inside me. When you love with that power, you don't need
logic. As my belly grew, my thoughts diminished. I stopped working.
I became incurious, passive. I rested from being myself, preparing
to create a new life. I did not want my womb cancered with misery.
So I taught myself to wonder about nothing, except how my baby
would look.

I was dimly aware that trouble was afoot in Albania. Ali Pasha's
old enemies, Ibrahim Pasha and the Pasha of Sutari, encircled
Tepelene, and the smell of blood was in the air. There was murder
and cutting of throats in the mountains all around. The Pasha himself was with his men, in their encampments.

The only dramas that punctuated my day were the arrivals of
merchants and envoys from Greece and Turkey, for they brought the
stories which I fed on, of Byron and Hobhouse and their progress
through the East. I sat for hours in the window-sill that I had once
shared with Byron. I looked out on Albania, waiting for riders to
come with news of my lover. It occurred to me, one long, idle day,
that even if I did not paint, I was in the process of giving Byron a
portrait of himself for immortality. This portrait of him would be
made of his own flesh, and mine.

Part Three

1

L'amor se cazza in tuti i busi.

Love inserts itself in every hole.

VENETIAN PROVERB

I know this all now because Love made me a spy.

My obsession with Angelica Kauffman had taught me the honest ways and clean-handed work of research. But Love made me a shameful, shameless thief of information. Love made me a secret reader of other people's letters. Love taught me to refine my French and to speak English well enough to read the scurrilous English newspapers. Love taught me to make friends of English clients who might have information about him, and who might be relied on to keep it flowing to me, even after they left Venice and returned to London. Love taught me to charm his friends, Hobhouse and Mary Shelley, when I met them later, and to forage for their confidences about him. Love taught me to take a comment from Hobhouse or a comical phrase from his manservant Fletcher, add it to a sigh of Mary Shelley's and stitch it to a line in Byron's poetry or the draft of a note I stole from his desk. And from this, I could assemble a piece of Byron's history in my mind in the same way that I could assemble someone's life on canvas with only their face to give me clues.

But what kind of love is this, which is so greedy and so needy? Which feeds not on caresses but second-hand stories and gossip from the street? Which muses alone for quiet hours and acts stealthily in the night? It is an unrequited love, of course, a love that is not satisfied in the ways that demand satisfaction.

Hobhouse would tell me much later – and I believed him – that he for one had not wanted to abandon me at Tepelene, at least not furtively. '"Do the decent thing with Cecilia," I said to Byron, "Let her know that we are leaving at least, man!"' But Hobhouse had been rewarded with a Vathek-like stare.

'Perhaps he felt guilty?' I wondered. 'Perhaps he regretted it? Was he miserable after he left Tepelene?' I asked.

Hobhouse tried to be both tactful and honest but it was impossible to be both. He settled for silence, from which I knew the truth – that Byron had barely given me another thought, and that kindly, honest Hobhouse felt badly about it. All these years later, when everything is clearer to me, I marvel at the unshakeable decency of the man, and still try to understand why he allied himself to Byron. Was it just an instinct to not, for once, be boring? Was he in love with Byron like the rest of us? He too would one day know what it was to be abused and left by Byron. But on this occasion he had left with him.

What I know now, as a result of my spying, is this: sated with comfort, with palace life, and with me, Byron had renewed his desire for an intoxicating adventure. Perhaps he also feared the consequences of staying longer. I was not the only creature in Tepelene who clung to him. Nor was I the most demanding. Ali Pasha's velvety attentions had become so enclosing as to be threatening. When he heard of Byron's resolve, the Pasha, though disappointed to lose his beautiful young lord, offered him guides and an armed escort for the onward journey. All this had been negotiated, in the most extravagant and flourishing French, while I stood in my studio, cleaning my brushes two nights before.

On the morning of their departure the Pasha rose early to bid farewell to his guests, and the harems of both sexes were summoned, twittering under their veils, their jewels scintillating in the dawn light, to support their lord in his moment of loss. The little princesses were left alone in their beds, untended by their maids and midwives, who leant over the serried balconies to watch this strange leave-taking.

One of the midwives told me how Ali Pasha and Byron stood alone for a moment in the echoing courtyard. The light was as yet cold, but it gilded the bells on the horses and the chestnut curls of the English milord. It was a long time since Byron had seen the dawn but that day he had pressing reasons to be gone before the sun rose. The Pasha whispered something in his delicate ear. Byron pulled away and swallowed visibly. But he drew back to the Pasha and held out both his arms. Their last embrace seemed to be passionate to the point of pain. Breaking free, Byron limped to his horse.

All this happened while I lay sleeping, or trying to sleep in my room at the other side of the palace. While I soothed myself thinking that nothing worse could happen to me than to be abandoned by Byron for a night, the horses had been caparisoned, fowls slaughtered and boiled, sticky puddings wrapped in muslin and servant boys instructed how best to serve the English milord. While I rose and washed my face in rose-petal water at a marble bowl, on the other side of the palace Byron's horse stood steaming at the mouth and nosing the mare who was to carry Hobhouse. When I returned to my bed and lay there, schooling myself to forgive him for his night's absence, Byron was prancing out of the Pasha's courtyard with a sheaf of my portraits in his saddlebag.

By the time I was awakened by the little princess with the news of Byron's departure, the rest of the palace had gone back to bed, Ali Pasha with three of the harem boys and a dangerous pout. And when I lay on Byron's bed, filling my mouth with his linen, he was already far away in the tufted olive-green hills.

However, I do now know every detail of what happened next, not only from the lips of Hobhouse himself but from his book. When the worthy Hobhouse wrote his *Travels In Albania And Other Provinces Of Turkey, in 1809 & 1810*, he had no idea how much speculation he saved me. For I would be able to read between his rather pedantic lines – how well I remembered his obsession with detail! – and see the unsavoury side of every genteel romp that he described in their onward journey. Free from the cloying love he had drawn to himself in Tepelene, Byron rushed on towards new stringless experiences like a schoolboy released from lessons.

From Albania they planned to go to Greece by sea but their vessel was driven ashore in a tempest. They thought they would perish. Hobhouse would describe the gnashing of the waves and the death rattle of the timbers, and Byron's excitement. 'He seemed not to care whether we lived or died. He just stood on the deck in the moonlight, while the waves crashed around him. He kept saying to me, "This is life, Hob, this is really it."'

In the event, they were rescued by the Suliotes, barbarous subjects of the Pasha, and brought to their camp. 'We sat around the night fire watching them roast a goat, dance, and sing. When Byron offered them a few coins, the chief answered him, to his delight, "I wish you to love me, not to pay me."'

Hobhouse recalled, 'Byron asked me *how much* he should love the hairy chief. I advised him to calm himself. We were not yet out of the Pasha's territories.'

The sea had rejected them. They decided now to go by land to

Greece, a magnificent but bandit-infested ride through the mountains. At last they reached the plains and stopped in a small town with the haunting name of Missolonghi. It cast the shadow of its church spire on the edge of a vast sea lake. They were in Greece, at last, and bound for the East. Byron was alive with excitement, Hobhouse told me. 'He barely slept, would wake me at all hours and talk wildly of nothing at all.'

Athens, Cape Sunium, Smyrna, Constantinople . . . the journey turned even the sensible Hobhouse into a species of poet, travelling in the realm of his own senses as much as in this exotic new world. He described how they voyaged on amid the delicious perfumes of orange, citron and jasmine flowers. Windblown fragments of thyme and the sharp prickle of rosemary dilated their nostrils. The blood of the bougainvillaea dripped into their hair in the gardens of white-painted tavernas in the ports. Everything was alight with sensuality; at night, on the ship, they both heard unmistakable shufflings in neighbouring cabins. As they travelled along the Mediterranean coasts, they watched the sun drop into the arms of the olive trees every night. Merely to breathe was prodigiously fine poetry.

'And was Byron writing poetry?' I would ask Hobhouse one day. *Love poetry? The poetry of love, regret and loss?* I wondered silently.

'No, he was being a poet. There is a difference, you know.'

I knew. Instead of poetry, Byron made graffiti. He was much given to it. Hobhouse told me how Byron inscribed his name on a column at the monastery of the Panagia at Delphi and on the temple of Cape Sunium. At school, he had left his mark on wood and stone. I remembered my palette, on which he had etched his name. And I had tried to think this a shy declaration of love! The day Byron left Albania I had thrown the palette from the palace walls. I was afraid that in my obsession I might make it a votive object. He had left me nothing else that was tangible to worship.

And I was afraid that it would make bad portraits, that the paint I scooped from its surface would be tainted with the pain which he had caused me.

If Byron thought about me at all during this period, it was not manifest. I received no letter, no message and no payment for my paintings. He was not, it seemed, even curious about what had happened to me. He knew nothing of my uncontainable pain, of my sorrowful days and darker nights while his child grew inside me.

In Athens, Byron and Hobhouse saw the Parthenon, and witnessed the looting of her stones by Lord Elgin. Hobhouse told me how the Greeks suffered to see their marbles carried away, some even refused to load the crates onto the boat that was to take them to England. 'They believed that the statues contained spirits wailing in lament,' he explained, laboriously. The Greek workmen stood rapt on the quay, listening to the cries of the stones sentenced to exile. Byron stood with them. I wonder if he thought of me, looking at those other portraits wrought of ancient marble. I doubt it.

Hobhouse stumbled over the next part of the story. In fact, I already knew by the time he told me about it. An Albanian merchant, self-important and trussed up with gossip, had brought tales of Byron to the Palace of Tepelene, where everyone, from the Pasha to the serving girls, was eager to hear about the progress of the beautiful English milord in his onward journey.

Even now I find it hard to tell it, because this is how I was replaced. I bear Byron's next lover no ill-will, but I still burn for the fact that within weeks of leaving me, Byron fell in Greek love with a beautiful French boy, Nicolo Giraud. It seems that Nicolo's firm, sweet charms dispelled any lingering wisps of Byron's feelings for me. Nicolo, who was bilingual, completed the Italian lessons I had begun. By the time I next saw Byron we were able to talk entirely in my native tongue. This always gave me pain, for I was never able to forget how it had happened. I preferred to talk French or English with him.

No, Hobhouse would never talk to me of Nicolo, and perhaps he had reasons of his own for that too. I tried to question him later, and he begged me, 'Do not ask, please, Cecilia.'

Thinking of Nicolo, the pain swelled up inside me. I could no longer spare Hobhouse.

'Then tell me this. Did I mean anything to him?'

'Yes, Cecilia, yes.'

'How do you know?'

'Because he told me years ago, "Never mention Albania to me again."'

Hobhouse was more comfortable telling me how Byron had flirted with Teresa Macri, the twelve-year-old daughter of his land-lady, who had hopes of selling the girl for a high sum to the English milord.

'But he scorned the very thought. For it was some time since Byron had needed to pay for his pleasures,' said Hobhouse, and then blushed on realising what he had implied. He changed the subject hurriedly.

'Don't worry. Tell me the truth. Anything else insults me,' I said, vehemently.

'Byron was in rut, in Greece,' Hobhouse admitted. 'There was no shortage of willing flesh for him. He boasted that he had made love two hundred times since we left England.' Again, Hobhouse dissolved in blushes. What a war went on in his head when he was with me, poor man: a war between honorable honesty and gentle-manly modesty. I patted his large arm to show him that he had not behaved badly. But my head was filled with unwanted images and involuntary calculations. Of the two hundred acts of love, some were surely women. A dozen, if you could call them acts of love, had been with me.

After ten weeks in Greece, Byron and Hobhouse left on the *Pylades* for Smyrna. They arrived on March 6th. Travelling past caravans of camels and to the accompaniment of a hundred thousand noisy frogs, they saw Ephesus, and were haunted by the wail of jackals amongst the fallen columns. They witnessed the Albanians in their retinue being sold into slavery. They watched whirling dervishes in a coffee house and the dancing troupes, unfettered by decency, on the streets.

'This is the real thing,' Byron told Hobhouse.

Onwards and eastwards went Byron and Hobhouse. Back came the messengers and merchants to tell the inhabitants of the Palace of Tepelene all about it. On the way to Constantinople, they were delayed at the entrance to the Dardanelles, the narrow cleft that separates two continents, Asia and Europe. Byron spent hours diving for turtles. He was eager to imitate Leander, who had swum across the Hellespont to join his lover Hero, in the great tale. He made two attempts, failing the first time. The four miles throbbed to a strong, cold and dangerous current. Then, on May 3rd, he succeeded, swimming – an elegant breast-stroke, we were told – from Europe to Asia, in an hour and a half.

In Constantinople Byron dedicated himself to cultural and erotic explorations. Again he watched the young boys engaged in lustful dances in the wine shops – 'Disgusting!' Hobhouse would tell me later – and listened to the whirling dervishes howling in their ecstasy. 'You never heard such an unearthly caterwaul! And the smells that rose from those filthy skirts!'

Byron rode along the European side of the Bosphorus to the village of Belgrade where his heroine Lady Mary Wortley Montagu had once lived. He circumnavigated the walls of the Sultan's *seraglio*, a four-mile journey along triple ivy walls, past Turkish burial grounds tall with strange tombstones and cypresses. He was presented to the young Sultan Mahmoud II. Byron dressed in his red regimental splendour and an elaborate feathered hat for this ceremony as he had for Ali Pasha.

'He looked such a sight, Cecilia. I never saw him look so well. The travelling had suited him, and he seemed to have acquired a kind of Oriental grace. The sultan afterwards declared that he thought Byron was really a woman inside the fur coat. I never told him that, of course. Please don't say anything!' Hobhouse would implore.

'There is a feminine side to him,' I said.

'And never say that either, Cecilia. Better to say that there was something of the Levant or the Orient about him. He would prefer that. It was at this point that he started to say that he could not see not much difference between Englishmen and Turks, save that we have – excuse me, Cecilia – foreskins and they have none, that they have long dresses and we short, and that we talk much and they little. In England, he pointed out, the vices in fashion are whoring and drinking, in Turkey sodomy and smoking, we prefer a girl and a bottle, they a pipe and a pathic.

'You know what an addict he is for new languages. He swallows them whole. I don't know how he does it. I expected him to be talking fluent Turk in a week. However, in Turkey he noticed that the men take their pleasures silently, apart from the usual horrid grunts and foul eructations.' Hobhouse wrinkled his nose. 'So the only words of Turk he mastered were those for "bread", "water" and "pimp".'

After Constantinople, Hobhouse and Byron sailed back to Greece, where the two friends parted. Hobhouse was returning to England to face his financial affairs. The parting with Byron could make even the sensible Hobhouse wax sentimental. 'I admit it, I cried. I even divided a little nosegay of flowers with him. At the time, as he seemed bent on destroying himself with pleasure, it seemed the last thing perhaps I would ever share with him.'

'Was he not sad to see you go?' I asked. Perhaps Byron could not manage proper partings. Perhaps it cost him too much pain? Perhaps this was why he had run away from me?

If Hobhouse saw the direction of my thoughts he did not pursue them. He said, 'No, he was not sad to see the back of me. He was well ready for me to leave. I was holding him back. He wanted to try things he could not "taste" with me around him all the time. In Turkey, he was continually disappearing, and when he came back he did not seem to have the words to tell me where he had been. He did not want an Englishman, even me, as witness. He did not want to have to explain any more.'

This is what Hobhouse would not tell me, but because of what he did tell me, and because of what I know about Byron, I can tell you. After he left me, Byron took a darker turn in his life.

Sometimes, I know certainly, he went a little deeper. Not just the Grand Coital Tourist, but more. Sometimes he renounced the Oriental Bazaar and the donkey ride, and trod in things unintended for tourist feet. Passing doorways that gaped at him darkly, he breathed forbidden perfumes and private decays. His tongue was coated with dust. Nobody asked him where he came from, likened him to Semiramis, offered camels for him. Suddenly it would become quiet among the orange peel, lettuce, mud, offal, sawdust, date stones, children and flies. Slowly, stupidly, he would begin to perceive the quiet sounds of Greeks not performing satires of self-abasement. He had strayed into streets where the people sat without curiosity, wanting nothing from him, not even his story. He heard a drummer's rhythmic sussuration, curving around the urgent notes of a flute-player. The noise tugged at his groin like a hand.

Byron couldn't hear music without a lover to fondle. He didn't like the way it disentangled him. He took steps, with the music still in his ears. He bought a whore for the afternoon, and, as an afterthought, the musicians as well. In moments like this, he could almost love the whore whose tunic

he pulled up in the carriage on the way home, while the musicians perched
on the baggage-rack behind them, still warbling and whispering to their
instruments.

And if that ripe smell was the incense of a love disease, did he care? He
drew her onto his lap and unfastened his trousers, cupping the lush soft but-
tocks almost tenderly. He slid easily inside her. He had to bite her nipple to
make her acknowledge his entrance. As she cried out in pain, he finished. Ten
minutes later, he took her again, more slowly, more pleasurably, in a place
where there was more resistance, where he didn't have to bite to make her
weep.

What I know about Byron from the next period, I heard later from
his comical manservant Fletcher, for Byron was now left alone with
his paid retinue. Fletcher never learnt much Italian, and very little
French, but by the time I called him in as witness, my English had
become good enough for spying purposes. Sometimes, as I have
said, I tussled with Fletcher's language, which had come freshly
minted from the back alleys of London, but somehow, when we met
again years later, I was able to distil more truth, and more pain for
myself, from it.

So it is from Fletcher that I have the eye-witness accounts of
Byron's second sojourn in Greece. It lasted eight months. While
I was preparing for my confinement, dragging my swollen body
back and forth across the marble floors every long haunted night,
Byron was falling for a beautiful Greek youth, Eustathios
Georgiori, whose long curls hung down his back, and who sulked
and flounced.

'You should have seen that boy,' said Fletcher. 'From behind, he
was a perfect woman, but slimmer in the hips. Yooothatteeoss!
What a name! What a great big girl! He carried a *parasol*! Byron put
up with what-all from him. Obstropulous is not the word for it! I
would have given him a souse across the chops and filliped his

snout. What I was *puling* to do, though, was to whop him a kick where milord was most tender to him.'

Byron did not know that the Pasha soon disappeared to conduct his innumerable small wars in the north. He did not know that I stayed in Tepelene till my time came in the heats of July 1810. He knew nothing of the hours of white pain before Girolamo's birth or of the kind brisk hands and hypnotic incantations of the Albanian midwife, or of the extravagant and unsuitable birth-gifts from Ali Pasha. He did not know how I converted my bath into a luxurious crib for my baby. He knew nothing of Girolamo, of course. He did not know that I decided to name our son for Casanova, taking my old lover's soft liquid middle name, for comfort, for luck. I wanted the child to belong in some way to Casanova, who had known how to love properly.

The Albanians offered to keep my little Girolamo. His provenance was obvious, and a little wild milord might have flourished in the palace of Ali Pasha. The Albanians also offered a hundred other solutions for the problem of an inconvenient baby, each more barbarous than the next. There need be no trace of the child, I was told. I could pretend nothing had happened: that I had come to Albania, that I had painted, that I had accepted the Pasha's gold, and returned home; that I had not met Byron, and that I had not lost him.

But when the midwife handed me my son the world had turned upside down. A perfect being smiled at me with Byron's pale blue eyes. I could not leave him in Albania. I found another solution. I would take him back with me to Venice and give him to the Armenian monks on the island of San Lazzaro. A brief exchange of letters sealed the fate of my child. The Armenians were kind and direct. They would take the child. Their terms: I could see him whenever I wanted; to pay for his keep I would work on their frescoes, save them from the damp, pulverising breath of our lagoon. The monks would care for him, educate him, bring him to manhood as one of their own. Their final and unbreakable condition was this: Girolamo was never to know that I was his mother.

I would give him to the Armenians, but not before I had got to know my little baby. I allowed myself three months in Albania with him before I returned to Venice. I declined the offers of a wet-nurse and fed Girolamo from my own breasts. While Byron ran wild amongst the Oriental boys, I nursed his son, and found all my thoughts absorbed in him.

From the earliest days my little Girolamo was a creature of the most outrageously sophisticated sensuality. I swear he fondled my breasts with tenderness. They were no longer the wrong breasts. They were exactly and utterly the right breasts, and Girolamo smiled up at me over them every hour of the day. I swear he kissed them when he had drunk his full.

But surprisingly soon my baby also reached out for peach juice and hot chocolate, not milk pottages. He loved the nectar of oysters! What a palate he had, how unlike his father's and how like his namesake Casanova's! In my room at the palace, one day I saw the baby sniffing and smiling. I realised that he was lying near my box of pungent mussel shells. In those times I used the old method to store gold paint: ground to powder with sugar and stored inside those purple shells. Girolamo wanted the flesh of the shellfish. 'One day,' I told him, 'you will drink crab soup in Venice.' His exquisite little nostrils dilated and he smiled at me, trusting me to deliver whatever I promised.

'And I will give you peacock flesh,' I told him. 'It never rots.'

For three months I had Girolamo to love, and the pain of Byron's parting could not penetrate the milky, sleepy little world of joy I inhabited when the baby was in my arms. But one day, I already knew in the small of my back and in the pit of my stomach and in the palms of my hands, one day it would be otherwise.

And as Girolamo lay sleeping, my thoughts sometimes took flight, took me to the East, where I knew Byron journeyed, took me to his mouth, his eyes, his white hands, the nights he had spent with me here in Tepelene and the moment he betrayed me.

While I played with Girolamo, Byron moved into the monastery of the Capuchins. He tired of Eustathios and renewed his passionate friendship with the sweet Nicolo Giraud. He rescued a Turkish girl who was to be drowned in a sack in the sea after being caught *in flagrante* with a lover during Ramadan. This incident would become part of his poem *The Giaour*, as would memories of Ali Pasha, whose son, Veli Pasha, came to meet Byron, and became infatuated with him, embracing him in public with more than brotherly warmth.

Of course, Byron swam the Piraeus. Perhaps the polluted water swam into his veins because Byron caught malaria and, maltreated, nearly died of it. 'It was a near thing,' Fletcher would tell me. 'I even started a letter to his ma, to tell her what had happened. But he got better. Thinner, but better. The flesh fell off him.'

'Perhaps he was a little sad?' I asked. *Perhaps he thought of me, and missed me?*

'Oh no, he was happy as a French chicken! He liked himself skinny as what-have-you. He wanted to stay that way. After that he became the very devil to feed.'

Of course. I understood that Byron would have been pleased to have become emaciated with the illness. On his recovery he observed a strict regimen to preserve his ethereal beauty. 'The only thing he would eat was rice, great boiled nasty lumps of it – unchristian, I told him it was. And no more wine. He sucked all day on a bottle of vinegar and water.'

I could imagine that in Athens, where every young man was supposed to look like a Greek god, it must have been hard work for Byron to be the most beautiful of all.

Fletcher told me, 'He didn't eat enough proper food to feed an eel, and it went to his head. His guts must have been wondering if his throat had been cut. It was a big drama looking after his body. We all knew our parts. We were there to listen. He would talk forever about a single fallen hair or a hole in his tooth. He was forever writing to his friends to send him that bilious red toothpaste he liked.' Fletcher spat.

The other side of this coin, it seemed, was an intense self-consciousness. 'When he walked in public,' Fletcher recounted, 'and he heard footsteps approaching, he would stop dead and stand motionless, in case some stranger happened to see him limping. It was as if the stranger's opinion of him mattered more than the opinions of the people who really knew him.'

This, too, made sense to me.

On April 21st, Byron and Fletcher boarded the *Hydra* to leave Athens. But the boat remained becalmed for three days – the unwilling wind reflecting his own feelings about leaving the place where he had been happy. His mood was bitter. 'He was writing nasty stuff, about Lord Elgin and the marbles, about Scotland, about everything really. I kept out of his way,' said Fletcher. 'When he's gut-foundered like that, I'm better off out of it.' I realised that Byron must have been gnawing at his own roots as the return to Britain, where his affairs languished in dire disorder, loomed ever closer. Fulminate as he did, the *Hydra* still bore in her hold the last large consignment of the Elgin Marbles on their journey to the British Museum in London.

'Then we set sail and he got sick as a dog,' said Fletcher. 'Malaria, piles and, pardon me, Madam, a little gentlemanly disorder in the lower regions. He took to his berth and kept on scribbling.' As the

Hydra finally pulled out of Piraeus harbour, Byron made notes on his miserable state of mind, 'Four or Five Reasons in Favour of a Change.' They stretched to seven.

Many years later I found them in his desk. They had never stopped being true. Even now, thinking on them, I see the misery inside Byron, and my tenderness wells out of a soft part of me. Even now, when I read them, I cannot really hate him.

Reasons in Favour of a Change,
by George Gordon, Lord Byron

1st At twenty-three the best of life is over and its bitters double.

2ndly I have seen mankind in various countries and find them equally despicable, if anything the Balance is rather in favour of the Turks.

3rdly I am sick at heart . . .

4thly A man who is lame of one leg is in a state of bodily inferiority, which increases with years and must render his old age more peevish & intolerable. Besides, in another existence I expect to have two if not four legs by way of compensation.

5th I grow selfish & misanthropical . . .

6th My affairs at home and abroad are gloomy enough.

7th I have outlived all my appetites and most of my vanities, aye even the vanity of authorship.

2

I too knew what it was to make a weary homecoming.

While Byron abandoned himself to his second Athenian idyll, in the late October of 1810, Girolamo and I made our way back to Venice, first with horse-carts through the mountain passes, then in a carriage on the kinder roads and finally, blessedly, over water. Mouchar accompanied me all the way to the boat, taking care of every practicality. I was happy to have his soothing presence, and for the graceful scent of his hair oil, which blocked the uglier stenches of our travels. But I barely talked to him. I had eyes and ears only for Girolamo, who had lived three months in this world now, never more than seconds from my side. All this while Girolamo was learning different ways to laugh at me: slow, bubbling chuckles, short staccato cries, silent laughs with his eyes crinkled up like cowry shells.

As we boarded the boat, I embraced Mouchar, and held him close to me with Girolamo between us. Mouchar kissed the top of Girolamo's head.

'Goodbye, little God,' he said to my son.

'Go, be great again, Cecilia!' he said. There were no tears in his eyes, or in mine, but in his dark pupils I read a potent blessing.

I waved to him as the boat slid from the dock into the milky evening sea. I held up Girolamo like a triumphal goblet. For a moment it seemed that I had come to Albania only to acquire him.

But I had acquired him only to lose him.

During the past months I had tried to negotiate further with the fathers on San Lazzaro by letter. They informed me that the same restrictions applied to all their novices. They remained adamant that my son must not know his parentage. He was to join the monastery as an anonymous foundling. As a special concession to me, he might keep the name Girolamo, but his *cognome* would be the same as that of all the other foundlings. Another of their strange conditions was that he must never come to the city. He must be brought directly to them on the island. He should not spend a night under my Venetian roof with me. They would take the child from me at Mestre, before I entered Venice. I was to expect someone, and I was to be as discreet as possible in the transaction, so as not to draw attention to myself or the child. It would be better that way, they wrote.

How different was this voyage to the one that had brought me to Albania. I could not bear to look upon the alien landscapes now: I was too vulnerable. I am sure that the unrelenting sun continued to rise on the black sea as before, but I did not see it. I had no curiosity to spare. For the entire journey, lying on my berth with the baby breathing quietly beside me, I imagined other scenarios. I imagined arriving at our *palazzo* at Miracoli with Girolamo. I imagined Sofia taking my baby tenderly to her breast. I imagined a gentlemanly thump on the back from Giovanni. But at this thought reality always intruded. Quite apart from the scandal he would bring, little Girolamo would not be welcome at our *palazzo*.

Giovanni and Sofia had never managed to make a son. My baby would pose a threat to Giovanni's cherished plans for his favourite young brother's inheritance. But more importantly, it was his paternity that made it impossible for me to keep him. If his father was discovered, and he *would* be discovered if Girolamo stayed with me – I had already seen how swiftly and vividly gossip about Byron was relayed even to far Tepelene – then there would be no peace for the child. Better anonymity, a life of scholarship and decency at San Lazzaro, than the dark opportunities that would await another abandoned Byron bastard.

Disembarking at Mestre just before dawn, I stood among my possessions on the quay with Girolamo asleep in my arms. I saw the outlines of huge coils of frayed ropes, like the greasy plaits of giantesses. Living silhouettes of the world and his wife jostled past us. They seemed phantoms to me. Only Girolamo glowed with life in the emerging frail pink light. He was full of my milk, so full that a little dribbled from his tiny soft mouth. When I pulled him gently from my breast he was already asleep. *Better that way*, I thought. To look into his pale blue eyes just now would be more than I could bear. I leant against the rim of the bath that carried my canvases, in which Girolamo had slept, and looked around me. From which direction would the great pain come? My stomach had already started to ossify. I could not move. But I waited patiently. Every moment was another moment with Girolamo.

I did not know what to expect of myself. When Byron abandoned me, I had screamed and wept. When Girolamo was taken from me, would I be able to shuffle away, noiselessly, discreetly? I am an Italian. There is drama in my blood. But I had promised the Fathers that I would be as inscrutable as a nun. I held my baby closer, and took long breaths of the perfume of his head. I kissed the soft shells of his sleeping eyes. I licked his nose.

There was tap on my shoulder. I turned to see a tall, cadaverous
and long-bearded Father behind me. He was dressed in the familiar robes of the San Lazzaro monks. How often Casanova and I had
seen them all those years ago! I clutched at a memory of a dark
habit approaching us through the olive trees as we sat talking on the
sweet grass, and kind hands pouring water for us from an earthenware jug. They had welcomed us without comment to their island,
the old sinner and the young hoyden as I must have seemed then, all
splashed with paint and wild of hair. God knows what they thought
we were doing together, but whatever it was, they forgave us. Now
they would welcome Girolamo the same way, and absorb him into
their kind community.

'Cecilia Cornaro?' the Father asked in the knotty accent of his
race. His consonants butted against each other. 'You have something
for me?'

Girolamo stirred in my arms. I put my little finger in his mouth
and he sucked on it gently, without opening his eyes, making little
burbles of satisfied desire. The Father held out his hands. The
expression on his large, sunken face was kind, sympathetic, forgiving. I knew that all the Fathers on San Lazzaro had suffered their
own tragedies, refugees to a man, witnesses and victims of violence
and horror in the homeland from which they had fled. I knew he
understood my pain; he knew its strength if not its style.

Still, I temporised, like a child who does not want to go to bed.
'But it's early . . .' The Father gently shook his head. His honey-
coloured eyes regarded me as softly and moistly as a dog's.

Girolamo did not wake as I handed him over. I too closed my
eyes on the sight of his body leaving mine. I wanted no such
memory to knife my heart. Afterwards, I stood for a moment,
cradling the air, the warmth of his body still tangible in the cavity of
my arms. It had been done, as the Fathers insisted, secretly. I had
given away my baby and no one would ever know. I waited until the

Father had disappeared in the crowd before sitting down on my bath and letting go of my tears, my screams, my oaths and my whispers. I spilled all my pain as if it might flow away once I evacuated it from my body. I had kept my part of the bargain. I had nothing to lose now. People came running. Kind hands were laid on my shoulder. Soothing words were said to me. I did not look up. I screamed louder. I shook, I squealed like a rodent; I took tearing breaths; I roared. I vomited yellow bile on someone's knee. Milk from my breasts darkened my bodice. 'Is she a lunatic?' someone asked. Eventually I lost consciousness, just after someone had said to someone else, 'My God! That's Cecilia Cornaro, the artist. Her family's at Miracoli. She's been in Albania for over a year, poor soul. What have they done to her, the savages?'

And that was how I was delivered to my family's *palazzo*: delirious, journey-stained, stinking and childless. Sofia took one look at me and sent the servants away. She herself sponged the sweat and tears from my body and put me to bed in my old room on the *mezzanino*. When I had rested, and was less shocking to the eye, she brought my mother and my young niece to bid me welcome. I took the girl in my arms. This girl was Girolamo's cousin; she was flesh of my flesh. I saw something alive in her face, something of Girolamo. I held her to me until she gasped. I did not care. I no longer had my own child.

The Cat Speaks

It's a long time since the reader has had word from his obedient servant, the cat.

Imagine how it has been for *me*.

As for Cecilia – she came back, just like that, without a word to explain her absence.

A year she had left me alone.

And all those unfinished canvases rotting in her studio. I had guarded them, as if I knew her return was imminent, and that everything must be *a posto*.

She looked different. I knew something had happened to her. There was a smell of sour milk about her that told me that she had obviously birthed quite recently, though there was no sign of a single kitten. But it was more than that. Something else had happened to her.

She painted like a lunatic. She squeezed the water out of those brushes so hard I almost thought to see blood spurt out of them.

Her paintings were different when she came back. All those canvases I had guarded? She just painted them over with white gesso and started again. For a while, there were no portraits. She painted suicidal lady-saints and weeping Madonnas, and small babies, their toes curling with pleasure as they suckled with their eyes wide open. They tugged at their gentle mothers' mantles with fat, delicious fingers. When Cecilia returned, her Madonnas grew heavy breasts and knees which could actually support a baby.

Anyway, I was happy when she came back. I dribbled on her hand and purred against her cheek.

She was so happy to see me that I thought she would squeeze me to death. I had to remind her, with a little scrape of my claw, that I, too, could be hurt.

3

Dime che so, ma non me dir chi gero.

Tell me who I am, but not who I was.

VENETIAN PROVERB

There was another homecoming.

In July 1811, two years after he had left it, Byron returned to the tight little island of his birth. Hobhouse resumed his post as my spy for this period of Byron's life.

'Was he happy to be home?' I would ask. 'To be with his people again?'

'It did not feel like coming home for Byron. It felt like slinking back to a cave. He was neither fish nor fowl. He could not live forever in exotic lands. Nor could he ever again resume his Englishness, which he had so easily sloughed off in the East. As for "people", there was only his mother.'

I said, 'And his half-sister, Augusta.'

'Ah yes, Augusta.'

There were more practical reasons to come home. Byron was penniless, worn out and plagued with an itch where no true English gentleman would scratch in polite society. This consideration would no longer restrain him. He considered himself freed from gentlemanly constraints, indeed antipathetical to them. 'I shall become the sworn enemy of English etiquette,' he had declared to me in Albania, as if formulating state policy. Now he was to put the theory into action.

He was annoyed to find that he had lost along the way some of his favourite portraits, the ones I had made for him, the images of love he had stolen from me. Hobhouse had told me that Byron would never use my name after we left Albania, but it seems that he wanted to recreate the image I had made of him. So he had himself painted again in the garb of an Albanian buccaneer. I saw an engraving later. I believe the artist – I think he was called Phillips – executed a competent likeness. But can he have painted Byron as I did? I doubt it.

Soon afterwards, Hobhouse told me, Byron gave away the Albanian costume to a friend, muttering that it cost him some deranging memories. 'He told her to use it for a fancy-dress ball and then for whatever she wanted, so long as he never had to see it again.'

Unlike me, Byron tried to preserve some dignity about his return, a little grace. Unlike me, his deepest problem was money.

'Byron came home with a shawl and attar of roses for his mother, some marbles for me and for himself a phial of Attic hemlock, four Athenian skulls and four Greek tortoises he had found in an ancient sarcophagus,' Hobhouse told me. 'But his affairs were so dire that he did not have the money for a journey to Newstead.'

Byron dallied in London, waiting for funds to be sent by his lawyer and hoping that all his old creditors were dead or jailed. Inconveniently, this was not so. 'They were closing in around him, politely but relentlessly,' Hobhouse recalled. 'The thing they did not know was that even if he had wanted to, he could not pay them. All he had were his outlandish souvenirs, his pistols, and a fat sheaf of poetry.'

I asked, 'But the poetry was worth something, surely?'

'Remember, in those days it was the custom that no true aristocrat would stoop to accept payment for his writings.'

'Marvellous creatures, the English,' I had observed then, thinking of the theft of my work. 'Among the Venetians the indignity lies in *not* being paid.'

Eventually Byron set off for Newstead, but his mother, who had fought off bailiffs and serious illness during his two-year voyage, did not manage to survive his delayed journey from the capital. She died, probably of a cancerous growth in the stomach, or so it seems to me from the cruel symptoms Hobhouse described. Hobhouse thought that her final throes were possibly brought on by fear of seeing her son again. 'She had heard some of the stories,' he said, shaking his head. 'If she had seen his face, it would have confirmed them.'

'Was he devastated to lose her?' I asked. 'Did he feel guilty at his treatment of her?'

'He did not show it. Byron had abused her so consistently during her life that he was now unable to demonstrate any grief for her. No one would have believed him,' Hobhouse explained, as if that answered my question.

'You never saw such a strange funeral. Her coffin bore no affectionate message and merely recorded that she was the mother of George, Lord Byron. He refused to attend his mother's funeral procession.' Byron had watched the cortège grimly from the front door and then called for his boxing gloves.

Byron was now officially an orphan. And it was a time of other, more painful deaths. Byron heard that his beloved, exquisite chorister, John Edelston, had perished of tuberculosis the previous May, but Byron only now received the letter which told him. And his friend Charles Skinner Matthew had drowned in the Cam; his body was found later entwined in reeds. Byron's own element, water, had killed his great friend. Hobhouse was shaken, too. He told me, 'It seemed too terrible a coincidence: water had already claimed another of the Harrow boys, for Edward Noel Long had drowned in 1809.'

Byron's reaction was hysterical, Hobhouse told me. Greek love, the message came loud and clear, was dangerous for him. 'He felt himself one of a set of doomed, beautiful young men,' Hobhouse said. 'So he cultivated the role of victim.'

'You are cynical about him!' I exclaimed.

'No, he was not pretending, just dramatising. He empathised excessively with the extinction of those young flames. He took them all into himself. He spent hours moping at Newstead, staring at those four Greek skulls. He reshaped himself as a man who attracted untold sorrows to himself and carried a superhuman burden of pain. And he drew up an extraordinary will in which he insisted that he should have no funeral and be buried with his dog, Boatswain, in the family vault at Newstead.'

Back at Newstead, he was chewing tobacco to stave off hunger and retain his slender figure. He was bored. Rural entertainments, after the excitement of the East, offered little. Hobhouse had watched him with concern. 'He took to exploding soda water bottles with his pistols, and jumping into the lake, and rowing over it, and shooting wildfowl he had no intention of eating.'

Byron resumed correspondence with his half-sister Augusta, now unhappily married, and started to think of marriage himself. Hobhouse explained, 'He saw no other way out of his debts. The thought of wedlock made him shudder. He told me that when he imagined himself married, there ranged across his imagination vague but distasteful scenes of domesticity, the smell of milk, the prospect of the same ageing face across the table, endlessly.'

Needs must, however. Like his father before him, Byron set off heiress-hunting.

'I always remember how he described his quest for a bride,' Hobhouse told me. 'It was hardly a romantic quest! He said that he was "pledged to find some wealthy dowdy to ennoble the dirty puddle of mercantile blood". Those were his exact words. I pitied his bride already.'

There were no wealthy dowdies in the vicinity of Newstead. Byron became bored with conjugating the verb *ennuyer* at Newstead and moved back down to London.

Like Byron, I returned home and became motherless.

A sweating fever swept through Venice in 1810, just after I arrived back from Albania. It carried away my mother, already weakened by lung disorder, in a week.

I faced Sofia over my mother's deathbed. Humbly she handed the priest a salver with lemon and an ampulla of holy oil. I watched her praying, blowing her nose delicately into a silk handkerchief, tenderly spooning a fragrant julap of honey and water onto my mother's dry lips. I found myself thinking, suddenly, that when my time came to die she would do the same for me, as gracefully and sweetly.

Returning from San Lazzaro that day, I had run up the stairs to my mother's sick room. I could see, in an instant, that her condition was graver, even without the presence of the mumbling priest. I looked at the outline of Sofia's cheek, inclined towards my mother, and her hands, both grasping one of my mother's wasted claws. I retreated to the doorway, where I stood, stricken, excluded. Sofia turned to me and reached a hand out, her face suffused with hope and slick with tears, but I stumbled away muttering excuses. I simply could not feel I deserved the dispensation of Sofia's tenderness, and I did not know how to accept it.

I had buried what was left of my capacity to love in Girolamo, and it was rationed to minutes at a time when I went to San Lazzaro to work on the frescoes. The Fathers would let me look at Girolamo in the sunny nursery, where he lay with three other baby boys, clearly well-fed and well-loved. They kicked their little legs in unison. I thought Girolamo's by far the shapeliest. I was not permitted even a quick caress, but I could look.

Girolamo and the sadness of him had made me sensitive to my family. I felt the need to re-attach myself to the roots of the tree which bore me. It seemed that from Girolamo I had learnt to be a daughter as well as a mother. But I had lost my opportunity; my timing could not have been worse. It was too late. My mother would die before I could have one of the many conversations I planned. I realised, hunching my shoulders in misery, that I would be an orphan before I could learn to touch her again, the way she had touched me as a child, in the days before I made myself remote from her.

Before I had Girolamo, my mother had already ceased to be, years before, the flesh that bore me. She had become simply flesh, simply an education in chromatic intensity and texture. It was not that I did not love her; it was that I had not thought that love precious or worthy of remark. I invested myself elsewhere. I was entirely occupied in my passion for painting and my pursuit of novelty. I knew her love for me hung around my life like the air I breathed. I did not question it. But we were shy with one another, overly courteous, as if to compensate for the absence of the more normal, sweeter ties which bound her to Sofia.

Now, too late, I wanted to give and receive affection from her, the way Sofia did. I envied the way they fed each other with kisses and small touches of the hand. I nursed a wild fantasy of presenting Girolamo to my mother and so receiving the same butterfly kisses she had given Sofia at her confinements. I now knew how nourishing that could be.

I have wasted love, I thought, *I did not love my mother properly*.

These were my thoughts as I watched my mother pass from life to death, to the quiet sound of Sofia's tears.

When my mother died Sofia and her husband took over our *palazzo* at Miracoli. They had come to live with us after my father died, but under the fluttering rule of my mother. Now they were officially the householders. We now lived in a state of utmost elegance. Sofia was, of course, attentive to every nuance of each modish ruling: every puffed sleeve, ribband and ruffle was an object of as much anxiety to her as might be the choice of pistols for a soldier at duel. She could barely wait for the cold weather to sport her muffs of sea otter and Muscovy sable. For Sofia, ostrich feathers were positively mundane. She must have egret plumes or nothing. In this alone she was suited to her husband. Giovanni strutted about in a waistcoat of bottle green and claret-coloured silk.

As I have said, there had been no heir born to them, and now there would not be, for Giovanni had all but abandoned Sofia for his mistresses. He came home for meals, which Sofia superintended with all the skills but little of the anxiety of my mother. At first it seemed inconceivable that life should go on as before, with both my parents dead, but I soon realised that Sofia had been the backbone of the household for some time before my mother died. She fell smoothly into the role she was in fact already playing, pale with grief for the loss of our mother, but never too frail to undertake her duties. She made sure that all the right foods were served on the right days, salmon and eels with cabbage on Christmas Day, duck on the first day of August and so on. The rest of us accepted this as if it were our right.

I continued to live with them. I stayed in my room on the *mezzanino*. I gave them most of what I earned, and Giovanni treated me as a gentleman-equal, in a comradely asexual way. I lived with them peaceably enough, and left Sofia to busy herself with the astonishingly complicated domestic details that did not interest me.

My old maid, with whom Casanova had done business, was long dead. Now I dropped my clothes where I shed them for anonymous backs to stoop over and hands to pick up. There was always a fragrant pile of freshly laundered *fisiù* for me to tie around my bodice. I sometimes wondered what happened to the little white shawls when I threw them on the floor, stained with paint and oil. Were they thrown away or did the maids hate me, straining their fingers to remove the colours with stiff brushes? Did a laundry woman boil them in a vat as she had once boiled the little Casanova's blood-soaked handkerchiefs? From knowledge of all these things I was protected. This felt right to me. I had no child to tend to, so let them tend to me, I thought.

I was not much disturbed. I spent a great deal of time at the studio. I lived ferally, often arriving home too late to dine *in famiglia*, and foraging in the kitchen for cold pasta, which I ate, standing up, reading letters and books sent by my fond clients. The family became accustomed to my strange ways, and obliged me where they could. If I had allowed it, I think they would have shown me affection, but I remained rigid in my pain and isolation. I had been denied my two great loves, Girolamo and Byron, and I refused to accept what seemed to me to be the lesser joys of domesticated, familial love.

The only way I could join myself with them was with painting. When I wanted to try a new technique, I would ask Sofia's daughter or our servants to sit for me. Often I painted our *ballerino*, the *major-domo* who regulated the deportment of the whole household. He was a ridiculous little man, an exercise in pomposity. I painted him teaching my niece and the upper servants to kiss hands, to dance, when to smile, how to do so capriciously but with dignity, which is how we do these things in Venice. Sofia, I one day noticed, had beautiful hands, as beautiful as I had once thought my own. Perhaps they were not beautiful before. Perhaps it was the stroking of human flesh, her husband's, her child's – for she was as tender as a kitten with everyone around her – that had made them so soft and sweet. I developed the habit of using her hands as studies for those of my noble lady-clients. And so we sat, almost companionably, in the evenings, in the *soggiorno*, with Sofia sewing and me sketching and my niece singing to us in the firelight. *I am here only for the hands*, I told myself.

I came and went. Unless I entertained a lover in my studio, I would spend the evenings at home. For when the day dimmed, when the light leached away, that was when I became needy. These were the times I tried not to be out on the streets, when I tried not to be alone. It is the time when humans incline towards the comfort of loving arms. They come in from the cold and want more than the fire's warmth. These are the dangerous times for someone to be alone. They can hurt a fragile heart. At these times I went back home, and let my family surround me with the clatter of tongues, plates and knitting needles. I would eat with them, sharing the food that Sofia had chosen, knowing my preferences were respected, that breast of duck with marmalade sauce would be served at least once a week, that a fresh *torta al cioccolato* would always be cooling on a rack in the kitchen and that the best *fragolino* would always be glowing in the crystal decanter. Sometimes Sofia would come to me where I sat sketching by the fire after supper and place beside me a little bowl of pistachio nuts, which she knew I loved. She had already pulled the pale green nuggets from their shells, with her own soft fingers, because she knew I liked them fresh and moist.

I was part of the household and yet not part of it. I had the freedom of the *piano nobile* and all the reception rooms. But my little pink niece was forbidden to descend to the *mezzanino*. Sofia, no doubt remembering her own experiences with my early attempts at pornography, did not want her to see what she might find in my room.

In general, I kept away from my brother-in-law. He had already tried to humiliate Sofia by bringing two of his mistresses to my studio for a cheap portrait. I sent him away with a lash of my *lingua biforcuta*. According to my Libran sense of justice, Sofia did not deserve this. She was a tender wife to Giovanni, and never thought to take on her own *cavalier servente*. She never criticised me, and bore my outbursts without comment. She always turned instinctively to my portrait of her little dead child when I was cruel to her, as if to remind herself of my goodness to her. For in this portrait I had made a living likeness so the child was never absent from her. I was silenced by this. For me, it had been a piece of work, like any other. That was then, before Girolamo. Now I knew what it meant to her.

I still went to church with them, and still gave confessions I stole from my sitters. These days it was because my own story was too painful to tell. And I had no need of penance from a priest for those things. I had already been punished for both Byron and Girolamo. My sins were too deep for any number of Our Fathers to erase. But once I tried to see how God might reckon my behaviour with Sofia.

That day I told the Father Confessor, 'I am a bad sister.'

'In what way, my child?'

I was silent. There was too much to say. In no way was I a good sister.

Sometimes I wondered if Sofia had guessed something of what had happened to me in Albania. She had become so gentle towards me after that. She was not stupid. She could count months. When she undressed me the day I returned, raving and delirious, she must have seen certain marks on my belly and the milk spilling from my breasts. She knew what it was to lose a little child.

My portrait of my little dead niece was hung above the prayer table in her parlour instead of a Madonna. Sofia never talked to me of it, but I knew she suffered. I watched her. I knew it from her thinning body inside her luxurious clothes, from her pale face, from the droplets on her lashes when she returned from prayers, from the way she coddled her remaining daughter as if she was a jewel whom the very gods envied her and might at any moment snatch away.

And I know that Sofia watched me, secretly when she thought I was unaware of it, and openly when she dared.

But she never asked me, never mentioned Albania. For that tact alone, I blessed her. And these days I watched her over the break-fast table, no longer with disdain but with wonder.

Meanwhile, in London, wonderful things were afoot.

Childe Harold's Pilgrimage, A Romaunt, was published and Byron, famously, woke up famous. A thousand copies a day flew out of the bookstores. The gazettes were full of it.

From what I read in the English newspapers, Byron was now the only topic of conversation among London society. Certainly none of the English visitors in Venice wanted to talk of anyone else. No one saw the poem as anything other than autobiography. The press was convulsed by the tale of a moody young nobleman, sick at heart, of his journey from a stately but dilapidated pile to far Constantinople, of the wildness of the protagonist as he ran through Sin's long labyrinth, of his splendid isolation, of his grim and tender desper-ation, of his stiff upper lip. For his English peers, he was the cipher for all that was hot, forbidden, and exotic: all such things they lusted after in the drowsy hush of their cold drawing rooms.

Within a fortnight, I had a copy in my own hands, the gift of a kindly English client with whom I had practised English while I painted her. The little book, smelling in a male leathery way of London, was affectionately inscribed by my client, 'To Mademoiselle Cornaro, so that you may read English at its very best.' I tore out that page, so as not to be distracted, and settled down with the book.

I tried to recognise in this little volume the Byron I knew from our time in Albania. But there were more clues to be found outside *Childe Harold* than within it. I saw how Byron's celebrity enveloped the book. The poem and Byron's person fed upon each other. The poem now defined him – a sad, rebellious romantic with a heart of veined marble. Proud, moody, cynical, implacable in revenge, capable of diabolic eroticism, but incapable of deep or lasting love. In his preface, he insisted that Harold resembled no real personage – *Harold is the child of imagination* . . . but I was sure that no one, least of all Byron, wanted to believe this. I realised that he would now have to live up to it. From the moment *Childe Harold* was published, he could no longer be Byron; he had to become Byronic.

Mary Shelley would say later, 'When I wrote *Frankenstein*, perhaps I had the birth of Lord Byron in the back of my mind. Not his physical birth in 1788, but the moment he birthed *himself* when *Childe Harold* was published.'

The new Byron, 1812 edition: wanted, envied, accepted by the fashionable society, he was their literary lion of the moment. I saw the accounts in the papers, how the street in front of his house was solidly crammed with carriages bearing invitations to more parties than he could attend.

But underneath, I saw that the London literary community wondered about Byron. I saw the small demurs emerging in the newspapers. I saw the niggling complaints from the conservative press that Byron lacked the technical perfection of the great old Englishmen like Alexander Pope and John Dryden. I saw the feverish sniping by the young writers: they claimed that Byron lacked the deeper spiritual penetration of the new men, of a Wordsworth or a Coleridge. I saw all that, in the midst of the general lionisation, and I took it in.

But I relied more on the feeling in my gut. By the time I finished the book, I had my own thoughts about it. I know I am a painter, and it ill becomes me to wander into the *campo* of the writers. I know I am Italian, that English is only my third language. But I do not believe that anyone read that poem with more attention to every nuance than I did. And, excuse me, but I must point this out: sometimes it takes an innocent to see the real cut of the Emperor's new clothes.

If you ask me, *Childe Harold*'s verse was fluent, yes, and spectacularly flamboyant. It had verve. It glittered at the surface like enamel. I could see that Byron was making poetry erotic, desirable and the subject of conversation. No wonder the literary community was aroused: they could all profit from that. Yes, his poetry flowed over the page and its rhythms were delicious. But for all that, I have to say that I was disappointed by it. All those facile verses, all that relentless, bathetic hyperbole! It seemed to me that they were always ringing the changes on the same thing: the monstrous misery and voluptuous self-indulgence of the hero. I hate to say it, and I shall be pilloried for it, but is it not almost *monotonous*? Is its range not rather *tiny*? Is there not something *missing*?

I felt deep inside me that Byron lacked an emotional dimension to his language. His words said what they said, and no more. There was no magical suggestion, no mystery, no emotional illumination, no half-tones, no overtones, no undertones, all the things I understood to be required by poetry. Sitting in my studio, with the book on my lap, I fondled my cat while I turned the pages. I read slowly. Eventually the cat stretched out an elegant paw and knocked the book to floor. I leant down to pick it up but changed my mind. I left it there and walked over to the window with the cat in my arms.

'You are right, *signor*, let us not read any more of this. It cannot do us any good.'

You see, I had understood the problem with *Childe Harold*. It had strong sinews and scented flesh, that poem, but it was feeble at its core. I stroked the cat's head and whispered in his ear, 'I know what's wrong with it.'

The cat looked into my face, waiting for the answer.

I told him, 'It's the *heart* of his poetry that is impotent.'

4

I saw babies and children everywhere. It was an affliction to me. I pulsed with pain every time I saw a little child pull a nodding wooden duck on a string across a *campo*. It galled my ears to hear the mothers of little children calling *dammi la tua manina*, 'give me your little hand', to their fallen, squalling children, and it hurt my eyes to see those mothers tenderly excavate the grit of the street from those tiny fingernails. I saw children raising their arms to the sun like flowers in the park. From the windows of humble houses I heard little voices mourning a lost *caramella* as if the world had ended. I ached and hungered for Girolamo. Such craving for his arms around me muttered in my belly! I saw baby linen hanging on lines fed out from shabby shutters. I thought, *Blessed house, a baby lives there.*

Girolamo's precocious, joyful greed haunted me. When I passed the pastry shops I wanted to rush in and buy armfuls of sweetness for him. I wanted to give him all the good things, the Venetian delicacies: 'Kisses in a Gondola', the little white meringues cemented in pairs with chocolate; the sour sweet fish dishes like *sarde in saor*. At the fish market I found myself wondering how I might make crab soup for him, even though I had never cooked anything in my life. I saw mother birds returning to their nests with worms. I turned my head away from them, sick with sorrow. They had young to feed. Why them, and not me?

Venice had fallen in 1797. Like Venice, I had my period of confusion. The Austrian soldiers had taken possession in 1798 but Napoleon had claimed us back again in 1805. Then he gave us back to the Habsburgs. Our heads were spinning. The reminders of our indignity were everywhere around me: the tidy buildings left by Napoleon, the new system of street numbers and the many new Austrian street names, the waltz tunes played a little louder in the cafés than our own Venetian folk-song. For the first time I felt our subjection personally. We had been a happy city, and now we were not. I had been a happy woman, and now I was not.

When I returned to Venice in 1810, after the hell I had known in Albania, Venice was no longer home because it no longer knew me, the creature I had become. I had a bitter taste in my mouth. The *lingua biforcuta* hung limp inside it. Sofia was no longer so frightened of me. There was nothing to fear. I was pathetic to know. After I gave away Girolamo and came home, I collapsed into myself. It was days before I left my room. I was dizzy and spent. I told them I was well again but I was unconvincing. Sofia insisted on accompanying me when I took my first *passeggiata* to San Marco. How different my world looked now that I had been humbled and hurt! It was only when it was too late that I understood how my family's little *palazzo* at Miracoli, Casanova's love and Venice herself had sheltered me.

I thought I would feel calmer when I came home but it was not like that. Coming home, I found, had merely confirmed my loss. I had left Venice confident and curious. I had returned home damaged and closed up inside myself. I looked at Salute and remembered how, in Casanova's arms, I had enjoyed the beauty of her white domes against an eggshell dawn sky. There was a such a distance between that time and now, between my state of happiness then and my present broken state.

When I went to my studio, I sat staring at my old work. I did not believe in it any longer. I did not believe I had painted anything real. In my ignorant arrogance I had thought I knew how to paint Venetians. I thought I had captured their joys and their sorrows in the *sfumatura* of their skin. Now I realised that I had known nothing about it. The Venetians had deceived me: I had painted only what they wanted me to see. Even without their masks the Venetians are always masked. We wear a veil of self-absorption on our faces, as when we dance the *furlana*. The pageant is always being performed. We are outside ourselves, watching ourselves. See that far-off look we have – it excludes outsiders. It is Venetians turning into puppets in their great puppet theatre. The play is not for the benefit of the audience. It is the play we create of ourselves, in that beautiful theatre, that floating theatre. Now I knew that I had not really known my sitters because I had never understood how brave they were. I guessed at how many of them must carry inside them a pain as great as mine, for how few of them were ever loved properly?

Clients started to come, tapping nervously on the door. For a long time, I sent them away. I only wanted to go to San Lazzaro and work on the frescoes, so that I could see my baby.

Eventually, after a period of oblivion, I, like Venice, lifted my pale head and carried on. I walked mechanically to my studio. Soon I was working again. At first I painted Madonnas and babies but soon I hungered for new faces and let it be known that Cecilia Cornaro was accepting clients again. I worked faster than before to leave the truth behind. As I laid the paint on canvas the old alchemy started to work upon me. I had learnt to accept that even unhappy people

and unhappy cities have their desires; these desires are still beautiful and can be painted. Indeed the artist can excavate them and
bring them forth. My portraits from this period are among my best.
They show, for the first time, the compassion I had learnt to feel for
my fellow creatures because I was in need of it myself. They show
an acceptance of weakness; they show the fragile beauty of hope. I
became infected with a desire to be happy myself, to rewrite my
story and to repaint the features on my own mask. I did not want
to be an abandoned woman. In my new story, Byron had been my
sexual adventure; I was the great sexual adventuress. With this
fable, I escaped the pain of his abandonment most of the time.

But sometimes, when I felt the old skin-hunger, I took another
lover. Then I would remember Byron and his usage. I lay wakeful on
the divan, full of emptiness, while an uncomprehending man dozed
beside me. I would rouse him roughly and send him away. I was
more lonely beside him than on my own. When he had gone, I
faced the truth. In those long nights I would be forced to see what
had really happened to me. It was then that the suffering would
come back to visit. It was as if Byron had just left me. The feelings
were as fresh as ever. Such feelings are more dangerous in the dark,
when the stars hang fat in the sky. I thought of how those same stars
hung over the palace of Tepelene and over Byron somewhere in
London, perhaps at Newstead, but certainly not thinking of me.
Those nights I ran back to Miracoli, weeping through the streets, a
solitary maddened figure, shameful as a rat. I threw myself upon my
bed and I would rise in the morning, diminished in my own eyes.

But by day I would not acknowledge it. I was not able to swallow
the fact of how he stopped loving me. It was as if I had no right to
think about him, because he had withdrawn my heart's rights, my
rights to feel, to claim love. Stripped, nameless, voiceless, I
crouched in an unnumbered cell, without the means to absorb or
record what he had done to me. Even while I wove my new story in

my mind, my body told me how to feel. A head of curled chestnut hair glimpsed in a crowd could still twist my liver before I even realised why. A couple embracing in a gondola could force tears from my eyes. I was too much alone and too sad with it. The beauty of Venice showed me an unbeautiful nullity inside me.

For years after that I tore through my days in order to sleep like the dead. While I slept memories of Byron circled round my bed like sharks. I hated waking. In that first moment of consciousness Byron was always there, plucking at my eyelids, prodding at my heart with a skewer. He crouched over my face, slapping his lazy erection on my eyelids while I pushed the hilt of his hips away from me. I never had enough sleep. He always forced me out of bed after a few hours. He was my last thought, too, leaking sadness into my dreams. I chased people out of my life in order to be alone. When I was alone, my loneliness spilled out of me like black blood. Scenting it, the cat would nuzzle my hand, jump on my lap, put his paws upon my shoulders and look into my eyes with Casanova's tenderness. But Casanova's love could not mend what Byron had broken.

Why did I still love Byron? I told you before. Because he emptied me. It felt like fainting. After being with him, I was depleted. I was too weak not to love him.

I am not stupid. I read what I have written about him. I know that I describe a monster. I would have liked him to be dead. But I was still in love with him, and frightened of his annihilating indifference to me. I still wanted him to die, with my name upon his lips.

I was not alone in this.

5

*So no ghe fusse vento, né fèmena mata,
non ghe sarìa mal tempo né mala giornata.*

If there was no wind, and no crazy women,
there would be no bad weather or bad days.

VENETIAN PROVERB

Unlike the Venetians, the English have no secrets. It must be easy for their spies. The whole shabby spectacle of their lives is played out upon the stage: in their newspapers. Their gossip and scandal are not mischievous and light, as they are here in Venice, but cold and deadly for the English. Their gossip columns run with the blood and the misery of their victims. I am not surprised to hear of the number of suicides that result.

Until I saw him again, the rest of Byron's story was played out for me in the newspapers, with their 'eye-witness' narratives and their anonymous letters from distressed gentlewomen – and in a dreadful novel by one Lady Caroline Lamb. Byron's story was also recounted to me *viva voce* by my English clients who came to Venice full of fresh tales about him. Some of them had even met him. Mostly, though, they got their information as I did, hovering breathlessly over the accounts of others and listening to the word-of-mouth legend-making that seemed to occupy all of London.

So Byron's style of lovemaking was wrenched from the privacy of my memory and put on the stage for all to see. 'I am at your mercy,' he would say sometimes, to the women, apparently. But he meant, 'I am, for the moment, at your service. And you are at my disposal.' He would not be denied. It was always urgent, the ladies reported. He could not bear to be rejected.

You see, there is this other side to the Byronic hero. It is the motherless child, in search of a tender feminine hand to stroke his wild hair and wrap his wounds. She alone can cut a chasm through the flinty breast and rescue the tender lover weeping inside. She is at once mother and lover, ministering angel and submissive mistress. The persona of this woman, whom he painted again and again, was what sold Byron's books in their thousands. Every woman who read about her wanted to be her, and to perform the gentle sacrifice for him.

'Me! Me!' exclaimed a thousand women, ten thousand women after *Childe Harold* was published. 'Let it be me!'

Women, women. Byron was no longer frightened of them. He frightened them instead. He had developed a famous 'underlook' to assault feminine sensibilities. One woman, at least, complained of being unable to breathe after five minutes in his devastating company. Another droplet was added to the rich brew of his reputation. The men were jealous of him, the women of each other. It was put about that Lady Caroline Lamb, upon meeting him, wrote in her diary, 'Mad, bad, and dangerous to know.' A few days later, apparently, she wrote underneath, 'That beautiful pale face is my fate.' I felt a bolt in my stomach when I read about this. I had thought the same thing when I saw him for the first time. Instead of writing it in a diary I had painted it on canvas.

Lady Caroline lived with her husband and her mother-in-law, Lady Melbourne, whom Byron, apparently, greatly admired. My London informants told me that Byron was always in Lady Melbourne's clever, cool company. Caro acted, drew, loved Latin and Greek,

French and Italian. I studied an engraving of her: she appeared almost androgynous with her short curls and large dark eyes. I wondered if she resembled young Nicolo Giraud. She was, it seemed, a celebrated eccentric, given to rages and odd behaviours. Normally I have little use for women like that – professional *prime donne*. If I had met her, Caro Lamb would have felt the sting of my tongue. I might well have refused to paint her. I'm sure she could never sit still. Of course, I never met her, but she was the next woman in Byron's life, so I included her in my researches. And the more I heard about her, the more my opinion of her softened. Finally I saw her as someone to pity. After all, she was not so different from me.

Even so, I could never understand what perversity drew Byron into her bed. I knew that a woman who took the initiative in the intellectual passions was a horror to him. Caroline did not seem to be his type. Nevertheless, provoked, it seems that he took her, though in perfect coolness. The affair was the sensation of London. Both lovers played to the public gallery. Caroline followed him around, sent him a *ciuffo* of pubic hair, made scenes, twice ran away from home in one-sided elopements. Hobhouse was forced to intervene to save his friend from being carried off. He would turn terracotta with embarrassment when I asked him about the *ciuffo* later.

'Really? She really did that?'

'Yes, and she expected the same in exchange. She told him to be careful with the scissors in the process.'

Byron quickly tired of Lady Caroline's histrionics and conspired with her family to have her exiled to Ireland. He began what seems to have been a languid affair with the forty-year-old Lady Oxford, wife of Edward Harley, fashionable and voluble in pink pearls, so voluble that she was given the nickname of 'Silence'. Byron was just one of a series of lovers – a fact so well-known that her brood of assorted children were sometimes described as the Harleian Miscellany.

I heard it all, every whisper, every drop of malice. All this time, my English lords and ladies came rustling stiffly into my studio in Venice for portraits. They knew nothing of my relationship with Byron, but, given a glass of *vin santo* and a comfortable chair, they began to talk, and it was always of London's great triangular scandal, that of Lord Byron, Lady Caroline Lamb and Lady Oxford. It seemed to me that Byron was living inside a malevolent bubble. Like Venice, he had only transparent walls to protect him. Against London's ravening gossips he had no defence.

From Lady Oxford's house, Byron sent Caroline a definitively cool letter, insultingly fastened with his new lover's seal. Caroline had plans for that letter. Meanwhile, her behaviour worsened. In her rustic exile, Caroline burned an effigy of Byron while village girls, dressed in white, danced around the pyre. She herself, dressed as a page, placed on the fire a basket containing his books, his ring, copies of his letters, a lock of his hair. It was not his hair, in fact. It was a servant's chestnut curl she had cherished since the day he sent it at the height of their affair. Even then, he had begrudged her a hair of his head. When she asked for another curl, he sent her one of Lady Oxford's. Caroline had the buttons of her servants' livery inscribed with the motto: *Ne 'Crede B'* – *Don't Believe Byron*.

Caroline came back to London. A confrontation was inevitable, and it came. At a ball, Caroline approached Byron. He spoke to her negligently and turned away. Shortly afterwards Caroline was seen to pick up a pair of scissors. Accounts were confused. The one I heard most often was that Byron suggested that Caroline turn the blade on herself rather than on him, having already struck his heart. *That sounded like him*, I thought, *yes, he would say that*. Caroline ran away with the scissors, and returned spattered with blood, having been cut slightly in a scuffle with some ladies who tried to remove her weapon from her. Other stories were circulated that she had cut herself on a custard-dish.

I soon realised that Hobhouse hated Caroline. Describing the excesses of her behaviour truly pained him. With some difficulty, he explained to me that Byron had made one dreadful mistake with Caroline. In the time of their intimacy she had squeezed the truth out of him. She knew of the Greek love. When the time came for revenge, she was ready with potentially fatal revelations.

Hobhouse told me how Caro assaulted Byron with threatening letters. Knowing Byron, I doubt if he bothered to read them. His desk was heaped every morning with other, less predictable, and more entertaining correspondence. He had started to receive hundreds of *billets-doux* – from respectable married women offering to flee their husbands, from aristocratic ladies, from provincial spinsters, from chorus girls and actresses. He kept these letters in a trunk labelled 'Anonymous Effusions'. Miss MacDonald of Clifton begged a lock of his hair. Miss Baldry of Pimlico confessed, 'I adore you.' Meanwhile Henrietta d'Ussières beseeched him in letters, and in agony columns, to let her be his 'sister'.

Even with Caroline out of the picture, Byron was still on everyone's lips. He fuelled the flames. He published a new poem, *The Giaour*, an Oriental tale of a Venetian-style Harold; the hero bore the same pale, haunted face and the same bitter smile. My faithful English clients sent me a first edition 'to continue your education, Madame Cecilia, in the beauties of the English imagination'.

I seized the book and took it to my chair by the window. Hours later, I looked up, drained. I realised that I had not once reached for my dictionary. For *The Giaour* Byron had merely retraced his old steps. I knew the vocabulary already from *Harold*. So did the English public. They adored it. Byron's *Giaour* would run through fourteen editions by 1815.

Again, it would be Hobhouse who eventually explained to me what happened next in the astonishing drama that Byron lived out apart from me.

Byron's half-sister, Augusta, came to see him. Her marriage to her feckless cousin George Leigh had left her destitute and with a tribe of unruly children. She appealed to Byron for help. No one was less able to give it. His own debts were on the point of forcing him to flee to the Continent a second time.

Byron had not seen Augusta for years. It seems that the reunion was ecstatic, excessively so. I can well imagine that Byron was physically delighted by her. Later, I saw her portrait, which was full-face, and I thought it might have been a painting of Byron himself in a long wig. Hobhouse would tell me that Augusta had the Byron profile, the frowning eyebrows, the same chestnut curls, the full chin, the pouting, flexible lips. 'She was as shy as he was,' said Hobhouse. 'She had the same talent for mimicry and she loved, she adored, to laugh. She even affected a little lisp on her "r" just like him.'

If you ask me, Byron's love for Augusta was less incest and more an extreme form of narcissism. With this thought, of course, I preserved myself from jealousy. I theorised that it was natural for him to love someone who was the image of himself. Augusta was the nearest creature in existence to Byron, in blood, style and spirit. *Why, if I saw her*, I said to myself, *I might well conceive a passion for her too!* And perhaps, for Byron, there was a touch of exoticism in having her – yet another way for him to make himself an outlaw. Hobhouse would explain that in England, at that time, incest was the fashionable aristocratic vice. It carried a maximum six-months sentence, and even its social stigma was tinged with romance. It was part of the taboo-breaking, passion-sweltering, love-beyond-control spirit of the age, the spirit defined by *Childe Harold*. So incest was not excluded from the drawing rooms of English society. I thought that it was perhaps a peculiarly *English* tendency: a delicious *frisson* to refresh the native dullness without contaminating the blood of the aristocracy.

'I am not over-fond of resisting temptations,' Byron had often quoted from *Vathek*. In fact, I doubt if he ever resisted a single one. Within days, it seemed, the love between sister and brother ignited into sensuality. Byron knew no other way to be intimate with a woman, and from Augusta, it seems, he craved the most intense intimacy, the most extravagant proofs of love. With the Byron features, it was rumoured that Augusta had also inherited the irritable, unreliable and urgent Byron libido, and the inability to restrain herself, and, more importantly, an inability to see *why* she should restrain herself.

Hobhouse, of course, watched with concern, warned Byron of disaster. This new, old, unique love was hard to shake, but, eventually, perhaps exhausted, Byron tried. He sent Augusta away and, according to my English clients, now toyed with another married woman, Lady Frances Webster. He was writing a new Turkish tale, *The Bride of Abydos*, in which his heroine Zuleika loves her brother, Selim. *The Bride* was dashed off, Byron boasted, to anyone who would listen, in just four desperate days. *Vathek*, I recalled, had taken Beckford just three. I remembered Byron's keen interest in this feverish feat of creativity.

Augusta was pregnant, and still he could not keep away from her. He stopped trying. With Augusta to tempt and soothe him, Byron wrote pages of verse every day. The public was still hungry for Byronic heroes who were adepts of the jewelled sword and disastrously dextrous also with the ladies. Byron kept them breathless with a series of swashbuckling love-stories, starting with *The Corsair*. Written in ten days, it sold ten thousand copies upon publication, and twenty-five thousand within a month. I didn't bother to read my copy, which arrived with the predictable affectionate inscription from my client. I knew what I would see and I did not like it well enough to repeat the experience.

Byron took Augusta to Newstead, but her increasing pregnancy made it necessary for her to go home. Newstead, slipping ever further into ruin, was no place for a confinement. I saw in *The Times* that a daughter, Medora (the heroine of *The Corsair*), was born on April 15th 1815. I realised that it was exactly nine months after the reunion of the brother and sister.

The new father now wrote *Lara*, the eponymous hero of which resembled Conrad, who resembled Childe Harold, who resembled Byron.

It was all just a little too obvious.

Then, suddenly, the mood of Society changed. I heard a different, reproachful tone of voice among my English clients. I saw the querulous comments emerging in the press. I received uncertain letters from my English clients. Byron had gone too far. It seemed to me that the fashionable world of London felt slapped in its stiff powdered face. Its indulgence had been abused. Byron's poetry, which had seemed so fresh and brave, in this new light looked shameless and mocking. The whispering chorus in the gallery fed on all the evidence that Byron carelessly scattered in their path and puffed up its collective chest in indignation. It was no longer, it seemed, quite the thing, to be slavishly devoted to the works of George Gordon, Lord Byron.

But a poet – even an outlaw poet – has a poetic existence to support.

The poet's debts piled upon themselves. His new extravagances ran deep into his few remaining lines of credit. I realised that he was trapped in his unaffordable opulence.

It was part of the legend. He *had* to spend money like water. A Byronic hero does not go begging, does not economise, does not go about in a second-hand carriage. Reading between the lines of the letters I received, and the newspapers I read, I saw that Byron was slipping, floundering and drowning in his debt.

6

I did not need to worry about money, unless I wanted to do so, for I had lately acquired an aristocratic suitor, Maurizio, who for his pains truly loved me. He was the son of the elderly nobleman Maurizio Mocenigo, into whose care Casanova had tried to consign me when he left Venice for the last time. I had, of course, refused the father, but the son walked into my studio one day, and in a weak moment I decided, belatedly, to accept the kindness that Casanova had meant for me. I did not need Maurizio's financial protection, but I needed to know that I was loved, whether I triumphed or failed. Or so I thought.

There are so many ways to be loved badly! Maurizio was tall, handsome, well-built with the wide green eyes and the outspread cheekbones of north Italy. His torso was perfectly triangular, like that of an ancient Greek athlete. But he was the anemone style of lover − inanimate apart from wildly flailing limbs, eternally and ineffectually swishing nourishment towards itself. Wherever I was, Maurizio wanted to be there too. And he took the concept of 'being with' to extremes. In my presence he seemed bound to me with an inflexible short cord, so that if I moved an inch, he would move an inch and a half in the same direction, sincerely believing, in the warm sludge of his brain, that I would not notice the encroachment.

I had a feeling that he would stop being lonely for me only when his blood was forcing mine around my heart and his fingernails were neatly inserted under mine. Even then he would still be needy. He could not understand how unlovely this was for me, and how it made my blood and fingernails tingle with loathing sometimes. I was not flattered. I had been loved properly, and I knew the difference.

Predators come in all forms. No one is as hunted as those who feel under sexual pressure. I kept telling myself that Maurizio filled the great vacancy in my life for tenderness and fidelity. Indeed the gap had existed since Albania, as I was not even allowed to be Girolamo's mother in any demonstrable sense. I was so certain that I needed, that I was due, emotional nourishment.

But Maurizio, by his behaviour, forced me to think that to be alone was the thing I longed for above all others. Of course it was true that I needed love, but the screaming of my blood and fingernails when Maurizio loomed around me made me unable to think clearly. I so much wanted to love him and accept his dogged love, but his engulfing greed for me forced me to hate him when he was with me.

When he was away from me, I would rehabilitate the memory of his presence, tell myself I was fortunate to be loved by a decent person, and I would arrange to be with him again. And so we continued.

Maurizio was a kind man, but he had been bred for uselessness. It was not his fault. Sometimes, I thought I could teach him how to make love to me, but when I ventured a few suggestions, he was so

nervous that he was unable to retain the information, too convul-
sive in his gratitude. He was unable to keep my words and his joy in
the same place. When he touched me, it was with hard, sweating
fingers, which did not so much stroke as prod me, not to gain
pleasure but to reassure himself that I was there. He could not
kiss. He knew that his tongue had something to do with the act, but
when it jabbed at my mouth in little sorties from his pursed lips, I
was simply repulsed and turned my head. It was easier to distract
him with a more basic manoeuvre. He was too agitated to be able
to take more than the most primitive pleasure, and had little control of his own climactic events. Sometimes, when I was away from
him, I planned a simple voluptuous education for him, but, when he
was with me, I balked at the humiliation for both of us.

Maurizio was difficult. But I had my work. And that didn't fail
me. Since Albania, I had painted more crowned and plumed heads
from the East to the West. I travelled, I met people who pressed
their love and friendship upon me. I had painted the celebrated Mrs
Thrale in 1789, and Stendhal in 1815. I had, of course, painted
Napoleon, and anyone who was anyone in Venice. Into my studio
had walked Goethe, once, as you know, in 1786, and then again this
same year of 1815. Later he would write to me about Byron's
Manfred, complaining loudly about Byron's rape and pillage of his
great *Faustus*. 'The English poet has taken my Faustus for himself
and sucked out of it a fine nourishment for his own hypochondriac
humour!' Grudgingly, though, he admired what Byron had done, for
his audacity and his methodical stripping of all that was useful, and
the dark turn of his mind on what he had stolen.

The foreign sitters were fascinating but I still preferred to paint
Venetians. I did not think to leave Venice now: I would not leave
Girolamo. Fortunately, as Casanova had foretold, the clients came to
me. Venice is a wonderful place for a portrait painter because there
are few trees to cast their variegated shadows into our light. For my

portraits of Venetians, I would try to find out where the portrait would be hung, and make it harmonise with that space. So during the day, I inhabited the great *palazzi* of the Grand Canal, painting their owners, the wives of their owners, and their children, surrounded by the emblems of their wealth and nobility: treasure chests, model boats and family jewels.

But in my studio, at night, I painted the same owners, with their lovers, surrounded by red roses and flesh-coloured silk. And when I finished them, I took out my old Albanian portrait of Byron, and caressed it with my brush.

7

Quando Dio vol castigar un omo,
el ghe mete in mente de maridarse.

When God wants to punish a man,
he puts him in mind to get married.

VENETIAN PROVERB

I t is only now that I can tell you everything. It has taken years to
piece this picture together. You already know that I have had all
the best sources. By the time I met Hobhouse again, years after
Albania, he was stuffed with useful information. He seemed to feel
he owed it to me to tell me everything I wanted to know about
Byron. As you know, there were others, too. Through what they
wrote, which I later read, I also became the unknown confidante of
Lady Caroline Lamb, and even Annabella Milbanke herself, in matters regarding the man they both loved, almost to their destruction,
as I did.

I took it all, this information flavoured with love, jealousy and
hatred, and I distilled a more piquant truth when I mixed it with
my own knowledge of Byron. What did I want to do with this
truth? Nothing good. In my heart, I had not parted company with
Byron.

I still had that one unfinished painting of him from Albania. Every
year, as my skills increased, I added just a little to it. I considered it

my masterpiece. So those mere days of intoxication, followed by seven years of pain, had birthed one great portrait – a bargain, some would say, looking to the wider scheme of things. No matter how often I told myself that the portrait was finished, I always went back to it. I had not been able to let him go. Now, starved of his presence, I tried to find a more distant and accurate perspective. After all, it is only when your lover unwraps his hands from round your eyes that you really start to see again. So, unwittingly and involuntarily, every-one who knew Byron helped me to see more clearly.

From my various witnesses, I now saw Byron in trouble and heading towards catastrophe. When not with Augusta, Byron was yet again with the beautiful young men of his youth. To the reper-toire of his rumoured perversions with his half-sister was added this new one, subject of crude jokes in the places of men and whispered horror in the drawing rooms of London.

I knew from the English newspapers, that, unlike incest, Greek Love was neither fashionable nor remotely acceptable. Sodomy was a capital crime, as brutal and abhorred as rape. I read one account of a low-life sodomite who was hanged on separate gallows so as not to contaminate other condemned prisoners. Murderers all, the others were still to be spared the presence of a homosex-ual in their midst. And after the Greek Lover was cut down, they burned the rope. Greek Love, it was becoming clear to me, was the one allegation that Byron could not survive. I realised that it would blight the romance of his misery. The secretive remorse of the Byronic hero would be rendered sordid if it turned out to be shielding a mere sodomite from the rightful disgust and revenge of the world.

Now the whispers were of Byron's homosexual initiation at Harrow, where, it was rumoured, fifty pubescent boys were locked up in their dormitory at night without supervision. The gossip was that Byron had personally initiated three schoolfellows there.

Byron did nothing to mitigate the case against him. He was still writing poems about the beating of his heart at the sound of the word 'Clare'. Everyone knew that it was not a feminine Clare of whom he wrote: it was the lovely Earl of Clare, one of his great teenage passions.

At Cambridge, Byron had shown great interest in all matters of Greek Love. Stories of this time were now excavated and re-presented, in leering innuendo, in the gossip columns. There was more. New tales emerged of the lovely John Edelston, angelic chorister and undoubted bedfellow. There was the journey to Albania, the months in Greece and Turkey. Why else, the scandalmongers asked, had Byron gone to the barbaric East, avoiding the normal Grand Tour highlights of Paris and Rome, if not to satisfy his addiction to the 'revolting passion' that flourished there?

The hornets' nest of rumour started to fashion itself into an arrow pointing at Byron. It seemed obvious, even to me, thousands of miles away, that Byron was about to be exposed. He needed to act. He needed a wife, quickly. Marriage was the only thing that could protect him from the threatened scandal. I heard from my English clients of the various heiresses who were proffered and considered, on a more urgent basis than before.

In the end, Byron married Caro's cousin, Annabella Milbanke, a neat, clever, self-satisfied personage, whom he later dubbed *the Princess of Parallelograms*. She was chaste – prudish, in fact. She even wrote a few poems. She presented nothing unknown, nothing out of control, no challenge, no excitement: she seemed a safe haven. He was fond of her, I believe, and mildly attracted, that is, until she became his bride. It appeared that he had even proposed to her once or twice before. Annabella had turned him down, as had other heiresses, when he was running around London with the shameless, mad Caro Lamb. She had watched his relationship with Caroline, and pursed her lips, blaming her cousin, and not Byron. But now, with Caro discarded, Annabella apparently felt herself ready to 'do her duty', and bring the mad, bad Byron to heel.

'But how did he feel about it?' I would ask Hobhouse.

'Byron had a healthy inkling of her resolve. At first he joked that he had resigned himself to becoming *Lord Annabella*.'

'But why her?'

'For years,' Hobhouse told me, 'Annabella had seemed the only woman in London capable of keeping Byron at arm's length. I think he liked that.' Hobhouse shook his head and added, 'But even Annabella was not capable of leaving him alone.'

'How did they become close?'

'They did not. Instead of getting to know each other, they wrote letters.'

An arch, fey correspondence had grown between them, in which Annabella hinted delicately at a position vacant – saviour of his immortal soul – and in which he revelled in his depravity, enjoying shocking her. 'There is no doubt that Annabella was one of the many women who fell in love with Childe Harold, and looked for him in Byron,' said Hobhouse. 'She just suffered for it more than most.'

'Was she beautiful?' I asked Hobhouse. 'Was she *fascinating*?'

Hobhouse was not a portrait painter, nor even a man to revel in the beauty of women. From him, I gleaned merely that Annabella was pretty enough to be enjoyed but not so glaringly beautiful as to attract rivals in the case of neglect. Hobhouse confirmed this, in his ponderous way, concluding, 'No, Annabella was not unworthy of attention.' Such lukewarm descriptions! Attention would not be Annabella's portion, however. Byron's matrimonial creed, I already knew from our conversations in Albania – and Hobhouse would have known it too – was that one should marry a woman of good birth and fortune, whom one did not love, and breed children with her. And then leave her alone, to pursue one's passions and one's destiny.

'Did Annabella not read what he wrote of Conrad, or Harold?' I asked Hobhouse, wonderingly. 'Did she not see what was in store for her?'

'Oh, Annabella was full of self-confidence. She thought that, being with such a good person as herself, he would start to become good by association. She thought decent family life would soon help him forsake his bad ways.

'Or so she justified it. I think the truth was that Annabella, despite herself, had fallen in love with Byron, just like every other girl. Then, when the engagement became public, for the first time in her life she found herself envied and talked about.' Hobhouse added, thoughtfully, 'She had taken first prize in the great shooting match of London high society: she had scored Lord Byron. I think that much of what happened afterwards can be explained by Annabella's need for the kind of attention that warmed her in the engagement. Certainly, she had need of warmth, later.'

Compliments and congratulations had flooded in. Even Lady Caroline wrote to Byron. It was a letter heavy with sarcasm. Hobhouse told me, 'She claimed to love him like a sister, like Augusta. Evil woman!' (*Ecco quà!* I thought, a sister, an English *lingua biforcuta!*) Caro spread the word in the gossip columns that 'a certain Lord B would not be able to survive his marriage to a certain mathematical Miss A, it not being his style to pull with a woman who went to church punctually, and understood statistics and had a bad figure'.

Secretly, Caroline was preparing an explosive wedding gift for the couple. She was putting the finishing touches to a masterpiece of her own, an expansive work of 'fiction', entitled *Glenarvon*. She had written the novel in four weeks, while locked up in disgrace for injuring a servant by throwing a hard ball at his head.

'If you want to know about Byron's marriage to Miss Milbanke, you should read *Glenarvon*,' Hobhouse told me. 'There you have it: how it came to be, and how it would be. Caroline is a worthless writer, but she knows her subject.' I had my own green-bound copy, of course, within days of publication, with the usual affectionate dedication from my English client – 'Here's what all London is talking about now, Madame Cecilia, with love.'

Slowly, I made my way through Caro Lamb's *Glenarvon*. It was a melodrama, but even its excesses brought me to tears. I cannot describe it better than to say it was like reading my own diary transcribed by some effeminate buffoon and set in a far-off country. The names were changed, but the pain was the same. So much of it, albeit expressed so badly, was true to my own experience.

In *Glenarvon*, Caroline left nothing to the imagination. As a lover, and now as a writer, she had always scorned subtlety. She depicted herself as Calantha, a wayward but innocent young woman swept up in the corrupt society of London hostesses and their nibbling poetic parasites. Poor, wild Calantha is seduced by the evil but fascinating Glenarvon. *He* is depicted as a mad anti-hero, complete with demoniacal laugh and sweeping black cape. Murder, kidnapping and seduction are his *modi operandi*. After ruining Calantha, Glenarvon abandons her with the coldest of cruelty for a cynical affair with a sophisticated married woman. (Caroline interspersed her story with extracts from the real letter Byron had sent her when he was staying with Lady Oxford.) Finally, Glenarvon sends Calantha to her death with the news that he is about to marry a prim little heiress, Miss Monmouth.

Caroline wrote:

Her youth, her innocence, a certain charm of manner and of person, rare and pleasing, had already, apparently, made some impression upon Glenarvon. He had secretly paid her

every most marked attention. He had even made her
repeatedly the most honourable offers. At first, trembling
and suspicious, she repulsed the man of whom rumour had
spoken much . . . but alas! too soon she was over-reached by
the same fascination and disguise which had imposed upon
every other.

As yet happily ignorant of Caroline's literary exertions, Lord
Byron and Miss Milbanke continued with the extensive formalities.
The engaged couple were nearly strangers to each other.

'How could they let it go on like that?' I asked Hobhouse.

'Ah Cecilia, remember that we are not Italians. Annabella
remained absorbed in her fantasy of redemption, Byron in excesses
he felt justified by the coming sacrifice of his liberty. It seems to me
now that neither wanted to break the shell of their remoteness:
what lay beneath was too troubling to contemplate. Annabella did
not want to know that he did not love her. He did not want to know
that she adored him. So they hid their secrets in letters. It was fatal
for both of them.'

'So they hung themselves on their separate gallows?'

'Yes, you could say that,' said Hobhouse, with a sad smile. 'It certainly seemed more like a public execution than a wedding.' Even
the proposal and the acceptance had been made by post, and Byron
did not hurry to the side of his new fiancée. It was clear to everyone that he had no desire to take physical possession of her, or to
rejoice in that possession. Post-engagement letters from her were
frequent, as if to reassure herself of the decision. His were sparse,
superficial, theatrical. I read in an English newspaper that people
had started laying bets at Newmarket as to whether the marriage
would actually take place.

But the deed was to be done. Byron ('to the utter disbelief of his
friends,' commented Hobhouse) moved slowly, slowly towards his

shackles. Via pilgrimages to Augusta, and Newstead, Byron made his way to his fiancée. At Newstead he carved his initials, entwined with those of Augusta, upon an elm in the ancestral park. Finally, there was nothing else to be done. Byron set off for his marriage. Never, as Hobhouse observed, was a bridegroom in less haste to claim his bride.

8

La mare sèmena, la morte tol su.

What the mother sows, death reaps.

VENETIAN PROVERB

From the first, my customers were surprised to see the profusion of Madonnas in my studio. They soon became accustomed to it. I had become obsessed with copying the great Madonnas of La Serenissima. Giovanni Bellini I copied, and Tiziano, and Veronese. I copied the Greek icons from our churches: Madonnas of Tenderness with their hands cupped around little knees or around the faces of the little babies who swarmed up to their cheeks.

The Christ child always had Girolamo's face.

Other than that, I copied them faithfully, absorbing the Madonnas' beauty. I did not paint my own face, indeed I felt I did not deserve to be among them. My image with Girolamo's should not hang anywhere, should it? I had abandoned my baby. Painted Madonnas keep their colourless tears in the well of their pale round eyes. A good painter will make you feel them beneath the surface. And so I tried to keep mine inside me. But it did not always work out like that. Sometimes I erupted in noisy tears while I painted, and stood sobbing in front of my own work.

When I painted my son, I gave him everything. I gave him kings to visit him, I gave him the soft warm stench of beasts to surround him. I gave him frankincense, gold and myrrh. Then I read somewhere that myrrh was used for embalming. *This child of mine was not born to die*, I told myself. So when I painted the container of the myrrh it was empty inside. My baby would not die. I painted him '*argento vivo*' – silvery with life.

The Armenians had no wealth. They had only their minds, but of those they gave exhaustively to my son. They fed his brain with good thoughts and fine words. I saw him becoming wise, alight with knowledge. I knew they saw him as one of the chosen ones. This worried me, in view of the sad history of their faith. Did they think that this baby of mine was born to suffer and die for humanity's sins?

Girolamo had been baptised by the monks. I was allowed to watch from behind a curtain as my little son was passed from hand to hand. I saw the gold cup arch over his head, turn and drop the arc of water upon his tiny head. He had never known rain, my baby, in the high skies of Albania. I prayed he never would. I saw a solemn young altar-boy attending with a long white taper. He was absorbed in his ceremony, concentrating on his role. This was my little Girolamo's fate. I already knew that I would not be allowed to watch his acceptance into the novitiate.

My desires and aversions developed as Girolamo grew older. At first, I could not bear mothers with babies. Then I could not bear mothers with little stumbling children; then mothers with little boys who walked upright and could argue with their mamas. I never had that luxury with Girolamo. From Girolamo I had the most perfect crystalline courtesy. The manners of San Lazzaro were so decorous as to desex us all. Girolamo bowed to me as he bowed to the Fathers. He *respected* me. I was an adult, and my art was a special kind of religion in his eyes, I think.

But there was such grace about him! Such fervour in his polite-
ness! Such a winning modesty! Such a delectable crinkle around the
eyes when he smiled! Such a sweet moue of the lips when he
returned to gravity! At all these times, and when he bowed to me,
he reminded me of Casanova.

But he was better than me. He was better than both of us. He
had been born with an inner grace, a light inside. Byron had the
same thing in a physical way; I still envisioned an alabaster lamp
when I thought of him. Girolamo's light was truer because it came
from his soul.

I was less than Girolamo, because I had not learnt to bite my flay-
ing tongue. I still hurt Sofia and Maurizio with irony and worse.

I was less than Girolamo because I had not conquered my love
for Byron. I still wanted him, and I still burned for him. I had not
learnt to renounce him. I was still weak, infected by my stubborn
useless desire.

9

El matrimonio nasce da l'amore
come l'azéto dal vin.

Marriage comes from love
the way vinegar comes from wine.

VENETIAN PROVERB

When he finally arrived, Annabella told everyone afterwards, she found her fiancé coarser, somehow sullied since they last met. *As well she might*, I thought, when I read her account years later. Moreover, she was disturbed by the dark and frequent self-reproachful allusions he muttered in their few stilted conversations. He had not brought an engagement ring or a gift. A prenuptial agreement was signed and its embarrassing details were circulated in gleeful whispers.

It was Hobhouse, of course, who would describe the wedding to me and the pathos of Byron's terror, which he had tried to disguise with an acrid graveyard humour. Byron had wanted Hobhouse and other friends to find their own brides, and share his torture. He fantasised about all his friends being bound together, as if to receive a simultaneous electric shock. 'I could not oblige,' said Hobhouse, ignoring my interrogatively arched eyebrows, 'but I came, with all the support I could give him. He seemed like a man condemned to the cruellest death.'

Hobhouse, as you know, had an abiding love of plodding detail. His brain was a vast repository with no classification system. When he described the wedding, he omitted no detail, visual or emotional. If I were the kind of artist who did wedding portraits, I could have painted a picture of the supposedly happy couple, from his words alone.

Byron wore black to his wedding, rejecting the traditional English blue. He refused to be married in a church, so the wedding took place at his new wife's family home. Byron had to be called away from target practice to say his vows.

Annabella appeared in a muslin gown trimmed with lace at the hem, a white muslin jacket, and nothing on her head. She was plain as a shepherdess. She looked steadily at Byron as the parson intoned the rites. Her answers fell like peals of small bells. She had achieved her conquest, an innocent conquest. 'I am sure that is just how she felt,' said Hobhouse. 'She meant no harm.'

Throughout the ceremony, Byron muttered his responses, as if confessing a small and shameful felony. When he vowed to endow his wife with all his worldly goods, he smiled ironically at Hobhouse, and they telepathically added up his total debts. When it was over, Byron gave no sign of pleasure at the deed being done, or of affection for his new wife. He bolted to a corner like a wronged animal, where he stood pale and glowering. No one dared approach him to offer congratulations.

It was January 2nd 1815, dark and stormy. The guests proceeded silently to the reception chamber, as if to a wake. Hobhouse, for one, felt as if he had buried a friend. Certainly, Byron looked a walking corpse. He was, said Hobhouse, so pale as to be a species of light blue. 'He looked inhuman.'

The wedding cake was stale, having been baked a month before, and kept waiting for the reluctant bridegroom.

'Apparently, no one had thought it worthwhile to bake a new one, as there was every chance that he would not appear at all,' explained Hobhouse. 'As I remember it, Annabella's hand shook as she tried to pour the tea, and the rattling of the silver teapot was the only noise for a very long time. No one had anything to say. It was the most silent party you ever saw, even in England.'

After trying in vain to masticate the cake, the guests left as soon as they could. Byron, sitting in the carriage about to depart on his honeymoon journey, would not let go of Hobhouse's hand. The wedding, it seemed, had indeed electrified Byron. Hours later, he still appeared spectral, unreal, unlike himself.

'Everything was finished,' remembered Hobhouse. 'The horses were snorting and chafing. I believe that Byron's dangerous quietness had infected them with anxiety. Everyone else looked away in embarrassment. At the last minute, Byron stared at his hands enclosing mine, and said to me, "Look, these small white hands are sold into slavery now." He would never have left. It was Annabella who signalled to the coachman to pull away. My hands slipped out of his grasp. He looked straight ahead, not at her. I wondered then what lay in store for the poor lady, who seemed at that moment so much in charge of her destiny.'

The horses started off. Hobhouse became a pin-prick in the distance. Annabella sat patiently by the stranger she had married.

The Cat Speaks

The yellow silk coverlet in Cecilia's studio is a diary of my comings and goings, my triumphs over fur and feather at either end of my digestive tract. Look at my work! Blood, mud, small regurgitated skeletons and skulls, pale ornamental paw prints upon the yellow silk.

By the records I keep here Cecilia may know that I am happy and successful.

Cecilia is my woman. We are married.

I could purr and fawn around her to reassure her about this, but I know a better way to keep her love and attention. I treat her coolly and this keeps her passionate, and this keeps us both happy.

I don't often look her in the face when she talks to me. Sometimes it is just too much effort to mew so I open my mouth silently to show that it has occurred to me to address her. Cecilia understands. We are married.

Cecilia is important to me. It is against her backdrop that I enact my daily dramas of murder, disappointment, sleep and sex. I share my fleas with her. I sing my special Chicken Song to her when she comes to the studio with a damp parcel from the butcher. I sneer at her only when she behaves incongruously. I am deliberately rude to her only when she leaves me no choice.

When all is *a posto* I reward her with *passive* approval. I love her a little more in the winter when it is cold outside. Sometimes she eats something luscious and then I sniff her mouth as if kissing it. I would love her more if we were not married, but that is my nature.

I am sorry about the coverlet. It's simply that when my feet are clean they don't feel like walking on silk. That, too, is my nature.

10

Matrimoni e macaroni —
se non i xe caldi no i xe boni.

Marriage and macaroni —
if they are not hot, they are not good.

<small>VENETIAN PROVERB</small>

Annabella's own account of their honeymoon makes sad reading. For her, the joy closed up the moment it should have blossomed. In the carriage, it seemed that Byron remained eerily silent for several hours, and then burst into an Albanian dirge, howling as if at the malevolent fate which had married him to Annabella Milbanke. It must have been the same savage noise that he had made as we sat together on the window-sill in Tepelene.

As the light failed and the snow closed in, he vented all his bitterness against his bride and her family.

'You are a fool to have married me,' were the first words Annabella, apparently, heard from her new husband.

They arrived in the evening at Halnaby, the house where they were to begin their married life. It seems, from her coy chronicle, that Byron deflowered Annabella, peremptorily, on the sofa before dinner. *Yes*, I thought, *he would not make a ceremony of it*. He ate in silence, with his arm around his plate, as if she might steal the very food from his fork. He told her that she could sleep with him if she must, but he preferred his own company. Before he lay down, facing away from her, he placed a dagger and two pistols beside the bed. Annabella climbed in beside him. He did not turn to her. She did not know yet that he hated to sleep with his women. She reported later that when he awoke in the middle of the night, and saw the firelight flickering on the red curtains, he screamed that he was in Hell.

But it was Annabella who had fallen from grace. Byron tortured his wife with words and with black, frigid silence, and with a clear and insatiable desire for the presence of Augusta. 'Annabella was not stupid,' Hobhouse told me. 'Her suspicions about the true nature of his relationship with Augusta were surely thrust upon her with her own first physical experience. Byron *wanted* her to know.

'He wanted to punish her as much as possible for taking his liberty. And he wanted to test her.'

'He was testing her love? To see if it came with conditions? Like a naughty child with his mother?'

'You could be right, Cecilia. You Italians know about mother-love, don't you?'

And so Byron tested Annabella, it seems from her recitals, to the full extent of her capacity to suffer, and her proud determination to love him.

The day after the wedding he announced to Annabella, 'I have done that for which I can never forgive myself.' She gently urged him to unburden himself, but he replied that she 'could know nothing of the things to which he alluded – good women could know nothing'. Finally, he mocked her with terrifying tales of insanity on both sides of his family.

Caroline Lamb, deep in chapter XIX of the second volume of *Glenarvon*, described what may have happened to Annabella. When

I read this page, I felt the warmth of truth rising from it. In Byron's own copy of the book, I later found he had underlined in red crayon the following passages:

> Glenarvon said there was a horrid secret, which weighed upon his mind. He would start at times, and gaze on vacancy; then turn to Calantha, and ask her what she had heard and seen. His gestures, his menaces were terrific. He would talk to the air; then laugh with convulsive horror; and gazing wildly around, enquire of her, if there were not blood upon the earth, and if ghosts of departed men had not been seen by some.
>
> Calantha thought that madness had fallen upon his mind, and wept to think that talents such as his were darkened and shrouded over by so heavy a calamity. But when the fierce moment was passed, tears would force their way into his eyes, and placing her hand upon his burning head, he would call her his sole comforter, the only hope that was left him upon earth, his dearest, his only friend . . .

'But Annabella broke him down in the end,' said Hobhouse. 'He had not really been in possession of himself since the wedding.'

Finally, exhausted by his own performance, Byron started to talk to his wife. After bottles of claret, he must have raved to her of his childhood abuse at the hands of Nurse May and his ungentle mother. As if to compensate, he let Annabella mother him, tenderly, like the women of his poems. 'She was allowed to tend his little foot,' said Hobhouse, wonderingly, 'bathe his head with eau-de-cologne, or feel his pulse when his hypochondria persuaded him of some deadly ailment.' I could hear the jealousy growing in Hobhouse's voice. I realised, too, that though he tried to be fair, Hobhouse could not make himself actually like Annabella. Maybe he envied her these intimate ministrations she was so briefly allowed.

Annabella nursed him back to physical health. But she made him strong enough to hurt her. When he was well again, he turned on her. Annabella would suffer for the freedom she had stolen from him. Byron revolted at husbandhood. He revolted at her vision of his redemption. And every cloying 'dearest' and every clinging touch at his elbow would be punished. She had only to wait and see.

When the couple visited Augusta's home, it seems that Byron subjected Annabella to endless humiliation. Early one night, he dismissed her as the siblings sat cosily together: 'We don't want you, my charmer.' Hours later, when he came to bed, he told her, 'Now I have *her*, you will find that I can do without *you*.' Night after night, Annabella lay in bed listening to their intimate laughter downstairs. Byron, who had confessed sympathies for Herod, changed his attitude and showed great affection to little Medora, and called her his child. I imagined Annabella leaning over the cradle and looking from the baby to her husband. I saw her suddenly growing white and rigid, taking a step backwards, her eyes ablaze with tears.

She would have been shocked when he alluded with great authority to the fact that Augusta wore the new-fangled drawers. She would have borne in silence their giggles and knowing smiles. It must have seemed to her that her silent suffering somehow added to their complicit pleasures, which otherwise excluded her. But every night, when he finished with Augusta, he performed his nuptial duties with Annabella, without words and without gentleness.

In the early hours, Byron would leave both women, to sleep alone. Both Annabella and Augusta must have suffered equally from Byron's horrendous moods, and drew, in some ways, closer together, to shelter themselves from the fire. And in the middle of this heat, Annabella conceived a child.

The Byrons moved to London. *Number 13, Piccadilly Terrace*, I read in the newspapers. I guessed from the description of its style that it was a house well beyond their means. Ten days later Augusta arrived. Again, Annabella lay upstairs in bed, listening to the intimate laughter late in the night. Annabella, disgusted and terrified, must have begun, at this point, to discard her romantic notions of herself as gentle saviour of her husband's soul. Nowadays, I imagined, she thought more often of Byron's dagger by her lonely bedside, and wished to plunge it into her sister-in-law's heart.

In Caroline's *Glenarvon*, a discarded lover warns the poor Calantha about what she should expect from the man in whom she has placed her faith and entrusted her reputation. When I read this passage, I thought of Annabella, and wondered at which moment she allowed herself to see the truth about her marriage.

But there will come a time when you will draw his character
with darker shades, and taking from it all the romance and
mystery of guilt, see him, as I do, a cold malignant heart,
which the light of genius, self-love and passion, have warmed
at intervals; but which, in all the detail of every-day life,
sinks into hypocrisy and baseness. Crimes have been
perpetrated in the heat of passion, even by noble minds; but
Glenarvon is little, contemptible and mean. He unites the
malice and petty vices of a woman, to the perfidy and villainy
of a man. You do not know him as I do.

Byron, it seemed, was violently allergic to his marriage. In London, his behaviour, if possible, worsened. The debts mounted, and it looked as if the bailiffs and the midwife would be calling on Annabella at the same time. Byron was scarcely at home. He had taken up with an actress, Susan Boyce. He was open in his infidelity and announced to Annabella that he intended to continue with Susan and anyone else who took his fancy. He seemed not to be married at all. The days when she bathed his forehead and tended his feet were long forgotten. She must have almost missed the days when he had hated her with violence. Now the neglect was comprehensive.

As Annabella went into labour, Byron was shooting the tops of soda bottles in the pantry. When first shown the child, a girl, he said to the squalling infant, 'Oh! what an implement of torture I have acquired in you!'

Hobhouse told me, between ponderous lines, that Byron attempted to sodomise Annabella after the baby was born. Hobhouse could never bring himself to address this issue in clear words in any language. In fact, even before he told me, I had already guessed. We women, in the end, have the more physical grasp of the world.

Poor Annabella! Worse than his affront to her person, Byron must have also violated her intellectual innocence. As he raged around the bed where she lay recovering from the birth, I am sure that he subjected her to the same shocking revelations that Caro Lamb had heard, including, no doubt, the crime of which good women could know nothing. Annabella no longer wished to know, but that was no reason to spare her. She had dared to trap him in marriage. Byron was taking his revenge. He laughed at her tears.

Caroline wrote, just in case Byron had withheld anything:

Deeds of guilt concealed from other eyes, he now dwelt
upon to Calantha with hórrid pleasure. 'Shrink not, start
not,' he exclaimed, when she trembled at each new
confession. 'Proud, even of my crimes, shall thou become,
poor victim of thy mad infatuation . . .'

'Oh must I become as hardened as wicked,' she said,
bursting into tears. He pressed her mournfully to his bosom.

'Weep,' he replied, 'I like to see your tears; they are the last tears of expiring virtue . . .'

Shortly after the birth of the baby, christened Augusta Ada, Annabella left Byron.

There were convulsions in the English and even the Italian press. Annabella fuelled them. She was once again at the centre of attention. The journalists feasted on the story. Even in Venice I was able to read intimate 'eye-witness accounts' of the unspeakable sufferings of poor young Lady Byron, and put together the story as I knew it would have happened.

Annabella announced to all that he was insane.

'Byron? Rejected? . . . How . . .?' I would ask Hobhouse. It seemed to me unlikely that he could swallow this concept, in fact or thought, he thought. Hobhouse told me, 'You are right, Cecilia. He was devastated.'

'Did he try to get her back?'

'Briefly. His life was spinning out of control, and Annabella had seemed a safe haven. Even in moments of worst abuse, he had trusted her to stand by him. In a fair world, of course, he should expect her to expose him, but he was used to living a blessed life. Even with Caroline he had got away with it. Or he thought he had. Of course, he did not know about *Glenarvon* yet.

'And there was another thing. His debts were terrifying.'

'How did he manage?'

'He went back to Augusta, who at least loved him. And he started to accept money from his publisher, John Murray. It was a moment of the deepest shame for him.'

I understood very well. Byron had become a species of courtesan: paid for giving pleasure to people he despised. I could picture him, full of self-loathing, still penniless, besieged, taking comfort with

Augusta. I knew already that he had vented his anger in the written word. Accounts of his verbal fireworks were widely available. Byron wrote insultingly of his wife and in-laws, in memorable phrases that were repeated everywhere. He invariably referred to his wedding day as his funeral.

I could well understand that Byron's 'domestic destruction' had opened him to the world, making him vulnerable, an object of derision, a person who had been rejected. He would never forgive Annabella for that. It would be possible for him to construct in his mind a scenario whereby she stood guilty of everything he did afterwards – everything wicked, cruel or violent, that is. He no longer had a reputation to defend, thanks to Annabella. He would go to the dogs. Let his peers, and worse, the public, whisper behind their hands, he was now free to do what he wished. He had declared war on the world.

Somehow people must have scented his dangerous attitude. The scandals of Annabella and Augusta were bad enough, but what was worse was that Byron did not seem to be ashamed. The sensation was appalling. Rooms emptied when he and Augusta entered them. The fall from grace was absolute. It was time to leave England again.

'I shall go to Venice,' said Byron, and a thousand miles away, the sea wall of my studio lurched. Gondolas shivered in the disturbed water.

11

I monti xe monti senza bisogno d'essar monti.

Mountains are mountains without needing
to be mountains.

VENETIAN PROVERB

Hobhouse was summoned. They were on the road again.
'I was to meet up with him later, but of course he
needed my help with the practicalities. He was too busy
in his domestic drama to have a care for such trivialities as passports
and tickets.'

Byron was not too busy to deepen his debts. Not the least of the
final extravagances was a travelling coach, a replica of Napoleon's.
Byron had acquired the family name Noel through his marriage to
Annabella, so the doors were decorated with the initials N. B.,
those of his French hero. The coach was fitted with every conceivable luxury including a bed, a small library and a dinner service.

It was the end of April 1816. Byron left home, his separation
papers in hand. He was taking his manservant Fletcher and a young
doctor, John William Polidori. Hobhouse could not bear Doctor
Polly-dolly, who was full of himself in the diary that John Murray
had commissioned him to write about Byron's new life. 'He was a
cretin,' said Hobhouse. 'A clown.'

As they left, the bailiffs moved in, seizing everything they could. 'They even took Byron's tame squirrel, which he had abandoned in a bedroom,' Hobhouse told me.

Curiosity at Dover was peaking . . . It was reported in the English papers that a number of well-born ladies disguised themselves as chambermaids so they could watch Byron limp down the passages of the inn.

'Was he sad to leave England, at the last minute?' I asked Hobhouse.

'Who can tell? All I can tell you is that Byron left England with a stupendous hangover. He boarded the boat, like a condemned man, and waved to us on the shore until he was invisible among the waves. He seemed to be calm, but I for one was choked with emotion at what felt to be a final farewell.'

I pictured Byron on the deck, pale and vulnerable, hatred, bile and wine swilling together in his stomach. Byron was Childe Harold again, though this time embittered and older, and in search of the second half of his story. If his own poems were to be believed, it was certain to end in excesses of every kind and the misery of women.

But as the English shores receded, the new exile improved in spirit and health, and within hours had shrugged off any last remaining English restraint. Polidori recorded in his diary that when the party reached their hotel at Ostend, Byron fell like a thunderbolt upon the chambermaid.

Polidori spied intimately. There were other spies close on his heels. The English papers followed him, reporting all his new misdoings. Byron's every act seemed to show that he was indeed an enemy of everything English. He insisted on sightseeing at Waterloo, where his hero Napoleon had been vanquished, much to the poet's regret. Byron galloped over the field in an imaginary cavalry charge. He carved his name in the chapel at Hougoumont.

They stopped at Dejean's hotel at Sécheron. He entered his name in the guest book, and his age, '100'.

Within a few days I knew all these things. A whole new breed of journalist seemed to have been spawned to feed off the depravities of George Gordon, Lord Byron. He could not lift a glass of wine to his lips, it seemed, without someone finding something to insinuate about the act. He may have left England behind, but he was still selling newspapers for them, so they would not let him out of their grasp — not now, or ever.

However, for the following part of Byron's story, I have the most scrupulous of witnesses. I have never known what it is to have a female friend, but the closest I ever came to such a thing was with Mary Shelley, who was to spend the next few months with Byron.

While Byron raged around the battlefields, by the shores of Lake Geneva a previous London innamorata, plump, pretty, silly Claire Claremont, was already waiting for him, plying him with letters offering consolations of various kinds. A more interesting offer of intellectual entertainment came from Claire's hosts, Mary and Percy Bysshe Shelley. Claire was Mary's step-sister. She had come with them to the Lakes to pursue Byron.

When I met Shelley later, I found him beautiful but shy, and clearly consumptive. He was high-born, but entirely without Byron's excessive pride in his birth. Shelley was more purely political, more purely idealistic. He had deserted his first wife, Harriet, and two children to elope with Mary. Thereafter Shelley found himself the object of intense hatred. Like Byron, debts and scandal had forced him into Continental exile. Harriet would later drown herself. Like Byron, Shelley stood in danger of losing his children as a result of his unrespectable life. But London society had counted for nothing with Shelley, who lived for more abstract and intellectual pursuits.

The exiles huddled together. The Shelleys rented a little cottage by the lake, and Byron took the charming Villa Diodati nearby. Mary told me that the two households merged most days. She observed, 'It suited him. Byron had Claire at his disposal when he wanted a certain kind of comfort, or someone to make a fair copy of a manuscript. He ignored her when he did not.'

At the villa late-night discussions turned to talks of ghosts. Byron declaimed from Coleridge's *Christabel*: a description of the witch's hideous pallid breast. Shelley succumbed to the dramatic performance, and ran screaming from the room. He fainted, and when revived with cold water, told of a vision of a woman with eyes where her nipples should be. 'My poor Shelley never completely escaped that vision afterwards,' said Mary, narrowing her eyes. She blamed Byron.

Byron suggested that they each write a ghost story. He himself tired after a few pages, but, using his idea, Polidori wrote *The Vampyre*, which was eventually published (and did well on the false rumour that it was Byron's. When I read it, I could see that he had written it in Byron's company or under his influence). But Mary Shelley, herself over-stimulated in the candlelight, suffered the waking nightmare that turned into her first novel *Frankenstein*.

It seems that the three-month idyll exerted a profound influence on Byron, who, though he could never emulate it, found charming and touching Shelley's single-minded devotion to the imagination and simplicity. 'With Shelley,' Mary explained, 'Byron did not flounce or sulk or behave badly. There was no point. Shelley would not be shocked or impressed, he would not notice, except as a strange irrelevant distraction from the serious matters of life and art. His great concern was to interest Byron in the higher ethics of poetry. Byron listened, but in the end he would not be bothered with the higher ground. Poetry? – I don't think it was in him. He would always confine himself to *verse*.'

In the presence of the Shelleys, Byron continued to write, 'sometimes on the walls,' Mary said pointedly, 'but also in his manuscripts.' Byron carved his name upon the wall in Chateau Chillon, the stone fortress beside the Lake, where the sixteenth-century adventurer Bonivard had been confined. After seeing the picturesque dungeon, Byron was moved to write *The Prisoner of Chillon*, a dramatic monologue about the adventurer Bonivard who languished hopeless years inside it. Mary observed, 'He told us he could well understand Bonivard's misery after being married to Annabella for a year.'

He was also finishing the third canto of *Childe Harold*. 'You could not stop him scribbling,' said Mary. 'I think he was writing in order to escape the desolation he really felt. It was one thing to be Childe Harold, a romantic traveller, another thing to be rejected and hated, the object of gossip, and penniless. He looked at the implacable purity of the mountains and the lakes as an escape from the delinquencies for which he felt himself so violently punished.'

Then came the news that Caro Lamb had actually published *Glenarvon*. London convulsed. It flew out of the shops as if – as if it were an original Byron. Society husbands and wives stayed at home in the evenings to read it. People stood on street corners talking about it. Now everyone thought they knew everything about Byron. Caroline Lamb had known Byron *intimately*, after all.

'Was he horrified?' I asked Mary.

'Not really. It was attention. But he took the opportunity to say some terrible things about Caroline, and to throw cold water on the idea that their love-affair had been of any importance or duration. He compared it to a portrait, and told everyone that the likeness could not be very good because he did not sit for it long enough.'

I flinched at this. Poor Caroline! With me, of course, it had been the same. In fact, my time with him had been even briefer than hers.

'Did he read it?' I asked.

'He pretended not to, but he did. Madame de Stäel lent it to him. I saw a copy of it at the Villa Diodati and the spine was creased. I read it myself, of course. It just took a day or so – really, the woman writes like a guttersnipe. I can see that it would not have distressed him too much. You see, it scarcely harmed his reputation as a dangerously attractive, melancholy villainous hero.'

'What did Annabella think?'

'Oh, she was vengeful as ever, Annabella. She thought Caroline had been too kind. Apparently, she told everyone that *Glenarvon* was over-indulgent.'

My sources double at this point.

Hobhouse arrived at the Villa Diodati bringing fresh news of the demonising going on in England. He had actually been to see Caroline, who responded to his admonitions by showing him some bawdy sketches she had made of Byron. She threatened to expose them to a public clamorous for more Byron abominations. He had persuaded her against it.

'What were they saying about him?' I asked him.

'Oh, the usual mixture of truth and malice. He was supposed to be enjoying himself in the arms of not just Claire and Mary Shelley but also those of young Robert Rushton, his page. When we told him, Byron just nodded impatiently. He held out his hand for a letter from Augusta. I had none, so he turned away from us, and picked up his book. He was reading *Faust* and writing *Manfred*.'

I repeated from memory three lines, about the love of Manfred's life:

> She was like me in lineaments – her eye –
> Her hair – her features – all, to the very tone
> Even of her voice, they said were like to mine.

'So you know already?' Hobhouse said.

'Of course. I have read *Manfred*. So has everyone in Venice. But why did he hear nothing from Augusta?'

'I am afraid the reasons were most wounding. You see Annabella had got Augusta in her clutches. Augusta was sweet and weak. Annabella was cunning and subtle. And of course she thought she had God's will on her side. Byron had been gone only a few months before Annabella had extracted some kind of confession from Augusta and made her promise to hand over all the letters she received from Byron.'

'But why didn't Augusta write to him herself?'

'I think she was shamed into silence. When she did write, it was always in a strange, oblique style, as if she was writing to a stranger. It drove him mad. But he kept writing to her. Without her, he was telling her, he was doomed to wander the earth alone. And, imagine, Annabella was reading every word!'

At the end of September, Byron and Hobhouse left the Villa Diodati to travel to Milan by way of the Simplon. In Milan Byron was delighted by the Ambrosiana Library, and the letters of Lucrezia Borgia and Cardinal Bembo. He found a lock of Lucrezia's hair – so long and fair, and the letters so beautiful, that he said it made him feel wretched not to have been born sooner and at least to have seen her.

'Of course,' said Hobhouse, 'he turned it all into a pretty letter to Augusta. He could not resist mentioning a rumoured whiff of incest around the lovely Lucrezia. There was some story about her father, Pope Alexander, and her brother Cesare Borgia. Think what Annabella made of that! Byron learnt some of the Borgia letters by heart, and stole a single hair as a relic.'

'He stole Lucrezia Borgia's *hair*? From a *library*?'

'Remember, he thought he was a dangerous outlaw. In any case, he just took a single hair, which he wrapped around his finger.'

At the beginning of November, Byron and Hobhouse set off for Venice, via Brescia and Verona. Byron was in a feverish state, grey and giddy. Hobhouse remembered, 'He kept writing to Augusta, but her responses were so strange. Or course, we know why now, but at the time it was incomprehensible. Trying to fathom her words, Byron said to me, "I feel as if my head is decaying. I only wish my memory would . . ."'

In a night of rain, they arrived in Mestre and embarked in a gondola. Swaddled inside the black *felze* they drowsed, as the beak of the gondola sliced through the snakeskin water. They did not wake until they reached Cannaregio. They stirred and roused themselves as the gondola slipped past the Palazzo Labia and into the Grand Canal.

I can picture it. It would have been a soft, rocking awakening, amid the reflections of dim haloed lights, blooming fungally with vitreous petals, and the tapping of soft footsteps overhead. The echo of the oars would have told them that they were under another bridge. 'The Rialto,' their gondolier would have answered their question. Byron would have repeated 'Rialto' softly, memorising every nuance of the Venetian intonation.

They disembarked at Hotel de la Grande Bretagne, and were shown up a splendid staircase to rooms of chipped gilding and painted silks. It was seedy, and it was magnificent: it was theatre. The city and the dwelling, that first night, must have spoken to them of happy people in happier times, of mouldy sensuality and slow, delicious corruption. Byron must have passed gently from waking dreams to sleeping dreams that first night on the Grand Canal, half a mile from my studio in the Palazzo Balbi Valier.

I had not been so close to Byron for seven years.

A Gondolier Writes

It was only later that I found out who that little man was. The one with the limp and that strange white light around his pudgy little mug. He was the wicked English milord who could have had all the women in Venice, and eventually had most of them, by all accounts.

Stupid bitches. He was just a small fellow, with bad breath and a face like uncooked bread dough. Big lips like a Moor. They tell me — even my sainted mother tells me — that he writes poems to make you burst inside your breast. But how would she know? She's a washerwoman. What time has she for English poetry? She's only repeating what they say in the newspapers.

I, of course, have learnt a few lines now. I can say my piece of Byron for the English tourists and the gold drops nicely into my hand.

But when I say it — it tastes like old fruit in my mouth, that poetry of his.

He got his own gondolier soon. That dangerous Tita Falcieri. Too simple for him to limp down to the canal and hail one like an ordinary citizen. Oh no, not him. *Ma Morti!*

Remember me. I was the first gondolier to bring him into Venice. What if I had tipped him and that homely friend of his quietly into the lagoon? What if the beak of my gondola had quarrelled with his drowning limbs? How many Venetian women would have remained pure? How many hearts unbroken? How many little bastards unborn?

Part Four

1

Tosa smemorada, tosa inamorada.

The forgetful girl is the girl who has fallen in love.

VENETIAN PROVERB

Ah Casanova, here are some more numbers for you, for I know how you love them.

Now I write of a time thirty-four years since I first fell into your arms, since I slept a night of my life without your sweat upon my skin and mine upon yours. I have painted eight hundred and three portraits since I last saw you. Your cat has sired and grandsired more than nine hundred times and the silkworms have toiled in their thousands to make the velvet collars I have bought. My memoirs, though neither written nor painted, are now etched more deeply on my skin. My catalogue of sensual and artistic disasters has not been much enriched. And yes, they still speak of you in Venice. But your memoirs, no, they are not yet published.

You might not recognise me, Casanova. The fashions have changed and I with them, for I must remain pleasing to the eyes of my sitters. I know you would be fascinated with such details. The powder and paint are nearly vanished – now the fine ladies use them discreetly to enhance their complexions rather than to encrust them — not that I ever used them excessively, as you know. Hair powder is seen hardly at all now, but perfume is still the very thing. Sofia wafts about leaving a trail of 'Royal Tincture of Peach Kernels'. Our dresses have changed. No longer is the lower extreme of the waist nipped in to the narrowness of an orange and a half. Now we are tightened just beneath the breasts, which are thrust upwards and barely covered. Instead there is a great volume of fabric over our bellies, so that we all, maid and matron alike, look to be with child now. I am told that in these draperies we emulate the ancient Greek and Roman Ladies, whose Republican past is of course so much in fashion these days. Sofia, naturally, takes the concept to its outer limitation: she sports laurel leaves and cameos in her hair and san- dals à la Sappho, without having the least idea of why, except that it is all the rage.

The style of this new century is most curious also in the realm of the heart. We have become excessively polite in our speech. It is as if we no longer have bodies. It is years since I heard someone men- tion their bowels or their womb, the conditions of which we used to share in such vivid and enjoyable 'organ recitals'. Even intimate garments may not be referred to in polite conversation, or, if it is inevitable, they are described, with a little flush, as 'unmention- ables'. But it has become fashionable to be excessively sentimental. No love letter is considered sincere unless it has been spattered with counterfeit tears, applied with a sponge and rose-water. Even the hoariest of my lady-sitters wants to be depicted as a sweet victim expiring of love, or the mother of tragic sons. The men want to be shown as alabaster lamps lit from within, pale, luminous, with something erotic and something of the grave about them.

But all this fades to insignificance before the most singular and important fact of my life. I have a little son, Casanova. He is seven years old and as sweet as cream. I have named him Girolamo, for you, Casanova.

The news is not all good. I had to give my baby away. His father did not love me. I have been hurt, grievously hurt, by this man who prizes love not at all, but finds his *frissons* in a dark and chilly breed of cynicism. He does not seek lovers; he seeks victims to share the darkness inside him. He is the style of man who puts pins through butterflies, and then writes a sonnet upon the sadness of the act. The women rush to comfort him . . . And now that man has come to Venice. Yes, Byron is here. I know he will seek me out.

He will want to compare his seven-years-older physique and face with my 1809 painting of him. He takes it for granted that I will have kept – no, *treasured* – the one portrait he left me after his robbery. He will also want to compare the sensations of seven years ago, with those of today. After abusing his body in every possible way, I can be sure that Byron is no longer well. He needs to remember, against someone else's body, how strong he was before.

Since those days and nights in Tepelene, I have never seen nor heard Byron's name without a commotion in my belly. For years I have been drinking in, thirstily, all that was said in my presence respecting him. I have become a spy for him. I have scrabbled in desks and eavesdropped on conversations. With cynical motives I have befriended useful people. All this I have done to keep the thread of intelligence about him unrolling.

I tell you this too. If I have even seen a volume of his upon a table, it has awoken a wasp-barbed sixth sense of danger, a frail fire scuttling under my skin. But that has not stopped me reaching for it. I have glazed the pages of his books with my clammy fingers. I have understood every word. You would be proud of my English. How well I speak it now! Well enough to know his failings as a poet, as I know his failings as a lover. But my tongue clatters dryly in my throat if I try to explain him to you. So I will not try. I am no longer talking to you, Casanova, for now I must tell things that you could not bear to hear.

*

Since Albania, I had learnt to be afraid of Scots, of their honey-salted accents and their underwater eyes. I swam against the stream in that; for Scots and Italians have ever been attracted to each other. The Italians are drawn to the wild cruel simplicity of the Scots; theirs is a life pared down to a solitary cloud mirrored in a loch, a ruined cottage, a single blow. The solitariness, the flintiness of the Scots is something we Italians cannot understand. We cannot live outside our families. The Scots simply do not acknowledge the pain of solitude. They will put a single rock as a monument in a far field; the very opposite of our crowded *campi*. The first Scottish cloth merchant seems to have found his way to Siena in around 1430. The Sienese churches are now crammed with tiny interior scenes from the lives of the saints, each bed sporting its fashionable plaid blanket. Under these blankets, for centuries, Scots and Italians have tried to love each other.

But it doesn't work, it will never work, a Scot and an Italian. At least not a Scottish man, with rocks in his heart, and an Italian woman, with soft carboniferous substances smouldering inside.

There are kisses a Scot can give you that are not worth the saliva they're etched on. Scots are not naturally good kissers: their lips tend to be thin, and their teeth prominent. They don't know, or care, to make their lips into eels, starfish, petals. They don't know how to turn their fingers into lips.

They know the bones of the act, and sorry little climaxes. Byron didn't know or care when women cried out under his kisses, whether it was the laceration of their gums under his teeth or their thighs under his elbow that caused it, and that their sobbing afterwards was the sense of loss released by their bruises. There was no shelter under his eyes, even in his embrace, and afterwards your smile would take flight in the chill wind of his choler.

For he hated to find you there when he returned from wherever his orgasm had taken him. He did not like to lie with his women; no, not even the carnal somnolence between caresses.

That's how it was for me and for the other poor *donne*. I heard it on the streets later about Marianna Segati and Margarita Cogni, about how they suffered. The muses in the casinos, the *faxoléti* in the gutters, they all cried for Byron because they could not hold him. She who came after me – she could not hold him either. She lost even her claim to be Byron's last lover. Nobody could possess him: he never loved enough to give up his liberty. Indeed, when the world was running mad after Byron, clamouring to be his lover, that was just when he despised the world the most.

In November 1816, the night Byron arrived in Venice, I was working in my studio. I had changed during the past seven years. By now I had learnt to live with the pain he had given me. I had reshaped my space in the world. I sometimes woke without thinking of him, though I never lay down without wishing him in my arms. I found that I had been allocated a certain amount of love, the most of it crowded into my fourteenth year. I was not always unhappy. I had my son, albeit at a distance. I had my success to warm me: I saw myself pointed out on the street. I could now pick and choose my commissions. My arrival was anticipated with excitement in every noble house in Venice. I had found many ways to outrun the griefs that stalked me.

There were still times when I painted to escape the pain of Byron's abandonment. There were also times when I used the pain to intensify the painting. These times became confused, and I became afraid to stop painting. On canvas, great pain informs great joy. I know that I am not unique in this, being a painter. I think we all like to put our pain on the wall so that we may observe it – and then walk past it.

But I refused to walk past. I stayed in front of my work, in dialogue with it. It was the only place I could be. Everything else bored or distressed me. I was bored with drawing breath! There seemed little point to an activity that only maintained my unhappiness and did nothing to restore my happiness. It seemed, sometimes, that every moment I did not spend painting was merely time I spent waiting, indifferently, to die. I could not always be in the studio when the pain broke out. Sometimes I slashed a wall with a charcoal outline of my pain as I passed it. We have a saying in Venice: *Muro bianco, carta da mati* — *White walls, the paper of the mad.*

Flake White, Titanium White, Zinc White . . . for the wretched, white is not beautiful; it is not pure; it is not good. It merely serves to display darkness in better relief.

A painter is a listener. Within two days of his arrival, in all the *soggiorni* in all the *palazzi*, I heard the same tidings of my old lover: *Byron is in Venice!*

A painter is an entertainer. Think how even the process of painting conspires to make this possible: many artists hold conversations as they work, with their sitters, with visitors. An artist's mind has room to roam while she works; she can simultaneously order dinner while stroking Rose Madder onto a child's cheek, all the while keeping that child still and spellbound making shadow puppets on the wall with her left hand. She can hear the words, 'Byron is in Venice!' and continue to flick her brush calmly in the gallipot as if someone had said to her, 'It's good weather in Perugia, lately.'

My Albanian portrait of Byron had never been seen, and my connection with him was not known in Venice. Remember, he was just an obscure English nobleman in 1809, before *Childe Harold* and the subsequent scandals made him conspicuous in the eyes of the world. In this way I had been able to preserve the secrecy of Girolamo's birth. Byron's celebrity had changed everything. Had my relations with him been known now, every noble and merchant of Venice would be demanding a portrait, if only for the opportunity to cross-examine me, and the chance to show the portrait, saying casually, 'Of course, this artist – Cecilia Cornaro, you know – also painted the English milord. She said that there was something about me – the eyes, the strong chin – that reminded her of him.'

I knew I should feel outraged that Byron could invade my city, take possession of my refuge, and not even show me the respect of warning me. I knew I should make it my object to avoid him, to leave Venice if necessary, until he did. I knew I should think on the seven years' silence and remember his usage of me. Whether I consented to it or not, it was ill-usage, and it should not be excused. But what I felt was much simpler: excitement, and fear. With every hour, the excitement clotted in my belly, and I began to anticipate the moment when he would come to me.

It took Byron just two days to find me.

I had been that morning to my old tree-lined boudoir of San Michele. It was where I always went to be closer to Casanova. I felt the need of his protection that day. I could not sleep, with the thought of Byron besieging the fragile peace of my mind. I left Miracoli so early that the sparrows were still nodding in their sparrow-sized niches in the walls. There was a gentle sleepy chittering as I walked past and then they sighed and resumed their early-morning dreams.

At the island I had paced backwards and forwards among the graves, imagining how Byron would commence his new assault upon my happiness. Would it be with indifference or with passion?

I thought of Casanova. *Povero*. I hoped that his dematerialised spirit had made the journey from that cold graveyard at Dux home

to Venice. I had left a rose, of course, upon the grave of little
Fortunato, and carried home with me the impression of him on my
palm.

> Con culto d'amore
> spargono fiori e pregano pace . . .
>
> In the name of love,
> Scatter flowers and beg for peace . . .

I must have stayed some hours. In my absence it had been a
strange day in Venice. When I returned from San Michele I found
the city convulsed by a new phenomenon. There was everywhere
a deafening din of unseen birds. Meanwhile tiny black feathers
floated in the thick golden air. They did not seem to settle to the
ground, but remained suspended in the ether, not so much floating
as flying of their own will. When people talked the little fronds
became tangled in their teeth. I snatched a fistful of feathers from
the air and took them to my studio. In a French manual of art
symbols I found the answer: these were baby blackbird feathers,
tokens of the dark nature of sin. The bird's alluring voice embodied the beckoning temptations of the flesh. Saint Benedict had
recognised the bird as a little devil who tried to distract him from
his devotions.

Byron is here, I thought. I tested myself for pain with the memory
of his face. Yes, the pain was still there, rich and strident. So I
turned my back on the thought of him, as I had taught myself to do,
and continued with the portrait in hand.

Hours later, in the dark of the night, I was still working in my
studio in the Palazzo Balbi Valier. I did not hear him enter. He was
so slight, that in the long shadows of the room, I did not see him
until he was standing with his hand on the back of my chair. His
touch vibrated even through the senseless wood into my heart. The

air suddenly curdled around me. Then he took my neck in his hand, hard.

'Show me your Casanova,' he said.

You know the rest. You know how he pincered my neck, made me open my portfolio, threw my Casanovas on the floor, and me after them, how I inhaled the vinegar of his breath, and how he re-entered my body and my life.

'Now you can finish that portrait of me, Cecilia,' Byron said as he left the studio.

After Byron had gone, I picked up the stained and soiled Casanovas. I did not put on my clothes. I stood naked and looked at myself in my sitters' tall mirror. I gazed at myself, and my paintings of Casanova, which I held tenderly in my arms as if to comfort them for the violence they had just sustained.

'Why did you not spare me this?' I asked an oil sketch of Casanova's face, unreasonably. 'Why did you not protect me from him?'

But I was being less than honest. I was alive with sensation. I was truly animate for the first time in seven years. It had hardly been an apology, a settling of accounts or a loving reunion, that violent rut on the floor of my studio. But I was filled with something like happiness, for I could not help feeling, with a corrupt kind of triumph, that Byron had returned a little of what he had stolen. He had not been able to come to Venice without coming back to me. It was an involuntary gift, this proof of continuing desire for me. It had been delivered gracelessly and without the intention of giving pleasure. But it was a gift.

The cat came out of the shadows and nudged my ankle inter-rogatively. If a cat can look displeased, he looked displeased. What he had just seen was not the kind of lovemaking he knew or could approve of.

'You are right,' I told him. 'That was not pretty.'

At the word 'pretty', the cat rolled on his back and showed me his beautiful belly of blond and grey stripes stippled with white, chocolate browns and terracottas.

'But I know what I am doing,' I told him, smoothing his stomach. 'I will not just lie down and die for him. I will not let him ruin me again.'

The cat stretched until he was the longest cat he could be. He looked as if he were staked out upon the ground.

'No, you are wrong,' I told him. 'I am not going to allow myself to be hurt again. I am a Libran. The sign of the scales. I simply need more time with him in order to hurt him as badly as he hurt me in Albania. I need to make him feel pain as I felt it. My sense of balance requires it.'

The cat turned his back upon me, his tail erect in the air. He presented his posterior, clean and pink as a baby's ear.

'I know you don't believe a word of it,' I told him. 'But I am stronger now, really.'

It was not true. When Byron came back to me it seemed that I had carried inside me all these years a phial of his essence, a cloudy dangerous perfume like the dread poison of the Doges. When he limped into my studio again, the phial broke open and I was flooded with the old weakness, the old love and the old pain. It was as if he had never been absent.

The cat had lain down and was sleeping. His little paws rippled and his teeth chattered. He dribbled a little. Finally, he relaxed. I knew not to interrupt him when he was dreaming, so I left him there and went home to my bedroom, where I lay in my bath for a long time, soaking the bruises Byron had given me, telling myself lies.

The Cat Speaks
of the Pedigree of
George Gordon,
Lord Byron

A deformed cat like Byron is known to occur in nature, but not often.

He was right when he said that worst animals bear only one progeny at a time. A whole litter like *him* is inconceivable in our world. We manage things better than that. When she smelt the style of him, a mother cat might well nip him in the neck or despatch him with a cleansing paw.

A cat like Byron would be avoided by the she-cats in their season and so his cripple-seed would silt up in his loins, like his anger. Then it would die out.

Good.

No matter how dramatically or poetically he declaimed his love songs from the roof tiles, none of us would believe a word of it. We would stare at his leg, hard.

We would not encourage him with a surfeit of flattery and notoriety. We would not hold his badness up to admiration and reproach at the same time. We would not leave his few actual virtues unremarked on. Cats like Byron *want* to appear worse than they actually are.

Cats like Byron pretend to hate the world but they cannot survive without its attention. The whole world is their mirror, and when they look into it they see a better cat than they really are.

In fact, they are nothing more than schoolboys with their pockets stuffed full of firecrackers. They make a big noise, but can they catch a sparrow in their teeth? Can they nurture a family? No.

A cat like Byron might live a while, though. Soft-hearted human females would be tricked into pity by his limp, and take him to their laps.

I am not happy that Byron has come to Venice.

It is not a good thing.

2

Chi ga dentro 'l fogo, manda fora el fumo.

If you have fire inside, you send out smoke.

VENETIAN PROVERB

Y ou never see Venice for the first time. She is already floating inside you. She is waiting to pour herself into your
heart when it opens.

Byron, the Aquarian, the swimmer, loved our beaver-republic
before he ever saw her. She was one of those places he already
knew in his mind's eye, the greenest island of his imagination. How
often, in Albania, he had questioned me about our city! Even then
I had sometimes found myself thinking that in making love to me he
tried to pull Venice into his arms.

But Byron came growling into Venice. Exit London, pursued by
unbearable ostracism. Enter Venice, which had been chastened by
defeat. She was a city in exile from herself, denatured, chagrined.
Her empire had been confiscated, her lottery dismantled. The
Doges' Palace had been looted. The invaders had stripped the
Doges' boat, the *Bucentoro*, of its gold and turned it into a prison
hulk. Byron arrived in a city branded by Napoleon, who had demys-
tified those dark streets that once confounded Beckford. Each

dwelling now had its neat lozenge of a number. It was no longer possible to be lost, to lose someone, or to disappear. La Serenissima's shameless nobility had been shamed. Her arcane laws had been dismantled. Even the mouths of the stone lions in the walls had been stopped up: the secret processes of Venice were now themselves proscribed. Napoleon had paved over our *campi dei morti*: the dead were now deported to the island of San Cristoforo, and were no longer permitted to lie among us. The city was ruled as efficiently and transparently as possible by an Austrian governor. We were left gasping in the great cull of our happiness.

But Venice was not humbled, not really. If you looked beneath the surface, we were still a happy city. The four bronze horses of San Marco, once shipped off to graze in ignominy in the gardens of the Tuileries in Paris, had just been restored to us. Although our golden rule was vanquished, our warehouses still bulged with silks and stuffs from the corners of our former empire. Our churches were still crammed like magpies' nests with the jewelled masterpieces of the world. In our cafés we still served the most flagrant scoundrels of the epoch, the most extravagant lovers, the most rapacious cheats, the most monstrous murderers. Sumptuous sinning continued in the casinos. Most of all, our ancient beauty was as impudent as ever. A deep mist or a dark night could still undo all Napoleon's work, and restore her mystery to Venice.

And the city still behaved according to her nature – she sent little waves to stroke the stairs, made dark smells in alleyways, breathed her opulent sadness against Byron's cheek. Nor would the stones of Venice leave his feelings alone. I knew, because I knew Venice and Byron, how she would act on him. He would wake to find himself in love, with all the pain of a new love, with the seductive city outside his window. The *palazzi*, except the rough-hewn Byzantine ones, would appear feminine to him – delicate virgins or ruined sluts, all of them just out of his grasp. Her drowning colours and her sinuous waters would whisper to him. I knew that Venice would drive him mad with desires.

Byron had brought my descriptions of Venice with him. They were secreted in his memory, somewhere quite apart from the thoughts of me, which he had sweated into oblivion on the skins of other lovers. Now my Venetian pictures in his mind would, I knew, fuse with all five of his senses and take possession of him. That first morning, Venice must have entered Byron through his ears and his nose. I know this because I experienced the same things every morning myself. It is always a festival for the senses merely to wake up, breathe and listen in Venice.

Byron must have woken, of course, to the sound of water snickering around stone and wood and the splat of the green soil of the seagulls who laughed as they flew away. While Byron lay in bed, the orchestra of the street would have tuned itself for the day's performance, commencing with the cries of the vegetable-sellers and the answering calls of their quarry, the housewives. Everyone would be laughing, at themselves or someone else. Byron must have listened to the robust Venetian dialect, compelling to his sensitive ear. One could distinguish the sellers' wares merely from the sounds of their voices: the cries of the flower-sellers soft-tongued as petals; the grating rasps of the onion-sellers; the seductive mewing of the women who sold catmeat. There were the dangerous clipped barks of the seller of rat's bane and the cat-castrator. 'L-a-t-t-e?' lapped the milkwomen, swinging their pails on the yoke. The knife-grinder played percussionist, trundling over the cobbles with his barrow, his knives twittering on their leather straps. A lighter beat came from the stuttering of the crutches as the beggars arrived for their day's importuning. The water-borne barrel-organs competed with the music of the caged canaries, sparrows and turtle-doves.

The morning would be thick with noise and warm air dis-
placed by a thousand vibrant bodies. Any potential for collision
would be fully realised, and the laughter and apologies would
come floating through the air to Byron's ears. And how they sang,
the Venetians! A song would start on someone's lips and the
refrain would spread, until a whole *calle* was alight with music and
applause.

And the smells! The stinks and the perfumes must have coiled
around each other in Byron's fine nostrils: the scent of crisp new
laundry mixed with buttery pastry; the hot, rich stench of the
candle-makers' wares; casks on the quay breathing peppermint and
musk, which would have joined with the incense floating from the
dark-scented phials of nostrum uncorked and flourished by the
quack doctors selling eternal beauty and erotic vigour. He would
have sniffed the grainy sweet-dirt smell of potatoes being shaved of
their skins by men rocking on hundred-year-old wooden stools in
doorways. The *acquaoli* must have wafted upwards the intoxicating
fumes of chilled water opalescent with liqueurs. Below all this
would have hovered the soft salty fragrance that seeps from sun-
warmed stones in the morning and the sharp breath of the seaweed
lolling on the sea-steps at the low tide.

As he lay in bed, I knew that Byron would have read aloud from
his guidebook the euphonious names of the *palazzi*. He would have
heard the beating of wings and watched a pair of pigeons trying to
mate on a narrow ledge, snatching the least opportunity – a flurry
of feathers and a dizzy recovery. He would have listened to the
unexpected gush of lark-song from gardens hidden behind tall walls.
Then the beckoning songs of the boatmen would have begun to
invade the morning.

I was right. Later Hobhouse would tell me how Byron had leapt
from his bed that first morning and come limping to rouse him.

'I was stupefied,' said Hobhouse. 'It was an unspeakably early hour for him, who never saw the morning light if he could help it.

'But he had a belly full of fire that morning. He said, "Come, Hobhouse, let us show this deadly city how *we* live. I have a taste for *Plen & opt C*, today, Venetian style. Let us go and rock some gondolas. No? Don't look at me with those fish-eyes. Well, I shall go forth alone."

'I said to him, "Why not simply just go out?"

'He wasn't to be put off. He laughed at me: "Oh no! Hobhouse, what are you saying? I, Byron, shall *go forth*."

'I had correspondence to attend to, I refused to join him, so he thundered off alone. He pulled on a dark cloak that covered him to the ground and ran down the stairs. I went to my window to watch. After a second, Byron had slipped into the crowd and disappeared. When he came back he was full of stories, happier than I had seen him in years.'

On that first morning, Byron must have continued to hear the Venice I could not describe for him for it is necessary to experience it for one's self. As he passed through the markets he would have heard the thud of hatchets decapitating a thousand artichokes in a single morning, the struggles of boiling water in kettles. He would have heard the wooden spatulas raking through hot nuts roasting in tin drums. From open doors in the laundrywomen's houses would have issued the hiss of irons nosing through the ruffles of the ladies' linen. He must have heard the early violins musing through the windows of the *Conservatorio*. He would have stopped for a moment, there, looking up at the graceful windows.

In the morning-blooming cafés the waiters would have unfurled their tablecloths with a flourish as he passed, and the fragrance of soap dried in sunshine would have flown up to meet his twitching nose. The waiters would have bowed to him, prouder than dukes in their clean frock-coats. I know that he passed through the Merceria, tapestried with cloth-of-gold, rich damasks and silks which the shops draped from their first floors. He must have breathed in the perfumes and savoury scents from the apothecary shops. He must have dandled a finger in at least one of the shopkeepers' noisy cages of nightingales. He probably stood at a marble counter and drank a glass of orange juice red as blood. As he crossed bridges he would have trailed his fingers along elaborate railings warmed by the sun.

Byron walked into seduction. Venice is a city that likes to *fare la civetta* – make owl eyes at you, flirt. And it instils those wiles in its people – you soon learn the art of casting long looks as you pass someone land-bound when you are in a boat. You learn how to make them turn their heads and follow you with voracious eyes. And in Venice, small as she is, you learn to await the reliable joy of meeting that same person soon afterwards in some dark passageway, and remembering. It's up to you how much you grant of what you promised with your eyes from the water.

And Venice likes to laugh at you while she flirts. She plays tricks on you with her beauty. A delicate arch draws your eye up and then you see a mysterious sleeve of lace among the flowers on a balcony. And is that a stone lion perched among the geraniums? . . . But look! you have slipped in a puddle and lie sprawling on the sweating stones. Venice is laughing at you again, but so affectionately!

Byron went to the Basilica. He went alone, unwitnessed, that first time.

So I have to imagine him dragging his leg over the sunken floor all inlaid with achats, lazulis, chalcedonies, jaspers and porphyries. I must picture him in my mind's fervent eye, gazing at the sumptuous encrustations of the walls. I see him lifting his gaze to the roof, a vast inverted and undulating field of variegated gold mosaic, like a crop of corn set on fire by a sunset. I see him running his finger down cool columns of blond alabaster, rumoured to have been brought from King Solomon's mines.

I am sure he enjoyed its Oriental opulence for itself and for the memories it stirred in him of his own Eastern pleasures seven years before. He would have noted, contemptuously, a small flock of English tourists huddling together with nervous smiles. The English never know how to conduct themselves in our church, because San Marco is barbaric and intensely spiritual all at once. The bodies of stolen saints rest in disturbingly intimate proximity to the visitor. The golden cupolas are strung with dim lamps and swaying red-eyed censers that only intensify the shadows. From behind the columns come whiffs of unknowable perfumes, mixed with potent miasmas from our ancient drains. Perhaps it is this smell that makes some people fall spontaneously to their knees in San Marco's dark alcoves, smitten with sudden remorse or grief, or perhaps an uncontainable joy.

Byron did not stay long, he told me afterwards. On closer inspection, the Basilica must have troubled him. It had been built from a love he could not conceive. The enormity of the work must have stupefied him. He must have thought uncomfortably of the facility with which he threw together his verses, his own great monument, himself. San Marco, *invece*, showed the sweat, hopes and prayers – but most of all the love – of a thousand artists, giving everything of themselves, holding back nothing, and content to work in eternal anonymity.

It would have been then that he would have started to find the Oriental-looking Madonnas disturbing. The concept of worshipping a mother and child must have filled him with disgust. He could not have helped thinking of the puffy pink maternity of Annabella, and the smell of fresh milk-vomit on Ada, from those few weeks he had known his daughter. 'Miss Milbanke did not give birth. She *calved*,' he told me afterwards. In the left transept,

I imagine that the far-away eyes of the Virgin must have made him think of Annabella's staring at him, wet with tears forced out by the shock of their final encounter in the bedroom.

He dragged his leg up the Campanile in Piazza San Marco, almost to the top, where an angel turned with the wind. From there, he saw the prospect down the Adriatic as far as Istria, and our miraculous city, floating in the sea the shape of a mandolin laced with bridges. Afterwards, he told me later, he sat at a café in San Marco, and let the bells of the great Campanile enter him, until they sounded in his gut. He sat so long that the pigeons surrounded him as if he were one of their own. Perhaps he felt at home with their nodding walk on feet like branches of coral. It was not unlike his own undulating step. A nun walked past, tearing into shreds a small piece of paper. Lines of voluptuous excess crossed her face.

'I love your town, Cecilia,' he told me, after describing his first day in all its minutiae. He had held forth as if I myself had never seen Venice.

'I shall find what I want here,' he told me.

Byron loved Venice, and soon Venice began to love him back. In him Venice had, as usual, obtained the *crème de la crème*. Venice has a great taste for allegory, and she inclines towards the East. When Byron came to Venice, it was as if Vathek himself had arrived. La Serenissima was perturbed, though as delightfully as possible. An English milord, suspected of crimes against God and the flesh, a mysterious deformed person, delicate and depraved, who secreted himself in the heart of Venice – *Che delizia!*

But there were few confirmed sightings to gratify the curiosity whipped up by the rumours. Byron's sightseeing had been accomplished discreetly, before the news of his arrival was quite out. Once his presence had become known, Byron cultivated his celebrity with rarity, knowing that to make one's self too available is to allow one's charm to evaporate. He knew that his short stature, his limp, his as yet imperfect grasp of Italian would undermine the enormity of his unknown persona. So, as the rumours of his presence spread, he hid himself, allowing carefully groomed incidents to become public. He sat in his parlour, waiting to be mythologised.

Those days the defiant remnants of the Venetian intelligentsia congregated in the salon of Countess Albrizzi. Byron, of course, was introduced, making a rare excursion abroad in the dark of the evening. At the Albrizzi *conversazione* he listened to the Venetian nobles reading aloud their refined little poems in languid voices. The men stood in one part of the room. At the other, the ladies sat in a semi-circle. This was the most elegant entertainment offered by Venice. He took his place amongst our aristocrats as a matter of course. His literary legend would have gained him entry, even without his personal notoriety. Murray had published the third canto of *Childe Harold* just weeks before Byron arrived here, closely followed by *The Prisoner of Chillon and Other Poems*. Seven thousand of each were sold in one evening at a dinner for booksellers. Byron triumphed again, and spume of the adulation in London floated to Venice within days.

Byron's stock only increased when a Venetian newspaper published a review of Caroline Lamb's *Glenarvon*, along with a breathless description of the attempted suicide of the noble authoress in the sad throes of her hopeless passion for the English milord. Byron made an attempt to appear livid – describing the drama to the Albrizzi guests as 'the scratching attempt at canicide of that two-handed whore'. Still, he kept the Venetian newspaper, along with another, labelling him a supporter of the hated Bonaparte. 'As curiosities,' he told me.

Byron-fever increased. His gondola was chased through the narrow canals by hooded black boats from which issued soft gusts of giggles and feminine sighs. Noble ladies were said to have bribed his laundry women for a rag of his linen. Everyone was desperate for a glimpse of Glenarvon/Byron's fatal beauty. Byron infected the dreams of Venetian women, humble and noble, for he was known to take his pleasure among both extremes of society. Virgins and matrons, nuns and courtesans tossed and turned in their beds, whispering his name; they closed their eyes in the arms of their lovers and pretended to be tending to the poor maimed foot or smoothing down the famous chestnut curls. In their sleep they tore their sheets from their moorings and bathed them in sweat.

It was all Caro Lamb's fault. She had described his face just as he loved to have it described: as one of those faces that, once seen, cannot be forgotten. The soul of passion, according to Caro, was stamped upon his every feature. His eyes threw up an ardent gaze. The proud curl of the upper lip expressed haughtiness and bitter contempt, but an air of melancholy shaded and softened every harsher expression.

'Was it possible to behold him unmoved?' cried Caroline's long-suffering heroine, Calantha. 'Oh! was it in woman's nature to hear him, and not cherish every word he uttered? . . . What woman upon earth exists who had not wished to please Glenarvon?' All Venice wanted to see that face for themselves, and hear those words and please Glenarvon/Byron, to make him more pleased than he ever was in his life.

His conversation was made up of a thousand nothings; yet all his phrases *seemed* somehow so different from what others had said before. He could speak home to the human heart, for he knew it in all its turnings and windings, and he could rouse and tame the passions of those he wished to dominate. He could appear, without being subservient, to be possessed of a rare gentleness and sweetness, combined with the powers of imagination, vigour of intellect, and brilliance of wit. But it was all a cruel disguise, wrote Caroline. *Beware*.

Caroline had written thrillingly, and dreadfully, of his cold, cold heart. Did he ever love anyone? *Never*, according to Caro. Even in the midst of his most passionate conquest, he despised the victim of his art. Even while he soothed her softly panting breast with loving vows, he was planning his escape from the unbearable thraldom of her charms.

She should know, thought everyone who read *Glenarvon*. Fortunate, unfortunate Caroline Lamb, writing from experience! She knew what it was to feel his hand upon her neck, hard.

I set upon my easel my 1809 Albanian portrait of Byron. I found that it had grown apart from its subject. Those intervening years, when I had continued to work on it, had preserved my vision of him as I knew him first.

The 1809 Byron was fearless, and still had something to seek. The 1816 Byron was greater and lesser. He was famous now, as famous as Casanova had ever been, but he was less easy in his skin.

Now I remembered all the questions he had asked about Casanova. Why did it matter so much to him here in Venice when in Albania it had seemed to mean so little? What loss in Byron had made him need to compare himself to my poor Casanova, so vindictively?

I picked up my copy of *Glenarvon* and dipped into it again.

The Cat Speaks

The thing about Byron and Cecilia is this – she knows his faults but she accepts him back into her life anyway. She shows that she loves him despite the horror that he is. He despises her for that. She despises herself for that.

But she sits there painting him again as if nothing had happened, as if he had not fathered a living creature on her (for I have worked it out, you see), as if he were not the author of the pain that made all those terrible Madonnas she painted for years after she came back from Albania.

I let him know what I think. When he comes to the studio I allow him to approach. 'Come here, you hairy little egotist,' he says. 'Animals love me,' he tells Cecilia. I do not come. I make him come to me. Then I capsize my guts for him just when he bends down to stroke me.

Cecilia has her *lingua biforcuta*. I have my *culo*. I make a fearsome smell, a real warm and vibrant distillation of the contents of my intestines which that day included some ripe fish and the last soft organs of a small mouse.

Byron recoils, groaning, squeezing his nose.

'That cat has a Sicilian vendetta,' he tells Cecilia.

3

Non ghe xe Pasqua senza fogia,
né dona senza vogia.

There's no Easter without leaves,
and no woman without desires.

VENETIAN PROVERB

In December Hobhouse departed for Rome, leaving Byron to the frenzy that Caroline had whipped up in Venice.

He took apartments in the home of 'a Merchant of Venice', il Signor Segati, in the Calle della Piscina, off the Frezzeria, by coincidence, under the sign of *Il Corno*. In Venice this was soon known as *Il Corno Inglese*. For Marianna Segati, the merchant's wife, was within days on intimate terms with her new lodger.

'I see mischief coming of this,' Hobhouse told me, shaking his head. He had come to my studio to say goodbye, and to express, in his fumbling, thorough way, his regrets for what had happened in Albania, or at least for what he knew of what had happened in there.

I waved my hand in a dismissive gesture. It was not the kind of pain for which Hobhouse could apologise so it was best to leave it alone. Instead, I took the opportunity to bring my knowledge of his friend up to date. Of course, I had heard episodes from the mythology already, on the streets and in my studio and via all my multifarious channels of research. Hobhouse helped me distinguish truth from malice.

From this long conversation with him I distilled all the small facts that had thus far eluded me. I asked Hobhouse all the questions that no one else could answer. I refined what I already knew of Nicolo, Caroline, Augusta and Annabella. Hobhouse fed my obsession with delicacies, tiny details, and with more substantial fare: his long account of Byron's marriage. His intended brief farewell stretched to a conversation of some five hours' duration. He seemed to feel he owed me the intelligence I craved. It was as if he was trying to make amends to me for the deprivation of it in Albania. Shamelessly, I exploited the decency in him that made him feel that way.

'Is it better to know?' Hobhouse asked, as he left. I nodded.

From now on, until Hobhouse came back to Venice, I would have to rely on what I saw myself in the Segati household and what I heard from Byron or read when I made my private investigations of his desk. I kept no written dossier. Every fact about him was classified and catalogued in the large part of my consciousness which was devoted to him. I thought that what I knew about Byron raised my love for him above that of other women. It was one way, I thought, of loving him properly.

I was not unduly worried about the new development in Byron's domestic life, which was fortunate because Byron did not spare my feelings when explaining the situation to me. When he came to my studio, which was nearly every day, he liked to tell me about Marianna while I was painting him.

I already knew about Marianna Segati. Who didn't, in Venice? I had even met her a few times at various *conversazione*. I had not been insensible to her rather obvious attractions. I had heard her sing: her rich voice was of the kind that acted notably on the men in the audience but she did not penetrate the emotion of the words she sang. I knew the style of woman she was. I told myself that Signora Marianna Segati lacked the intelligence to love properly. She was merely, I felt, the animal vessel of love – the low kind of love needed by this new, weakened Byron. Anyway, he was not obsessed with her. He merely enjoyed her, and enjoyed talking about it. An official Venetian lover was an essential accessory to him at this moment, like a gondola, to weld him to his new city. Marianna had one more attraction: she was safely married, with a small daughter.

As Byron told me – he had not yet realised how we all know each other in this town – Marianna was twenty-one years old, with large, black, beckoning Oriental eyes, the grace of an antelope, and a variety of subsidiary charms. She had a hectic colour – a real Cochineal – to her soft velutinous complexion. She was fond of the bedchamber, and, I heard on the streets, fond of Byron's purse. She was generally good-natured, as she would soon have need to be. The naiveté of the Venetian dialect was sweet, Byron told me, in the mouth of such a woman.

Il Signor Segati proved a very accommodating kind of man, with a discreet blind eye and the tact to occupy himself elsewhere. Within a month, Byron was boasting to me and everyone else that he and Marianna were one of the happiest unlawful couples on the south side of the Alps. A month later, Byron was still entangled with his Adriatic nymph. For a while he was even faithful – apart from the time he spent with me.

I, for my part, was not jealous of Marianna, any more than I had been of Annabella or Caroline. I looked upon these women as devoid of real significance. Not one of them could stir the core of my relationship with Byron. We merely operated around Marianna, as Casanova and I had done with Francesca Buschini, the way I now did with Maurizio. And it did not occur to Marianna to be jealous of me. She had the glory of strutting the town on Byron's arm, his public and licensed lover. If she suspected what Byron did in those long private hours in my studio, it did not disturb her as it did not ruffle her vanity. She was not suffering, as yet, from a lack of Byron's attention.

Byron sat in my studio, filling the air with unwanted information: 'She is insatiable. There never pass twenty-four hours without us giving and receiving from one to three (and occasionally an extra or two) pretty unequivocal proofs of our mutual good contentment.' And he was, for once, free of physical debility, as he told me 'thank Heaven above – and woman beneath . . .' He had no illusions about Marianna's intellectual finesse. *Conversazione* was not the point of this relationship.

Byron was highly diverted by the moral universal he found in Venice. Despite the fall of the Republic and our public humiliation, married life in La Serenissima was still an affair of merry intrigue. It was normal for a Venetian woman to wait a year after marriage before taking a *moroso*, also known as a *cavalier servente* or a *cicisbeo*. (The mellifluous word '*cicisbeo*' comes from '*bisbigliare*' – to whisper, which is what lovers do.) The *cicisbeo* might or might not be the physical lover of his mistress, but he would offer her the constant stimulation of unconsecrated love and secrecy. Titillation, of course, is more exciting than fulfilment, which is enervating. And the Venetians were utterly enervated after a century of happy dissipation. In Byron's case the chastity of the old-time *cicisbeo* was set aside. He was the new nineteenth-century protagonist, who took his own pleasures rather than serving his lady.

It was all played out for us at the Fenice one night. Byron and I went together to the opera, Marianna being engaged in a family matter. Byron delighted in a local production with a traditional storyline in which one hundred and fifty ladies of quality poison their husbands. This extraordinary mortality, in the eyes of the world, is at first explained as merely the common effect of matrimony. The wickedness of the ladies is eventually uncovered, in a paroxysm of shrieks, tears, groans and fainting. 'I never saw anything I enjoyed so much,' said Byron to me, when the last sturdy corpse was dragged off behind the velvet curtains.

Not all the melodramas were enacted upon the stage at the Fenice. That night Byron asked me to come to his apartments. He wanted to show me a letter from Hobhouse and some raw white silk that might make a flattering cravat for the next painting. In the entrance hall, Marianna's young sister-in-law was lying in wait. Ignoring me, she approached Byron, smiling in an unmistakable way. She was stroking the buttons of his waistcoat – Byron looking down upon her in stupefied fascination – when Marianna made a timely arrival. Without a single word, she seized her rival by her blond hair and bestowed some sixteen violent slaps upon her pretty face.

Screaming ensued from both parties. The vanquished pretender took flight, pursued by Marianna, intent on murder or at least mutilation. With difficulty, Byron and I restrained his lover. She fell into convulsions on a bench with all the apparatus of confusion, dishevelled hair, hat, handkerchief, salts, at which point her ever-understanding husband arrived. Calmly, Signor Segati took his wife back to their apartments, and I went back, with Byron, to his.

Then *Carnevale*, universal madness, came to Venice. We donned our masks and threw away our modesty. The gondolas, like sinuous coffins, held white-faced sinners bound for hell by virtue of their excesses. The air fizzled with wanton excitement. All places, all orifices were free to enter. There seemed, Byron grinned to me, to be almost a competition to see how many sins one could commit, so that the Lenten confessions would be worth hearing.

Carnevale had faded since the fall of the Republic. No longer did we hurl twelve live pigs from the top of the Campanile. Nor did we fire small dogs from the city's cannons, as we had done previously. But some of the old pleasures remained to us, and they were still extreme and picturesque. Not even Napoleon had been able to stamp out the spirit of mischief in Venice.

Byron asked me about the old days, about the way *Carnevale* used to happen.

'Let me *show* you,' I said.

I took him to the Querini *palazzo* at Santa Maria Formosa. The family was away; a servant, bowing deeply, welcomed us in, and we climbed the stairs to the *piano nobile* alone. The walls were alive with the Querinis' peerless collection of paintings by Gabriel Bella and Pietro Longhi. Those two artists had recorded, better than anyone, how we used to live when we were a happy city.

As we walked through the painted rooms, I told him how in the old days we had *Carnevale* six months of the year and how we spent the other six months pining for it and looking forward to it. I stopped at different pictures to show him how.

'The *Compagnie della Calza* – see their striped stockings here – were the masters of ceremony. They organised balls and readings of erotic poetry. There's the *mattacino* flinging eggs filled with sweet water – but sometimes with something rather nasty instead. These boys are hunting bulls through tiny alleys, with no escape. This picture shows one of our mock regattas at Rialto. Instead of boats, we ran about with decorated wheelbarrows.

'You see here how noblemen dressed as country bumpkins. Maids dressed as great ladies and were treated as such. Then there were all the characters of the *Commedia dell'Arte*: That's Arlecchino in his chequerboard costume with the hare's foot flopping on his cap. That's Doctor Graziano in the black robe, and here's Pulcinella playing the bagpipes. Here are some satyrs, dervishes, Indians in their feathers and wooden muffs, a few Roman emperors.

'As you can see, you could be whomever you wanted. In their

masks, everyone took on the personality of the mask, aggressively so, so there was no possibility of walking the streets unmolested. These maskers are dressed as lawyers. They're buttonholing passers-by to inform them of disastrous law-suits against their families. Of course, it was always a complete fiction.

'Even people who *looked* ordinary were not so. You see those two apparently respectable gentlemen walking together, deep in serious conversation? Look behind them . . . See they are carrying fishing rods baited with sugar almonds. Those small boys following behind them would nibble at the sweetmeats like fish.'

I drew him to a painting of the Riva degli Schiavoni.

'This was the side-show of the *Carnevale*. This was where you came if you wanted to watch mountebanks, ballad singers, rope-dancers, jugglers, snake-charmers and conjurers. Once the Irish giant, Magrat, came here. He was seven foot tall and forty stones in weight. That's a fortune-teller whispering his predictions down a long silver trumpet. Those are the quack doctors with their noxious nostrums.

'And those are the animal enclosures. We had a rhinoceros there once. Every kind of dancing dog and bear. Imagine how noisy it was! The crowds swayed from stall to stall, chattering above the noise of the entertainers. Then you would hear the roll of the drum that announced that the tooth-puller was about to make an extraction. At that, everyone stopped, and clutched their own jaws, unconsciously.'

I showed him a picture of the Piazza San Marco at the height of the revelry.

'Now this is the *forza d'Ercole*, a human pyramid of twenty-six men with a tiny child on top. That flying figure is the *saltamartino*. On Maundy Thursday he slid face-down a rope from the top of the Campanile. You must imagine the intake of five thousand breaths as he leapt off the tower.

'People even changed sexes. It was common for men to dress in full female costume, not neglecting the airiest of underwear. Or they would hire a dressmaker to graft luxurious female clothes into male ones.'

I gestured to a pair of figures, 'See – male and female silks and satins are torn apart and thrust in amongst each other. Flame-coloured satin peeks out of lilac floss silk. Sulphur-yellow short-nap velvet is rent to reveal blue and white satin. The ladies' dresses are torn at the bosom, and slashed to reveal half a leg. There are holes everywhere you want to look! The men's batiste shirts and cuffs are shredded, their hair unravelled. They both wear naturalistic masks expressing ardent desperation. Under their masks, you can be sure that they are starting to feel the emotions painted upon them. They bear begging-bowls and they have clearly rehearsed themselves in how to hold their heads in the convincing abjection of poverty.'

I told him how the Venetians made love during *Carnevale*, how everywhere you looked were huge lunging shadows projected upon the wall: lovers and strangers in the grip of the fever that had seized us all. 'Nine months after *Carnevale*, it was always the busy season for our midwives,' I told him.

I told him how, at the end of the *Carnevale*, the Calabresi with their lighted caps would carry the coffin of the old feast to San Marco, followed by wheelbarrows of limp bodies wearing the hideous death mask of a face covered with syphilitic sores, baring their rosy knees to show the world the symptoms of the disease that killed them. Even Lent would be interrupted by the *segaveccia*: a decrepit dummy of an old woman, symbolising famine and depri-vation, would be put on trial on a stage. She stood accused of killing the *Carnevale* and was condemned to be sawn in two. As the saws sliced through her torso, sweets and fruit fell from her belly and the crowd would fight for them.

Byron had been curiously silent while I talked and pointed. Now we sat among the paintings while he rested his leg.

Byron said suddenly, 'You have the *Carnevale* inside you, Cecilia.' He drew my head to his and kissed me on the lips.

Carnevale. Farewell to meat. Byron had long since bidden farewell to meat in his endless quest to starve himself. But he was not about to say farewell to flesh. The picturesque rituals of the past were gone but *Carnevale* still provided endless new carnality. Byron found women. It seemed that he was never free of the smell and moisture of them. Later, he told me that his first *Carnevale* was his best. He ticked off the places where he had spent himself in Venice, the places and the pieces – a woman's anterior orifice in Campo San Barnaba; her saltiness disappearing in the mouth of a young boy in Campo Santa Margarita half an hour later; then the boy's saliva sucked inside the great belly of a mooress on the Schiavoni, riding him almost to death with her monstrous weight; and her silt rammed into the posterior of a sailor who resembled sweet Robert Rushton.

'I might have just outstripped your Casanova this time,' he told me. He smirked like a schoolboy. 'But then, I have more choice of where to put my parts.'

Then he looked around him. 'What's that stink from hell?'

The cat rippled into the shadows waving a tail that fanned his fumes in Byron's direction.

Byron loved *Carnevale* but he didn't want to lose himself in Venice. His image depended upon being the exotic outsider, no matter how exotic the place. Certainly, after Annabella, he wanted his one thousand and one nights of lovers to be enjoyed and then despatched the next morning. But in Venice there was too much competition. He had been used to being alone in the farther promontories of bad behaviour. And the Venetians were too expert and too energetic in their excesses. He was worn out, self-abused almost to oblivion. He was almost grateful when it ended, with a masked ball at the Fenice, on February 28th.

With the end of *Carnevale* had come a scourging for Byron, too: a violent attack upon him in the *Edinburgh Review*. I saw him throw the newspaper across the room, but later he picked it up again. In the eyes of his countrymen he felt damned, and worse, demeaned. The exile in Venice now seemed to be forced upon him, and it lost thereby some of its initial lustre. At twenty-nine, Byron was starting to find his sword outwearing the scabbard. Augusta had not written to him. Marianna's uses were limited. I kissed his eyes each day. But he was alone. One evening I watched him sitting on my sea-steps, listening to the echo chorus. He put his head in his hands.

It is a particular thing, the echo chorus. The gondoliers perform it only occasionally these days. One boatman stands upon the shore of an island, on the canal-bank or in his gondola, and sings at the top of his voice, pushing the sound as far as he can over the mirroring water. Far away, another gondolier hears it. He knows the words and answers with the next verse. The first singer replies . . . and so it continues, mouth to mouth. If you are sitting halfway in between, the effect is magical, and more so if the singers are far away. Most tender and haunting of all are the voices of the women of Malamocco and Pellestrina. They too sing the verses of Tasso, and they sit upon the shore when their men are sea-fishing, singing as penetratingly as they can, until, far out at sea, but nearing home, the men start to hear them and begin to reply. In this way, the amorous reunion commences before the lovers are unseparated, and when flesh touches flesh it is already alight.

4

Verze riscaldà e mugér ritornà
no xe mai bone.

Reheated cabbage and women who come back
are never good.

VENETIAN PROVERB

After we consummated the Casanova portraits, Byron and I met, ostensibly for portrait sessions, nearly every day. Sometimes it was at my studio at the Balbi Valier, sometimes at his own apartments in the Segati house in the Frezzaria.

I was his private mirror. In front of me, Byron changed his costumes and his looks almost daily. He favoured, of course, a romantic *figura*. His extravagant white linen posed problems in the filth of our Venetians streets, slimy with the leavings of the canals and the exhalations of the porous stones. Flakes of pastry whirling through the air, chimney smuts floating in droplets of humidity, small insects were all attracted to Byron's clothes, it seemed.

'Like women,' he would say, 'sticky.' He slapped at the specks of dirt and smeared them on his linen.

'Paint it as if it were still white,' he bade, flexing a soiled sleeve. 'Paint me as if I were still pure!' he laughed. He never tired of sitting. If I ever expressed concern for the length of time he must hold his pose, he would snap, 'Oh blood and guts, get on with it, woman.'

I never knew what to expect when I heard his dragging step in the courtyard. Sometimes it was a long skirmish on my divan and a quick sketch. Sometimes it was a short, brutal act of love and just time to apply some colour in oils before an abrupt, unaffectionate departure.

'I'd have fucked you better if I'd been drunk,' he said once, staggering from the divan. 'Sorry Cecilia. Don't take it personally.'

'It would be a reckless woman who tried to extract a compliment from you,' I retorted. We still played these dangerous word games. I felt as if he were testing me for vulnerability. Any sign of weakness on my part and he would be gone. For my part, I was determined to act like a man, a worse man even than Byron. It seemed the only way to gain a different kind of treatment to that that he gave other women. Amusing wickednesses tumbled constantly from my tongue, just as they did from his. Some days I thought we were in competition as to who could be the most outrageous and most hurtful. Now, when I painted myself, as I did quite often, to test a new pigment or brush, my double-tipped tongue was always there inside my mouth. If you looked closely you would see *two* ruby snippets between my lips instead of one. I would also paint in a feinting distraction – the cat on my lap with a paw draped comfortably but distractingly between my legs, or a pomegranate seed of a nipple between a pair of unidentifiable thumbs (unless you were fortunate enough to have known Casanova's thumbs) attached to a smooth male arm.

Sometimes Byron would come to me with melancholy hanging upon him. He seemed unsure of himself, looking around the studio at my other subjects who gazed down upon us with their lucent, knowing eyes.

'I feel asexual,' he told me on one of these bad days. Naked on the divan he nursed himself in the palm of his hand. He complained as if I should pity him and feel guilty of rendering him so lonely in his own skin by my own unattractiveness. Somehow it was my fault, or the fault of all the women.

'It's for the inventory of my *pieces* that I shall be known,' he said gloomily.

'Not your poetry? You don't think of that?' *I am one of those pieces*, I thought, *I hope that fact is never known.*

'No, and nor will anyone else when I am not rutting the world and his wife. They think they can learn to do that from reading the poems. See how they sell! It's not my metaphor they pay for. It's the life I've lived. And the face I've got,' he said, gesturing at my portrait.

If you ask me, Byron's beauty was not yet ruined. Certainly the last seven years had extracted a toll from his features, but he had retained the physical arrogance of his youth. It was a confidence trick, like our Venetian walls of water. Byron thought himself beautiful, and by force of his personality created a collective illusion, among his friends and acquaintances, that he was so. You probably think I write as a woman who loves, and you are right. As long as Byron looked at me, sometimes, with desire in his eyes, I myself was vain enough to believe that he was overspilling with beauty.

Byron still wanted to personify the adventures of 1809, to be Childe Harold, the buccaneer, the *homme fatal*, the eternal foreigner. Nothing had since happened to him in England to make him want to be depicted as an Englishman. He already knew that so long as he paid for his portraits, or commanded the love of the artist, he had a choice of his immortal image. Of course, each portrait had one other essential gift for him: in it, he was always physically perfect. Portraits did not show his diminutive height, and they could not show his limp.

He knew my trick with sensual symbols. He was desperate that we should find the right one for him. He would bring me a dead eagle, stuffed, or a jewelled sword. 'This?' he would ask, 'Is this me?' He insisted on no quill pen or book. 'That would look like *Trade*,' he said, wrinkling his nose. In the end I found a symbol for him. He would never have accepted it, so I inserted it secretly into every picture. He was much too busy checking for a fading bloom in the cheek or a crow's foot beside the eye to notice that I had tucked into his pocket a silk handkerchief exquisitely embroidered with a nodding, coral-footed pigeon. When he finally saw the bird, he reddened with anger at this reference to his gait.

'Would you have preferred a wingless animal, perhaps?' I dared. 'A hyena?'

'Hyenas hunt in packs.' The door slammed, and I was left alone.

Byron never asked again to see the pictures of Casanova. That weakness was buried more deeply inside him now. He was making his own place in Venice. But he demanded to see my studies and copies of all the portraits I had made of other famous people. First and foremost, he had wanted to see William Beckford.

'Let us see how you have rendered Lord Vathek, Prince of the Pederasts,' he said. 'You flinch, Cecilia? You know he loved little boys?'

'It's an ugly word,' I said. Since becoming the mother of a son, I had become sensitive to that word; I hated it, in any language.

I showed him my still-unframed portrait of Beckford, removing it from my cupboard and placing it upon the easel as carefully as if it were still wet. I felt a sudden warmth of fondness as I looked at the vanished young man again after all these years. Knowing my tricks, Byron identified the Cornaro crest on the porcelain buttons, and the leering *putto* in the mirror. He saw the chess-piece palaces and the terracotta camel – 'Alboufaki!' – on the desk. But he was disappointed by Beckford himself. Or perhaps he was a little gratified, in these reduced days of his own confidence, to see that Beckford presented no competition. He examined every feature separately.

'What a long nose! What stupid hair! I thought he would be a great beauty in spite of what you said the last time.' The word 'Albania' would never pass his lips in my company.

I stood defensively in front of my portrait, as if to protect Beckford from Byron's scorn.

'He was not a *conventionally* beautiful man, and that was not important to him. He lived for inner rather than outer sensations. His portrait is not his monument.'

'You are right, *Vathek* is. And rammed to the fundament with sensations it is, too. Such a waste it is that he's become a hermit. We'll never know if he has another *Vathek* in him, I suppose. Well, it's up to the young men to carry on with what he started! Now show me what you are doing with *my* face here.'

I unveiled the current work: a profile of the poet with his chin resting upon his hand. While we gazed at the glistening portrait together his arm stole around me. He nuzzled my ear and whispered, 'I love the way you make the light shine out of me.'

While he wanted me, Byron wanted everything I did, everything I thought of. He seemed to offer a thousand loves in exchange for the one I had to offer. But one day I knew it would be otherwise. Already I asked myself, *But what am I that I should have your love a second time? Can I hold it? Will it last?*

I talked to my heart. I reminded it of our old campaign in 1809, and the stripes we had earned together then. I reasoned with my heart about Byron. I reminded it that there was always something about him that was not good enough. Since when had Byron known or cared how to love properly? I had betrayed everything I believed in when I first gave my love to him and consented to the kind of love he gave me. I had been cruelly punished for it. Yet I found myself re-enacting my old crime in the full knowledge of the probable consequences.

The most scarring knowledge of all was that he was not afraid to lose me. Byron controlled his desires; he was not controlled by them. He liked love, but he could always be sure of getting it elsewhere. Without that fear, there was nothing to civilise him in his treatment of me or any other woman. Knowing this, perversely, just made me more desperate to keep him. As I am certain all his lovers did, I pictured myself dead, and him keening over my pale corpse. I dreamt of his pain and regret, but I knew what his true reaction would be: *What good luck I did not invest too much in her.*

But I soothed away the worries and ignored the affronts to my own strong sense of what was right in love. I put my heart's shoulders back, and swelled my heart's breast out. What kind of peace had my heart known without him? Those grey years alone, what had they been but a period of recuperative numbness? Was I not a professional heart-soldier like Casanova? Well then, I would go to war with Byron, again.

I told my heart such dreadful lies! I told it that it was better to love extraordinarily than never to love. I rang in so many changes on this one simple theme. It was good for my work, I told myself, to understand what lighted up the flesh I painted. I worked on lovers and abandoned lovers every day. Everyone was one or the other: by experiencing these things, I was researching my craft.

I transfigured my memories of Albania. I traduced them.

I clenched my fists, my stomach and my womb and drew in the first breath of the new battle. I unloved my emotionally celibate state. I unsheathed my tongue, and I dipped it in *fragolino*. I heard inside me a stomach-growl of sadness, a metallic pincing in the womb, a bad bell in my ears.

When Byron was in my studio the cat often erected his tail and shook it as if spraying his stink. It seemed a threatening gesture. Byron preferred dogs, but he would bend to stroke my cat. The cat looked at him cynically, but allowed himself to be pleasured.

'*Bravo gatto*! That is how to handle him,' I told myself, listening to his even purring.

But Byron himself was already listening to something else.

Learning a foreign language is like making a erotic conquest. The more foreign and exotic, the more intractable the challenge, the greater is the thrill of penetration. The greater the intimacy, the deeper is the gratification.

Byron *inhaled* language with the kisses he took. By the time we were reunited in Venice, Byron, he told me, had come to know eleven languages and approximately five hundred women. Who can guess at the number of boys? And does it count if you do not actually talk to them?

The seeds of Byron's linguistic success were planted early. He had told me the story when we were still in Albania. At seven, Byron had exposed his appalling doctor, Lavender, who had encased his little foot in an agonising wooden trap that was supposed to straighten it. Lavender, in reality little more than a part-time truss-maker, posed as a great linguist. Little Byron did not believe a word of it. One day, the boy had scribbled out random letters of the alphabet, as if in sentences, on a scrap of paper. He laid the sheet in front of Lavender, and asked, mildly, 'What language, sir, is this?'

The foolish Lavender, who should have been more attentive to the uncharacteristic gentleness, had replied unwarily, 'Italian, of course.'

After the doctor was shamed and sent away, Byron was left with a free, naked leg and a lasting fondness for the Italian language that had liberated it. By the time he arrived in Venice, Byron already spoke Italian with a picturesque fluency rather than accuracy — learnt from the *Divine Comedy*, but more, he boasted, from the young Nicolo Giraud, the young man with whom he had been besotted in Athens. Of course, he had also taken the opportunity, for a few days in 1809, to learn a little Venetian from me. Once Hobhouse had filled in the missing pieces, I calculated that Byron went directly from my bed to Nicolo's with only anonymous whores along the way. So he probably made use of my Venetian endearments within a few weeks.

Now Byron enjoyed Marianna Segati's Venetian dialect, though it took him a little time to get his lithe tongue around our strange elongated vowels. He described the Venetian style of Italian as something like the Somersetshire version of English. Marianna taught Byron how to swear in both Venetian and Italian. His ear was excellent; he could mimic both sound and cadence, and so, forever after, when he said such things, even to me, it was in her accent.

Byron loved Italian. He tried to goad me, 'Why did your Casanova always write in French? Did he have no feeling for his own language? When I hear he used French I think he lacked all sensual feelings in his mouth. Italian is the finest language, even though it's just bastard Latin at heart. It still melts like kisses on the tongue. It should be written upon satin, not on paper.'

But, as ever, Byron was not faithful to his latest passion. Italian and Venetian conquered, he felt restless, in need of a challenge, perhaps an activity to mask the fact that he was not really writing. Marianna was demanding. Living in the same home as his mistress was not something he had tried to do before. He needed a place where she could not follow him with her caresses, her tears and her eager fingers.

So he took another language-mistress, too.

Every day, Byron went to the Armenian convent on the Island of San Lazzaro, the island where, with Casanova's encouragement, I had learnt to paint landscapes, the island where, though Byron had no idea of his existence, our son Girolamo was now a seven-year-old novice, living in peace, safety and ignorance. I saw him often, always monitored by the Fathers. Few women came to San Lazzaro, so

Girolamo was growing up under the impression that all of them must be as tender as I was. For me, seeing Girolamo had these days become a mixed pleasure, as his father's features fastened ever more distinctly onto his face. I was still caught short with fierce impulses to embrace him, but knew that should I weaken, even once, I would be denied further access to him.

San Lazzaro had escaped Napoleon's dissolution of the monasteries by virtue of the great works of science and scholarship undertaken by the Armenian scholar-priests there. As I have told you, the island had been a leper colony, a *lazzaretto*, in the thirteenth century, after which it had languished into ruins. But the industrious holy Fathers, once granted this refuge, had ploughed their gratitude into its soil. Now it was beautiful, fertile and immaculate, as the paradises created by exiles usually are, uncontaminated by the old or the disreputable, or by the weight of the past.

It was always glorious weather inside the Armenian church, with its arched corridor of peacock-blue paint and bright gilt stars, its chequerboard floor in coral-coloured and white marble. The cupolas glittered with mosaics in turquoise, olive green and gold, each glinting chip brought from the glass island of Murano. The frescoes I had repainted for them in 1810 were in a little room, screened off from the rest. My colours were inspired by Carpaccio's paintings in the Schiavoni Chapel, which Casanova had once shown me by candlelight. When I first heard that he had been there, I imagined Byron, limping through the church, lifting the curtain on my pictures. I knew he would be struck and disturbed by them. I could picture the Father Superior, watching his face change. He would not answer the questions that Byron did not ask. Instead, he would have guided him gently towards the library. I imagined Girolamo tripping past him, laden as usual, with heavy books. In my mind's eye I saw Byron turn to watch him, curiously: such a beautiful little boy! He might have said as much to the Father who would have smiled in embarrassment and hurried him to the library.

The library, rich and deep, with a pearly stucco ceiling, reflected a kindly love of even seditious literature. Byron would have seen there the lascivious works of Catullus and Propertius; he could read Horace and even *The Letters of Lord Chesterfield* in gold-stamped olive green. Lovingly tended by the monks were four thousand manuscripts, many from the dawn of Armenian civilisation, thousands of years before. There was plenty to remind him of his beloved exotic East – he would have sat in winged Oriental chairs and at octagonal tables inlaid with camel bones; he would have peered into cabinets of Egyptian antiquities.

He came back to me with stories of his discoveries. Byron, like Napoleon before him, was impressed with the Father Superior, a fine old fellow with a beard like a meteor. Byron quickly made friends among the ninety monks who lived there. Within weeks, Byron was helping Father Paschal Archer to compose an English–Armenian grammar. The brutal difficulty of the language was strangely restorative for Byron. He explained to me, 'My mind needs something craggy to break upon, and this – as the most difficult thing I could discover here for an amusement – I have chosen, to torture me into attention.'

San Lazzaro quickly became a sacred place for Byron, perhaps the only place in the world he acknowledged as such. Byron could not be cynical about the Armenian monks, no matter how he railed and sneered at everything else. He found that they manifested all the joy and beauty of religion and religious life, with none of the faults. They lived in aesthetic and physical comfort, but in sincere piety. They could teach the world, he declared, that there could be a different, a better kind of life. Indeed, by accepting him, when the rest of the world had cast him as the devil, the Armenian Fathers showed him a kind of faith in which he could almost believe.

'Remember,' Byron told me, as if this was his personal discovery, 'that it was in Armenia that God planted the terrestrial paradise, and it was in this Armenia that the waters of the great flood subsided and where the dove found land to rest his legs.'

I asked him, 'Do you believe, then, as the Armenians believe? I could almost think your soul saved, when you talk about them.'

'I do not know what to believe or disbelieve. All sense, and senses, are against it . . . It's like walking in the dark over a rabbit warren.'

'It gives comfort to many.'

'Let it, more fools them. Let them pay for their comfort with discomfort. Let them contort themselves to be "good"! I am too indolent to be so unnatural. Anyway, I believe they enjoy the guilt, take baths in it. Damn me if there isn't a rivalry among the God-botherers to suffer the most for their sins. Everybody may be damned, as they seem fond of it. So let them wallow in their brimstone and scream under the lashing of the devil's tail on their private parts for all eternity.'

When he found that I was the author of the glowing colours in the shrouded frescoes at San Lazzaro he shouted with delight. 'Cecilia, Cecilia, Cecilia! I knew it! I knew there was something about them! How typical that you should have been there before me.'

Then his face darkened. 'I suppose you came here with *him*.'

I did not answer.

Back in Venice, in my studio, Byron continued his language studies, in his preferred way. '*Sangue di Dio, faccia da maladetti*, God's blood, face of the damned,' Byron would whisper in my ear as he pulled me to the floor. '*Sei le mie viscere*,' he would moan, 'you're my guts.' Later, as he grew more excited, 'I would go for you into the midst of a hundred knives,' and finally, '*Mazza ben*,' which means literally, 'I wish you well even to killing.' He loved to recite to me the

intimate alphabet of physical love, in Venetian, all the picturesque
obscenities he could muster, one after another.

He is more of a little boy than Girolamo, I thought.

Eventually, with Armenian tamed to almost conversational level,
Byron started to write poetry again. He brought his manuscripts to
the island. Byron reclined in an olive grove at San Lazzaro, and
wrote the fourth canto of *Childe Harold*, and I painted him as he did
so. The Fathers had granted permission for him to continue with
his work, and I with mine, in the pleasant sanctuary of their island.
In those hours we sat in happy amity. Sometimes, when Byron
came to look at my work, he would kiss my ear, a rare gratuitous
kiss. He would smile at me and I would begin to believe again in the
possibility of happiness.

Byron, as always, seized any portraits which he considered complete. I kept the unfinished canvases I painted at San Lazzaro in my
studio. Together we presented one portrait to the monks, to com-
memorate the Armenian–English grammar.

You can still see it on the island of Saint Lazzaro of the
Armenians. Byron wears a white shirt, with a jewel at the throat, a
brocaded jacket. Look at how I have Italianised him! That pale skin
has an olive hue. The blue eyes look brown. The small ears, too, are
somehow Italian. Except in his unavoidable resemblance to little
Girolamo, there are no secret details in this painting. I owed that
courtesy to the Armenian Fathers, who had raised our son to be an
angel.

Venetian
Intimate Alphabet

Male

bìgolo: spaghetti

coa: the tail

bapi: 'Jamey'

oselo: the little bird

mànego: the handle

creapòpoli: the people-maker

tubo: the pipe

ghigno: the sneering one

spàreso: the asparagus

pìfero: the flute

gobo: the hunchback

tega: the seed pod

Female

sfesa: the crack

mona: the silly thing

màndola: the almond

frìtola: the pancake

gnoca: the pretty one

buso: the hole

sportela: the little shopping bag

meneghela: the Two of Spades

mustaciona: the moustachioed one

mónega: the nun, or the warming pan

mosca: the fly

pantegana: the water rat

musina: the money box

barbatoe: the one with big lips

Quando le fémene se barufa,
el diavolo se pètena la coa.

When females fight,
the devil combs his tail.

Venetian proverb

January 2nd, 1817 was Byron's second wedding anniversary. He commemorated it with *Plen & opt Cs* with Marianna, with a whore at Arsenale and with me: one for each year, and one for luck.

'Aha! Miss Milbanke!' he gasped at the last moment. *He has not got over it*, I thought, *her rejection of him*. He was already asleep, or unconscious, breathing heavily through his nose. I sat on the edge of the divan in my studio, gazing down upon him. He looked most like Girolamo when he was sleeping, when his tongue was still, when he was not on his guard. I stroked his hair, and his eyes rolled open like a doll's. He caught my hand and kissed it. I was knitted to him again.

Another Byron daughter, a half-sister to Annabella's 'Little Legitimacy', had been born in England. This was Byron's child by Claire Claremont, conceived at the Villa Diodati among the chastened exiles and their febrile ghost stories. When I heard, I thought, *What kind of child will this be, the half-sister of my son? A little ghoul? A little devil? A little angel like Girolamo?* Byron was curious, as usual,

about another Byron coming into the world, though he continued
to vilify her mother in the ugliest terms, Venetian, English and now
Armenian.

Shelley had written to him about the Claremont child, he told
me.

'It seems that it's a great beauty. I shall have it brought here. I
shall acknowledge and breed it myself.'

'What is she called?'

The Shelleys had called the baby Alba, drawn from his own nickname among them, Albé. But Byron decided to give her a Venetian
name, Allegra, drawing his blood closer to our city. It had been my
suggestion.

'Why not, Cecilia?' he had said. 'And you shall paint her when she
comes. I should like to see how you paint a child of mine.'

The advent of the new child and the thought of her arrival clearly
discomposed Byron. Outside on the streets the *Carnevale* swarmed
and glittered but he took to his bed, indefinably ill, still musing
about Augusta's strange remoteness. Marianna fussed around him,
creating more melodrama about his frail condition than even Byron
could withstand. It was not the low and vulgar typhus, I heard him
snap at her, but a sharp gentlemanly fever that, with his noble
blood, he would survive. While ill, he finished the third act of
Manfred, in which, he told me, the hero confronts death.

Hobhouse would tell me later that when *Manfred* was published in
June 1817, it pointed such an unequivocal a finger at Augusta, as
Astarte, the incestuous lover of the hero, that there was no hope but
for it to be denounced. Augusta did not respond. Byron thought of
a new way to extort her attention. In the ebb of his fever, Byron
summoned me to the house in the Frezzaria, where he lay in bed
pale and flaccid as a fading lily. Marianna flounced and pouted, but,
during a fortnight, I painted two miniatures of him. They showed

Byron as blanched and wasted as he wanted to be. These were despatched to Augusta, and he anxiously awaited her comments on his appearance, now but the shadow of her twin self. He was devastated when Augusta, still in Annabella's thrall, did not give him satisfaction. The bruised look on his face was more than I could bear.

'Why do you want to be so thin?' I asked.

'I want the women to say, "Poor sweet Lord Byron. How *interesting* he looked when dying."'

Then *Carnevale* itself died and the town went into mourning for it. The Venetians were buried alive in their black veils and dark clothes. Byron emerged from his bed, restless. Venice had not given him the refuge from himself he thought he would find here. Neither the wildness of *Carnevale* nor the jaded peace afterwards had given him satisfaction, or even the ease of exhaustion this year. The poetry had started to flow again, in its usual facile way, but not the *estro*.

Seeking distraction, he went travelling south. But Venice had taken hold of him. He took the mist and glare of the Canal with him to Rome and saw everything through Venetian eyes, darkly. He wrote to me, short, vivid, discontented letters. After reading them once, I threw them away. I did not like the feel of them bristling in the corners of the studio when I was working. He found Rome swarming with the pestilential English. There he watched, from close quarters, the guillotining of three robbers. He described to me the horrific ceremony – the masked priests, the half-naked executioners, the bandaged criminals, the black Christ and his banner, the soldiers, the slow procession, the fall of the axe and the splash of blood. It turned him hot and thirsty and made him shake so he could hardly see through the opera glass. Though close, he had not wanted to miss a detail.

As I read the letters, I told myself that Byron's outer being was becoming more and more Childe Harold. He had become more absorbent of the tragedy around him. The execution of the robbers, he wrote to me, had besmeared a patina of doom upon his own soul. Now, being addicted to portraiture, it did not surprise me to hear that he wanted his transmogrification recorded in a new painting. He called me to Rome, but I would not come. For once, I had something more important than Byron to occupy me.

Girolamo was ill with typhus, and I could not leave him. The Fathers at San Lazzaro let me tend him while he was delirious. I placed my hands over the pale blue eyes and tried to draw out his pain. I stroked his perfect limbs, and held his small, hot hands, frail and lifeless as dead sparrows.

So this is what it is to be a mother, I thought. *How do women survive the joy and the pain?*

Girolamo doubled himself up like a little clam in the bed. When the Fathers were absent from the room, I quickly lay down on the bed behind him and folded myself around his motionless body, smoothing his skin and his curls, listening to him breathing as I had listened in the cabin on the boat that brought us back from Albania eight years before. *Eight years is a long time to wait to hold your child in your arms*, I thought to myself. *There is something extremely wrong in the world.*

When it seemed certain that he would die I blamed myself with all the colours of hatred. I had left him to grow up as an anonymous little slave for the aged scholars of this island. Perhaps they had worked him too hard; I did not even know. I had left him in an ascetic environment where there were few comforts to protect him from infections. As the doctor shuffled in and out, I sat hunched and stiff beside the bed, waiting for him to leave so that I might take Girolamo in my arms again. Late at night, the Fathers would come to me with a candle, and tell me that a boatman was waiting to take me back to Miracoli. I sat in the boat, without seeing the lagoon. When I came home I rushed to my room to record

Girolamo's changing features. While he lay unconscious they were changing subtly. He seemed to be growing up at an accelerated rate, as if snatching at years he might not ever have upon this earth.

One morning, I arrived and confronted closed faces.

'Is he dead?'

'No, he is recovered, so you may not tend to him any longer.'

I packed my heart back into my breast and returned to Venice. I would not go to Rome, however, in case Girolamo needed me again.

Without me, Byron decided to risk a three-dimensional portrait. The Danish sculptor Thorwaldson, for whom he posed at the recommendation of Countess Albrizzi, was ordered to capture the translation from Byron to Childe Harold.

Thorwaldson proved rather indiscreet, and news about the sittings leaked out to Rome agog for information about the wicked Lord Byron. One of my English clients told me about it, in authoritative detail.

It was said that when he sat down to pose, Byron had frozen his features into a tortured expression.

Thorwaldson told him, laconically, 'You need not put on that look, my Lord.'

'That is my expression,' Byron said.

'Indeed?' replied the sculptor, and portrayed Byron as he himself saw him: a little sulky.

I did not hear of this incident from Byron himself, and dared not ask, but it had the ring of truth. He gave himself away when he wrote to tell me that he was horribly disappointed in the bust.

'It does not look like me at all,' he complained. 'My expression is far more melancholic.'

The new attempt to immortalise himself was a failure. Byron was disconsolate, feeling himself in exile, even from Venice. He was

bored. He missed Marianna. He summoned her and then returned
with her to Venice. And came back to me.

I continued to paint Byron, as I always had, as I was ordered or persuaded to do. The current portrait was of the compleat Romantic
poet, expiring tragically young, of excesses that I could suggest but
not name with the nuances of my brush. Suicide seemed but a
dagger-thrust away, in the pictures he wanted painted of himself
now. Let the world and Miss Milbanke see what they had done to
him!

'Paint me,' he said, 'so that they can see that I have been more
ravished than anybody since the Trojan War. Paint me vanquished
and at peace.'

Then he astonished me. He whispered under his breath, with the
catch of tears in his throat,

> 'Con culto d'amore
> spargono fiori e pregano pace . . .'
>
> In the name of love,
> Scatter flowers and beg for peace . . .

He had been to San Michele, to the grave of little Fortunato. Did he
know? How could he know? Was he still thinking of Casanova? I
dared not ask. He had all but stopped talking about my old lover. I
believed that was because he could not stomach the softness on my
face when Casanova's name was mentioned. I was moved by the
misery and curiosity that might have prompted Byron to go to our
island.

I asked him, gently, 'Do you ever contemplate suicide, Byron?'
Not stirring an eyelash to disturb his tragic pose, Byron mocked my
tenderness.

He said, 'I should, many a good day, have blown my brains out, but for the recollection of the pleasure it would have given to that bitch my mother-in-law.'

He leapt from his chair and fastened his lips to mine.

Then it was summer. How quiet Venice is without nature! Never the lowing of a cow or the clopping of a horse. In the stillness of summer, there is just the tolling of the bells to punctuate the groaning of the sick and old in the heavy air and the tugging of boats against their moorings. This fitful silence is rent by the cruel laughter of the seagulls along the Schiavoni as the fishing boats come in. There is a dangerous quiet in the narrow alleyways. Typhus spreads silently, from *campo* to *campo*, and island to island. Two novices had died on San Lazzaro. When I think of that summer my memories are of the funeral gondolas lurching like sobs in the silent heat of afternoons, and the keening of women under black veils. I remember how the clear green of the Grand Canal seemed to clot and thicken into some kind of pestilential abscess. I remember heavy, wan clouds bearing down upon us, and the stickiness of my own skin.

Girolamo was now pale but strong. I worried for his immoderate grief at the loss of his friends. One of the Fathers told me, 'He takes it hard; he seems to take on the pain of the whole community.' I realised that they were proud of his ability to suffer like that. I did not know what to make of this, but it somehow disquieted me.

Byron feared the fever. He hated the sight of the funeral gondolas in procession and the dark-robed doctors hurrying through the streets. He complained to me that he smelt sickness in every alley. The very walls seemed to be sweltering a poisonous threat; he saw infection in every droplet that coursed down them. He fled. He rented for the summer the Villa Foscarini at La Mira, on the Brenta, some distance out of Venice. He took Marianna there. Hobhouse joined him. They rode horses on the long sands of the Lido. They watched beautiful sunsets. They passed happy months. Byron wrote till the early hours of the morning and came by gondola into Venice to see me on cooler days. While the typhus raged there, he avoided San Lazzaro.

At La Mira, under high clean skies, he enjoyed the effects of the heat; it lessened his appetite. His pallor, by careful management, increased. Hobhouse was at his side, Marianna in his arms. The only clouds on his horizon were those strange letters from Augusta, full of hints of melancholy and mysterious apprehensions, disorder and broken hearts.

'What does she *mean* by these runes and imprecations?' he asked me, flinging down another letter, pacing around my studio. 'With all these megrims and mysteries I cannot understand whether she has a broken heart or earache. I give up on her.' I think he was starting to guess at the truth, though he could not quite stomach the thought that Annabella had infiltrated his intimacy with Augusta.

Byron was floating like a bubble upon the water. He was not quite Venetian, but he was not quite anything else either. He was tired of himself, of the old tragic identity, of the constant confessional of his poetry. I think he had cleared his arteries of the poison of the past and he was bored with bleeding from the heart. I watched him changing. Even his posture was different – freer and looser. His face was in flux, too. He no longer looked out from under hunched eyebrows but cast careless glances and mischievous grins.

Byron was working on *Beppo*. He had been convulsed by a new poem by John Hookham Fere, a light satire imitated from the Italian poets. He seized upon a story recounted, ironically enough, by Marianna's amiable spouse, about a lady who thinks she has lost her husband at sea, and takes a *cavalier servente*, or vice-husband, to deputise for him in every important little thing. A delicious dilemma ensues when the husband returns.

Into this story Byron poured all his cruel good humour, his old delight at Venetian amorality. In the process, he freed himself from the fetters of high tragedy that enveloped the living embodiment of Childe Harold. *Beppo* is an amoral, sensuous and cool romp. He read lines to me while I worked, and they entered my paintings, too. I was bemused to see him in this new state. It was like entertaining a new lover inside a body I already adored.

> The moment night with dusky mantle covers
> The skies (and the more duskily the better)
> The time less liked by husbands than by lovers
> Begins, and prudery flings aside her fetter;
> And gaiety on restless tiptoe hovers,
> Giggling with all the gallants who beset her;
> And there are songs and quavers, roaring, humming,
> Guitars, and every other sort of strumming.

I strummed the paintbrush and Maurizio. Byron strummed Marianna Segati, me, and the muses of the casino. Marianna was still queen of his household, but he had begun to detach himself from her. He mused on the awful notions of constancy he had witnessed in some Italian women. He had seen some ancient figures of eighty pointed out as *morosi* of forty, fifty and sixty years' standing. This did not bear thinking about. For all her tiny size, Marianna was imperious, and she dared to criticise. Perhaps, I thought to myself, she lacked the intelligence not to do so. She was not delighted when Byron started to write poetry again. She did not want to philosophise about love, she just wanted to make it. I heard her shout at him, 'If you loved me properly you would not make so many fine reflections, which are only good for *birsi i sçarpi*' – cleaning shoes with, a versatile Venetian proverb.

Marianna started to misbehave. She sold the diamonds Byron had given her. He bought them back and gave them to her again. She was not at all embarrassed. I think she was scenting, in her primitive way, the end of Byron's protection; she was laying her hands upon what she could in the time she had left. Bribing Signor Segati for the loan of his wife was also becoming expensive for Byron. Worse still, Marianna was beginning to display symptoms of jealousy. Well, she had reason for it, for apart from me, the nine muses at the casino, and random couplings on dark canals, Byron had found something else to capture his attention.

It was now the talk of Venice that Byron had made a new conquest. During a ride along the canal, it was reported, Byron had caught sight of a dark beauty. She caught sight of him too, and called out, in dialect.

'*Carissimo*, you're so kind to others – why don't you give me a hand, too?'

'You're too pretty to need help, *Signorina*,' laughed Byron.

'You wouldn't say that if you could see where I live. And it's *Signora*, by the way. Not that I have a husband you'd say was worth the name. He's never at home. In fact, I'd say there was a spare room to rent.' She gave a low, throaty laugh, and looked boldly at Byron.

Margarita Cogni was twenty-two years old, illiterate, dramatically beautiful. Her sobriquet in her own family was La Mora, from her colour, which was very dark, dark as Othello, prince of murderous jealousy. When Byron proposed a rendezvous, she stared hard at his pocket. All married women had a lover in Venice, it seemed, whatever their class. It was just a question of the price. Margarita's husband was a baker. Byron dubbed her 'La Fornarina', the baker's wife. As such, she was not expensive. Marianna, a middle-class matron, had been more so.

It was all over Venice in days. There were a dozen witnesses to the memorable morning when Marianna sought out Margarita and insulted her. Margarita was unperturbed and returned the slight, with interest. The two women stood in the street and entertained all Venice with their exchange. Margarita told Marianna, 'You are not his wife. You are his whore. I am his whore. What of it?'

Marianna spat, eloquently, but Margarita continued, 'Your husband is a cuckold. Mine is another.'

Marianna raised her hand to slap her rival, but thought the better of it. Margarita was twice her size, a known brawler, and her voice was louder. Margarita pronounced finally, 'And for the rest – why should you reproach me? If he prefers what is mine to what is yours – is it my fault?'

It's all over with La Segati, was the word in the streets from that day forth. *She's priced herself out of a cosy income. The baker's wife's the one to watch.*

The subject of this and many other discussions returned from La Mira to Venice late in the autumn, and plunged back into a social life lived out in the *conversazione* of Countess Marina Benzoni. Everything was changing. In January Hobhouse left again for England. On his last night they hired a gondola and two singers, who sat one at the prow and one at the stern of the boat. They embarked from the Piazzetta, and stopped at my studio to entice me to join them. The night was freezing but I wrapped myself in my cloak and slipped into the boat.

We flowed past all Byron's favourite haunts, while the musicians strummed and sang fragments of lowlife street songs, which were absorbed into the fervent darkness like coins dropping into water. Everyone pulled on a bottle of *fragolino*, scuffling for it like puppies for a teat. The singing slipped into the bottle. Then there was just the quiet gulp of the water and the cradle-rocking of the benches where the friends were taking leave of each other, and taking stock of what was left. They talked quietly and seriously, side by side upon the narrow bench.

How different they were to look at — Hobhouse so ungainly, Byron so graceful — and how different they were to hear. I drifted in and out of their conversations, watching for the moments when I could see Girolamo's face in Byron's, the sweet moments when he was at peace.

As we passed San Vio, Byron said, 'Love? I rather think of it as a hostile transaction.'

'It can be otherwise.'

'You think you shall find a better "otherwise" in England?'

'Neither of us shall find it here.'

'I shall not be looking.'

When Byron said this, Hobhouse looked at me, to see how I survived the insult. I smiled at him to show him that I took it well, in the spirit that it was meant, in the spirit that I was woman enough to understand when Byron needed his moments of drama and self-pity and that I must not take them personally. *Venice makes him even sadder*, I thought to myself.

Byron, after Hobhouse left, abandoned himself to the next *Carnevale*. Day became night for him. For weeks he never saw the sun. During the height of the revelry, he found himself consumed by a new *amore* with an unknown masked woman. She clutched the button of her *moretta* mask between her teeth so that she could not cry out even in her moments of dissolving joy. Byron told me, as if it meant nothing to me, 'I don't know exactly whom or what she is except that she is an insatiate of love, and won't take money . . .'

He found out who she was when he discovered his symptoms.

The Gondolier Speaks

Can you imagine how it is to sleep like a milord? Never rising before the supper hour?

They said that he would not sleep with his women, even after *you know what*.

'Out!' he'd say, even before he was outside of them, if you know what I mean. *Mi Morti!*

Didn't he ever worry that one day the tears might come round to himself?

He knew how to sleep, the milord. He never saw the morning light. I think it was probably deliberate. He didn't want to see himself in it.

And it was probably that bastard milord looking to himself in another way, as well. He didn't want to see the women then. Their faces are thinner-skinned in the mornings. You know what I mean. Their tears are closer to their eyes. So he kept his own eyes shut until they had put themselves back together.

After whatever he had done to them in the dead of the night before.

6

L'amor fa passar el tempo,
e el temp fa passar l'amor.

Love makes the time pass,
but time makes love pass, too.

<small>VENETIAN PROVERB</small>

*C*arnevale 1818 left Byron with a love-disease, haemorrhoids
and a fever.

I saw the letter he wrote to Hobhouse, 'Elena da Mosta,
a Gentil Donna, was clapt, and she has clapt me; to be sure it was
gratis, the first gonorrhoea I have not paid for.'

Carnevale ended again. The Venetians once more carried a black
coffin round the city to show that the beast that had possessed
them had now expired. Byron encoffined himself in a new home.

After he broke with Marianna it was obvious that Byron could no
longer inhabit the Segati house in the Frezzeria. In June, he agreed
to take one of the four Mocenigo *palazzi* on the *volta*, the crook, of
the Grand Canal, at an annual rent of 4800 francs.

When I heard this news my heart somersaulted inside me. Yes,
it was the same Palazzo Mocenigo where I had comforted Casanova
after his night of losses at the table, and where I had memorised
the guests' faces to paint a *Biribissi* board of noble portraits blos-
soming from tulips and pineapples. Yes, it was the same Palazzo

Mocenigo where Casanova and I had disported so lovingly behind
the empty frame. In part of that *palazzo* still lived the now very elderly Maurizio Mocenigo, whom Casanova had suggested as my
protector, with such disastrous results. And in another apartment
in the same building lived his son Maurizio, who still loved me like
an anemone.

'So what do you know about the Palazzo Mocenigo?' Byron asked
me. The papers for the lease had just been signed. Fletcher was
packing up his books and Marianna's sobs could be heard in a distant room.

What did I know? At first, I told him what I was prepared to tell
him.

I told him that the Mocenigos were one of the ancient and opulent families of Venice. As it grew the Mocenigo family had divided
into more than twenty branches, as my own Cornaro family had
done. Predominant, in their case, were the Mocenigos of San Stae
and the Mocenigos of San Samuele. It was the latter seat that had
been my haven with Casanova, and that was now to become Byron's
home.

I told him that Mocenigos were politicians, soldiers, patrons of
the arts and sciences. Their portraits had been painted by
Giorgione, Tiziano and Tintoretto. The Mocenigo dynasties gave
Venice seven doges, Tommaso, Pietro and Alvise winning great battles against the Turks. Alvise had been a man of such noble courage
that when he died the Ottomans decked their ships in black and
dipped their crescent banners in the sea.

I told him that the house of Mocenigo was also disgraced. The
great shame of the house hung over Giovanni Mocenigo, who had,
in 1591, invited the saintly philosopher Giordano Bruno to be his
guest, hoping to learn from him the secrets of alchemy. When the
formula was not forthcoming, Giovanni denounced his guest as a

heretic. Bruno was burned at the stake in the Campo dei Fiori in Rome.

Byron was not satisfied with my recitation. He drummed his fingers while I recited my history like a schoolgirl. 'You have not told me everything, Cecilia. Tell me more. I want the *dirty laundry*.'

So I told him about the dark times when noble Venetians cultivated the habit of murdering their debtors. Domenigo Mocenigo stabbed the brother of one of his, and his name was erased from the *Libro d'oro*. I told him about the notorious beauty Marina Mocenigo. I told him about Lucrezia Basadonna, a Mocenigo wife, who had been betrayed by her English lover. Rosalba Carriera painted her with the Mocenigo pearls heavy upon her neck. I told him about Giustiniana Gussoni, the eighteen-year-old bride of a Mocenigo, who eloped in a gondola with the Count de Tassis.

'That's more like it,' said Byron. 'Any more scandal?'

'English scandal?'

'Any kind of scandal will serve, so long as it's filthy.'

So I told him about the eccentric Lady Mary Wortley Montagu, who had lived there before I was born, the great friend of Antonio Mocenigo – 'Yes! I've read her letters! What a lively old piece!' – and I told him about another scandalous Englishwoman, Lady Arundel, who had been implicated in the alleged treason of her supposed Venetian lover, Antonio Foscarini.

'So it's seen some passion in its time, that *palazzo*!' Byron exclaimed.

'And such parties!' I said. I told them how Pietro Mocenigo once spent, in one night alone, 40,000 *ducati* on wine, food and showers of gold. I told him about the rose essence sent by Madame de Pompadour and how it wafted over noble heads gathered around the gaming table at sumptuous parties in the last days of the Republic.

I still did not tell him about my magical night behind the empty frame with Casanova.

In acquiring the Palazzo Mocenigo, Byron acquired a palatial way of life. He now lived like a Venetian aristocrat, with his own gondola moored to his own blue and white *paline*, and his own gondolier, Tita Falcieri, a huge man with extravagant black moustachios. When not poling the gondola, Tita acted as both butler and pimp.

The first time I returned to the Palazzo Mocenigo I was almost afraid to approach it. I came by gondola along the Canal. It was a day when a strata of clear water seemed to hang above the green mud like a banner of silk. I stood sniffing the air on the sea-steps. The water was brighter than the sky that day. The right and proper tonal hierarchy of the world was reversed. It felt uneasy. Everything loomed out of its own mist, the way a *sfumato* outline gives every head a halo in certain paintings. The whole world is pulsing with the disturbances of souls in paintings like that and on days like this one. It has to be found, a language for this. I find it in my paint.

I asked myself how I would paint the Mocenigo now. The fall of the Republic, it seemed, had dragged the Mocenigo down with it. The *palazzo* looked frailer, less prosperous than before. Its lion-coloured pigment still clung to the exterior, but it was dirty and faded, licked and clawed by the mist and the sea. The twelve lion heads still loomed above the windows of the *piano nobile* but they seemed diminished, shabbier. Gone were the sea-porter in his velvet doublet and the ten gondolas that used to be tethered there. Now, if I were painting it, I would add more Lead White to the Burnt Terra di Sienna than I would have done thirty years before. I would thereby make it look less substantial and more dangerous. I would add grey to the blue of the *paline*, as time had done. With Lamp Black on a dry brush I would eat away the feet of the sea-doors, as the tiny insects had done since I was last there.

I opened what was left of the sea-doors. There was a lurch and a splintering inside the heavy wood. I walked inside, feeling the damp air in my lungs, running my eyes over its unchecked depredations on the red velvet and mirrors I had last seen so many years before. I climbed the stairs. Yes, the lanterns on the out-thrust arms still lit the stone corridors. But now mummified flies swayed in thick cob-webs in high corners. Trails of moisture bled down the walls.

At the door to Byron's apartments I stopped for a moment. I closed my eyes and travelled back in my memories. They were still so rich, so vivid! I indulged in a sudden fantasy that I might open the door and find inside that party of 1782 still in flow. I wanted to see the men gay as butterflies and powdered as pastry. I wanted to see the courtesans and the great ladies, the luxuriant plates piled high with delicacies, to hear the clink of the counters on the gaming tables, to see the men leaning over their lovers with the silk embroidery of their frock-coats lambent in the candlelight. I wanted to hear the confection of elegant voices, the high-bred buzz of gossip and flirtation. Most of all I wanted to see Casanova, opening his arms to me.

Instead, when I tapped the door, ugly little Fletcher came strutting out to greet me. Inside was emptiness and silence, darkness and dust.

'My Lord is waiting for you Missis Cecilia. He said you'd know the way. I'll warn you, His Numps is a sad dog today.'

I walked through the deserted reception rooms, following my instinct and my memory. I found Byron sitting surrounded by books. He had chosen for his study the same room where I had spent those unforgettable moments with Casanova; I had not seen it in the daylight before. It was revealed now as a dark room with a *terrazzo* floor inlaid with the colours of topaz and lapis. It was an intimidating room, slanted as if sidling away, but looming thirty feet high above me. In 1782 it had seemed a quiet haven from the glitter of the party. Now it was noisy with faded luxury.

I recognised the gold frame behind which Casanova and I had made love: now it housed a Canaletto and was hung between two effete little French landscapes. The room was crowded with small ornamental objects, like a bazaar. The walls were lined with gold and red brocade, up to a heavy frieze, from which projected little gold buttresses. High above were beams the colour of bruises. In permanent shadow, between the two Grand Canal windows, writhed a mass of stucco work now stained with smoke from the fireplace. There was a mirror between the two eyes of the windows. Reflected in this, when I entered the room, I could see Byron reclining gracefully on his sofa among columns of leather tomes.

On the table in front of him was the *Biribissi* board I had painted all those years ago, the faces peeling and the animals mere ghosts of themselves.

'Welcome back, Cecilia,' he said, in an unwelcoming tone. I could see his anger boiling under his skin. 'Look what I found in this Nicknackatorium. I discover that you have been somewhat lacking in candour. I think you have more to tell me about the Palazzo Mocenigo, Cecilia.' He pushed the board towards me.

He had recognised my work.

In my new relationship with the Mocenigo I discovered more about the *palazzo*. When I went there as a girl with Casanova my experiences had revolved around him. I accepted everything for its surface beauty and fairy-tale qualities, as a child does. Now, after all my experiences, I was more sensitive. I found the *palazzo* both more beautiful and more threatening. There were things about the Mocenigo that I still could not tell Byron. He would have to find out for himself.

Byron, who had broken every taboo, now found himself amongst violators of a different hue: the unresting, warm-blooded spirits of the Palazzo Mocenigo disturbing the air with the guilt and pain of crimes performed and suffered there.

For the Mocenigo also sheltered the anonymous ghosts of unhappy lovers, servant-girls nursing big bellies from their masters, idiot sons poisoned in their beds, hushed-up homosexual suicides, malformed heirs quietly flushed into the canal at birth, ugly daughters shaved and tipped into convents, the beautiful ones married off against their will to decrepit noble satyrs. No, the Mocenigos were no different from any other high Venetian family.

And yet there was also laughter in the air, and sometimes a sublime heat beat against the window. The gates swung languidly on their hinges in the breezeless garden. As the sun set, the walls bulged with phantoms like a cat in a bag. The charred phantom of the betrayed Bruno was known to stalk the dark corridors at night; petals of ash were to be found there in the mornings and strange spillages of water: his ghost was known to search everywhere for liquid to moisten his smouldering flesh as he writhed upon the stake. The beautiful women who had lived there – their beauty persevered in the mirrors, even when they died, and sometimes little gushes of perfume came forth from uninhabited corners. Their hearts were preserved in their family crypts but their transparent joys remained floating around the house. Some days, there were buds on the floor of flowers that had not been brought in, the gloves of women who had not visited. Byron tried not to eat, and thereby doubled his receptivity to the phantoms the Mocenigo offered him.

Sodden with self-pity, drooping like a flower watered by every member of the family, Byron succumbed. Cowering in the back of the room, he tried to write. Meanwhile the ghosts of the Palazzo Mocenigo screamed at him and pushed the wine glass closer to his hand.

7

Tre done in casa, inferno verto.

Three women in the house, hell opens.

VENETIAN PROVERB

That spring, an elephant went on the rampage in Venice. It had been the stellar attraction of a circus on the Riva degli Schiavoni. It escaped through the Campo Bandiera e Moro, disappeared round the far corner into the Salizzada, and thundered into the church of San Antonin. The Austrian soldiers could not induce it to come out, so they dragged a cannon to the door, and shot it. The elephant's forequarters exploded, festooning the beams with viscera, and it finally lay down to die, bellowing like a hundred women in childbirth.

Byron described it to Hobhouse, reading aloud to me as he wrote.

> We have had, a fortnight ago, the devil's own row with an elephant who broke loose, ate up a fruit shop, killed his keeper; broke into a church and was at last killed by a cannon-shot brought from the Arsenale. I saw him the day he broke open his own house; he was standing in the Riva,

and his keepers trying to persuade him with peck loaves to go on board a sort of ark they had got. I went close up to him that afternoon in my gondola, and he amused himself with flinging great beams that flew about over the water in all directions; he was then not very angry, but towards midnight he became furious, and displayed the most extraordinary strength, pulling down everything before him. All musketry proved in vain; and when he charged, the Austrians threw down their muskets and ran. At last they broke a hole and brought a field piece, the first shot missed, the second entered behind, and came out all but the skin at his shoulder. I saw him dead the next day, a stupendous fellow. He went mad for want of She, it being his rutting month.

I went with Byron to see the stinking corpse. He asked me to make a portrait of the elephant but I refused. I was afraid of its hulk, even in death. I knew why Byron wanted me to paint it. He saw in it a metaphor for himself: painting the vanquished giant would teach me to capture better the savage pathos of Byron himself.

Byron liked any kind of animal. For all I know, he even shared his ancestor's passion for cockroaches. On the whole, Byron was kinder to four-legged beasts than to his servants and his women. The animals at least never felt the scorn of his words or the dismissal in his voice. The rest of us wore his contempt like a shameful smell that clung about our persons.

The Palazzo Mocenigo itself now growled and snarled with Byron's own bizarre menagerie.

At the dark heart of the *palazzo* crouched the covered courtyard with its stone flagged floor, odd blackened panelling and empty architraves. The air was curiously thin there, unbreathable. As if to show his new merman state, Byron ordered the wheels taken off his carriages, which had been carried to the *palazzo*. Their carcasses lay there, dismembered, like the ribs of ancient beasts. There was a lower chamber near the canal, which was set with columns – here Byron housed his living animals: two monkeys, several cats, three or four dogs, a wolf, a fox, a crow and an eagle. The red walls were still inset with the harlequin mirrors, so the animals were duplicated and triplicated. Their strange doppelgängers kept them in a constant state of lust and fear. Through the dim mullioned windows and the flares of light in the cracks of the door, the wretched prisoners could see and even smell the water. But, chained, caged or tethered, they could not escape their terror and misery.

It was now the talk of Venice that the English milord was keeping a small zoo on the Grand Canal. Byron was not unaware of the appearance they made when unsuspecting guests arrived at the wooden gates which opened out to the Canal. As he had done with the entrance to Newstead Abbey, with its chained wolf and bear, Byron enjoyed making his visitors run the gamut of the screaming animals and their infernal stench before coming up to pay their respects to him, the King of all the Beasts.

The neighbours, including Maurizio, were in despair. But what could they do? Maurizio was afraid to say anything to Byron, whom he occasionally encountered in the courtyard. It was hard for me to imagine the two of them together, even for an instant.

After we saw the elephant, Byron became curious about the fate of other animals in Venice. So, while I painted him, I told him stories about them, as they came to my mind. He was like a child listening to a fairy tale. 'More!' he cried, every time I finished a description or an anecdote. At my studio I showed him vignettes and drawings from my sketchbook.

I described the *Casotto de leone*, a wooden stage where a tethered lion lay, watching delicious little Maltese poodles in full mask and party dress dancing minuets on their back legs to the strains of a charlatan's violin. The she-dogs clutched perfect miniature fans in their coral-enamelled claw-nails. The he-dogs in their frock-coats attended their bitches solicitously.

I showed him my sketch of the famous canary who could count to thirty.

I told him about the horrible ceremony of cat-butting in Santa Maria Formosa, which used to take place every February, and about the way, at the same *festa*, the men leapt to strangle a goose suspended above the canal before sliding down its slippery body to the water.

I showed him engravings of the bull-baiting, how the trained dogs were set upon bulls and leapt for their ears where they hung on until death. They could only be removed when the dog-pullers bit their tails or clamped their testicles. At bullfights in the very court-yard of the Doges' Palace, the bulls had their heads severed with a single blow. I told him of the bear-tormenting, when the dogs were set on the tethered beast. When the bear caught one of his yapping attackers in his jaws they were levered open with jagged wooden spades, ripping his mouth apart.

I showed Byron a pen and ink sketch of men leaning over tubs of water, catching live eels in their teeth. I showed him boys tying fire-crackers to the feet of dogs.

I told him about the terrible horse tournament when my father lost his life.

'Poor horse!' sighed Byron. 'Poor beasts.'

To complete the household, Byron now imported his bastard daughter, Allegra, by Claire Claremont. I was nervous as a deer the first time I met the child, but I searched her features in vain for a resemblance to Girolamo, or even Byron himself. She was a pretty blonde cherub, plump and solid, with nothing airy or graceful to her.

Byron watched me. 'I know what you are thinking. Not much like me, is she? The damnedest thing is that she doesn't even look like her mother, which is a relief. However, she is more like me in spirit.'

It was true. Allegra was wilful and I often heard her scream, several times saw her kick at a servant or a cat. But she preferred to laugh. Byron was affectionate towards the child, as he was towards the other beasts. Every time I saw him stoop to ruffle her hair or smile at her, I imagined him doing the same thing to Girolamo. *This is how he is as a father*, I thought. *And this.* I realised that I was, pointlessly, jealous on my son's behalf.

Byron liked to have Allegra around him. She was often playing in the room where I painted him. She sang incomprehensible tunes to herself, and treated her father like any other adult. After a while Byron accepted her presence without comment and absorbed her personality into his circle so that it no longer disturbed him. He stopped noticing her. Little Allegra tottered unsupervised down grimy staircases and lay under tables like a dog.

Byron bought Allegra a *velocimano*, a little wooden horse mounted on wheels. Its ears flared straight out from its head. Allegra plucked at its mane, made of real horse hair. She steered the toy with little handles behind his head. One day, unnoticed by her father, she opened the great doors and steered the *velocimano* right down the stairs to the pit of the beasts, any one of which might have devoured her.

Byron's friends, the Hoppners, found this atmosphere too dangerous for a child. Allegra was moved to the English Consul's house.

Byron had one more beast to add to his zoo: the baker's wife, Margarita Cogni.

I think that it was probably Margarita's primitive animal nature that attracted him. 'She is one of these women who can be made to do anything. I am sure if I put a poniard in her hand, she would plunge it where I told her – and into me, if I offended her. I like this kind of beast, particularly . . .'

'Pythoness,' he called her. 'Tiger.' 'Lioness with a cub.'

I had to agree with him: Margarita Cogni was a terrifying animal. It had taken her just a few months to separate him from Marianna Segati, and claim him for her own. When she knew her moment of triumph, her inhuman shrieks of joy could be heard echoing down the Grand Canal. Byron dared not clap his hand over her mouth. He might lose a finger. I felt about her much as I had felt about Marianna, except that I, too, was physically frightened of her.

One night in August 1818, Margarita Cogni sat upon the steps of the palace and refused to go home to her husband, that *becco etico*, consumptive cuckold, as she called him. She was not to be removed, neither by the intervention of the police nor the parish priest, so Byron made her his housekeeper. He was a little embarrassed with his unexpected acquisition. However, she kept the household in rare order and saved him money. She believed, as an Italian, that everyone was cheating him, and treated them accordingly: with screams and blows. Soon the Mocenigo was being run on a shoe-string. Margarita had found another way into Byron's heart.

'But how do you manage her?' I asked, when he came to my studio.

'I don't even try. I let her rampage. It's amusing to watch. She has already frightened the learned Fletcher out of his remnants of wits more than once . . . Don't worry, Cecilia, I can deal with anything but a cold-blooded animal such as the never-to-be-sufficiently-damned-and-confounded Miss Milbanke.'

Margarita was beyond control, despite what Byron had said to me. In order to spy on him, she learnt to read. Byron had not exaggerated: she terrified both Tita and Fletcher. At the sound of her step, they cringed like hyenas. Margarita would not allow

another woman inside the Mocenigo unless she was old and frightful. She would wait for Byron through the night on the steps of the
palazzo, her eyes phosphorescent with burning tears and her dark
hair coiling as tumultuously over her brow and breasts as the snakes
of the Medusa. When Byron eventually came home, he found her
welcome almost dangerously enthusiastic. She bore him away in triumph.

When Margarita became a fixture, I was merely philosophical, and
went back to my studio. I had no wish to be disfigured by
Margarita's fingernails. Byron had already left his mark on me –
and, more importantly, I had already realised that to become a part
of his everyday life would rob me forever of any attraction Byron
still felt for me. He visited the studio most days, and we continued
to meet at San Lazzaro.

Sometimes, however, I would come to the Mocenigo, where my
easel was still permanently in place in his study. We devised a way to
placate Margarita: I painted a quick study of her in the finery she
insisted on wearing now that she was living *la vita di palazzo*. She had
renounced her white *faxoléto* for a ridiculously long train that she
dragged around behind her. She gave herself a comical parcel of airs,
looked a walking caricature of a great lady. I painted her as one, but
kindly, without irony. When she saw her likeness she snatched it
from my easel and ran away with it. But after that she would nod at
me almost amicably. She had accepted me as part of the household,
like Fletcher or Tita: another diligent and devoted creature in service to her master.

After that I could paint Byron while he worked on the first canto
of his new poem *Don Juan*, which he had commenced at the beginning of September 1816. He declared, from the first stanza, that it
would be his masterpiece. Although he often affected to scorn it, he
was still hungry for fame. 'Its fumes are frankincense to human

thought,' he told me. It was true, I reflected. My own worldly success hung about me like spun sugar, sweetening my life.

Apart from the times when Byron read aloud from his work,
these days we sat in silence. We were still afraid of Margarita. Every
now and then, from one of the three doors that punctuated the
study walls, La Fornarina would dart in. Finding all in order, she
would run to Byron, straddle him briefly. He caught my eye over her
shoulder. This was part of his pleasure. Under my canvas, I reached
for the paper and charcoal. These moments would not go
unrecorded, on the page or inside me.

One day, while we were working, a calamitous noise erupted
downstairs among the servants. Eventually, Fletcher came pattering
upstairs to explain. Margarita had found a pretty Rialto girl lingering in the kitchen after delivering some potatoes for one of Byron's
horrid boil-ups. The girl had been attacked and lay unconscious on
the floor. Margarita was circling her prey, and seemed about to be
deliver the *coup de grâce*.

'Bring her to me,' Byron told Fletcher. 'Then endeavour to resus-
citate the victim.'

Hair streaming, colour roused, blood under her fingernails,
Margarita came spitting into the room, with the stiff-legged gait of
a dog in its courting display.

'Margarita, you are a bitch,' Byron told her. Now, *cagna* in Italian
is a filthy insult, like *lingua biforcuta*, but worse. I drew in my breath,
waiting for the tall girl to crumple or erupt in screams.

But Margarita merely curtsied and answered, '*Sì, la tua cagna* —
your bitch. *Sono sempre in calore.* I am always on heat.'

Byron laughed and dismissed her. Margarita first took his head
between her hands and engulfed his mouth with hers. He pulled
away and at this she rushed off, quick tears wetting her cheeks, a
howl in the air. Byron turned to me, wiping his mouth. 'You know
what we say in England about women, "the more they cry the less

they piss."' He added, 'I hate to see a woman cry like I hate to see a goose go barefoot.'

I said nothing. Margarita's noisy sobs and hiccups and loud imprecations to God could be heard from a distant room. Byron inclined his head towards the sad noise. 'You know she crosses herself when she hears the prayer-bell, *no matter what we are doing*. Sometimes, I can tell you, there is some incongruity with the activities of the other parts of her body. She's a fine rammish animal. I like her energy. I overhear her with the servants: I like the way she boasts about me. She amuses me – she can always get round me by making me laugh with some Venetian pantaloonery or other. And I love her little names for me.'

Yes, I heard them all the time. Margarita called them out in moments of frenzy from the bedroom or the study. *Uvetta mia*, my little grape, she called him, and *pasta di marzapane*. La Fornarina, I thought disdainfully to myself, was after all a baker's wife, so naturally she took her imagery from the kitchen. I had always pictured Marianna Segati flopping sweetly around him, more liquid than solid. She would keep those inky eyes open on him; he would be afloat inside her. I could not help imagining la Fornarina working Byron's flesh like pastry, flipping him over, forcing her fingers into all the yielding places. Afterwards she would lie next to him breathing like bread rising. In the time it took to put a knife through a warm loaf, she would be ready again, her face as greasy as a buttered veal-chop and greedy as rising dough to engulf him.

8

Xe più le done che varda i òmeni
che le stele che varda la tera.

There are more women looking at men
than there are stars looking at the earth.

VENETIAN PROVERB

I have said this before. I never had a female friend.

I am a woman who prefers to be with men. I am not at my
ease with other women. Until Casanova died in 1798 I had in
him the only friend I needed. Our letters were my gossip, my safe
vent for mischief, my cosiness. When Casanova died, I became
harder and colder. After Byron left me in Albania, I suppose that I
became softer and kinder, having been battered by pain, but not
warmer. The pain made me nicer, I suppose. I was very slightly
kinder to Sofia. In fact, I was more amiable with all women. I no
longer felt myself above them so I had more compassion for their
sorrows. But it was too late in my life then to start trusting women.

I have said this before, too, I suppose that Mary Shelley is the
closest thing to a woman friend that I have ever known.

The Shelleys – Percy and Mary – came to Venice that summer. I
was working on a portrait of Byron when they arrived at the Palazzo
Mocenigo one morning. Shelley, pink and blond as an angel, looked
the Romantic poet to his every inch. He had Byron's luminous

quality, but in him it had not been dimmed with sulking or bitterness. I itched with an intemperate craving to paint him; I knew I could make the poetry shine out of him. *How Byron would hate that idea*, I thought. I asked myself if I was attracted to Shelley, but I found that I was not. He did not seem to make a human connection with anyone: it was all spiritual and intellectual for him. Anyway, the image of Byron was imprinted upon my soul. It was his mouth I wanted on mine, not a mouth even somewhat like it.

Mary, I thought plain, at first glance. *She would not make a fine portrait*, I thought. Her charm was to be found in the unseen things and not in her pale features. She was dressed simply. I thought that her facial skin was unpleasantly transparent and that it hung shapelessly on her skull. Her figure was unexceptional. Her hands were good.

'Who is she?' asked Shelley, in his high-pitched, anxious voice, looking at me, distractedly. He had come here to talk about poetry. He feared, as always with Byron, trivial and vulgar pursuits.

'No one. An artist,' said Byron, carelessly.

Mary said, soft and sibilant, 'But an artist is surely someone, Albé. An artist is a kind of god! He or She' – and she bowed to me – 'creates life, in a *thinking*, skilful way.'

As she spoke I noticed the liveliness of Mary's pupils under her thick eyelids. Her shining hair was parted in the middle and ringletted at the sides. She had a gesture of bringing her left arm up to her shoulder with the hand curled around, like a little child stretching before bedtime. *It is quite affecting, in an unaffected way*, I thought.

Byron sneered, 'God help us if the artists start to *think*!'

But Mary continued, as if she had not heard him. 'I am not talking about mere likeness, the correct measurement of the eyelid or the faithful rendering of a complexion. I am talking about a tension that is rendered like life itself, a kind of alchemy to recreate the personal essence of the sitter. With colour and life and depth, the artist creates something that can be *felt*, in other words, *life*.'

She came over to the easel, looked at my portrait, and smiled at me, then at Byron. 'This picture, Albé, is you, to the eyelash. She has created life, your life, and I can read everything I know about you on your face here.'

Byron hated bluestockings, and Mary's, he had always told me, were of the deepest indigo. He had no respect for her *Frankenstein* theories of life forces and reanimation. He did not grace her with an answer. Shelley looked embarrassed. It was not a subject with which his brain currently teemed. Byron did not introduce me. He swept Shelley off to the drawing room and slammed the door like a slap in the face. I understood that he was showing off for Shelley. Mary and I closed our eyes for a second with the shock of the noise. When we opened them we were looking at each other. I was conscious of some kind of transaction, some kind of marching out of souls to greet each other. I did not know how to be this way with women and I felt confused and diffident.

We have in common famous Romantic poets in our beds, I thought. But how different they were! I could imagine Shelley tender and tearful in ways that Byron would never be. I wondered, and I shall always wonder, what Mary herself was thinking at that moment as we gazed at each other.

Our ocular negotiations, which I would now call the early stirring of a friendship, were interrupted. The study door was flung open. Suddenly, Byron returned and threw some papers towards us. They thumped on the floor and a cloud of dust made a short-lived halo around them.

'My memoirs,' he said, over his shoulder.

'Your confessions?' Mary challenged. 'Just these few pages?'

He did not answer her. The door slammed again.

The reverberations of the door faded to silence. Mary and I looked at each other again. Now I thought my first impression might have been wrong. There was quite definitely something alive in her face. I might, after all, enjoy painting it.

Mary came to sit with me. She spoke excellent Italian, she was knowledgeable about art, and she knew everything about Byron. We talked like flowers opening together on one branch. The packet of thrown papers lay behind us, temporarily forgotten. Mary had fascinating things to tell me.

After a very short while it became clear to me that Mary hated Byron. She felt he had cost her the life of her daughter. She told me how Shelley had summoned her urgently to Venice to help him reason with Byron about poor little Allegra. Mary told me that the child's mother Claire — at the name, she compressed her lips — unbeknownst to Byron, was lurking in wait for him here in Venice. She wanted her baby, but she was also using Allegra as bait to see her former lover. Byron, it seemed, was equally determined not to see Claire or to give up the child. From what I had heard of Claire, she was grotesque, and Mary's unsaid words confirmed this. But why would Byron not give up Allegra? Mary said, 'He was afraid that people would say that he had grown tired of her. He already has a reputation here for being capricious, I understand.' I nodded. 'Still, everyone must think of the child.' Reluctantly, Mary had set off across Italy to support her husband and Claire. But the hard journey killed her own ailing little daughter, Clara, who died in Mary's arms within an hour of their arrival in Venice.

Mary felt that Shelley had put Byron's and Claire's interests above those of herself and their own child. And this, because of Shelley's insistence that there was a thread of gold running through the vulgar weave of Byron's mind. He knew that Byron was no intellectual but he also knew that Byron was chosen from all other men to draw attention to the heat and light he made. Shelley saw

Byron throwing it away, wasting its precious luminosity. Shelley wanted to help the poetry come forth, whatever the human expense. It was also possible – I realised from Mary's sourness – that Shelley, too, had betrayed her with the incorrigible Claire.

The story raised a storm inside me. Here were other women deprived of their children because of Byron. Here was Shelley, a man as fascinated with him as the women were. I let Mary talk, asking just a question here or there. *Why is she telling me this?* I wondered at one point. At other times it seemed perfectly clear.

Fletcher brought us tea. La Fornarina darted in for a quick look and then hurtled into the study where Byron and Shelley were sequestered. Moments later she emerged streaming with tears and rushed away, shaking a large fist at Mary, who flinched.

'Don't worry,' I told her. 'When she is violent it is only with her own kind. That amuses Byron. Beating you would not amuse him.'

'Can you be so sure?' Mary had the measure of him. But we did not see Margarita again.

The men stayed shut up together all day. Enclosed with Mary, I gradually forgot about my own work. After some hours, I gave up the paintbrush and sat with my hands folded on my lap like a schoolgirl. This plain young woman had hypnotised me with her charm and intelligence.

She set out to answer my every question. She omitted no detail, like a conscientious biographer afraid to sacrifice a fact that posterity might later judge vital. From her I learnt the things about Byron that Hobhouse, in his lumbering kindness, had spared me, and Byron himself had omitted, thinking them deleterious to his legend. Hobhouse thought I was not strong enough to hear it. Mary, knowing women, knew better. And she knew more. She told me of his childhood, and his growing up. Mary's account made sense of Byron's. In Albania he had told me the facts as he saw them. Mary told me what others had seen. She spoke intimately of the aspects of his marriage that a man wouldn't know how to explain to a woman. She had been an industrious distiller of information herself, it seemed. All that he had shared with Shelley, and Shelley with her, after those long, unguarded evenings at the Villa Diodati, when his hurts were fresh and angry, Mary now shared with me.

She concluded, 'Byron is not yet an Italian, though he pretends to be. Nor is he as happy as he pretends to be, or as tragic as he pretends to be. He is heartily and deeply discontented with himself. That's why he behaves so badly.'

She said nothing I could deny, but nothing I cared to corroborate. I was absorbed in what she had told me about the last seven years of Byron's life, the ones in which he had not missed me. The stories of Caroline, of Augusta, of Claire, of Annabella were now intertwined with my own, as were the stories of Edelston, Claire and Rushton. I saw my own place in the great scheme of Byron's life. I saw how it was likely to end. I fell to silence again, looking at the floor.

'Ah,' Mary said, 'we have forgotten the famous memoirs.' We turned to them, raked up the sheets and examined them together in silence. As we read, Mary's hand strayed out of its sleeve, like a turtle's head emerging from a shell, to cover mine. I had never been touched like this, in tenderness, by a woman. Sofia would not dare. But I found myself aching to accept Mary's sweetness. I had need of it. When we reached his account of Albania, she took my hand in hers, and stroked its trembling fingers.

There was not much in those so-called memoirs of Byron's. What we read were just notes and scrawls. He had not cared to leave the world too much information. The stories of Greek Love were confirmed, but in no way could that be called titillating. He felt more for his boy-loves than for the women, yes, but still he treated them badly when they bored him.

Mary and I read pages together in silence, marvelling at how little we had meant to him. At one point she turned to me and said, 'Cecilia, there is not enough scorn in all the world for him, is there?'

I shook my head, mutely. Mary, with my hand still in hers, looked into my face.

'But please remember this, Cecilia: just because Byron scorns a creature, that creature is not unworthy. Similarly a creature whom he praises is not necessarily a great one. One should not let his scorn discolour and pervert what is good in this life. We must live apart from his malicious opinions, which have no basis in the truth, only in the weakness in him.'

I was too distressed to understand her. I took the words into my head and stored them up for later, when I would be calmer. In my case, the memoirs had this to say:

In Albania, I had my portrait painted by a famous Venetian artist, a woman. I do not remember her name, but I made sure, as you may imagine, that she got a good likeness of me.

Shelley and Byron finally emerged from their colloquy, and the former reclaimed his wife. At the last moment, Mary leant over to kiss me twice in the Italian style.

'It's a beautiful portrait,' she said, pointing at the canvas. 'I knew immediately that you were his lover,' she whispered, without a smile, but with infinite gentleness. 'You have painted the pain into your picture.'

'Let me paint you,' I offered suddenly. The words had entered my mouth without negotiating with my brain. I realised that for some time now I had been studying her, memorising her features.

'Ah, Cecilia, but I am plain. It's scarcely worth your talent to render my face. My children were the beautiful ones. Look.'

She pulled from her pocket a miniature wrapped in silk and wool. It was a glass-mounted pastel of the little dead Clara as a baby, truly the image of her angelic-looking father.

'A sweet child,' I said, and I felt for Mary deeply. I had never felt such compassion for another human being before. My little Girolamo was not mine to hold any longer, but at least he still lived. I could not quite imagine surviving Mary's pain. I no longer saw her as plain, but as beautiful, as the image of intelligence and sweetness inscribed on human flesh. In her eyes now I saw diamonds of light, and in the tilt of her head an enviable grace. Yet from that gentle head had come the horrors of *Frankenstein*. Mary Shelley was truly a fascinating woman, but it was not the fascination that drew me. It was her warmth.

'Let me keep this for a day,' I asked her, with the miniature still in my hand. 'I shall make you a copy of it.'

'No, no! I cannot ask it!' But she was blushing with pleasure at the thought.

Shelley and Byron had gone out to the terrace to watch the sunset. Mary looked over her shoulder and drew closer to me.

'I have a gift for you, too, Cecilia,' she said. 'It is a thought.'

'A thought?'

'A thought that might help you.' Mary leant over to me. The light of the mullioned windows was tender upon her face. She started to talk, looking at the figures of the two men silhouetted on the terrace. With their nipped-in waists and their curls, they looked like little boys. Then Byron turned and I saw his profile suddenly, cruel as a subtle gargoyle.

I heard Mary say, 'People can become addicted not just to wine, or even a lover, but to their mistakes. People can fall in love with an unworthy object, but they cannot admit that they have made a mistake. And so they weld themselves to it with love, knit themselves to it with desire. They start to admire it, their great passion. They step outside it and look at it, and think, "What a masterpiece of love this is, on my side, at least!"'

I looked at Mary. I could not speak. She went on.

'But what they have made is a Frankenstein monster, a dangerous hybrid given life by their dangerous fantasies. They allow themselves to be savaged by it, rather than admit that they have made a mistake, that they have taken up with something that they should have left alone. They would like to see it as the great tragedy in their life, as something romantic and fated, but in reality it was merely a lapse of taste, and nothing grander than that.'

I turned away from her then. She rose and stood above me. She reached out to me and was not discouraged when I instinctively flinched away from her. For just an instant, she stroked my hair with gentle fingers. I let her. It felt strange but pleasing to be touched like that.

Then she said, 'That was important, Cecilia, but what I really want to say to you is this: you do not need to die of your addiction. There are other ways to cure addiction. It's important to remember that it is the *vice* that should die and not the poor creature who suffers from it.

'But few can do it alone. We need to turn to another human being, and accept help. Perhaps you are not ready yet, Cecilia. But keep this thought inside you and perhaps you will come to accommodate it in your heart.'

'What were you two talking about all that time?' Byron asked me, the next day, at my studio, where he had come to avoid Margarita's wrath. La Fornarina had not been happy to learn that Mary Shelley, homely as she was, had spent a whole day in what she saw as her house. Me, she had accepted as a nearly sexless object, an artist. But Mary, in Margarita's primitive reasoning, posed a real threat. She was a woman, after all, with a husband, and therefore a vacancy for a lover.

Byron hated to be disapproved of by the Shelleys as much as he adored it from more respectable folk. But he needed to know. He tried to draw me out. 'Shelley's woman has the eyes of a cow. Did you see her face when Margarita came in? She is without the smallest element of attraction. She's a bracket-faced, stiff-rumped piece if I ever saw one. What does she call that hairstyle – curls à la blowze? She is stuffed to the gills with impacted *merde*. Why does Shelley pule around her so? What is it with her?' I winced at these insults.

'What did you think of my memoirs, then?'

I was silent. I knew how to hurt him.

He knew how to hurt me too. 'Not much like Casanova's? Have I not had as many pieces? Of course, I am a fraction of his age when he came hobbling into your bed.'

I turned away from him. Byron was still ruminating about Mary. 'I suppose she told you that my memoirs should be burned? I suppose Shelley thinks that now he is married, he doesn't get anyone else. Of course he has Claire when he wants, but then who doesn't? Mary won't open her legs to anyone else, we can be sure. But I am sure that she *thinks* of me on top of her.'

He strode around my studio, kicking at stacked canvases, too restless to pose. I quietly picked up the canvases. He had not kicked them hard: they might have been pictures of himself. *Anyway, canvas is durable*, I thought, *tougher than human skin*. And there was only one canvas that was still wet, and he would not see that. I had hidden it away when I heard his dragging steps upon my threshold.

When he saw that my resolve was impermeable, both to threats and kisses, he left, looking for easier sport. I turned back to my thoughts of Mary.

I took the small wet canvas from its hiding place and resumed work. Within a few hours, it was ready. I sent it, along with the miniature of Clara, to the *palazzo* where Mary and Shelley were staying.

The Shelleys left Venice very soon. Allegra was briefly restored to her mother. I never saw Mary Shelley again, so I do not know how she received her gift. Of course she wrote to me, and ever after wrote to me. Her letters, great bundles of them, are almost as precious as Casanova's are to me. But I did not see the moment when she unwrapped my canvas and first held it to the light. I can only imagine her gasp of delight and the soft tears that would have fallen from those fine eyes.

My gift was a little painting in the *cinquecento* style that she adored. It was a clever pastiche; one would look twice before realising that it was a modern piece. Even then, unless you knew Mary, and Clara, you might not guess the truth. For I had painted them as the Madonna and Child, using the miniature for Clara's likeness and my vibrant warm memories of Mary for hers.

9

El segreto de le fémene no lo sa nissum,
altri che mi e vu, e tuto 'l Comun.

No one knows the women's secret,
except me, you and the whole city.

VENETIAN PROVERB

Even when Margarita Cogni was installed at the Palazzo Mocenigo, Byron continued to find his low-life women in casinos. He knew that Margarita was rabid enough to disfigure or possibly murder them, so he kept them secret.

When Byron expanded his court from the Countess Albrizzi's salon to include that of the Countess Benzona, a wider circle of noble women had opened to him. He also foraged in the markets, shops and gutters for useful, usable women. The prostitutes from San Stae to San Marco came to know his dragging step. The retailers of love were required to dispense their favours at keen prices to the English milord. He would be offered the choicest of young flesh at every establishment at a fraction of the normal cost, and sometimes he took the madam as well.

Of course they compared experiences. The diseased, malnourished women of the slums were privileged with information longed for by half the respectable women of England and nearly all the men. It was generally agreed that his lame foot was no impediment in matters of pleasure for the milord, unless you happened to touch it accidentally, or worse still, with tenderness. Then would follow a storm of silence, an agonised '*vattene*' ('get away from me'), no tip, and quite possibly a bruise.

Some women cherished the belief that with correct handling the deformed limb could become an organ of pleasure for the milord, but he did not interest himself in this fashion of creativity. When he had limped away, they discussed him with familiarity, the way two women of the same family discuss the bowel movements of their babies. Had he known! When he took them, and felt their little hearts beating like birds under their translucent narrow skins, I am certain that he thought himself powerful. But it was the women who felt themselves strong.

Lover by lover, Byron continued to scandalise and enchant Venice, a city that adores debauchery done in style. An acquaintance who had visited him in Venice carried news of Byron's escapades back to London. Byron was annoyed to hear what was being said: it was not bad enough.

He raged at me, pacing around my studio. 'Which "piece" does he mean? . . . Is it the Tarruscelli, the Da Mosto, the Spinola, the Lotti, the Rizzato, the Eleanor, the Carlotta, the Giulietta, the Alvisi, the Zambieri, the Eleonora de Bezzi, the Theresina of the Mazzurati, the Glettenheim and her sister, the Luigia and her mother, the Fornarina, the Santa, the Caligara, the Portiera Vedova, the Bolognese figurante, the Tentora and her sister? . . . I have had them all and thrice as many to boot since I got here. There were also some courtesans and some cobblers' wives. Pushing schools and nunneries – what's the difference in Venice? One thing I will tell you: middling, high or low, they were all of them whores. Even the virgins were whores.'

I too heard it all, of course, relayed by my sitters, who sometimes brought a favoured courtesan with them to gaze upon while I painted them. These men believed that the yellow light of lust in their eyes, captured in my painting, would make a more potent picture for the future to admire. 'What a lover he must have been!' they wanted their descendants to say.

I had a curious relationship with the *puttane*, the whores. They dipped and wove around my studio in quick graceless movements, like parrots in vulgar plumage. I usually painted the mistresses themselves in the morning light, when their noble lovers were asleep. In this way I sought to avoid embarrassing encounters on my stairs between wives and mistresses.

I smiled to myself at the cross-grained fidelity of the men: they were faithful to me in that they sent both their wives and mistresses to me. However, the wives and lovers were required to adopt different poses in the studio. The mistresses would be portrayed in movement – dancing, laughing, holding aloft baskets of tempting fruit. The wives were usually painted still as death, as well-tended expensive dolls on which to display the family jewels.

When they were not accompanied by the patrons, the *puttane* sighed after the English milord. They appealed to me: 'You know how it is, Madame . . .' I would not talk to them about Byron – I hated to think that our liaison was discussed on the streets – but I could not hide my discomposure. And this satisfied them. Shamelessly, they would watch my lips compress to a thin line that would not allow even a whisper to break out, until, at the end of the session, I would say, 'The portrait is finished.' Later I would tell their wealthy lovers, 'Don't send her again.'

Afterwards, cleaning my brushes, examining my work, I would take my revenge. In some small subtle way, I would spoil the portrait, not the work of art but the image of the woman. I would add a little yellow feather on a lapel, an eggstain on the lace. I pinked their knees (for I painted the *puttane* in lascivious poses) to indicate the early stages of syphilis. Most people cannot bear to gaze directly at their own portrait at first sight. So I knew that they would not notice my malice till they had grown accustomed to their image, long after their protector had paid for it, and then they would be too embarrassed to ask me to paint out the blemish.

I continued to go to the Mocenigo to work on the permanent portrait of Byron. Sometimes I arrived by gondola, and took my chances with the beasts in the courtyard. Sometimes I walked to his *palazzo*, for the pleasure of arriving at the narrow entrance down the Calle Mocenigo Ca' Nova – so narrow that even a small man could touch both sides with barely outstretched hands. From the alley you saw the strange vine-covered first-floor pergola that hung over the garden gate – resembling nothing so much as engravings I had seen of the *seraglio* in Constantinople. At the gate itself the Mocenigo family crest reared above the fanlight. I walked under the pergola into Byron's strange kingdom.

Perhaps I imagined it, but it always seemed to me that all was not well in the statue-haunted garden, stretching away from me in both directions, like a vindictive smile. There was a choked well in the centre, and at least one rape taking place in marble in the undergrowth where also nestled startling dwarves of stone where your eye longed for cupids.

I took the left path (the right one led to Maurizio's apartments) and let myself into the dark inner courtyard, sour with the smell of miserable beasts imprisoned at the other end and tortured with their howls. They were diminished in number now, following the elopement of one cat and the decease of two monkeys and a crow by indigestion. But the beasts that remained seemed louder and their stink worse, as if they were abandoned in grief for their lost companions. I spoke kindly to the poor caged cats, and then I mounted the stone steps, with their lanterns on out-thrust arms, and ascended to the *piano nobile*.

Sometimes Fletcher told me to wait in the dark entrance hall, where I studied the painted ceiling, with its circular central panel and four medallions. Little light fed through the leaded windows. While I waited, I mentally repaired the ravaged faces of the frescoes, adding roses and cream to the pale grey buttocks of the *putti* and the chipped nipples of the nymphs.

Eventually I was summoned to Byron's study, walking first through the *soggiorno*, with its pink marble walls veined like the heart of a freshly killed bull. He rarely acknowledged my arrival, so I went straight to my easel. I always sat by the fire that burned between the two windows on the Grand Canal. Byron was ensconced towards the back of the room.

I found it hard to breathe in there. I felt the weight of the stucco's suffering figures pressed against my shoulders, and Byron's simmering humours pressed against my breast. If the window was open, from time to time I reeled when an upward breeze puffed the stench of the trapped animals up into my face. Sometimes, when the Canal was quiet, a strain of their sad cries would reach my ears. Perhaps this was why Byron sat so far back in the room: to avoid the mournful reminder of their plight. He seemed oblivious to their manifest miseries.

When I painted him, he reclined on his sofa in a writing attitude. He often actually started to write. But, as *Beppo* and *Don Juan* show, he did not lose himself in his verse. He stood some feet away from it and was at once audience, performer and author – miming the words and at the same time watching for the effect.

He read me pieces of the poetry while I painted. The lines gave me ideas. Little phrases of verse, small images, fell into my paintings. I listened to Byron making use of his life, and my life, sometimes. I saw him draw on William Beckford, the Ali Pasha, Hobhouse, for his characters. I flinched as he invested each of us with his scorn. Sometimes I laughed, but I was ashamed of my laughter. Sometimes I had no desire to laugh at all. It was a physical blow to read the lines that defined us, his intimates, secretly and not so secretly, inside the public poetry. Of course he started with himself and he was no less savagely ironical on that count.

I want a hero, he commenced . . .

Byron needed all his heroism to deal with Margarita. Their battles seemed to be unto the death. The merest perceived slight threw her into a combustion. In her fury there was nothing she dared not say to him. I witnessed bruising scenes that made me pity both of them.

La Fornarina would scream, 'Is this how you treat your wife?'

Byron clawed the air. 'Stop it! Don't ask me about Annabella. Everyone wants to know about her! Why don't they ask about me? About how I felt? Everyone talks to me the way Caroline *writes*. I cannot bear it.' He put his face in his hands.

'I'm not interested in that. I'm interested in how you are with me,' said Margarita. 'It's good, no, with me? Better than with her?'

For a moment, I thought she was talking about me. Then I realised that Margarita was defying him. She was still talking about Annabella. I held my breath.

Margarita said, 'Anyway, Missis Byron have own *moroso*, yes?'

Byron slithered to his feet and said, with a dangerous quietness, 'Go.'

It was the one thing calculated to break her. Margarita could not survive his coldness any more than I could. She fled, screams erupting like a haemorrhage.

Byron turned to me. His face was raw. Little grey pearls of sweat were distilling above his lips, which were set in a thin, ugly line.

'No, Cecilia,' he said, 'in case you are thinking it. The state of cuckoldry in England is not so flourishing as it is here in Venice. Annabella Milbanke will not replace me in her bed. Damn her and Ada and all the other brats I might have begot out of her.'

Then he clawed the air again, as he had done with Margarita, a gesture of such pain that I felt the ghostly laceration of his nails in my stomach.

'Do you know how much I hate Miss Milbanke?' he asked me. 'I hate her *professionally*. I hate her the way the grave-digger hates the gases that come from corpses, I hate her the way the fisherman hates the rotten oyster for which he has put his life in danger. When she is dead, I will hate her *dust*.'

I quickly sketched him as he spoke, and slid the picture into my portfolio before he noticed it. This portrait was different from the ones I let him see. But I thought it was also important to record them, the moments like these.

By autumn, the heroic poet's health finally collapsed again – the natural and perhaps looked-for result of his recent regime of relentless self-abuse. His stringent diet changed again. Now he ate nothing but *scampi*, claiming that the expensive little crustaceans performed rare purgative miracles inside him.

Under the cowardly mantle of the doctor's orders, La Fornarina was told to leave. I was there when Byron called her into the study. He announced, as if talking to a departing tradeswoman, that he had made financial provision for herself and her mother. He spoke in a conversational tone of voice, emphasising the generosity of the settlement. Margarita ran screaming from the room. She had not listened to his words, merely the drab tone of his voice. She left some words in the air for us, words about knives and revenge.

The next day, at the dinner hour, she was back. She smashed a glass door on the staircase and ran babbling like a madwoman up to Byron's apartments. She burst into the study where we were working. She stood there silently, her arms folded in front of her. Byron looked up at her with exasperation. 'I was entirely serious, Margarita. You no longer have a position here. I shall not change my mind.'

Margarita pulled a knife from her apron. The glint of it whisked the air as she rushed at Byron. I stood helpless as she pulled him out of his chair and into her arms. She fastened her lips upon his and he screamed, a high-pitched animal noise. She started backwards and I could see Byron gazing at a slight wound to his thumb. He put it to his mouth and turned his back on her. I was astounded at his temerity, but he seemed to know that Margarita could not really hurt him, or perhaps he did not care if she did.

'Look at me!' she shrieked. He refused to respond. I saw her turn the blade in her hand and ram it into her own breast, as Caroline Lamb had done. When I could bear to look again I saw that her gesture had been as futile as her predecessor's. For all her bellowing she had done little more than sever the lace from her bodice. By now the entire staff had come running to us, but when they saw Margarita with the knife in her hand and the vicious light in her eye, they would not enter the room. They stood in the doorway, crossing themselves.

Byron ordered Tita to see her out, but Margarita was too agile for the frightened gondolier. She leapt through the door and launched herself from the balcony with a great flapping of linen, cawing like a seagull. We heard a splash.

'She's thrown herself in the Canal,' said Byron. 'Good God! I imagine that she will float in all that get-up. Go and fish her out, Tita. Fletcher doesn't know the right end of a woman from the wrong one.'

A few minutes later Margarita was carried limp and dripping up the stairs. By this time Byron was sitting at the dinner table, gorging upon scampi. He continued to eat while directing Tita and Fletcher on the techniques of resuscitation. 'Female suicides,' he observed, ripping shells from pink flesh, 'are seldom conclusive.'

He added, 'In my experience.'

I watched all this sadly from behind my easel. It seemed only a crude puppet-play of what had happened to me in Albania, and could happen to me again at any minute. I did not feel much more dignified than Margarita. I did not love Byron any less than she did, either, or hate him any less. When she had hurtled towards him, with the knife alive in her hand, I had half-wished her well, I realised now, and perhaps that was why I had done nothing to help him in the moment of apparent danger.

While La Fornarina reigned, Byron never touched me at the Mocenigo. We both feared death at her ungovernable hands. But after she left, I would stay, and wake in the night, not with him, for of course he hated to sleep or eat with us, but in a smaller room with two windows on the Canal. I would glide to my painting, naked, with a candle and work on it with the ardour he would not allow me to show him. He never woke early, but sometimes he came home in the middle of the night from a rout at a casino, and he would find me working there. He would discard all his clothes apart from the silk trousers that hid the withered leg, and walk straight to the painting as if he wished to walk right into this beautiful version of himself. He would take me on the floor, while he looked into the eyes of his portrait.

'Do you think she has made me handsome enough?' Byron would ask Fletcher, pointing at my work. 'Do you think she has caught my best features?' he demanded, thrusting his groin into the air.

Fletcher would be in difficulties. He would stammer something equivocal, carefully staring over my left shoulder. Byron always laughed. 'It's not a trap, you nigit. If it were a difficult question I would not expect you to understand it.'

Tita the gondolier would be summoned. A few minutes later I would smell his sweat and perfumed hair oil behind me, as he crossed his arms and pronounced gravely on the painting with all the weight of a Venetian born into a city of art he never looked at but absorbed as he did the winter mist that rotted all our bones. (We Venetians click and snap as we bend our joints – just listen to us, like castanets. The city exacts this physical tax and we pay more each year of our lives.) Byron would then satirise them both, cruelly, in English and Italian, so that each suffered for himself and snickered at the humiliation of the other.

'You know Fletcher has grand plans to establish a *pasta* factory in Knightsbridge, Cecilia?' he told me. 'I remember when he was too nice-gutted to dip his tongue in a bowl of macaroni! Look at him now! His impudence has a kind of monstrous elegance to it, doesn't it? He tells me, by the way, that I myself may never return to London because of my little "fox's paw" regarding my wife. I see you knitting your brow, Cecilia. A "fox's paw" is what the French, in their ignorance, call a *faux pas*.'

I watched him tormenting them and I burned at the injustice. It was thin amusement to watch them struggle, ensnared in his sarcasm. I, with my *lingua biforcuta*, could at least engage in equal, or almost equal hostilities with him.

I asked myself why I neglected my own good work to spend time with this man, who made my nostrils steam? Why did I want to spend a night, an evening, an hour with this man? Mary Shelley's words came crowding into my head: *addicted not just to wine, or even a lover, but to their mistakes . . . a dangerous hybrid . . . a lapse of taste*.

Over these thoughts, I superimposed my own.

Perhaps Girolamo knitted me to him.

Perhaps he was my way of taking responsibility: he was the nemesis of the men I had used for the shape of their bodies on my canvas and discarded. But no, I thought, they did not require avenging. They had left my studio happy, rubbing their eyes, sniffing their fingers.

Perhaps, as I had told my cat, I was still waiting for my chance to avenge myself for the treatment I had received in Albania.

But even this was a self-deception. I saw him because I still loved him and because I was flattered that he still came to me and called me to himself. But the rules of our engagement had changed now to be even more in his favour. In Venice he allowed me to align my life with his, but it was all one to him what I did. At times he was available to me; at others not. I gave myself wholly to him, but he picked at me querulously, like a spoilt invalid at a plate of delicacies.

He had taken residence in my imagination like a tapeworm in the gut. I did not know how to expel him. It seemed that this style of tapeworm fed ferociously on neglect. So he grew inside me. Yes, he was malignant as a parasite, but I was addicted to my mistake. I thought of Mary Shelley's words but I did not have the strength to act on them. My desire for Byron still enfeebled me.

I did the only thing I could: I committed my pain to paper.

None of them, not even Byron, ever saw my private sketches – the ones I made when his back was turned or when he was engaged with La Fornarina. These were the ones that showed the extra chin, the flesh squeezing out over the rings on his hands, the watering eyes I saw early in the morning when he returned from the *casino*. But I recorded it all, when Byron wasn't looking: the dark shadows under his eyes and the early grey hairs behind his ears, the stooped shoulders, and the emptiness.

The Gondolier Speaks
Again

Remember me? I was the one who brought that English milord into
La Serenissima. She was never quite so serene after that. The town
was rocked with oaths. I should know. We gondoliers are the treasure house of the vulgar tongue here. I could teach you a thing or
two!

I brought a pestilence here, if you ask me. Venice exiles all her
own best men – my grandfather, by the way, served Casanova when
he escaped from the Leads – and welcomes in the leavings and
refuse from every other land in Europe. *Mi Morti!* They roost in our
palazzi and foul our canals with the English Overcoats they fill with
their slimy seed.

I heard that Byron could make a girl love him just by ignoring
her. Just by pretending she did not exist. He could turn a sweet *fan-
ciulla* into a stinking heap of moans.

I want to tell you what Byron did to my brother-in-law's cousin's
wife. You probably knew her. Wild woman, that Margarita Cogni.
She would tear off her blood-rag to strangle a woman who came

near her Byron. But he almost killed her by not loving her enough.
She was not the only one. That artist, Cecilia Cornaro, the one who
does portraits, she was sick for love of him, too. Don't tell me it
takes TWO years to make a portrait of one ugly little English lord.

I wonder if she or Margarita or any of the other bitches ever
knew that what he really wanted was his own kind?

We did, we gondoliers. Because we carry people every day to
their secret desires. We carry messages; the great and good use us to
fare l'ambasciata. We know all the hidden staircases and the niches in
walls where love letters are kept. We know the ladies' maids. We
know their mistresses. They think we are anonymous. Welded to
the boat, like horse-heads onto black horses. But we are not. We see
everything.

And I saw Byron with his boys. He did not take *them* to the
Albrizzi or the Benzona *conversazione*. And what he did at Arsenale
with the sailor boys, well, that is between him and his conscience.

Nor could he take Margarita to the Albrizzi's or the Benzona's.
She'd have bitten the leg off any of those so-called ladies who hung
on his words. She'd have taken off her clothes in the middle of the
conversazione and shown them exactly what it was that endeared her
to Byron.

She showed all Venice during the Historical Regatta – there they
were, the two of them, with her petticoats flung over his shoulder,
on the balcony at the Palazzo Mocenigo while the noblemen's barge
sailed past, and the Princess of Madagascar on board, too.

He got rid of her. Perhaps she was too much like him. Byron was
the kind, and Margarita was the kind, too, to make *Carnevale* boil
over.

10

Chi va col porco impara a sgrugnar.

He who runs with the pigs learns to grunt.

VENETIAN PROVERB

B yron's solicitor Hanson arrived from London, with a new will to sign.

Hanson and his son disembarked from their gondola at the sea-steps of the Palazzo Mocenigo. As they walked into the covered courtyard, the stink of manure must have assaulted them. From upstairs we heard the dogs and birds make a cacophony around them. They must have stumbled, disbelievingly, past the fox and the wolf and Byron's graveyard of dismantled carriages until they found the dim marble staircase to Byron's apartments. But of all the beasts, I suspect that it was Byron himself who shocked Hanson the most. I read it in the older man's reaction as he was ushered into the study where I was at work on my painting, and Byron on his writing. Hanson's startled face made me look at my lover in a new way.

It was true. Byron's skin was now bloated and sallow. He looked ten years older than his thirty. He had lately grown very fat again. His shoulders were round and the knuckles of his hands were lost in pink flesh. His eyes looked boiled, lacking in lustre. Even his hair looked dead. The copper lights of it had vanished and now it hung about his pale face like faded silk curtains. That day I realised that he now looked, as he had dreaded all his life to look, like his mother. Hanson did not dare say as much, but the fact that he mentioned Lady Catherine Byron so often, and so unnecessarily, in the course of the conversation, utterly gave him away. I would look later at the miniature of her that Byron kept hidden in the lowest drawer of his desk and understand. The family face had indeed caught up with Byron.

Byron signed all the papers quickly, with Fletcher and myself as the witnesses. They included a new codicil to his will which vouchsafed 5000 pounds to Allegra provided that she did not marry a native of Great Britain. The Hansons left as soon as they could. They were visibly afraid of corruption. They seemed nervous of Byron's new, dangerous laugh, and the excesses of his conversation. I saw them exchange glances when Byron savaged his nails, already gnawed to the quick, and I saw them take note of the tears of wine on his silk waistcoat. Venice, the Hansons seemed to think, was rotting Byron's soul. I watched them hurry out of the door, accompanied by an unsteady Byron, and I knew that they would not be back, despite his slurred invitations and aggressive *bonhomie*.

I followed them down to the courtyard. As the Hansons stepped into their gondola, Byron shouted at Fletcher, 'Spooney and Young Spooney have left. Now go up and count the silver. And get me a couple of good-natured girls from the nugging-shop – you know what I mean. The kind who when you ask them to sit down will lie down.'

Bleary-eyed, he staggered back into the *palazzo*.

'*Inglese italianizzato, diavolo incarnato*,' I said quietly to the Hansons, 'Italianised Englishman, the devil incarnate.'

They looked at me in terror. For them, I was part of the problem, as were the dozens of my portraits of himself that Byron now kept disposed about him. To Hanson and young Hanson, I was nothing more than a lying, corrupting Venetian mirror. Their gondola slid away into the water and they did not look back.

Like the original Venetians, fleeing persecution at the hands of the barbarians, Byron had come to Venice when the world turned hostile against him. He had chosen a floating refuge with walls of water and a secret language as soft and treacherous as the curve of a wave. Never mind the Fall of the Republic, Byron rejoiced in the fact that the whole city of Venice had twice been excommunicated by the Pope.

Venice laid on a noble kind of exile. One of the things Byron liked most about exile was that in Europe his title received greater deference than it did at home. In England, he was just a minor aristocrat hanging on to the coat-tails of high society. His claims were slight, his ancestry compromised with scandal. As a result he carried his aristocracy like a raised fist in front of him. He had felt the cold contempt of his superiors: as a result his own slender silver spoon had left a nasty taste in his mouth. But on the Continent, as in the East, he could reinvent himself as a prince. What is more, in his own eyes he was still a beautiful prince distinguished by his small ears and exquisite hands.

Byron was reading Voltaire and revelling in his cool, satiric spirit. He was still writing his comedy of *Don Juan*, applying his new ideas. His letters had always been cruelly funny. Now he presented that side of himself to the public. Childe Harold had grown up into a cynical adolescent, lashing out at every constraint that offended him and at others merely to shock.

'What do you think of this?' he asked as he read me pieces of *Don Juan*. Byron was writing about shipwreck, lingering death, the devouring of a pet dog, and finally cannibalism, with *humour*. The blackest core of the comedy, in which the cannibals go mad, was based on the true tale of the wreck of the *Medusa*, which went down off the coast of Senegal in 1816.

I shall always think that *Don Juan* was a faster's fantasy, which explains some of its excesses. Since the Hansons had left, and perhaps with the memory of their faces in his mind, Byron was dieting again, trying to scrape loose the tallow that had gathered on his bones. He would exist upon dry biscuits and soda water for days on end. Finally, driven by the buzzing in his ears and the thunder in his belly, he would stride into the kitchen and scrape into one bowl a disgusting mess of fish, rice, old vegetables. He deluged it all with vinegar, bolting it down in gagging swallows. 'I have no palate,' he told me, when I remonstrated. 'It all tastes the same to me. But the vinegar – that I can hear on my tongue, at least.' He measured his waist and his wrists every morning. The tiniest increase brought forth the glass jar of Epsom salts. This was followed by his usual basin of pitchy green tea, unmilked and unsweetened.

By now, Byron had only one English friend left in Venice, the English Consul, Richard Hoppner, who had rescued Allegra. In April 1818, Byron's exile was further confirmed: news of Lady Melbourne's death arrived. I was with him when the letter came.

'I have always dreaded this,' he told me. 'She was my mentor, my muse, the companion of my spirit. Now I am alone in the world.' *What about me?* I clamoured silently.

With Lady Melbourne dead, there was one less attachment to England. For years now, Byron had been referring to England, in letters to friends, as *your island*. Byron nursed a sore reason to stay away from his birthplace. Annabella was still there, manufacturing poison against him.

One day he came rampaging triumphantly into my studio waving a piece of paper. He dropped it in my lap. Newstead Abbey had been sold for 94,500 pounds. This was an unimaginable sum of *lire*.

'You sold your *home*?' I asked. 'Are you not sad today?'

'I am happy, because I am free now.'

'To me, you look sad. And I know about your face.'

Byron sat in the window of the Mocenigo and watched women in slow gondolas passing back and forwards with copies of *Childe Harold* ostentatiously open upon their laps. Very occasionally he would summon one inside. At night, he sat brooding on his terrace with the candles extinguished. He was beginning to understand what was happening to Augusta. In hours like these, he could not stop thinking of the virtuous monster Annabella lurking in London, poisoning Augusta's mind against him.

Don Juan gave Byron a chance to take revenge on Annabella for all he had suffered. He depicted Annabella, Princess of Parallelograms, as Donna Inez, *perfect past all parallel*. But in Byron's newly created world, where values were turned upside down, such perfection was insipid and pretentious. Byron ridiculed Annabella's superficial grasp of the classics and modern languages. Crueller still, he mocked her face. He wrote that she 'look'd a lecture', with each eye a sermon and her brow a homily. 'A walking calculation,' he taunted her. 'Morality's prim personification.'

Murray was afraid to publish *Don Juan*. As delicately as possible, he explained that Byron, in his exile, might have distanced himself just a little too far from the *mores* of the English. Byron, who had been idolised for the waywardness of the earlier poems, disagreed. He swore that England was clamouring for a fresh, robust humour. This might be so, the publisher conceded, but the English would not stomach the indecency and irreverence of *Don Juan*. He asked Byron to remove some of the indelicacies. He would receive a dusty reply. 'You shall not make Canticles of my Cantos . . . I will have none of your damned cutting and slashing,' declared Byron in a letter he read aloud to me as he scratched it across the page. Finally, he threw down the pen.

'Cecilia, he's pathetic. He wants to cut the bollocks off my Donny Jonny because he has none of his own.'

'Perhaps he looks also at the poetry?' I asked, mildly.

'But the poetry is *the thing*! It may be bawdy, but is it not good English? It may be profligate, but is it not *life*, is it not *the thing*? Could any man have written it who has not lived in the world? – and tooled in a post-chaise?– in a hackney coach? – in a gondola? – against a wall? – in a court carriage? – in a vis-à-vis? – on a table? – and under it?'

'That is true,' I said. 'But is it necessary to offend them so? Could you not extract the passion, the *estro*, and sublimate it, cleverly and subtly, into something that would make them think on themselves, rather than something that makes them afraid?'

'Damn them, they need me, Cecilia, to blow the dust off their privates. At least to give them something new to read while they finger their equipment, or to think about when they go about the grim exercise of begetting heirs on their ugly wives.'

'The poem will need to be published – publishable – before they can do that. I have some portraits at the studio that I shall never sell because of the offence that they give. I painted them in anger. I was foolish because my work is thereby lost.'

'If people cannot bear the sight of genius, they don't deserve it. Anyway, I hate the thought of them reading and reciting, no, *vomiting* up my poetry.'

Then my *lingua biforcuta* darted out of my mouth. I regretted it an instant later. 'Sometimes I wonder if what you think of as genius may just be bile.' Having uttered these words, I looked at Byron fearfully.

But today Byron chose to laugh with me. 'Ha, ha, Cecilia. We are both of us rather bilious these days. But it's our anger that the world needs. The hypocrites and moralists are winning. Cant is so much stronger than cunt these days that I fear my experience in all the vital monosyllables must be lost to despairing posterity. Shame. The women would love it. And the more scandal they talk of it, the more women would buy it.'

'You do not really believe that.'

'Perhaps not. The only thing I know is that reading or not reading it would never keep down a single petticoat. That last, by the way, was a good phrase. I shall use it. Though never on English soil.'

'Do you not want to go back, ever?' I asked him.

'You know, I have already passed more than half of my time out of it.'

Like Casanova, I thought, *no, not like Casanova at all*.

I asked him, 'With no regrets?'

'None, except that I ever returned to it at all and sold myself to the accursed bitch I married.'

'Do you not wish to be buried there, with your family?'

'You Venetians, always thinking of death! I hope that whoever may survive me shall see me put in the foreigners' burying-ground on the Lido. I trust they won't think of chopping and pickling me, for the edification of the doctors and the told-you-sos – looking for my heart, I suppose – and bring me home to Clod or Blunderbuss Hall. I would not even feed their English worms, if I could help it. Let me enrich the soil of Italy, where I have also spread my seed.'

I thought of Girolamo, and quietly agreed with him.

Exile is more attractive when it can be achieved in style. For the first time in his life, Byron was now wealthy as an Oriental potentate, rich as Vathek. There were the proceeds of the sale of Newstead at his disposal, as well as the remittances from Murray for the books. In *lire*, he was a millionaire.

'I have imbibed a great love of this stuff, money,' he told me one day. We had been looking at the English papers, reading the habitual dire conglomeration of idolatry and abuse about him. 'With every word they write about me, the worse the better, I get richer.'

It was at this moment that Byron started to pine for something that was not for sale.

11

Se Dio voleva che i veneziani fusse pessi,
el gavarìa dà un aquario, non una cità.

If God had wanted Venetians to be fish,
He would have given us an aquarium and not a city.

V<small>ENETIAN PROVERB</small>

I am sure that the Fathers at San Lazzaro did not deliberately put Girolamo in Byron's way.

The Fathers knew Girolamo was special. They had some idea of Byron's tendencies. They had some suspicions of Girolamo's provenance, too, I am sure.

I was torn between wanting to tell the Fathers that they must keep him away from Byron and wanting my son and his father to be together. How would I frame the impure words to corrupt the Fathers' minds, how to explain the pollution I feared, without violating the sanctity of the island?

So I said nothing, and I hoped. I hoped that in Girolamo Byron had met his match. I hoped that he had met a soul he could not corrupt. I had confidence in Girolamo's strength. It surprised and amazed me. It was greater than my own.

There were only eleven novices on the island, pitting their slender bodies against the Herculean tasks imposed upon them. Byron loved to be among the boys. He would sit in the arbour, looking out

at the lagoon, with each arm around one boy. He had already nom-
inated his favourites, though they never offered their names. They
were trained not to think of themselves as individuals. They were
erasing their sinful humanity in the course of becoming living
angels. For Byron, it was Harrow all over again. He even found
fleeting resemblances to little Lords Clare and Delawarr among the
boys.

He swam with them, walked with them. He did not seem to
realise that the eyes of Venice were upon him, that the lagoon is an
aquarium for the gossips of the *conversazione*, the gondoliers and
the hairdressers. Everyone has their face pressed against the glass,
hoping for transgressions to be performed in front of them.

Girolamo was not shy, but he was unaware of his beauty. One of
Byron's arms always rested on his shoulder.

Girolamo's personality showed none of his father's perversity or
darkness. He was full of joy and curiosity. Sometimes I wondered if
the trajectory of Byron's seed had simply nudged into life a procreative cell of Casanova's stored somewhere inside me, for truly he
was more Casanova's son than anyone's. His only fault was greed,
and even his greed had a subtle artistry, and he enjoyed delicious
things only if he shared them with others.

Each time I saw him I carried his features home with me and
smoothed them on to the canvas after each of my visits, hardly
releasing my breath, my memory, until I had caught his new likeness. I kept my Girolamos, dozens of them, in my *armadio*. My
portfolio of Casanovas hid and protected them. In my mind now, I
always saw my son standing in front of Byron, pigeon-toed like a
little crucified Christ.

And I remembered when he was only a thrust of Byron's thigh,
an agonised intake of breath and a slump upon my breast.

12

E chi no sa nuar?

Is there anyone who doesn't know how to swim?

VENETIAN PROVERB

B orn in January, straddling the year and indeed the centuries, Byron was an Aquarian. Water was his natural element, and he loved it, even though it had drowned two of the boys he adored in his youth.

Water is beautiful and dangerous. It undulates, as he did. Yes, Byron knew the water, its suck and pull, its slap and tickle, the float and sink of it.

Now Byron lived in a floating palace.

Venice is a swimming and a drowning city. Byron was rarely seen to walk her streets. If he must go forth on foot, he donned such long robes that he seemed to be floating. Only his creamy throat and face appeared above the dark waves of his cloak like a luminous alabaster pebble just before it sinks into a dark pond. He must hide his deformity, at all costs. In Venice he had created a hallucinatory vision of himself: it swam through the unconscious minds of the Venetian women. It was as a sea-creature that we accepted him, as one of our own.

Those of us who fell in love with him found his limp more of a grace than a defect. There was a certain light and gentle undulation when he entered a room, of which strangers hardly felt tempted to enquire the cause. There was something about him, a quiet dark menace flowing from him, that forbade it. When Byron burst on the London scene in 1812, he had one rival for the feverish attention of Society – a newfangled German dance called the Waltz. He could never do it; to try to do so would have drawn attention to his deformity and his ungainly gait.

(Like Byron, I hated to dance, but for different reasons. My breasts attracted too much attention on the dance floor. They responded to the music in their own way. Also, I despised the polite hypocrisy of most modern dances. I particularly hated the Waltz, where a man leads and the woman must trust him, continually taking polite small backwards steps at his direction! I did not dance but I loved to watch. When I watched I preferred the dances that pace out the desires of the blood: the *fandango*, the *furlana*, where men and women are equal partners, where the limbs flash and the eyes widen and afterwards everyone is out of breath, their hearts beating and their skin alive with lust.)

Like me, but for different reasons, Byron skulked in corners pretending not to look while the waltzing women swirled around like blousy tulips.

On the land, he must hide. But in the water, Byron was a hero, from the duckpond at Harrow to the Grand Canal. He took his epic swims dressed in silk trousers to hide the withered leg. When he felt the water enclose the damaged limb, he relaxed inside his skin and a different smile would come to his lips.

At Cambridge, he swam in the Cam. At nineteen, he swam three miles down the Thames. After that triumph, every stretch of water must be conquered, and was: the Hellespont, the Tagus, the Piraeus, rivers, seas. Another Byron legend was born upon the spume of the water: he became a kind of male Venus, rising in beauty from the waves.

In Venice, on hot nights, Byron was seen to leave palaces on the Grand Canal, and fling himself fully clothed into the water. He then swam home, holding aloft a torch in his left hand to avoid the oars of passing gondolas.

In the sultry summer of 1818, the Cavalier Angelo Mengaldo, a boastful and vainglorious soldier of the Napoleonic wars, with literary ambitions, formed a niggling relationship with Byron. Their rivalry was bound to culminate in a swimming contest, for both men loved to boast of their aquatic triumphs. Mengaldo had swum the Danube and the Beresina, in the latter case with the added glamour of doing so under enemy fire.

'I have to do this, Cecilia,' Byron told me, lolling on the divan in my studio. 'This is important. It's Age against Beauty. It's Military against Poetry.'

'It is dangerous vanity,' I muttered under my breath. People could become sick from the strange tiny beasts and stinks that floated on the compromised waves of the lagoon and the canals. Think how many chamber pots, cooking pots, laundry barrels, fish guts and worse were thrown into the forgiving water every day!

The competition took place on June 25th. The swimmers left from the Lido, at precisely the same moment. Byron won easily, leaving Mengaldo to give up before they even reached the Grand Canal. For days, he could talk of nothing else, of how he had beaten the Italian 'all to bubbles'.

Byron had risen from the water, dimpled like a plucked chicken, and came directly to me. He was not even tired. With the salt of the water still on his body, he had thrown himself upon me and made love to me with pounding thrusts and strokes, as if he was still swimming.

*

I had watched the swimmers pass me from the steps of the Balbi Valier. I wondered what Byron was thinking. Afterwards, he told me.

Mostly, he thought of winning and that it would be another victory against Annabella in some obscure but satisfying way. One by one, as he swam past them now, his eyes discovered all the *palazzi* in which he had enjoyed his pleasures.

His exhaustion had peeled layers from his thoughts and the memories were crystalline as if suspended in drops of water. In those drops he saw Marianna and Margarita, he saw his favourite among the nine muses, he saw the masked lover who had tainted his blood during that first *Carnevale*. It seemed that naked pink women were suspended in each droplet he shook from his eyes.

He passed a private garden with a decapitated Satyr and for some reason thought of Casanova, and, fleetingly, of me.

He passed a mother and child on a window-sill, feeding upon nuts like pretty little apes. He thought of his daughters, the unknown Ada and the unseen Allegra.

He passed the Contarini degli Scrovegni, the *palazzo* of the money-chests, and thought of the remittances to come from Murray.

Water invaded his mouth. He remembered how he had taught his dog, Boatswain, to save him from drowning when he pretended to need help in the lake at Newstead. One dank autumn, a thousand years ago it seemed, Boatswain had caught rabies. Byron nursed him himself and sponged the froth from the dying dog's mouth with his own hand. Boatswain was gentle in his disease, biting no one but himself, and at the memory of him Byron had felt the warmth of tenderness. The cold water had sealed Byron's warmth inside him. The thought of Boatswain belonged in there.

These random thoughts had taken him almost without effort to the *volta* of the Grand Canal. Not for the first time, Byron told me, he then found himself wondering what he meant to Venice. As he passed the circus of the Rialto he realised he was just a prize exhibit in this most beautiful of zoos.

'Surely you are more than that?' I asked. 'What about the poetry?'

'That's all *merde*,' he said. '*Merde* that flows.'

13

Servo de do paròni, servo dei miei cogioni.

I am a servant of two masters: my two testicles.

VENETIAN PROVERB

At San Lazzaro, Byron crouched over his Armenian–English grammar, but he could not concentrate. The beautiful boy was gently dead-heading the roses in a pot on his desk. I was painting Byron while he worked. Yes, we were alone in the study, we three, unless you count the cicada whose throbbing song invaded the room and our thoughts. In another world we would be a family. The Fathers had left us alone together again. I wondered why. I still wonder.

'Why do you cut the heads of the flowers?' Byron asked Girolamo.

'They are no longer alive, and they are stealing strength from the rest of the plant.' Girolamo smiled. His affection for Byron was written openly upon his face. Byron was a hero among all the novices, a glamorous figure from a world they would never know.

'Who are you, little man?'

'You know me, signor, I am Girolamo, the novice.' Now the child was troubled. The smile was spent. He knew that Byron wanted something more of him, but he did not understand the need. From the depths of his generous nature, he tried to do so.

'Where do you come from, Girolamo?'

'From Our Heavenly Father.'

'You are so sure?' With this, my Girolamo's face flowered into a smile again.

'Of course. Why are you so sad, my Lord?'

Byron rested his head in his hands, stretched his eyes till he looked as Oriental as Ali Pasha. When had he ever seen anything as beautiful as Girolamo? Probably not since he gazed in his own mirror twenty years previously. When had he wanted something more? Augusta? Nicolo? Could he name his wants? I doubted it. The manifestation of his darker desires could exile him even from Venice. What happens when you defile even the place of exile? Had he become addicted to a need for violation? Or was it simply that Girolamo was so beautiful?

I was almost sorry for Byron. For so many years the erotic impulse had been tied to the love impulse that Byron was no longer able to separate the two. But with Girolamo I saw him struggle to do so. He could not want to ruin Girolamo's purity: ruined, Girolamo would no longer be the creature of light that drew Byron to him. Byron would not hurt my son, I was sure of it. Something in his blood would keep him from hurting the boy. Girolamo himself would make it so. I had such faith in the infectious goodness of my child.

Suddenly a desperate pigeon stumbled into the window, followed by a shrieking white seagull. We watched a swift and bloody murder. When the pigeon was dead and limp, the seagull moaned its victory, raising its beak to the sky as if to thank God for its grisly meal. Then it seized its prey and swooped out of the window. None of us spoke during the hideous incident. My phantom arms reached out to comfort both Girolamo and Byron, their faces contorted in exactly the same grimace of horror. I wanted to cover their eyes, rock them both against me, take the evil to myself and protect them from it.

Finally, Byron said, bitterly, 'You see how Venice is torn apart: her sea-self devours her land-self.'

Girolamo looked at his father with infinite tenderness, spreading his hands, just as Casanova would have done, to show that he understood, that he felt Byron's pain, that he knew the darkness of his soul and that he forgave him for it.

And I looked at Girolamo, hoping that he was not too good for this world.

14

Da dona dei altri, a da cavai scampai,
libera nos Domine.

From other men's women, and from frisky horses,
O Lord, save us!

VENETIAN PROVERB

At the Mocenigo, Byron fumed and paced the terrace, watched with interest by a crowd of sightseers in the gondolas below.

The tourists were eager for some visible act of depravity from the English milord. Sometimes La Fornarina had used to oblige, waving an intimate garment at them in a threatening manner. He missed her, in some ways. Her pugilism had at least entertained him. He was bored without her daily melodramas. He was recovered from the wound of his marriage and tired of the disease and disappointment of promiscuous concubinage with strangers. He could not go every day to San Lazzaro. The Fathers had begun to be cool with him, he told me.

'Damn them to hell, then, and their grammar with them. I will find myself another diversion,' he said.

I rather hoped he would, even if it took him away from me. These days I could not be sure that Byron's temper would not erupt in the face of Girolamo's unshakeable serenity. My son had never heard a hard or evil word. I wanted it to stay that way.

Byron's satiety with Venice had slid into a dangerous lassitude from which, I knew, only a dramatic act of effrontery could rescue him. His ennui was so painful to him that I was sorry for him. He yawned hugely; he continually stretched. He seemed unable to contain himself within his own skin. I would see him shudder, after lovemaking, the way the cat shook his back legs at an unsatisfactory plateful of food, before stalking off.

Then something happened that swept his boredom off the table.

In April 1819, Byron met Teresa Guiccioli.

It happened, as most noteworthy things did in those days, at La Benzona's *conversazione*.

Marina Benzoni was a loquacious ageing beauty with full confidence in her charms, even at sixty. The nobleman Giuseppe Rangone had been her *cavalier servente* for thirty years, and finally married her just before his seventieth birthday. Byron told me how he had asked Rangone after La Benzona one morning. The *cavalier*, who had just come from her bed, replied that his mistress was *rugiadosa*, 'dewy'.

Not far from the Mocenigo, Marina Benzoni kept a luxurious house. She was famous for the pieces of hot polenta she used to carry between her breasts on cold days. One of her nicknames was El Fumeto – the Steaming Lady. Another was La Biondina in Gondola, after the famous song composed in her honour. She had been known in her time as the sweetest and loosest woman in Venice. I remembered her from the parties at the Mocenigo and other *palazzi* when Casanova was still with me in Venice. I could never forget her dancing round the 'liberty tree' in San Marco at the fall of the Republic. She acknowledged with a nod that she too remembered those times, and my witnessing of them. Byron adored her wit, and called her the Venetian Lady Melbourne. There could be no higher compliment from him.

It was the dewy Benzona herself who told me what happened that night, as I was at that time in the middle of a portrait of her. She was one of the few old ladies in Venice who still loved to be painted. You could still see the outlines Longhi had painted in her old, proud face. Like Longhi, to capture her, I was mixing Lead White, Naples Yellow and Rose Madder. I cooled passages of her complexion that had become too foxy using tones of French Ultramarine. Where her aged skin had become extremely thin, under her eyes and around her nose, I dotted in Purple Lake.

I still remember how that long, high-arched and bird-like nose quivered at the memory of the night Byron met Teresa Guiccioli.

It should not have happened as it did. Teresa was pregnant, tired and she had come only reluctantly to La Benzona's *conversazione* that evening. Nor was Byron, in his bearish mood, particularly interested in being introduced to a clever young bride from Ravenna.

'Leave me,' he had told La Benzona, gracelessly, when she proposed to introduce him to Teresa. 'I do not want to make any new acquaintances with women; if they are ugly because they are ugly – and if they are beautiful, because they are beautiful.'

'But I prevailed,' smiled the hostess, recalling that night. 'I always do.

'He loved to shock me, the naughty boy! He said, "Very well then. How desperate is she? How willing is she to perform acts of unspeakable degradation with me?"'

La Benzona giggled at the memory.

But then, from across the room, Byron had seen a petite but voluptuous version of himself – chestnut curls, full lips, large luminous eyes, a fully realised femininity beyond her years.

'I presented Byron to Teresa,' said La Benzona, 'simply as "Peer of England and its greatest poet". The extraordinary thing was, when I saw them together, they seemed immediately to be just like brother and sister.' She winked at me.

I knew what La Benzona meant about Teresa. I had myself met her when she was in Venice a year before, on her honeymoon. She had seemed to me a woman who was over-ripe without ever having matured. Titian-haired, with a beautiful mouth, and rather short legs, Teresa was convent-educated, spoke French as well as Italian, quoted the Latin historians and could even paint small flower studies – all charmingly. We had all looked at one of her pictures, in a locket on her breast, and she had no reason to be embarrassed by it.

For twelve months now, she had been married to a sixty-year-old count from Ravenna. Her husband was a pleasant old man, though rumoured to have murdered his first wife. He seemed fond of Teresa and she did not appear to be repulsed by him. Until she met Byron, it might have been considered a successful aristocratic marriage.

'Of course,' continued La Benzona, 'it was an instant love. No woman could look at Byron without falling for him. Teresa can never have met such an enchanting man. None of us had. But in this case, it was mutual. He looked at her, and saw what he wanted.'

La Benzona continued, 'Byron was talking, and he included Teresa in the conversation in the subtlest of ways. Small secret smiles and little gestures, you know. I saw it all. He spoke brilliantly that evening, too. Normally, he was quiet; he often sat in the corner glowering, especially if English people turned up. But that night, with Teresa, he took to the stage. He was so eloquent that I seized a pencil and started immediately to write it down. Here is my transcription; I keep it rolled up in the spine of my fan.'

In an instant she had extracted the roll of paper from the ivory stem and handed it to me. I smoothed it out and read what Byron had said, the words he had used to win Teresa Guiccioli.

'But, ladies and gentlemen, and in particular ladies, you must realise that passion gives a strength above nature, we see it in mad people; true love always shows a refined degree of madness.

'It must be madness to discard everything but that single person whom you love, to lose all the repose in one's life in hunting after them, when there is so little likelihood of ever gaining them.'

I rolled up the paper and handed it back to her. I could imagine it all: the inflections of his voice, the inclining of her head, the moment he put his white hand upon her shoulder.

What happened next is now known to everyone in Venice.

As he left the *conversazione*, Byron had slipped a note into Teresa's fingers. It was an assignation.

She told her husband that she would take a gondola expedition with her companion-governess, Fanny Silvestrini, to practise her French. As arranged, Teresa's gondola crossed with Byron's, and the precious cargo was exchanged. Feverish and no doubt delightful negotiations took place over several days.

Lord Byron, Teresa had observed to anyone who would listen, was not a man to confine himself to sentiment. A few nights later she became his mistress, at one of Byron's convenient casinos, Santa Maria Zobenigo, where he had always pursued his stray loves away from the wrath of La Fornarina. For ten days, Fanny waited patiently while they tried to exhaust their passion for each other. The lovers often went as far as the Lido, or islands beyond.

Byron did not appear in my studio during this whole period. I went to the Mocenigo and found it deserted. I went to the desk and read the letters there. I found words that made me afraid.

I saw Byron's letter to Kinnaird, which explained it all, including his fears: 'She is as fair as the sunrise, and warm as noon . . . She is the queerest woman I ever met with, for in general they cost one something one way or other, whereas by an odd combination of circumstances, I have proved an expense to her, which is not my custom, but an accident; however, it don't matter. She is a sort of Italian Caroline Lamb, except that she is much prettier, and not so savage. But she has the same red-hot head, the same noble disdain of public opinion, with the superstructure of all that Italy can add to such natural dispositions. To be sure, they go much further here with Impunity . . .'

Byron's letter to Hobhouse frightened me even more. He was serious, it seemed, so serious that he had doubts already: 'I should not like to be frittered down to a regular *cicisbeo*. What shall I do? I am in love, and tired of promiscuous concubinage, and have now an opportunity of settling for life.'

Hobhouse tried pleading for me, bless him. A week later I saw his swift response. I saw how worried he was by the levity he affected, ponderously as ever. 'Don't you go after that terra firma lady: they are very vixens in those parts especially, and I recollect when I was at Ferrara hearing of two women in the hospital who had stabbed one another in the guts and all *por gelosia*. Take a fool's advice for once and content with your Naids – your amphibious fry – you make a very pretty splashing with them in the Lagune and I recommend constancy to the neighbourhood.'

Byron, as always, ignored his earnest friend.

He did not see, as I did, the pattern: how he had rushed to Annabella to save himself from Augusta, and darker secrets; now he rushed to Teresa to save himself from something he could not name.

15

Se l'invidia fusse freve, tuto el mondo scotaria.

If jealousy was a fever the world would burn up.

VENETIAN PROVERB

I had watched him every day, in the gondola with Teresa. Sometimes I had followed them in my own gondola, hidden under the *felze*. I had trailed him to the Lido where he kept his horses. I had spied on them at the opera, where he sat, scandalously, in a box with his mistress and her husband. From his fish-eyes and his fixed gaze upon Teresa, his dreamer's stumble and the damp sheen on his skin, I had seen the truth and the malaise of his love for her.

His latest portrait was not finished, but Byron, I already understood, would not come back to sit for me again. He was hypnotised by his reflection in La Guiccioli's eyes and no longer cared for his immortality in the hands of an artist.

After ten days of silence, Byron came whistling into my studio. He greeted me affectionately, by name, like an old friend or a favoured servant. I understood from this use of my name the collapse of all intimacy between us. Until now he had always entered my studio wordlessly, as if it were his own habitation, and he had led me silently to the divan or to the easel. Now he leant towards me, in an unfamiliar confidential manner, and, in the most casual of tones, asked me to paint Teresa Guiccioli's portrait.

'She's an artist, herself, Cecilia. You should see her work. She has something, you know, a great delicacy, a penetration. But of course she cannot paint her own likeness. I told her that I would commission the best artist in Venice to paint her for me.'

In one moment, I saw it. My position in his life had become entirely functional. I said nothing, waiting for the feeling to reach my tongue and allow me to answer.

Meanwhile Byron strolled around the studio, picking up small objects of his and pocketing them. 'You're quiet, Cecilia. But think about it. You know how much it would please me. Think how *gratifying* it would be for me to have a picture of Teresa, painted by you.'

I clicked back my ears, but still I said nothing. Eventually, he left, whistling again. My cat came out of the shadows and nudged my cold hand. A client came, sat for two hours. I worked. Another client came to discuss terms. I agreed to what he offered, dully, and made notes in my sitters' book. I soaked canvases in my bath. I cleaned my brushes, even those that I had not used. I stupefied myself to continue.

Finally, I walked out to the terrace in front of my studio. The canal steamed like hot milk under the full moon. I stopped where Casanova had stood in 1782, shaped like an exclamation mark of pain. I wished that someone was watching me with love now, as I had watched him.

Until Teresa, my rival had never really been another woman. It had been Byron himself, as we competed to love him the most intensely. I had known that the women, Marianna, Margarita, the muses of the Casino, were irrelevant.

But Teresa, who looked like Augusta, who looked like Byron, had entered a place that I had reserved for myself.

I do not know how I knew it, but I knew that I had lost my place in the world. The truth invaded me that evening. The betrayal, having entered my body, sent its agents — nausea, faintness, trembling, an intense and sour coldness — in all directions. Like a house in an earthquake, I bided my time, waiting for everything that was insecure and fragile to crash and break inside me. Clattering down came my faith in myself, my sexual self-confidence. Falling gently on their wrecks, then came my hazy hopes and dreams, dislodged like cobwebs, torn and dirty.

I spent the evening with Maurizio, looking across the table at him as if through a pane of mullioned glass. That night he was afraid of me, but he stayed, watching me pace around the studio. He smelt my febrile humour, and I imagined, vindictively, he felt there might be something in it for him. Maurizio still hungered for attention from me, any kind of attention, and still followed me to the corners of every room, till I turned on him, snarling. He loved that, too. For once, it seemed to him that I was really looking at him, really thinking about him. For him, this was as close an approximation of passion as he had known from me. He had never been loved properly, poor Maurizio. He did not know the difference.

But that night, finally, I told him about Byron. I told him the whole story in simple words so that he could understand it. He listened in silence for hours. When it was all out there hanging in the air between us — all the ugly truth, the rancid pain, the lies and the secrets — my studio suddenly felt unsafe, a contaminated place. I did not feel relieved, only more tired than I had ever felt. Then Maurizio put his head in his hands. I saw tears sliding between his thick fingers, heard them dripping on the table. I saw his shoulders tremble. Once he thumped his fist ineffectually upon the table. Then he became quiet. We sat in silence for a long time.

Finally Maurizio said, 'Cecilia, the way you feel about Byron — that is how I love you.'

'I am very sorry,' I said.

I did not reach out to comfort him. It was not in me. I watched him and absorbed his pain like a Vampyre, as if it might cancel out my own. I had no kindness left for him. Our separate pains could not combine to soothe each other. Finally, I grew bored. I told him to go home. He laid his hand upon mine with what seemed to be unselfish tenderness.

'You should not be alone, Cecilia. At least let me stay here to comfort you.'

'I shall be safer alone,' I flinched away. 'Go. I don't deserve you.'

I was not safer alone. Later that night it came to me: the fury and the pain. I was kneeling to stroke the cat one minute, and the next I was raging up and down inside the *cortile*, too agitated to sit down. If I did, my misery would enclose me, so I kept walking away from it, in little feinting steps. *He had asked me to paint Teresa.*

The ferocity of my bitterness took me by surprise. In a way, it was a relief. Anger about Teresa's portrait was something into which I could sink my teeth. It was more satisfying than the years of tiny insults and hurts overlaying and somehow obscuring the fundamental pain Byron had given me when he abandoned me in Albania. I strode around the studio shouting at the walls, shaking my fists at the painted *putti* on the ceiling, running my fingernails along the marble walls so that they made an unbearable noise, like painted canvas being torn.

I calmed myself, eventually.

But I could not swallow the insult, so I allowed it to sit in my throat.

After the rage, came misery.

For comfort, I turned, unwisely, to my latest portrait of Byron. I picked up my brush. I allowed my memory to guide my hand, as if across his real flesh. I permitted myself to succumb once again to my addiction for thinking of him. The memories bled a subtly sweet poison into my heart. I argued to myself that these memories were better than the pain, but I lied. I did not accept the widowhood of my heart.

In the end, I couldn't work any more. Everything in the studio reminded me of Byron. Everything was the same, but Byron was not there.

I put down my paintbrush and ran through the dark streets back home. I pounded across Campo San Stefano, Campo San Angelo, Campo San Luca, Campo San Bartolomeo. I did not see a living being. My footsteps echoed in the hollow squares as if my pain was in pursuit of me. How strange Venice looked to me that night! The air was still; the water seemed solid in the canals. I thudded through the streets, afraid of the moon, which dipped in and out of clouds. The moon, it seemed to me, was to be looked upon by women who were loved. Women like me must hide from it. Familiar buildings looked dangerous in the excluding moonlight. When I reached Campiello Santa Maria Nova I gratefully let myself into our *palazzo*. I panted up to the *piano nobile*, hoping to find Sofia still at her needlework. I would not have any words for her; I merely hoped to find some serenity in her quiet presence. But it was the middle of the night. She had gone to bed.

Passing through the house I seized a large candelabra from the dining table and returned to my bedroom. Sofia had made sure that a small fire still burned there, despite the dark hour. I imagined her in my room, tending to it quietly herself, rather than keeping the servants up late, before gliding up the stairs to her bed. I took a taper to the fire and lit all eight candles, which rose up in tall tumultuous flames, casting red shadows over my painted walls, as if to devour the gondola, the palaces of *Vathek* and the Mocenigo. Even in the haven of my bedroom, I could not escape from Byron and the images we shared.

He would not be erased from my mind.

I held the candelabra to the mirror and looked at myself. I barely recognised myself in the dark glass. I seemed a foreign creature, bleached of blood, an indecent creature, who loved without being loved.

How did this happen to me? I asked myself.

I tried to think back to the beginning of everything, to the moment when I had consented to live like this.

At every stage, I identified my mistakes, my misconceptions and my false moves.

It had started in Albania. I had fallen in love not with Byron's soul, but with his skin. Then I had painted it as if it were capable of loving properly. I had fallen irrevocably in love with the lie I had painted. I had wished the face in my portrait to love me back. As long as he still had that skin, it seemed, I was condemned to love it.

I had fallen in love with a look that Byron gave me, in which I saw something that seemed native to myself. That glimpse of a life he showed me then was embedded in my imagination like a falling star swallowed by the sea. For those few moments of intimacy, I had made a life that was welded to his. I had offered him, however, a servitude for which he had no use.

I reckoned up Byron's cruelties and his small mean acts. I listed for myself his bad breath, his awkward body, his unloving way of making love. I counted the women – seventeen of whom I knew – he had ruined in Venice. I knew that Byron was a lie that walked around; he seemed to personify romantic love but he was its enemy. Hate was closer to love than the poor fare that he offered hearts hungry for his love. He did not even bestir himself to hate. But, by his very indifference, he roused a tempest of hate and love in others. I knew Byron was the wrong man to love. I had spent too many years loving as wrong a man as I could have found, had I travelled the whole world looking for ways to hurt myself.

I had betrayed things that I believed in to accept his bad style of love, the stale air in his heart. I had lost the right of complaint by my very own forbearance. I had been so passive that I had consented tacitly to acts against the heart. In the hellish light of the candelabra it suddenly seemed to me that I had given up my son because of the narrowness of his father's soul. Because of Byron, because of Byron's inability to love me, I had become an unnatural kind of mother.

But it was my own mistake, my love for Byron. I had created it and I had made it monstrous all by myself, with only a little help from him. He was *my* mistake, the mistake I had coddled and cherished, humoured, succoured, delivered in all his painted beauty to the world.

But because I had made it myself, my love for him would not change now, whatever he did. My love had long ceased to depend upon the way he treated me or the kind of man he was.

For I was addicted to my old mistake, as I had once been addicted to novelty. I still could not let go of it. There is no cure for a love like this; there is no disgust, no pain and no outrage strong enough to strangle it. I did not have it in me to destroy it. I had been made too weak by it to fight against it. Nor could I hurt him: I would be circumvented by my own senseless tenderness for him, and because he was indifferent to me. Worse, he was at heart indifferent to love itself.

I knew all these things. But I remained a slave enfeebled by my desire. When I thought of Byron I still felt like fainting. Now that weakness made me long for his hard hand on my back. It was Byron who had authored this enfeebled version of myself. I thought that only he could restore me.

I went to my desk and picked up a pen. I wrote to Byron.

I had been the one woman with the dignity not to crawl after him. Now I joined those legions on their knees. I wrote. I sent the words scrabbling over the paper, looking for cover, longing for a beloved shadow to fall over them as it leant to steal a kiss. No shadow came, and the words scrabbled on in the pitiless light, like the ants that boys burn with magnifying glasses.

I signed the letter and sealed it with a vivid splotch of wax. The droplets looked like solid tears upon the creamy paper.

The Cat Speaks

I never saw her do such a thing before. Put herself on her knees like that! It ill becomes our Cecilia, if you ask me, to behave like another pathetic victim-mistress, whimpering on paper, begging him to return to her, selling herself like a side-show attraction!

'Will you not be alone on this earth, in some ways that are intrinsic to your soul, if we are not together?' . . . 'Without you, I have gone out like a flaming brand deprived of air. I need you.' . . . 'I need your love to move my fingers properly, to hold my brush.'

Hardly like to win him back, is it? A man like that.

She should not have said that about Teresa Guiccioli, either – doesn't she realise that when she says ugly things about that woman she is insulting Byron's own image and likeness?

And how is he going to respond to that, then?

It was badly done, the whole thing. It was not a good letter. Cecilia is unskilled in the ways of grovelling. That is one of the reasons that I like her.

Anyway, soon she will forget about that letter because I shall be bringing her a more important one.

I hear the *acqua alta* rising in the bowels of the lagoon. The humans have no idea yet, but the cats always know. When did you ever see an accidentally drowned cat?

It is an exceptional *acqua alta*, this time. There will be death and damage and the smell of damp carpets and the crying of women for a long time after this one.

I go every day to the grille where Casanova's letter to Cecilia fell all those years ago. The water comes closer and closer.

16

Chi tropo se inchina, mostra 'l culo.

He who bows too low shows his arsehole.

VENETIAN PROVERB

After ten days in Venice, Teresa's husband Count Guiccioli announced that business called him back to Ravenna. They would leave immediately. Teresa, as all Venice knew in an hour, had rushed to the theatre, and, flouting every graceful law of *cicisbeo* etiquette, burst into Byron's box to tell him the lamentable news. The Guicciolis were gone within twenty-four hours.

Teresa left, unpainted, but Byron did not come back to me. He had thrown in his lot with Teresa. The formalities had commenced.

A Greek chorus of gossip, with its strident authority, informed me that Teresa was demanding of Byron that he become her *cavalier servente*, a lover who would attend her according to the very definite etiquette of Italian married life, from which Byron had already profited with Marianna and Margarita, amongst dozens of others. But Teresa was a high-born girl, with greater expectations. Byron, with Teresa's grip on his loins, contemplated a relationship that could bind him in decorous chivalry to a society that took its hypocrisy very seriously.

Under the laws of aristocratic *serventismo*, he would be expected to pretend a platonic and moral relationship with his *morosa*, and a civilised friendship with her husband. He would be expected to treat Teresa with extreme gallantry at all times. The trouble with this system, he had said many times, was that it seemed like polygamy, *but on the woman's side*. Listening to the gossip, I found myself doubting if Byron was ready to be a mere amatory appendage, a real *cicisbeo*. Could he descend to being a high-class fan-and-shawl-carrying gigolo? He would not want to be tamed to house-stallion. The little Scottish boy who had unexpectedly become a lord was ever nervous of undignifying himself. He was afraid of bowing too low, of exposing himself.

At the beginning of June Byron set off for Ravenna to find his lover. By all accounts he found her in bed, seriously ill. She had suffered a miscarriage. Now the rumours in Venice were that Byron himself had been the involuntary cause, by the violence of his copulations with her. Everyone knew that he was not the father of the foetus, for Teresa was three months' pregnant at the time of their first encounter. It was reported to the breathless *conversazione* in Venice that Byron and the count feared for Teresa's life. They waited in corridors while nuns and doctors rushed past with fearful basins and crucifixes.

Byron need not have worried. Soon we heard that Teresa had recovered enough to resume her sexual duties. A maid, a Negro boy and a female friend conspired to create opportunities for them. Count G was perfectly aware of what was going on but continued to extend the utmost courtesy to Byron.

Byron and Teresa had their portrait painted together. Perhaps my curses swam into the brain of the artist. For the painting of Teresa pleased her so ill that she scratched out her own face. We heard in Venice that Byron, though disliking the expense of her caprice, laughed at her vanity. It resembled his own, so he would indulge it.

*

I had written the wrong letter to him. I heard nothing from Byron.

The waters were rising. There was a surge in the belly of the lagoon, a force I had not felt previously. I stood by the Canal, watching the rain pierce its thick transparent skin. At night I dreamt of sand dunes and camels, as all Venetians do when the water threatens us in our sleep.

I waited for Byron. I tried to forget. I forgot him every hour. Wherever I was, whatever I did, I only killed the remembering time. I wished for darkness to come so that I might sleep in the hope that the next day would bring me word from Byron. But I had written the wrong letter.

When he came into my thoughts I tried to refuse him admission. I tried to purge him. I tried to think of him in the ugly moments, which were suitable to contain and define him; I thought of him when I passed water or when I threw the sludge of my gallipot into the Grand Canal. I tried to evacuate Byron in the same way.

I had a dream that he was dead, and for a while it really felt as if he were dead, and that felt better than before. In my dream Byron's death was something ignominious in a cold English town, not a dramatic death with glory, but something slight and regrettable, involving drink, a scuffle, a shabby carriage. He was lying there in the gutter, like a dog tossed off the road by a horse, with empty eyes and legs inelegantly splayed. It seemed appropriate that he had left life the way he left me.

Of course, he never quite left me. He did something worse. He returned to Venice with Teresa. They lived at La Mira. The word on the streets was that La Guiccioli did not like the Palazzo Mocenigo. Byron had filled it with too many feminine ghosts. The next thing we heard was that while Teresa waited for him at La Mira, Byron had resumed his visits to San Lazzaro.

He never came to me now, but I still inhabited a part of Byron's soul, and I very often knew where he was. I knew, always, the moment he woke, with Teresa's curls in his mouth, and the moment he thought, *I must go to Venice today*. Then I would be waiting, under my own black *felze*, and would follow him as he performed his careless errands. I watched him fondling the other neglected animals at the Mocenigo. I watched him limping into La Benzona's, and later, entering the casino of the nine enthusiastic and forgiving muses.

I did not follow him to San Lazzaro. My work there was finished. The frescoes could not be more immaculate. I had no excuse to revisit them, not for many years. You can overplay a fresco, and I had already worked the walls to the extent that they had lost the careless grace I intended for them. The Fathers knew, but they were kind to me, as they had been kind to Byron, when he least deserved it. They still let me visit Girolamo on the pretext of giving lessons in art and calligraphy to all the novices. I hoped every day that I might meet Byron's eyes over Girolamo's head. But it would not happen. I had written the wrong letter. The Fathers, as if complicit in my punishment, seemed to have arranged it so that Byron and I never arrived at San Lazzaro at the same time.

The Gondolier Speaks

You should have seen him after La Guiccioli left that first time. Moping and dragging himself around town like a sick dog. Eyes like dead beetles you find in drawers. A great stupid expression on his face like a sheep looking over a fence. I am sure he thought he was some kind of tragic hero, but to us he looked like something stuffed and put on a post to scare the seagulls.

I heard that her husband hired someone to beat him up. Should have finished the job, but I think they were ashamed to murder a little cripple like him.

Then off he went to Ravenna, like a dog on the trail. He soon came back, with La Guiccioli in tow. He put her at La Mira, so he could carry on as he liked in Venice, pulling the pieces at the Zobenigo casino, and lording it over the ladies at the Benzona *conversazione*.

For all he took from our women, if you ask me – and even if you don't – the milord was a *finocchio*. In fact I think he really hated women and just found a cunning way to hide it. He hid his hatred inside them, if you know what I mean. (Though the word from the *faxoléti* was that he didn't exactly have the *equipment* to go deep. Those girls have filthy mouths. But sweet, too, sometimes!)

I saw him soon after at San Lazzaro, walking by the shore with a couple of young boys. The kids couldn't have been more than nine. He was bending over the boys, as if trying to choose the most delicious one from a tray of little cakes, and even from a hundred yards away I could smell the musk. I never saw him looking at a woman like that, though I saw his bitches trying to eat him with their eyes. *They* always looked hungry. Probably there's some truth in that rumour that he wouldn't let his women eat in front of him. I ask you – what kind of man is that who won't share his dinner with his woman? No kind of man, I say.

Now, look, he gets away with anything, because he's a *lord, because he's a poet*.

So he was still hanging around San Lazzaro even after he'd brought Teresa Guiccioli back to Venice with him. Looked more like his sister than his *morosa*, that one. D'you think she was pleased to see him go back to the Armenian island? Don't you think she begged him, in that porridgy Ravenna accent, 'Oh, why do you leave me, my Biron?' D'you think he told her why? *Che sboro!*

And what were they about, those so-called Sacred Fathers? Were they stupid? Couldn't they see what he was like? I'm a father myself; it teaches you to look out for these things. Venice has always been full of *recioni*, shirt-lifters, looking for a tasty young morsel to impale on their nasty sticks. I remember when they had to hire whores to stand on bridges showing their tits to keep the men off each other and doing the decent business of getting the women with child. We had a better idea about his type in the old days. We'd burn them alive between the columns in the Piazzetta and all Venice would turn out to spit and cheer.

We gondoliers knew the names of all the novices at San Lazzaro, because they would come to the water's edge to collect the parcels and provisions we brought to the island. That Girolamo was the sweetest child. It shone out of him. There are a few kids in the world like that, and he was one of them. He is special, that child. He really could be Our Redeemer in certain lights.

I couldn't believe my eyes when I saw that the Armenian Fathers let pretty little Girolamo walk around the island with the English milord. *Mi morti! Che sulsi!* What idiots! They were dangling that kid like fish bait in front of the English milord. Didn't they know it?

Maybe, damn them, they did. Maybe they were sending that poor little kid to his fate, like Jesus before him. Ruin a kid and save a lord, I can see them thinking that. They act all holy, those Armenians, but I tell you that in my book they are not above human sacrifice like those heathens in the East.

You see, I saw it all. It was hot, and water was what we call *limpida* that day. It was the day before the big *acqua alta* put Venice on her knees. I was just leaving the island. I had made my delivery and I was poling back towards San Marco. I was about two hundred yards away when I saw the two of them taking their *passeggiata* on the foreshore. I saw the way the English milord gripped the little boy's shoulder. It must have hurt a lot. The kid looked up in surprise. I saw the milord taking off all his clothes, and gesturing at Girolamo to do the same.

It was not a pretty sight, the fat English milord, white as lard, one leg shrivelled like a length of dried cod, and the little boy, wading into the water together. I saw those puffy arms closing around the boy in the water and a strange set to the milord's body. If you had blinked you would have missed it. It's not that he *did* anything, it's just that he was in the state to do it. Anyway, before anything could happen, I saw Girolamo start out of Byron's arms like a rabbit.

Girolamo turned around to face Byron. The kid stayed there, without moving, just looking into the milord's eyes. He did not seem frightened. He seemed, well, intent. I don't know what they were saying to each other. All I could hear was the waves in my ears. The milord straightaway dropped his empty arms and staggered backwards into the deeper water.

By this time I was poling towards them as fast as I could. The tide was against me. From a hundred yards away I made violent gestures and yelled obscenities at the milord. The wind carried my voice away. They couldn't hear me over the water.

Do you know the most astonishing thing? The next thing that happened was that instead of running away, the little boy held out his hand to the milord.

After a moment, they walked together to the shore. Girolamo never let go of his hand. Byron came ploughing out of the water, shaking like an old wet dog. Then Girolamo – I can scarcely ask you to believe this – reached up to Byron's shoulders and gently pushed him to kneel down on the sand. Then the kid kneeled down beside him. He took the milord's two hands – it was as if he were the one in charge – and he placed them together.

Then I got closer. I heard the kid praying, and I heard the milord repeating his words. By now they had their backs to me, two naked backs, one grey, the other rosy and perfect as a cherub on a church ceiling. They did not see me, but I heard them pray.

I should have grabbed that bastard and killed him on the spot. But there was something going on there that I did not understand. I was way out of my depth. Nothing had really happened, and yet . . .

So I left them. I poled away. I did not tell anyone. Maybe the Fathers were right. Maybe the little boy is some kind of Jesus-child. I have to say that it seemed to me as if I had witnessed a miracle.

But why, for fuck's sake, did the little boy have to face that, for a worthless piece of mud like Byron? Did he have to be shamed like that? Even Christ on his cross had the dignity of his loincloth, and his loins, more to the point, left alone.

To the end of my days I myself shall feel dirty for what I have seen. Byron is luckier than me. He had Girolamo to protect him from himself and forgive him.

But I – I can never tell anyone. Not my wife, not the priest, not the Fathers. How can I say that I saw what I did, and did nothing to stop it?

17

Aqua turbia no fa specio.

Turbulent water doesn't make a mirror.

VENETIAN PROVERB

One night the sea rose in the lagoon and swept silently into the city. By morning Venice had fallen apart, humbled to a string of small islands barely holding their heads above the water. It was an *acqua alta* such as I had never seen. Venice fell under her old enemy, her old love, a wordless but obliterating crime of passion. Noiselessly, the sea reclaimed her own. Bridges disappeared. The tall *palazzi* were foreshortened by the rising water. A great democracy of little boats, torn from their moorings, rabbled in the Piazza. The muted percussion of prow against prow was the only sound. Markets, cafés and convents had been struck dumb. The city lay hushed with its hand over its mouth. The Venetians waited, feeling the nervous throb of vestigial gills in our throats. This was what we had always feared. The strange silence only made the threat seem more palpable, like a deep breath before a scream.

Then, indeed, the water forswore its silence and became loud and angry. Now it pulsed and thrashed like the scales of a dragon.

People climbed higher up inside their buildings, sent messages of safety to their families in other quarters. Others sent more tragic messages, *We have lost our darling Gentile, the waters swept him away.* Our losses, perversely, comforted us. After a day of drowning, we felt we had been punished enough, this time. We waited for the sea to subside.

But the low tide did not come. The waters rose higher. The canals flowed towards us in tumultuous ridges, as if the Seven Plagues were writhing beneath their skins. Until now the sky had hung low and heavy, silent and empty, breathing a sick, dry light upon us. Now it bared its breast; bruised clouds were strung up like a sudden ugly gesture. A quick tongue of rain lolled down on us and a sudden slapping wind rattled over the sea just as the first roll of thunder struck. Within seconds we were besieged. Gibbets of lightning held up a swinging silver mirror to the sea. The canals boiled white with rain. The water hurled itself against our walls, was rebuffed, exploded in anger, slunk back into the dark mouth of the lagoon. There it glowered, coiled, sprang up. Again and again this happened.

At Miracoli, the water flooded our *magazzino*. Sofia and Giovanni pleaded with me to evacuate my room on the lower floor and move up to the *piano nobile* with the rest of the family. I had no hope of getting to my studio at the Palazzo Balbi Valier. No boatman would be mad or venal enough to take me through the surging water. I had no way of knowing if Girolamo and the Fathers were safe on San Lazzaro. I chafed and lurched around the house. Sofia and my niece kept out of my way.

Darkness came suddenly and earlier than it should, as if the voracious waters had also swallowed up the light. We sat around the table in the dining room listening to the roar outside. No one spoke much. We thought of the drowned souls floating out to sea. We went to bed early, to be alone with the troubled thoughts we could not share. Sofia had disposed a pretty bedroom for me on the *piano nobile*. Sweeping aside the silk curtains I looked down at the dark churning water. It snarled up at me, spitting spray in my face from the waves that threw themselves against the wall below.

I lay on the soft bed Sofia had prepared for me and lost consciousness in the folds of an embroidered crimson coverlet. In my sleep I heard the satiny surge and swell of the water under my window and absorbed it into my dreams without waking. I dreamt of Casanova's cat, the grandfather of the cat who now guarded my studio. In my dream he came swimming in calm, graceful strokes to me. I dreamt he mewed at me and shook diamonds of water from his whiskers onto my face.

I woke to find the cat on my belly, kneading the crimson coverlet to its ruination. His claws, dripping with vivid filaments of silk, tore right through the shredded fabric to my skin. His moist fur was flattened down on his spare body. 'Stop!' I begged him. Delicately, he stepped on to my pillow, shook himself, and sat upon it, looking down on me. I traced on his features the lines of his ancestor, Casanova's cat. How had the brave little beast got himself across the flooded city to my family *palazzo*? I had imagined him safe in the studio, perched high above the waters and looking down disdainfully upon them.

As I smoothed his wet feathery breast, the cat dribbled onto my hand. I wiped the stickiness back onto his fur, and, as I did so, I found the smallest imaginable packet tucked inside the velvet collar I had presented to him the day he killed his first rat. I pulled it out. The tiny letter was addressed to me: *Signorina Cecilia Cornaro*.

I sat up in bed. My candle from the night before still flickered on the table. It was just before dawn and another strange light had invaded the room. With a sick surge in my belly I realised that it was the dull white reflection of the water that had risen even further while I lay sleeping. Now I heard it groping and muttering through the lower regions of the house. I thought of the water cascading into my room on the *mezzanino*, I thought of it gathering in a dark pool and rising. I thought of it scouring the walls. I thought of my colours bleeding into it, of my painted *palazzi* and the gondola and the landscapes of *Vathek* and the *Biribissi* board, all washed into the same dappled distillation, swirling together with the refuse of the flood. When the waters receded, they would take my old life with them. They would take the Mocenigo, where I had suffered such humiliations, with them. They would take Beckford's dark fantasies with them.

Maybe it is for the best, I thought. *It is all gone, anyway.*

There was nothing I could do. I turned to the little letter in my hand. The handwriting on the outside of the packet looked familiar.

Then, at the back of my neck, the hairs started to rise.

For this was Casanova's handwriting, which I had loved so well! *From Giacomo Girolamo Casanova, San Michele*, was written on the back. On the front, under my own name, was the address of the studio at the Palazzo Balbi Valier.

At first I thought the cat had retrieved one of Casanova's old love letters from their hiding place in the wall of my studio. For years I had not looked at them. I knew them by heart, and they were beginning to suffer, like over-fondled children, and become transparent and weak. They were becoming impregnated with damp, and with the sadness that dripped from my fingers. They were becoming contaminated with the sorry little griefs of my unwanted lovers, their lost lovers, their lost potency, the rejected kisses they tried to give their wives that morning, their lost glove floating down the Grand Canal, the jewel squandered on an unloving mistress. All these sadnesses had come to my studio to be painted, and they were starting to infect Casanova's letters. Years ago I had realised that I had to stop touching them and hide them away. I had put them in a safe place to recover themselves. I knew that their goodness, like the milky kernel of a nut, would be available to me if I needed it. It gave me pleasure to think of my letters to him and his letters to me interleaved in their soft packet, intimate as the feathers of a bird.

This letter must be one of them, I thought. I pictured the cat scrabbling at my secret place in the wall to dig them all out. But how could I be angry with him? I looked at the letter again. The paper was discoloured and wrinkled, as if it had been immersed in water. There was no seal, just the stain of one, as if the wax had been washed away. I opened it, hoping to re-live a moment of tenderness with Casanova, to glean some more comfort from those words I had already read a thousand times.

'Tell me, little hero,' I said to the cat, who arched his back up to meet my cupped hand. 'Did you think this old letter might save me from the flood? *Grazie, signor.* It was a noble thought.'

The cat shook his head. There must have been a flea in his muzzle. I stroked him. Poor cat, why do fleas not drown? Then my hand slid off his back as I realised that I had not read this letter before. It was entirely new to my eyes. It was dated September 21st 1782, the day Casanova had left me; the day I had used my hard tongue against him; the day the cat had sung with his mouth like a cathedral; the last time I had seen Casanova in my life.

I felt the inebriation of discovery: a curious mingling of joy and anxiety. The paper was rattling in my hands. The cat looked at me with concern, but he nudged my fingers, as if urging me to read what he had brought me. I took a pin from my hair and slid it under the softened folds of the letter. It opened like a flower, and from between its petals there spilled a tiny coil of pearls, wedding pearls.

The cat put his paw upon them and looked up at me.

I read.

My darling Cecilia,

Your words were hard, my soul, but they were true. When I examined them afterwards I found you had accused me justly of hiding the truth from myself. My exiles, like everything else in my life, are my own fault. If I had loved you better – not more, because that is not possible, but better – I would not have written that dangerous, senseless book. I would still be there with you. You were cruel, but you were right. You have dared, of all the women I have loved, to tell me the truth about myself. I thank you for that.

Now I ask of you a very great thing.

I await you at San Michele, beside the sweet tomb of our little Fortunato. Come with me. Live with me, share my fortunes. Do you know I have never asked this of any woman before? I have offered indefinite and infinite pleasures, moments, experiences. Now I offer you this, such as it is, me, Giacomo Girolamo Casanova, in my entirety.

I hardly dare to ask you this. You are scarcely more than a child. You have never yet left Venice. I offer you a vagabond future with only our talents and our love to feed us. But I dare to, because I want to, so much.

There is something between us that neither differences of age nor fortune can displace. I knew it before I took you from your bath. We are the same, we want the same things. In your arms I am myself, the best possible rendering of myself. In my arms, you are loved as much as a woman can be loved.

You always asked me why: why I chose you, how I found you. Now I feel that I owe you an explanation. In the eyes of the superficial world, it was simple. I saw you eating *torta al cioccolato* at Florian with your father. The way you ate it, pushing the velvety cream into your mouth like a lover's

fingers, I knew you were ready for me. So I made it my
business to find out everything about you and I infiltrated
the good will of your maid. But before I came to claim you, I
consulted the esoteric forces. I read your future in the
cabbala. The numbers confirmed it. They told me that you
were the woman of my life.

There is another thing. To my surprise the numbers
strayed into danger as well as joy. They also told me that
unless I took you to me you would suffer not just the loss of
our perfect love, but something else as well. If we were not
together, I saw, then you would meet a darker fate alone.

I write this not as a threat, but to offer you the
intelligence you should have when you make your decision
to come to me – or not. If you can believe in the numbers
then you must see that you need me as much as I need you.
Let me look after you, and protect you from the things I saw
in your future.

Come to me. I love you.

Casanova.

I lay back on the bed and closed my eyes. Reading his words, I had felt
Casanova's warm breath on my neck. I felt the hair on his wrists again.
I felt the curl of his tongue in my mouth and the nudge of the steed
against my thigh. Every part of my body longed to embrace him.

A waking part of my mind told me that Casanova had been dead
now for twenty-one years.

A thinking part of my mind asked: how many years, how many
letters had passed between us in the false shadow of this one unde-
livered packet?

I clenched in my hand the piece of paper that could have rescued
our lives. Casanova had never needed to know loneliness. I had
never needed to know Byron.

I knew the invitation had died with Casanova.

But he had invited me to join him. He was still inviting me to join him. But now the invitation was to a safe place, a place beyond pain.

I turned the letter in my hand. I walked to the window and looked out on the hungry water. It winked back at me, full of treacherous complicity.

I thought of Girolamo with a melting in my stomach.

But Casanova had the prior claim to me.

I would accept, I decided, as I had always meant to.

I picked up the wedding pearls and fastened them around my neck.

18

Dio ne vol ferii, ma no morti.

God wants us hurt but not dead.

<small>Venetian proverb</small>

The waters subsided. We cleaned our houses and counted our dead.

Venice offered me a palette for my sorrows: after the flood she was grey and pale pink, the colour of her corpses. Something had drowned inside me too, it seemed. Casanova's letter had released my misery from my day-to-day habit of taut discipline. I cried all the tears I had held inside me. I lay on my bed with my nose in the belly-fur of the cat, fingering the pearls at my throat, exhausted beyond anything I had known. I felt weaker than a newborn. I was in limbo, a state of sorrow in paralysis. But I needed the misery to ferment a little more. Then, I thought, I would go to Casanova. For the moment I was just too tired to take the actions needed.

Eventually I rose from my bed and went to my studio. There is a boredom that insinuates itself into the most tragic of dramas. Now I was even tired of my own pain, of the dull rhythmic torments of my losses beating inside my brain. *Girolamo, Byron, Casanova.*

Wherever my thoughts went, they recoiled in dolorous echoes. As I left the house, I saw how the canals clenched themselves in the cold, drinking in the light and steaming as if Hell itself would soon bubble to their chilly surfaces. The waves were swishing petulantly, like the train of a noblewoman's balldress. The sick pallor of the clouds and the clamminess of the walls conspired; the whole city seemed victim to a wasting malaise. A rotten smell came up from the water that the storm had disturbed, like the sour gas of a sad old stomach. I walked past the Palazzo Mocenigo. I did not enter, but leant for a moment against the railings, the cold iron branding my forehead.

As I walked through the *calle*, the sound of Byron's name floated out from cafés where the nobles and the *borghese* huddled, gossiping and sipping their coffee and *prosecco*. Like a Greek chorus, they intoned Byron's name in incantatory repetition. *Byron, Byron*, I heard everywhere, *the English milord!*

Crede Biron, I thought. They wouldn't believe it if they knew the truth about us, about Cecilia Cornaro, Byron, and the existence of our son, Girolamo. Instead, with portentous phrases layered in canonic imitation, the chorus was weaving a new thread into the fantastical chronicles of the English milord. As I paced the misty city, I absorbed the new tidings along with the white vapour heavy with the scent of smouldering damp wood. The words of the chorus seemed intensified by the cold and were carried entire to me across water and stone. Venice was a-whisper and a-mumble with the rumour that Byron was already becoming restless again.

Byron, I heard, had found a public way to express this agitation. I supposed, as I listened to these new litanies, that he must be feeling the need to make a dramatic gesture to La Serenissima, whom he had ruffled so wildly for the last three years. Or maybe he wished to purify himself in some kind of cold, strenuous cleansing. Perhaps it was his way of saluting the city and those of us whose hearts he had filled with tears. Whatever his motives, the chorus, with its overlapping harmonies and sibilant assents, now made it known to all Venice that Byron had decided to repeat his triumphant swim from the Lido to the Grand Canal, this time alone and in the dangerous swell that had followed the great flood. In two days' time, when the tide was favourable, he would perform again.

I knew what was in his mind. Since I had received Casanova's letter I felt in a heightened state of perception. I could read Byron's thoughts as if he were lying next to me, muttering in his dreams. Byron's ideas floated across the water to me and I absorbed them easily. So I knew when and where to be the night he would make his last swim. I would be trailing him in my gondola while Tita poled him in his.

And so Byron's plans became my plans. So his intentions nourished my own parallel resolves and his timing became my own. My feelings did not enter into the operation; I remained frozen in the pain of the night of the flood. Like a mechanical doll, I made my small arrangements, in jerky motions. My teeth felt numb. I did not need to eat. I did not wash myself; in any case I bore no odour. I was aware that Sofia watched me with concern, but I ignored her. I was not even angry at the intrusion. The range of my feelings was tiny in those days. Nothing penetrated the waxen cocoon of my introspection. I was like a patient made tranquil before an amputation by a heady mixture of pain and liquor. *Not much longer now*, I told myself, soothingly, when an occasional weak and fluttering acrid thought rose up inside me like bile in my throat.

It was necessary, I realised, to preserve this curious state of inanimation. It requires, I understood, an intense stilled energy to exterminate the light of one soul before its time. In order to die, you must be a little dead for some time beforehand.

Byron chose a night so quiet that the waters moved no more than the surface of a jellyfish stirred by its own slight heart. It was three hours after midnight when he set out for the Lido. Following in my own gondola, I looked at the moonlit stones of Venice in a careful way, not as someone who lived there, but as someone who *had* lived there. I saw old walls studded with crumbling stone peacocks and griffins. I saw faded *paline* looming spectrally from the smoky water. I saw little reliefs of Saint George prodding a boneless dragon. A lazy eyelid of a blind blinked at me over a slanting window; its wrinkles seemed old and malevolent. The Gothic windows, with their shutters open, looked like hooded angels flexing their wings. But the *palazzi* seemed to hold their glass eyes averted from me, reflecting a point just over my shoulder, which did not include me. I saw the gargoyles, sipping the silvery broth of the canals at the water's edge; suddenly, just as Beckford had done, I saw all the horror woven into the silky pleasures of our lives in Venice.

I clutched Casanova's letter in my hand and drew the curtain of my *felze* around me. I watched my gondolier arching his neck to drink from the bottle of *fragolino* I had given him. After he had drunk a few more mouthfuls, the drugs would start to work.

At the Lido, Byron slips from his gondola with a subtle splash. He is wearing white silk trousers and nothing else. The water takes his limbs in its soft jaws.

He swims for two hours and ten minutes, into the dawn.

In the last ten minutes, when Byron reaches the *Basino*, I see that the opium in the *fragolino* has had its effect: my gondolier is swaying. He droops over his pole. By the time we reach the church of Santa Maria della Salute, at the mouth of the Grand Canal, he has slumped down upon his knees. A moment later, he is lying on the prow of the boat, oblivious to everything. All is as I planned it. The current has taken possession of the boat, and we now float down the Canal without the gondolier's help. I slip out from under the *felze* and lay a carpet over him. I look around. There is no one on the shore to see me. I think of Casanova in the dismal streets of

London, his pockets weighted with lead, on his way to the Thames. I think of La Charpillon, the cold whore who brought him to that. But I have trained myself well; I am still insensate. I feel no inner agitation, only a vague sense of meetness.

Byron is still swimming, bobbing above the water like a toy horse. He is just a hundred yards ahead of me now. How strange it is to see him from this distance. I think how often I have smoothed the hair now flattened against his head. My hand remembers the soft lustre of his curls but the memory does not connect with any feeling of pain or pleasure.

I sit on the edge of the gondola and I kick off my shoes. I do not hesitate for an instant as I slip into the Canal and start to swim after him. The water closes round me like an angry fist. In the shock of the cold, I experience a moment of clarity. Memories spill into my head, tickling at my dormant emotions like little fish.

I remember La Fornarina, who threw herself into the Canal for love of Byron. I know that Byron is a man who lures people to their deaths. I think of Saint Cecilia singing in her boiling bath. I remember myself in the bath sipping *fragolino*. But here, in the Canal, the water holds me silently in a freezing embrace and I refuse to allow my feelings to be roused. Only a technicality, a matter of minutes, separate me from what I desire.

I am a Venetian. I can swim. My hands and feet perform the requisite actions without interior commands. It will take an effort for me to desist from this slow, cold dance. But now the water has crept into my clothes and their weight starts to drag me downwards. I am losing sight of him.

It doesn't matter. I move my arms and legs as little as possible.

Nonetheless, there come more clear moments to interrupt me. I am invaded by thoughts.

Life is too short, I think, and the time in which we love is too short, to make pronouncements about happy and unhappy love. I only know this, that when I was with Byron, it was this way, and when I was with Casanova, it was otherwise. Between them I have known both extremes of felicity. I have known Venice, too, as a happy and an unhappy city.

Perhaps these are my last thoughts, I think.

My clothes are too heavy now, but I welcome the weight. Underwater, the light is kind. I am as ageless as a fish. I remember an old letter of Casanova's, *the sea is hungry* . . . but I cannot remember what it hungers for.

I give myself to the water, which seems disposed to accept the gift. It starts to bite inside my nose. Its greasy saltiness has entered my mouth. I let my head loll back so that a wave rolls over it. The spray pricks my eyes. I sink just a little lower into the water. *I have started to drown*, I think. *It does not hurt; it does not hurt as much as Byron has hurt me.* The moments when my head is above the waves have become shorter and my eyes have glazed with the brackish wash. Water shuttles down the back of my throat and I swallow it.

Crede Biron.

Then, over the water, comes a sudden and intense gust of warmth, fragrant with the hot smell of chocolate. My tongue hears the roasting of the pine nuts, and the air expanding in soft sighs inside a *torta al cioccolato*.

I raise my head above the waves, sniffing. I find myself treading water and kneading my hands against the dragging current. My numb teeth begin to chatter like cicadas.

The aroma of melted chocolate grows stronger and warmer, wafting towards me, potent as incense swung in a censer. It fills my lungs where the sea-water is supposed to be.

Girolamo, I think . . .

In the roots of my teeth, in the cave of my belly, in the cap of my scalp, I feel the fierce pulse of hot blood. And this is nothing to the eruptions of my heart and the pictures swarming in vivid colour into my mind. I gasp with recognition, like someone who has fallen in love at first sight. There is a kaleidoscope revolving inside me. I think of the butter-soft chestnuts folded into the chocolate cream. I think of Girolamo's hot little hands, as beautiful as mine. I think of the love in Casanova's letter, in all his letters. I think of Mary Shelley's eyes, and of Sofia's quiet, tender voice. I think of the things I have not yet experienced, warm, sweet novelties for the mouth, hands and eyes.

Suddenly I feel fear, a healthful rumbling in my gut. I am afraid that I shall lose these things because I have made myself blind, and unable to hear.

I think of Mary's last words to me: *There are other ways to cure addiction. It's important to remember that it is the* vice *that should die and not the poor creature who suffers from it.*

Now I thrash like a fish in a net. I struggle for air. I take great gulps of it. It tastes sweet to me.

Suddenly, I feel anger, a ripeness in my breast and a clenching of my fists. I punch the water and I feel it shrinking from me, as if afraid of my righteous rage.

I think: *Where is it written that I must have a lover as odious as Byron? And that I should die of it?*

My anger empowers my arms. I swim strong, deliberate strokes. I turn towards the shore. The waves part for me, as if respecting my wishes. I think, *The sea is hungry, but it is not me that it hungers for now.*

A sudden tug of happiness nudges away my anger. I feel inspired, as if all solutions are possible to me. I find myself laughing in delight. I catch the cynical eye of a seagull floating in the water near me. *Know your element*, it seems to say to me. *My own elements*, I think, *what are they? Air and oil paint and* torta al cioccolato *and that delicious smell at the top of Girolamo's head.*

These thoughts carry me to the shore. At Campo San Vio I rise from the water like Botticelli's Venus. I walk straight to the bakery and beat on the door with my wet hands. The old wood makes a pulpy noise as if I am bruising it. The baker, seeing my mermaid form in the dawn light, crosses himself. He thinks I am a beggar and that I am mad. He gives me a big slice of the hot *torta al cioccolato*. I devour it on his doorstep like an animal.

I am weak with cravings for the chocolate cake, for the colours of the dawn, for the joys I have known through this wet but still living skin. *Girolamo*, I think, *yes, even he was made with joy.*

I draw myself up to my full height and look at San Vio, where Casanova's gondola used to rock with our love and laughter. I smile. I look at the rising sun gilding the roof of the Accademia galleries. I know that one day my paintings will hang in there. I have more love poems to write to the faces of Venice. And there are Girolamo's future faces to record!

Girolamo, I think . . .

But first there are less lovely things to attend to.

I think that addicts have been cured. I think that the poison can be excavated from the blood. Once I thought that it was essential to my happiness to be near Byron. Now I have realised that the necessary thing is never to see him again.

I think we are all redeemable, at a price. Sometimes it is cruel price: exposure. Sometimes it is a dangerous price: revenge. Sometimes it is even more exacting: the truth. In my new omnipotent, omniscient state, I know a way to make Byron leave Venice, leave me and my son in peace, to let us find our happiness. I know two ways in fact. There is one thing I can do immediately.

I ask the baker for a piece of paper. I write on it, address it, and hand it to the baker's boy with a wet coin from my pocket. I explain what I want, precisely. 'Run!' I tell him.

I watch the boy skimming off down the street. I raise my arm to salute him on his way. I feel light and bright as a goddess. I feel certain that I have saved both Byron and my son from danger, and that I have done so just in time.

I walk towards my studio, dripping along the stones. The baker watches me, shaking his head.

As I enter my courtyard I stand for a moment looking at the Grand Canal between the three graceful arches. I know that Byron is still immersed in that green water, still dipping in and out of it. I know that the baker's boy is pounding through Campo San Vidal and in a few moments he will arrive, panting, at the rear gates of the Palazzo Mocenigo.

A few minutes later, Byron himself will arrive at the sea-doors of the Mocenigo. He will drag himself from the water and push his way inside. Still dripping from his swim, he will walk past his howling beasts in the courtyard to the staircase. On the very first step he will find a letter in my handwriting, still warm from the baker boy's humid little hand. He will hear the echoes of the boy's thudding footsteps fading away.

He will unfold the letter as he walks up the steps. By the time he reaches the landing the packet will be open. He will hold it to the light of that lantern-bearing arm that seems to have punched its way through the wall.

He will see that my letter contains just one line, and he will fall to his knees on the stone steps when he reads it.

My letter says this:

But can she ever be as beautiful as our son, Girolamo?

19

La lontananza l'è fiola de la dimenticanza.

Distancing is the child of forgetting.

VENETIAN PROVERB

I take the damp key out of my pocket and unlock my door.

The cat greets me loudly and I kneel down to caress him.

Over his head, I look around my studio. Inside, from floor to ceiling, I gaze upon my painted faces of Venetians. In the harsh clamour of dawn light they look flushed and slightly surprised, as if put out of breath by a sudden clout upon the back. But nothing can stifle their happiness! I have preserved it here forever in my oils and pastels. The perfervid joy of the happy city lives on here in my studio, in that delicate *sfumatura* of desire on their skin, those cloudy loves inscribed in the lustre of their eyes, the soft laughter haunting the corners of their mouths.

Among these ghostly faces of the once happy city sits my last beautiful portrait of Byron. Before I left my studio that evening for the swim that had ended differently from the way I had expected, I placed Byron on my easel with a pair of pale candles burning in front of him. *Are you still here?* I want to say to him, now. I turn away from the painting.

A flickering light calls my attention back to him.

When I opened the door to my studio a quick sigh of wind rushed in ahead of me. Now it teases the flames of the candles so they dance crazily on their wicks. Soon the candles start rocking on their silver sticks; from side to side they go. Unless I close the door, they will topple and fall. The flames would caress Byron's face on the canvas. But first they would devour his breast. They would eat him from the heart up.

I consider the scene. It would make a fine, fragrant blaze, that painting of Byron. It would give out more warmth than he did in his whole life. The canvas would writhe like driftwood in the fire. I imagine the delicate features withering and dying, as I suspect they never will in real life. *Byron has lived too fast, he has already swallowed his story in gulps. He will not live long*, I think. *The world will be sweeter without him*, I think.

However, I close the door, for the moment. The flames gasp quietly and become calm, for the moment. This is not the way I wish to spend my new-born power: no, not in destruction.

I slither from my wet clothes and into dry ones. I do not remove the pearls: I am married to my happiness, now. I am vibrating with vigour like a harp in the wind, and I know exactly what I must do. I take a leather portfolio from the top of the cupboard and spill its contents out on the table. I contemplate my other portraits of Byron, the secret ones, the hideous ones. I fan them out and choose six of them, the ones that best express the moments that almost killed my happiness.

I begin to work. I have much to do. The pictures must be stretched and mounted. Some of the pastels must be fixed with fine coats of varnish and given time to dry. The boat for England leaves at noon and I must have them ready.

I hum as I work, a Venetian love song. The beauty of the words seems out of place as I run my hands over my grotesque pictures of

Byron. I glaze his double chins and his fat wrists. I anoint the wrinkles round his eyes with a preservative oil. I dust his vapid cheeks with desiccating powder to preserve their sick pallor on the long journey.

I wonder, briefly, what Caroline Lamb will make of them. Will it hurt her to see her lover like this? Then I think of *Glenarvon*. Caroline Lamb will know what to do with my pictures.

When I have mounted the last portrait I gather them all together in careful folds of silk that I bind inside narrow, strong widths of board. I address the parcel. I know where to send it. I have seen the address on his and Hobhouse's letters to Caroline's mother-in-law, Lady Melbourne.

I think, *I am sorry, Hobhouse. You will feel betrayed. It is a necessary sacrifice.*

I look in the mirror and see that my swim has brought a bloom to my skin. I sweep up my hair so that the pearls can be seen against my throat. I meet my eyes in the mirror and smile. I put on my cloak and salute the cat, who brandishes his tail at me. Quickly, I carry the parcel to the docks and I negotiate with a sailor. I give him certain monies and certain looks that will ensure that he will come back to Venice and tell me of the safe delivery of my work.

As I walk back from the docks I hear the voices in the cafés again, the chanting of a Greek chorus. *Byron!* I hear, *the English milord!*

'Pale as death, you never saw anything like it,' I hear.

'The Mocenigo is abandoned. They say he ran out with just a valise of poems. He has sworn never to return.'

I let the voices fade behind me.

Girolamo, I think . . .

The winter sun, a frail little petal floating in the sky, begins to lower itself. I go home. There is one more thing to do.

I walk through the streets I love. Everywhere I smell the savoury joys of the Venetians at their tables: sage, butter, rosemary, crab soups, sour *parmigiano*. I inhale the rich stinks of the seaweed and the soft breath of the stones. I see tall finials unfurling like white buds above the terracotta rooftops. I notice the sinuous black fissures in the white Istrian stone of the paving. I see the flowers blushing on window-sills. I hear the crunch of the waves under the prows of the gondolas. I press coins into the beggars' curved palms, which bloom up like pale pink tulips as I pass. I hear the gondoliers singing and the children at their nursery rhymes. I look at the striped *paline* and hear the clicking of the iridescent beasts who devour them at the water-line. I hold my arms open, as if to claim it all. I walk for a long time, until it is almost dark.

I go home.

I go to my *campo*, and lift my eyes to the delicate cupolas, the airy arches and the pale marble ribs of the church of Miracoli. I pass through the courtyard where once upon a time I fell into the arms of Casanova and I climb the stairs to Sofia's little parlour, to wait for her. When she has finished the duties of her day, she comes here to sit with my portrait of her dead baby, and to repose a little.

I imagine how I will take her hand and talk to her.

I will tell Sofia everything and I will embrace her.

I think of how we shall go to Giovanni together and how we shall, with our hands uplifted and our eyes fixed upon him, make him see our point of view.

I think of how Sofia and I shall walk together to the Fondamenta Nuova, with our arms linked and our heads close together. One of us will hold the lamp to light our way. We will ask the boatman to take us to San Lazzaro and we will bring Girolamo home.

Postscript

Dr Julius Millingen's Report

I, Dr Julius Millingen, who attended Lord Byron during his final days at Missolonghi, performed an autopsy after the poet died on April 19th 1824, of a malarial infection, at the age of thirty-six years. This is my account of it. There is nothing I have done, in my long life, and what has been, I may say, a distinguished career, about which I have been asked more.

It behoves me first, for the sake of my conscience, to make it clear that Lord Byron would have been horrified at our actions. He believed in the sanctity of the body. At least, he believed fervently in the sanctity of his own. In a premonition of his death, he told me, while I placed the leeches on his forehead, 'Let my body not be hacked, or be sent to England.' I promised him, I admit it, that we would leave his carcass entire and that it would rest in Greece, for whose liberation he was, apparently, sacrificing his life. He had no love of his own country, vowing never to return, alive or dead, whole or in pieces, to what he consistently referred to, with loathing, as that 'tight little island'. He also seemed violently opposed to the idea of returning to his adopted home, Italy, or at least to Venice. 'Venice, no . . .!' he would whisper, from time to time. It was as if there was something there which frightened him.

Lord Byron was mostly delirious in those last days. He believed that he had been cursed by the evil eye. He asked if I would do him the favour of finding an old and ugly witch to exorcise the curse! I regret to say that I did not hear him make any, not even the smallest, mention of the Christian religion. He spoke several times in Italian at the last, something incomprehensible. I believe I heard the word 'ritratto'. I understand this means 'portrait'. He said several times, 'My son, my son,' and this distressed all those attending him, for it is well known that he had no legitimate male issue.

He continually referred to the fate of his corpse. 'Let it just be laid in a corner,' he said at one point, 'without pomp or nonsense.' I think, in his delirium, that he believed he could trick us out of an autopsy.

However, I regret to say that Lord Byron was thoroughly 'hacked' in the autopsy by five doctors, including myself. What else could we do? The world was clamouring for information.

It is true that two of us burst into tears as we approached his beautiful corpse with our saws. As soon as we had done our grim work, I departed from the bloody scene with my eyes streaming. I left the others to put him back together. I could not look on his dismembered body for a moment longer.

I own that I should have stayed in the room. For when I returned I found that the body had been spliced back together as crudely as a rag doll, like Mary Shelley's Frankenstein monster. Feeling guilty, I supervised the final rites rigorously: the remains were preserved in spirits, sealed in a tin packing case, there being no lead coffins available, and shipped back to England, accompanied by the organs in four separate jars. The lungs were an exception. In response to an earnest request from the Greeks, they were placed in an urn in the church of San Spiridione at Missolonghi, from where they subsequently disappeared.

I know that I promised that the carcass should remain in Greece. But you must understand our position. Greece was at war. We were afraid that if left there his remains might one day become the sport of insulting barbarians. Our greatest poet! I could not permit it. The fate of the lungs alone seems to me to justify my decision.

I understand that when Lord Byron's body arrived in England, his friend John Cam Hobhouse forced himself to bid farewell to his friend, now laid out in state in London. But the parts had been assembled wrongly and he could not recognise him. It was to my eternal regret that poor Hobhouse had to identify the corpse by lifting the pall to look at his deformed foot. I understand that Lord Byron's half-sister Augusta also went to view the body, as did immense numbers of members of the public on the two days when it was available for them to file past.

There was talk of it, but permission was refused to bury him in Westminster Abbey. He was put in the family vault in Hucknall Torkard. I read in the papers that Byron's funeral cortège was followed by dozens of fine carriages. These belonged to great families – the peers of the Realm, Lord Byron's peers.

But for all their funeral finery, for all the plumed horses and black-garbed footmen, the carriages were empty. The English aristocracy did not wish to offer more than token grief for the death of the man who had scorned and scandalised them. The ghost carriages arrived at the church, barely waited outside, and cantered off.

This I learnt later. My hands were the last to touch Lord Byron when he was still warm, and I shall never forget that feeling. I was undone by it.

In my distressed state I was indiscreet enough to talk to the journalists sent from the local newspapers, foraging for lurid details about the passing of the great poet. I was not myself, I admit it, and I said more than I meant to, but it was no less than the truth.

And so it was that the *Greek Telegraph* justly reported that Byron's autopsy revealed a remarkable quantity of brains, at least a quarter more than average, and extremely saturated in blood. But the bones in his head – they were like those of an old man, the sutures of the skull fused together. The texture of the cranium was as hard as ivory. In his body, we saw that the adipose tissue was everywhere predominant, a proof of his congenital predisposition to corpulence. It was noted that the liver was beginning to undergo the alterations usually observed in those who have indulged in the abuse of alcoholic liquors. Its bulk was smaller, its texture harder and its colour much lighter than a healthy liver.

Lord Byron's heart, I told them – to my eternal regret, for I was forever after hounded for my words – was also very large, far larger than a normal man's.

But I had to say, in all honesty, that the pale bloated heart displayed on the chopping board lacked the musculature one would expect. It was as flabby as that of someone who had died of old age. In truth, I must admit, though I mislike to do so, that Lord Byron's heart was but a feeble organ.

Author's note

Only truth can be invented.

JOHN RUSKIN

The invented characters in this book are Cecilia and her family, Mouchar, Maurizio Mocenigo, the gondolier and the cat.

The others are real: Casanova and his family, Byron and his, Francesca Buschini, William Beckford, Johann Wolfgang von Goethe, Ambassador Alvise Mocenigo, Count Waldstein of Dux and his servant Feldkirchner, Lorenzo da Ponte, Ali Pasha of Albania, William Fletcher, John Cam Hobhouse, Nurse Gray, Caroline Lamb, Annabella Milbanke, Marianna Segati, Margarita Cogni, Tita Falcieri, Mary and Percy Bysshe Shelley, Claire Claremont, Ada and Allegra Byron, Marina Benzoni, Teresa Guiccioli, Julius Millingen, Angelica Kauffman and Rosalba Carriera, Lady Mary Wortley Montagu, Lady Arundel and Giordano Bruno.

All the literary works of Casanova are real. Casanova's theories about love, women, Venice and portrait-painting and the anecdotes of his life are based on various allusions and anecdotes in his *Histoire de Ma Vie*. These memoirs, three thousand and six hundred pages of them, were written in French during his exile in Dux. They first appeared in German in 1822 and were not published in Italian till 1882. They are now translated into twenty-four languages and considered one of the most fascinating accounts of European life in the eighteenth century. Casanova's letters from exile are invented, but partly based on some he sent to Francesca Buschini.

The camp Gothic masterpiece *Vathek* is real, as was Byron's passion for Beckford's book. When Byron set off for his last journey to Greece in 1823, he ordered all his books and other property to be sold, except for his copy of *Vathek*. Also real are Byron's 'Reasons In Favour of a Change' and his description of the demented elephant despatched by the Austrians. Many of Byron's more colourful comments are culled from his letters to Hobhouse, his publisher John Murray, and his sister, Augusta. Caroline Lamb's dire *Glenarvon* really exists and the 1816 edition may still be borrowed from the London Library. The *Poupée de France* did indeed dictate Venetian fashion for many years from her shop window in the Merceria. The descriptions of the *Carnevale* in Venice are drawn from the Gabriel Bella paintings in the Palazzo Querini Stampalia, where they may still be seen. The island of San Michele was in 1782 the home of the Camadolese monastery. It became the cemetery island of Venice early in the next century.

Byron really was in Albania in 1809 and in Venice between 1816 and 1819. He lived at the Segati house in the Frezzeria and the Palazzo Mocenigo at San Samuele. He did indeed swim from the Lido to the Grand Canal, though only one occasion is recorded. He also studied Armenian on the island of San Lazzaro. (By coincidence, Casanova had also been involved with the Armenian community on the island. He was asked by the Venetian state to mediate with a fugitive cell of Armenian monks: this was one of the tasks assigned to him in the period before he returned from exile in 1774.)

William Beckford's connection with Casanova is imagined but entirely possible. They were both friends of William Hamilton. Beckford and Casanova were both in Venice at the dates described. Beckford's letters of introduction in Venice were addressed to the Countess Giustiniana d'Orsini Rosenberg, at that time a respectable widow. But thirty years before she had been one of Casanova's most picaresque lovers. Giustiniana, whom he called Miss XCV in his memoirs, was pregnant by a friend of Casanova's; he tried to help her to abort the child. The attempt, involving the repeated application of a honeyed ointment called Paracelsus' Aroph to the mouth of womb via the agent of Casanova's ever-willing 'steed', was, though pleasurable, a failure. Casanova smuggled Giustiniana to a convent where the baby was born in secrecy. She returned to her family with her reputation more or less intact. By the time Casanova returned from his eighteen-year exile, Giustiniana had married the Count d'Orsini Rosenberg and set up her own salon in Venice. It was in this same salon that Beckford was entertained.

Byron left Venice in 1819 and attached himself to the household of Teresa Guiccioli. Teresa's family drew Byron into the Italian nationalist movement and he became interested in the parallel Greek cause. In 1823, he was elected to the Greek Committee formed to free Greece from Turkish rule. He joined the liberation forces personally at Missolonghi in January 1824. He died of malaria there on April 19th 1824, attended by Julius Millingen.

Byron did write some memoirs of his own but they were ceremonially burned in his publisher's offices in Albemarle Street on May 17th 1824, four weeks after his death. It was thought by his friends that the sexual revelations therein rendered them too dangerous to be allowed to survive. Hobhouse was among those who urged their destruction, even without having read them. To refute malicious allegations about him, years later, Teresa Guiccioli wrote her adoring *Vie de Lord Byron*, but this was considered too intimate to be published during her lifetime. However, Annabella also had her say: she persuaded Harriet Beecher Stowe to write her account of the disastrous marriage. It appeared in 1870, ten years after her death, as *Lady Byron Vindicated*.

Byron's autopsy and funeral were indeed as described. Mary Shelley was in London at the time. She watched Byron's hearse ascend Highgate Hill, and recorded a wave of affection for the man who had cost her so much. Caroline Lamb, by chance, also encountered the funeral procession. When told who lay in the hearse, it is said that she became mentally deranged and that she never fully recovered.

Finally, there is, as described in Part Four, a portrait of Byron on the island of Saint Lazzaro.

The name of the artist remains unknown.

A c k n o w l e d g e m e n t s

With great thanks to my editors, Sally Abbey and Jill Foulston, for their indispensable help and immaculate instincts about Cecilia, and to my agent, Tanja Howarth, particularly for finding them for me. Thanks also to Rebecca Kerby for fine-tuning the text and timeline.

With deep thanks to Wendy and Fred Oliver for absolutely everything, to Joanna Skepers, Melissa Stein, James Tipton, Donna Martin, Kristina Blagojevitch and Jenny Lovric for reading the original manuscript, and to Susanna Geoghegan, Nancy Starr and Bart and Marilyn Stoner for their continual support.

I'm grateful to Ornella Tarantola, Clara Caleo-Green, Cinzia Viviani and Lucio Sponsa for help with the Italian and Venetian vocabulary and iconography. Thank you to David Swift and Lynne Curran for help with the bizarre aspects of the eighteenth century and cat life; to Reggie Pennington for agricultural advice.

Profound thanks to Alison Fell, Nicolette Hardee, Val Lee, Janie Mitchell, Susannah Rickards, Angela Robson and Katri Skala, for their generous, skilful commentaries on the text over the year it took to refine it.

Thanks to June Mendoza for help with the technical aspects of portraiture; to Cynthia Craig for her kind and detailed help with Casanova; and to Tom Holland for his with Byron.

With thanks also to the staff at the British and the London Libraries and the Marciana Library in Venice and to the National Portrait Gallery and National Gallery in London.

And in Venice, deep gratitude to Donatella and Paolo Asta for their infinite kindness in allowing me to write the Palazzo Mocenigo scenes in Byron's former apartments; to Michele Sammartini for the use of the Palazzo Molin Balbi Valier della Trezza, both as my Venetian domicile and as the setting for Cecilia's studio in the book; to Paola and Pitagora Zoffoli for an insight into the feline life of Venice; to Alessandra Angelini and Diego Vianello and to Franco Gasperin for introducing me to the flavoursome world of Venetian proverbs; and to Ada Gasperin for the *minestre*.

And warmest thanks to Sergio and Roberta Grandesso for the *fragolino*, and to Graziella, Emilio and Valentina Scarpa for the hundreds of 6 a.m. *ottimi capucci non troppo schiuma* at the Bar da Gino at San Vio, without which this novel would not have been written.

Select Textual Acknowledgements

The following books were invaluable in research for this novel:

The Story Of My Life, by Giacomo Casanova, Chevalier de Seingalt, translated by Willard R. Trask, Johns Hopkins Paperbacks edition, 1997. English translation copyright © by Harcourt, Brace & World, Inc. Originally published as *Histoire de Ma Vie*, Edition intégrale, by Jacques Casanova de Seingalt, Vénitien, by F. A. Brockhaus, Wiesbaden, Librairie Plon, Paris, 1960. © F. A. Brockhaus, Wiesbaden, 1960.

Glenarvon, by Lady Caroline Lamb, Henry Colburn, London, 1816.

Byron: A Self-Portrait Letters and Diaries 1798 To 1824, edited by Peter Quennell, John Murray, London, 1950.

Dreams, Waking Thoughts And Incidents, by William Beckford of Fonthill, edited by Robert J. Gemmett, Fairleigh University Press. © 1971 Associated University Presses Inc, Cranbury, New Jersey.

Vathek, by William Beckford, London, 1786.